HENRY JAMES

HENRY JAMES

Selected Works

DAISY MILLER: A STUDY
THE PORTRAIT OF A LADY
THE ASPERN PAPERS
THE TURN OF THE SCREW

LEOPARD

This edition published in 1995 by Leopard Books
Random House, 20 Vauxhall Bridge Road, London SW1V 2SA

ISBN 0 7529 0016 1

Printed and bound in Great Britain by
Mackays of Chatham

CONTENTS

Introduction	vii
Daisy Miller: A Study	1
The Portrait of a Lady	47
The Aspern Papers	497
The Turn of the Screw	571

INTRODUCTION

Henry James led a single-minded life. He wrote more than twenty novels, a hundred and twelve novellas and short stories, and numerous essays, as well as reviews and travel pieces. Never married, he was able to devote his undivided attention to writing—his art, what he termed his "sacred rage." For James art was the focus and the most stimulating part of his existence. As he wrote to H. G. Wells: "It is art that makes life, makes interest, makes importance . . . and I know no substitute for the force and beauty of its process."

Although James achieved limited commercial success in his lifetime, his influence on American fiction in the twentieth century has been profound. The resurgence of interest in his writing, beginning in the period between the two world wars, has made true his prediction that "some day, all my buried prose will kick off its various tombstones at once." His emphasis on portraying his characters realistically and describing the psychological reasons for their attitudes and motivations made his works forerunners to the modernist stream-of-consciousness novels.

James also brought a new level of craftsmanship to American fiction. He was meticulous in his choice of words, carefully weighing their placement and rhythmic nuance. He believed in the formal conception of fiction as practiced by such European writers as Gustav Flaubert and Ivan Turgenev, who influenced him greatly. James's fiction was in marked contrast to that of the popular American writers of the day like Mark Twain, who epitomized the then popular vernacular and folksy mode of writing. James, in contrast, wedded a European sophistication to his American outlook that greatly influenced such writers as F. Scott Fitzgerald, Ernest Hemingway, and William Faulkner, who followed him in the flowering of American fiction in the twentieth century.

Henry James was born in New York City on April 15, 1843. His father, Henry James, Sr., was independently wealthy and rather eccentric. He had no occupation, but spent his time studying philosophy and religion—especially the teachings of Emanuel Swedenborg, the eighteenth-century Swedish scientist, philosopher, theologian, and mystic. Henry's older brother William, whom he called "the Ideal Elder Brother," would become America's first important psychologist and philosopher. Other members of the family included two younger brothers, Garth Wilkinson and Robertson, their brilliant younger sister, Alice, and their mother, Mary Walsh, who used self-sacrifice as a means of ruling the family.

In 1855, when Henry was twelve, the family left for Europe because the elder James believed that the American school system was inadequate, and wanted his children to have a "sensuous education." He concluded that broad-based schooling, involving travel and tutors, would better serve his sons and daughter. For the next four years the family traveled to Paris, London, and Switzerland in search of the best schools and tutors. They also visited countless galleries and museums, libraries, and theaters.

James's unsystematic education resulted in his being largely self-taught. His father observed, "Henry is not so fond of study properly so-called, as of reading. He is a devourer of libraries." He was, indeed, extremely well-read in nineteenth-century fiction, and learned French adequately enough to engage in a lifelong study of its literature. His only conventional studies were at Harvard Law School, which he briefly attended in 1862 before he decided to commit himself to writing.

An "obscure hurt," as James described it, probably to his back, prevented him from serving in the American Civil War with his brothers Wilkinson and Robertson. In the early 1860s he began to publish stories and reviews in such leading magazines as the *Atlantic Monthly* and the *Nation*. James remained close to his family, especially to his older brother William, and it was not until he was in his thirties, when he decided to move to England, that he permanently left home.

In December 1876, Henry James settled in London, where he would remain for the rest of his life. There he was quickly accepted by English society, and he formed lasting friendships with many of the important writers on the international literary scene, including: George Eliot, H. G. Wells, Joseph Conrad, Edith Wharton, Robert Louis Stevenson, Émile Zola, Ivan Turgenev, and Gustav Flaubert. He enjoyed a busy social life, even boasting that one winter he dined out one hundred and seven times.

Many American critics have accused James of disloyalty to his own country by choosing to live abroad. But he had positive feelings about the United States and had chosen to live in London in part because he felt alienated from his generation of Americans since he had spent so many of his formative years abroad. In addition, he had not served in the Civil War. But it was primarily on an artistic level that he needed Europe. He wrote: "The burden is necessarily greater for an American—for he *must* deal . . . with Europe; whereas no European is obliged to deal in the least with America." With London as his base he could easily travel all over the Continent. In Europe he discovered things he felt America lacked, things essential to his interests as a writer. James said that America had "no sovereign, no court . . . no aristocracy, no church, no clergy, no army, no diplomatic service, no country gentleman, no palaces, no castles, no manors, nor old country houses . . . no literature, no novels, no museums, no pictures, no political society, no sporting class." Although clearly humorously exaggerated, during James's lifetime the statement had some validity, since culturally the United States was still barely beyond its formative stages.

According to Leon Edel, who is considered one of foremost James scholars, Henry James's writing career can be divided into three periods. The first, from the beginning of James's career until 1881, is marked by his interest in the so-called "international theme," his depiction of the interaction of Europeans and Americans and the cultural tensions and conflicts that result. His major works from this period include *Roderick Hudson*, published in 1875, and *The American*, published two years later. This phase culminated with the publication in 1878 of *Daisy Miller: A Study* and, in 1881, *The Portrait of a Lady*, both of which are included in this collection.

When *Daisy Miller: A Study* was first published it caused controversy in the United States because it appeared to many to be a satiric attack on the heroine who was an ill-mannered American girl. Today it serves as a marvelous introduction to Henry James's milieu, the world of upper-class society and its manners, which has largely disappeared. (The novelist Joseph Conrad once commented that James was "the historian of finer consciences.") In this novella James uses one of his most important technical devices, the restricted point of view. The reader follows the events of the story through Winterbourne, a young American living abroad. Without a formal introduction he meets Daisy Miller in a hotel in Switzerland. His aunt labels her "a dreadful girl." Later in Rome, he again meets Daisy in the company of Giovanelli, an Italian gigolo. She causes a scandal for what society deems "loose" behavior. But as Giovanelli says at the end of the story, Daisy "was the most beautiful young lady I ever saw, and the most amiable. . . . Also—naturally—the most innocent." James said that "the keynote of her *character* is her innocence." The focus of the story is the disparity between appearance and reality, but James is also exploring the theme in the social context of Americans confronting Europe's cultural milieu when the appearance of virtue was more important than the reality.

The Portrait of a Lady expands upon the theme of *Daisy Miller*. It is one of James's longest, as well as one of his best and most perennially popular, novels. The central character is Isabel Archer, an impoverished American who is introduced to European society by her aunt, Lydia Touchett, the wife of a retired wealthy banker, Daniel Touchett. Isabel is perhaps James's most glamorous character, whose natural charm and grace were inspired by his beloved cousin, Mary Temple, who died of tuberculosis in 1870 at the age of twenty-four. Isabel is a true innocent abroad who slowly learns about the society she has entered and the malevolence that lurks beneath its rich and pleasing surface. Like a character in a fairy tale she is rewarded for her goodness with an inheritance, but ensuing consequences are evidence of James's doubt that lasting happiness or freedom can be realized or maintained.

The second period of James's career, which roughly covers 1881 to 1895, is more experimental in subject matter as well as form. James was interested in such social issues of the day as women's rights, the subject of *The Bostonians*, and the class struggle in England, the subject of *The Princess Casamassima*—both published in 1886. Although James lived comfortably he never became rich from his writing, and in the 1890s, prompted by a desire for popular acclaim, he tried his hand at drama. He wrote seven plays, but only two were produced. In 1895, as a result of the humiliating and hostile opening-night response to *Guy Domville*, he gave up his aspirations to be a playwright. He then returned full-time to fiction with a series of short stories and novellas that explored the relationship of artists to society as well as with some bizarre tales of obsessed and haunted men, women, and children. Two stories from this period are included in this book—*The Aspern Papers* (1888) and *The Turn of the Screw* (1898).

The Aspern Papers is one of Henry James's best tales and is based on a story he heard in Florence in 1887 about a Captain Silsbee's attempt to get some papers of Byron's and Shelley's that were in the possession of Claire Clairmont, one of Byron's mistresses. James set the story in Venice, and created a dead fictional American poet, Jeffrey Aspern, in place of Byron and Shelley. The tale is narrated by a publisher who learns that some of Aspern's papers are in the hands of the poet's now aged mistress, Miss Bordereau. In hopes of making a fortune with the manuscripts, the publisher cons his way into Miss Bordereau's household as a lodger and charms her spinster niece, Miss Tita, into helping him to get the papers. But, in the end, Miss Tita's price is too high.

Oscar Wilde called *The Turn of the Screw* "a most wonderful, lurid, poisonous little tale, like an Elizabethan tragedy." It remains one of James's most popular works and one of the greatest ghost stories ever written. It is a marvel of ambiguity. Are the ghosts that the governess sees and believes to be haunting her two young charges, Miles and Flora, real or figments of her overactive imagination? James never makes it clear, allowing either possibility and leaving it to the reader to puzzle over the answer.

In the final period, the "major phase," from 1896 until the end of his career, James returned to the international theme with the novels that are considered to be among his masterpieces—*The Wings of the Dove* (1902), *The Ambassadors* (1903), and *The Golden Bowl* (1904).

By the end of his career, Henry James was an honored literary figure, much admired by his fellow writers, two hundred and seventy of whom presented him with a "golden bowl" on his seventieth birthday. He received honorary degrees from Harvard and Oxford and in January 1916 was awarded the Order of Merit by King George V for his efforts on behalf of England during the first years of World War I. To protest America's reluctance to enter the war, James became a British subject shortly before he suffered a stroke in December 1915. He died on February 28, 1916.

In the years since his death, American fiction has followed the course that James plotted, conveying a more psychologically complex and realistic conception of life, as well as bringing forth a more sophisticated and highly crafted novel. Shortly after James's death, the American poet Ezra Pound wrote: "Peace comes of communication. No man of our time has so labored to create means of communication as did the late Henry James. The whole of great art is a struggle for communication." It remains a fitting tribute to one of America's greatest novelists.

CHRISTOPHER MOORE

New York
1994

DAISY MILLER:
A STUDY

I

At the little town of Vevey, in Switzerland, there is a particularly comfortable hotel. There are, indeed, many hotels; for the entertainment of tourists is the business of the place, which, as many travellers will remember, is seated upon the edge of a remarkably blue lake—a lake that it behooves every tourist to visit. The shore of the lake presents an unbroken array of establishments of this order, of every category, from the "grand hotel" of the newest fashion, with a chalk-white front, a hundred balconies, and a dozen flags flying from its roof, to the little Swiss *pension* of an elder day, with its name inscribed in German-looking lettering upon a pink or yellow wall, and an awkward summer-house in the angle of the garden. One of the hotels at Vevey, however, is famous, even classical, being distinguished from many of its upstart neighbors by an air both of luxury and of maturity. In this region, in the month of June, American travelers are extremely numerous; it may be said, indeed, that Vevey assumes at this period some of the characteristics of an American watering place. There are sights and sounds which evoke a vision, an echo, of Newport and Saratoga. There is a flitting hither and thither of "stylish" young girls, a rustling of muslin flounces, a rattle of dance music in the morning hours, a sound of high-pitched voices at all times. You receive an impression of these things at the excellent inn of the Trois Couronnes, and are transported in fancy to the Ocean House or to Congress Hall. But at the Trois Couronnes, it must be added, there are other features that are much at variance with these suggestions: neat German waiters, who look like secretaries of legation; Russian princesses sitting in the garden; little Polish boys walking about, held by the hand, with their governors; a view of the snowy crest of the Dent du Midi and the picturesque towers of the Castle of Chillon.

I hardly know whether it was the analogies or the differences that were uppermost in the mind of a young American, who, two or three years ago, sat in the garden of the Trois Couronnes, looking about him, rather idly, at some of the graceful objects I have mentioned. It was a beautiful summer morning, and in whatever fashion the young American looked at things, they must have seemed to him charming. He had come from Geneva the day before, by the little steamer, to see his aunt, who was staying at the hotel—Geneva having been for a long time his place of residence. But his aunt had a headache—his aunt had almost always a headache—and now she was shut up in her room, smelling camphor, so that he was at liberty to wander about. He was some seven-and-twenty years of age; when his friends spoke of him, they usually said that he was at Geneva, "studying." When his enemies spoke of him they said—but, after all, he had no enemies; he was an extremely amiable fellow, and universally liked. What I should say is, simply, that when certain persons spoke of him they affirmed that the reason of his spending so much time at Geneva was that he was extremely devoted to a lady who lived there—a foreign lady—a person older than himself. Very few Americans—indeed I think none—had ever seen this lady, about whom there were some singular stories. But Winterbourne had an old attachment for the little metropolis of Calvinism; he had been put to school there as a boy, and he had afterward gone to college there—circumstances which had led to his forming a great many youthful friendships. Many of these he had kept, and they were a source of great satisfaction to him.

After knocking at his aunt's door and learning that she was indisposed, he had taken a walk about the town, and then he had come in to his breakfast. He had now finished his breakfast; but he was drinking a small cup of coffee, which had been served to him on a little table in the garden by one of the waiters who looked like an *attaché*. At last he finished his coffee and lit a cigarette. Presently a small boy came walking along the path—an urchin of nine or ten. The child, who was diminutive for his years, had an aged expression of countenance, a pale complexion, and sharp little features. He was dressed in knickerbockers, with red stockings, which displayed his poor little spindle-shanks; he also wore a brilliant red cravat. He carried in his hand a long alpenstock, the sharp point of which he thrust into everything that he approached—the flower beds, the garden benches, the trains of the ladies' dresses. In front of Winterbourne he paused, looking at him with a pair of bright, penetrating little eyes.

"Will you give me a lump of sugar?" he asked, in a sharp, hard little voice—a voice immature, and yet, somehow, not young.

Winterbourne glanced at the small table near him, on which his coffee service rested, and saw that several morsels of sugar remained. "Yes, you may take one," he answered; "but I don't think sugar is good for little boys."

This little boy stepped forward and carefully selected three of the coveted fragments, two of which he buried in the pocket of his knickerbockers, depositing the other as promptly in another place. He poked his alpenstock, lance-fashion, into Winterbourne's bench, and tried to crack the lump of sugar with his teeth.

"Oh, blazes; it's har-r-d!" he exclaimed, pronouncing the adjective in a peculiar manner.

Winterbourne had immediately perceived that he might have the honor of claiming him as a fellow countryman. "Take care you don't hurt your teeth," he said, paternally.

"I haven't got any teeth to hurt. They have all come out. I have only got seven teeth. My mother counted them last night, and one came out right afterward. She said she'd slap me if any more came out. I can't help it. It's this old Europe. It's the climate that makes them come out. In America they didn't come out. It's these hotels."

Winterbourne was much amused. "If you eat three lumps of sugar, your mother will certainly slap you," he said.

"She's got to give me some candy, then," rejoined his young interlocutor. "I can't get any candy here—any American candy. American candy's the best candy."

"And are American little boys the best little boys?" asked Winterbourne.

"I don't know. I'm an American boy," said the child.

"I see you are one of the best!" laughed Winterbourne.

"Are you an American man?" pursued this vivacious infant. And then, on Winterbourne's affirmative reply—"American men are the best," he declared.

His companion thanked him for the compliment; and the child, who had now got astride of his alpenstock, stood looking about him, while he attacked a second lump of sugar. Winterbourne wondered if he himself had been like this in his infancy, for he had been brought to Europe at about this age.

"Here comes my sister!" cried the child, in a moment. "She's an American girl."

Winterbourne looked along the path and saw a beautiful young lady advancing. "American girls are the best girls," he said, cheerfully, to his young companion.

"My sister ain't the best!" the child declared. "She's always blowing at me."

"I imagine that is your fault, not hers," said Winterbourne. The young lady meanwhile had drawn near. She was dressed in white muslin, with a hundred frills and flounces, and knots of pale-colored ribbon. She was bareheaded; but she balanced in her hand a large parasol, with a deep border of embroidery; and she was strikingly, admirably pretty. "How pretty they are!" thought Winterbourne, straightening himself in his seat, as if he were prepared to rise.

The young lady paused in front of his bench, near the parapet of the garden, which overlooked the lake. The little boy had now converted his alpenstock into a vaulting pole, by the aid of which he was springing about in the gravel, and kicking it up not a little.

"Randolph," said the young lady, "what *are* you doing?"

"I'm going up the Alps," replied Randolph. "This is the way!" And he gave another little jump, scattering the pebbles about Winterbourne's ears.

"That's the way they come down," said Winterbourne.

"He's an American man!" cried Randolph, in his little hard voice.

The young lady gave no heed to this announcement, but looked straight at her brother. "Well, I guess you had better be quiet," she simply observed.

It seemed to Winterbourne that he had been in a manner presented. He got up and stepped slowly toward the young girl, throwing away his cigarette. "This little boy and I have made acquaintance," he said, with great civility. In Geneva, as he had been perfectly aware, a young man was not at liberty to speak to a young unmarried lady except under certain rarely occurring conditions; but here at Vevey, what conditions could be better than these?—a pretty American girl coming and standing in front of you in a garden. This pretty American girl, however, on hearing Winterbourne's observation, simply glanced at him; she then turned her head and looked over the parapet, at the lake and the opposite mountains. He wondered whether he had gone too far; but he decided that he must advance farther, rather than retreat. While he was thinking of something else to say, the young lady turned to the little boy again.

"I should like to know where you got that pole," she said.

"I bought it!" responded Randolph.

"You don't mean to say you're going to take it to Italy."

"Yes, I am going to take it to Italy!" the child declared.

The young girl glanced over the front of her dress, and smoothed out a knot or two of ribbon. Then she rested her eyes upon the prospect again. "Well, I guess you had better leave it somewhere," she said, after a moment.

"Are you going to Italy?" Winterbourne inquired, in a tone of great respect.

The young lady glanced at him again.

"Yes, sir," she replied. And she said nothing more.

"Are you—a—going over the Simplon?" Winterbourne pursued, a little embarrassed.

"I don't know," she said. "I suppose it's some mountain. Randolph, what mountain are we going over?"

"Going where?" the child demanded.

"To Italy," Winterbourne explained.

"I don't know," said Randolph. "I don't want to go to Italy. I want to go to America."

"Oh, Italy is a beautiful place!" rejoined the young man.

"Can you get candy there?" Randolph loudly inquired.

"I hope not," said his sister. "I guess you have had enough candy, and mother thinks so too."

"I haven't had any for ever so long—for a hundred weeks!" cried the boy, still jumping about.

The young lady inspected her flounces and smoothed her ribbons again; and Winterbourne presently risked an observation upon the beauty of the view. He was ceasing to be embarrassed, for he had begun to perceive that she was not in the least embarrassed herself. There had not been the slightest alteration in her charming complexion; she was evidently neither offended nor fluttered. If she looked another way when he spoke to her, and seemed not particularly to hear him, this was simply her habit, her manner. Yet, as he talked a little more, and pointed out some of the objects of interest in the view, with which she appeared quite unacquainted, she gradually gave him more of the benefit of her glance; and then he saw that this glance was perfectly direct and unshrinking. It was not, however, what would have been called an immodest glance, for the young girl's eyes were singularly honest and fresh. They were wonderfully pretty eyes; and, indeed, Winterbourne had not seen for a long time anything prettier than his fair countrywoman's various features—her complexion, her nose, her ears, her teeth. He had a great relish for feminine beauty; he was addicted to observing and analyzing it; and as regards this young lady's face he made several observations. It was not at all insipid, but it was not exactly expressive; and though it was eminently delicate Winterbourne mentally accused it—very forgivingly—of a want of finish. He thought it very possible that Master Randolph's sister was a coquette; he was sure she had a spirit of her own; but in her bright, sweet, superficial little visage there was no mockery, no irony. Before long it became obvious that she was much disposed toward conversation. She told him that they were going to Rome for the winter—she and her mother and Randolph. She asked him if he was a "real American"; she wouldn't have taken him for one; he seemed more like a German—this was said after a little hesitation, especially when he spoke. Winterbourne, laughing, answered that he had met Germans who spoke like Americans; but that he had not, so far as he remembered, met an American who spoke like a German. Then he asked her if she would not be more comfortable in sitting upon the bench which he had just quitted. She answered that she liked standing up and walking about; but she presently sat down. She told him she was from New York State—"if you know where that is." Winterbourne learned more about her by catching hold of her small, slippery brother and making him stand a few minutes by his side.

"Tell me your name, my boy," he said.

"Randolph C. Miller," said the boy, sharply. "And I'll tell you her name"; and he leveled his alpenstock at his sister.

"You had better wait till you are asked!" said this young lady, calmly.

"I should like very much to know your name," said Winterbourne.

"Her name is Daisy Miller!" cried the child. "But that isn't her real name; that isn't her name on her cards."

"It's a pity you haven't got one of my cards!" said Miss Miller.

"Her real name is Annie P. Miller," the boy went on.

"Ask him *his* name," said his sister, indicating Winterbourne.

But on this point Randolph seemed perfectly indifferent; he continued to supply information with regard to his own family. "My father's name is Ezra B. Miller," he announced. "My father ain't in Europe; my father's in a better place than Europe."

Winterbourne imagined for a moment that this was the manner in which the child had been taught to intimate that Mr. Miller had been removed to the sphere of celestial rewards. But Randolph immediately added, "My father's in Schenectady. He's got a big business. My father's rich, you bet."

"Well!" ejaculated Miss Miller, lowering her parasol and looking at the embroidered border. Winterbourne presently released the child, who departed, dragging his alpenstock along the path. "He doesn't like Europe," said the young girl. "He wants to go back."

"To Schenectady, you mean?"

"Yes; he wants to go right home. He hasn't got any boys here. There is one boy here, but he always goes round with a teacher; they won't let him play."

"And your brother hasn't any teacher?" Winterbourne inquired.

"Mother thought of getting him one, to travel round with us. There was a lady told her of a very good teacher; an American lady—perhaps you know her—Mrs. Sanders. I think she came from Boston. She told her of this teacher, and we thought of getting him to travel round with us. But Randolph said he didn't want a teacher travelling round with us. He said he wouldn't have lessons when he was in the cars. And we *are* in the cars about half the time. There was an English lady we met in the cars—I think her name was Miss Featherstone; perhaps you know her. She wanted to know why I didn't give Randolph lessons—give him "instruction," she called it. I guess he could give me more instruction than I could give him. He's very smart."

"Yes," said Winterbourne; "he seems very smart."

"Mother's going to get a teacher for him as soon as we get to Italy. Can you get good teachers in Italy?"

"Very good, I should think," said Winterbourne.

"Or else she's going to find some school. He ought to learn some more. He's only nine. He's going to college." And in this way Miss Miller continued to converse upon the affairs of her family, and upon other topics. She sat there with her extremely pretty hands, ornamented with very brilliant rings, folded in her lap, and with her pretty eyes now resting upon those of Winterbourne, now wandering over the garden, the people who passed by, and the beautiful view. She talked to Winterbourne as if she had known him a long time. He found it very pleasant. It was many years since he had heard a young girl talk so much. It might have been said of this unknown young lady, who had come and sat down beside him upon a bench, that she chattered. She was very quiet, she sat in a charming tranquil attitude; but her lips and her eyes were constantly moving. She had a soft, slender, agreeable voice, and her tone was decidedly sociable. She gave Winterbourne a history of her movements and intentions, and those of her mother and brother, in Europe, and enumerated, in particular, the various hotels at which they had stopped. "That English lady in the cars," she said—"Miss Featherstone—asked me if we didn't all live in hotels in America. I told her I had never been in so many hotels in my life as since

I came to Europe. I have never seen so many—it's nothing but hotels." But Miss Miller did not make this remark with a querulous accent; she appeared to be in the best humor with everything. She declared that the hotels were very good, when once you got used to their ways, and that Europe was perfectly sweet. She was not disappointed—not a bit. Perhaps it was because she had heard so much about it before. She had ever so many intimate friends that had been there ever so many times. And then she had had ever so many dresses and things from Paris. Whenever she put on a Paris dress she felt as if she were in Europe.

"It was a kind of a wishing cap," said Winterbourne.

"Yes," said Miss Miller, without examining this analogy; "it always made me wish I was here. But I needn't have done that for dresses. I am sure they send all the pretty ones to America; you see the most frightful things here. The only thing I don't like," she proceeded, "is the society. There isn't any society, or, if there is, I don't know where it keeps itself. Do you? I suppose there is some society some-where, but I haven't seen anything of it. I'm very fond of society, and I have always had a great deal of it. I don't mean only in Schenectady, but in New York. I used to go to New York every winter. In New York I had lots of society. Last winter I had sev-enteen dinners given me; and three of them were by gentlemen," added Daisy Miller. "I have more friends in New York than in Schenectady—more gentlemen friends; and more young lady friends too," she resumed in a moment. She paused again for an instant; she was looking at Winterbourne with all her prettiness in her lively eyes and in her light, slightly monotonous smile. "I have always had," she said, "a great deal of gentlemen's society."

Poor Winterbourne was amused, perplexed, and decidedly charmed. He had never yet heard a young girl express herself in just this fashion; never, at least, save in cases where to say such things seemed a kind of demonstrative evidence of a cer-tain laxity of deportment. And yet was he to accuse Miss Daisy Miller of actual or potential *inconduite*, as they said at Geneva? He felt that he had lived at Geneva so long that he had lost a good deal; he had become dishabituated to the American tone. Never, indeed, since he had grown old enough to appreciate things, had he encountered a young American girl of so pronounced a type as this. Certainly she was very charming, but how deucedly sociable! Was she simply a pretty girl from New York State—were they all like that, the pretty girls who had a good deal of gen-tlemen's society? Or was she also a designing, an audacious, an unscrupulous young person? Winterbourne had lost his instinct in this matter, and his reason could not help him. Miss Daisy Miller looked extremely innocent. Some people had told him that, after all, American girls were exceedingly innocent, and others had told him that, after all, they were not. He was inclined to think Miss Daisy Miller was a flirt—a pretty American flirt. He had never, as yet, had any relations with young ladies of this category. He had known, here in Europe, two or three women—persons older than Miss Daisy Miller, and provided, for respectability's sake, with husbands—who were great coquettes—dangerous, terrible women, with whom one's relations were liable to take a serious turn. But this young girl was not a coquette in that sense; she was very unsophisticated; she was only a pretty American flirt. Winterbourne was almost grateful for having found the formula that applied to Miss Daisy Miller. He leaned back in his seat; he remarked to himself that she had the most charming nose he had ever seen; he wondered what were the regular conditions and limitations of one's intercourse with a pretty American flirt. It presently became apparent that he was on the way to learn.

"Have you been to that old castle?" asked the young girl, pointing with her parasol to the far gleaming walls of the Château de Chillon.

"Yes, formerly, more than once," said Winterbourne. "You too, I suppose, have seen it?"

"No, we haven't been there. I want to go there dreadfully. Of course I mean to go there. I wouldn't go away from here without having seen that old castle."

"It's a very pretty excursion," said Winterbourne, "and very easy to make. You can drive, you know, or you can go by the little steamer."

"You can go in the cars," said Miss Miller.

"Yes, you can go in the cars," Winterbourne assented.

"Our courier says they take you right up to the castle," the young girl continued. "We were going last week, but my mother gave out. She suffers dreadfully from dyspepsia. She said she couldn't go. Randolph wouldn't go either; he says he doesn't think much of old castles. But I guess we'll go this week, if we can get Randolph."

"Your brother is not interested in ancient monuments?" Winterbourne inquired, smiling.

"He says he don't care much about old castles. He's only nine. He wants to stay at the hotel. Mother's afraid to leave him alone, and the courier won't stay with him; so we haven't been to many places. But it will be too bad if we don't go up there." And Miss Miller pointed again at the Château de Chillon.

"I should think it might be arranged," said Winterbourne. "Couldn't you get someone to stay—for the afternoon—with Randolph?"

Miss Miller looked at him a moment, and then, very placidly—"I wish *you* would stay with him!" she said.

Winterbourne hesitated a moment. "I would much rather go to Chillon with you."

"With me?" asked the young girl, with the same placidity.

She didn't rise, blushing, as a young girl at Geneva would have done, and yet Winterbourne, conscious that he had been very bold, thought it possible she was offended. "With your mother," he answered very respectfully.

But it seemed that both his audacity and his respect were lost upon Miss Daisy Miller. "I guess my mother won't go, after all," she said. "She don't like to ride round in the afternoon. But did you really mean what you said just now; that you would like to go up there?"

"Most earnestly," Winterbourne declared.

"Then we may arrange it. If mother will stay with Randolph, I guess Eugenio will."

"Eugenio?" the young man inquired.

"Eugenio's our courier. He doesn't like to stay with Randolph; he's the most fastidious man I ever saw. But he's a splendid courier. I guess he'll stay at home with Randolph if mother does, and then we can go to the castle."

Winterbourne reflected for an instant as lucidly as possible—"we" could only mean Miss Daisy Miller and himself. This program seemed almost too agreeable for credence; he felt as if he ought to kiss the young lady's hand. Possibly he would have done so—and quite spoiled the project, but at this moment another person— presumably Eugenio—appeared. A tall, handsome man, with superb whiskers, wearing a velvet morning coat and a brilliant watch chain, approached Miss Miller, looking sharply at her companion. "Oh, Eugenio!" said Miss Miller, with the friendliest accent.

Eugenio had looked at Winterbourne from head to foot; he now bowed gravely to the young lady. "I have the honor to inform mademoiselle that luncheon is upon the table."

Miss Miller slowly rose. "See here, Eugenio," she said. "I'm going to that old castle, anyway."

"To the Château de Chillon, mademoiselle?" the courier inquired. "Mademoiselle has made arrangements?" he added, in a tone which struck Winterbourne as very impertinent.

Eugenio's tone apparently threw, even to Miss Miller's own apprehension, a slightly ironical light upon the young girl's situation. She turned to Winterbourne, blushing a little—a very little. "You won't back out?" she said.

"I shall not be happy till we go!" he protested.

"And you are staying in this hotel?" she went on. "And you are really an American?"

The courier stood looking at Winterbourne, offensively. The young man, at least, thought his manner of looking an offence to Miss Miller; it conveyed an imputation that she "picked up" acquaintances. "I shall have the honor of presenting to you a person who will tell you all about me," he said smiling, and referring to his aunt.

"Oh, well, we'll go someday," said Miss Miller. And she gave him a smile and turned away. She put up her parasol and walked back to the inn beside Eugenio. Winterbourne stood looking after her and as she moved away, drawing her muslin furbelows over the gravel, said to himself that she had the *tournure* of a princess.

II

He had, however, engaged to do more than proved feasible, in promising to present his aunt, Mrs. Costello, to Miss Daisy Miller. As soon as the former lady had got better of her headache he waited upon her in her apartment and, after the proper inquiries in regard to her health, he asked her if she had observed, in the hotel, an American family—a mamma, a daughter, and a little boy.

"And a courier?" said Mrs. Costello. "Oh, yes, I have observed them. Seen them—heard them—and kept out of their way." Mrs. Costello was a widow with a fortune; a person of much distinction, who frequently intimated that, if she were not so dreadfully liable to sick-headaches, she would probably have left a deeper impress upon her time. She had a long pale face, a high nose, and a great deal of very striking white hair, which she wore in large puffs and *rouleaux* over the top of her head. She had two sons married in New York, and another who was now in Europe. This young man was amusing himself at Homburg, and, though he was on his travels, was rarely perceived to visit any particular city at the moment selected by his mother for her own appearance there. Her nephew, who had come up to Vevey expressly to see her, was therefore more attentive than those who, as she said, were nearer to her. He had imbibed at Geneva the idea that one must always be attentive to one's aunt. Mrs. Costello had not seen him for many years, and she was greatly pleased with him, manifesting her approbation by initiating him into many of the secrets of that social sway which, as she gave him to understand, she exerted in the American capital. She admitted that she was very exclusive, but, if he were acquainted with New York, he would see that one had to be. And her picture of the minutely hierarchical constitution of the society of that city, which she presented to him in many different lights, was, to Winterbourne's imagination, almost oppressively striking.

He immediately perceived, from her tone, that Miss Daisy Miller's place in the social scale was low. "I am afraid you don't approve of them," he said.

"They are very common," Mrs. Costello declared. "They are the sort of Americans that one does one's duty by not—not accepting."

"Ah, you don't accept them?" said the young man.

"I can't, my dear Frederick. I would if I could, but I can't."

"The young girl is very pretty," said Winterbourne, in a moment.

"Of course she's pretty. But she is very common."

"I see what you mean, of course," said Winterbourne, after another pause.

"She has that charming look that they all have," his aunt resumed. "I can't think where they pick it up; and she dresses in perfection—no, you don't know how well she dresses. I can't think where they get their taste."

"But, my dear aunt, she is not, after all, a Comanche savage."

"She is a young lady," said Mrs. Costello, "who has an intimacy with her mamma's courier."

"An intimacy with the courier?" the young man demanded.

"Oh, the mother is just as bad! They treat the courier like a familiar friend—like a gentleman. I shouldn't wonder if he dines with them. Very likely they have never seen a man with such good manners, such fine clothes, so like a gentleman. He probably corresponds to the young lady's idea of a Count. He sits with them in the garden, in the evening. I think he smokes."

Winterbourne listened with interest to these disclosures; they helped him to make up his mind about Miss Daisy. Evidently she was rather wild. "Well," he said, "I am not a courier, and yet she was very charming to me."

"You had better have said at first," said Mrs. Costello with dignity, "that you had made her acquaintance."

"We simply met in the garden, and we talked a bit."

"*Tout bonnement!* And pray what did you say?"

"I said I should take the liberty of introducing her to my admirable aunt."

"I am much obliged to you."

"It was to guarantee my respectability," said Winterbourne.

"And pray who is to guarantee hers?"

"Ah, you are cruel!" said the young man. "She's a very nice girl."

"You don't say that as if you believed it," Mrs. Costello observed.

"She is completely uncultivated," Winterbourne went on. "But she is wonderfully pretty, and, in short, she is very nice. To prove that I believe it, I am going to take her to the Château de Chillon."

"You two are going off there together? I should say it proved just the contrary. How long had you known her, may I ask, when this interesting project was formed? You haven't been twenty-four hours in the house."

"I had known her half-an-hour!" said Winterbourne, smiling.

"Dear me!" cried Mrs. Costello. "What a dreadful girl!"

Her nephew was silent for some moments.

"You really think, then," he began, earnestly, and with a desire for trustworthy information—"you really think that—" But he paused again.

"Think what, sir?" said his aunt.

"That she is the sort of young lady who expects a man—sooner or later—to carry her off?"

"I haven't the least idea what such young ladies expect a man to do. But I really think that you had better not meddle with little American girls that are uncultivated, as you call them. You have lived too long out of the country. You will be sure to make some great mistake. You are too innocent."

"My dear aunt, I am not so innocent," said Winterbourne, smiling and curling his moustache.

"You are too guilty, then!"

Winterbourne continued to curl his moustache, meditatively. "You won't let the poor girl know you then?" he asked at last.

"Is it literally true that she is going to the Château de Chillon with you?"

"I think that she fully intends it."

"Then, my dear Frederick," said Mrs. Costello, "I must decline the honor of her acquaintance. I am an old woman, but I am not too old—thank Heaven—to be shocked!"

"But don't they all do these things—the young girls in America?" Winterbourne inquired.

Mrs. Costello stared a moment. "I should like to see my granddaughters do them!" she declared, grimly.

This seemed to throw some light upon the matter, for Winterbourne remembered to have heard that his pretty cousins in New York were "tremendous flirts." If, therefore, Miss Daisy Miller exceeded the liberal license allowed to these young ladies, it was probable that anything might be expected of her. Winterbourne was impatient to see her again, and he was vexed with himself that, by instinct, he should not appreciate her justly.

Though he was impatient to see her, he hardly knew what he should say to her about his aunt's refusal to become acquainted with her, but he discovered, promptly enough, that with Miss Daisy Miller there was no great need of walking on tiptoe. He found her that evening in the garden, wandering about in the warm starlight, like an indolent sylph, and swinging to and fro the largest fan he had ever beheld. It was ten o'clock. He had dined with his aunt, had been sitting with her since dinner, and had just taken leave of her till the morrow. Miss Daisy Miller seemed very glad to see him; she declared it was the longest evening she had ever passed.

"Have you been all alone?" he asked.

"I have been walking round with mother. But mother gets tired walking round," she answered.

"Has she gone to bed?"

"No, she doesn't like to go to bed," said the young girl. "She doesn't sleep—not three hours. She says she doesn't know how she lives. She's dreadfully nervous. I guess she sleeps more than she thinks. She's gone somewhere after Randolph; she wants to try to get him to go to bed. He doesn't like to go to bed."

"Let us hope she will persuade him," observed Winterbourne.

"She will talk to him all she can, but he doesn't like her to talk to him," said Miss Daisy, opening her fan. "She's going to try to get Eugenio to talk to him. But he isn't afraid of Eugenio. Eugenio's a splendid courier, but he can't make much impression on Randolph! I don't believe he'll go to bed before eleven." It appeared that Randolph's vigil was in fact triumphantly prolonged, for Winterbourne strolled about with the young girl for some time without meeting her mother. "I have been looking round for that lady you want to introduce me to," his companion resumed. "She's your aunt." Then, on Winterbourne's admitting the fact, and expressing some curiosity as to how she had learned it, she said she had heard all about Mrs. Costello from the chambermaid. She was very quiet and very *comme il faut;* she wore white puffs; she spoke to no one, and she never dined at the *table d'hôte*. Every two days she had a headache. "I think that's a lovely description, headache and all!" said Miss Daisy, chattering along in her thin, gay voice. "I want to know her ever so much. I know just what *your* aunt would be; I know I should like her. She would be very exclusive. I like a lady to be exclusive; I'm dying to be exclusive myself. Well, we *are* exclusive, mother and I. We don't speak to everyone—or they don't speak to us. I suppose it's about the same thing. Anyway, I shall be ever so glad to know your aunt."

Winterbourne was embarrassed. "She would be most happy," he said; "but I am afraid those headaches will interfere."

The young girl looked at him through the dusk. "But I suppose she doesn't have a headache every day," she said, sympathetically.

Winterbourne was silent a moment. "She tells me she does," he answered at last—not knowing what to say.

Miss Daisy Miller stopped and stood looking at him. Her prettiness was still visible in the darkness; she was opening and closing her enormous fan. "She doesn't want to know me!" she said, suddenly. "Why don't you say so? You needn't be afraid. I'm not afraid!" And she gave a little laugh.

Winterbourne fancied there was a tremor in her voice; he was touched, shocked, mortified by it. "My dear young lady," he protested, "she knows no one. It's her wretched health."

The young girl walked on a few steps, laughing still. "You needn't be afraid," she repeated. "Why should she want to know me?" Then she paused again; she was close to the parapet of the garden, and in front of her was the starlit lake. There was a vague sheen upon its surface, and in the distance were dimly seen mountain forms. Daisy Miller looked out upon the mysterious prospect, and then she gave another little laugh. "Gracious! she *is* exclusive!" she said. Winterbourne wondered whether she was seriously wounded, and for a moment almost wished that her sense of injury might be such as to make it becoming in him to attempt to reassure and comfort her.

He had a pleasant sense that she would be very approachable for consolatory purposes. He felt then, for the instant, quite ready to sacrifice his aunt, conversationally; to admit that she was a proud, rude woman, and to declare that they needn't mind her. But before he had time to commit himself to this perilous mixture of gallantry and impiety, the young lady, resuming her walk, gave an exclamation in quite another tone. "Well, here's mother! I guess she hasn't got Randolph to go to bed." The figure of a lady appeared, at a distance, very indistinct in the darkness, and advancing with a slow and wavering movement. Suddenly it seemed to pause.

"Are you sure it is your mother? Can you distinguish her in this thick dusk?" Winterbourne asked.

"Well!" cried Miss Daisy Miller, with a laugh, "I guess I know my own mother. And when she has got on my shawl, too! She is always wearing my things."

The lady in question, ceasing to advance, hovered vaguely about the spot at which she had checked her steps.

"I am afraid your mother doesn't see you," said Winterbourne. "Or perhaps," he added—thinking, with Miss Miller, the joke permissible—"perhaps she feels guilty about your shawl."

"Oh, it's a fearful old thing!" the young girl replied, serenely. "I told her she could wear it. She won't come here, because she sees you."

"Ah, then," said Winterbourne, "I had better leave you."

"Oh no; come on!" urged Miss Daisy Miller.

"I'm afraid your mother doesn't approve of my walking with you."

Miss Miller gave him a serious glance. "It isn't for me; it's for you—that is, it's for *her*. Well, I don't know who it's for! But mother doesn't like any of my gentlemen friends. She's right down timid. She always makes a fuss if I introduce a gentleman. But I *do* introduce them—almost always. If I didn't introduce my gentlemen friends to mother," the young girl added, in her little soft, flat monotone, "I shouldn't think I was natural."

"To introduce me," said Winterbourne, "you must know my name." And he proceeded to pronounce it.

"Oh, dear; I can't say all that!" said his companion, with a laugh. But by this time they had come up to Mrs. Miller, who, as they drew near, walked to the parapet of the garden and leaned upon it, looking intently at the lake and turning her back upon them. "Mother!" said the young girl, in a tone of decision. Upon this the elder lady turned round. "Mr. Winterbourne," said Miss Daisy Miller, introducing the young man very frankly and prettily. "Common" she was, as Mrs. Costello had pronounced her; yet it was a wonder to Winterbourne that, with her commonness, she had a singularly delicate grace.

Her mother was a small, spare, light person, with a wandering eye, a very exiguous nose, and a large forehead, decorated with a certain amount of thin, much-frizzled hair. Like her daughter, Mrs. Miller was dressed with extreme elegance; she had enormous diamonds in her ears. So far as Winterbourne could observe, she gave him no greeting—she certainly was not looking at him. Daisy was near her, pulling her shawl straight. "What are you doing, poking round here?" this young lady inquired, but by no means with that harshness of accent which her choice of words may imply.

"I don't know," said her mother, turning toward the lake again.

"I shouldn't think you'd want that shawl!" Daisy exclaimed.

"Well—I do!" her mother answered, with a little laugh.

"Did you get Randolph to go to bed?" asked the young girl.

"No, I couldn't induce him," said Mrs. Miller, very gently. "He wants to talk to the waiter. He likes to talk to that waiter."

"I was telling Mr. Winterbourne," the young girl went on, and to the young man's ear her tone might have indicated that she had been uttering his name all her life.

"Oh, yes!" said Winterbourne; "I have the pleasure of knowing your son."

Randolph's mamma was silent; she turned her attention to the lake. But at last she spoke. "Well, I don't see how he lives!"

"Anyhow, it isn't so bad as it was at Dover," said Daisy Miller.

"And what occurred at Dover?" Winterbourne asked.

"He wouldn't go to bed at all. I guess he sat up all night—in the public parlor. He wasn't in bed at twelve o'clock; I know that."

"It was half-past twelve," declared Mrs. Miller, with mild emphasis.

"Does he sleep much during the day?" Winterbourne demanded.

"I guess he doesn't sleep much," Daisy rejoined.

"I wish he would!" said her mother. "It seems as if he couldn't."

"I think he's real tiresome," Daisy pursued.

Then, for some moments, there was silence. "Well, Daisy Miller," said the elder lady, presently, "I shouldn't think you'd want to talk against your own brother!"

"Well, he *is* tiresome, mother," said Daisy, quite without the asperity of a retort.

"He's only nine," urged Mrs. Miller.

"Well, he wouldn't go to that castle," said the young girl. "I'm going there with Mr. Winterbourne."

To this announcement, very placidly made, Daisy's mamma offered no response. Winterbourne took for granted that she deeply disapproved of the projected excursion, but he said to himself that she was a simple, easily-managed person, and that a few deferential protestations would take the edge from her displeasure. "Yes," he began; "your daughter has kindly allowed me the honor of being her guide."

Mrs. Miller's wandering eyes attached themselves, with a sort of appealing air, to Daisy, who, however, strolled a few steps farther, gently humming to herself. "I presume you will go in the cars," said her mother.

"Yes; or in the boat," said Winterbourne.

"Well, of course, I don't know," Mrs. Miller rejoined. "I have never been to that castle."

"It is a pity you shouldn't go," said Winterbourne, beginning to feel reassured as to her opposition. And yet he was quite prepared to find that, as a matter of course, she meant to accompany her daughter.

"We've been thinking ever so much about going," she pursued; "but it seems as if we couldn't. Of course Daisy—she wants to go round. But there's a lady here—I don't know her name—she says she shouldn't think we'd want to go to see castles *here;* she should think we'd want to wait till we got to Italy. It seems as if there would be so many there," continued Mrs. Miller, with an air of increasing confidence. "Of course, we only want to see the principal ones. We visited several in England," she presently added.

"Ah, yes! in England there are beautiful castles," said Winterbourne. "But Chillon, here, is very well worth seeing."

"Well, if Daisy feels up to it—," said Mrs. Miller, in a tone impregnated with a sense of the magnitude of the enterprise. "It seems as if there was nothing she wouldn't undertake."

"Oh, I think she'll enjoy it!" Winterbourne declared. And he desired more and more to make it a certainty that he was to have the privilege of a *tête-à-tête* with the young lady, who was still strolling along in front of them, softly vocalizing. "You are not disposed, madam," he inquired, "to undertake it yourself?"

Daisy's mother looked at him, an instant, askance, and then walked forward in silence. Then—"I guess she had better go alone," she said, simply.

Winterbourne observed to himself that this was a very different type of maternity from that of the vigilant matrons who massed themselves in the forefront of social intercourse in the dark old city at the other end of the lake. But his meditations were interrupted by hearing his name very distinctly pronounced by Mrs. Miller's unprotected daughter.

"Mr. Winterbourne!" murmured Daisy.

"Mademoiselle!" said the young man.

"Don't you want to take me out in a boat?"

"At present?" he asked.

"Of course!" said Daisy.

"Well, Annie Miller!" exclaimed her mother.

"I beg you, madam, to let her go," said Winterbourne, ardently, for he had never yet enjoyed the sensation of guiding through the summer starlight a skiff freighted with a fresh and beautiful young girl.

"I shouldn't think she'd want to," said her mother. "I should think she'd rather go indoors."

"I'm sure Mr. Winterbourne wants to take me," Daisy declared. "He's so awfully devoted!"

"I will row you over to Chillon, in the starlight."

"I don't believe it!" said Daisy.

"Well!" ejaculated the elderly lady again.

"You haven't spoken to me for half-an-hour," her daughter went on.

"I have been having some very pleasant conversation with your mother," said Winterbourne.

"Well, I want you to take me out in a boat!" Daisy repeated. They had all stopped, and she had turned round and was looking at Winterbourne. Her face wore a charming smile, her pretty eyes were gleaming, she was swinging her great fan about. No, it's impossible to be prettier than that, thought Winterbourne.

"There are half-a-dozen boats moored at that landing place," he said, pointing to certain steps which descended from the garden to the lake. "If you will do me the honor to accept my arm, we will go and select one of them."

Daisy stood there smiling; she threw back her head and gave a little light laugh. "I like a gentleman to be formal!" she declared.

"I assure you it's a formal offer."

"I was bound I would make you say something," Daisy went on.

"You see it's not very difficult," said Winterbourne. "But I am afraid you are chaffing me."

"I think not, sir," remarked Mrs. Miller, very gently.

"Do, then, let me give you a row," he said to the young girl.

"It's quite lovely, the way you say that!" cried Daisy.

"It will be still more lovely to do it."

"Yes, it would be lovely!" said Daisy. But she made no movement to accompany him; she only stood there laughing.

"I should think you had better find out what time it is," interposed her mother.

"It is eleven o'clock, madam," said a voice, with a foreign accent, out of the neighboring darkness, and Winterbourne, turning, perceived the florid personage who was in attendance upon the two ladies. He had apparently just approached.

"Oh, Eugenio," said Daisy, "I am going out in a boat!"

Eugenio bowed. "At eleven o'clock, mademoiselle?"

"I am going with Mr. Winterbourne. This very minute."

"Do tell her she can't," said Mrs. Miller to the courier.

"I think you had better not go out in a boat, mademoiselle," Eugenio declared.

Winterbourne wished to heaven this pretty girl were not so familiar with her courier, but he said nothing.

"I suppose you don't think it's proper!" Daisy exclaimed. "Eugenio doesn't think anything's proper."

"I am at your service," said Winterbourne.

"Does mademoiselle propose to go alone?" asked Eugenio of Mrs. Miller.

"Oh, no, with this gentleman!" answered Daisy's mamma.

The courier looked for a moment at Winterbourne—the latter thought he was smiling—and then, solemnly, with a bow, "As mademoiselle pleases!" he said.

"Oh, I hoped you would make a fuss!" said Daisy. "I don't care to go now."

"I myself shall make a fuss if you don't go," said Winterbourne.

"That's all I want—a little fuss!" And the young girl began to laugh again.

"Mr. Randolph has gone to bed!" the courier announced, frigidly.

"Oh, Daisy, now we can go!" said Mrs. Miller.

Daisy turned away from Winterbourne, looking at him, smiling and fanning herself. "Good night," she said; "I hope you are disappointed, or disgusted, or something!"

He looked at her, taking the hand she offered him. "I am puzzled," he answered.

"Well, I hope it won't keep you awake!" she said, very smartly, and, under the escort of the privileged Eugenio, the two ladies passed toward the house.

Winterbourne stood looking after them; he was indeed puzzled. He lingered beside the lake for a quarter of an hour, turning over the mystery of the young girl's sudden familiarities and caprices. But the only very definite conclusion he came to was that he should enjoy deucedly "going off" with her somewhere.

Two days afterward he went off with her to the Castle of Chillon. He waited for her in the large hall of the hotel, where the couriers, the servants, the foreign tourists were lounging about and staring. It was not the place he would have chosen, but she had appointed it. She came tripping downstairs, buttoning her long gloves, squeezing her folded parasol against her pretty figure, dressed in the perfection of a soberly elegant traveling costume. Winterbourne was a man of imagination and, as our ancestors used to say, of sensibility; as he looked at her dress and, on the great staircase, her little rapid, confiding step, he felt as if there were something romantic going forward. He could have believed he was going to elope with her. He passed out with her among all the idle people that were assembled there; they were all looking at her very hard; she had begun to chatter as soon as she joined him. Winterbourne's preference had been that they should be conveyed to Chillon in a carriage, but she expressed a lively wish to go in the little steamer; she declared that she had a passion for steamboats. There was always such a lovely breeze upon the water, and you saw such lots of people. The sail was not long, but Winterbourne's companion found time to say a great many things. To the young man himself their little excursion was so much of an escapade—an adventure— that, even allowing for her habitual sense of freedom, he had some expectation of seeing her regard it in the same way. But it must be confessed that, in this particular, he was disappointed. Daisy Miller was extremely animated, she was in charming spirits, but she was apparently not at all excited; she was not fluttered; she avoided neither his eyes nor those of anyone else; she blushed neither when she looked at him nor when she saw that people were looking at her. People continued to look at her a great deal, and Winterbourne took much satisfaction in his pretty companion's distinguished air. He had been a little afraid that she would talk loud, laugh overmuch, and even, perhaps, desire to move about the boat a good deal. But he quite forgot his fears; he sat smiling, with his eyes upon her face, while, without moving from her place, she delivered herself of a great number of original reflections. It was the most charming garrulity he had ever heard. He had assented to the idea that she was "common," but was she so, after all, or was he simply getting used to her commonness? Her conversation was chiefly of what metaphysicians term the objective cast, but every now and then it took a subjective turn.

"What on *earth* are you so grave about?" she suddenly demanded, fixing her agreeable eyes upon Winterbourne's.

"Am I grave?" he asked. "I had an idea I was grinning from ear to ear."

"You look as if you were taking me to a funeral. If that's a grin, your ears are very near together."

"Should you like me to dance a hornpipe on the deck?"

"Pray do, and I'll carry round your hat. It will pay the expenses of our journey."

"I never was better pleased in my life," murmured Winterbourne.

She looked at him a moment, and then burst into a little laugh. "I like to make you say those things! You're a queer mixture!"

In the castle, after they had landed, the subjective element decidedly prevailed. Daisy tripped about the vaulted chambers, rustled her skirts in the corkscrew staircases, flirted back with a pretty little cry and a shudder from the edge of the *oubliettes,* and turned a singularly well-shaped ear to everything Winterbourne told her about the place. But he saw that she cared very little for feudal antiquities, and that the dusky traditions of Chillon made but a slight impression upon her. They had the good fortune to have been able to walk about without other companionship than that of the custodian, and Winterbourne arranged with this functionary that they should not be hurried—that they should linger and pause wherever they chose. The custodian interpreted the bargain generously—Winterbourne, on his side, had been generous—and ended by leaving them quite to themselves. Miss Miller's observations were not remarkable for logical consistency; for anything she wanted to say she was sure to find a pretext. She found a great many pretexts in the rugged embrasures of Chillon for asking Winterbourne sudden questions about himself—his family, his previous history, his tastes, his habits, his intentions—and for supplying information upon corresponding points in her own personality. Of her own tastes, habits and intentions Miss Miller was prepared to give the most definite, and indeed the most favorable, account.

"Well, I hope you know enough!" she said to her companion, after he had told her the history of the unhappy Bonivard. "I never saw a man that knew so much!" The history of Bonivard had evidently, as they say, gone into one ear and out of the other. But Daisy went on to say that she wished Winterbourne would travel with them and "go round" with them; they might know something, in that case. "Don't you want to come and teach Randolph?" she asked. Winterbourne said that nothing could possibly please him so much, but that he had unfortunately other occupations. "Other occupations? I don't believe it!" said Miss Daisy. "What do you mean? You are not in business." The young man admitted that he was not in business, but he had engagements which, even within a day or two, would force him to go back to Geneva. "Oh, bother!" she said, "I don't believe it!" and she began to talk about something else. But a few moments later, when he was pointing out to her the pretty design of an antique fireplace, she broke out irrelevantly, "You don't mean to say you are going back to Geneva?"

"It is a melancholy fact that I shall have to return to Geneva tomorrow."

"Well, Mr. Winterbourne," said Daisy; "I think you're horrid!"

"Oh, don't say such dreadful things!" said Winterbourne—"just at the last."

"The last!" cried the young girl; "I call it the first. I have half a mind to leave you here and go straight back to the hotel alone." And for the next ten minutes she did nothing but call him horrid. Poor Winterbourne was fairly bewildered; no young lady had as yet done him the honor to be so agitated by the announcement of his movements. His companion, after this, ceased to pay any attention to the curiosities of Chillon or the beauties of the lake; she opened fire upon the mysterious charmer in Geneva, whom she appeared to have instantly taken it for granted that he was hurrying back to see. How did Miss Daisy Miller know that there was a charmer in Geneva? Winterbourne, who denied the existence of such a person, was quite unable to discover, and he was divided between amazement at the rapidity of her induction and amusement at the frankness of her *persiflage*. She seemed to him, in all this, an extraordinary mixture of innocence and crudity. "Does she never allow you more than three days at a time?" asked Daisy, ironically. "Doesn't she give you a vacation in summer? There's no one so hard worked but they can get leave to go off somewhere at this season. I suppose, if you stay another day, she'll come after you in the boat. Do wait over till Friday, and I will go down to the landing to see her arrive!" Winterbourne began to think he had been wrong to feel disappointed in the temper in which the young lady had embarked. If he had missed the personal accent, the personal accent was now making its appearance. It sounded very distinctly, at last, in her telling him she would stop "teasing" him if he would promise her solemnly to come down to Rome in the winter.

"That's not a difficult promise to make," said Winterbourne. "My aunt has taken an apartment in Rome for the winter, and has already asked me to come and see her."

"I don't want you to come for your aunt," said Daisy; "I want you to come for me." And this was the only allusion that the young man was ever to hear her make to his invidious kinswoman. He declared that, at any rate, he would certainly come. After this Daisy stopped teasing. Winterbourne took a carriage, and they drove back to Vevey in the dusk; the young girl was very quiet.

In the evening Winterbourne mentioned to Mrs. Costello that he had spent the afternoon at Chillon, with Miss Daisy Miller.

"The Americans—of the courier?" asked this lady.

"Ah, happily," said Winterbourne, "the courier stayed at home."

"She went with you all alone?"

"All alone."

Mrs. Costello sniffed a little at her smelling bottle. "And that," she exclaimed, "is the young person you wanted me to know!"

III

Winterbourne, who had returned to Geneva the day after his excursion to Chillon, went to Rome towards the end of January. His aunt had been established there for several weeks, and he had received a couple of letters from her. "Those people you were so devoted to last summer at Vevey have turned up here, courier and all," she wrote. "They seem to have made several acquaintances, but the courier continues to be the most *intime*. The young lady, however, is also very intimate with some third-rate Italians, with whom she rackets about in a way that makes much talk. Bring me that pretty novel of Cherbuliez's—*Paule Méré*—and don't come later than the 23rd."

In the natural course of events, Winterbourne, on arriving in Rome, would presently have ascertained Mrs. Miller's address at the American banker's and have gone to pay his compliments to Miss Daisy. "After what happened at Vevey I certainly think I may call upon them," he said to Mrs. Costello.

"If, after what happens—at Vevey and everywhere—you desire to keep up the acquaintance, you are very welcome. Of course a man may know everyone. Men are welcome to the privilege!"

"Pray what is it that happens—here, for instance?" Winterbourne demanded.

"The girl goes about alone with her foreigners. As to what happens farther, you must apply elsewhere for information. She has picked up half-a-dozen of the regular Roman fortune hunters, and she takes them about to people's houses. When she comes to a party she brings with her a gentleman with a good deal of manner and a wonderful moustache."

"And where is the mother?"

"I haven't the least idea. They are very dreadful people."

Winterbourne meditated a moment. "They are very ignorant—very innocent only. Depend upon it they are not bad."

"They are hopelessly vulgar," said Mrs. Costello. "Whether or not being hopelessly vulgar is being 'bad' is a question for the metaphysicians. They are bad enough to dislike, at any rate, and for this short life that is quite enough."

The news that Daisy Miller was surrounded by half-a-dozen wonderful moustaches checked Winterbourne's impulse to go straightway to see her. He had perhaps not definitely flattered himself that he had made an ineffaceable impression upon her heart, but he was annoyed at hearing of a state of affairs so little in harmony with an image that had lately flitted in and out of his own meditations; the image of a very pretty girl looking out of an old Roman window and asking herself urgently when Mr. Winterbourne would arrive. If, however, he determined to wait a little before reminding Miss Miller of his claims to her consideration, he went very soon to call upon two or three other friends. One of these friends was an American lady who had spent several winters at Geneva, where she had placed her children at school. She was a very accomplished woman and she lived in the Via Gregoriana. Winterbourne found her in a little crimson drawing room, on a third floor; the room was filled with southern sunshine. He had not been there ten minutes when the servant came in, announcing "Madame Mila!" This announcement was presently followed by the entrance of little Randolph Miller, who stopped in the middle of the room and stood staring at Winterbourne. An instant later his pretty sister crossed the threshold and then, after a considerable interval, Mrs. Miller slowly advanced.

"I know you!" said Randolph.

"I'm sure you know a great many things," exclaimed Winterbourne, taking him by the hand. "How is your education coming on?"

Daisy was exchanging greetings very prettily with her hostess, but when she heard Winterbourne's voice she quickly turned her head. "Well, I declare!" she said.

"I told you I should come, you know," Winterbourne rejoined smiling.

"Well—I didn't believe it," said Miss Daisy.

"I am much obliged to you," laughed the young man.

"You might have come to see me!" said Daisy.

"I arrived only yesterday."

"I don't believe that!" the young girl declared.

Winterbourne turned with a protesting smile to her mother, but this lady evaded his glance, and seating herself, fixed her eyes upon her son. "We've got a bigger place than this," said Randolph. "It's all gold on the walls."

Mrs. Miller turned uneasily in her chair. "I told you if I were to bring you, you would say something!" she murmured.

"I told *you!*" Randolph exclaimed. "I tell *you,* sir!" he added jocosely, giving Winterbourne a thump on the knee. "It *is* bigger, too!"

Daisy had entered upon a lively conversation with her hostess; Winterbourne judged it becoming to address a few words to her mother. "I hope you have been well since we parted at Vevey," he said.

Mrs. Miller now certainly looked at him—at his chin. "Not very well, sir," she answered.

"She's got the dyspepsia," said Randolph. "I've got it too. Father's got it. I've got it worst!"

This announcement, instead of embarrassing Mrs. Miller, seemed to relieve her. "I suffer from the liver," she said. "I think it's the climate; it's less bracing than Schenectady, especially in the winter season. I don't know whether you know we reside at Schenectady. I was saying to Daisy that I certainly hadn't found any one like Dr. Davis, and I didn't believe I should. Oh, at Schenectady, he stands first; they think everything of him. He has so much to do, and yet there was nothing he wouldn't do for me. He said he never saw anything like my dyspepsia, but he was bound to cure it. I'm sure there was nothing he wouldn't try. He was just going to try something new when we came off. Mr. Miller wanted Daisy to see Europe for herself. But I wrote to Mr. Miller that it seems as if I couldn't get on without Dr. Davis. At Schenectady he stands at the very top, and there's a great deal of sickness there, too. It affects my sleep."

Winterbourne had a good deal of pathological gossip with Dr. Davis's patient, during which Daisy chattered unremittingly to her own companion. The young man asked Mrs. Miller how she was pleased with Rome. "Well, I must say I am disappointed," she answered. "We had heard so much about it; I suppose we had heard too much. But we couldn't help that. We had been led to expect something different."

"Ah, wait a little, and you will become very fond of it," said Winterbourne.

"I hate it worse and worse every day!" cried Randolph.

"You are like the infant Hannibal," said Winterbourne.

"No, I ain't!" Randolph declared, at a venture.

"You are not much like an infant," said his mother. "But we have seen places," she resumed, "that I should put a long way before Rome." And in reply to Winterbourne's interrogation, "There's Zurich," she observed; "I think Zurich is lovely, and we hadn't heard half so much about it."

"The best place we've seen is the City of Richmond!" said Randolph.

"He means the ship," his mother explained. "We crossed in that ship. Randolph had a good time on the City of Richmond."

"It's the best place I've seen," the child repeated. "Only it was turned the wrong way."

"Well, we've got to turn the right way some time," said Mrs. Miller, with a little laugh. Winterbourne expressed the hope that her daughter at least found some gratification in Rome, and she declared that Daisy was quite carried away. "It's on account of the society—the society's splendid. She goes round everywhere; she has made a great number of acquaintances. Of course she goes round more than I do. I must say they have been very sociable; they have taken her right in. And then she knows a great many gentlemen. Oh, she thinks there's nothing like Rome. Of course, it's a great deal pleasanter for a young lady if she knows plenty of gentlemen."

By this time Daisy had turned her attention again to Winterbourne. "I've been telling Mrs. Walker how mean you were!" the young girl announced.

"And what is the evidence you have offered?" asked Winterbourne, rather annoyed at Miss Miller's want of appreciation of the zeal of an admirer who on his way down to Rome had stopped neither at Bologna nor at Florence, simply because of a certain sentimental impatience. He remembered that a cynical compatriot had once told him that American women—the pretty ones, and this gave a largeness to the axiom—were at once the most exacting in the world and the least endowed with a sense of indebtedness.

"Why, you were awfully mean at Vevey," said Daisy. "You wouldn't do anything. You wouldn't stay there when I asked you."

"My dearest young lady," cried Winterbourne, with eloquence, "have I come all the way to Rome to encounter your reproaches?"

"Just hear him say that!" said Daisy to her hostess, giving a twist to a bow on this lady's dress. "Did you ever hear anything so quaint?"

"So quaint, my dear?" murmured Mrs. Walker, in the tone of a partisan of Winterbourne.

"Well, I don't know," said Daisy, fingering Mrs. Walker's ribbons. "Mrs. Walker, I want to tell you something."

"Motherr," interposed Randolph, with his rough ends to his words, "I tell you you've got to go. Eugenio'll raise something!"

"I'm not afraid of Eugenio," said Daisy, with a toss of her head. "Look here, Mrs. Walker," she went on, "you know I'm coming to your party."

"I am delighted to hear it."

"I've got a lovely dress."

"I am very sure of that."

"But I want to ask a favor—permission to bring a friend."

"I shall be happy to see any of your friends," said Mrs. Walker, turning with a smile to Mrs. Miller.

"Oh, they are not my friends," answered Daisy's mamma, smiling shyly, in her own fashion. "I never spoke to them!"

"It's an intimate friend of mine—Mr. Giovanelli," said Daisy, without a tremor in her clear little voice or a shadow on her brilliant little face.

Mrs. Walker was silent a moment, she gave a rapid glance at Winterbourne. "I shall be glad to see Mr. Giovanelli," she then said.

"He's an Italian," Daisy pursued, with the prettiest serenity. "He's a great friend of mine—he's the handsomest man in the world—except Mr. Winterbourne! He knows plenty of Italians, but he wants to know some Americans. He thinks ever so much of Americans. He's tremendously clever. He's perfectly lovely!"

It was settled that this brilliant personage should be brought to Mrs. Walker's party, and then Mrs. Miller prepared to take her leave. "I guess we'll go back to the hotel," she said.

"You may go back to the hotel, mother, but I'm going to take a walk," said Daisy.

"She's going to walk with Mr. Giovanelli," Randolph proclaimed.

"I am going to the Pincio," said Daisy, smiling.

"Alone, my dear at this hour?" Mrs. Walker asked. The afternoon was drawing to a close—it was the hour for the throng of carriages and of contemplative pedestrians. "I don't think it's safe, my dear," said Mrs. Walker.

"Neither do I," subjoined Mrs. Miller. "You'll get the fever as sure as you live. Remember what Dr. Davis told you!"

"Give her some medicine before she goes," said Randolph.

The company had risen to its feet; Daisy, still showing her pretty teeth, bent over and kissed her hostess. "Mrs. Walker, you are too perfect," she said. "I'm not going alone, I am going to meet a friend."

"Your friend won't keep you from getting the fever," Mrs. Miller observed.

"Is it Mr. Giovanelli?" asked the hostess.

Winterbourne was watching the young girl; at this question his attention quickened. She stood there smiling and smoothing her bonnet ribbons; she glanced at Winterbourne. Then, while she glanced and smiled, she answered without a shade of hesitation, "Mr. Giovanelli—the beautiful Giovanelli."

"My dear young friend," said Mrs. Walker, taking her hand, pleadingly, "don't walk off to the Pincio at this hour to meet a beautiful Italian."

"Well, he speaks English," said Mrs. Miller.

"Gracious me!" Daisy exclaimed. "I don't want to do anything improper. There's an easy way to settle it." She continued to glance at Winterbourne. "The Pincio is only a hundred yards distant, and if Mr. Winterbourne were as polite as he pretends he would offer to walk with me!"

Winterbourne's politeness hastened to affirm itself, and the young girl gave him gracious leave to accompany her. They passed downstairs before her mother, and at

the door Winterbourne perceived Mrs. Miller's carriage drawn up, with the orna-
mental courier whose acquaintance he had made at Vevey seated within. "Goodbye, Eugenio!" cried Daisy, "I'm going to take a walk." The distance from the Via
Gregoriana to the beautiful garden at the other end of the Pincian Hill is, in fact,
rapidly traversed. As the day was splendid, however, and the concourse of vehicles,
walkers, and loungers numerous, the young Americans found their progress much
delayed. This fact was highly agreeable to Winterbourne, in spite of his consciousness of his singular situation. The slow-moving, idly-gazing Roman crowd bestowed
much attention upon the extremely pretty young foreign lady who was passing
through it upon his arm, and he wondered what on earth had been in Daisy's mind
when she proposed to expose herself, unattended, to its appreciation. His own mission, to her sense, apparently, was to consign her to the hands of Mr. Giovanelli, but
Winterbourne, at once annoyed and gratified, resolved that he would do no such
thing.

"Why haven't you been to see me?" asked Daisy. "You can't get out of that."

"I have had the honor of telling you that I have only just stepped out of the
train."

"You must have stayed in the train a good while after it stopped!" cried the young
girl, with her little laugh. "I suppose you were asleep. You have had time to go to see
Mrs. Walker."

"I knew Mrs. Walker——" Winterbourne began to explain.

"I knew where you knew her. You knew her at Geneva. She told me so. Well, you
knew me at Vevey. That's just as good. So you ought to have come." She asked him
no other question than this; she began to prattle about her own affairs. "We've got
splendid rooms at the hotel; Eugenio says they're the best rooms in Rome. We are
going to stay all winter—if we don't die of the fever, and I guess we'll stay then. It's
a great deal nicer than I thought; I thought it would be fearfully quiet; I was sure it
would be awfully poky. I was sure we should be going round all the time with one of
those dreadful old men that explain about the pictures and things. But we only had
about a week of that, and now I'm enjoying myself. I know ever so many people, and
they are all so charming. The society's extremely select. There are all kinds—
English, and Germans, and Italians. I think I like the English best. I like their style
of conversation. But there are some lovely Americans. I never saw anything so hospitable. There's something or other every day. There's not much dancing, but I must
say I never thought dancing was everything. I was always fond of conversation. I
guess I shall have plenty at Mrs. Walker's—her rooms are so small." When they had
passed the gate of the Pincian Gardens, Miss Miller began to wonder where Mr.
Giovanelli might be. "We had better go straight to that place in front," she said,
"where you look at the view."

"I certainly shall not help you to find him," Winterbourne declared.

"Then I shall find him without you," said Miss Daisy.

"You certainly won't leave me!" cried Winterbourne.

She burst into her little laugh. "Are you afraid you'll get lost—or run over? But there's Giovanelli, leaning against that tree. He's staring at the women in the carriages: did you ever see anything so cool?"

Winterbourne perceived at some distance a little man standing with folded arms, nursing his cane. He had a handsome face, an artfully poised hat, a glass in one eye and a nosegay in his button-hole. Winterbourne looked at him a moment and then said, "Do you mean to speak to that man?"

"Do I mean to speak to him? Why, you don't suppose I mean to communicate by signs?"

"Pray understand, then," said Winterbourne, "that I intend to remain with you."

Daisy stopped and looked at him, without a sign of troubled consciousness in her face; with nothing but the presence of her charming eyes and her happy dimples. "Well, she's a cool one!" thought the young man.

"I don't like the way you say that," said Daisy. "It's too imperious."

"I beg your pardon if I say it wrong. The main point is to give you an idea of my meaning."

The young girl looked at him more gravely, but with eyes that were prettier than ever. "I have never allowed a gentleman to dictate to me, or to interfere with anything I do."

"I think you have made a mistake," said Winterbourne. "You should sometimes listen to a gentleman—the right one."

Daisy began to laugh again. "I do nothing but listen to gentlemen!" she exclaimed. "Tell me if Mr. Giovanelli is the right one."

The gentleman with the nosegay in his bosom had now perceived our two friends, and was approaching the young girl with obsequious rapidity. He bowed to Winterbourne as well as to the latter's companion; he had a brilliant smile, an intelligent eye; Winterbourne thought him not a bad-looking fellow. But he nevertheless said to Daisy—"No, he's not the right one."

Daisy evidently had a natural talent for performing introductions; she mentioned the name of each of her companions to the other. She strolled along with one of them on each side of her; Mr. Giovanelli, who spoke English very cleverly—Winterbourne afterward learned that he had practiced the idiom upon a great many American heiresses—addressed her a great deal of very polite nonsense; he was extremely urbane, and the young American, who said nothing, reflected upon that profundity of Italian cleverness which enables people to appear more gracious in proportion as they are more acutely disappointed. Giovanelli, of course, had counted upon something more intimate; he had not bargained for a party of three. But he kept his temper in a manner which suggested far-stretching intentions.

Winterbourne flattered himself that he had taken his measure. "He is not a gentle-man," said the young American; "he is only a clever imitation of one. He is a music-master, or a penny-a-liner, or a third-rate artist. Damn his good looks!" Mr. Giovanelli had certainly a very pretty face, but Winterbourne felt a superior indig-nation at his own lovely fellow countrywoman's not knowing the difference between a spurious gentleman and a real one. Giovanelli chattered and jested and made himself wonderfully agreeable. It was true that if he was an imitation the imi-tation was very skillful. "Nevertheless," Winterbourne said to himself, "a nice girl ought to know!" And then he came back to the question whether this was in fact a nice girl. Would a nice girl—even allowing for her being a little American flirt—make a rendezvous with a presumably low-lived foreigner? The rendezvous in this case, indeed, had been in broad daylight, and in the most crowded corner of Rome, but was it not impossible to regard the choice of these circumstances as a proof of extreme cynicism? Singular though it may seem, Winterbourne was vexed that the young girl, in joining her *amoroso*, should not appear more impatient of his own company, and he was vexed because of his inclination. It was impossible to regard her as a perfectly well-conducted young lady; she was wanting in a certain indis-pensable delicacy. It would therefore simplify matters greatly to be able to treat her as the object of one of those sentiments which are called by romancers "lawless passions." That she should seem to wish to get rid of him would help him to think more lightly of her, and to be able to think more lightly of her would make her much less perplexing. But Daisy, on this occasion, continued to present herself as an inscrutable combination of audacity and innocence.

She had been walking some quarter of an hour, attended by her two cavaliers, and responding in a tone of very childish gaiety, as it seemed to Winterbourne, to the pretty speeches of Mr. Giovanelli, when a carriage that had detached itself from the revolving train drew up beside the path. At the same moment Winterbourne perceived that his friend Mrs. Walker—the lady whose house he had lately left—was seated in the vehicle and was beckoning to him. Leaving Miss Miller's side, he hastened to obey her summons. Mrs. Walker was flushed; she wore an excited air. "It is really too dreadful," she said. "That girl must not do this sort of thing. She must not walk here with you two men. Fifty people have noticed her."

Winterbourne raised his eyebrows. "I think it's a pity to make too much fuss about it."

"It's a pity to let the girl ruin herself!"

"She is very innocent," said Winterbourne.

"She's very crazy!" cried Mrs. Walker. "Did you ever see anything so imbecile as her mother? After you had all left me, just now, I could not sit still for thinking of it. It seemed too pitiful, not even to attempt to save her. I ordered the carriage and put on my bonnet, and came here as quickly as possible. Thank heaven I have found you!"

"What do you propose to do with us?" asked Winterbourne, smiling.

"To ask her to get in, to drive her about here for half-an-hour, so that the world may see she is not running absolutely wild, and then to take her safely home."

"I don't think it's a very happy thought," said Winterbourne; "but you can try."

Mrs. Walker tried. The young man went in pursuit of Miss Miller, who had simply nodded and smiled at his interlocutrix in the carriage and had gone her way with her own companion. Daisy, on learning that Mrs. Walker wished to speak to her, retraced her steps with a perfect good grace and with Mr. Giovanelli at her side. She declared that she was delighted to have a chance to present this gentleman to Mrs. Walker. She immediately achieved the introduction, and declared that she had never in her life seen anything so lovely as Mrs. Walker's carriage rug.

"I am glad you admire it," said this lady, smiling sweetly. "Will you get in and let me put it over you?"

"Oh, no, thank you," said Daisy. "I shall admire it much more as I see you driving round with it."

"Do get in and drive with me," said Mrs. Walker.

"That would be charming, but it's so enchanting just as I am!" and Daisy gave a brilliant glance at the gentlemen on either side of her.

"It may be enchanting, dear child, but it is not the custom here," urged Mrs. Walker, leaning forward in her victoria with her hands devoutly clasped.

"Well, it ought to be, then!" said Daisy. "If I didn't walk I should expire."

"You should walk with your mother, dear," cried the lady from Geneva, losing patience.

"With my mother dear!" exclaimed the young girl. Winterbourne saw that she scented interference. "My mother never walked ten steps in her life. And then, you know," she added with a laugh, "I am more than five years old."

"You are old enough to be more reasonable. You are old enough, dear Miss Miller, to be talked about."

Daisy looked at Mrs. Walker, smiling intensely. "Talked about? What do you mean?"

"Come into my carriage and I will tell you."

Daisy turned her quickened glance again from one of the gentlemen beside her to the other. Mr. Giovanelli was bowing to and fro, rubbing down his gloves and laughing very agreeably; Winterbourne thought it a most unpleasant scene. "I don't think I want to know what you mean," said Daisy presently. "I don't think I should like it."

Winterbourne wished that Mrs. Walker would tuck in her carriage-rug and drive away, but this lady did not enjoy being defied, as she afterward told him. "Should you prefer being thought a very reckless girl?" she demanded.

"Gracious me!" exclaimed Daisy. She looked again at Mr. Giovanelli, then she turned to Winterbourne. There was a little pink flush in her cheek; she was tremendously pretty. "Does Mr. Winterbourne think," she asked slowly, smiling, throwing back her head and glancing at him from head to foot, "that—to save my reputation—I ought to get into the carriage?"

Winterbourne colored; for an instant he hesitated greatly. It seemed so strange to hear her speak that way of her "reputation." But he himself, in fact, must speak in accordance with gallantry. The finest gallantry, here, was simply to tell her the truth; and the truth, for Winterbourne, as the few indications I have been able to give have made him known to the reader, was that Daisy Miller should take Mrs. Walker's advice. He looked at her exquisite prettiness; and then he said very gently, "I think you should get into the carriage."

Daisy gave a violent laugh. "I never heard anything so stiff! If this is improper, Mrs. Walker," she pursued, "then I am all improper, and you must give me up. Good-bye; I hope you'll have a lovely ride!" and, with Mr. Giovanelli, who made a triumphantly obsequious salute, she turned away.

Mrs. Walker sat looking after her, and there were tears in Mrs. Walker's eyes. "Get in here, sir," she said to Winterbourne, indicating the place beside her. The young man answered that he felt bound to accompany Miss Miller; whereupon Mrs. Walker declared that if he refused her this favor she would never speak to him again. She was evidently in earnest. Winterbourne overtook Daisy and her companion and, offering the young girl his hand, told her that Mrs. Walker had made an imperious claim upon his society. He expected that in answer she would say something rather free, something to commit herself still farther to that "recklessness" from which Mrs. Walker had so charitably endeavored to dissuade her. But she only shook his hand, hardly looking at him, while Mr. Giovanelli bade him farewell with a too emphatic flourish of the hat.

Winterbourne was not in the best possible humor as he took his seat in Mrs. Walker's victoria. "That was not clever of you," he said candidly, while the vehicle mingled again with the throng of carriages.

"In such a case," his companion answered, "I don't wish to be clever, I wish to be *earnest!*"

"Well, your earnestness has only offended her and put her off."

"It has happened very well," said Mrs. Walker. "If she is so perfectly determined to compromise herself, the sooner one knows it the better; one can act accordingly."

"I suspect she meant no harm," Winterbourne rejoined.

"So I thought a month ago. But she has been going too far."

"What has she been doing?"

"Everything that is not done here. Flirting with any man she could pick up; sitting in corners with mysterious Italians; dancing all the evening with the same partners; receiving visits at eleven o'clock at night. Her mother goes away when visitors come."

"But her brother," said Winterbourne, laughing, "sits up till midnight."

"He must be edified by what he sees. I'm told that at their hotel everyone is talking about her, and that a smile goes round among the servants when a gentleman comes and asks for Miss Miller."

"The servants be hanged!" said Winterbourne angrily. "The poor girl's only fault," he presently added, "is that she is very uncultivated."

"She is naturally indelicate," Mrs. Walker declared. "Take that example this morning. How long had you known her at Vevey?"

"A couple of days."

"Fancy, then, her making it a personal matter that you should have left the place!"

Winterbourne was silent for some moments; then he said, "I suspect, Mrs. Walker, that you and I have lived too long at Geneva!" And he added a request that she should inform him with what particular design she had made him enter her carriage.

"I wished to beg you to cease your relations with Miss Miller—not to flirt with her—to give her no farther opportunity to expose herself—to let her alone, in short."

"I'm afraid I can't do that," said Winterbourne. "I like her extremely."

"All the more reason that you shouldn't help her to make a scandal."

"There shall be nothing scandalous in my attentions to her."

"There certainly will be in the way she takes them. But I have said what I had on my conscience," Mrs. Walker pursued. "If you wish to rejoin the young lady I will put you down. Here, by the way, you have a chance."

The carriage was traversing that part of the Pincian Garden which overhangs the wall of Rome and overlooks the beautiful Villa Borghese. It is bordered by a large parapet, near which there are several seats. One of the seats, at a distance, was occupied by a gentleman and a lady, toward whom Mrs. Walker gave a toss of her head. At the same moment these persons rose and walked toward the parapet. Winterbourne had asked the coachman to stop; he now descended from the carriage. His companion looked at him a moment in silence, then, while he raised his hat, she drove majestically away. Winterbourne stood there; he had turned his eyes toward Daisy and her cavalier. They evidently saw no one; they were too deeply occupied with each other. When they reached the low garden wall they stood a moment looking off at the great flat-topped pine clusters of the Villa Borghese; then Giovanelli seated himself familiarly upon the broad ledge of the wall. The western sun in the opposite sky sent out a brilliant shaft through a couple of cloud bars, whereupon Daisy's companion took her parasol out of her hands and opened it. She came a little nearer and he held the parasol over her, then, still holding it, he let it rest upon her shoulder, so that both of their heads were hidden from Winterbourne. This young man lingered a moment, then he began to walk. But he walked—not toward the couple with the parasol, toward the residence of his aunt, Mrs. Costello.

IV

He flattered himself on the following day that there was no smiling among the servants when he, at least, asked for Mrs. Miller at her hotel. This lady and her daughter, however, were not at home; and on the next day after, repeating his visit, Winterbourne again had the misfortune not to find them. Mrs. Walker's party took place on the evening of the third day, and in spite of the frigidity of his last interview with the hostess Winterbourne was among the guests. Mrs. Walker was one of those American ladies who, while residing abroad, make a point, in their own phrase, of studying European society, and she had on this occasion collected several specimens of her diversely born fellow mortals to serve, as it were, as textbooks. When Winterbourne arrived Daisy Miller was not there, but in a few moments he saw her mother come in alone, very shyly and ruefully. Mrs. Miller's hair, above her exposed-looking temples, was more frizzled than ever. As she approached Mrs. Walker, Winterbourne also drew near.

"You see I've come all alone," said poor Mrs. Miller. "I'm so frightened; I don't know what to do; it's the first time I've ever been to a party alone—especially in this country. I wanted to bring Randolph or Eugenio, or someone, but Daisy just pushed me off by myself. I ain't used to going round alone."

"And does not your daughter intend to favor us with her society?" demanded Mrs. Walker, impressively.

"Well, Daisy's all dressed," said Mrs. Miller, with that accent of the dispassionate, if not of the philosophic, historian with which she always recorded the current incidents of her daughter's career. "She got dressed on purpose before dinner. But she's got a friend of hers there; that gentleman—the Italian—that she wanted to bring. They've got going at the piano; it seems as if they couldn't leave off. Mr. Giovanelli sings splendidly. But I guess they'll come before very long," concluded Mrs. Miller hopefully.

"I'm sorry she should come—in that way," said Mrs. Walker.

"Well, I told her that there was no use in her getting dressed before dinner if she was going to wait three hours," responded Daisy's mamma. "I didn't see the use of her putting on such a dress as that to sit round with Mr. Giovanelli."

"This is most horrible!" said Mrs. Walker, turning away and addressing herself to Winterbourne. "*Elle s'affiche.* It's her revenge for my having ventured to remonstrate with her. When she comes I shall not speak to her."

Daisy came after eleven o'clock, but she was not, on such an occasion, a young lady to wait to be spoken to. She rustled forward in radiant loveliness, smiling and chattering, carrying a large bouquet and attended by Mr. Giovanelli. Every one stopped talking, and turned and looked at her. She came straight to Mrs. Walker. "I'm afraid you thought I never was coming, so I sent mother off to tell you. I wanted to make Mr. Giovanelli practice some things before he came; you know he sings beautifully, and I want you to ask him to sing. This is Mr. Giovanelli; you know I introduced him to you; he's got the most lovely voice and he knows the most charming set of songs. I made him go over them this evening, on purpose; we had the greatest time at the hotel." Of all this Daisy delivered herself with the sweetest, brightest audibleness, looking now at her hostess and now round the room, while she gave a series of little pats, round her shoulders, to the edges of her dress. "Is there any one I know?" she asked.

"I think every one knows you!" said Mrs. Walker pregnantly, and she gave a very cursory greeting to Mr. Giovanelli. This gentleman bore himself gallantly. He smiled and bowed and showed his white teeth, he curled his moustaches and rolled his eyes, and performed all the proper functions of a handsome Italian at an evening party. He sang, very prettily, half-a-dozen songs, though Mrs. Walker afterward declared that she had been quite unable to find out who asked him. It was apparently not Daisy who had given him his orders. Daisy sat at a distance from the piano, and though she had publicly, as it were, professed a high admiration for his singing, talked, not inaudibly, while it was going on.

"It's a pity these rooms are so small; we can't dance," she said to Winterbourne, as if she had seen him five minutes before.

"I am not sorry we can't dance," Winterbourne answered; "I don't dance."

"Of course you don't dance; you're too stiff," said Miss Daisy. "I hope you enjoyed your drive with Mrs. Walker."

"No, I didn't enjoy it; I preferred walking with you."

"We paired off, that was much better," said Daisy. "But did you ever hear anything so cool as Mrs. Walker's wanting me to get into her carriage and drop poor Mr. Giovanelli—and under the pretext that it was proper? People have different ideas! It would have been most unkind; he had been talking about that walk for ten days."

"He should not have talked about it at all," said Winterbourne; "he would never have proposed to a young lady of this country to walk about the streets with him."

"About the streets?" cried Daisy, with her pretty stare. "Where then would he have proposed to her to walk? The Pincio is not the streets, either, and I, thank goodness, am not a young lady of this country. The young ladies of this country have a dreadfully pokey time of it, so far as I can learn; I don't see why I should change my habits for *them*."

"I am afraid your habits are those of a flirt," said Winterbourne gravely.

"Of course they are," she cried, giving him her little smiling stare again. "I'm a fearful, frightful flirt! Did you ever hear of a nice girl that was not? But I suppose you will tell me now that I am not a nice girl."

"You're a very nice girl, but I wish you would flirt with me, and me only," said Winterbourne.

"Ah! thank you, thank you very much; you are the last man I should think of flirting with. As I have had the pleasure of informing you, you are too stiff."

"You say that too often," said Winterbourne.

Daisy gave a delighted laugh. "If I could have the sweet hope of making you angry, I would say it again."

"Don't do that; when I am angry I'm stiffer than ever. But if you won't flirt with me, do cease at least to flirt with your friend at the piano; they don't understand that sort of thing here."

"I thought they understood nothing else!" exclaimed Daisy.

"Not in young unmarried women."

"It seems to me much more proper in young unmarried women than in old married ones," Daisy declared.

"Well," said Winterbourne, "when you deal with natives you must go by the custom of the place. Flirting is a purely American custom; it doesn't exist here. So when you show yourself in public with Mr. Giovanelli and without your mother—"

"Gracious! poor mother!" interposed Daisy.

"Though you may be flirting, Mr. Giovanelli is not; he means something else."

"He isn't preaching, at any rate," said Daisy with vivacity. "And if you want very much to know, we are neither of us flirting; we are too good friends for that; we are very intimate friends."

"Ah!" rejoined Winterbourne, "if you are in love with each other it is another affair."

She had allowed him up to this point to talk so frankly that he had no expectation of shocking her by this ejaculation; but she immediately got up, blushing visibly, and leaving him to exclaim mentally that little American flirts were the queerest creatures in the world. "Mr. Giovanelli, at least," she said, giving her interlocutor a single glance, "never says such very disagreeable things to me."

Winterbourne was bewildered; he stood staring. Mr. Giovanelli had finished singing; he left the piano and came over to Daisy. "Won't you come into the other room and have some tea?" he asked, bending before her with his decorative smile.

Daisy turned to Winterbourne, beginning to smile again. He was still more perplexed, for this inconsequent smile made nothing clear, though it seemed to prove, indeed, that she had a sweetness and softness that reverted instinctively to the pardon of offences. "It has never occurred to Mr. Winterbourne to offer me any tea," she said, with her little tormenting manner.

"I have offered you advice," Winterbourne rejoined.

"I prefer weak tea!" cried Daisy, and she went off with the brilliant Giovanelli. She sat with him in the adjoining room, in the embrasure of the window, for the rest of the evening. There was an interesting performance at the piano, but neither of these young people gave heed to it. When Daisy came to take leave of Mrs. Walker, this lady conscientiously repaired the weakness of which she had been guilty at the moment of the young girl's arrival. She turned her back straight upon Miss Miller and left her to depart with what grace she might. Winterbourne was standing near the door; he saw it all. Daisy turned very pale and looked at her mother, but Mrs. Miller was humbly unconscious of any violation of the usual social forms. She appeared, indeed, to have felt an incongruous impulse to draw attention to her own striking observance of them. "Good night, Mrs. Walker," she said; "we've had a beautiful evening. You see if I let Daisy come to parties without me, I don't want her to go away without me." Daisy turned away, looking with a pale, grave face at the circle near the door; Winterbourne saw that, for the first moment, she was too much shocked and puzzled even for indignation. He on his side was greatly touched.

"That was very cruel," he said to Mrs. Walker.

"She never enters my drawing room again," replied his hostess.

Since Winterbourne was not to meet her in Mrs. Walker's drawing room, he went as often as possible to Mrs. Miller's hotel. The ladies were rarely at home, but when he found them the devoted Giovanelli was always present. Very often the polished little Roman was in the drawing room with Daisy alone, Mrs. Miller being apparently constantly of the opinion that discretion is the better part of the surveillance. Winterbourne noted, at first with surprise, that Daisy on these occasions was never embarrassed or annoyed by his own entrance, but he very presently began to feel that she had no more surprises for him; the unexpected in her behavior was the only thing to expect. She showed no displeasure at her *tête-à-tête* with Giovanelli being interrupted; she could chatter as freshly and freely with two gentlemen as with one; there was always in her conversation, the same odd mixture of audacity and puerility. Winterbourne remarked to himself that if she was seriously interested in Giovanelli it was very singular that she should not take more trouble to preserve the sanctity of their interviews, and he liked her the more for her innocent-looking indifference and her apparently inexhaustible good humor. He could hardly have said why, but she seemed to him a girl who would never be jealous. At the risk of exciting a somewhat derisive smile on the reader's part, I may affirm that with regard to the women who had hitherto interested him it very often seemed to Winterbourne among the possibilities that, given certain contingencies, he should be afraid—literally afraid—of these ladies. He had a pleasant sense that he should never be afraid of Daisy Miller. It must be added that this sentiment was not altogether flattering to Daisy; it was part of his conviction, or rather of his apprehension, that she would prove a very light young person.

But she was evidently very much interested in Giovanelli. She looked at him whenever he spoke; she was perpetually telling him to do this and to do that; she was constantly "chaffing" and abusing him. She appeared completely to have forgotten that Winterbourne had said anything to displease her at Mrs. Walker's little party. One Sunday afternoon, having gone to St. Peter's with his aunt, Winterbourne perceived Daisy strolling about the great church in company with the inevitable Giovanelli. Presently he pointed out the young girl and her cavalier to Mrs. Costello. This lady looked at them a moment through her eyeglass, and then she said:

"That's what makes you so pensive in these days, eh?"

"I had not the least idea I was pensive," said the young man.

"You are very much preoccupied, you are thinking of something."

"And what is it," he asked, "that you accuse me of thinking of?"

"Of that young lady's—Miss Baker's, Miss Chandler's—what's her name?—Miss Miller's intrigue with that little barber's block."

"Do you call it an intrigue," Winterbourne asked—"an affair that goes on with such peculiar publicity?"

"That's their folly," said Mrs. Costello, "it's not their merit."

"No," rejoined Winterbourne, with something of that pensiveness to which his aunt had alluded. "I don't believe that there is anything to be called an intrigue."

"I have heard a dozen people speak of it; they say she is quite carried away by him."

"They are certainly very intimate," said Winterbourne.

Mrs. Costello inspected the young couple again with her optical instrument. "He is very handsome. One easily sees how it is. She thinks him the most elegant man in the world, the finest gentleman. She has never seen anything like him; he is better even than the courier. It was the courier probably who introduced him, and if he succeeds in marrying the young lady, the courier will come in for a magnificent commission."

"I don't believe she thinks of marrying him," said Winterbourne, "and I don't believe he hopes to marry her."

"You may be very sure she thinks of nothing. She goes on from day to day, from hour to hour, as they did in the Golden Age. I can imagine nothing more vulgar. And at the same time," added Mrs. Costello, "depend upon it that she may tell you any moment that she is 'engaged.'"

"I think that is more than Giovanelli expects," said Winterbourne.

"Who is Giovanelli?"

"The little Italian. I have asked questions about him and learned something. He is apparently a perfectly respectable little man. I believe he is in a small way a *cavaliere avvocato*. But he doesn't move in what are called the first circles. I think it is really not absolutely impossible that the courier introduced him. He is evidently immensely charmed with Miss Miller. If she thinks him the finest gentleman in the world, he, on his side, has never found himself in personal contact with such splendor, such opulence, such expensiveness, as this young lady's. And then she must seem to him wonderfully pretty and interesting. I rather doubt whether he dreams of marrying her. That must appear to him too impossible a piece of luck. He has nothing but his handsome face to offer, and there is a substantial Mr. Miller in that mysterious land of dollars. Giovanelli knows that he hasn't a title to offer. If he were only a count or a *marchese!* He must wonder at his luck at the way they have taken him up."

"He accounts for it by his handsome face, and thinks Miss Miller a young lady *qui se passe ses fantaisies!*" said Mrs. Costello.

"It is very true," Winterbourne pursued, "that Daisy and her mamma have not yet risen to that stage of—what shall I call it?—of culture, at which the idea of catching a count or a *marchese* begins. I believe that they are intellectually incapable of that conception."

"Ah! but the *cavaliere* can't believe it," said Mrs. Costello.

Of the observation excited by Daisy's "intrigue," Winterbourne gathered that day at St. Peter's sufficient evidence. A dozen of the American colonists in Rome came to talk with Mrs. Costello, who sat on a little portable stool at the base of one of the great pilasters. The vesper service was going forward in splendid chants and organ-tones in the adjacent choir, and meanwhile, between Mrs. Costello and her friends, there was a great deal said about poor little Miss Miller's going really "too far." Winterbourne was not pleased with what he heard, but when, coming out upon the great steps of the church, he saw Daisy, who had emerged before him, get into an open cab with her accomplice and roll away through the cynical streets of Rome, he could not deny to himself that she was going very far indeed. He felt very sorry for her—not exactly that he believed that she had completely lost her head, but because it was painful to hear so much that was pretty and undefended and natural assigned to a vulgar place among the categories of disorder. He made an attempt after this to give a hint to Mrs. Miller. He met one day in the Corso a friend—a tourist like himself—who had just come out of the Doria Palace, where he had been walking through the beautiful gallery. His friend talked for a moment about the superb portrait of Innocent X by Velasquez, which hangs in one of the cabinets of the palace, and then said, "And in the same cabinet, by the way, I had the pleasure of contemplating a picture of a different kind—that pretty American girl whom you pointed out to me last week." In answer to Winterbourne's inquiries, his friend narrated that the pretty American girl—prettier than ever—was seated with a companion in the secluded nook in which the great papal portrait is enshrined.

"Who was her companion?" asked Winterbourne.

"A little Italian with a bouquet in his buttonhole. The girl is delightfully pretty, but I thought I understood from you the other day that she was a young lady *du meilleur monde.*"

"So she is!" answered Winterbourne, and having assured himself that his informant had seen Daisy and her companion but five minutes before, he jumped into a cab and went to call on Mrs. Miller. She was at home, but she apologized to him for receiving him in Daisy's absence.

"She's gone out somewhere with Mr. Giovanelli," said Mrs. Miller. "She's always going round with Mr. Giovanelli."

"I have noticed that they are very intimate," Winterbourne observed.

"Oh! it seems as if they couldn't live without each other!" said Mrs. Miller. "Well, he's a real gentleman, anyhow. I keep telling Daisy she's engaged!"

"And what does Daisy say?"

"Oh, she says she isn't engaged. But she might as well be!" this impartial parent resumed. "She goes on as if she was. But I've made Mr. Giovanelli promise to tell me, if *she* doesn't. I should want to write to Mr. Miller about it—shouldn't you?"

Winterbourne replied that he certainly should, and the state of mind of Daisy's mamma struck him as so unprecedented in the annals of parental vigilance that he gave up as utterly irrelevant the attempt to place her upon her guard.

After this Daisy was never at home, and Winterbourne ceased to meet her at the houses of their common acquaintance, because, as he perceived, these shrewd people had quite made up their minds that she was going too far. They ceased to invite her, and they intimated that they desired to express to observant Europeans the great truth that, though Miss Daisy Miller was a young American lady, her behavior was not representative—was regarded by her compatriots as abnormal. Winterbourne wondered how she felt about all the cold shoulders that were turned toward her, and sometimes it annoyed him to suspect that she did not feel at all. He said to himself that she was too light and childish, too uncultivated and unreasoning, too provincial, to have reflected upon her ostracism or even to have perceived it. Then at other moments he believed that she carried about in her elegant and irresponsible little organism a defiant, passionate, perfectly observant consciousness of the impression she produced. He asked himself whether Daisy's defiance came from the consciousness of innocence or from her being, essentially, a young person of the reckless class. It must be admitted that holding oneself to a belief in Daisy's "innocence" came to seem to Winterbourne more and more a matter of fine-spun gallantry. As I have already had occasion to relate, he was angry at finding himself reduced to chopping logic about this young lady; he was vexed at his want of instinctive certitude as to how far her eccentricities were generic, national, and how far they were personal. From either view of them he had somehow missed her, and now it was too late. She was "carried away" by Mr. Giovanelli.

A few days after his brief interview with her mother, he encountered her in that beautiful abode of flowering desolation known as the Palace of the Cæsars. The early Roman spring had filled the air with bloom and perfume, and the rugged surface of the Palatine was muffled with tender verdure. Daisy was strolling along the top of one of those great mounds of ruin that are embanked with mossy marble and paved with monumental inscriptions. It seemed to him that Rome had never been so lovely as just then. He stood looking off at the enchanting harmony of line and color that remotely encircles the city, inhaling the softly humid odors and feeling the freshness of the year and the antiquity of the place reaffirm themselves in mysterious interfusion. It seemed to him also that Daisy had never looked so pretty, but this had been an observation of his whenever he met her. Giovanelli was at her side, and Giovanelli, too, wore an aspect of even unwonted brilliancy.

"Well," said Daisy, "I should think you would be lonesome!"

"Lonesome?" asked Winterbourne.

"You are always going round by yourself. Can't you get anyone to walk with you?"

"I am not so fortunate," said Winterbourne, "as your companion."

Giovanelli, from the first, had treated Winterbourne with distinguished politeness; he listened with a deferential air to his remarks; he laughed, punctiliously, at his pleasantries, he seemed disposed to testify to his belief that Winterbourne was a superior young man. He carried himself in no degree like a jealous wooer; he had obviously a great deal of tact, he had no objection to your expecting a little humility of him. It even seemed to Winterbourne at times that Giovanelli would find a certain mental relief in being able to have a private understanding with him—to say to him, as an intelligent man, that, bless you, *he* knew how extraordinary was this young lady, and didn't flatter himself with delusive—or at least *too* delusive— hopes of matrimony and dollars. On this occasion he strolled away from his companion to pluck a sprig of almond blossom, which he carefully arranged in his button-hole.

"I know why you say that," said Daisy, watching Giovanelli. "Because you think I go round too much with *him!*" And she nodded at her attendant.

"Every one thinks so—if you care to know," said Winterbourne.

"Of course I care to know!" Daisy exclaimed seriously. "But I don't believe it. They are only pretending to be shocked. They don't really care a straw what I do. Besides, I don't go round so much."

"I think you will find they do care. They will show it—disagreeably."

Daisy looked at him a moment. "How—disagreeably?"

"Haven't you noticed anything?" Winterbourne asked.

"I have noticed you. But I noticed you were as stiff as an umbrella the first time I saw you."

"You will find I am not so stiff as several others," said Winterbourne, smiling.

"How shall I find it?"

"By going to see the others."

"What will they do to me?"

"They will give you the cold shoulder. Do you know what that means?"

Daisy was looking at him intently; she began to color. "Do you mean as Mrs. Walker did the other night?"

"Exactly!" said Winterbourne.

She looked away at Giovanelli, who was decorating himself with his almond-blossom. Then looking back at Winterbourne—"I shouldn't think you would let people be so unkind!" she said.

"How can I help it?" he asked.

"I should think you would say something."

"I do say something;" and he paused a moment. "I say that your mother tells me that she believes you are engaged."

"Well, she does," said Daisy very simply.

Winterbourne began to laugh. "And does Randolph believe it?" he asked.

"I guess Randolph doesn't believe anything," said Daisy. Randolph's scepticism excited Winterbourne to farther hilarity, and he observed that Giovanelli was coming back to them. Daisy, observing it too, addressed herself again to her country-man. "Since you have mentioned it," she said, "I *am* engaged." . . . Winterbourne looked at her; he had stopped laughing. "You don't believe it!" she added.

He was silent a moment; and then, "Yes, I believe it!" he said.

"Oh, no, you don't," she answered. "Well, then—I am not!"

The young girl and her cicerone were on their way to the gate of the enclosure, so that Winterbourne, who had but lately entered, presently took leave of them. A week afterward he went to dine at a beautiful villa on the Cælian Hill, and, on arriving, dismissed his hired vehicle. The evening was charming, and he promised himself the satisfaction of walking home beneath the Arch of Constantine and past the vaguely lighted monuments of the Forum. There was a waning moon in the sky, and her radiance was not brilliant, but she was veiled in a thin cloud curtain which seemed to diffuse and equalize it. When, on his return from the villa (it was eleven o'clock), Winterbourne approached the dusky circle of the Colosseum, it occurred to him, as a lover of the picturesque, that the interior, in the pale moonshine, would be well worth a glance. He turned aside and walked to one of the empty arches, near which, as he observed, an open carriage—one of the little Roman street-cabs—was stationed. Then he passed in among the cavernous shadows of the great structure, and emerged upon the clear and silent arena. The place had never seemed to him more impressive. One-half of the gigantic circus was in deep shade, the other was sleeping in the luminous dusk. As he stood there he began to murmur Byron's famous lines, out of *Manfred*; but before he had finished his quotation he remembered that if nocturnal meditations in the Colosseum are recommended by the poets, they are deprecated by the doctors. The historic atmosphere was there, certainly, but the historic atmosphere, scientifically considered, was no better than a villainous miasma. Winterbourne walked to the middle of the arena, to take a more general glance, intending thereafter to make a hasty retreat. The great cross in the center was covered with shadow; it was only as he drew near it that he made it out distinctly. Then he saw that two persons were stationed upon the low steps which formed its base. One of these was a woman, seated; her companion was standing in front of her.

Presently the sound of the woman's voice came to him distinctly in the warm night air. "Well, he looks at us as one of the old lions or tigers may have looked at the Christian martyrs!" These were the words he heard, in the familiar accent of Miss Daisy Miller.

"Let us hope he is not very hungry," responded the ingenious Giovanelli. "He will have to take me first; you will serve for dessert!"

Winterbourne stopped, with a sort of horror, and, it must be added, with a sort of relief. It was as if a sudden illumination had been flashed upon the ambiguity of Daisy's behaviour and the riddle had become easy to read. She was a young lady whom a gentleman need no longer be at pains to respect. He stood there looking at her—looking at her companion, and not reflecting that though he saw them vaguely, he himself must have been more brightly visible. He felt angry with himself that he had bothered so much about the right way of regarding Miss Daisy Miller. Then, as he was going to advance again, he checked himself; not from the fear that he was doing her injustice, but from a sense of the danger of appearing unbecomingly exhilarated by this sudden revulsion from cautious criticism. He turned away toward the entrance of the place; but as he did so he heard Daisy speak again.

"Why, it was Mr. Winterbourne! He saw me—and he cuts me!"

What a clever little reprobate she was, and how smartly she played an injured innocence! But he wouldn't cut her. Winterbourne came forward again, and went toward the great cross. Daisy had got up; Giovanelli lifted his hat. Winterbourne had now begun to think simply of the craziness, from a sanitary point of view, of a delicate young girl lounging away the evening in this nest of malaria. What if she *were* a clever little reprobate? That was no reason for her dying of the *perniciosa*. "How long have you been there?" he asked, almost brutally.

Daisy, lovely in the flattering moonlight, looked at him a moment. Then—"All the evening," she answered gently . . . "I never saw anything so pretty."

"I am afraid," said Winterbourne, "that you will not think Roman fever very pretty. This is the way people catch it. I wonder," he added, turning to Giovanelli, "that you, a native Roman, should countenance such a terrible indiscretion."

"Ah," said the handsome native, "for myself, I am not afraid."

"Neither am I—for you! I am speaking for this young lady."

Giovanelli lifted his well-shaped eyebrows and showed his brilliant teeth. But he took Winterbourne's rebuke with docility. "I told the Signorina it was a grave indiscretion, but when was the Signorina ever prudent?"

"I never was sick, and I don't mean to be!" the Signorina declared. "I don't look like much, but I'm healthy! I was bound to see the Colosseum by moonlight; I shouldn't have wanted to go home without that, and we have had the most beautiful time, haven't we, Mr. Giovanelli? If there has been any danger, Eugenio can give me some pills. He has got some splendid pills."

"I should advise you," said Winterbourne, "to drive home as fast as possible and take one!"

"What you say is very wise," Giovanelli rejoined. "I will go and make sure the carriage is at hand." And he went forward rapidly.

Daisy followed with Winterbourne. He kept looking at her; she seemed not in the least embarrassed. Winterbourne said nothing; Daisy chattered about the beauty of the place. "Well, I *have* seen the Colosseum by moonlight!" she exclaimed. "That's one good thing." Then, noticing Winterbourne's silence, she asked him why he didn't speak. He made no answer; he only began to laugh. They passed under one of the dark archways; Giovanelli was in front with the carriage. Here Daisy stopped a moment, looking at the young American. "*Did* you believe I was engaged the other day?" she asked.

"It doesn't matter what I believed the other day," said Winterbourne, still laughing.

"Well, what do you believe now?"

"I believe that it makes very little difference whether you are engaged or not!"

He felt the young girl's pretty eyes fixed upon him through the thick gloom of the archway; she was apparently going to answer. But Giovanelli hurried her forward. "Quick, quick," he said; "if we get in by midnight we are quite safe."

Daisy took her seat in the carriage, and the fortunate Italian placed himself beside her. "Don't forget Eugenio's pills!" said Winterbourne, as he lifted his hat.

"I don't care," said Daisy, in a little strange tone, "whether I have Roman fever or not!" Upon this the cabdriver cracked his whip, and they rolled away over the desultory patches of the antique pavement.

Winterbourne—to do him justice, as it were—mentioned to no one that he had encountered Miss Miller, at midnight, in the Colosseum with a gentleman, but nevertheless, a couple of days later, the fact of her having been there under these circumstances was known to every member of the little American circle, and commented accordingly. Winterbourne reflected that they had of course known it at the hotel, and that, after Daisy's return, there had been an exchange of jokes between the porter and the cabdriver. But the young man was conscious at the same moment that it had ceased to be a matter of serious regret to him that the little American flirt should be "talked about" by low-minded menials. These people, a day or two later, had serious information to give: the little American flirt was alarmingly ill. Winterbourne, when the rumor came to him, immediately went to the hotel for more news. He found that two or three charitable friends had preceded him, and that they were being entertained in Mrs. Miller's salon by Randolph.

"It's going round at night," said Randolph—"that's what made her sick. She's always going round at midnight. I shouldn't think she'd want to—it's so plaguey dark. You can't see anything here at night, except when there's a moon. In America there's always a moon!" Mrs. Miller was invisible; she was now, at least, giving her daughter the advantage of her society. It was evident that Daisy was dangerously ill.

Winterbourne went often to ask for news of her, and once he saw Mrs. Miller, who, though deeply alarmed, was—rather to his surprise—perfectly composed, and, as it appeared, a most efficient and judicious nurse. She talked a good deal about Dr. Davis, but Winterbourne paid her the compliment of saying to himself that she was not, after all, such a monstrous goose. "Daisy spoke of you the other day," she said to him. "Half the time she doesn't know what she's saying, but that time I think she did. She gave me a message: she told me to tell you. She told me to tell you that she never was engaged to that handsome Italian. I am sure I am very glad; Mr. Giovanelli hasn't been near us since she was taken ill. I thought he was so much of a gentleman, but I don't call that very polite! A lady told me that he was afraid I was angry with him for taking Daisy round at night. Well, so I am, but I suppose he knows I'm a lady. I would scorn to scold him. Anyway, she says she's not engaged. I don't know why she wanted you to know, but she said to me three times—'Mind you tell Mr. Winterbourne.' And then she told me to ask if you remembered the time you went to that castle, in Switzerland. But I said I wouldn't give any such messages as that. Only, if she is not engaged, I'm sure I'm glad to know it."

But, as Winterbourne had said, it mattered very little. A week after this the poor girl died; it had been a terrible case of the fever. Daisy's grave was in the little Protestant cemetery, in an angle of the wall of imperial Rome, beneath the cypresses and the thick spring flowers. Winterbourne stood there beside it, with a number of other mourners; a number larger than the scandal excited by the young lady's career would have led you to expect. Near him stood Giovanelli, who came nearer still before Winterbourne turned away. Giovanelli was very pale; on this occasion he had no flower in his buttonhole, he seemed to wish to say something. At last he said, "She was the most beautiful young lady I ever saw, and the most amiable." And then he added in a moment, "And she was the most innocent."

Winterbourne looked at him, and presently repeated his words, "And the most innocent?"

"The most innocent!"

Winterbourne felt sore and angry. "Why the devil," he asked, "did you take her to that fatal place?"

Mr. Giovanelli's urbanity was apparently imperturbable. He looked on the ground a moment, and then he said, "For myself, I had no fear; and she wanted to go."

"That was no reason!" Winterbourne declared.

The subtle Roman again dropped his eyes. "If she had lived, I should have got nothing. She would never have married me, I am sure."

"She would never have married you?"

"For a moment I hoped so. But no. I am sure."

Winterbourne listened to him; he stood staring at the raw protuberance among the April daisies. When he turned away again Mr. Giovanelli, with his light slow step, had retired.

Winterbourne almost immediately left Rome, but the following summer he again met his aunt, Mrs. Costello, at Vevey. Mrs. Costello was fond of Vevey. In the interval Winterbourne had often thought of Daisy Miller and her mystifying manners. One day he spoke of her to his aunt—said it was on his conscience that he had done her injustice.

"I am sure I don't know," said Mrs. Costello. "How did your injustice affect her?"

"She sent me a message before her death which I didn't understand at the time. But I have understood it since. She would have appreciated one's esteem."

"Is that a modest way," asked Mrs. Costello, "of saying that she would have reciprocated one's affection?"

Winterbourne offered no answer to this question, but he presently said, "You were right in that remark that you made last summer. I was booked to make a mistake. I have lived too long in foreign parts."

Nevertheless, he went back to live at Geneva, whence there continue to come the most contradictory accounts of his motives of sojourn: a report that he is "studying" hard—an intimation that he is much interested in a very clever foreign lady.

THE PORTRAIT
OF A LADY

❧ 1 ❧

U nder certain circumstances there are few hours in life more agreeable
than the hour dedicated to the ceremony known as afternoon tea. There
are circumstances in which, whether you partake of the tea or not—
some people of course never do—the situation is in itself delightful. Those that I
have in mind in beginning to unfold this simple history offered an admirable setting to an innocent pastime. The implements of the little feast had been disposed
upon the lawn of an old English country house, in what I should call the perfect
middle of a splendid summer afternoon. Part of the afternoon had waned, but much
of it was left, and what was left was of the finest and rarest quality. Real dusk would
not arrive for many hours; but the flood of summer light had begun to ebb, the air
had grown mellow, the shadows were long upon the smooth, dense turf. They
lengthened slowly, however, and the scene expressed that sense of leisure still to
come which is perhaps the chief source of one's enjoyment of such a scene at such
an hour. From five o'clock to eight is on certain occasions a little eternity; but on
such an occasion as this the interval could be only an eternity of pleasure. The persons concerned in it were taking their pleasure quietly, and they were not of the sex
which is supposed to furnish the regular votaries of the ceremony I have mentioned. The shadows on the perfect lawn were straight and angular; they were the
shadows of an old man sitting in a deep wicker chair near the low table on which
the tea had been served, and of two younger men strolling to and fro, in desultory
talk, in front of him. The old man had his cup in his hand; it was an unusually large
cup, of a different pattern from the rest of the set, and painted in brilliant colors.
He disposed of its contents with much circumspection, holding it for a long time
close to his chin, with his face turned to the house. His companions had either finished their tea or were indifferent to their privilege; they smoked cigarettes as they
continued to stroll. One of them, from time to time, as he passed, looked with a certain attention at the elder man, who, unconscious of observation, rested his eyes
upon the rich red front of his dwelling. The house that rose beyond the lawn was a
structure to repay such consideration, and was the most characteristic object in
the peculiarly English picture I have attempted to sketch.

It stood upon a low hill, above the river—the river being the Thames, at some forty miles from London. A long gabled front of red brick, with the complexion of which time and the weather had played all sorts of picturesque tricks, only, however, to improve and refine it, presented itself to the lawn, with its patches of ivy, its clustered chimneys, its windows smothered in creepers. The house had a name and a history; the old gentleman taking his tea would have been delighted to tell you these things: how it had been built under Edward the Sixth, had offered a night's hospitality to the great Elizabeth (whose august person had extended itself upon a huge, magnificent, and terribly angular bed which still formed the principal honor of the sleeping apartments), had been a good deal bruised and defaced in Cromwell's wars, and then, under the Restoration, repaired and much enlarged; and how, finally, after having been remodeled and disfigured in the eighteenth century, it had passed into the careful keeping of a shrewd American banker, who had bought it originally because (owing to circumstances too complicated to set forth) it was offered at a great bargain; bought it with much grumbling at its ugliness, its antiquity, its incommodity, and who now, at the end of twenty years, had become conscious of a real æsthetic passion for it, so that he knew all its points, and would tell you just where to stand to see them in combination, and just the hour when the shadows of its various protuberances—which fell so softly upon the warm, weary brickwork—were of the right measure. Besides this, as I have said, he could have counted off most of the successive owners and occupants, several of whom were known to general fame; doing so, however, with an undemonstrative conviction that the latest phase of its destiny was not the least honorable. The front of the house, overlooking that portion of the lawn with which we are concerned, was not the entrance-front; this was in quite another quarter. Privacy here reigned supreme, and the wide carpet of turf that covered the level hilltop seemed but the extension of a luxurious interior. The great still oaks and beeches flung down a shade as dense as that of velvet curtains; and the place was furnished, like a room, with cushioned seats, with rich-colored rugs, with the books and papers that lay upon the grass. The river was at some distance; where the ground began to slope, the lawn, properly speaking, ceased. But it was nonetheless a charming walk down to the water.

The old gentleman at the tea table, who had come from America thirty years before, had brought with him, at the top of his baggage, his American physiognomy; and he had not only brought it with him, but he had kept it in the best order, so that, if necessary, he might have taken it back to his own country with perfect confidence. But at present, obviously, he was not likely to displace himself; his journeys were over, and he was taking the rest that precedes the great rest. He had a narrow, clean-shaven face, with evenly distributed features, and an expression of placid acuteness. It was evidently a face in which the range of expression was not large; so that the air of contented shrewdness was all the more of a merit. It seemed to tell that he had been successful in life, but it seemed to tell also that his success had not been exclusive and invidious, but had had much of the inoffensiveness of failure. He had certainly had a great experience of men; but there was an almost rustic simplicity in the faint smile that played upon his lean, spacious cheek, and lighted up his humorous eye, as he at last slowly and carefully deposited his big teacup upon the table. He was neatly dressed, in well-brushed black; but a shawl was folded upon his knees, and his feet were encased in thick, embroidered slippers. A beautiful collie dog lay upon the grass near his chair, watching the master's face almost as tenderly as the master contemplated the still more magisterial physiognomy of the house; and a little bristling, bustling terrier bestowed a desultory attendance upon the other gentlemen.

One of these was a remarkably well-made man of five-and-thirty, with a face as English as that of the old gentleman I have just sketched was something else; a noticeably handsome face, fresh-colored, fair, and frank, with firm, straight features, a lively gray eye, and the rich adornment of a chestnut beard. This person had a certain fortunate, brilliant exceptional look—the air of a happy temperament fertilized by a high civilization—which would have made almost any observer envy him at a venture. He was booted and spurred, as if he had dismounted from a long ride; he wore a white hat, which looked too large for him; he held his two hands behind him, and in one of them—a large, white, well-shaped fist—was crumpled a pair of soiled dog-skin gloves.

His companion, measuring the length of the lawn beside him, was a person of quite another pattern, who, although he might have excited grave curiosity, would not, like the other, have provoked you to wish yourself, almost blindly, in his place. Tall, lean, loosely and feebly put together, he had an ugly, sickly, witty, charming face—furnished, but by no means decorated, with a straggling moustache and whisker. He looked clever and ill—a combination by no means felicitous; and he wore a brown velvet jacket. He carried his hands in his pockets, and there was something in the way he did it that showed the habit was inveterate. His gait had a shambling, wandering quality; he was not very firm on his legs. As I have said, whenever he passed the old man in the chair, he rested his eyes upon him; and at this moment, with their faces brought into relation, you would easily have seen that they were father and son.

The father caught his son's eye at last, and gave him a mild, responsive smile.

"I am getting on very well," he said.

"Have you drunk your tea?" asked the son.

"Yes, and enjoyed it."

"Shall I give you some more?"

The old man considered, placidly.

"Well, I guess I will wait and see."

He had, in speaking, the American tone.

"Are you cold?" his son inquired.

The father slowly rubbed his legs.

"Well, I don't know. I can't tell till I feel."

"Perhaps someone might feel for you," said the younger man, laughing.

"Oh, I hope someone will always feel for me! Don't you feel for me, Lord Warburton?"

"Oh yes, immensely," said the gentleman addressed as Lord Warburton, promptly. "I am bound to say you look wonderfully comfortable."

"Well, I suppose I am, in most respects." And the old man looked down at his green shawl, and smoothed it over his knees. "The fact is, I have been comfortable so many years that I suppose I have got so used to it I don't know it."

"Yes, that's the bore of comfort," said Lord Warburton. "We only know when we are uncomfortable."

"It strikes me that we are rather particular," said his companion.

"Oh yes, there is no doubt we're particular," Lord Warburton murmured.

And then the three men remained silent a while; the two younger ones standing looking down at the other, who presently asked for more tea.

"I should think you would be very unhappy with that shawl," said Lord Warburton, while his companion filled the old man's cup again.

"Oh no, he must have the shawl!" cried the gentleman in the velvet coat. "Don't put such ideas as that into his head."

"It belongs to my wife," said the old man, simply.

"Oh, if it's for sentimental reasons——" And Lord Warburton made a gesture of apology.

"I suppose I must give it to her when she comes," the old man went on.

"You will please to do nothing of the kind. You will keep it to cover your poor old legs."

"Well, you mustn't abuse my legs," said the old man. "I guess they are as good as yours."

"Oh, you are perfectly free to abuse mine," his son replied, giving him his tea.

"Well, we are two lame ducks; I don't think there is much difference."

"I am much obliged to you for calling me a duck. How is your tea?"

"Well, it's rather hot."

"That's intended to be a merit."

"Ah, there's a great deal of merit," murmured the old man, kindly. "He's a very good nurse, Lord Warburton."

"Isn't he a bit clumsy?" asked his lordship.

"Oh no, he's not clumsy—considering that he's an invalid himself. He's a very good nurse—for a sick-nurse. I call him my sick-nurse because he's sick himself."

"Oh, come, daddy!" the ugly young man exclaimed.

"Well, you are; I wish you weren't. But I suppose you can't help it."

"I might try: that's an idea," said the young man.

"Were you ever sick, Lord Warburton?" his father asked.

Lord Warburton considered a moment.

"Yes, sir, once, in the Persian Gulf."

"He is making light of you, daddy," said the other young man. "That's a sort of joke."

"Well, there seem to be so many sorts now," daddy replied, serenely. "You don't look as if you had been sick, anyway, Lord Warburton."

"He is sick of life; he was just telling me so; going on fearfully about it," said Lord Warburton's friend.

"Is that true, sir?" asked the old man gravely.

"If it is, your son gave me no consolation. He's a wretched fellow to talk to—a regular cynic. He doesn't seem to believe anything."

"That's another sort of joke," said the person accused of cynicism.

"It's because his health is so poor," his father explained to Lord Warburton. "It affects his mind, and colors his way of looking at things; he seems to feel as if he had never had a chance. But it's almost entirely theoretical, you know; it doesn't seem to affect his spirits. I have hardly ever seen him when he wasn't cheerful—about as he is at present. He often cheers me up."

The young man so described looked at Lord Warburton and laughed.

"Is it a glowing eulogy or an accusation of levity? Should you like me to carry out my theories, daddy?"

"By Jove, we should see some queer things!" cried Lord Warburton.

"I hope you haven't taken up that sort of tone," said the old man.

"Warburton's tone is worse than mine; he pretends to be bored. I am not in the least bored; I find life only too interesting."

"Ah, *too* interesting; you shouldn't allow it to be that, you know!"

"I am never bored when I come here," said Lord Warburton. "One gets such uncommonly good talk."

"Is that another sort of joke?" asked the old man. "You have no excuse for being bored anywhere. When I was your age, I had never heard of such a thing."

"You must have developed very late."

"No, I developed very quick; that was just the reason. When I was twenty years old, I was very highly developed indeed. I was working, tooth and nail. You wouldn't be bored if you had something to do; but all you young men are too idle. You think too much of your pleasure. You are too fastidious, and too indolent, and too rich."

"Oh, I say," cried Lord Warburton, "you're hardly the person to accuse a fellow creature of being too rich!"

"Do you mean because I am a banker?" asked the old man.

"Because of that, if you like; and because you are so ridiculously wealthy."

"He isn't very rich," said the other young man, indicating his father. "He has given away an immense deal of money."

"Well, I suppose it was his own," said Lord Warburton; "and in that case could there be a better proof of wealth? Let not a public benefactor talk of one's being too fond of pleasure."

"Daddy is very fond of pleasure—of other people's."

The old man shook his head.

"I don't pretend to have contributed anything to the amusement of my contemporaries."

"My dear father, you are too modest!"

"That's a kind of joke, sir," said Lord Warburton.

"You young men have too many jokes. When there are no jokes, you have nothing left."

"Fortunately there are always more jokes," the ugly young man remarked.

"I don't believe it—I believe things are getting more serious. You young men will find that out."

"The increasing seriousness of things—that is the great opportunity of jokes."

"They will have to be grim jokes," said the old man. "I am convinced there will be great changes; and not all for the better."

"I quite agree with you, sir," Lord Warburton declared. "I am very sure there will be great changes, and that all sorts of queer things will happen. That's why I find so much difficulty in applying your advice; you know you told me the other day that I ought to 'take hold' of something. One hesitates to take hold of a thing that may the next moment be knocked sky-high."

"You ought to take hold of a pretty woman," said his companion. "He is trying hard to fall in love," he added, by way of explanation, to his father.

"The pretty women themselves may be sent flying!" Lord Warburton exclaimed.

"No, no, they will be firm," the old man rejoined; "they will not be affected by the social and political changes I just referred to."

"You mean they won't be abolished? Very well, then, I will lay hands on one as soon as possible, and tie her round my neck as a life-preserver."

"The ladies will save us," said the old man; "that is, the best of them will—for I make a difference between them. Make up to a good one and marry her, and your life will become much more interesting."

A momentary silence marked perhaps on the part of his auditors a sense of the magnanimity of this speech, for it was a secret neither for his son nor for his visitor that his own experience in matrimony had not been a happy one. As he said, however, he made a difference; and these words may have been intended as a confession of personal error; though of course it was not in place for either of his companions to remark that apparently the lady of his choice had not been one of the best.

"If I marry an interesting woman, I shall be interested: is that what you say?" Lord Warburton asked. "I am not at all keen about marrying—your son misrepresented me; but there is no knowing what an interesting woman might do with me."

"I should like to see your idea of an interesting woman," said his friend.

"My dear fellow, you can't see ideas—especially such ethereal ones as mine. If I could only see it myself—that would be a great step in advance."

"Well, you may fall in love with whomsoever you please; but you must not fall in love with my niece," said the old man.

His son broke into a laugh. "He will think you mean that as a provocation! My dear father, you have lived with the English for thirty years, and you have picked up a good many of the things they say. But you have never learned the things they don't say!"

"I say what I please," the old man declared, with all his serenity.

"I haven't the honor of knowing your niece," Lord Warburton said. "I think it is the first time I have heard of her."

"She is a niece of my wife's; Mrs. Touchett brings her to England."

Then young Mr. Touchett explained. "My mother, you know, has been spending the winter in America, and we are expecting her back. She writes that she has discovered a niece, and that she has invited her to come with her."

"I see—very kind of her," said Lord Warburton. "Is the young lady interesting?"

"We hardly know more about her than you; my mother has not gone into details. She chiefly communicates with us by means of telegrams, and her telegrams are rather inscrutable. They say women don't know how to write them, but my mother has thoroughly mastered the art of condensation. 'Tired America, hot weather awful, return England with niece, first steamer, decent cabin.' That's the sort of message we get from her—that was the last that came. But there had been another before, which I think contained the first mention of the niece. 'Changed hotel, very bad, impudent clerk, address here. Taken sister's girl, died last year, go to Europe, two sisters, quite independent.' Over that my father and I have scarcely stopped puzzling; it seems to admit of so many interpretations."

"There is one thing very clear in it," said the old man; "she has given the hotel clerk a dressing."

"I am not sure even of that, since he has driven her from the field. We thought at first that the sister mentioned might be the sister of the clerk; but the subsequent mention of a niece seems to prove that the allusion is to one of my aunts. Then there was a question as to whose the two other sisters were; they are probably two of my late aunt's daughters. But who is 'quite independent,' and in what sense is

the term used?—that point is not yet settled. Does the expression apply more particularly to the young lady my mother has adopted, or does it characterise her sisters equally?—and is it used in a moral or in a financial sense? Does it mean that
they have been left well off, or that they wish to be under no obligations? or does it
simply mean that they are fond of their own way?"

"Whatever else it means, it is pretty sure to mean that," Mr. Touchett remarked.

"You will see for yourself," said Lord Warburton. "When does Mrs. Touchett
arrive?"

"We are quite in the dark; as soon as she can find a decent cabin. She may be
waiting for it yet; on the other hand, she may already have disembarked in England."

"In that case she would probably have telegraphed to you."

"She never telegraphs when you would expect it—only when you don't," said the
old man. "She likes to drop on me suddenly; she thinks she will find me doing something wrong. She has never done so yet, but she is not discouraged."

"It's her independence," her son explained, more favorably. "Whatever that of
those young ladies may be, her own is a match for it. She likes to do everything for
herself, and has no belief in anyone's power to help her. She thinks me of no more
use than a postage-stamp without gum, and she would never forgive me if I should
presume to go to Liverpool to meet her."

"Will you at least let me know when your cousin arrives?" Lord Warburton asked.

"Only on the condition I have mentioned—that you don't fall in love with her!"
Mr. Touchett declared.

"That strikes me as hard. Don't you think me good enough?"

"I think you too good—because I shouldn't like her to marry you. She hasn't
come here to look for a husband, I hope; so many young ladies are doing that, as if
there were no good ones at home. Then she is probably engaged; American girls are
usually engaged, I believe. Moreover, I am not sure, after all, that you would be a
good husband."

"Very likely she is engaged; I have known a good many American girls, and they
always were; but I could never see that it made any difference, upon my word! As
for my being a good husband, I am not sure of that either; one can but try!"

"Try as much as you please, but don't try on my niece," said the old man, whose
opposition to the idea was broadly humorous.

"Ah, well," said Lord Warburton, with a humor broader still, "perhaps, after all,
she is not worth trying on!"

❧ 2 ❧

While this exchange of pleasantries took place between the two, Ralph Touchett wandered away a little, with his usual slouching gait, his hands in his pockets, and his little rowdyish terrier at his heels. His face was turned toward the house, but his eyes were bent, musingly, upon the lawn; so that he had been an object of observation to a person who had just made her appearance in the doorway of the dwelling for some moments before he perceived her. His attention was called to her by the conduct of his dog, who had suddenly darted forward, with a little volley of shrill barks, in which the note of welcome, however, was more sensible than that of defiance. The person in question was a young lady, who seemed immediately to interpret the greeting of the little terrier. He advanced with great rapidity, and stood at her feet, looking up and barking hard; whereupon, without hesitation, she stooped and caught him in her hands, holding him face to face while he continued his joyous demonstration. His master now had had time to follow and to see that Bunchie's new friend was a tall girl in a black dress, who at first sight looked pretty. She was bareheaded, as if she were staying in the house—a fact which conveyed perplexity to the son of its master, conscious of that immunity from visitors which had for some time been rendered necessary by the latter's ill-health. Meantime the two other gentlemen had also taken note of the newcomer.

"Dear me, who is that strange woman?" Mr. Touchett had asked.

"Perhaps it is Mrs. Touchett's niece—the independent young lady," Lord Warburton suggested. "I think she must be, from the way she handles the dog."

The collie, too, had now allowed his attention to be diverted, and he trotted toward the young lady in the doorway, slowly setting his tail in motion as he went.

"But where is my wife, then?" murmured the old man.

"I suppose the young lady has left her somewhere: that's a part of the independence."

The girl spoke to Ralph, smiling, while she still held up the terrier. "Is this your little dog, sir?"

"He was mine a moment ago; but you have suddenly acquired a remarkable air of property in him."

"Couldn't we share him?" asked the girl. "He's such a little darling."

Ralph looked at her a moment; she was unexpectedly pretty. "You may have him altogether," he said.

The young lady seemed to have a great deal of confidence, both in herself and in others; but this abrupt generosity made her blush. "I ought to tell you that I am probably your cousin," she murmured, putting down the dog. "And here's another!" she added quickly, as the collie came up.

"Probably?" the young man exclaimed, laughing. "I supposed it was quite settled! Have you come with my mother?"

"Yes, half-an-hour ago."

"And has she deposited you and departed again?"

"No, she went straight to her room; and she told me that, if I should see you, I was to say to you that you must come to her there at a quarter to seven."

The young man looked at his watch. "Thank you very much; I shall be punctual." And then he looked at his cousin. "You are very welcome here," he went on. "I am delighted to see you."

She was looking at everything, with an eye that denoted quick perception—at her companion, at the two dogs, at the two gentlemen under the trees, at the beautiful scene that surrounded her. "I have never seen anything so lovely as this place," she said. "I have been all over the house; it's too enchanting."

"I am sorry you should have been here so long without our knowing it."

"Your mother told me that in England people arrived very quietly; so I thought it was all right. Is one of those gentlemen your father?"

"Yes, the elder one—the one sitting down," said Ralph.

The young girl gave a laugh. "I don't suppose it's the other. Who is the other?"

"He is a friend of ours—Lord Warburton."

"Oh, I hoped there would be a lord; it's just like a novel!" And then—"O you adorable creature!" she suddenly cried, stooping down and picking up the little terrier again.

She remained standing where they had met, making no offer to advance or to speak to Mr. Touchett, and while she lingered in the doorway, slim and charming, her interlocutor wondered whether she expected the old man to come and pay her his respects. American girls were used to a great deal of deference, and it had been intimated that this one had a high spirit. Indeed, Ralph could see that in her face.

"Won't you come and make acquaintance with my father?" he nevertheless ventured to ask. "He is old and infirm—he doesn't leave his chair."

"Ah, poor man, I am very sorry!" the girl exclaimed, immediately moving forward. "I got the impression from your mother that he was rather—rather strong."

Ralph Touchett was silent a moment.

"She has not seen him for a year."

"Well, he has got a lovely place to sit. Come along, little dogs."

"It's a dear old place," said the young man, looking sidewise at his neighbor.

"What's his name?" she asked, her attention having reverted to the terrier again.

"My father's name?"

"Yes," said the young lady, humorously; "but don't tell him I asked you."

They had come by this time to where old Mr. Touchett was sitting, and he slowly got up from his chair to introduce himself.

"My mother has arrived," said Ralph, "and this is Miss Archer."

The old man placed his two hands on her shoulders, looked at her a moment with extreme benevolence, and then gallantly kissed her.

"It is a great pleasure to me to see you here; but I wish you had given us a chance to receive you."

"Oh, we were received," said the girl. "There were about a dozen servants in the hall. And there was an old woman curtseying at the gate."

"We can do better than that—if we have notice!" And the old man stood there, smiling, rubbing his hands, and slowly shaking his head at her. "But Mrs. Touchett doesn't like receptions."

"She went straight to her room."

"Yes—and locked herself in. She always does that. Well, I suppose I shall see her next week." And Mrs. Touchett's husband slowly resumed his former posture.

"Before that," said Miss Archer. "She is coming down to dinner—at eight o'clock. Don't you forget a quarter to seven," she added, turning with a smile to Ralph.

"What is to happen at a quarter to seven?"

"I am to see my mother," said Ralph.

"Ah, happy boy!" the old man murmured. "You must sit down—you must have some tea," he went on, addressing his wife's niece.

"They gave me some tea in my room the moment I arrived," this young lady answered. "I am sorry you are out of health," she added, resting her eyes upon her venerable host.

"Oh, I'm an old man, my dear; it's time for me to be old. But I shall be the better for having you here."

She had been looking all round her again—at the lawn, the great trees, the reedy, silvery Thames, the beautiful old house; and while engaged in this survey, she had also narrowly scrutinized her companions; a comprehensiveness of observation easily conceivable on the part of a young woman who was evidently both intelligent and excited. She had seated herself, and had put away the little dog; her white hands, in her lap, were folded upon her black dress; her head was erect, her eye brilliant, her flexible figure turned itself lightly this way and that, in sympathy with the alertness with which she evidently caught impressions. Her impressions were numerous, and they were all reflected in a clear, still smile. "I have never seen anything so beautiful as this," she declared.

"It's looking very well," said Mr. Touchett. "I know the way it strikes you. I have been through all that. But you are very beautiful yourself," he added with a politeness by no means crudely jocular, and with the happy consciousness that his advanced age gave him the privilege of saying such things—even to young girls who might possibly take alarm at them.

What degree of alarm this young girl took need not be exactly measured; she instantly rose, however, with a blush which was not a refutation.

"Oh yes, of course, I'm lovely!" she exclaimed quickly, with a little laugh. "How old is your house? Is it Elizabethan?"

"It's early Tudor," said Ralph Touchett.

She turned toward him, watching his face a little. "Early Tudor? How very delightful! And I suppose there are a great many others."

"There are many much better ones."

"Don't say that, my son!" the old man protested. "There is nothing better than this."

"I have got a very good one; I think in some respects it's rather better," said Lord Warburton, who as yet had not spoken, but who had kept an attentive eye upon Miss Archer. He bent toward her a little smiling; he had an excellent manner with women. The girl appreciated it in an instant; she had not forgotten that this was Lord Warburton. "I should like very much to show it to you," he added.

"Don't believe him," cried the old man; "don't look at it! It's a wretched old barrack—not to be compared with this."

"I don't know—I can't judge," said the girl, smiling at Lord Warburton.

In this discussion, Ralph Touchett took no interest whatever; he stood with his hands in his pockets, looking greatly as if he should like to renew his conversation with his new-found cousin.

"Are you very fond of dogs?" he inquired, by way of beginning; and it was an awkward beginning for a clever man.

"Very fond of them indeed."

"You must keep the terrier, you know," he went on, still awkwardly.

"I will keep him while I am here, with pleasure."

"That will be for a long time, I hope."

"You are very kind. I hardly know. My aunt must settle that."

"I will settle it with her—at a quarter to seven." And Ralph looked at his watch again.

"I am glad to be here at all," said the girl.

"I don't believe you allow things to be settled for you."

"Oh yes; if they are settled as I like them."

"I shall settle this as I like it," said Ralph. "It's most unaccountable that we should never have known you."

"I was there—you had only to come and see me."

"There? Where do you mean?"

"In the United States: in New York, and Albany, and other places."

"I have been there—all over, but I never saw you. I can't make it out."

Miss Archer hesitated a moment.

"It was because there had been some disagreement between your mother and my father, after my mother's death, which took place when I was a child. In consequence of it, we never expected to see you."

"Ah, but I don't embrace all my mother's quarrels—Heaven forbid!" the young man cried. "You have lately lost your father?" he went on, more gravely.

"Yes; more than a year ago. After that my aunt was very kind to me; she came to see me, and proposed that I should come to Europe."

"I see," said Ralph. "She has adopted you."

"Adopted me?" The girl stared, and her blush came back to her, together with a momentary look of pain, which gave her interlocutor some alarm. He had underestimated the effect of his words. Lord Warburton, who appeared constantly desirous of a nearer view of Miss Archer, strolled toward the two cousins at the moment, and as he did so, she rested her startled eyes upon him. "Oh, no; she has not adopted me," she said. "I am not a candidate for adoption."

"I beg a thousand pardons," Ralph murmured. "I meant—I meant——" He hardly knew what he meant.

"You meant she has taken me up. Yes; she likes to take people up. She has been very kind to me; but," she added, with a certain visible eagerness of desire to be explicit, "I am very fond of my liberty."

"Are you talking about Mrs. Touchett?" the old man called out from his chair. "Come here, my dear, and tell me about her. I am always thankful for information."

The girl hesitated a moment, smiling.

"She is really very benevolent," she answered; and then she went over to her uncle, whose mirth was excited by her words.

Lord Warburton was left standing with Ralph Touchett, to whom in a moment he said—

"You wished a while ago to see my idea of an interesting woman. There it is!"

❧ 3 ❧

Mrs. Touchett was certainly a person of many oddities, of which her behavior on returning to her husband's house after many months was a noticeable specimen. She had her own way of doing all that she did, and this is the simplest description of a character which, although it was by no means without benevolence, rarely succeeded in giving an impression of softness. Mrs. Touchett might do a great deal of good, but she never pleased. This way of her own, of which she was so fond, was not intrinsically offensive—it was simply very sharply distinguished from the ways of others. The edges of her conduct were so very clear-cut that for susceptible persons it sometimes had a wounding effect. This purity of outline was visible in her deportment during the first hours of her return from America, under circumstances in which it might have seemed that her first act would have been to exchange greetings with her husband and son. Mrs. Touchett, for reasons which she deemed excellent, always retired on such occasions into impenetrable seclusion, postponing the more sentimental ceremony until she had achieved a toilet which had the less reason to be of high importance as neither beauty nor vanity were concerned in it. She was a plain-faced old woman, without coquetry and without any great elegance, but with an extreme respect for her own motives. She was usually prepared to explain these—when the explanation was asked as a favor; and in such a case they proved totally different from those that had been attributed to her. She was virtually separated from her husband, but she appeared to perceive nothing irregular in the situation. It had become apparent, at an early stage of their relations, that they should never desire the same thing at the same moment, and this fact had prompted her to rescue disagreement from the vulgar realm of accident. She did what she could to erect it into a law—a much more edifying aspect of it—by going to live in Florence, where she bought a house and established herself; leaving her husband in England to take care of his bank. This arrangement greatly pleased her; it was so extremely definite. It struck her husband in the same light, in a foggy square in London, where it was at times the most definite fact he discerned; but he would have preferred that discomfort should have a greater vagueness. To agree to disagree had cost him an effort; he was ready to agree to almost anything but that, and saw no reason why either assent or dissent should be so terribly consistent. Mrs. Touchett indulged in no regrets nor speculations, and usually came once a year to spend a month with her husband, a period during which she apparently took pains to convince him that she had adopted the right system. She was not fond of England, and had three or four reasons for it to which she currently alluded; they bore upon minor points of British civilization, but for Mrs. Touchett they amply justified nonresidence. She detested bread-sauce, which, as she said, looked like a poultice and tasted like soap; she objected to the consumption of beer by her maid-servants; and she affirmed that the British laundress (Mrs. Touchett was very particular about the appearance of her linen) was not a mistress of her art. At fixed intervals she paid a visit to her own country; but this last one had been longer than any of its predecessors.

She had taken up her niece—there was little doubt of that. One wet afternoon, some four months earlier than the occurrence lately narrated, this young lady had been seated along with a book. To say that she had a book is to say that her solitude did not press upon her; for her love of knowledge had a fertilizing quality and her imagination was strong. There was at this time, however, a want of lightness in her situation, which the arrival of an unexpected visitor did much to dispel. The visitor had not been announced; the girl heard her at last walking about the adjoining room. It was an old house at Albany—a large, square, double house, with a notice of sale in the windows of the parlor. There were two entrances, one of which had long been out of use, but had never been removed. They were exactly alike—large white doors, with an arched frame and wide sidelights, perched upon little "stoops" of red stone, which descended sidewise to the brick pavement of the street. The two houses together formed a single dwelling, the party-wall having been removed and the rooms placed in communication. These rooms, above stairs, were extremely numerous, and were painted all over exactly alike, in a yellowish white which had grown sallow with time. On the third floor there was a sort of arched passage, connecting the two sides of the house, which Isabel and her sisters used in their childhood to call the tunnel, and which, though it was short and well-lighted, always seemed to the girl to be strange and lonely, especially on winter afternoons. She had been in the house, at different periods, as a child; in those days her grandmother lived there. Then there had been an absence of ten years, followed by a return to Albany before her father's death. Her grandmother, old Mrs. Archer, had exercised, chiefly within the limits of the family, a large hospitality in the early period, and the little girls often spent weeks under her roof—weeks of which Isabel had the happiest memory. The manner of life was different from that of her own home—larger, more plentiful, more sociable; the discipline of the nursery was delightfully vague, and the opportunity of listening to the conversation of one's elders (which with Isabel was a highly valued pleasure) almost unbounded. There was a constant coming and going; her grandmother's sons and daughters, and their children, appeared to be in the enjoyment of standing invitations to stay with her, so that the house offered, to a certain extent, the appearance of a bustling provincial inn, kept by a gentle old landlady who sighed a great deal and never presented a bill. Isabel, of course, knew nothing about bills; but even as a child she thought her grandmother's dwelling picturesque. There was a covered piazza behind it, furnished with a swing, which was a source of tremulous interest; and beyond this was a long garden, sloping down to the stable, and containing certain capital peach trees. Isabel had stayed with her grandmother at various seasons; but, somehow, all her visits had a flavor of peaches. On the other side, opposite, across the street, was an old house that was called the Dutch House—a peculiar structure, dating from the earliest colonial time, composed of bricks that had been painted yellow, crowned with a gable that was pointed out to strangers, defended by a rickety wooden paling, and standing sidewise to the street. It was occupied by a primary school for children of both sexes, kept in an amateurish manner by a demonstrative lady, of whom Isabel's chief recollection was that her hair was puffed out very much at the temples and that she was the widow of someone of consequence. The little girl had been offered the opportunity of laying a foundation of knowledge in this establishment; but having spent a single day in it, she had expressed great disgust with the place, and had been allowed to stay at home, where in the September days, when the windows of the Dutch House were open, she used to hear the hum of childish voices repeating the multiplication table—an incident in which the elation of liberty and the pain of exclusion were indistinguishably mingled. The foundation of her knowledge was really laid in the idleness of her grandmother's house, where, as most of the other inmates were not reading people, she had uncontrolled use of a library full of books with frontispieces, which she used to climb upon a chair to take down. When she had found one to her taste—she was guided in the selection chiefly by the frontispiece—she carried it into a mysterious apartment which lay beyond the library, and which was called, traditionally, no one knew why, the office. Whose office it had been, and at what period it had flourished, she never learned; it was enough for her that it contained an echo and a pleasant musty smell, and that it was a chamber of disgrace for old pieces of furniture, whose infirmities were not always apparent (so that the disgrace seemed unmerited, and rendered them victims of injustice), and with which, in the manner of children, she had established relations almost human, or dramatic. There was an old haircloth sofa, in especial, to which she had confided a hundred childish sorrows. The place owed much of its mysterious melancholy to the fact that it was properly entered from the second door of the house, the door that had been condemned, and that was fastened by bolts which a particularly slender little girl found it impossible to slide. She knew that this silent, motionless portal opened into the street; if the sidelights had not been filled with green paper, she might have looked out upon the little brown stoop and the well-worn brick pavement. But she had no wish to look out, for this would have interfered with her theory that there was a strange, unseen place on the other side—a place which became, to the child's imagination, according to its different moods, a region of delight or of terror.

It was in the "office" still that Isabel was sitting on that melancholy afternoon of early spring which I have just mentioned. At this time she might have had the whole house to choose from, and the room she had selected was the most joyless chamber it contained. She had never opened the bolted door nor removed the green paper (renewed by other hands) from its sidelights; she had never assured herself that the vulgar street lay beyond it. A crude, cold rain was falling heavily; the springtime presented itself as a questionable improvement. Isabel, however, gave as little attention as possible to the incongruities of the season; she kept her eyes on her book and tried to fix her mind. It had lately occurred to her that her mind was a good deal of a vagabond, and she had spent much ingenuity in training it to a military step, and teaching it to advance, to halt, to retreat, to perform even more complicated maneuvers, at the word of command. Just now she had given it marching orders, and it had been trudging over the sandy plains of a history of German thought. Suddenly she became aware of a step very different from her own intellectual pace; she listened a little, and perceived that someone was walking about the library, which communicated with the office. It struck her first as the step of a person from whom she had reason to expect a visit; then almost immediately announced itself as the tread of a woman and a stranger—her possible visitor being neither. It had an inquisitive, experimental quality, which suggested that it would not stop short of the threshold of the office; and, in fact, the doorway of this apartment was presently occupied by a lady who paused there and looked very hard at our heroine. She was a plain, elderly woman, dressed in a comprehensive waterproof mantle: she had a sharp, but not an unpleasant, face.

"Oh," she said, "is that where you usually sit?" And she looked about at the heterogeneous chairs and tables.

"Not when I have visitors," said Isabel, getting up to receive the intruder.

She directed their course back to the library, and the visitor continued to look about her. "You seem to have plenty of other rooms; they are in rather better condition. But everything is immensely worn."

"Have you come to look at the house?" Isabel asked. "The servant will show it to you."

"Send her away; I don't want to buy it. She has probably gone to look for you, and is wandering about upstairs; she didn't seem at all intelligent. You had better tell her it is no matter." And then, while the girl stood there, hesitating and wondering, this unexpected critic said to her abruptly, "I suppose you are one of the daughters?"

Isabel thought she had very strange manners. "It depends upon whose daughters you mean."

"The late Mr. Archer's—and my poor sister's."

"Ah," said Isabel, slowly, "you must be our crazy Aunt Lydia!"

"Is that what your father told you to call me? I am your Aunt Lydia, but I am not crazy. And which of the daughters are you?"

"I am the youngest of the three, and my name is Isabel."

"Yes; the others are Lilian and Edith. And are you the prettiest?"

"I have not the least idea," said the girl.

"I think you must be." And in this way the aunt and the niece made friends. The aunt had quarreled, years before, with her brother-in-law, after the death of her sister, taking him to task for the manner in which he brought up his three girls. Being a high-tempered man, he had requested her to mind her own business; and she had taken him at his word. For many years she held no communication with him, and after his death she addressed not a word to his daughters, who had been bred in that disrespectful view of her which we have just seen Isabel betray. Mrs. Touchett's behavior was, as usual, perfectly deliberate. She intended to go to America to look after her investments (with which her husband, in spite of his great financial position, had nothing to do), and would take advantage of this opportunity to inquire into the condition of her nieces. There was no need of writing, for she should attach no importance to any account of them that she should elicit by letter; she believed, always, in seeing for one's self. Isabel found, however, that she knew a good deal about them, and knew about the marriage of the two elder girls; knew that their poor father had left very little money, but that the house in Albany, which had passed into his hands, was to be sold for their benefit; knew, finally, that Edmund Ludlow, Lilian's husband, had taken upon himself to attend to this matter, in consideration of which the young couple, who had come to Albany during Mr. Archer's illness, were remaining there for the present, and, as well as Isabel herself, occupying the mansion.

"How much money do you expect to get for it?" Mrs. Touchett asked of the girl, who had brought her to sit in the front parlor, which she had inspected without enthusiasm.

"I haven't the least idea," said the girl.

"That's the second time you have said that to me," her aunt rejoined. "And yet you don't look at all stupid."

"I am not stupid; but I don't know anything about money."

"Yes, that's the way you were brought up—as if you were to inherit a million. In point of fact, what have you inherited?"

"I really can't tell you. You must ask Edmund and Lilian; they will be back in half-an-hour."

"In Florence we should call it a very bad house," said Mrs. Touchett; "but here, I suspect, it will bring a high price. It ought to make a considerable sum for each of you. In addition to that, you *must* have something else; it's most extraordinary your not knowing. The position is of value, and they will probably pull it down and make a row of shops. I wonder you don't do that yourself; you might let the shops to great advantage."

Isabel stared; the idea of letting shops was new to her.

"I hope they won't pull it down," she said; "I am extremely fond of it."

"I don't see what makes you fond of it; your father died here."

"Yes; but I don't dislike it for that," said the girl, rather strangely. "I like places in which things have happened—even if they are sad things. A great many people have died here; the place has been full of life."

"Is that what you call being full of life?"

"I mean full of experience—of people's feelings and sorrows. And not of their sorrows only, for I have been very happy here as a child."

"You should go to Florence if you like houses in which things have happened—especially deaths. I live in an old palace in which three people have been murdered; three that were known, and I don't know how many more besides."

"In an old palace?" Isabel repeated.

"Yes, my dear; a very different affair from this. This is very *bourgeois.*"

Isabel felt some emotion, for she had always thought highly of her grandmother's house. But the emotion was of a kind which led her to say—

"I should like very much to go to Florence."

"Well, if you will be very good, and do everything I tell you, I will take you there," Mrs. Touchett rejoined.

The girl's emotion deepened; she flushed a little, and smiled at her aunt in silence.

"Do everything you tell me? I don't think I can promise that."

"No, you don't look like a young lady of that sort. You are fond of your own way; but it's not for me to blame you."

"And yet, to go to Florence," the girl exclaimed in a moment, "I would promise almost anything!"

Edmund and Lilian were slow to return, and Mrs. Touchett had an hour's uninterrupted talk with her niece, who found her a strange and interesting person. She was as eccentric as Isabel had always supposed; and hitherto, whenever the girl had heard people described as eccentric, she had thought of them as disagreeable. To her imagination the term had always suggested something grotesque and inharmonious. But her aunt infused a new vividness into the idea, and gave her so many fresh impressions that it seemed to her she had overestimated the charms of conformity. She had never met anyone so entertaining as this little thin-lipped, bright-eyed, foreign-looking woman, who retrieved an insignificant appearance by a distinguished manner, and, sitting there in a well-worn waterproof, talked with striking familiarity of European courts. There was nothing flighty about Mrs. Touchett, but she was fond of social grandeur, and she enjoyed the consciousness of making an impression on a candid and susceptible mind. Isabel at first had answered a good many questions, and it was from her answers apparently that Mrs. Touchett derived a high opinion of her intelligence. But after this she had asked a good many, and her aunt's answers, whatever they were, struck her as deeply interesting. Mrs. Touchett waited for the return of her other niece as long as she thought reasonable, but as at six o'clock Mrs. Ludlow had not come in, she prepared to take her departure.

"Your sister must be a great gossip," she said. "Is she accustomed to staying out for hours?"

"You have been out almost as long as she," Isabel answered; "she can have left the house but a short time before you came in."

Mrs. Touchett looked at the girl without resentment; she appeared to enjoy a bold retort, and to be disposed to be gracious to her niece.

"Perhaps she has not had so good an excuse as I. Tell her, at any rate, that she must come and see me this evening at that horrid hotel. She may bring her husband if she likes, but she needn't bring you. I shall see plenty of you later."

❧ 4 ❧

Mrs. Ludlow was the eldest of the three sisters, and was usually thought the most sensible; the classification being in general that Lilian was the practical one, Edith the beauty, and Isabel the "intellectual" one. Mrs. Keyes, the second sister, was the wife of an officer in the United States Engineers, and as our history is not further concerned with her, it will be enough to say that she was indeed very pretty, and that she formed the ornament of those various military stations, chiefly in the unfashionable West, to which, to her deep chagrin, her husband was successively relegated. Lilian had married a New York lawyer, a young man with a loud voice and an enthusiasm for his profession; the match was not brilliant, any more than Edith's had been, but Lilian had occasionally been spoken of as a young woman who might be thankful to marry at all—she was so much plainer than her sisters. She was, however, very happy, and now, as the mother of two peremptory little boys, and the mistress of a house which presented a narrowness of new brownstone to Fifty-third Street, she had quite justified her claim to matrimony. She was short and plump, and, as people said, had improved since her marriage; the two things in life of which she was most distinctly conscious were her husband's force in argument and her sister Isabel's originality. "I have never felt like Isabel's sister, and I am sure I never shall," she had said to an intimate friend; a declaration which made it all the more creditable that she had been prolific in sisterly offices.

"I want to see her safely married—that's what I want to see," she frequently remarked to her husband.

"Well, I must say I should have no particular desire to marry her," Edmund Ludlow was accustomed to answer, in an extremely audible tone.

"I know you say that for argument; you always take the opposite ground. I don't see what you have against her, except that she is so original."

"Well, I don't like originals; I like translations," Mr. Ludlow had more than once replied. "Isabel is written in a foreign tongue. I can't make her out. She ought to marry an Armenian, or a Portuguese."

"That's just what I am afraid she will do!" cried Lilian, who thought Isabel capable of anything.

She listened with great interest to the girl's account of Mrs. Touchett's visit, and in the evening prepared to comply with her commands. Of what Isabel said to her no report has remained, but her sister's words must have prompted a remark that she made to her husband in the conjugal chamber as the two were getting ready to go to the hotel.

"I do hope immensely she will do something handsome for Isabel; she has evidently taken a great fancy to her."

"What is it you wish her to do?" Edmund Ludlow asked; "make her a big present?"

"No, indeed; nothing of the sort. But take an interest in her—sympathize with her. She is evidently just the sort of person to appreciate Isabel. She has lived so much in foreign society; she told Isabel all about it. You know you have always thought Isabel rather foreign."

"You want her to give her a little foreign sympathy, eh? Don't you think she gets enough at home?"

"Well, she ought to go abroad," said Mrs. Ludlow. "She's just the person to go abroad."

"And you want the old lady to take her, is that it?" her husband asked.

"She has offered to take her—she is dying to have Isabel go! But what I want her to do when she gets her there is to give her all the advantages. I am sure that all we have got to do," said Mrs. Ludlow, "is to give her a chance!"

"A chance for what?"

"A chance to develop."

"O Jupiter!" Edmund Ludlow exclaimed. "I hope she isn't going to develop any-more!"

"If I were not sure you only said that for argument, I should feel very badly," his wife replied. "But you know you love her."

"Do *you* know I love you?" the young man said, jocosely, to Isabel a little later, while he brushed his hat.

"I am sure I don't care whether you do or not!" exclaimed the girl, whose voice and smile, however, were sweeter than the words she uttered.

"Oh, she feels so grand since Mrs. Touchett's visit," said her sister.

But Isabel challenged this assertion with a good deal of seriousness.

"You must not say that, Lily. I don't feel grand at all."

"I am sure there is no harm," said the conciliatory Lily.

"Ah, but there is nothing in Mrs. Touchett's visit to make one feel grand."

"Oh," exclaimed Ludlow, "she is grander than ever!"

"Whenever I feel grand," said the girl, "it will be for a better reason."

Whether she felt grand or no, she at any rate felt busy; busy, I mean, with her thoughts. Left to herself for the evening, she sat awhile under the lamp, with empty hands, heedless of her usual avocations. Then she rose and moved about the room, and from one room to another, preferring the places where the vague lamplight expired. She was restless, and even excited; at moments she trembled a little. She felt that something had happened to her of which the importance was out of pro-portion to its appearance; there had really been a change in her life. What it would bring with it was as yet extremely indefinite; but Isabel was in a situation which gave a value to any change. She had a desire to leave the past behind her, and, as she said to herself, to begin afresh. This desire, indeed, was not a birth of the present occa-sion; it was as familiar as the sound of the rain upon the window, and it had led to her beginning afresh a great many times. She closed her eyes as she sat in one of the dusky corners of the quiet parlor; but it was not with a desire to take a nap. On the contrary, it was because she felt too wide-awake, and wished to check the sense of seeing too many things at once. Her imagination was by habit ridiculously active; if the door were not opened to it, it jumped out of the window. She was not accus-tomed, indeed, to keep it behind bolts; and, at important moments, when she would have been thankful to make use of her judgment alone, she paid the penalty of hav-ing given undue encouragement to the faculty of seeing without judging. At present, with her sense that the note of change had been struck, came gradually a host of images of the things she was leaving behind her. The years and hours of her life came back to her, and for a long time, in a stillness broken only by the ticking of the big bronze clock, she passed them in review. It had been a very happy life and she had been a very fortunate girl—this was the truth that seemed to emerge most vividly. She had had the best of everything, and in a world in which the circumstances of so many people made them unenviable, it was an advantage never to have known anything particularly disagreeable. It appeared to Isabel that the disagreeable had been even too absent from her knowledge, for she had gathered from her acquaintance with literature that it was often a source of interest, and even of instruction. Her father had kept it away from her—her handsome, much-loved father, who always had such an aversion to it. It was a great good fortune to have been his daughter; Isabel was even proud of her parentage. Since his death she had gathered a vague impression that he turned his brighter side to his children, and that he had not eluded discomfort quite so much in practice as in aspiration. But this only made her tenderness for him greater; it was scarcely even painful to have to think that he was too generous, too good-natured, too indifferent to sordid considerations. Many persons thought that he carried this indifference too far; especially the large number of those to whom he owed money. Of their opinions, Isabel was never very definitely informed; but it may interest the reader to know that, while they admitted that the late Mr. Archer had a remarkably handsome head and a very taking manner (indeed, as one of them had said, he was always taking something), they declared that he had made a very poor use of his life. He had squandered a substantial fortune, he had been deplorably convivial, he was known to have gambled freely. A few very harsh critics went so far as to say that he had not even brought up his daughters. They had had no regular education and no permanent home; they had been at once spoiled and neglected; they had lived with nursemaids and governesses (usually very bad ones), or had been sent to strange schools kept by foreigners, from which, at the end of a month, they had been removed in tears. This view of the matter would have excited Isabel's indignation, for to her own sense her opportunities had been abundant. Even when her father had left his daughters for three months at Neufchâtel with a French *bonne,* who eloped with a Russian nobleman, staying at the same hotel—even in this irregular situation (an incident of the girl's eleventh year) she had been neither frightened nor ashamed, but had thought it a picturesque episode in a liberal education. Her father had a large way of looking at life, of which his restlessness and even his occasional incoherency of conduct had been only a proof. He wished his daughters, even as children, to see as much of the world as possible; and it was for this purpose that, before Isabel was fourteen, he had transported them three times across the Atlantic, giving them on each occasion, however, but a few months' view of foreign lands; a course which had whetted our heroine's curiosity without enabling her to satisfy it. She ought to have been a partisan of her father, for among his three daughters she was quite his favorite, and in his last days his general willingness to take leave of a world in which the difficulty of doing as one liked appeared to increase as one grew older was sensibly modified by the pain of separation from his clever, his superior, his remarkable girl. Later, when the journeys to Europe ceased, he still had shown his children all sorts of indulgence, and if he had been troubled about money matters, nothing ever disturbed their irreflective consciousness of many possessions. Isabel, though she danced very well, had not the recollection of having been in New York a successful member of the choreographic circle; her sister Edith was, as everyone said, so very much more popular. Edith was so striking an example of success that Isabel could have no illusions as to what constituted this advantage, or as to the moderate character of her own triumphs. Nineteen persons out of twenty (including the younger sister herself) pronounced Edith infinitely the prettier of the two; but the twentieth, besides reversing the judgment, had the entertainment of thinking all the others a parcel of fools. Isabel had in the depths of her nature an even more unquenchable desire to please than Edith; but the depths of this young lady's nature were a very out-of-the-way place, between which and the surface communication was interrupted by a dozen capricious forces. She saw the young men who came in large numbers to see her sister; but as a general thing they were afraid of her; they had a belief that some special preparation was required for talking with her. Her reputation of reading a great deal hung about her like the cloudy envelope of a goddess in an epic; it was supposed to engender difficult questions, and to keep the conversation at a low temperature. The poor girl liked to be thought clever, but she hated to be thought bookish; she used to read in secret, and, though her memory was excellent, to abstain from quotation. She had a great desire for knowledge, but she really preferred almost any source of information to the printed page; she had an immense curiosity about life, and was constantly staring and wondering. She carried within herself a great fund of life, and her deepest enjoyment was to feel the continuity between the movements of her own heart and the agitations of the world. For this reason she was fond of seeing great crowds and large stretches of country, of reading about revolutions and wars, of looking at historical pictures—a class of efforts to which she had often gone so far as to forgive much bad painting for the sake of the subject. While the Civil War went on, she was still a very young girl; but she passed months of this long period in a state of almost passionate excitement, in which she felt herself at times (to her extreme confusion) stirred almost indiscriminately by the valor of either army. Of course the circumspection of the local youth had never gone the length of making her a social proscript; for the proportion of those whose hearts, as they approached her, beat only just fast enough to make it a sensible pleasure, was sufficient to redeem her maidenly career from failure. She had had everything that a girl could have: kindness, admiration, flattery, bouquets, the sense of exclusion from none of the privileges of the world she lived in, abundant opportunity for dancing, the latest publications, plenty of new dresses, the London *Spectator*, and a glimpse of contemporary aesthetics.

These things now, as memory played over them, resolved themselves into a multitude of scenes and figures. Forgotten things came back to her; many others, which

she had lately thought of great moment, dropped out of sight. The result was kalei-
doscopic; but the movement of the instrument was checked at last by the servant's
coming in with the name of a gentleman. The name of the gentleman was Caspar
Goodwood; he was a straight young man from Boston, who had known Miss Archer
for the last twelvemonth, and who, thinking her the most beautiful young woman of
her time, had pronounced the time, according to the rule I have hinted at, a foolish
period of history. He sometimes wrote to Isabel, and he had lately written to her
from New York. She had thought it very possible he would come in—had, indeed, all
the rainy day been vaguely expecting him. Nevertheless, now that she learned he
was there, she felt no eagerness to receive him. He was the finest young man she had
ever seen, was, indeed, quite a magnificent young man; he filled her with a certain
feeling of respect which she had never entertained for anyone else. He was supposed
by the world in general to wish to marry her; but this of course was between themselves. It at least may be affirmed that he had traveled from New York to Albany
expressly to see her; having learned in the former city, where he was spending a few
days and where he had hoped to find her, that she was still at the capital. Isabel
delayed for some minutes to go to him; she moved about the room with a certain
feeling of embarrassment. But at last she presented herself, and found him standing
near the lamp. He was tall, strong, and somewhat stiff; he was also lean and brown.
He was not especially good-looking, but his physiognomy had an air of requesting
your attention, which it rewarded or not, according to the charm you found in a blue
eye of remarkable fixedness and a jaw of the somewhat angular mould, which is supposed to bespeak resolution. Isabel said to herself that it bespoke resolution
tonight; but, nevertheless, an hour later, Caspar Goodwood, who had arrived hopeful
as well as resolute, took his way back to his lodging with the feeling of a man
defeated. He was not, however, a man to be discouraged by a defeat.

❧ 5 ❧

R alph Touchett was a philosopher, but nevertheless he knocked at his
mother's door (at a quarter to seven) with a good deal of eagerness. Even
philosophers have their preferences, and it must be admitted that of his
progenitors his father ministered most to his sense of the sweetness of filial dependence. His father, as he had often said to himself, was the more motherly; his mother,
on the other hand, was paternal, and even, according to the slang of the day, guber-

natorial. She was nevertheless very fond of her only child, and had always insisted on his spending three months of the year with her. Ralph rendered perfect justice to her affection, and knew that in her thoughts his turn always came after the care of her house and her conservatory (she was extremely fond of flowers). He found her completely dressed for dinner, but she embraced her boy with her gloved hands, and made him sit on the sofa beside her. She inquired scrupulously about her husband's health and about the young man's own, and receiving no very brilliant account of either, she remarked that she was more than ever convinced of her wisdom in not exposing herself to the English climate. In this case she also might have broken down. Ralph smiled at the idea of his mother breaking down, but made no point of reminding her that his own enfeebled condition was not the result of the English climate, from which he absented himself for a considerable part of each year.

He had been a very small boy when his father, Daniel Tracy Touchett, who was a native of Rutland, in the state of Vermont, came to England as subordinate partner in a banking house, in which some ten years later he acquired a preponderant interest. Daniel Touchett saw before him a lifelong residence in his adopted country, of which, from the first, he took a simple, cheerful, and eminently practical view. But, as he said to himself, he had no intention of turning Englishman, nor had he any desire to convert his only son to the same sturdy faith. It had been for himself so very soluble a problem to live in England, and yet not be of it, that it seemed to him equally simple that after his death his lawful heir should carry on the bank in a pure American spirit. He took pains to cultivate this spirit, however, by sending the boy home for his education. Ralph spent several terms in an American school, and took a degree at an American college, after which, as he struck his father on his return as even redundantly national, he was placed for some three years in residence at Oxford. Oxford swallowed up Harvard, and Ralph became at last English enough. His outward conformity to the manners that surrounded him was nonetheless the mask of a mind that greatly enjoyed its independence, on which nothing long imposed itself, and which, naturally inclined to jocosity and irony, indulged in a boundless liberty of appreciation. He began with being a young man of promise; at Oxford he distinguished himself, to his father's ineffable satisfaction, and the people about him said it was a thousand pities so clever a fellow should be shut out from a career. He might have had a career by returning to his own country (though this point is shrouded in uncertainty), and even if Mr. Touchett had been willing to part with him (which was not the case), it would have gone hard with him to put the ocean (which he detested) permanently between himself and the old man whom he regarded as his best friend. Ralph was not only fond of his father, but he admired him—he enjoyed the opportunity of observing him. Daniel Touchett to his perception was a man of genius, and though he himself had no great fancy for the banking business, he made a point of learning enough of it to measure the great figure his father had played. It was not this, however, he mainly relished, it was the old man's effective simplicity. Daniel Touchett had been neither at Harvard nor at Oxford, and it was his own fault if he had put into his son's hands the key to modern criticism. Ralph, whose head was full of ideas which his father had never guessed, had a high esteem for the latter's originality. Americans, rightly or wrongly, are commended for the ease with which they adapt themselves to foreign conditions; but Mr. Touchett had given evidence of this talent only up to a certain point. He had made himself thoroughly comfortable in England, but he had never attempted to pitch his thoughts in the English key. He had retained many characteristics of Rutland, Vermont; his tone, as his son always noted with pleasure, was that of the more luxuriant parts of New England. At the end of his life, especially, he was a gentle, refined, fastidious old man, who combined consummate shrewdness with a sort of fraternizing good-humor, and whose feeling about his own position in the world was quite of the democratic sort. It was perhaps his want of imagination and of what is called the historic consciousness; but to many of the impressions usually made by English life upon the cultivated stranger his sense was completely closed. There were certain differences he never perceived, certain habits he never formed, certain mysteries he never understood. As regards these latter, on the day that he had understood them his son would have thought less well of him.

Ralph, on leaving Oxford, spent a couple of years in traveling; after which he found himself mounted on a high stool in his father's bank. The responsibility and honor of such positions is not, I believe, measured by the height of the stool, which depends upon other considerations; Ralph, indeed, who had very long legs, was fond of standing, and even of walking about, at his work. To this exercise, however, he was obliged to devote but a limited period, for at the end of some eighteen months he became conscious that he was seriously out of health. He had caught a violent cold, which fixed itself upon his lungs and threw them into extreme embarrassment. He had to give up work and embrace the sorry occupation known as taking care of one's self. At first he was greatly disgusted; it appeared to him that it was not himself in the least that he was taking care of, but an uninteresting and uninterested person with whom he had nothing in common. This person, however, improved on acquaintance, and Ralph grew at last to have a certain grudging tolerance, and even undemonstrative respect, for him. Misfortune makes strange bedfellows, and our young man, feeling that he had something at stake in the matter—it usually seemed to him to be his reputation for common sense—devoted to his unattractive *protégé* an amount of attention of which note was duly taken, and which had at least the effect of keeping the poor fellow alive. One of his lungs began to heal, the other promised to follow its example, and he was assured that he might outweather a dozen winters if he would betake himself to one of those climates in which consumptives chiefly congregate. He had grown extremely fond of

London, and cursed this immitigable necessity; but at the same time that he
cursed, he conformed, and gradually, when he found that his sensitive organ was
really grateful for such grim favors, he conferred them with a better grace. He win-
tered abroad, as the phrase is; basked in the sun, stopped at home when the wind
blew, went to bed when it rained, and once or twice, when it snowed, almost never
got up again. A certain fund of indolence that he possessed came to his aid and
helped to reconcile him to doing nothing; for at the best he was too ill for anything
but a passive life. As he said to himself, there was really nothing he had wanted very
much to do, so that he had given up nothing. At present, however, the perfume of
forbidden fruit seemed occasionally to float past him, to remind him that the finest
pleasures of life are to be found in the world of action. Living as he now lived was
like reading a good book in a poor translation—a meager entertainment for a
young man who felt that he might have been an excellent linguist. He had good winters and poor winters, and while the former lasted he was sometimes the sport of a
vision of virtual recovery. But this vision was dispelled some three years before the
occurrence of the incidents with which this history opens; he had on this occasion
remained later than usual in England, and had been overtaken by bad weather
before reaching Algiers. He reached it more dead than alive, and lay there for several weeks between life and death. His convalescence was a miracle, but the first
use he made of it was to assure himself that such miracles happen but once. He
said to himself that his hour was in sight, and that it behoved him to keep his eyes
upon it, but that it was also open to him to spend the interval as agreeably as might
be consistent with such a preoccupation. With the prospect of losing them, the simple use of his faculties became an exquisite pleasure; it seemed to him that the
delights of observation had never been suspected. He was far from the time when
he had found it hard that he should be obliged to give up the idea of distinguishing
himself; an idea nonetheless importunate for being vague, and nonetheless delightful for having to struggle with a good deal of native indifference. His friends at present found him much more cheerful, and attributed it to a theory, over which they
shook their heads knowingly, that he would recover his health. The truth was that
he had simply accepted the situation.

It was very probable this sweet-tasting property of observation to which I allude
(for he found himself in these last years much more inclined to notice the pleasant
things of the world than the others) that was mainly concerned in Ralph's quickly-
stirred interest in the arrival of a young lady who was evidently not insipid. If he
were observantly disposed, something told him, here was occupation enough for a
succession of days. It may be added, somewhat crudely, that the liberty of falling in
love had a place in Ralph Touchett's programme. This was of course a liberty to be
very temperately used; for though the safest form of any sentiment is that which is
conditioned upon silence, it is not always the most comfortable, and Ralph had for-

bidden himself the art of demonstration. But conscious observation of a lovely woman had struck him as the finest entertainment that the world now had to offer him, and if the interest should become poignant, he flattered himself that he could carry it off quietly, as he had carried other discomforts. He speedily acquired a conviction, however, that he was not destined to fall in love with his cousin.

"And now tell me about the young lady," he said to his mother. "What do you mean to do with her?"

Mrs. Touchett hesitated a little. "I mean to ask your father to invite her to stay three or four weeks at Gardencourt."

"You needn't stand on any such ceremony as that," said Ralph. "My father will ask her as a matter of course."

"I don't know about that. She is my niece; she is not his."

"Good Lord, dear mother; what a sense of property! That's all the more reason for his asking her. But after that—I mean after three months (for it's absurd asking the poor girl to remain but for three or four paltry weeks)—what do you mean to do with her?"

"I mean to take her to Paris, to get her some clothes."

"Ah yes, that's of course. But independently of that?"

"I shall invite her to spend the autumn with me in Florence."

"You don't rise above detail, dear mother," said Ralph. "I should like to know what you mean to do with her in a general way."

"My duty!" Mrs. Touchett declared. "I suppose you pity her very much," she added.

"No, I don't think I pity her. She doesn't strike me as a girl that suggests compassion. I think I envy her. Before being sure, however, give me a hint of what your duty will direct you to do."

"It will direct me to show her four European countries—I shall leave her the choice of two of them—and to give her the opportunity of perfecting herself in French, which she already knows very well."

Ralph frowned a little. "That sounds rather dry—even giving her the choice of two of the countries."

"If it's dry," said his mother with a laugh, "you can leave Isabel alone to water it! She is as good as a summer rain, any day."

"Do you mean that she is a gifted being?"

"I don't know whether she is a gifted being, but she is a clever girl, with a strong will and a high temper. She has no idea of being bored."

"I can imagine that," said Ralph; and then he added, abruptly, "How do you two get on?"

"Do you mean by that that I am a bore? I don't think Isabel finds me one. Some girls might, I know; but this one is too clever for that. I think I amuse her a good deal. We get on very well, because I understand her; I know the sort of girl she is. She is very frank, and I am very frank; we know just what to expect of each other."

"Ah, dear mother," Ralph exclaimed, "one always knows what to expect of you! You have never surprised me but once, and that is today—in presenting me with a pretty cousin whose existence I had never suspected."

"Do you think her very pretty?"

"Very pretty indeed; but I don't insist upon that. It's her general air of being someone in particular that strikes me. Who is this rare creature, and what is she? Where did you find her, and how did you make her acquaintance?"

"I found her in an old house at Albany, sitting in a dreary room on a rainy day, reading a heavy book, and boring herself to death. She didn't know she was bored, but when I told her, she seemed very grateful for the hint. You may say I shouldn't have told her—I should have let her alone. There is a good deal in that; but I acted conscientiously; I thought she was meant for something better. It occurred to me that it would be a kindness to take her about and introduce her to the world. She thinks she knows a great deal of it—like most American girls; but like most American girls she is very much mistaken. If you want to know, I thought she would do me credit. I like to be well thought of, and for a woman of my age there is no more becoming ornament than an attractive niece. You know I had seen nothing of my sister's children for years; I disapproved entirely of the father. But I always meant to do something for them when he should have gone to his reward. I ascertained where they were to be found, and, without any preliminaries, went and introduced myself. There are two other sisters, both of whom are married; but I saw only the elder, who has, by the way, a very uncivil husband. The wife, whose name is Lily, jumped at the idea of my taking an interest in Isabel; she said it was just what her sister needed—that someone should take an interest in her. She spoke of her as you might speak of some young person of genius, in want of encouragement and patronage. It may be that Isabel is a genius; but in that case I have not yet learned her special line. Mrs. Ludlow was especially keen about my taking her to Europe; they all regard Europe over there as a sort of land of emigration, a refuge for their superfluous population. Isabel herself seemed very glad to come, and the thing was easily arranged. There was a little difficulty about the money question, as she seemed averse to being under pecuniary obligations. But she has a small income, and she supposes herself to be traveling at her own expense."

Ralph had listened attentively to this judicious account of his pretty cousin, by which his interest in her was not impaired. "Ah, if she is a genius," he said, "we must find out her special line. Is it, by chance, for flirting?"

"I don't think so. You may suspect that at first, but you will be wrong."

"Warburton is wrong, then!" Ralph Touchett exclaimed. "He flatters himself he has made that discovery."

His mother shook her head. "Lord Warburton won't understand her; he needn't try."

"He is very intelligent," said Ralph; "but it's right he should be puzzled once in a while."

"Isabel will enjoy puzzling a lord," Mrs. Touchett remarked.

Her son frowned a little. "What does she know about lords?"

"Nothing at all; that will puzzle him all the more."

Ralph greeted these words with a laugh, and looked out of the window a little. Then—"Are you not going down to see my father?" he asked.

"At a quarter to eight," said Mrs. Touchett.

Her son looked at his watch. "You have another quarter of an hour, then; tell me some more about Isabel."

But Mrs. Touchett declined his invitation, declaring that he must find out for himself.

"Well," said Ralph, "she will certainly do you credit. But won't she also give you trouble?"

"I hope not; but if she does, I shall not shrink from it. I never do that."

"She strikes me as very natural," said Ralph.

"Natural people are not the most trouble."

"No," said Ralph; "you yourself are a proof of that. You are extremely natural, and I am sure you have never troubled anyone. But tell me this; it just occurs to me. Is Isabel capable of making herself disagreeable?"

"Ah," cried his mother, "you ask too many questions! Find that out for yourself."

His questions, however, were not exhausted. "All this time," he said, "you have not told me what you intend to do with her."

"Do with her? You talk as if she were a yard of calico. I shall do absolutely nothing with her, and she herself will do everything that she chooses. She gave me notice of that."

"What you meant then, in your telegram, was that her character was independent."

"I never know what I mean by my telegrams—especially those I send from America. Clearness is too expensive. Come down to your father."

"It is not yet a quarter to eight," said Ralph.

"I must allow for his impatience," Mrs. Touchett answered.

Ralph knew what to think of his father's impatience; but making no rejoinder, he offered his mother his arm. This put it into his power, as they descended together, to stop her a moment on the middle landing of the staircase—the broad, low, wide-armed staircase of time-stained oak which was one of the most striking ornaments of Gardencourt.

"You have no plan of marrying her?" he said, smiling.

"Marry her? I should be sorry to play her such a trick! But apart from that, she is perfectly able to marry herself; she has every facility."

"Do you mean to say she has a husband picked out?"

"I don't know about a husband, but there is a young man in Boston——"

Ralph went on; he had no desire to hear about the young man in Boston. "As my father says," he exclaimed, "they are always engaged!"

His mother had told him that he must extract his information about his cousin from the girl herself, and it soon became evident to him that he should not want for opportunity. He had, for instance, a good deal of talk with her that same evening, when the two had been left alone together in the drawing room. Lord Warburton, who had ridden over from his own house, some ten miles distant, remounted and took his departure before dinner; and an hour after this meal was concluded, Mr. and Mrs. Touchett, who appeared to have exhausted each other's conversation, withdrew, under the valid pretext of fatigue, to their respective apartments. The young man spent an hour with his cousin; though she had been traveling half the day she appeared to have no sense of weariness. She was really tired; she knew it, and knew that she should pay for it on the morrow; but it was her habit at this period to carry fatigue to the furthest point, and confess to it only when dissimulation had become impossible. For the present it was perfectly possible; she was interested and excited. She asked Ralph to show her the pictures; there were a great many of them in the house, most of them of his own choosing. The best of them were arranged in an oaken gallery of charming proportions, which had a sitting room at either end of it, and which in the evening was usually lighted. The light was insufficient to show the pictures to advantage, and the visit might have been deferred till the morrow. This suggestion Ralph had ventured to make; but Isabel looked disappointed—smiling still, however—and said, "If you please, I should like to see them just a little." She was eager, she knew that she was eager and that she seemed so; but she could not help it. "She doesn't take suggestions," Ralph said to himself; but he said it without irritation; her eagerness amused and even pleased him. The lamps were on brackets, at intervals, and if the light was imperfect it was genial. It fell upon the vague squares of rich color and on the faded gilding of heavy frames; it made a shining on the polished floor of the gallery. Ralph took a candle-stick and moved about, pointing out the things he liked; Isabel, bending toward one picture after another, indulged in little exclamations and murmurs. She was evidently a judge; she had a natural taste; he was struck with that. She took a candle-stick herself and held it slowly here and there; she lifted it high, and as she did so, he found himself pausing in the middle of the gallery and bending his eyes much less upon the pictures than on her figure. He lost nothing, in truth, by these wandering glances; for she was better worth looking at than most works of art. She was thin, and light, and middling tall; when people had wished to distinguish her from the other two Miss Archers, they always called her the thin one. Her hair, which was dark even to blackness, had been an object of envy to many women; her light gray eye, a little too keen perhaps in her graver moments, had an enchanting softness when she smiled. They walked slowly up one side of the gallery and down the other, and then she said—

"Well, now I know more than I did when I began!"

"You apparently have a great passion for knowledge," her cousin answered, laughing.

"I think I have; most girls seem to me so ignorant," said Isabel.

"You strike me as different from most girls."

"Ah, some girls are so nice," murmured Isabel, who preferred not to talk about herself. Then, in a moment, to change the subject, she went on, "Please tell me— isn't there a ghost?"

"A ghost?"

"A specter, a phantom; we call them ghosts in America."

"So we do here, when we see them."

"You do see them, then? You ought to, in this romantic old house."

"It's not a romantic house," said Ralph. "You will be disappointed if you count on that. It's dismally prosaic; there is no romance here but what you may have brought with you."

"I have brought a great deal; but it seems to me I have brought it to the right place."

"To keep it out of harm, certainly; nothing will ever happen to it here, between my father and me."

Isabel looked at him a moment.

"Is there never anyone here but your father and you?"

"My mother, of course."

"Oh, I know your mother; she is not romantic. Haven't you other people?"

"Very few."

"I am sorry for that; I like so much to see people."

"Oh, we will invite all the county to amuse you," said Ralph.

"Now you are making fun of me," the girl answered, rather gravely. "Who was the gentleman that was on the lawn when I arrived?"

"A county neighbor; he doesn't come very often."

"I am sorry for that; I liked him," said Isabel.

"Why, it seemed to me that you barely spoke to him," Ralph objected.

"Never mind, I like him all the same. I like your father, too, immensely."

"You can't do better than that; he is a dear old man."

"I am so sorry he is ill," said Isabel.

"You must help me to nurse him; you ought to be a good nurse."

"I don't think I am; I have been told I am not; I am said to be too theoretic. But you haven't told me about the ghost," she added.

Ralph, however, gave no heed to this observation.

"You like my father, and you like Lord Warburton. I infer also that you like my mother."

"I like your mother very much, because—because——" And Isabel found herself attempting to assign a reason for her affection for Mrs. Touchett.

"Ah, we never know why!" said her companion, laughing.

"I always know why," the girl answered. "It's because she doesn't expect one to like her; she doesn't care whether one does or not."

"So you adore her, out of perversity? Well, I take greatly after my mother," said Ralph.

"I don't believe you do at all. You wish people to like you, and you try to make them do it."

"Good heavens, how you see through one!" cried Ralph, with a dismay that was not altogether jocular.

"But I like you all the same," his cousin went on. "The way to clinch the matter will be to show me the ghost."

Ralph shook his head sadly. "I might show it to you, but you would never see it. The privilege isn't given to everyone; it's not enviable. It has never been seen by a young, happy, innocent person like you. You must have suffered first, have suffered greatly, have gained some miserable knowledge. In that way your eyes are opened to it. I saw it long ago," said Ralph, smiling.

"I told you just now I was very fond of knowledge," the girl answered.

"Yes, of happy knowledge—of pleasant knowledge. But you haven't suffered, and you are not made to suffer. I hope you will never see the ghost!"

Isabel had listened to him attentively, with a smile on her lips, but with a certain gravity in her eyes. Charming as he found her, she had struck him as rather presumptuous—indeed it was a part of her charm; and he wondered what she would say.

"I am not afraid," she said; which seemed quite presumptuous enough.

"You are not afraid of suffering?"

"Yes, I am afraid of suffering. But I am not afraid of ghosts. And I think people suffer too easily," she added.

"I don't believe you do," said Ralph, looking at her with his hands in his pockets.

"I don't think that's a fault," she answered. "It is not absolutely necessary to suffer; we were not made for that."

"You were not, certainly."

"I am not speaking of myself." And she turned away a little.

"No, it isn't a fault," said her cousin. "It's a merit to be strong."

"Only, if you don't suffer, they call you hard," Isabel remarked. They passed out of the smaller drawing room, into which they had returned from the gallery, and paused in the hall, at the foot of the staircase. Here Ralph presented his companion with her bedroom candle, which he had taken from a niche. "Never mind what they call you," he said. "When you do suffer, they call you an idiot. The great point is to be as happy as possible."

She looked at him a little; she had taken her candle, and placed her foot on the oaken stair. "Well," she said, "that's what I came to Europe for, to be as happy as possible. Good night."

"Good night! I wish you all success, and shall be very glad to contribute to it!"

She turned away, and he watched her, as she slowly ascended. Then, with his hands always in his pockets, he went back to the empty drawing room.

❦ 6 ❦

I sabel Archer was a young person of many theories; her imagination was remarkably active. It had been her fortune to possess a finer mind than most of the persons among whom her lot was cast; to have a larger perception of surrounding facts, and to care for knowledge that was tinged with the unfamiliar. It is true that among her contemporaries she passed for a young woman of extraordinary profundity; for these excellent people never withheld their admiration from a reach of intellect of which they themselves were not conscious, and spoke of Isabel as a prodigy of learning, a young lady reputed to have read the classic authors—in translations. Her paternal aunt, Mrs. Varian, once spread the rumor that Isabel was writing a book—Mrs. Varian having a reverence for books—and averred that Isabel would distinguish herself in print. Mrs. Varian thought highly of literature, for which she entertained that esteem that is connected with a sense of privation. Her own large house, remarkable for its assortment of mosaic tables and decorated ceilings, was unfurnished with a library, and in the way of printed volumes contained nothing but half-a-dozen novels in paper, on a shelf in the apartment of one of the Miss Varians. Practically, Mrs. Varian's acquaintance with literature was confined to the *New York Interviewer*; as she very justly said, after you had read the *Interviewer*, you had no time for anything else. Her tendency, however, was rather to keep the *Interviewer* out of the way of her daughters; she was determined to bring them up seriously, and they read nothing at all. Her impression with regard to Isabel's labors was quite illusory; the girl never attempted to write a book, and had no desire to be an authoress. She had no talent for expression, and had none of the consciousness of genius; she only had a general idea that people were right when they treated her as if she were rather superior. Whether or no she were superior, people were right in admiring her if they thought her so; for it seemed to her often that her mind moved more quickly than theirs, and this encouraged an impatience that might easily be confounded with superiority. It may be affirmed without delay that Isabel was probably very liable to the sin of self-esteem; she often surveyed with complacency the field of her own nature; she was in the habit of taking for granted, on scanty evidence, that she was right; impulsively, she often admired her-self. Meanwhile her errors and delusions were frequently such as a biographer interested in preserving the dignity of his heroine must shrink from specifying. Her thoughts were a tangle of vague outlines, which had never been corrected by the judgment of people who seemed to her to speak with authority. In matters of opin-ion she had had her own way, and it had led her into a thousand ridiculous zigzags. Every now and then she found out she was wrong, and then she treated herself to a week of passionate humility. After this she held her head higher than ever again; for it was of no use, she had an unquenchable desire to think well of herself. She had a theory that it was only on this condition that life was worth living; that one should be one of the best, should be conscious of a fine organization (she could not help knowing her organization was fine), should move in a realm of light, of natu-ral wisdom, of happy impulse, of inspiration gracefully chronic. It was almost as unnecessary to cultivate doubt of oneself as to cultivate doubt of one's best friend; one should try to be one's own best friend, and to give oneself, in this manner, dis-tinguished company. The girl had a certain nobleness of imagination which ren-dered her a good many services and played her a great many tricks. She spent half her time in thinking of beauty, and bravery, and magnanimity; she had a fixed determination to regard the world as a place of brightness, of free expansion, of irresistible action; she thought it would be detestable to be afraid or ashamed. She had an infinite hope that she should never do anything wrong. She had resented so strongly, after discovering them, her mere errors of feeling (the discovery always made her tremble, as if she had escaped from a trap which might have caught her and smothered her), that the chance of inflicting a sensible injury upon another person, presented only as a contingency, caused her at moments to hold her breath. That always seemed to her the worst thing that could happen to one. On the whole, reflectively, she was in no uncertainty about the things that were wrong. She had no taste for thinking of them, but whenever she looked at them fixedly she recog-nized them. It was wrong to be mean, to be jealous, to be false, to be cruel; she had seen very little of the evil of the world, but she had seen women who lied and who tried to hurt each other. Seeing such things had quickened her high spirit; it seemed right to scorn them. Of course the danger of a high spirit is the danger of inconsistency—the danger of keeping up the flag after the place has surrendered; a sort of behavior so anomalous as to be almost a dishonor to the flag. But Isabel, who knew little of the sorts of artillery to which young ladies are exposed, flattered herself that such contradictions would never be observed in her own conduct. Her life should always be in harmony with the most pleasing impression she should produce; she would be what she appeared, and she would appear what she was. Sometimes she went so far as to wish that she should find herself some day in a difficult position, so that she might have the pleasure of being as heroic as the occasion demanded. Altogether, with her meager knowledge, her inflated ideals, her confidence at once innocent and dogmatic, her temper at once exacting and indulgent, her mixture of curiosity and fastidiousness, of vivacity and indifference, her desire to look very well and to be if possible even better; her determination to see, to try, to know; her combination of the delicate, desultory, flame-like spirit and the eager and personal young girl; she would be an easy victim of scientific criticism, if she were not intended to awaken on the reader's part an impulse more tender and more purely expectant.

It was one of her theories that Isabel Archer was very fortunate in being independent, and that she ought to make some very enlightened use of her independence. She never called it loneliness; she thought that weak; and besides, her sister Lily constantly urged her to come and stay with her. She had a friend whose acquaintance she had made shortly before her father's death, who offered so laudable an example of useful activity that Isabel always thought of her as a model. Henrietta Stackpole had the advantage of a remarkable talent; she was thoroughly launched in journalism, and her letters to the *Interviewer*, from Washington, Newport, the White Mountains, and other places, were universally admired. Isabel did not accept them unrestrictedly, but she esteemed the courage, energy, and good-humor of her friend, who, without parents and without property, had adopted three of the children of an infirm and widowed sister, and was paying their school-bills out of the proceeds of her literary labor. Henrietta was a great radical, and had clear-cut views on most subjects; her cherished desire had long been to come to Europe and write a series of letters to the *Interviewer* from the radical point of view—an enterprise the less difficult as she knew perfectly in advance what her opinions would be, and to how many objections most European institutions lay open. When she heard that Isabel was coming, she wished to start at once; thinking, naturally, that it would be delightful the two should travel together. She had been obliged, however, to postpone this enterprise. She thought Isabel a glorious creature, and had spoken of her, covertly, in some of her letters, though she never mentioned the fact to her friend, who would not have taken pleasure in it and was not a regular reader of the *Interviewer*. Henrietta, for Isabel, was chiefly a proof that a woman might suffice to herself and be happy. Her resources were of the obvious kind; but even if one had not the journalistic talent and a genius for guessing, as Henrietta said, what the public was going to want, one was not therefore to conclude that one had no vocation, no beneficent aptitude of any sort, and resign oneself to being trivial and superficial. Isabel was resolutely determined not to be superficial. If one should wait expectantly and trustfully, one would find some happy work to one's hand. Of course, among her theories, this young lady was not without a collection of opinions on the question of marriage. The first on the list was a conviction that it was very vulgar to think too much about it. From lapsing into a state of eagerness on this point she earnestly prayed that she might be delivered; she held that a woman ought to be able to make up her life in singleness, and that it was perfectly possible to be happy without the society of a more or less coarse-minded person of another sex. The girl's prayer was very sufficiently answered; something pure and proud that there was in her—something cold and stiff, an unappreciated suitor with a taste for analysis might have called it—had hitherto kept her from any great vanity of conjecture on the subject of possible husbands. Few of the men she saw seemed worth an expenditure of imagination, and it made her smile to think that one of them should present himself as an incentive to hope and a reward of patience. Deep in her soul—it was the deepest thing there—lay a belief that if a certain light should dawn, she could give herself completely; but this image, on the whole, was too formidable to be attractive. Isabel's thoughts hovered about it, but they seldom rested on it long; after a little it ended by frightening her. It often seemed to her that she thought too much about herself; you could have made her blush, any day in the year, by telling her that she was selfish. She was always planning out her own development, desiring her own perfection, observing her own progress. Her nature had for her own imagination a certain gardenlike quality, a suggestion of perfume and murmuring boughs, of shady bowers and lengthening vistas, which made her feel that introspection was, after all, an exercise in the open air, and that a visit to the recesses of one's mind was harmless when one returned from it with a lapful of roses. But she was often reminded that there were other gardens in the world than those of her virginal soul, and that there were, moreover, a great many places that were not gardens at all—only dusky, pestiferous tracts, planted thick with ugliness and misery. In the current of that easy eagerness on which she had lately been floating, which had conveyed her to this beautiful old England and might carry her much further still, she often checked herself with the thought of the thousands of people who were less happy than herself—a thought which for the moment made her absorbing happiness appear to her a kind of immodesty. What should one do with the misery of the world in a scheme of the agreeable for oneself? It must be confessed that this question never held her long. She was too young, too impatient to live, too unacquainted with pain. She always returned to her theory that a young woman whom after all everyone thought clever, should begin by getting a general impression of life. This was necessary to prevent mistakes, and after it should be secured she might make the unfortunate condition of others an object of special attention.

England was a revelation to her, and she found herself as entertained as a child at a pantomime. In her infantine excursions to Europe she had seen only the Continent, and seen it from the nursery window; Paris, not London, was her father's Mecca. The impressions of that time, moreover, had become faint and remote, and the old-world quality in everything that she now saw had all the charm of strangeness. Her uncle's house seemed a picture made real; no refinement of the agreeable was lost upon Isabel; the rich perfection of Gardencourt at once revealed a world and gratified a need. The large, low rooms, with brown ceilings and dusky corners, the deep embrasures and curious casements, the quiet light on dark, polished panels, the deep greenness outside, that seemed always peeping in, the sense of well-ordered privacy, in the center of a "property"—a place where sounds were felicitously accidental, where the tread was muffled by the earth itself, and in the thick mild air all shrillness dropped out of conversation—these things were much to the taste of our young lady, whose taste played a considerable part in her emotions. She formed a fast friendship with her uncle, and often sat by his chair when he had had it moved out to the lawn. He passed hours in the open air, sitting placidly with folded hands, like a good old man who had done his work and received his wages, and was trying to grow used to weeks and months made up only of off-days. Isabel amused him more than she suspected—the effect she produced upon people was often different from what she supposed—and he frequently gave himself the pleasure of making her chatter. It was by this term that he qualified her conversation, which had much of the vivacity observable in that of the young ladies of her country, to whom the ear of the world is more directly presented than to their sisters in other lands. Like the majority of American girls, Isabel had been encouraged to express herself; her remarks had been attended to; she had been expected to have emotions and opinions. Many of her opinions had doubtless but a slender value, many of her emotions passed away in the utterance; but they had left a trace in giving her the habit of seeming at least to feel and think, and in imparting, moreover, to her words, when she was really moved, that artless vividness which so many people had regarded as a sign of superiority. Mr. Touchett used to think that she reminded him of his wife when his wife was in her teens. It was because she was fresh and natural and quick to understand, to speak—so many characteristics of her niece—that he had fallen in love with Mrs. Touchett. He never expressed this analogy to the girl herself, however; for if Mrs. Touchett had once been like Isabel, Isabel was not at all like Mrs. Touchett. The old man was full of kindness for her; it was a long time, as he said, since they had had any young life in the house; and our rustling, quickly-moving, clear-voiced heroine was as agreeable to his sense as the sound of flowing water. He wished to do something for her, he wished she would ask something of him. But Isabel asked nothing but questions; it is true that of these she asked a great many. Her uncle had a great fund of answers, though interrogation sometimes came in forms that puzzled him. She questioned him immensely about England, about the British constitution, the English character, the state of politics, the manners and customs of the royal family, the peculiarities of the aristocracy, the way of living and thinking of his neighbors; and in asking to be enlightened on these points she usually inquired whether they corresponded with the descriptions in the books. The old man always looked at her a little, with his fine dry smile, while he smoothed down the shawl that was spread across his legs.

"The books?" he once said; "well, I don't know much about the books. You must ask Ralph about that. I have always ascertained for myself—got my information in the natural form. I never asked many questions even; I just kept quiet and took notice. Of course, I have had very good opportunities—better than what a young lady would naturally have. I am of an inquisitive disposition, though you mightn't think it if you were to watch me; however much you might watch me, I should be watching you more. I have been watching these people for upwards of thirty-five years, and I don't hesitate to say that I have acquired considerable information. It's a very fine country on the whole—finer perhaps than what we give it credit for on the other side. There are several improvements that I should like to see introduced; but the necessity of them doesn't seem to be generally felt as yet. When the necessity of a thing is generally felt, they usually manage to accomplish it; but they seem to feel pretty comfortable about waiting till then. I certainly feel more at home among them than I expected to when I first came over; I suppose it's because I have had a considerable degree of success. When you are successful you naturally feel more at home."

"Do you suppose that if I am successful I shall feel at home?" Isabel asked.

"I should think it very probable, and you certainly will be successful. They like American young ladies very much over here; they show them a great deal of kindness. But you mustn't feel too much at home, you know."

"Oh, I am by no means sure I shall like it," said Isabel, somewhat judicially. "I like the place very much, but I am not sure I shall like the people."

"The people are very good people; especially if you like them."

"I have no doubt they are good," Isabel rejoined; "but are they pleasant in society? They won't rob me nor beat me; but will they make themselves agreeable to me? That's what I like people to do. I don't hesitate to say so, because I always appreciate it. I don't believe they are very nice to girls; they are not nice to them in the novels."

"I don't know about the novels," said Mr. Touchett. "I believe the novels have a great deal of ability, but I don't suppose they are very accurate. We once had a lady who wrote novels staying here; she was a friend of Ralph's, and he asked her down. She was very positive, very positive; but she was not the sort of person that you could depend on her testimony. Too much imagination—I suppose, that was it. She afterwards published a work of fiction in which she was understood to have given a representation—something in the nature of a caricature, as you might say—of my unworthy self. I didn't read it, but Ralph just handed me the book, with the principal passages marked. It was understood to be a description of my conversation; American peculiarities, nasal twang, Yankee notions, stars and stripes. Well, it was not at all accurate; she couldn't have listened very attentively. I had no objection to her giving a report of my conversation, if she liked; but I didn't like the idea that she hadn't taken the trouble to listen to it. Of course I talk like an American—I can't talk like a Hottentot. However I talk, I have made them understand me pretty well over here. But I don't talk like the old gentleman in that lady's novel. He wasn't an American; we wouldn't have him over there! I just mention that fact to show you that they are not always accurate. Of course, as I have no daughters, and as Mrs. Touchett resides in Florence, I haven't had much chance to notice about the young ladies. It sometimes appears as if the young women in the lower class were not very well treated; but I guess their position is better in the upper class."

"Dear me!" Isabel exclaimed; "how many classes have they? About fifty, I suppose."

"Well, I don't know that I ever counted them. I never took much notice of the classes. That's the advantage of being an American here; you don't belong to any class."

"I hope so," said Isabel. "Imagine one's belonging to an English class!"

"Well, I guess some of them are pretty comfortable—especially toward the top. But for me there are only two classes: the people I trust, and the people I don't. Of those two, my dear Isabel, you belong to the first."

"I am much obliged to you," said the young girl, quickly. Her way of taking compliments seemed sometimes rather dry; she got rid of them as rapidly as possible. But as regards this, she was sometimes misjudged; she was thought insensible to them, whereas in fact she was simply unwilling to show how infinitely they pleased her. To show that was to show too much. "I am sure the English are very conventional," she added.

"They have got everything pretty well fixed," Mr. Touchett admitted. "It's all settled beforehand—they don't leave it to the last moment."

"I don't like to have everything settled beforehand," said the girl. "I like more unexpectedness."

Her uncle seemed amused at her distinctness of preference. "Well, it's settled beforehand that you will have great success," he rejoined. "I suppose you will like that."

"I shall not have success if they are conventional. I am not in the least conventional. I am just the contrary. That's what they won't like."

"No, no, you are all wrong," said the old man. "You can't tell what they will like. They are very inconsistent; that's their principal interest."

"Ah well," said Isabel, standing before her uncle with her hands clasped about the belt of her black dress, and looking up and down the lawn—"that will suit me perfectly!"

❦ 7 ❦

The two amused themselves, time and again, with talking of the attitude of the British public, as if the young lady had been in a position to appeal to it; but in fact the British public remained for the present profoundly indifferent to Miss Isabel Archer, whose fortune had dropped her, as her cousin said, into the dullest house in England. Her gouty uncle received very little company, and Mrs. Touchett, not having cultivated relations with her husband's neighbors, was not warranted in expecting visits from them. She had, however, a peculiar taste; she liked to receive cards. For what is usually called social intercourse she had very little relish; but nothing pleased her more than to find her hall table whitened with oblong morsels of symbolic pasteboard. She flattered herself that she was a very just woman, and had mastered the sovereign truth that nothing in this world is got for nothing. She had played no social part as mistress of Gardencourt, and it was not to be supposed that, in the surrounding country, a minute account should be kept of her comings and goings. But it is by no means certain that she did not feel it to be wrong that so little notice was taken of them, and that her failure (really very gratuitous) to make herself important in the neighborhood, had not much to do with the acrimony of her allusions to her husband's adopted country. Isabel presently found herself in the singular situation of defending the British constitution against her aunt; Mrs. Touchett having formed the habit of sticking pins into this venerable instrument. Isabel always felt an impulse to pull out the pins; not that she imagined they inflicted any damage on the tough old parchment, but because it seemed to her that her aunt might make better use of her sharpness. She was very critical herself—it was incidental to her age, her sex, and her nationality; but she was very sentimental as well, and there was something in Mrs. Touchett's dryness that set her own moral fountains flowing.

"Now what is your point of view?" she asked of her aunt. "When you criticize everything here, you should have a point of view. Yours doesn't seem to be American—you thought everything over there so disagreeable. When I criticize, I have mine; it's thoroughly American!"

"My dear young lady," said Mrs. Touchett, "there are as many points of view in the world as there are people of sense. You may say that doesn't make them very numerous! American? Never in the world; that's shockingly narrow. My point of view, thank God, is personal!"

Isabel thought this a better answer than she admitted; it was a tolerable description of her own manner of judging, but it would not have sounded well for her to say so. On the lips of a person less advanced in life, and less enlightened by experience than Mrs. Touchett, such a declaration would savor of immodesty, even of arrogance. She risked it nevertheless, in talking with Ralph, with whom she talked a great deal, and with whom her conversation was of a sort that gave a large licence to violent statements. Her cousin used, as the phrase is, to chaff her; he very soon established with her a reputation for treating everything as a joke, and he was not a man to neglect the privileges such a reputation conferred. She accused him of an odious want of seriousness, of laughing at all things, beginning with himself. Such slender faculty of reverence as he possessed centered wholly upon his father; for the rest, he exercised his wit indiscriminately upon his father's son, this gentleman's weak lungs, his useless life, his anomalous mother, his friends (Lord Warburton in especial), his adopted and his native country, his charming new-found cousin. "I keep a band of music in my anteroom," he said once to her. "It has orders to play without stopping; it renders me two excellent services. It keeps the sounds of the world from reaching the private apartments, and it makes the world think that dancing is going on within." It was dance music indeed that you usually heard when you came within earshot of Ralph's band; the liveliest waltzes seemed to float upon the air. Isabel often found herself irritated by this perpetual fiddling; she would have liked to pass through the anteroom, as her cousin called it, and enter the private apartments. It mattered little that he had assured her that they were a very dismal place; she would have been glad to undertake to sweep them and set them in order. It was but half-hospitality to let her remain outside; to punish him for which, Isabel administered innumerable taps with the ferrule of her straight young wit. It must be said that her wit was exercised to a large extent in self-defense, for her cousin amused himself with calling her "Columbia," and accusing her of a patriotism so fervid that it scorched. He drew a caricature of her, in which she was represented as a very pretty young woman, dressed, in the height of the prevailing fashion, in the folds of the national banner. Isabel's chief dread in life, at this period of her development, was that she should appear narrow-minded; what she feared next afterwards was that she should be so. But she nevertheless made no scruple of abounding in her cousin's sense, and pretending to sigh for the charms of her native land. She would be as American as it pleased him to regard her, and if he chose to laugh at her, she would give him plenty of occupation. She defended England against his mother, but when Ralph sang its praises, on purpose, as she said, to torment her, she found herself able to differ from him on a variety of points. In fact, the quality of this small ripe country seemed as sweet to her as the taste of an October pear; and her satisfaction was at the root of the good spirits which enabled her to take her cousin's chaff and return it in kind. If her good-humor flagged at moments, it was not because she thought herself ill-used, but because she suddenly felt sorry for Ralph. It seemed to her that he was talking as a blind and had little heart in what he said.

"I don't know what is the matter with you," she said to him once; "but I suspect you are a great humbug."

"That's your privilege," Ralph answered, who had not been used to being so crudely addressed.

"I don't know what you care for; I don't think you care for anything. You don't really care for England when you praise it; you don't care for America even when you pretend to abuse it."

"I care for nothing but you, dear cousin," said Ralph.

"If I could believe even that, I should be very glad."

"Ah, well, I should hope so!" the young man exclaimed.

Isabel might have believed it, and not have been far from the truth. He thought a great deal about her; she was constantly present to his mind. At a time when his thoughts had been a good deal of a burden to him, her sudden arrival, which promised nothing and was an open-handed gift of fate, had refreshed and quickened them, given them wings and something to fly for. Poor Ralph for many weeks had been steeped in melancholy; his outlook, habitually somber, lay under the shadow of a deeper cloud. He had grown anxious about his father, whose gout, hitherto confined to his legs, had begun to ascend into regions more vital. The old man had been gravely ill in the spring, and the doctors had whispered to Ralph that another attack would be less easy to deal with. Just now he appeared tolerably comfortable, but Ralph could not rid himself of a suspicion that this was a sub-terfuge of the enemy, who was waiting to take him off his guard. If the maneuver should succeed, there would be little hope of any great resistance. Ralph had always taken for granted that his father would survive him—that his own name would be the first called. The father and son had been close companions, and the idea of being left alone with the remnant of a tasteless life on his hands was not gratifying to the young man, who had always and tacitly counted upon his elder's help in making the best of a poor business. At the prospect of losing his great motive, Ralph was indeed mightily disgusted. If they might die at the same time, it would be all very well; but without the encouragement of his father's society he should barely have patience to await his own turn. He had not the incentive of feeling that he was indispensable to his mother; it was a rule with his mother to have no regrets. He bethought himself, of course, that it had been a small kindness to his father to wish that, of the two, the active rather than the passive party should know the pain of loss; he remembered that the old man had always treated his own forecast of an uncompleted career as a clever fallacy, which he should be delighted to discredit so far as he might by dying first. But of the two triumphs, that of refuting a sophistical son and that of holding on a while longer to a state of being which, with all abatements, he enjoyed, Ralph deemed it no sin to hope that the latter might be vouchsafed to Mr. Touchett.

These were nice questions, but Isabel's arrival put a stop to his puzzling over them. It even suggested that there might be a compensation for the intolerable ennui of surviving his genial sire. He wondered whether he were falling in love with this spontaneous young woman from Albany; but he decided that on the whole he was not. After he had known her for a week, he quite made up his mind to this, and every day he felt a little more sure. Lord Warburton had been right about her; she was a thoroughly interesting woman. Ralph wondered how Lord Warburton had found it out so soon; and then he said it was only another proof of his friend's high abilities, which he had always greatly admired. If his cousin were to be nothing more than an entertainment to him, Ralph was conscious that she was an entertainment of a high order. "A character like that," he said to himself, "is the finest thing in nature. It is finer than the finest work of art—than a Greek bas-relief, than a great Titian, than a Gothic cathedral. It is very pleasant to be so well-treated where one least looked for it. I had never been more blue, more bored, than for a week before she came; I had never expected less that something agreeable would happen. Suddenly I receive a Titian, by the post, to hang on my wall—a Greek bas-relief to stick over my chimney piece. The key of a beautiful edifice is thrust into my hand, and I am told to walk in and admire. My poor boy, you have been sadly ungrateful, and now you had better keep very quiet and never grumble again." The sentiment of these reflections was very just; but it was not exactly true that Ralph Touchett had had a key put into his hand. His cousin was a very brilliant girl, who would take, as he said, a good deal of knowing; but she needed the knowing, and his attitude with regard to her, though it was contemplative and critical, was not judicial. He surveyed the edifice from the outside, and admired it greatly; he looked in at the windows, and received an impression of proportions equally fair. But he felt that he saw it only by glimpses, and that he had not yet stood under the roof. The door was fastened, and though he had keys in his pocket he had a conviction that none of them would fit. She was intelligent and generous; it was a fine free nature; but what was she going to do with herself? This question was irregular, for with most women one had no occasion to ask it. Most women did with themselves nothing at all; they waited, in attitudes more or less gracefully passive, for a man to come that way and furnish them with a destiny. Isabel's originality was that she gave one an impression of having intentions of her own. "Whenever she executes them," said Ralph, "may I be there to see!"

It devolved upon him of course to do the honors of the place. Mr. Touchett was confined to his chair, and his wife's position was that of a rather grim visitor; so that in the line of conduct that opened itself to Ralph, duty and inclination were harmoniously mingled. He was not a great walker, but he strolled about the grounds with his cousin—a pastime for which the weather remained favorable with a persistency not allowed for in Isabel's somewhat lugubrious prevision of the climate; and in the long afternoons, of which the length was but the measure of her gratified eagerness, they took a boat on the river, the dear little river, as Isabel called it, where the opposite shore seemed still a part of the foreground of the landscape; or drove over the country in a phaeton—a low, capacious, thick-wheeled phaeton formerly much used by Mr. Touchett, but which he had now ceased to enjoy. Isabel enjoyed it largely, and, handling the reins in a manner which approved itself to the groom as "knowing," was never weary of driving her uncle's capital horses through winding lanes and byways full of the rural incidents she had confidently expected to find; past cottages thatched and timbered, past ale-houses latticed and sanded, past patches of ancient common and glimpses of empty parks, between hedgerows made thick by midsummer. When they reached home, they usually found that tea had been served upon the lawn, and that Mrs. Touchett had not absolved herself from the obligation of handing her husband his cup. But the two for the most part sat silent; the old man with his head back and his eyes closed, his wife occupied with her knitting, and wearing that appearance of extraordinary meditation with which some ladies contemplate the movement of their needles.

One day, however, a visitor had arrived. The two young people, after spending an hour upon the river, strolled back to the house and perceived Lord Warburton sitting under the trees and engaged in conversation, of which even at a distance the desultory character was appreciable, with Mrs. Touchett. He had driven over from his own place with a portmanteau, and had asked, as the father and son often invited him to do, for a dinner and a lodging. Isabel, seeing him for half-an-hour on the day of her arrival, had discovered in this brief space that she liked him; he had made indeed a tolerably vivid impression on her mind, and she had thought of him several times. She had hoped that she should see him again—hoped too that she should see a few others. Gardencourt was not dull; the place itself was so delightful, her uncle was such a perfection of an uncle, and Ralph was so unlike any cousin she had ever encountered—her view of cousins being rather monotonous. Then her impressions were still so fresh and so quickly renewed that there was as yet hardly a sense of vacancy in the prospect. But Isabel had need to remind herself that she was interested in human nature, and that her foremost hope in coming abroad had been that she should see a great many people. When Ralph said to her, as he had done several times—"I wonder you find this endurable; you ought to see some of the neighbors and some of our friends—because we have really got a few, though you would never suppose it"—when he offered to invite what he called a "lot of people," and make the young girl acquainted with English society, she encouraged the hospitable impulse and promised, in advance, to be delighted. Little, however, for the present, had come of Ralph's offers, and it may be confided to the reader that, if the young man delayed to carry them out, it was because he found the labor of entertaining his cousin by no means so severe as to require extraneous help. Isabel had spoken to him very often about "specimens"; it was a word that played a considerable part in her vocabulary; she had given him to understand that she wished to see English society illustrated by figures.

"Well now, there's a specimen," he said to her, as they walked up from the riverside, and he recognized Lord Warburton.

"A specimen of what?" asked the girl.

"A specimen of an English gentleman."

"Do you mean they are all like him?"

"Oh no; they are not all like him."

"He's a favorable specimen, then," said Isabel; "because I am sure he is good."

"Yes, he is very good. And he is very fortunate."

The fortunate Lord Warburton exchanged a handshake with our heroine, and hoped she was very well. "But I needn't ask that," he said, "since you have been handling the oars."

"I have been rowing a little," Isabel answered; "but how should you know it?"

"Oh, I know *he* doesn't row; he's too lazy," said his lordship, indicating Ralph Touchett, with a laugh.

"He has a good excuse for his laziness," Isabel rejoined, lowering her voice a little.

"Ah, he has a good excuse for everything!" cried Lord Warburton, still with his deep, agreeable laugh.

"My excuse for not rowing is that my cousin rows so well," said Ralph. "She does everything well. She touches nothing that she doesn't adorn!"

"It makes one want to be touched, Miss Archer," Lord Warburton declared.

"Be touched in the right sense, and you will never look the worse for it," said Isabel, who, if it pleased her to hear it said that her accomplishments were numerous, was happily able to reflect that such complacency was not the indication of a feeble mind, inasmuch as there were several things in which she excelled. Her desire to think well of herself always needed to be supported by proof; though it is possible that this fact is not the sign of a milder egotism.

Lord Warburton not only spent the night at Gardencourt, but he was persuaded to remain over the second day; and when the second day was ended, he determined to postpone his departure till the morrow. During this period he addressed much of his conversation to Isabel, who accepted this evidence of his esteem with a very good grace. She found herself liking him extremely; the first impression he had made upon her was pleasant, but at the end of an evening spent in his society she thought him quite one of the most delectable persons she had met. She retired to rest with a sense of good fortune, with a quickened consciousness of the pleasantness of life. "It's very nice to know two such charming people as those," she said, meaning by "those" her cousin and her cousin's friend. It must be added, moreover, that an incident had occurred which might have seemed to put her good humor to the test. Mr. Touchett went to bed at half-past nine o'clock, but his wife remained in the drawing room with the other members of the party. She prolonged her vigil for something less than an hour, and then rising, she said to Isabel that it was time they should bid the gentlemen good night. Isabel had as yet no desire to go to bed; the occasion wore, to her sense, a festive character, and feasts were not in the habit of terminating so early. So, without further thought, she replied, very simply—

"Need I go, dear aunt? I will come up in half-an-hour."

"It's impossible I should wait for you," Mrs. Touchett answered.

"Ah, you needn't wait! Ralph will light my candle," said Isabel, smiling.

"I will light your candle; do let me light your candle, Miss Archer!" Lord Warburton exclaimed. "Only I beg it shall not be before midnight."

Mrs. Touchett fixed her bright little eyes upon him for a moment, and then transferred them to her niece.

"You can't stay alone with the gentlemen. You are not—you are not at Albany, my dear."

Isabel rose, blushing.

"I wish I were," she said.

"Oh, I say, mother!" Ralph broke out.

"My dear Mrs. Touchett," Lord Warburton murmured.

"I didn't make your country, my lord," Mrs. Touchett said majestically. "I must take it as I find it."

"Can't I stay with my own cousin?" Isabel inquired.

"I am not aware that Lord Warburton is your cousin."

"Perhaps I had better go to bed!" the visitor exclaimed. "That will arrange it."

Mrs. Touchett gave a little look of despair, and sat down again.

"Oh, if it's necessary, I will stay up till midnight," she said.

Ralph meanwhile handed Isabel her candlestick. He had been watching her; it had seemed to him that her temper was stirred—an accident that might be interesting. But if he had expected an exhibition of temper, he was disappointed, for the girl simply laughed a little, nodded good night, and withdrew, accompanied by her aunt. For himself he was annoyed at his mother, though he thought she was right. Abovestairs, the two ladies separated at Mrs. Touchett's door. Isabel had said nothing on her way up.

"Of course you are displeased at my interfering with you," said Mrs. Touchett.

Isabel reflected a moment.

"I am not displeased, but I am surprised—and a good deal puzzled. Was it not proper I should remain in the drawing room?"

"Not in the least. Young girls here don't sit alone with the gentlemen late at night."

"You were very right to tell me then," said Isabel. "I don't understand it, but I am very glad to know it."

"I shall always tell you," her aunt answered, "whenever I see you taking what seems to be too much liberty."

"Pray do; but I don't say I shall always think your remonstrance just."

"Very likely not. You are too fond of your liberty."

"Yes, I think I am very fond of it. But I always want to know the things one shouldn't do."

"So as to do them?" asked her aunt.

"So as to choose," said Isabel.

❧ 8 ❧

As she was much interested in the picturesque, Lord Warburton ventured to express a hope that she would come some day and see his house, which was a very curious old place. He extracted from Mrs. Touchett a promise that she would bring her niece to Lockleigh, and Ralph signified his willingness to attend upon the ladies if his father should be able to spare him. Lord Warburton assured our heroine that in the meantime his sisters would come and see her. She knew something about his sisters, having interrogated him, during the hours they spent together while he was at Gardencourt, on many points connected with his family. When Isabel was interested, she asked a great many questions, and as her companion was a copious talker, she asked him on this occasion by no means in vain. He told her that he had four sisters and two brothers, and had lost both his parents. The brothers and sisters were very good people—"not particularly clever, you know," he said, "but simple and respectable and trustworthy;" and he was so good as to hope that Miss Archer should know them well. One of the brothers was in the Church, settled in the parsonage at Lockleigh, which was rather a largeish parish, and was an excellent fellow, in spite of his thinking differently from himself on every conceivable topic. And then Lord Warburton mentioned some of the opinions held by his brother, which were opinions that Isabel had often heard expressed and that she supposed to be entertained by a considerable portion of the human family. Many of them, indeed, she supposed she had held herself, till he assured her that she was quite mistaken, that it was really impossible, that she had doubtless imagined she entertained them, but that she might depend that, if she thought them over a little, she would find there was nothing in them. When she answered that she had already thought several of them over very attentively, he declared that she was only another example of what he had often been struck with—the fact that, of all the people in the world, the Americans were the most grossly superstitious. They were rank Tories and bigots, every one of them; there were no conservatives like American conservatives. Her uncle and her cousin were there to prove it; nothing could be more medieval than many of their views; they had ideas that people in England nowadays were ashamed to confess to; and they had the impudence, moreover, said his lordship, laughing, to pretend they know more about the needs and dangers of this poor dear stupid old England than he who was born in it and owned a considerable part of it—the more shame to him! From all of which Isabel gathered that Lord Warburton was a nobleman of the newest pattern, a reformer, a radical, a contemner of ancient ways. His other brother, who was in the army in India, was rather wild and pig-headed, and had not been of much use as yet but to make debts for Warburton to pay—one of the most precious privileges of an elder brother. "I don't think I will pay anymore," said Warburton; "he lives a monstrous deal better than I do, enjoys unheard-of luxuries, and thinks himself a much finer gentleman than I. As I am a consistent radical, I go in only for equality; I don't go in for the superiority of the younger brothers." Two of his four sisters, the second and fourth, were married, one of them having done very well, as they said, the other only so-so. The husband of the elder, Lord Haycock, was a very good fellow, but unfortunately a horrid Tory; and his wife, like all good English wives, was worse than her husband. The other had espoused a smallish squire in Norfolk, and, though she was married only the other day, had already five children. This information, and much more, Lord Warburton imparted to his young American listener, taking pains to make many things clear and to lay bare to her apprehension the peculiarities of English life. Isabel was often amused at his explicitness and at the small allowance he seemed to make either for her own experience or for her imagination. "He thinks I am a barbarian," she said, "and that I have never seen forks and spoons;" and she used to ask him artless questions for the pleasure of hearing him answer seriously. Then when he had fallen into the trap—"It's a pity you can't see me in my war-paint and feathers," she remarked; "if I had known how kind you are to the poor savages, I would have brought over my national costume!" Lord Warburton had traveled through the United States, and knew much more about them than Isabel; he was so good as to say that America was the most charming country in the world, but his recollections of it appeared to encourage the idea that Americans in England would need to have a great many things explained to them. "If I had only had you to explain things to me in America!" he said. "I was rather puzzled in your country; in fact, I was quite bewildered, and the trouble was that the explanations only puzzled me more. You know I think they often gave me the wrong ones on purpose; they are rather clever about that over there. But when I explain, you can trust me; about what I tell you there is no mistake." There was no mistake at least about his being very intelligent and cultivated, and knowing almost everything in the world. Although he said the most interesting and entertaining things, Isabel perceived that he never said them to exhibit himself, and though he had a great good fortune, he was as far as possible from making a merit of it. He had enjoyed the best things of life, but they had not spoiled his sense of proportion. His composition was a mixture of good-humored manly force and a modesty that at times was almost boyish; the sweet and wholesome savor of which—it was as agreeable as something tasted—lost nothing from the addition of a tone of kindness which was not boyish, inasmuch as there was a good deal of reflection and of conscience in it.

"I like your specimen English gentleman very much," Isabel said to Ralph, after Lord Warburton had gone.

"I like him too—I love him well," said Ralph. "But I pity him more."

Isabel looked at him askance.

"Why, that seems to me his only fault—that one can't pity him a little. He appears to have everything, to know everything, to be everything."

"Oh, he's in a bad way," Ralph insisted.

"I suppose you don't mean in health?"

"No, as to that, he's detestably robust. What I mean is that he is a man with a great position, who is playing all sorts of tricks with it. He doesn't take himself seriously."

"Does he regard himself as a joke?"

"Much worse; he regards himself as an imposition—as an abuse."

"Well, perhaps he is," said Isabel.

"Perhaps he is—though on the whole I don't think so. But in that case, what is more pitiable than a sentient, self-conscious abuse, planted by other hands, deeply rooted, but aching with a sense of its injustice? For me, I could take the poor fellow very seriously; he occupies a position that appeals to my imagination. Great responsibilities, great opportunities, great consideration, great wealth, great power, a natural share in the public affairs of a great country. But he is all in a muddle about himself, his position, his power, and everything else. He is the victim of a critical age; he has ceased to believe in himself, and he doesn't know what to believe in. When I attempt to tell him (because if I were he, I know very well what I should believe in), he calls me an old-fashioned and narrow-minded person. I believe he seriously thinks me an awful Philistine; he says I don't understand my time. I understand it certainly better than he, who can neither abolish himself as a nuisance nor maintain himself as an institution."

"He doesn't look very wretched," Isabel observed.

"Possibly not; though, being a man of imagination, I think he often has uncomfortable hours. But what is it to say of a man of his opportunities that he is not miserable? Besides, I believe he is."

"I don't," said Isabel.

"Well," her cousin rejoined, "If he is not, he ought to be!"

In the afternoon she spent an hour with her uncle on the lawn, where the old man sat, as usual, with his shawl over his legs and his large cup of diluted tea in his hands. In the course of conversation he asked her what she thought of their late visitor.

"I think he is charming," Isabel answered.

"He's a fine fellow," said Mr. Touchett, "but I don't recommend you to fall in love with him."

"I shall not do it then; I shall never fall in love but on your recommendation. Moreover," Isabel added, "my cousin gives me a rather sad account of Lord Warburton."

"Oh, indeed? I don't know what there may be to say, but you must remember that Ralph is rather fanciful."

"He thinks Lord Warburton is too radical—or not radical enough! I don't quite understand which," said Isabel.

The old man shook his head slowly, smiled, and put down his cup.

"I don't know which, either. He goes very far, but it is quite possible he doesn't go far enough. He seems to want to do away with a good many things, but he seems to want to remain himself. I suppose that is natural; but it is rather inconsistent."

"Oh, I hope he will remain himself," said Isabel. "If he were to be done away with, his friends would miss him sadly."

"Well," said the old man, "I guess he'll stay and amuse his friends. I should certainly miss him very much here at Gardencourt. He always amuses me when he comes over, and I think he amuses himself as well. There is a considerable number like him, round in society; they are very fashionable just now. I don't know what they are trying to do—whether they are trying to get up a revolution; I hope at any rate they will put it off till after I am gone. You see they want to disestablish everything; but I'm a pretty big landowner here, and I don't want to be disestablished. I wouldn't have come over if I had thought they were going to behave like that," Mr. Touchett went on, with expanding hilarity. "I came over because I thought England was a safe country. I call it a regular fraud, if they are going to introduce any considerable changes; there'll be a large number disappointed in that case."

"Oh, I do hope they will make a revolution!" Isabel exclaimed. "I should delight in seeing a revolution."

"Let me see," said her uncle, with a humorous intention; "I forget whether you are a liberal or a conservative. I have heard you take such opposite views."

"I am both. I think I am a little of everything. In a revolution—after it was well begun—I think I should be a conservative. One sympathizes more with them, and they have a chance to behave so picturesquely."

"I don't know that I understand what you mean by behaving picturesquely, but it seems to me that you do that always, my dear."

"Oh, you lovely man, if I could believe that!" the girl interrupted.

"I am afraid, after all, you won't have the pleasure of seeing a revolution here just now," Mr. Touchett went on. "If you want to see one, you must pay us a long visit. You see, when you come to the point, it wouldn't suit them to be taken at their word."

"Of whom are you speaking?"

"Well, I mean Lord Warburton and his friends—the radicals of the upper class. Of course I only know the way it strikes me. They talk about the changes, but I don't think they quite realize. You and I, you know, we know what it is to have lived under democratic institutions; I always thought them very comfortable, but I was used to them from the first. But then, I ain't a lord; you're a lady, my dear, but I ain't a lord. Now, over here, I don't think it quite comes home to them. It's a matter of every day and every hour, and I don't think many of them would find it as pleasant as what they've got. Of course if they want to try, it's their own business; but I expect they won't try very hard."

"Don't you think they are sincere?" Isabel asked.

"Well, they are very conscientious," Mr. Touchett allowed; "but it seems as if they took it out in theories, mostly. Their radical views are a kind of amusement; they have got to have some amusement, and they might have coarser tastes than that. You see they are very luxurious, and these progressive ideas are about their biggest luxury. They make them feel moral, and yet they don't affect their position. They think a great deal of their position; don't let one of them ever persuade you he doesn't, for if you were to proceed on that basis, you would be pulled up very short."

Isabel followed her uncle's argument, which he unfolded with his mild, reflective, optimistic accent, most attentively, and though she was unacquainted with the British aristocracy, she found it in harmony with her general impressions of human nature. But she felt moved to put in a protest on Lord Warburton's behalf.

"I don't believe Lord Warburton's a humbug," she said; "I don't care what the others are. I should like to see Lord Warburton put to the test."

"Heaven deliver me from my friends!" Mr. Touchett answered. "Lord Warburton is a very amiable young man—a very fine young man. He has a hundred thousand a year. He owns fifty thousand acres of the soil of this little island. He has half-a-dozen houses to live in. He has a seat in Parliament as I have one at my own dinner-table. He has very cultivated tastes—cares for literature, for art, for science, for charming young ladies. The most cultivated is his taste for the new views. It affords him a great deal of entertainment—more perhaps than anything else, except the young ladies. His old house over there—what does he call it, Lockleigh?—is very attractive; but I don't think it is as pleasant as this. That doesn't matter, however—he has got so many others. His views don't hurt anyone as far as I can see; they certainly don't hurt himself. And if there were to be a revolution, he would come off very easily; they wouldn't touch him, they would leave him as he is; he is too much liked."

"Ah, he couldn't be a martyr even if he wished!" Isabel exclaimed. "That's a very poor position."

"He will never be a martyr unless you make him one," said the old man.

Isabel shook her head; there might have been something laughable in the fact that she did it with a touch of sadness.

"I shall never make anyone a martyr."

"You will never be one, I hope."

"I hope not. But you don't pity Lord Warburton, then, as Ralph does?"

Her uncle looked at her a while, with genial acuteness.

"Yes, I do, after all!"

❧ 9 ❧

The two Misses Molyneux, this nobleman's sisters, came presently to call upon her, and Isabel took a fancy to the young ladies, who appeared to her to have a very original stamp. It is true that, when she spoke of them to her cousin as original, he declared that no epithet could be less applicable than this to the two Misses Molyneux, for that there were fifty thousand young women in England who exactly resembled them. Deprived of this advantage, however, Isabel's visitors retained that of an extreme sweetness and shyness of demeanor, and of having, as she thought, the kindest eyes in the world.

"They are not morbid, at any rate, whatever they are," our heroine said to herself; and she deemed this a great charm, for two or three of the friends of her girlhood had been regrettably open to the charge (they would have been so nice without it), to say nothing of Isabel's having occasionally suspected that it might become a fault of her own. The Misses Molyneux were not in their first youth, but they had bright, fresh complexions, and something of the smile of childhood. Their eyes, which Isabel admired so much, were quiet and contented, and their figures, of a generous roundness, were encased in sealskin jackets. Their friendliness was great, so great that they were almost embarrassed to show it; they seemed somewhat afraid of the young lady from the other side of the world, and rather looked than spoke their good wishes. But they made it clear to her that they hoped she would come to lunch at Lockleigh, where they lived with their brother, and then they might see her very, very often. They wondered whether she wouldn't come over some day and sleep; they were expecting some people on the twenty-ninth, and perhaps she would come while the people were there.

"I'm afraid it isn't anyone very remarkable," said the elder sister; "but I daresay you will take us as you find us."

"I shall find you delightful; I think you are enchanting just as you are," replied Isabel, who often praised profusely.

Her visitors blushed, and her cousin told her, after they were gone, that if she said such things to those poor girls, they would think she was quizzing them; he was sure it was the first time they had been called enchanting.

"I can't help it," Isabel answered. "I think it's lovely to be so quiet, and reasonable, and satisfied. I should like to be like that."

"Heaven forbid!" cried Ralph, with ardor.

"I mean to try and imitate them," said Isabel. "I want very much to see them at home."

She had this pleasure a few days later, when, with Ralph and his mother, she drove over to Lockleigh. She found the Misses Molyneux sitting in a vast drawing room (she perceived afterwards it was one of several), in a wilderness of faded chintz; they were dressed on this occasion in black velveteen. Isabel liked them even better at home than she had done at Gardencourt, and was more than ever struck with the fact that they were not morbid. It had seemed to her before that, if they had a fault, it was a want of vivacity; but she presently saw that they were capable of deep emotion. Before lunch she was alone with them, for some time, on one side of the room, while Lord Warburton, at a distance, talked to Mrs. Touchett.

"Is it true that your brother is such a great radical?" Isabel asked. She knew it was true, but we have seen that her interest in human nature was keen, and she had a desire to draw the Misses Molyneux out.

"Oh dear, yes; he's immensely advanced," said Mildred, the younger sister.

"At the same time, Warburton is very reasonable," Miss Molyneux observed.

Isabel watched him a moment, at the other side of the room; he was evidently trying hard to make himself agreeable to Mrs. Touchett. Ralph was playing with one of the dogs before the fire, which the temperature of an English August, in the ancient, spacious room, had not made an impertinence. "Do you suppose your brother is sincere?" Isabel inquired with a smile.

"Oh, he must be, you know!" Mildred exclaimed, quickly; while the elder sister gazed at our heroine in silence.

"Do you think he would stand the test?"

"The test?"

"I mean, for instance, having to give up all this!"

"Having to give up Lockleigh?" said Miss Molyneux, finding her voice.

"Yes, and the other places; what are they called?"

The two sisters exchanged an almost frightened glance. "Do you mean—do you mean on account of the expense?" the younger one asked.

"I daresay he might let one or two of his houses," said the other.

"Let them for nothing?" Isabel inquired.

"I can't fancy his giving up his property," said Miss Molyneux.

"Ah, I am afraid he is an impostor!" Isabel exclaimed. "Don't you think it's a false position?"

Her companions, evidently, were rapidly getting bewildered. "My brother's position?" Miss Molyneux inquired.

"It's thought a very good position," said the younger sister. "It's the first position in the county."

"I suspect you think me very irreverent," Isabel took occasion to observe. "I suppose you revere your brother, and are rather afraid of him."

"Of course one looks up to one's brother," said Miss Molyneux, simply.

"If you do that, he must be very good—because you, evidently, are very good."

"He is most kind. It will never be known, the good he does."

"His ability is known," Mildred added; "everyone thinks it's immense."

"Oh, I can see that," said Isabel. "But if I were he, I should wish to be a conservative. I should wish to keep everything."

"I think one ought to be liberal," Mildred argued, gently. "We have always been so, even from the earliest times."

"Ah well," said Isabel, "you have made a great success of it; I don't wonder you like it. I see you are very fond of crewels."

When Lord Warburton showed her the house, after lunch, it seemed to her a matter of course that it should be a noble picture. Within, it had been a good deal modernized—some of its best points had lost their purity; but as they saw it from the gardens, a stout, gray pile, of the softest, deepest, most weather-fretted hue, rising from a broad, still moat, it seemed to Isabel a castle in a fairy tale. The day was cool and rather lusterless; the first note of autumn had been struck; and the watery sunshine rested on the walls in blurred and desultory gleams, washing them, as it were, in places tenderly chosen, where the ache of antiquity was keenest. Her host's brother, the Vicar, had come to lunch, and Isabel had had five minutes' talk with him—time enough to institute a search for theological characteristics and give it up as vain. The characteristics of the Vicar of Lockleigh were a big, athletic figure, a candid, natural countenance, a capacious appetite, and a tendency to abundant laughter. Isabel learned afterwards from her cousin that, before taking orders, he had been a mighty wrestler, and that he was still, on occasion—in the privacy of the family circle as it were—quite capable of flooring his man. Isabel liked him—she was in the mood for liking everything; but her imagination was a good deal taxed to think of him as a source of spiritual aid. The whole party, on leaving lunch, went to walk the grounds; but Lord Warburton exercised some ingenuity in engaging his youngest visitor in a stroll somewhat apart from the others.

"I wish you to see the place properly, seriously," he said. "You can't do so if your attention is distracted by irrelevant gossip." His own conversation (though he told Isabel a good deal about the house, which had a very curious history) was not purely archaeological; he reverted at intervals to matters more personal—matters personal to the young lady as well as to himself. But at last, after a pause of some duration, returning for a moment to their ostensible theme, "Ah, well," he said, "I am very glad indeed you like the old house. I wish you could see more of it—that you could stay here a while. My sisters have taken an immense fancy to you—if that would be any inducement."

"There is no want of inducements," Isabel answered; "but I am afraid I can't make engagements. I am quite in my aunt's hands."

"Ah, excuse me if I say I don't exactly believe that. I am pretty sure you can do whatever you want."

"I am sorry if I make that impression on you; I don't think it's a nice impression to make."

"It has the merit of permitting me to hope." And Lord Warburton paused a moment.

"To hope what?"

"That in future I may see you often."

"Ah," said Isabel, "to enjoy that pleasure, I needn't be so terribly emancipated."

"Doubtless not; and yet, at the same time, I don't think your uncle likes me."

"You are very much mistaken. I have heard him speak very highly of you."

"I am glad you have talked about me," said Lord Warburton. "But, all the same, I don't think he would like me to keep coming to Gardencourt."

"I can't answer for my uncle's tastes," the girl rejoined, "though I ought, as far as possible, to take them into account. But, for myself, I shall be very glad to see you."

"Now that's what I like to hear you say. I am charmed when you say that."

"You are easily charmed, my lord," said Isabel.

"No, I am not easily charmed!" And then he stopped a moment. "But you have charmed me, Miss Archer," he added.

These words were uttered with an indefinable sound which startled the girl; it struck her as the prelude to something grave; she had heard the sound before, and she recognized it. She had no wish, however, that for the moment such a prelude should have a sequel, and she said, as gaily as possible and as quickly as an appreciable degree of agitation would allow her, "I am afraid there is no prospect of my being able to come here again."

"Never?" said Lord Warburton.

"I won't say 'never'; I should feel very melodramatic."

"May I come and see you then some day next week?"

"Most assuredly. What is there to prevent it?"

"Nothing tangible. But with you I never feel safe. I have a sort of sense that you are always judging people."

"You don't of necessity lose by that."

"It is very kind of you to say so; but even if I gain, stern justice is not what I most love. Is Mrs. Touchett going to take you abroad?"

"I hope so."

"Is England not good enough for you?"

"That's a very Machiavellian speech; it doesn't deserve an answer. I want very much to see foreign lands as well."

"Then you will go on judging, I suppose."

"Enjoying, I hope, too."

"Yes, that's what you enjoy most; I can't make out what you are up to," said Lord Warburton. "You strike me as having mysterious purposes—vast designs!"

"You are so good as to have a theory about me which I don't at all fill out. Is there anything mysterious in a purpose entertained and executed every year, in the most public manner, by fifty thousand of my fellow-countrymen—the purpose of improving one's mind by foreign travel?"

"You can't improve your mind, Miss Archer," her companion declared. "It's already a most formidable instrument. It looks down on us all; it despises us."

"Despises you? You are making fun of me," said Isabel, seriously.

"Well, you think us picturesque—that's the same thing. I won't be thought picturesque, to begin with; I am not so in the least. I protest."

"That protest is one of the most picturesque things I have ever heard," Isabel answered with a smile.

Lord Warburton was silent a moment. "You judge only from the outside—you don't care," he said presently. "You only care to amuse yourself!" The note she had heard in his voice a moment before reappeared, and mixed with it now was an audible strain of bitterness—a bitterness so abrupt and inconsequent that the girl was afraid she had hurt him. She had often heard that the English were a highly eccentric people; and she had even read in some ingenious author that they were, at bottom, the most romantic of races. Was Lord Warburton suddenly turning romantic—was he going to make a scene, in his own house, only the third time they had met? She was reassured, quickly enough, by her sense of his great good manners, which was not impaired by the fact that he had already touched the furthest limit of good taste in expressing his admiration of a young lady who had confided in his hospitality. She was right in trusting to his good manners, for he presently went on, laughing a little, and without a trace of the accent that had discomposed her—"I don't mean, of course, that you amuse yourself with trifles. You select great materials; the foibles, the afflictions of human nature, the peculiarities of nations!"

"As regards that," said Isabel, "I should find in my own nation entertainment for a lifetime. But we have a long drive, and my aunt will soon wish to start." She turned back toward the others, and Lord Warburton walked beside her in silence. But before they reached the others—"I shall come and see you next week," he said.

She had received an appreciable shock, but as it died away she felt that she could not pretend to herself that it was altogether a painful one. Nevertheless, she made answer to this declaration, coldly enough, "Just as you please." And her coldness was not coquetry—a quality that she possessed in a much smaller degree than would have seemed probable to many critics; it came from a certain fear.

❧ 10 ❧

The day after her visit to Lockleigh she received a note from her friend, Miss Stackpole—a note of which the envelope, exhibiting in conjunction the postmark of Liverpool and the neat calligraphy of the quick-fingered Henrietta, caused her some liveliness of emotion. "Here I am, my lovely friend," Miss Stackpole wrote; "I managed to get off at last. I decided only the night before I left New York—the *Interviewer* having come round to my figure. I put a few things into a bag, like a veteran journalist, and came down to the steamer in a streetcar. Where are you, and where can we meet? I suppose you are visiting at some castle or other, and have already acquired the correct accent. Perhaps, even, you have married a lord; I almost hope you have, for I want some introductions to the first people, and shall count on you for a few. The *Interviewer* wants some light on the nobility. My first impressions (of the people at large) are not rose-colored; but I wish to talk them over with you, and you know that whatever I am, at least I am not superficial. I have also something very particular to tell you. Do appoint a meeting as quickly as you can; come to London (I should like so much to visit the sights with you), or else let me come to you, *wherever you are.* I will do so with pleasure; for you know everything interests me, and I wish to see as much as possible of the inner life."

Isabel did not show this letter to her uncle; but she acquainted him with its purport, and, as she expected, he begged her instantly to assure Miss Stackpole, in his name, that he should be delighted to receive her at Gardencourt. "Though she is a literary lady," he said, "I suppose that, being an American, she won't reproduce me, as that other one did. She has seen others like me."

"She has seen no other so delightful!" Isabel answered; but she was not altogether at ease about Henrietta's reproductive instincts, which belonged to that side of her friend's character which she regarded with least complacency. She wrote to Miss Stackpole, however, that she would be very welcome under Mr. Touchett's roof; and this enterprising young woman lost no time in signifying her intention of arriving. She had gone up to London, and it was from the metropolis that she took the train for the station nearest to Gardencourt, where Isabel and Ralph were in waiting to receive the visitor.

"Shall I love her, or shall I hate her?" asked Ralph, while they stood on the platform, before the advent of the train.

"Whichever you do will matter very little to her," said Isabel. "She doesn't care a straw what men think of her."

"As a man I am bound to dislike her, then. She must be a kind of monster. Is she very ugly?"

"No, she is decidedly pretty."

"A female interviewer—a reporter in petticoats? I am very curious to see her," Ralph declared.

"It is very easy to laugh at her, but it is not easy to be as brave as she."

"I should think not; interviewing requires bravery. Do you suppose she will interview me?"

"Never in the world. She will not think you of enough importance."

"You will see," said Ralph. "She will send a description of us all, including Bunchie, to her newspaper."

"I shall ask her not to," Isabel answered.

"You think she is capable of it, then."

"Perfectly."

"And yet you have made her your bosom friend?"

"I have not made her my bosom-friend; but I like her, in spite of her faults."

"Ah, well," said Ralph, "I am afraid I shall dislike her, in spite of her merits."

"You will probably fall in love with her at the end of three days."

"And have my love letters published in the *Interviewer?* Never!" cried the young man.

The train presently arrived, and Miss Stackpole, promptly descending, proved to be, as Isabel had said, decidedly pretty. She was a fair, plump person, of medium stature, with a round face, a small mouth, a delicate complexion, a bunch of light brown ringlets at the back of her head, and a peculiarly open, surprised looking eye. The most striking point in her appearance was the remarkable fixedness of this organ, which rested without impudence or defiance, but as if in conscientious exercise of a natural right, upon every object it happened to encounter. It rested in this manner upon Ralph himself, who was somewhat disconcerted by Miss Stackpole's gracious and comfortable aspect, which seemed to indicate that it would not be so easy as he had assumed to disapprove of her. She was very well dressed, in fresh, dove-colored draperies, and Ralph saw at a glance that she was scrupulously, fastidiously neat. From top to toe she carried not an ink-stain. She spoke in a clear, high voice—a voice not rich, but loud, though after she had taken her place, with her companions, in Mr. Touchett's carriage, she struck him, rather to his surprise, as not an abundant talker. She answered the inquiries made of her by Isabel, however, and in which the young man ventured to join, with a great deal of precision and distinctness; and later, in the library at Gardencourt, when she had made the acquaintance of Mr. Touchett (his wife not having thought it necessary to appear), did more to give the measure of her conversational powers.

"Well, I should like to know whether you consider yourselves American or English," she said. "If once I knew, I could talk to you accordingly."

"Talk to us anyhow, and we shall be thankful," Ralph answered, liberally.

She fixed her eyes upon him, and there was something in their character that reminded him of large, polished buttons; he seemed to see the reflection of surrounding objects upon the pupil. The expression of a button is not usually deemed human, but there was something in Miss Stackpole's gaze that made him, as he was a very modest man, feel vaguely embarrassed and uncomfortable. This sensation, it must be added, after he had spent a day or two in her company, sensibly diminished, though it never wholly disappeared. "I don't suppose that you are going to undertake to persuade me that *you* are an American," she said.

"To please you, I will be an Englishman, I will be a Turk!"

"Well, if you can change about that way, you are very welcome," Miss Stackpole rejoined.

"I am sure you understand everything, and that differences of nationality are no barrier to you," Ralph went on.

Miss Stackpole gazed at him still. "Do you mean the foreign languages?"

"The languages are nothing. I mean the spirit—the genius."

"I am not sure that I understand you," said the correspondent of the *Interviewer;* "but I expect I shall before I leave."

"He is what is called a cosmopolitan," Isabel suggested.

"That means he's a little of everything and not much of any. I must say I think patriotism is like charity—it begins at home."

"Ah, but where does home begin, Miss Stackpole?" Ralph inquired.

"I don't know where it begins, but I know where it ends. It ended a long time before I got here."

"Don't you like it over here?" asked Mr. Touchett, with his mild, wise, aged, innocent voice.

"Well, sir, I haven't quite made up my mind what ground I shall take. I feel a good deal cramped. I felt it on the journey from Liverpool to London."

"Perhaps you were in a crowded carriage," Ralph suggested.

"Yes, but it was crowded with friends—a party of Americans whose acquaintance I had made upon the steamer; a most lovely group, from Little Rock, Arkansas. In spite of that I felt cramped—I felt something pressing upon me; I couldn't tell what it was. I felt at the very commencement as if I were not going to sympathize with the atmosphere. But I suppose I shall make my own atmosphere. Your surroundings seem very attractive."

"Ah, we too are a lovely group!" said Ralph. "Wait a little and you will see."

Miss Stackpole showed every disposition to wait, and evidently was prepared to make a considerable stay at Gardencourt. She occupied herself in the mornings with literary labor; but in spite of this Isabel spent many hours with her friend, who, once her daily task performed, was of an eminently social tendency. Isabel speedily found occasion to request her to desist from celebrating the charms of their common sojourn in print, having discovered, on the second morning of Miss Stackpole's visit, that she was engaged upon a letter to the *Interviewer,* of which the title, in her exquisitely neat and legible hand (exactly that of the copy-books which our heroine remembered at school), was "Americans and Tudors—Glimpses of Gardencourt." Miss Stackpole, with the best conscience in the world, offered to read her letter to Isabel, who immediately put in her protest.

"I don't think you ought to do that. I don't think you ought to describe the place."

Henrietta gazed at her, as usual. "Why, it's just what the people want, and it's a lovely place."

"It's too lovely to be put in the newspapers, and it's not what my uncle wants."

"Don't you believe that!" cried Henrietta. "They are always delighted, afterward."

"My uncle won't be delighted—nor my cousin, either. They will consider it a breach of hospitality."

Miss Stackpole showed no sense of confusion; she simply wiped her pen, very neatly, upon an elegant little implement which she kept for the purpose, and put away her manuscript. "Of course if you don't approve, I won't do it; but I sacrifice a beautiful subject."

"There are plenty of other subjects, there are subjects all round you. We will take some drives, and I will show you some charming scenery."

"Scenery is not my department; I always need a human interest. You know I am deeply human, Isabel; I always was," Miss Stackpole rejoined. "I was going to bring in your cousin—the alienated American. There is a great demand just now for the alienated American, and your cousin is a beautiful specimen. I should have handled him severely."

"He would have died of it!" Isabel exclaimed. "Not of the severity, but of the publicity."

"Well, I should have liked to kill him a little. And I should have delighted to do your uncle, who seems to me a much nobler type—the American faithful still. He is a grand old man; I don't see how he can object to my paying him honor."

Isabel looked at her companion in much wonderment; it appeared to her so strange that a nature in which she found so much to esteem should exhibit such extraordinary disparities. "My poor Henrietta," she said, "you have no sense of privacy."

Henrietta colored deeply, and for a moment her brilliant eyes were suffused; while Isabel marveled more than ever at her inconsistency. "You do me great injustice," said Miss Stackpole, with dignity. "I have never written a word about myself!"

"I am very sure of that; but it seems to me one should be modest for others also!"

"Ah, that is very good!" cried Henrietta, seizing her pen again. "Just let me make a note of it, and I will put it in a letter." She was a thoroughly good-natured woman, and half an hour later she was in as cheerful a mood as should have been looked for in a newspaper-correspondent in want of material. "I have promised to do the social side," she said to Isabel; "and how can I do it unless I get ideas? If I can't describe this place, don't you know some place I can describe?" Isabel promised she would bethink herself, and the next day, in conversation with her friend, she happened to mention her visit to Lord Warburton's ancient house. "Ah, you must take me there—that is just the place for me!" Miss Stackpole exclaimed. "I must get a glimpse of the nobility."

"I can't take you," said Isabel; "but Lord Warburton is coming here, and you will have a chance to see him and observe him. Only if you intend to repeat his conversation, I shall certainly give him warning."

"Don't do that," her companion begged; "I want him to be natural."

"An Englishman is never so natural as when he is holding his tongue," Isabel rejoined.

It was not apparent, at the end of three days, that her cousin had fallen in love with their visitor, though he had spent a good deal of time in her society. They strolled about the park together, and sat under the trees, and in the afternoon, when it was delightful to float along the Thames, Miss Stackpole occupied a place in the boat in which hitherto Ralph had had but a single companion. Her society had a less insoluble quality than Ralph had expected in the natural perturbation of his sense of the perfect adequacy of that of his cousin; for the correspondent of the *Interviewer* made him laugh a good deal, and he had long since decided that abundant laughter should be the embellishment of the remainder of his days. Henrietta, on her side, did not quite justify Isabel's declaration with regard to her indifference to masculine opinion; for poor Ralph appeared to have presented himself to her as an irritating problem, which it would be superficial on her part not to solve.

"What does he do for a living?" she asked of Isabel, the evening of her arrival. "Does he go around all day with his hands in his pockets?"

"He does nothing," said Isabel, smiling; "he's a gentleman of leisure."

"Well, I call that a shame—when I have to work like a cotton-mill," Miss Stackpole replied. "I should like to show him up."

"He is in wretched health; he is quite unfit for work," Isabel urged.

"Pshaw! don't you believe it. I work when I am sick," cried her friend. Later, when she stepped into the boat, on joining the water-party, she remarked to Ralph that she supposed he hated her—he would like to drown her.

"Ah, no," said Ralph, "I keep my victims for a slower torture. And you would be such an interesting one!"

"Well, you do torture me, I may say that. But I shock all your prejudices; that's one comfort."

"My prejudices? I haven't a prejudice to bless myself with. There's intellectual poverty for you."

"The more shame to you; I have some delicious prejudices. Of course I spoil your flirtation, or whatever it is you call it, with your cousin; but I don't care for that, for I render your cousin the service of drawing you out. She will see how thin you are."

"Ah, do draw me out!" Ralph exclaimed. "So few people will take the trouble."

Miss Stackpole, in this undertaking, appeared to shrink from no trouble; resorting largely, whenever the opportunity offered, to the natural expedient of interrogation. On the following day the weather was bad, and in the afternoon the young man, by way of providing indoor amusement, offered to show her the pictures. Henrietta strolled through the long gallery in his society, while he pointed out its principal ornaments and mentioned the painters and subjects. Miss Stackpole looked at the pictures in perfect silence, committing herself to no opinion, and Ralph was gratified by the fact that she delivered herself of none of the little ready-made ejaculations of delight of which the visitors to Gardencourt were so frequently lavish. This young lady, indeed, to do her justice, was but little addicted to the use of conventional phrases; there was something earnest and inventive in her tone, which at times, in its brilliant deliberation, suggested a person of high culture speaking a foreign language. Ralph Touchett subsequently learned that she had at one time officiated as art critic to a transatlantic journal; but she appeared, in spite of this fact, to carry in her pocket none of the small change of admiration. Suddenly, just after he had called her attention to a charming Constable, she turned and looked at him as if he himself had been a picture.

"Do you always spend your time like this?" she demanded.

"I seldom spend it so agreeably," said Ralph.

"Well, you know what I mean—without any regular occupation."

"Ah," said Ralph, "I am the idlest man living."

Miss Stackpole turned her gaze to the Constable again, and Ralph bespoke her attention for a small Watteau hanging near it, which represented a gentleman in a pink doublet and hose and a ruff, leaning against the pedestal of the statue of a nymph in a garden, and playing the guitar to two ladies seated on the grass.

"That's my ideal of a regular occupation," he said.

Miss Stackpole turned to him again, and though her eyes had rested upon the picture, he saw that she had not apprehended the subject. She was thinking of something much more serious.

"I don't see how you can reconcile it to your conscience," she said.

"My dear lady, I have no conscience!"

"Well, I advise you to cultivate one. You will need it the next time you go to America."

"I shall probably never go again."

"Are you ashamed to show yourself?"

Ralph meditated, with a gentle smile.

"I suppose that, if one has no conscience, one has no shame."

"Well, you have got plenty of assurance," Henrietta declared. "Do you consider it right to give up your country?"

"Ah, one doesn't give up one's country any more than one gives up one's grandmother. It's antecedent to choice."

"I suppose that means that you would give it up if you could? What do they think of you over here?"

"They delight in me."

"That's because you truckle to them."

"Ah, set it down a little to my natural charm!" Ralph urged.

"I don't know anything about your natural charm. If you have got any charm, it's quite unnatural. It's wholly acquired—or at least you have tried hard to acquire it, living over here. I don't say you have succeeded. It's a charm that I don't appreciate, anyway. Make yourself useful in some way, and then we will talk about it."

"Well now, tell me what I shall do," said Ralph.

"Go right home, to begin with."

"Yes, I see. And then?"

"Take right hold of something."

"Well, now, what sort of thing?"

"Anything you please, so long as you take hold. Some new idea, some big work."

"Is it very difficult to take hold?" Ralph inquired.

"Not if you put your heart into it."

"Ah, my heart," said Ralph. "If it depends upon my heart——"

"Haven't you got any?"

"I had one a few days ago, but I have lost it since."

"You are not serious," Miss Stackpole remarked; "that's what's the matter with you." But for all this, in a day or two she again permitted him to fix her attention, and on this occasion assigned a different cause to his mysterious perversity. "I know what's the matter with you, Mr. Touchett," she said. "You think you are too good to get married."

"I thought so till I knew you, Miss Stackpole," Ralph answered; "and then I suddenly changed my mind."

"Oh, pshaw!" Henrietta exclaimed impatiently.

"Then it seemed to me," said Ralph, "that I was not good enough."

"It would improve you. Besides, it's your duty."

"Ah," cried the young man, "one has so many duties! Is that a duty too?"

"Of course it is—did you never know that before? It's everyone's duty to get married."

Ralph meditated a moment; he was disappointed. There was something in Miss Stackpole he had begun to like; it seemed to him that if she was not a charming woman she was at least a very good fellow. She was wanting in distinction, but, as Isabel had said, she was brave, and there is always something fine about that. He had not supposed her to be capable of vulgar arts; but these last words struck him as a false note. When a marriageable young woman urges matrimony upon an unencumbered young man, the most obvious explanation of her conduct is not the altruistic impulse.

"Ah, well now, there is a good deal to be said about that," Ralph rejoined.

"There may be, but that is the principal thing. I must say I think it looks very exclusive, going round all alone, as if you thought no woman was good enough for you. Do you think you are better than anyone else in the world? In America it's usual for people to marry."

"If it's my duty," Ralph asked, "is it not, by analogy, yours as well?"

Miss Stackpole's brilliant eyes expanded still further.

"Have you the fond hope of finding a flaw in my reasoning? Of course I have got as good a right to marry as anyone else."

"Well then," said Ralph, "I won't say it vexes me to see you single. It delights me rather."

"You are not serious yet. You never will be."

"Shall you not believe me to be so on the day that I tell you I desire to give up the practice of going round alone?"

Miss Stackpole looked at him for a moment in a manner which seemed to announce a reply that might technically be called encouraging. But to his great surprise this expression suddenly resolved itself into an appearance of alarm, and even of resentment.

"No, not even then," she answered, dryly. After which she walked away.

"I have not fallen in love with your friend," Ralph said that evening to Isabel, "though we talked some time this morning about it."

"And you said something she didn't like," the girl replied.

Ralph stared. "Has she complained of me?"

"She told me she thinks there is something very low in the tone of Europeans toward women."

"Does she call me a European?"

"One of the worst. She told me you had said to her something that an American never would have said. But she didn't repeat it."

Ralph treated himself to a burst of resounding laughter.

"She is an extraordinary combination. Did she think I was making love to her?"

"No; I believe even Americans do that. But she apparently thought you mistook the intention of something she had said, and put an unkind construction on it."

"I thought she was proposing marriage to me, and I accepted her. Was that unkind?"

Isabel smiled. "It was unkind to me. I don't want you to marry."

"My dear cousin, what is one to do among you all?" Ralph demanded. "Miss Stackpole tells me it's my bounden duty, and that it's hers to see I do mine!"

"She has a great sense of duty," said Isabel gravely. "She has, indeed, and it's the motive of everything she says. That's what I like her for. She thinks it's very frivolous for you to be single; that's what she meant to express to you. If you thought she was trying to—to attract you, you were very wrong."

"It is true it was an odd way; but I did think she was trying to attract me. Excuse my superficiality."

"You are very conceited. She had no interested views, and never supposed you would think she had."

"One must be very modest, then, to talk with such women," Ralph said, humbly. "But it's a very strange type. She is too personal—considering that she expects other people not to be. She walks in without knocking at the door."

"Yes," Isabel admitted, "she doesn't sufficiently recognise the existence of knockers; and indeed I am not sure that she doesn't think them a rather pretentious ornament. She thinks one's door should stand ajar. But I persist in liking her."

"I persist in thinking her too familiar," Ralph rejoined, naturally somewhat uncomfortable under the sense of having been doubly deceived in Miss Stackpole.

"Well," said Isabel, smiling, "I am afraid it is because she is rather vulgar that I like her."

"She would be flattered by your reason!"

"If I should tell her, I would not express it in that way. I should say it is because there is something of the 'people' in her."

"What do you know about the people? and what does she, for that matter?"

"She knows a great deal, and I know enough to feel that she is a kind of emanation of the great democracy—of the continent, the country, the nation. I don't say that she sums it all up, that would be too much to ask of her. But she suggests it; she reminds me of it."

"You like her then for patriotic reasons. I am afraid it is on those very grounds that I object to her."

"Ah," said Isabel, with a kind of joyous sigh, "I like so many things! If a thing strikes me in a certain way, I like it. I don't want to boast, but I suppose I am rather versatile. I like people to be totally different from Henrietta—in the style of Lord Warburton's sisters, for instance. So long as I look at the Misses Molyneux, they seem to me to answer a kind of ideal. Then Henrietta presents herself, and I am immensely struck with her; not so much for herself as what stands behind her."

"Ah, you mean the back view of her," Ralph suggested.

"What she says is true," his cousin answered; "you will never be serious. I like the great country stretching away beyond the rivers and across the prairies, blooming and smiling and spreading, till it stops at the blue Pacific! A strong, sweet, fresh odor seems to rise from it, and Henrietta—excuse my simile—has something of that odor in her garments."

Isabel blushed a little as she concluded this speech, and the blush, together with the momentary ardor she had thrown into it, was so becoming to her that Ralph stood smiling at her for a moment after she had ceased speaking.

"I am not sure the Pacific is blue," he said; "but you are a woman of imagination. Henrietta, however, is fragrant—Henrietta is decidedly fragrant!"

❧ 11 ❧

He took a resolve after this not to misinterpret her words, even when Miss Stackpole appeared to strike the personal note most strongly. He bethought himself that persons, in her view, were simple and homogeneous organisms, and that he, for his own part, was too perverted a representative of human nature to have a right to deal with her in strict reciprocity. He carried out his resolve with a great deal of tact, and the young lady found in her relations with him no obstacle to the exercise of that somewhat aggressive frankness which was the social expression of her nature. Her situation at Gardencourt, therefore, appreciated as we have seen her to be by Isabel, and full of appreciation herself of that fine freedom of composition which, to her sense, rendered Isabel's character a sister-spirit, and of the easy venerableness of Mr. Touchett, whose general tone, as she said, met with her full approval—her situation at Gardencourt would have been perfectly comfortable, had she not conceived an irresistible mistrust of the little lady to whom she had at first supposed herself obliged to pay a certain deference as mistress of the house. She presently discovered, however, that this obligation was of the lightest, and that Mrs. Touchett cared very little how Miss Stackpole behaved. Mrs. Touchett had spoken of her to Isabel as a "newspaperwoman," and expressed some surprise at her niece's having selected such a friend; but she had immediately added that she knew Isabel's friends were her own affair, and that she never undertook to like them all, or to restrict the girl to those she liked.

"If you could see none but the people I like, my dear, you would have a very small society," Mrs. Touchett frankly admitted; "and I don't think I like any man or woman well enough to recommend them to you. When it comes to recommending, it is a serious affair. I don't like Miss Stackpole—I don't like her tone. She talks too loud, and she looks at me too hard. I am sure she has lived all her life in a boardinghouse, and I detest the style of manners that such a way of living produces. If you ask me if I prefer my own manners, which you doubtless think very bad, I will tell you that I prefer them immensely. Miss Stackpole knows that I detest boardinghouse civilization, and she detests me for detesting it, because she thinks it is the highest in the world. She would like Gardencourt a great deal better if it were a boardinghouse. For me, I find it almost too much of one! We shall never get on together, therefore, and there is no use trying."

Mrs. Touchett was right in guessing that Henrietta disapproved of her, but she had not quite put her finger on the reason. A day or two after Miss Stackpole's arrival she had made some invidious reflections on American hotels, which excited a vein of counterargument on the part of the correspondent of the *Interviewer,* who in the exercise of her profession had acquired a large familiarity with the technical hospitality of her country. Henrietta expressed the opinion that American hotels were the best in the world, and Mrs. Touchett recorded a conviction that they were the worst. Ralph, with his experimental geniality, suggested, by way of healing the breach, that the truth lay between the two extremes, and that the establishments in question ought to be described as fair middling. This contribution to the discussion, however, Miss Stackpole rejected with scorn. Middling, indeed! If they were not the best in the world, they were the worst, but there was nothing middling about an American hotel.

"We judge from different points of view, evidently," said Mrs. Touchett. "I like to be treated as an individual; you like to be treated as a 'party.' "

"I don't know what you mean," Henrietta replied. "I like to be treated as an American lady."

"Poor American ladies!" cried Mrs. Touchett, with a laugh. "They are the slaves of slaves."

"They are the companions of freemen," Henrietta rejoined.

"They are the companions of their servants—the Irish chambermaid and the negro waiter. They share their work."

"Do you call the domestics in an American household 'slaves'?" Miss Stackpole inquired. "If that's the way you desire to treat them, no wonder you don't like America."

"If you have not good servants, you are miserable," Mrs. Touchett said, serenely. "They are very bad in America, but I have five perfect ones in Florence."

"I don't see what you want with five," Henrietta could not help observing. "I don't think I should like to see five persons surrounding me in that menial position."

"I like them in that position better than in some others," cried Mrs. Touchett, with a laugh.

"Should you like me better if I were your butler, dear?" her husband asked.

"I don't think I should; you would make a very poor butler."

"The companions of freemen—I like that, Miss Stackpole," said Ralph. "It's a beautiful description."

"When I said freemen, I didn't mean you, sir!"

And this was the only reward that Ralph got for his compliment. Miss Stackpole was baffled; she evidently thought there was something treasonable in Mrs.

Touchett's appreciation of a class which she privately suspected of being a mysterious survival of feudalism. It was perhaps because her mind was oppressed with this image that she suffered some days to elapse before she said to Isabel in the morning, while they were alone together,

"My dear friend, I wonder whether you are growing faithless?"

"Faithless? Faithless to you, Henrietta?"

"No, that would be a great pain; but it is not that."

"Faithless to my country, then?"

"Ah, that I hope will never be. When I wrote to you from Liverpool, I said I had something particular to tell you. You have never asked me what it is. Is it because you have suspected?"

"Suspected what? As a rule, I don't think I suspect," said Isabel. "I remember now that phrase in your letter, but I confess I had forgotten it. What have you to tell me?"

Henrietta looked disappointed, and her steady gaze betrayed it.

"You don't ask that right—as if you thought it important. You are changed—you are thinking of other things."

"Tell me what you mean, and I will think of that."

"Will you really think of it? That is what I wish to be sure of."

"I have not much control of my thoughts, but I will do my best," said Isabel.

Henrietta gazed at her, in silence, for a period of time which tried Isabel's patience, so that our heroine said at last—

"Do you mean that you are going to be married?"

"Not till I have seen Europe!" said Miss Stackpole. "What are you laughing at?" she went on. "What I mean is, that Mr. Goodwood came out in the steamer with me."

"Ah!" Isabel exclaimed, quickly.

"You say that right. I had a good deal of talk with him; he has come after you."

"Did he tell you so?"

"No, he told me nothing; that's how I knew it," said Henrietta, cleverly. "He said very little about you, but I spoke of you a good deal."

Isabel was silent a moment. At the mention of Mr. Goodwood's name she had colored a little, and now her blush was slowly fading.

"I am very sorry you did that," she observed at last.

"It was a pleasure to me, and I liked the way he listened. I could have talked a long time to such a listener; he was so quiet, so intense; he drank it all in."

"What did you say about me?" Isabel asked.

"I said you were on the whole the finest creature I know."

"I am very sorry for that. He thinks too well of me already; he ought not to be encouraged."

"He is dying for a little encouragement. I see his face now, and his earnest, absorbed look, while I talked. I never saw an ugly man look so handsome!"

"He is very simple-minded," said Isabel. "And he is not so ugly."

"There is nothing so simple as a great passion."

"It is not a great passion; I am very sure it is not that."

"You don't say that as if you were sure."

Isabel gave rather a cold smile.

"I shall say it better to Mr. Goodwood himself!"

"He will soon give you a chance," said Henrietta.

Isabel offered no answer to this assertion, which her companion made with an air of great confidence.

"He will find you changed," the latter pursued. "You have been affected by your new surroundings."

"Very likely. I am affected by everything."

"By everything but Mr. Goodwood!" Miss Stackpole exclaimed, with a laugh.

Isabel failed even to smile in reply; and in a moment she said—

"Did he ask you to speak to me?"

"Not in so many words. But his eyes asked it—and his handshake, when he bade me goodbye."

"Thank you for doing so." And Isabel turned away.

"Yes, you are changed; and have got new ideas over here," her friend continued.

"I hope so," said Isabel; "one should get as many new ideas as possible."

"Yes; but they shouldn't interfere with the old ones."

Isabel turned about again. "If you mean that I had any idea with regard to Mr. Goodwood——" And then she paused; Henrietta's bright eyes seemed to her to grow enormous.

"My dear child, you certainly encouraged him," said Miss Stackpole.

Isabel appeared for the moment to be on the point of denying this charge, but instead of this she presently answered—"It is very true; I did encourage him." And then she inquired whether her companion had learned from Mr. Goodwood what he intended to do. This inquiry was a concession to curiosity, for she did not enjoy discussing the gentleman with Henrietta Stackpole, and she thought that in her treatment of the subject this faithful friend lacked delicacy.

"I asked him, and he said he meant to do nothing," Miss Stackpole answered. "But I don't believe that; he's not a man to do nothing. He is a man of action. Whatever happens to him, he will always do something, and whatever he does will be right."

"I quite believe that," said Isabel. Henrietta might be wanting in delicacy; but it touched the girl, all the same, to hear this rich assertion made.

"Ah, you *do* care for him," Henrietta murmured.

"Whatever he does will be right," Isabel repeated. "When a man is of that supernatural mould, what does it matter to him whether one cares for him?"

"It may not matter to him, but it matters to one's self."

"Ah, what it matters to me, that is not what we are discussing," said Isabel, smiling a little.

This time her companion was grave. "Well, I don't care; you have changed," she replied. "You are not the girl you were a few short weeks ago, and Mr. Goodwood will see it. I expect him here any day."

"I hope he will hate me, then," said Isabel.

"I believe that you hope it about as much as I believe that he is capable of it."

To this observation our heroine made no rejoinder; she was absorbed in the feeling of alarm given her by Henrietta's intimation that Caspar Goodwood would present himself at Gardencourt. Alarm is perhaps a violet term to apply to the uneasiness with which she regarded this contingency; but her uneasiness was keen, and there were various good reasons for it. She pretended to herself that she thought the event impossible, and, later, she communicated her disbelief to her friend; but the next forty-eight hours, nevertheless, she stood prepared to hear the young man's name announced. The feeling was oppressive; it made the air sultry, as if there were to be a change of weather; and the weather, socially speaking, had been so agreeable during Isabel's stay at Gardencourt that any change would be for the worse. Her suspense, however, was dissipated on the second day. She had walked into the park, in company with the sociable Bunchie, and after strolling about for some time, in a manner at once listless and restless, had seated herself on a garden bench, within sight of the house, beneath a spreading beech, where, in a white dress ornamented with black ribbons, she formed, among the flickering shadows, a very graceful and harmonious image. She entertained herself for some moments with talking to the little terrier, as to whom the proposal of an ownership divided with her cousin had been applied as impartially as possible—as impartially as Bunchie's own somewhat fickle and inconstant sympathies would allow. But she was notified for the first time, on this occasion, of the finite character of Bunchie's intellect; hitherto she had been mainly struck with its extent. It seemed to her at last that she would do well to take a book; formerly, when she felt heavy-hearted, she had been able, with the help of some well-chosen volume, to transfer the seat of consciousness to the organ of pure reason. Of late, however it was not to be denied, literature had seemed a fading light, and even after she had reminded herself that her uncle's library was provided with a complete set of those authors which no gentleman's collection should be without, she sat motionless and empty-handed, with her eyes fixed upon the cool green turf of the lawn. Her meditations were presently interrupted by the arrival of a servant, who handed her a letter. The letter bore the London postmark, and was addressed in a hand that she knew—that she seemed to know all the better, indeed, as the writer had been present to her mind when the letter was delivered. This document proved to be short, and I may give it entire.

"MY DEAR MISS ARCHER—I don't know whether you will have heard of my coming to England, but even if you have not, it will scarcely be a surprise to you. You will remember that when you gave me my dismissal at Albany three months ago, I did not accept it. I protested against it. You in fact appeared to accept my protest, and to admit that I had the right on my side. I had come to see you with the hope that you would let me bring you over to my conviction; my reasons for entertaining this hope had been of the best. But you disappointed it; I found you changed, and you were able to give no reason for the change. You admitted that you were unreasonable, and it was the only concession you would make; but it was a very cheap one, because you are not unreasonable. No, you are not, and you never will be. Therefore it is that I believe you will let me see you again. You told me that I am not disagreeable to you, and I believe it; for I don't see why that should be. I shall always think of you; I shall never think of anyone else. I came to England simply because you are here; I couldn't stay at home after you had gone; I hated the country because you were not in it. If I like this country at present, it is only because you are here. I have been to England before, but I have never enjoyed it much. May I not come and see you for half-an-hour? This at present is the dearest wish of, yours faithfully,

"CASPAR GOODWOOD."

Isabel read Mr. Goodwood's letter with such profound attention that she had not perceived an approaching tread on the soft grass. Looking up, however, as she mechanically folded the paper, she saw Lord Warburton standing before her.

❧ 12 ❧

She put the letter into her pocket, and offered her visitor a smile of welcome, exhibiting no trace of discomposure, and half surprised at her self-possession.

"They told me you were out here," said Lord Warburton; "and as there was no one in the drawing room, and it is really you that I wish to see, I came out with no more ado."

Isabel had got up; she felt a wish, for the moment, that he should not sit down beside her. "I was just going indoors," she said.

"Please don't do that; it is much pleasanter here; I have ridden over from Lockleigh; it's a lovely day." His smile was peculiarly friendly and pleasing, and his whole person seemed to emit that radiance of good feeling and good fare which had formed the charm of the girl's first impression of him. It surrounded him like a zone of fine June weather.

"We will walk about a little, then," said Isabel, who could not divest herself of the sense of an intention on the part of her visitor, and who wished both to elude the intention and to satisfy her curiosity regarding it. It had flashed upon her vision once before, and it had given her on that occasion, as we know, a certain alarm. This alarm was composed of several elements, not all of which were disagreeable; she had indeed spent some days in analyzing them, and had succeeded in separating the pleasant part of this idea of Lord Warburton's making love to her from the painful. It may appear to some readers that the young lady was both precipitate and unduly fastidious; but the latter of these facts, if the charge be true, may serve to exonerate her from the discredit of the former. She was not eager to convince herself that a territorial magnate, as she had heard Lord Warburton called, was smitten with her charms; because a declaration from such a source would point to more questions that it would answer. She had received a strong impression of Lord Warburton's being a personage, and she had occupied herself in examining the idea. At the risk of making the reader smile, it must be said that there had been moments when the intimation that she was admired by a "personage" struck her as an aggression which she would rather have been spared. She had never known a personage before; there were no personages in her native land. When she had thought of such matters as this, she had done so on the basis of character—of what one liked in a gentleman's mind and in his talk. She herself was a character—she could not help being aware of that; and hitherto her visions of a completed life had concerned themselves largely with moral images—things as to which the question would be whether they pleased her soul. Lord Warburton loomed up before her, largely and brightly, as a collection of attributes and powers which were not to be measured by this simple rule, but which demanded a different sort of appreciation—an appreciation which the girl, with her habit of judging quickly and freely, felt that she lacked the patience to bestow. Of course, there would be a short cut to it, and as Lord Warburton was evidently a very fine fellow, it would probably also be a safe cut. Isabel was able to say all this to herself, but she was unable to feel the force of it. What she felt was that a territorial, a political, a social magnate had conceived the design of drawing her into the system in which he lived and moved. A certain instinct, not imperious, but persuasive, told her to resist—it murmured to her that virtually she had a system and an orbit of her own. It told her other things besides—things which both contradicted and confirmed each other; that a girl might do much worse than trust herself to such a man as Lord Warburton, and that it would be very interesting to see something of his system from his own point of view; that, on the other hand, however, there was evidently a great deal of it which she should regard only as an incumbrance, and that even in the whole there was something heavy and rigid which would make it unacceptable. Furthermore, there was a young man lately come from America who had no system at all; but who had a character of which it was useless for her to try to persuade herself that the impression on her mind had been light. The letter that she carried in her pocket sufficiently reminded her of the contrary. Smile not, however, I venture to repeat, at this simple young lady from Albany, who debated whether she should accept an English peer before he had offered himself, and who was disposed to believe that on the whole she could do better. She was a person of great good faith, and if there was a great deal of folly in her wisdom, those who judge her severely may have the satisfaction of finding that, later, she became consistently wise only at the cost of an amount of folly which will constitute almost a direct appeal to charity.

Lord Warburton seemed quite ready to walk, to sit, or to do anything that Isabel should propose, and he gave her this assurance with his usual air of being particularly pleased to exercise a social virtue. But he was, nevertheless, not in command of his emotions, and as he strolled beside her for a moment, in silence, looking at her without letting her know it, there was something embarrassed in his glance and his misdirected laughter. Yes, assuredly—as we have touched on the point, we may return to it for a moment again—the English are the most romantic people in the world, and Lord Warburton was about to give an example of it. He was about to take a step which would astonish all his friends and displease a great many of them, and which, superficially, had nothing to recommend it. The young lady who trod the turf beside him had come from a queer country across the sea, which he knew a good deal about; her antecedents, her associations, were very vague to his mind, except insofar as they were generic, and in this sense they revealed themselves with a certain vividness. Miss Archer had neither a fortune nor the sort of beauty that justifies a man to the multitude, and he calculated that he had spent about twenty-six hours in her company. He had summed up all this—the perversity of the impulse, which had declined to avail itself of the most liberal opportunities to subside, and the judgment of mankind, as exemplified particularly in the more quickly-judging half of it; he had looked these things well in the face, and then he had dismissed them from his thoughts. He cared no more for them than for the rosebud in his buttonhole. It is the good fortune of a man who for the greater part of a lifetime has abstained without effort from making himself disagreeable to his friends, that when the need comes for such a course it is not discredited by irritating associations.

"I hope you had a pleasant ride," said Isabel, who observed her companion's hesitancy.

"It would have been pleasant if for nothing else than that it brought me here," Lord Warburton answered.

"Are you so fond of Gardencourt?" the girl asked; more and more sure that he meant to make some demand of her; wishing not to challenge him if he hesitated, and yet to keep all the quietness of her reason if he proceeded. It suddenly came upon her that her situation as one which a few weeks ago she would have deemed deeply romantic; the park of an old English country house, with the foreground embellished by a local nobleman in the act of making love to a young lady who, on careful inspection, should be found to present remarkable analogies with herself. But if she were now the heroine of the situation, she succeeded scarcely the less in looking at it from the outside.

"I care nothing for Gardencourt," said Lord Warburton; "I care only for you."

"You have known me too short a time to have a right to say that, and I cannot believe you are serious."

These words of Isabel's were not perfectly sincere, for she had no doubt whatever that he was serious. They were simply a tribute to the fact, of which she was perfectly aware, that those he himself had just uttered would have excited surprise on the part of the public at large. And, moreover, if anything beside the sense she had already acquired that Lord Warburton was not a frivolous person had been needed to convince her, the tone in which he replied to her would quite have served the purpose.

"One's right in such a matter is not measured by the time, Miss Archer; it is measured by the feeling itself. If I were to wait three months, it would make no difference; I shall not be more sure of what I mean than I am today. Of course I have seen you very little; but my impression dates from the very first hour we met. I lost no time; I fell in love with you then. It was at first sight, as the novels say; I know now that is not a fancy phrase, and I shall think better of novels forevermore. Those two days I spent here settled it; I don't know whether you suspected I was doing so, but I paid— mentally speaking I mean—the greatest possible attention to you. Nothing you said, nothing you did, was lost upon me. When you came to Lockleigh the other day—or rather, when you went away—I was perfectly sure. Nevertheless, I made up my mind to think it over, and to question myself narrowly. I have done so; all these days I have thought of nothing else. I don't make mistakes about such things; I am a very judicious fellow. I don't go off easily, but when I am touched, it's for life. It's for life, Miss Archer, it's for life," Lord Warburton repeated in the kindest, tenderest, pleasantest voice Isabel had ever heard, and looking at her with eyes that shone with the light of a passion that had sifted itself clear of the baser parts of emotion—the heat, the violence, the unreason—and which burned as steadily as a lamp in a windless place.

By tacit consent, as he talked, they had walked more and more slowly, and at last they stopped, and he took her hand.

"Ah, Lord Warburton, how little you know me!" Isabel said, very gently; gently, too, she drew her hand away.

"Don't taunt me with that; that I don't know you better makes me unhappy enough already; it's all my loss. But that is what I want, and it seems to me I am taking the best way. If you will be my wife, then I shall know you, and when I tell you all the good I think of you, you will not be able to say it is from ignorance."

"If you know me little, I know you even less," said Isabel.

"You mean that, unlike yourself, I may not improve on acquaintance? Ah, of course, that is very possible. But think, to speak to you as I do, how determined I must be to try and give satisfaction! You do like me rather, don't you?"

"I like you very much, Lord Warburton," the girl answered; and at this moment she liked him immensely.

"I thank you for saying that; it shows you don't regard me as a stranger. I really believe I have filled all the other relations of life very creditably, and I don't see why I should not fill this one—in which I offer myself to you—seeing that I care so much more about it. Ask the people who know me well; I have friends who will speak for me."

"I don't need the recommendation of your friends," said Isabel.

"Ah now, that is delightful of you. You believe in me yourself."

"Completely," Isabel declared; and it was the truth.

The light in her companion's eyes turned into a smile, and he gave a long exhalation of joy.

"If you are mistaken, Miss Archer, let me lose all I possess!"

She wondered whether he meant this for a reminder that he was rich, and, on the instant, felt sure that he did not. He was thinking that, as he would have said himself; and indeed he might safely leave it to the memory of any interlocutor, especially of one to whom he was offering his hand. Isabel had prayed that she might not be agitated, and her mind was tranquil enough, even while she listened and asked herself what it was best she should say, to indulge in this incidental criticism. What she should say, had she asked herself? Her foremost wish was to say something as nearly as possible as kind as what he had said to her. His words had carried perfect conviction with them; she felt that he loved her.

"I thank you more than I can say for your offer," she rejoined at last; "it does me great honor."

"Ah, don't say that!" Lord Warburton broke out. "I was afraid you would say something like that. I don't see what you have to do with that sort of thing. I don't see why you should thank me—it is I who ought to thank you, for listening to me; a man whom you know so little, coming down on you with such a thumper! Of course it's a great question; I must tell you that I would rather ask it than have it to answer myself. But the way you have listened—or at least your having listened at all—gives me some hope."

"Don't hope too much," Isabel said.

"Oh, Miss Archer!" her companion murmured, smiling again in his seriousness, as if such a warning might perhaps be taken but as the play of high spirits—the coquetry of elation.

"Should you be greatly surprised if I were to beg you not to hope at all?" Isabel asked.

"Surprised? I don't know what you mean by surprise. It wouldn't be that; it would be a feeling very much worse."

Isabel walked on again; she was silent for some minutes.

"I am very sure that, highly as I already think of you, my opinion of you, if I should know you well, would only rise. But I am by no means sure that you would not be disappointed. And I say that not in the least out of conventional modesty; it is perfectly sincere."

"I am willing to risk it, Miss Archer," her companion answered.

"It's a great question, as you say; it's a very difficult question."

"I don't expect you, of course, to answer it outright. Think it over as long as may be necessary. If I can gain by waiting, I will gladly wait a long time. Only remember that in the end my dearest happiness depends upon your answer."

"I should be very sorry to keep you in suspense," said Isabel.

"Oh, don't mind. I would much rather have a good answer six months hence than a bad one today."

"But it is very probable that even six months hence I should not be able to give you one that you would think good."

"Why not, since you really like me?"

"Ah, you must never doubt of that," said Isabel.

"Well, then, I don't see what more you ask!"

"It is not what I ask; it is what I can give. I don't think I should suit you; I really don't think I should."

"You needn't bother about that; that's my affair. You needn't be a better royalist than the king."

"It is not only that," said Isabel; "but I am not sure I wish to marry anyone."

"Very likely you don't. I have no doubt a great many women begin that way," said his lordship, who, be it averred, did not in the least believe in the axiom he thus beguiled his anxiety by uttering. "But they are frequently persuaded."

"Ah, that is because they want to be!"

And Isabel lightly laughed.

Her suitor's countenance fell, and he looked at her for a while in silence.

"I'm afraid it's my being an Englishman that makes you hesitate," he said, presently. "I know your uncle thinks you ought to marry in your own country."

Isabel listened to this assertion with some interest; it had never occurred to her that Mr. Touchett was likely to discuss her matrimonial prospects with Lord Warburton.

"Has he told you that?" she asked.

"I remember his making the remark; he spoke perhaps of Americans generally."

"He appears himself to have found it very pleasant to live in England," said Isabel, in a manner that might have seemed a little perverse, but which expressed both her constant perception of her uncle's pictorial circumstances and her general disposition to elude any obligation to take a restricted view.

It gave her companion hope, and he immediately exclaimed, warmly—

"Ah, my dear Miss Archer, old England is a very good sort of country, you know! And it will be still better when we have furbished it up a little."

"Oh, don't furbish it, Lord Warburton; leave it alone; I like it this way."

"Well, then if you like it, I am more and more unable to see your objection to what I propose."

"I am afraid I can't make you understand."

"You ought at least to try; I have got a fair intelligence. Are you afraid—afraid of the climate? We can easily live elsewhere, you know. You can pick out your climate, the whole world over."

These words were uttered with a tender eagerness which went to Isabel's heart, and she would have given her little finger at that moment, to feel, strongly and simply, the impulse to answer, "Lord Warburton, it is impossible for a woman to do better in this world than to commit herself to your loyalty." But though she could conceive the impulse, she could not let it operate; her imagination was charmed, but it was not led captive. What she finally bethought herself of saying was something very different—something which altogether deferred the need of answering. "Don't think me unkind if I ask you to say no more about this today."

"Certainly, certainly!" cried Lord Warburton. "I wouldn't bore you for the world."

"You have given me a great deal to think about, and I promise you I will do it justice."

"That's all I ask of you, of course—and that you will remember that my happiness is in your hands."

Isabel listened with extreme respect to this admonition, but she said after a minute—"I must tell you that what I shall think about is some way of letting you know that what you ask is impossible, without making you miserable."

"There is no way to do that, Miss Archer. I won't say that, if you refuse me, you will kill me; I shall not die of it. But I shall do worse; I shall live to no purpose."

"You will live to marry a better woman than I."

"Don't say that, please," said Lord Warburton, very gravely. "That is fair to neither of us."

"To marry a worse one, then."

"If there are better women than you, then I prefer the bad ones; that's all I can say," he went on, with the same gravity. "There is no accounting for tastes."

His gravity made her feel equally grave, and she showed it by again requesting him to drop the subject for the present. "I will speak to you myself, very soon," she said. "Perhaps I shall write to you."

"At your convenience, yes," he answered. "Whatever time you take, it must seem to me long, and I suppose I must make the best of that."

"I shall not keep you in suspense; I only want to collect my mind a little."

He gave a melancholy sigh and stood looking at her a moment, with his hands behind him, giving short nervous shakes to his hunting whip. "Do you know I am very much afraid of it—of that mind of yours?"

Our heroine's biographer can scarcely tell why, but the question made her start and brought a conscious blush to her cheek. She returned his look a moment, and then, with a note in her voice that might almost have appealed to his compassion— "So am I, my lord!" she exclaimed.

His compassion was not stirred, however; all that he possessed of the faculty of pity was needed at home. "Ah! be merciful, be merciful," he murmured.

"I think you had better go," said Isabel. "I will write to you."

"Very good; but whatever you write, I will come and see you." And then he stood reflecting, with his eyes fixed on the observant countenance of Bunchie, who had the air of having understood all that had been said, and of pretending to carry off the indiscretion by a simulated fit of curiosity as to the roots of an ancient beech. "There is one thing more," said Lord Warburton. "You know, if you don't like Lockleigh—if you think it's damp, or anything of that sort—you need never go within fifty miles of it. It is not damp, by the way; I have had the house thoroughly examined; it is perfectly sanitary. But if you shouldn't fancy it, you needn't dream of living in it. There is no difficulty whatever about that; there are plenty of houses. I thought I would just mention it; some people don't like a moat, you know. Goodbye."

"I delight in a moat," said Isabel. "Goodbye."

He held out his hand, and she gave him hers a moment—a moment long enough for him to bend his head and kiss it. Then, shaking his hunting whip with little quick strokes, he walked rapidly away. He was evidently very nervous.

Isabel herself was nervous, but she was not affected as she would have imagined. What she felt was not a great responsibility, a great difficulty of choice; for it appeared to her that there was no choice in the question. She could not marry Lord Warburton; the idea failed to correspond to any vision of happiness that she had hitherto entertained, or was now capable of entertaining. She must write this to him, she must convince him, and this duty was comparatively simple. But what disturbed her, in the sense that it struck her with wonderment, was this very fact that it cost her so little to refuse a great opportunity. With whatever qualifications one would, Lord Warburton had offered her a great opportunity; the situation might have discomforts, might contain elements that would displease her, but she did her sex no injustice in believing that nineteen women out of twenty would accommodate themselves to it with extreme zeal. Why then upon her also should it not impose itself? Who was she, what was she, that she should hold herself superior? What view of life, what design upon fate, what conception of happiness, had she that pretended to be larger than this large occasion? If she would not do this, then she must do great things, she must do something greater. Poor Isabel found occasion to remind herself from time to time that she must not be too proud, and nothing could be more sincere than her prayer to be delivered from such a danger; for the isolation and loneliness of pride had for her mind the horror of a desert place. If it were pride that interfered with her accepting Lord Warburton, it was singularly misplaced; and she was so conscious of liking him that she ventured to assure herself it was not. She liked him too much to marry him, that was the point; something told her that she should not be satisfied, and to inflict upon a man who offered so much a wife with a tendency to criticize would be a peculiarly discreditable act. She had promised him that she would consider his proposal, and when, after he had left her, she wandered back to the bench where he had found her, and lost herself in meditation, it might have seemed that she was keeping her word. But this was not the case; she was wondering whether she were not a cold, hard girl; and when at last she got up and rather quickly went back to the house, it was because, as she had said to Lord Warburton, she was really frightened at herself.

❧ 13 ❧

It was this feeling, and not the wish to ask advice—she had no desire whatever for that—that led her to speak to her uncle of what Lord Warburton had said to her. She wished to speak to someone; she should feel more natural, more human, and her uncle, for this purpose, presented himself in a more attractive light than either her aunt or her friend Henrietta. Her cousin, of course, was a possible confidant; but it would have been disagreeable to her to confide this particular matter to Ralph. So, the next day, after breakfast, she sought her occasion. Her uncle never left his apartment till the afternoon; but he received his cronies, as he said, in his dressing room. Isabel had quite taken her place in the class so designated, which, for the rest, included the old man's son, his physician, his personal servant, and even Miss Stackpole. Mrs. Touchett did not figure in the list, and this was an obstacle the less to Isabel's finding her uncle alone. He sat in a complicated mechanical chair, at the open window of his room, looking westward over the park and the river, with his newspapers and letters piled up beside him, his toilet freshly and minutely made, and his smooth, speculative face composed to benevolent expectation.

Isabel approached her point very directly. "I think I ought to let you know that Lord Warburton has asked me to marry him. I suppose I ought to tell my aunt; but it seems best to tell you first."

The old man expressed no surprise, but thanked her for the confidence she showed him. "Do you mind telling me whether you accepted him?" he added.

"I have not answered him definitely yet; I have taken a little time to think of it, because that seems more respectful. But I shall not accept him."

Mr. Touchett made no comment upon this; he had the air of thinking that whatever interest he might take in the matter from the point of view of sociability, he had no active voice in it. "Well, I told you you would be a success over here. Americans are highly appreciated."

"Very highly indeed," said Isabel. "But at the cost of seeming ungrateful, I don't think I can marry Lord Warburton."

"Well," her uncle went on, "of course an old man can't judge for a young lady. I am glad you didn't ask me before you made up your mind. I suppose I ought to tell you," he added slowly, but as if it were not of much consequence, "that I have known all about it these three days."

"About Lord Warburton's state of mind?"

"About his intentions, as they say here. He wrote me a very pleasant letter, telling me all about them. Should you like to see it?" the old man asked, obligingly.

"Thank you; I don't think I care about that. But I am glad he wrote to you; it was right that he should, and he would be certain to do what was right."

"Ah, well, I guess you do like him!" Mr. Touchett declared. "You needn't pretend you don't."

"I like him extremely; I am very free to admit that. But I don't wish to marry anyone just now."

"You think someone may come along whom you may like better. Well, that's very likely," said Mr. Touchett, who appeared to wish to show his kindness to the girl by easing off her decision, as it were, and finding cheerful reasons for it.

"I don't care if I don't meet anyone else; I like Lord Warburton quite well enough," said Isabel, with that appearance of a sudden change of point of view with which she sometimes startled and even displeased her interlocutors.

Her uncle, however, seemed proof against either of these sensations.

"He's a very fine man," he resumed, in a tone which might have passed for that of encouragement. "His letter was one of the pleasantest letters I have received for some weeks. I suppose one of the reasons I liked it was that it was all about you; that is, all except the part which was about himself. I suppose he told you all that."

"He would have told me everything I wished to ask him," Isabel said.

"But you didn't feel curious?"

"My curiosity would have been idle—once I had determined to decline his offer."

"You didn't find it sufficiently attractive?" Mr. Touchett inquired.

The girl was silent a moment.

"I suppose it was that," she presently admitted. "But I don't know why."

"Fortunately, ladies are not obliged to give reasons," said her uncle. "There's a great deal that's attractive about such an idea; but I don't see why the English should want to entice us away from our native land. I know that we try to attract them over there; but that's because our population is insufficient. Here, you know, they are rather crowded. However, I suppose there is room for charming young ladies everywhere."

"There seems to have been room here for you," said Isabel, whose eyes had been wandering over the large pleasure-spaces of the park.

Mr. Touchett gave a shrewd, conscious smile.

"There is room everywhere, my dear, if you will pay for it. I sometimes think I have paid too much for this. Perhaps you also might have to pay too much."

"Perhaps I might," the girl replied.

This suggestion gave her something more definite to rest upon than she had found in her own thoughts, and the fact of her uncle's genial shrewdness being associated with her dilemma seemed to prove to her that she was concerned with the natural and reasonable emotions of life, and not altogether a victim to intellectual eagerness and vague ambitions—ambitions reaching beyond Lord Warburton's handsome offer to something indefinable and possibly not commendable. Insofar as the indefinable had an influence upon Isabel's behavior at this juncture, it was not the conception, however unformulated, of a union with Caspar Goodwood; for however little she might have felt warranted in lending a receptive ear to her English suitor, she was at least as far removed from the disposition to let the young man from Boston take complete possession of her. The sentiment in which she ultimately took refuge, after reading his letter, was a critical view of his having come abroad; for it was part of the influence he had upon her that he seemed to take from her the sense of freedom. There was something too forcible, something oppressive and restrictive, in the manner in which he presented himself. She had been haunted at moments by the image of his disapproval, and she had wondered—a consideration she had never paid in one equal degree to anyone else—whether he would like what she did. The difficulty was that more than any man she had ever known, more than poor Lord

Warburton (she had begun now to give his lordship the benefit of this epithet), Caspar Goodwood gave her an impression of energy. She might like it or not, but at any rate there was something very strong about him; even in one's usual contact with him one had to reckon with it. The idea of a diminished liberty was particularly disagreeable to Isabel at present, because it seemed to her that she had just given a sort of personal accent to her independence by making up her mind to refuse Lord Warburton. Sometimes Caspar Goodwood had seemed to range himself on the side of her destiny, to be the stubbornest fact she knew; she said to herself at such moments that she might evade him for a time, but that she must make terms with him at last—terms which would be certain to be favorable to himself. Her impulse had been to avail herself of the things that helped her to resist such an obligation; and this impulse had been much concerned in her eager acceptance of her aunt's invitation, which had come to her at a time when she expected from day to day to see Mr. Goodwood, and when she was glad to have an answer ready for something she was sure he would say to her. When she had told him at Albany, on the evening of Mrs. Touchett's visit, that she could not now discuss difficult questions, because she was preoccupied with the idea of going to Europe with her aunt, he declared that this was no answer at all; and it was to obtain a better one that he followed her across the seas. To say to herself that he was a kind of fate was well enough for a fanciful young woman, who was able to take much for granted in him; but the reader has a right to demand a description less metaphysical.

He was the son of a proprietor of certain well-known cotton mills in Massachusetts—a gentleman who had accumulated a considerable fortune in the exercise of this industry. Caspar now managed the establishment, with a judgment and a brilliancy which, in spite of keen competition and languid years, had kept its prosperity from dwindling. He had received the better part of his education at Harvard University, where, however, he had gained more renown as a gymnast and an oarsman than as a votary of culture. Later, he had become reconciled to culture, and though he was still fond of sport, he was capable of showing an excellent understanding of other matters. He had a remarkable aptitude for mechanics, and had invented an improvement in the cotton-spinning process, which was now largely used and was known by his name. You might have seen his name in the papers in connection with this fruitful contrivance; assurance of which he had given to Isabel by showing her in the columns of the New York *Interviewer* an exhaustive article on the Goodwood patent—an article not prepared by Miss Stackpole, friendly as she had proved herself to his more sentimental interests. He had great talent for business, for administration, and for making people execute his purpose and carry out his views—for managing men, as the phrase was; and to give its complete value to this faculty, he had an insatiable, an almost fierce, ambition. It always struck people who knew him that he might do greater things than carry on a cotton factory; there was nothing cottony about Caspar Goodwood, and his friends took for granted that he would not always content himself with that. He had once said to Isabel that, if the United States were only not such a confoundedly peaceful nation, he would find his proper place in the army. He keenly regretted that the Civil War should have terminated just as he had grown old enough to wear shoulder straps, and was sure that if something of the same kind would only occur again, he would make a display of striking military talent. It pleased Isabel to believe that he had the qualities of a famous captain, and she answered that, if it would help him on, she shouldn't object to a war—a speech which ranked among the three or four most encouraging ones he had elicited from her, and of which the value was not diminished by her subsequent regret at having said anything so heartless, inasmuch as she never communicated this regret to him. She liked at any rate this idea of his being potentially a commander of men—liked it much better than some other points in his character and appearance. She cared nothing about his cotton mill, and the Goodwood patent left her imagination absolutely cold. She wished him not an inch less a man than he was; but she sometimes thought he would be rather nicer if he looked, for instance, a little differently. His jaw was too square and grim, and his figure too straight and stiff; these things suggested a want of easy adaptability to some of the occasions of life. Then she regarded with disfavor a habit he had of dressing always in the same manner; it was not apparently that he wore the same clothes continually, for, on the contrary, his garments had a way of looking rather too new. But they all seemed to be made of the same piece; the pattern, the cut, was in every case identical. She had reminded herself more than once that this was a frivolous objection to a man of Mr. Goodwood's importance; and then she had amended the rebuke by saying that it would be a frivolous objection if she were in love with him. She was not in love with him, and therefore she might criticize his small defects as well as his great ones—which latter consisted in the collective reproach of his being too serious, or, rather, not of his being too serious, for one could never be that, but of his seeming so. He showed his seriousness too simply, too artlessly; when one was alone with him he talked too much about the same subject, and when other people were present he talked too little about anything. And yet he was the strongest man she had ever known, and she believed that at bottom he was the cleverest. It was very strange; she was far from understanding the contradictions among her own impressions. Caspar Goodwood had never corresponded to her idea of a delightful person, and she supposed that this was why he was so unsatisfactory. When, however, Lord Warburton, who not only did correspond with it, but gave an extension to the term, appealed to her approval, she found herself still unsatisfied. It was certainly strange.

Such incongruities were not a help to answering Mr. Goodwood's letter, and Isabel determined to leave it a while unanswered. If he had determined to persecute her, he must take the consequences; foremost among which was his being left to perceive that she did not approve of his coming to Gardencourt. She was already liable to the incursions of one suitor at this place, and though it might be pleasant to be appreciated in opposite quarters, Isabel had a personal shrinking from entertaining two lovers at once, even in a case where the entertainment should consist of dismissing them. She sent no answer to Mr. Goodwood; but at the end of three days she wrote to Lord Warburton, and the letter belongs to our history. It ran as follows.

"DEAR LORD WARBURTON—A great deal of careful reflection has not led me to change my mind about the suggestion you were so kind as to make me the other day. I do not find myself able to regard you in the light of a husband, or to regard your home—your various homes—in the light of my own. These things cannot be reasoned about, and I very earnestly entreat you not to return to the subject we discussed so exhaustively. We see our lives from our own point of view; that is the privilege of the weakest and humblest of us; and I shall never be able to see mine in the manner you proposed. Kindly let this suffice you, and do me the justice to believe that I have given your proposal the deeply respectful consideration it deserves. It is with this feeling of respect that I remain very truly yours,

"ISABEL ARCHER."

While the author of this missive was making up her mind to despatch it, Henrietta Stackpole formed a resolution which was accompanied by no hesitation. She invited Ralph Touchett to take a walk with her in the garden, and when he had assented with that alacrity which seemed constantly to testify to his high expectations, she informed him that she had a favor to ask of him. It may be confided to the reader that at this information the young man flinched; for we know that Miss Stackpole had struck him as indiscreet. The movement was unreasonable, however; for he had measured the limits of her discretion as little as he had explored its extent; and he made a very civil profession of the desire to serve her. He was afraid of her, and he presently told her so.

"When you look at me in a certain way," he said, "my knees knock together, my faculties desert me; I am filled with trepidation, and I ask only for strength to execute your commands. You have a look which I have never encountered in any woman."

"Well," Henrietta replied, good-humoredly, "if I had not known before that you were trying to turn me into ridicule, I should know it now. Of course I am easy game—I was brought up with such different customs and ideas. I am not used to your arbitrary standards, and I have never been spoken to in America as you have spoken to me. If a gentleman conversing with me over there, were to speak to me like that, I shouldn't know what to make of it. We take everything more naturally over there, and, after all, we are a great deal more simple. I admit that; I am very simple myself. Of course, if you choose to laugh at me for that, you are very welcome; but I think on the whole I would rather be myself than you. I am quite content to be myself; I don't want to change. There are plenty of people that appreciate me just as I am; it is true they are only Americans!" Henrietta had lately taken up the tone of helpless innocence and large concession. "I want you to assist me a little," she went on. "I don't care in the least whether I amuse you while you do so; or, rather, I am perfectly willing that your amusement should be your reward. I want you to help me about Isabel."

"Has she injured you?" Ralph asked.

"If she had I shouldn't mind, and I should never tell you. What I am afraid of is that she will injure herself."

"I think that is very possible," said Ralph.

His companion stopped in the garden walk, fixing on him a gaze which may perhaps have contained the quality that caused his knees to knock together. "That, too, would amuse you, I suppose. The way you do say things! I never heard anyone so indifferent."

"To Isabel? Never in the world."

"Well, you are not in love with her, I hope."

"How can that be, when I am in love with another?"

"You are in love with yourself, that's the other!" Miss Stackpole declared. "Much good may it do you! But if you wish to be serious once in your life, here's a chance; and if you really care for your cousin, here is an opportunity to prove it. I don't expect you to understand her; that's too much to ask. But you needn't do that to grant my favor. I will supply the necessary intelligence."

"I shall enjoy that immensely!" Ralph exclaimed. "I will be Caliban, and you shall be Ariel."

"You are not at all like Caliban, because you are sophisticated, and Caliban was not. But I am not talking about imaginary characters; I am talking about Isabel. Isabel is intensely real. What I wish to tell you is that I find her fearfully changed."

"Since you came, do you mean?"

"Since I came, and before I came. She is not the same as she was."

"As she was in America?"

"Yes, in America. I suppose you know that she comes from there. She can't help it, but she does."

"Do you want to change her back again?"

"Of course I do; and I want you to help me."

"Ah," said Ralph, "I am only Caliban; I am not Prospero."

"You were Prospero enough to make her what she has become. You have acted on Isabel Archer since she came here, Mr. Touchett."

"I, my dear Miss Stackpole? Never in the world. Isabel Archer has acted on me—yes; she acts on everyone. But I have been absolutely passive."

"You are too passive, then. You had better stir yourself and be careful. Isabel is changing every day; she is drifting away—right out to sea. I have watched her and I can see it. She is not the bright American girl she was. She is taking different views, and turning away from her old ideals. I want to save those ideals, Mr. Touchett, and that is where you come in."

"Not surely as an ideal?"

"Well, I hope not," Henrietta replied, promptly. "I have got a fear in my heart that she is going to marry one of these Europeans, and I want to prevent it."

"Ah, I see," cried Ralph; "and to prevent it, you want me to step in and marry her?"

"Not quite; that remedy would be as bad as the disease, for you are the typical European from whom I wish to rescue her. No; I wish you to take an interest in another person—a young man to whom she once gave great encouragement, and whom she now doesn't seem to think good enough. He's a noble fellow, and a very dear friend of mine, and I wish very much you would invite him to pay a visit here."

Ralph was much puzzled by this appeal, and it is perhaps not to the credit of his purity of mind that he failed to look at it at first in the simplest light. It wore, to his eyes, a tortuous air, and his fault was that he was not quite sure that anything in the world could really be as candid as this request of Miss Stackpole's appeared. That a young woman should demand that a gentleman whom she described as her very dear friend should be furnished with an opportunity to make himself agreeable to another young woman, whose attention had wandered and whose charms were greater—this was an anomaly which for the moment challenged all his ingenuity of interpretation. To read between the lines was easier than to follow the text, and to suppose that Miss Stackpole wished the gentleman invited to Gardencourt on her own account was the sign not so much of a vulgar, as of an embarrassed, mind. Even from this venial act of vulgarity, however, Ralph was saved, and saved by a force that I can scarcely call anything less than inspiration. With no more outward light on the subject than he already possessed, he suddenly acquired the conviction that it would be a sovereign injustice to the correspondent of the *Interviewer* to assign a dishonorable motive to any act of hers. This conviction passed into his mind with extreme rapidity; it was perhaps kindled by the pure radiance of the young lady's imperturbable gaze. He returned this gaze a moment, consciously, resisting an inclination to frown, as one frowns in the presence of larger luminaries. "Who is the gentleman you speak of?"

"Mr. Caspar Goodwood, from Boston. He has been extremely attentive to Isabel—just as devoted to her as he can be. He has followed her out here, and he is at present in London. I don't know his address, but I guess I can obtain it."

"I have never heard of him," said Ralph.

"Well, I suppose you haven't heard of everyone. I don't believe he has ever heard of you; but that is no reason why Isabel shouldn't marry him."

Ralph gave a small laugh. "What a rage you have for marrying people! Do you remember how you wanted to marry me the other day?"

"I have got over that. You don't know how to take such ideas. Mr. Goodwood does, however; and that's what I like about him. He's a splendid man and a perfect gentleman; and Isabel knows it."

"Is she very fond of him?"

"If she isn't she ought to be. He is simply wrapped up in her."

"And you wish me to ask him here," said Ralph, reflectively.

"It would be an act of true hospitality."

"Caspar Goodwood," Ralph continued—"it's rather a striking name."

"I don't care anything about his name. It might be Ezekiel Jenkins, and I should say the same. He is the only man I have ever seen whom I think worthy of Isabel."

"You are a very devoted friend," said Ralph.

"Of course I am. If you say that to laugh at me, I don't care."

"I don't say it to laugh at you; I am very much struck with it."

"You are laughing worse than ever; but I advise you not to laugh at Mr. Goodwood."

"I assure you I am very serious; you ought to understand that," said Ralph.

In a moment his companion understood it. "I believe you are; now you are too serious."

"You are difficult to please."

"Oh, you are very serious indeed. You won't invite Mr. Goodwood."

"I don't know," said Ralph. "I am capable of strange things. Tell me a little about Mr. Goodwood. What is he like?"

"He is just the opposite of you. He is at the head of a cotton factory; a very fine one."

"Has he pleasant manners?" asked Ralph.

"Splendid manners—in the American style."

"Would he be an agreeable member of our little circle?"

"I don't think he would care much about our little circle. He would concentrate on Isabel."

"And how would my cousin like that?"

"Very possibly not at all. But it will be good for her. It will call back her thoughts."

"Call them back—from where?"

"From foreign parts and other unnatural places. Three months ago she gave Mr. Goodwood every reason to suppose that he was acceptable to her, and it is not worthy of Isabel to turn her back upon a real friend simply because she has changed the scene. I have changed the scene too, and the effect of it has been to make me care more for my old associations than ever. It's my belief that the sooner Isabel changes it back again the better. I know her well enough to know that she would never be truly happy over here, and I wish her to form some strong American tie that will act as a preservative."

"Are you not a little too much in a hurry?" Ralph inquired. "Don't you think you ought to give her more of a chance in poor old England?"

"A chance to ruin her bright young life? One is never too much in a hurry to save a precious human creature from drowning."

"As I understand it, then," said Ralph, "you wish me to push Mr. Goodwood overboard after her. Do you know," he added, "that I have never heard her mention his name?"

Henrietta Stackpole gave a brilliant smile. "I am delighted to hear that; it proves how much she thinks of him."

Ralph appeared to admit that there was a good deal in this, and he surrendered himself to meditation, while his companion watched him askance. "If I should invite Mr. Goodwood," he said, "it would be to quarrel with him."

"Don't do that; he would prove the better man."

"You certainly are doing your best to make me hate him! I really don't think I can ask him. I should be afraid of being rude to him."

"It's just as you please," said Henrietta. "I had no idea you were in love with her yourself."

"Do you really believe that?" the young man asked, with lifted eyebrows.

"That's the most natural speech I have ever heard you make! Of course I believe it," Miss Stackpole answered, ingeniously.

"Well," said Ralph, "to prove to you that you are wrong, I will invite him. It must be, of course, as a friend of yours."

"It will not be as a friend of mine that he will come; and it will not be to prove to me that I am wrong that you will ask him—but to prove it to yourself!"

These last words of Miss Stackpole's (on which the two presently separated) contained an amount of truth which Ralph Touchett was obliged to recognize; but it so far took the edge from too sharp a recognition that, in spite of his suspecting that it would be rather more indiscreet to keep his promise than it would be to break it, he wrote Mr. Goodwood a note of six lines, expressing the pleasure it would give Mr. Touchett the elder that he should join a little party at Gardencourt, of which Miss Stackpole was a valued member. Having sent his letter (to the care of a banker whom Henrietta suggested) he waited in some suspense. He had heard of Mr. Caspar Goodwood by name for the first time; for when his mother mentioned to him on her arrival that there was a story about the girl's having an "admirer" at home, the idea seemed deficient in reality, and Ralph took no pains to ask questions, the answers to which would suggest only the vague or the disagreeable. Now, however, the native admiration of which his cousin was the object had become more concrete; it took the form of a young man who had followed her to London; who was interested in a cotton mill, and had manners in the American style. Ralph had two theories about this young man. Either his passion was a sentimental fiction of Miss Stackpole's (there was always a sort of tacit understanding among women, born of the solidarity of the sex, that they should discover or invent lovers for each other), in which case he was not to be feared, and would probably not accept the invitation; or else he would accept the invitation, and in this event would prove himself a creature too irrational to demand further consideration. The latter clause of Ralph's argument might have seemed incoherent; but it embodied his conviction, that if Mr. Goodwood were interested in Isabel in the serious manner described by Miss Stackpole, he would not care to present himself at Gardencourt on a summons from the latter lady. "On this supposition," said Ralph, "he must regard her as a thorn on the stem of his rose; as an intercessor he must find her wanting in tact."

Two days after he had sent his invitation he received a very short note from Caspar Goodwood, thanking him for it, regretting that other engagements made a visit to Gardencourt impossible, and presenting many compliments to Miss Stackpole. Ralph handed the note to Henrietta, who, when she had read it, exclaimed—

"Well, I never have heard of anything so stiff!"

"I am afraid he doesn't care so much about my cousin as you suppose," Ralph observed.

"No, it's not that; it's some deeper motive. His nature is very deep. But I am determined to fathom it, and I will write to him to know what he means."

His refusal of Ralph's overtures made this young man vaguely uncomfortable; from the moment he declined to come to Gardencourt Ralph began to think him of importance. He asked himself what it signified to him whether Isabel's admirers should be desperadoes or laggards; they were not rivals of his, and were perfectly welcome to act out their genius. Nevertheless he felt much curiosity as to the result of Miss Stackpole's promised inquiry into the causes of Mr. Goodwood's stiffness— a curiosity for the present ungratified, inasmuch as when he asked her three days later whether she had written to London, she was obliged to confess that she had written in vain. Mr. Goodwood had not answered her.

"I suppose he is thinking it over," she said; "he thinks everything over; he is not at all impulsive. But I am accustomed to having my letters answered the same day."

Whether it was to pursue her investigations, or whether it was in compliance with still larger interests, is a point which remains somewhat uncertain; at all events, she presently proposed to Isabel that they should make an excursion to London together.

"If I must tell the truth," she said, "I am not seeing much at this place, and I shouldn't think you were either. I have not even seen that aristocrat—what's his name?—Lord Washburton. He seems to let you severely alone."

"Lord Warburton is coming tomorrow, I happen to know," replied Isabel, who had received a note from the master of Lockleigh in answer to her own letter. "You will have every opportunity of examining him."

"Well, he may do for one letter, but what is one letter when you want to write fifty? I have described all the scenery in this vicinity, and raved about all the old women and donkeys. You may say what you please, scenery makes a thin letter. I must go back to London and get some impressions of real life. I was there but three days before I came away, and that is hardly time to get started."

As Isabel, on her journey from New York to Gardencourt, had seen even less of the metropolis than this, it appeared a happy suggestion of Henrietta's that the two should go thither on a visit of pleasure. The idea struck Isabel as charming; she had a great desire to see something of London, which had always been the city of her imagination. They turned over their scheme together and indulged in visions of aesthetic hours. They would stay at some picturesque old inn—one of the inns described by Dickens—and drive over the town in those delightful hansoms. Henrietta was a literary woman, and the great advantage of being a literary woman was that you could go everywhere and do everything. They would dine at a coffeehouse, and go afterwards to the play; they would frequent the Abbey and the British Museum, and find out where Doctor Johnson had lived, and Goldsmith and Addison. Isabel grew eager, and presently mentioned these bright intentions to Ralph, who burst into a fit of laughter, which did not express the sympathy she had desired.

"It's a delightful plan," he said. "I advise you to go to the Tavistock Hotel in Covent Garden, an easy, informal, old-fashioned place, and I will have you put down at my club."

"Do you mean it's improper?" Isabel asked. "Dear me, isn't anything proper here? With Henrietta, surely I may go anywhere; she isn't hampered in that way. She has traveled over the whole American continent, and she can surely find her way about this simple little island."

"Ah, then," said Ralph, "let me take advantage of her protection to go up to town as well. I may never have a chance to travel so safely!"

❧ 14 ❧

Miss Stackpole would have prepared to start for London immediately; but Isabel, as we have seen, had been notified that Lord Warburton would come again to Gardencourt, and she believed it to be her duty to remain there and see him. For four or five days he had made no answer to her letter; then he had written, very briefly, to say that he would come to lunch two days later. There was something in these delays and postponements that touched the girl, and renewed her sense of his desire to be considerate and patient, not to appear to urge her too grossly; a discretion the more striking that she was so sure he really liked her. Isabel told her uncle that she had written to him, and let Mr. Touchett know of Lord Warburton's intention of coming; and the old man, in consequence, left his room earlier than usual, and made his appearance at the lunch table. This was by no means an act of vigilance on his part, but the fruit of a benevolent belief that his being of the company might help to cover the visitor's temporary absence, in case Isabel should find it needful to give Lord Warburton another hearing. This personage drove over from Lockleigh, and brought the elder of his sisters with him, a measure presumably dictated by considerations of the same order as Mr. Touchett's. The two visitors were introduced to Miss Stackpole, who, at luncheon, occupied a seat adjoining Lord Warburton's. Isabel, who was nervous, and had no relish of the prospect of again arguing the question he had so precipitately opened, could not help admiring his good-humored self-possession, which quite disguised the symptoms of that admiration it was natural she should suppose him to feel. He neither looked at her nor spoke to her, and the only sign of his emotion was that he avoided meeting her eye. He had plenty of talk for the others, however, and he appeared to eat his luncheon with discrimination and appetite. Miss Molyneux, who had a smooth, nun-like forehead, and wore a large silver cross suspended from her neck, was evidently preoccupied with Henrietta Stackpole, upon whom her eyes constantly rested in a manner which seemed to denote a conflict between attention and alienation. Of the two ladies from Lockleigh, she was the one that Isabel had liked best; there was such a world of hereditary quiet in her. Isabel was sure, moreover, that her mild forehead and silver cross had a romantic meaning—that she was a member of a High Church sisterhood, had taken some picturesque vows. She wondered what Miss Molyneux would think of her if she knew Miss Archer had refused her brother; and then she felt sure that Miss Molyneux would never know—that Lord Warburton never told her such things. He was fond of her and kind to her, but on the whole he told her little. Such, at least, was Isabel's theory; when, at table, she was not occupied in conversation, she was usually occupied in forming theories about her neighbors. According to Isabel, if Miss Molyneux should ever learn what had passed between Miss Archer and Lord Warburton, she would probably be shocked at the young lady's indifference to such an opportunity; or no, rather (this was our heroine's last impression) she would impute to the young American a high sense of general fitness.

Whatever Isabel might have made of her opportunities, Henrietta Stackpole was by no means disposed to neglect those in which she now found herself immersed.

"Do you know you are the first lord I have ever seen?" she said, very promptly, to her neighbor. "I suppose you think I am awfully benighted."

"You have escaped seeing some very ugly men," Lord Warburton answered, looking vaguely about the table and laughing a little.

"Are they very ugly? They try to make us believe in America that they are all handsome and magnificent, and that they wear wonderful robes and crowns."

"Ah, the robes and crowns have gone out of fashion," said Lord Warburton, "like your tomahawks and revolvers."

"I am sorry for that; I think an aristocracy ought to be splendid," Henrietta declared. "If it is not that, what is it?"

"Oh, you know, it isn't much, at the best," Lord Warburton answered. "Won't you have a potato?"

"I don't care much for these European potatoes. I shouldn't know you from an ordinary American gentleman."

"Do talk to me as if I were one," said Lord Warburton. "I don't see how you manage to get on without potatoes; you must find so few things to eat over here."

Henrietta was silent a moment; there was a chance that he was not sincere.

"I have had hardly any appetite since I have been here," she went on at last; "so it doesn't much matter. I don't approve of *you*, you know; I feel as if I ought to tell you that."

"Don't approve of me?"

"Yes, I don't suppose anyone ever said such a thing to you before, did they? I don't approve of lords, as an institution. I think the world has got beyond that—far beyond."

"Oh, so do I. I don't approve of myself in the least. Sometimes it comes over me—how I should object to myself if I were not myself, don't you know? But that's rather good, by the way—not to be vainglorious."

"Why don't you give it up, then?" Miss Stackpole inquired.

"Give up—a—?" asked Lord Warburton, meeting her harsh inflection with a very mellow one.

"Give up being a lord."

"Oh, I am so little of one! One would really forget all about it, if you wretched Americans were not constantly reminding one. However, I do think of giving up— the little there is left of it—one of these days."

"I should like to see you do it," Henrietta exclaimed, rather grimly.

"I will invite you to the ceremony; we will have a supper and a dance."

"Well," said Miss Stackpole, "I like to see all sides. I don't approve of a privileged class, but I like to hear what they have got to say for themselves."

"Mighty little, as you see!"

"I should like to draw you out a little more," Henrietta continued. "But you are always looking away. You are afraid of meeting my eye. I see you want to escape me."

"No, I am only looking for those despised potatoes."

"Please explain about that young lady—your sister—then. I don't understand about her. Is she a Lady?"

"She's a capital good girl."

"I don't like the way you say that—as if you wanted to change the subject. Is her position inferior to yours?"

"We neither of us have any position to speak of; but she is better off than I, because she has none of the bother."

"Yes, she doesn't look as if she had much bother. I wish I had as little bother as that. You do produce quiet people over here, whatever you may do."

"Ah, you see one takes life easily, on the whole," said Lord Warburton. "And then you know we are very dull. Ah, we can be dull when we try!"

"I should advise you to try something else. I shouldn't know what to talk to your sister about; she looks so different. Is that silver cross a badge?"

"A badge?"

"A sign of rank."

Lord Warburton's glance had wandered a good deal, but at this it met the gaze of his neighbor.

"Oh, yes," he answered, in a moment; "the women go in for those things. The silver cross is worn by the eldest daughters of Viscounts."

This was his harmless revenge for having occasionally had his credulity too easily engaged in America.

After lunch he proposed to Isabel to come into the gallery and look at the pictures; and though she knew that he had seen the pictures twenty times, she complied without criticizing this pretext. Her conscience now was very easy; ever since she sent him her letter she had felt particularly light of spirit. He walked slowly to the end of the gallery, staring at the paintings and saying nothing; and then he suddenly broke out—

"I hoped you wouldn't write to me that way."

"It was the only way, Lord Warburton," said the girl. "Do try and believe that."

"If I could believe it, of course I should let you alone. But we can't believe by willing it; and I confess I don't understand. I could understand your disliking me; that I could understand well. But that you should admit what you do——"

"What have I admitted?" Isabel interrupted, blushing a little.

"That you think me a good fellow; isn't that it?" She said nothing, and he went on—"You don't seem to have any reason, and that gives me a sense of injustice."

"I have a reason, Lord Warburton," said the girl; and she said it in a tone that made his heart contract.

"I should like very much to know it."

"I will tell you some day when there is more to show for it."

"Excuse my saying that in the meantime I must doubt of it."

"You make me very unhappy," said Isabel.

"I am not sorry for that; it may help you to know how I feel. Will you kindly answer me a question?" Isabel made no audible assent, but he apparently saw something in her eyes which gave him courage to go on. "Do you prefer someone else?"

"That's a question I would rather not answer."

"Ah, you *do* then!" her suitor murmured with bitterness.

The bitterness touched her, and she cried out—

"You are mistaken! I don't."

He sat down on a bench, unceremoniously, doggedly, like a man in trouble; leaning his elbows on his knees and staring at the floor.

"I can't even be glad of that," he said at last, throwing himself back against the wall, "for that would be an excuse."

Isabel raised her eyebrows, with a certain eagerness.

"An excuse? Must I excuse myself?"

He paid, however, no answer to the question. Another idea had come into his head. "Is it my political opinions? Do you think I go too far?"

"I can't object to your political opinions, Lord Warburton," said the girl, "because I don't understand them."

"You don't care what I think," he cried, getting up. "It's all the same to you."

Isabel walked away, to the other side of the gallery, and stood there, showing him her charming back, her light slim figure, the length of her white neck as she bent her head, and the density of her dark braids. She stopped in front of a small picture, as if for the purpose of examining it; and there was something young and flexible in her movement, which her companion noticed. Isabel's eyes, however, saw nothing;

they had suddenly been suffused with tears. In a moment he followed her, and by this time she had brushed her tears away; but when she turned round, her face was pale, and the expression of her eyes was strange.

"That reason that I wouldn't tell you," she said, "I will tell it you, after all. It is that I can't escape my fate."

"Your fate?"

"I should try to escape it if I should marry you."

"I don't understand. Why should not that be your fate, as well as anything else?"

"Because it is not," said Isabel, femininely. "I know it is not. It's not my fate to give up—I know it can't be."

Poor Lord Warburton stared, with an interrogative point in either eye.

"Do you call marrying me giving up?"

"Not in the usual sense. It is getting—getting—getting a great deal. But it is giving up other chances."

"Other chances?" Lord Warburton repeated, more and more puzzled.

"I don't mean chances to marry," said Isabel, her color rapidly coming back to her. And then she stopped, looking down with a deep frown, as if it were hopeless to attempt to make her meaning clear.

"I don't think it is presumptuous in me to say that I think you will gain more than you will lose," Lord Warburton observed.

"I can't escape unhappiness," said Isabel. "In marrying you, I shall be trying to."

"I don't know whether you would try to, but you certainly would: that I must in candor admit!" Lord Warburton exclaimed, with an anxious laugh.

"I must not—I can't!" cried the girl.

"Well, if you are bent on being miserable, I don't see why you should make me so. Whatever charms unhappiness may have for you, it has none for me."

"I am not bent on being miserable," said Isabel. "I have always been intensely determined to be happy, and I have often believed I should be. I have told people that; you can ask them. But it comes over me every now and then that I can never be happy in any extraordinary way; not by turning away, by separating myself."

"By separating yourself from what?"

"From life. From the usual chances and dangers, from what most people know and suffer."

Lord Warburton broke into a smile that almost denoted hope.

"Why, my dear Miss Archer," he began to explain, with the most considerate eagerness, "I don't offer you any exoneration from life, or from any chances or dangers whatever. I wish I could; depend upon it I would! For what do you take me, pray? Heaven help me, I am not the Emperor of China! All I offer you is the chance of taking the common lot in a comfortable sort of way. The common lot? Why, I am devoted to the common lot! Strike an alliance with me, and I promise you that you shall have plenty of it. You shall separate from nothing whatever—not even from your friend Miss Stackpole."

"She would never approve of it," said Isabel, trying to smile and take advantage of this side issue; despising herself too, not a little, for doing so.

"Are we speaking of Miss Stackpole?" Lord Warburton asked, impatiently. "I never saw a person judge things on such theoretic grounds."

"Now I suppose you are speaking of me," said Isabel, with humility; and she turned away again, for she saw Miss Molyneux enter the gallery, accompanied by Henrietta and by Ralph.

Lord Warburton's sister addressed him with a certain timidity, and reminded him that she ought to return home in time for tea, as she was expecting some company. He made no answer—apparently not having heard her; he was preoccupied—with good reason. Miss Molyneux looked ladylike and patient, and awaited his pleasure.

"Well, I never, Miss Molyneux!" said Henrietta Stackpole. "If I wanted to go, he would have to go. If I wanted my brother to do a thing, he would have to do it."

"Oh, Warburton does everything one wants," Miss Molyneux answered, with a quick, shy laugh. "How very many pictures you have!" she went on, turning to Ralph.

"They look a good many, because they are all put together," said Ralph. "But it's really a bad way."

"Oh, I think it's so nice. I wish we had a gallery at Lockleigh. I am so very fond of pictures," Miss Molyneux went on, persistently, to Ralph, as if she were afraid that Miss Stackpole would address her again. Henrietta appeared at once to fascinate and to frighten her.

"Oh yes, pictures are very indispensable," said Ralph, who appeared to know better what style of reflection was acceptable to her.

"They are so very pleasant when it rains," the young lady continued. "It rains so very often."

"I am sorry you are going away, Lord Warburton," said Henrietta. "I wanted to get a great deal more out of you."

"I am not going away," Lord Warburton answered.

"Your sister says you must. In America the gentlemen obey the ladies."

"I am afraid we have got some people to tea," said Miss Molyneux, looking at her brother.

"Very good, my dear. We'll go."

"I hoped you would resist!" Henrietta exclaimed. "I wanted to see what Miss Molyneux would do."

"I never do anything," said this young lady.

"I suppose in your position it's sufficient for you to exist!" Miss Stackpole rejoined. "I should like very much to see you at home."

"You must come to Lockleigh again," said Miss Molyneux, very sweetly, to Isabel, ignoring this remark of Isabel's friend.

Isabel looked into her quiet eyes a moment, and for that moment seemed to see in their gray depths the reflection of everything she had rejected in rejecting Lord Warburton—the peace, the kindness, the honor, the possessions, a deep security and a great exclusion. She kissed Miss Molyneux, and then she said—

"I am afraid I can never come again."

"Never again?"

"I am afraid I am going away."

"Oh, I am so very sorry," said Miss Molyneux. "I think that's so very wrong of you."

Lord Warburton watched this little passage; then he turned away and stared at a picture. Ralph, leaning against the rail before the picture, with his hands in his pockets, had for the moment been watching him.

"I should like to see you at home," said Henrietta, whom Lord Warburton found beside him. "I should like an hour's talk with you; there are a great many questions I wish to ask you."

"I shall be delighted to see you," the proprietor of Lockleigh answered; "but I am certain not to be able to answer many of your questions. When will you come?"

"Whenever Miss Archer will take me. We are thinking of going to London, but we will go and see you first. I am determined to get some satisfaction out of you."

"If it depends upon Miss Archer, I am afraid you won't get much. She will not come to Lockleigh; she doesn't like the place."

"She told me it was lovely!" said Henrietta.

Lord Warburton hesitated a moment.

"She won't come, all the same. You had better come alone," he added.

Henrietta straightened herself, and her large eyes expanded.

"Would you make that remark to an English lady?" she inquired, with soft asperity.

Lord Warburton stared.

"Yes, if I liked her enough."

"You would be careful not to like her enough. If Miss Archer won't visit your place again, it's because she doesn't want to take me. I know what she thinks of me, and I suppose you think the same—that I oughtn't to bring in individuals."

Lord Warburton was at a loss; he had not been made acquainted with Miss Stackpole's professional character, and did not catch her allusion.

"Miss Archer has been warning you!" she went on.

"Warning me?"

"Isn't that why she came off alone with you here—to put you on your guard?"

"Oh, dear no," said Lord Warburton, blushing; "our talk had no such solemn character as that."

"Well, you have been on your guard—intensely. I suppose it's natural to you; that's just what I wanted to observe. And so, too, Miss Molyneux—she wouldn't commit herself. *You* have been warned, anyway," Henrietta continued, addressing this young lady, "but for you it wasn't necessary."

"I hope not," said Miss Molyneux, vaguely.

"Miss Stackpole takes notes," Ralph explained, humorously. "She is a great satirist; she sees through us all, and she works us up."

"Well, I must say I never have had such a collection of bad material!" Henrietta declared, looking from Isabel to Lord Warburton, and from this nobleman to his sister and to Ralph. "There is something the matter with you all; you are as dismal as if you had got a bad telegram."

"You do see through us, Miss Stackpole," said Ralph in a low tone, giving her a little intelligent nod, as he led the party out of the gallery. "There is something the matter with us all."

Isabel came behind these two; Miss Molyneux, who decidedly liked her immensely, had taken her arm, to walk beside her over the polished floor. Lord Warburton strolled on the other side, with his hands behind him, and his eyes lowered. For some moments he said nothing; and then—

"Is it true that you are going to London?" he asked.

"I believe it has been arranged."

"And when shall you come back?"

"In a few days; but probably for a very short time. I am going to Paris with my aunt."

"When, then, shall I see you again?"

"Not for a good while," said Isabel; "but some day or other, I hope."

"Do you really hope it?"

"Very much."

He went a few steps in silence; then he stopped, and put out his hand. "Goodbye."

"Goodbye," said Isabel.

Miss Molyneux kissed her again, and she let the two depart; after which, without rejoining Henrietta and Ralph, she retreated to her own room.

In this apartment, before dinner, she was found by Mrs. Touchett, who had stopped on her way to the drawing room.

"I may as well tell you," said her aunt, "that your uncle has informed me of your relations with Lord Warburton."

Isabel hesitated an instant.

"Relations? They are hardly relations. That is the strange part of it; he has seen me but three or four times."

"Why did you tell your uncle rather than me?" Mrs. Touchett inquired, dryly, but dispassionately.

Again Isabel hesitated.

"Because he knows Lord Warburton better."

"Yes, but I know you better."

"I am not sure of that," said Isabel, smiling.

"Neither am I, after all; especially when you smile that way. One would think you had carried off a prize! I suppose that when you refuse an offer like Lord Warburton's it's because you expect to do something better."

"Ah, my uncle didn't say that!" cried Isabel, smiling still.

❧ 15 ❧

It had been arranged that the two young ladies should proceed to London under Ralph's escort, though Mrs. Touchett looked with little favor upon the plan. It was just the sort of plan, she said, that Miss Stackpole would be sure to suggest, and she inquired if the correspondent of the *Interviewer* was to take the party to stay at a boardinghouse.

"I don't care where she takes us to stay, so long as there is local color," said Isabel. "That is what we are going to London for."

"I suppose that after a girl has refused an English lord she may do anything," her aunt rejoined. "After that one needn't stand on trifles."

"Should you have liked me to marry Lord Warburton?" Isabel inquired.

"Of course I should."

"I thought you disliked the English so much."

"So I do; but it's all the more reason for making use of them."

"Is that your idea of marriage?" And Isabel ventured to add that her aunt appeared to her to have made very little use of Mr. Touchett.

"Your uncle is not an English nobleman," said Mrs. Touchett, "though even if he had been, I should still probably have taken up my residence in Florence."

"Do you think Lord Warburton could make me any better than I am?" the girl asked, with some animation. "I don't mean that I am too good to improve. I mean— I mean that I don't love Lord Warburton enough to marry him."

"You did right to refuse him, then," said Mrs. Touchett, in her little spare voice. "Only, the next great offer you get, I hope you will manage to come up to your standard."

"We had better wait till the offer comes, before we talk about it. I hope very much that I may have no more offers for the present. They bother me fearfully."

"You probably won't be troubled with them if you adopt permanently the Bohemian manner of life. However, I have promised Ralph not to criticize the affair."

"I will do whatever Ralph says is right," Isabel said. "I have unbounded confidence in Ralph."

"His mother is much obliged to you!" cried this lady, with a laugh.

"It seems to me she ought to be," Isabel rejoined, smiling.

Ralph had assured her that there would be no violation of decency in their paying a visit—the little party of three—to the sights of the metropolis; but Mrs. Touchett took a different view. Like many ladies of her country who have lived a long time in Europe, she had completely lost her native tact on such points, and in her reaction, not in itself deplorable, against the liberty allowed to young persons beyond the seas, had fallen into gratuitous and exaggerated scruples. Ralph accompanied the two young ladies to town and established them at a quiet inn in a street that ran at right angles to Piccadilly. His first idea had been to take them to his father's house in Winchester Square, a large, dull mansion, which at this period of the year was shrouded in silence and brown holland; but he bethought himself that, the cook being at Gardencourt, there was no one in the house to get them their meals; and Pratt's Hotel accordingly became their resting-place. Ralph, on his side, found quarters in Winchester Square, having a "den" there of which he was very fond, and not being dependent on the local *cuisine*. He availed himself largely indeed of that of Pratt's Hotel, beginning his day with an early visit to his fellow-travelers, who had Mr. Pratt in person, in a large bulging white waistcoat, to remove their dish-covers. Ralph turned up, as he said, after breakfast, and the little party made out a scheme of entertainment for the day. As London does not wear in the month of September its most brilliant face, the young man, who occasionally took an apologetic tone, was obliged to remind his companion, to Miss Stackpole's high irritation, that there was not a creature in town.

"I suppose you mean that the aristocracy are absent," Henrietta answered; "but I don't think you could have a better proof that if they were absent altogether they would not be missed. It seems to me the place is about as full as it can be. There is no one here, of course, except three or four millions of people. What is it you call them—the lower-middle class? They are only the population of London, and that is of no consequence."

Ralph declared that for him the aristocracy left no void that Miss Stackpole herself did not fill, and that a more contented man was nowhere at that moment to be found. In this he spoke the truth, for the stale September days, in the huge half-empty town, borrowed a charm from his circumstances. When he went home at night to the empty house in Winchester Square, after a day spent with his inquisitive countrywomen, he wandered into the big dusky dining room, where the candle he took from the hall table, after letting himself in, constituted the only illumination. The square was still, the house was still; when he raised one of the windows of the dining room to let in the air, he heard the slow creak of the boots of a solitary policeman. His own step, in the empty room, seemed loud and sonorous; some of the carpets had been raised, and whenever he moved he roused a melancholy echo. He sat down in one of the armchairs; the big, dark, dining table twinkled here and there in the small candlelight; the pictures on the wall, all of them very brown, looked vague and incoherent. There was a ghostly presence in the room, as of dinners long since digested, of table talk that had lost its actuality. This hint of the supernatural perhaps had something to do with the fact that Ralph's imagination took a flight, and that he remained in his chair a long time beyond the hour at which he should have been in bed; doing nothing, not even reading the evening paper. I say he did nothing, and I maintain the phrase in the face of the fact that he thought at these moments of Isabel. To think of Isabel could only be for Ralph an idle pursuit, leading to nothing and profiting little to anyone. His cousin had not yet seemed to him so charming as during these days spent in sounding, tourist-fashion, the deeps and shallows of the metropolitan element. Isabel was constantly interested and often excited; if she had come in search of local color she found it everywhere. She asked more questions than he could answer, and launched little theories that he was equally unable to accept or to refute. The party went more than once to the British Museum, and to that brighter palace of art which reclaims for antique variety so large an area of a monotonous suburb; they spent a morning in the Abbey and went on a penny-steamer to the Tower; they looked at pictures both in public and private collections, and sat on various occasions beneath the great trees in Kensington Gardens. Henrietta Stackpole proved to be an indefatigable sightseer and a more good-natured critic than Ralph had ventured to hope. She had indeed many disappointments, and London at large suffered from her vivid remembrance of many of the cities of her native land; but she made the best of its dingy peculiarities and only heaved an occasional sigh, and uttered a desultory "Well!" which led no further and lost itself in retrospect. The truth was that, as she said herself, she was not in her element. "I have not a sympathy with inanimate objects," she remarked to Isabel at the National Gallery; and she continued to suffer from the meagerness of the glimpse that had as yet been vouchsafed to her of the inner life. Landscapes by Turner and Assyrian bulls were a poor substitute for the literary dinner-parties at which she had hoped to meet the genius and renown of Great Britain.

"Where are your public men, where are your men and women of intellect?" she inquired of Ralph, standing in the middle of Trafalgar Square, as if she had supposed this to be a place where she would naturally meet a few. "That's one of them on the top of the column, you say—Lord Nelson? Was he a lord too? Wasn't he high enough, that they had to stick him a hundred feet in the air? That's the past—I don't care about the past; I want to see some of the leading minds of the present. I won't say of the future, because I don't believe much in your future." Poor Ralph had few leading minds among his acquaintance, and rarely enjoyed the pleasure of buttonholing a celebrity; a state of things which appeared to Miss Stackpole to indicate a deplorable want of enterprise. "If I were on the other side I should call," she said, "and tell the gentleman, whoever he might be, that I had heard a great deal about him and had come to see for myself. But I gather from what you say that this is not the custom here. You seem to have plenty of meaningless customs, and none of those that one really wants. We *are* in advance, certainly. I suppose I shall have to give up the social side altogether;" and Henrietta, though she went about with her guide-book and pencil, and wrote a letter to the *Interviewer* about the Tower (in which she described the execution of Lady Jane Grey), had a depressing sense of falling below her own standard.

The incident which had preceded Isabel's departure from Gardencourt left a painful trace in the girl's mind; she took no pleasure in recalling Lord Warburton's magnanimous disappointment. She could not have done less than what she did; this was certainly true. But her necessity, all the same, had been a distasteful one, and she felt no desire to take credit for her conduct. Nevertheless, mingled with this absence of an intellectual relish of it, was a feeling of freedom which in itself was sweet, and which, as she wandered through the great city with her ill-matched companions, occasionally throbbed into joyous excitement. When she walked in Kensington Gardens, she stopped the children (mainly of the poorer sort) whom she saw playing on the grass; she asked them their names and gave them sixpence, and when they were pretty she kissed them. Ralph noticed such incidents; he noticed everything that Isabel did.

One afternoon, by way of amusing his companions, he invited them to tea in Winchester Square, and he had the house set in order as much as possible, to do honor to their visit. There was another guest, also, to meet the ladies, an amiable bachelor, an old friend of Ralph's, who happened to be in town, and who got on uncommonly well with Miss Stackpole. Mr. Bantling, a stout, fair, smiling man of forty, who was extraordinarily well dressed, and whose contributions to the conversation were characterized by vivacity rather than continuity, laughed immoderately at everything Henrietta said, gave her several cups of tea, examined in her society the *bric-à-brac*, of which Ralph had a considerable collection, and afterwards, when the host proposed they should go out into the square and pretend it was a *fête-champêtre*, walked round the limited inclosure several times with her and listened with candid interest to her remarks upon the inner life.

"Oh, I see," said Mr. Bantling; "I dare say you found it very quiet at Gardencourt. Naturally there's not much going on there when there's such a lot of illness about. Touchett's very bad, you know; the doctors have forbid his being in England at all, and he has only come back to take care of his father. The old man, I believe, has half-a-dozen things the matter with him. They call it gout, but to my certain knowledge he is dropsical as well, though he doesn't look it. You may depend upon it he has got a lot of water somewhere. Of course that sort of thing makes it awfully slow for people in the house; I wonder they have them under such circumstances. Then I believe Mr. Touchett is always squabbling with his wife; she lives away from her husband, you know, in that extraordinary American way of yours. If you want a house where there is always something going on, I recommend you to go down and stay with my sister, Lady Pensil, in Bedfordshire. I'll write to her tomorrow, and I am sure she'll be delighted to ask you. I know just what you want—you want a house where they go in for theatricals and picnics and that sort of thing. My sister is just that sort of woman; she is always getting up something or other, and she is always glad to have the sort of people that help her. I am sure she'll ask you down by return of post; she is tremendously fond of distinguished people and writers. She writes herself, you know; but I haven't read everything she has written. It's usually poetry, and I don't go in much for poetry—unless it's Byron. I suppose you think a great deal of Byron in America," Mr. Bantling continued, expanding in the stimulating air of Miss Stackpole's attention, bringing up his sequences promptly, and at last changing his topic, with a natural eagerness to provide suitable conversation for so remarkable a woman. He returned, however, ultimately to the idea of Henrietta's going to stay with Lady Pensil, in Bedfordshire. "I understand what you want," he repeated; "you want to see some genuine English sport. The Touchetts are not English at all, you know; they live on a kind of foreign system; they have got some awfully queer ideas. The old man thinks it's wicked to hunt, I am told. You must get down to my sister's in time for the theatricals, and I am sure she will be glad to give you a part. I am sure you act well; I know you are very clever. My sister is forty years old, and she has seven children; but she is going to play the principal part. Of course you needn't act if you don't want to."

In this manner Mr. Bantling delivered himself, while they strolled over the grass in Winchester Square, which, although it had been peppered by the London soot, invited the tread to linger. Henrietta thought her blooming, easy-voiced bachelor, with his impressibility to feminine merit and his suggestiveness of allusion, a very agreeable man, and she valued the opportunity he offered her.

"I don't know but I would go, if your sister should ask me," she said. "I think it would be my duty. What do you call her name?"

"Pensil. It's an odd name, but it isn't a bad one."

"I think one name is as good as another. But what is her rank?"

"Oh, she's a baron's wife; a convenient sort of rank. You are fine enough, and you are not too fine."

"I don't know but what she'd be too fine for me. What do you call the place she lives in—Bedfordshire?"

"She lives away in the northern corner of it. It's a tiresome country, but I daresay you won't mind it. I'll try and run down while you are there."

All this was very pleasant to Miss Stackpole, and she was sorry to be obliged to separate from Lady Pensil's obliging brother. But it happened that she had met the day before, in Piccadilly, some friends whom she had not seen for a year; the Miss Climbers, two ladies from Wilmington, Delaware, who had been traveling on the continent and were now preparing to reembark. Henrietta had a long interview with them on the Piccadilly pavement, and though the three ladies all talked at once, they had not exhausted their accumulated topics. It had been agreed therefore that Henrietta should come and dine with them in their lodgings in Jermyn Street at six o'clock on the morrow, and she now bethought herself of this engagement. She prepared to start for Jermyn Street, taking leave first of Ralph Touchett and Isabel, who, seated on garden chairs in another part of the inclosure, were occupied—if the term may be used—with an exchange of amenities less pointed than the practical colloquy of Miss Stackpole and Mr. Bantling. When it had been settled between Isabel and her friend that they should be reunited at some reputable hour at Pratt's Hotel, Ralph remarked that the latter must have a cab. She could not walk all the way to Jermyn Street.

"I suppose you mean it's improper for me to walk alone!" Henrietta exclaimed. "Merciful powers, have I come to this?"

"There is not the slightest need of your walking alone," said Mr. Bantling, in an off-hand tone expressive of gallantry. "I should be greatly pleased to go with you."

"I simply meant that you would be late for dinner," Ralph answered. "Think of those poor ladies, in their impatience, waiting for you."

"You had better have a hansom, Henrietta," said Isabel.

"I will get you a hansom, if you will trust to me," Mr. Bantling went on. "We might walk a little till we met one."

"I don't see why I shouldn't trust to him, do you?" Henrietta inquired of Isabel.

"I don't see what Mr. Bantling could do to you," Isabel answered, smiling; "but if you like, we will walk with you till you find your cab."

"Never mind; we will go alone. Come on, Mr. Bantling, and take care you get me a good one."

Mr. Bantling promised to do his best, and the two took their departure, leaving Isabel and her cousin standing in the square, over which a clear September twilight had now begun to gather. It was perfectly still; the wide quadrangle of dusky houses showed lights in none of the windows, where the shutters and blinds were closed;

the pavements were a vacant expanse, and putting aside two small children from a neighboring slum, who, attracted by symptoms of abnormal animation in the interior, were squeezing their necks between the rusty railings of the inclosure, the most vivid object within sight was the big red pillar-post on the south-east corner.

"Henrietta will ask him to get into the cab and go with her to Jermyn Street," Ralph observed. He always spoke of Miss Stackpole as Henrietta.

"Very possibly," said his companion.

"Or rather, no, she won't," he went on. "But Bantling will ask leave to get in."

"Very likely again. I am very glad they are such good friends."

"She has made a conquest. He thinks her a brilliant woman. It may go far," said Ralph.

Isabel was silent a moment.

"I call Henrietta a very brilliant woman; but I don't think it will go far," she rejoined at last. "They would never really know each other. He has not the least idea what she really is, and she has no just comprehension of Mr. Bantling."

"There is no more usual basis of matrimony than a mutual misunderstanding. But it ought not to be so difficult to understand Bob Bantling," Ralph added. "He is a very simple fellow."

"Yes, but Henrietta is simpler still. And pray, what am I to do?" Isabel asked, looking about her through the fading light, in which the limited landscape gardening of the square took on a large and effective appearance. "I don't imagine that you will propose that you and I, for our amusement, should drive about London in a hansom."

"There is no reason why we should not stay here—if you don't dislike it. It is very warm; there will be half-an-hour yet before dark; and if you permit it, I will light a cigarette."

"You may do what you please," said Isabel, "if you will amuse me till seven o'clock. I propose at that hour to go back and partake of a simple and solitary repast—two poached eggs and a muffin—at Pratt's Hotel."

"May I not dine with you?" Ralph asked.

"No, you will dine at your club."

They had wandered back to their chairs in the center of the square again, and Ralph had lighted his cigarette. It would have given him extreme pleasure to be present in person at the modest little feast she had sketched; but in default of this he liked even being forbidden. For the moment, however, he liked immensely being alone with her, in the thickening dusk, in the center of the multitudinous town; it made her seem to depend upon him and to be in his power. This power he could exert but vaguely; the best exercise of it was to accept her decisions submissively. There was almost an emotion in doing so.

"Why won't you let me dine with you?" he asked, after a pause.

"Because I don't care for it."

"I suppose you are tired of me."

"I shall be an hour hence. You see I have the gift of foreknowledge."

"Oh, I shall be delightful meanwhile," said Ralph. But he said nothing more, and as Isabel made no rejoinder, they sat some time in silence which seemed to contradict his promise of entertainment. It seemed to him that she was preoccupied, and he wondered what she was thinking about; there were two or three very possible subjects. At last he spoke again. "Is your objection to my society this evening caused by your expectation of another visitor?"

She turned her head with a glance of her clear, fair eyes.

"Another visitor? What visitor should I have?"

He had none to suggest; which made his question seem to himself silly as well as brutal.

"You have a great many friends that I don't know," he said, laughing a little awkwardly. "You have a whole past from which I was perversely excluded."

"You were reserved for my future. You must remember that my past is over there across the water. There is none of it here in London."

"Very good, then, since your future is seated beside you. Capital thing to have your future so handy." And Ralph lighted another cigarette and reflected that Isabel probably meant that she had received news that Mr. Caspar Goodwood had crossed to Paris. After he had lighted his cigarette he puffed it a while, and then he went on. "I promised a while ago to be very amusing; but you see I don't come up to the mark, and the fact is there is a good deal of temerity in my undertaking to amuse a person like you. What do you care for my feeble attempts? You have grand ideas—you have a high standard in such matters. I ought at least to bring in a band of music or a company of mountebanks."

"One mountebank is enough, and you do very well. Pray go on, and in another ten minutes I shall begin to laugh."

"I assure you that I am very serious," said Ralph. "You do really ask a great deal."

"I don't know what you mean. I ask nothing!"

"You accept nothing," said Ralph. She colored, and now suddenly it seemed to her that she guessed his meaning. But why should he speak to her of such things? He hesitated a little, and then he continued. "There is something I should like very much to say to you. It's a question I wish to ask. It seems to me I have a right to ask it, because I have a kind of interest in the answer."

"Ask what you will," Isabel answered gently, "and I will try and satisfy you."

"Well, then, I hope you won't mind my saying that Lord Warburton has told me of something that has passed between you."

Isabel started a little; she sat looking at her open fan. "Very good; I suppose it was natural he should tell you."

"I have his leave to let you know he has done so. He has some hope still," said Ralph.

"Still?"

"He had it a few days ago."

"I don't believe he has any now," said the girl.

"I am very sorry for him, then; he is such a fine fellow."

"Pray, did he ask you to talk to me?"

"No, not that. But he told me because he couldn't help it. We are old friends, and he was greatly disappointed. He sent me a line asking me to come and see him, and I rode over to Lockleigh the day before he and his sister lunched with us. He was very heavy-hearted; he had just got a letter from you."

"Did he show you the letter?" asked Isabel, with momentary loftiness.

"By no means. But he told me it was a neat refusal. I was very sorry for him," Ralph repeated.

For some moments Isabel said nothing; then at last, "Do you know how often he had seen me? Five or six times."

"That's to your glory."

"It's not for that I say it."

"What then do you say it for? Not to prove that poor Warburton's state of mind is superficial, because I am pretty sure you don't think that."

Isabel certainly was unable to say that she thought it; but presently she said something else. "If you have not been requested by Lord Warburton to argue with me, then you are doing it disinterestedly—or for the love of argument."

"I have no wish to argue with you at all. I only wish to leave you alone. I am simply greatly interested in your own sentiments."

"I am greatly obliged to you!" cried Isabel, with a laugh.

"Of course you mean that I am meddling in what doesn't concern me. But why shouldn't I speak to you of this matter without annoying you or embarrassing myself? What's the use of being your cousin, if I can't have a few privileges? What is the use of adoring you without the hope of a reward, if I can't have a few compensations? What is the use of being ill and disabled, and restricted to mere spectatorship at the game of life, if I really can't see the show when I have paid so much for my ticket? Tell me this," Ralph went on, while Isabel listened to him with quickened attention: "What had you in your mind when you refused Lord Warburton?"

"What had I in my mind?"

"What was the logic—the view of your situation—that dictated so remarkable an act?"

"I didn't wish to marry him—if that is logic."

"No, that is not logic—and I knew that before. What was it you said to yourself? You certainly said more than that."

Isabel reflected a moment and then she answered this inquiry with a question of her own. "Why do you call it a remarkable act? That is what your mother thinks, too."

"Warburton is such a fine fellow; as a man I think he has hardly a fault. And then, he is what they call here a swell. He has immense possessions, and his wife would be thought a superior being. He unites the intrinsic and the extrinsic advantages."

Isabel watched her cousin while he spoke, as if to see how far he would go. "I refused him because he was too perfect then. I am not perfect myself, and he is too good for me. Besides, his perfection would irritate me."

"That is ingenious rather than candid," said Ralph. "As a fact, you think nothing in the world too perfect for you."

"Do you think I am so good?"

"No, but you are exacting, all the same, without the excuse of thinking yourself good. Nineteen women out of twenty, however, even of the most exacting sort, would have contented themselves with Warburton. Perhaps you don't know he has been run after."

"I don't wish to know. But it seems to me," said Isabel, "that you told me of several faults that he has, one day when I spoke of him to you."

Ralph looked grave. "I hope that what I said then had no weight with you; for they were not faults, the things I spoke of; they were simply peculiarities of his position. If I had known he wished to marry you, I would never have alluded to them. I think I said that as regards that position he was rather a skeptic. It would have been in your power to make him a believer."

"I think not. I don't understand the matter, and I am not conscious of any mission of that sort.—You are evidently disappointed," Isabel added, looking gently but earnestly at her cousin. "You would have liked me to marry Lord Warburton."

"Not in the least. I am absolutely without a wish on the subject. I don't pretend to advise you, and I content myself with watching you—with the deepest interest."

Isabel gave a rather conscious sigh. "I wish I could be as interesting to myself as I am to you!"

"There you are not candid again; you are extremely interesting to yourself. Do you know, however," said Ralph, "that if you have really given Lord Warburton his final answer, I am rather glad it has been what it was. I don't mean I am glad for you, and still less, of course, for him. I am glad for myself."

"Are you thinking of proposing to me?"

"By no means. From the point of view I speak of that would be fatal; I should kill the goose that supplies me with golden eggs. I use that animal as a symbol of my insane illusions. What I mean is, I shall have the entertainment of seeing what a young lady does who won't marry Lord Warburton."

"That is what your mother counts upon too," said Isabel.

"Ah, there will be plenty of spectators! We shall contemplate the rest of your career. I shall not see all of it, but I shall probably see the most interesting years. Of course, if you were to marry our friend, you would still have a career—a very honorable and brilliant one. But relatively speaking, it would be a little prosaic. It would be definitely marked out in advance; it would be wanting in the unexpected. You know I am extremely fond of the unexpected, and now that you have kept the game in your hands I depend on your giving us some magnificent example of it."

"I don't understand you very well," said Isabel, "but I do so well enough to be able to say that if you look for magnificent examples of anything I shall disappoint you."

"You will do so only by disappointing yourself—and that will go hard with you!"

To this Isabel made no direct reply; there was an amount of truth in it which would bear consideration. At last she said, abruptly—"I don't see what harm there is in my wishing not to tie myself. I don't want to begin life by marrying. There are other things a woman can do."

"There is nothing she can do so well. But you are many-sided."

"If one is two-sided, it is enough," said Isabel.

"You are the most charming of polygons!" Ralph broke out, with a laugh. At a glance from his companion, however, he became grave, and to prove it he went on—"You want to see life, as the young men say."

"I don't think I want to see it as the young men want to see it; but I do want to look about me."

"You want to drain the cup of experience."

"No, I don't wish to touch the cup of experience. It's a poisoned drink! I only want to see for myself."

"You want to see, but not to feel," said Ralph.

"I don't think that if one is a sentient being, one can make the distinction," Isabel returned. "I am a good deal like Henrietta. The other day, when I asked her if she wished to marry, she said—'Not till I have seen Europe!' I too don't wish to marry until I have seen Europe."

"You evidently expect that a crowned head will be struck with you."

"No, that would be worse than marrying Lord Warburton. But it is getting very dark," Isabel continued, "and I must go home." She rose from her place, but Ralph sat still a moment, looking at her. As he did not follow her, she stopped, and they remained a while exchanging a gaze, full on either side, but especially on Ralph's, of utterances too vague for words.

"You have answered my question," said Ralph at last. "You have told me what I wanted. I am greatly obliged to you."

"It seems to me I have told you very little."

"You have told me the great thing: that the world interests you and that you want to throw yourself into it."

Isabel's silvery eyes shone for a moment in the darkness. "I never said that."

"I think you meant it. Don't repudiate it; it's so fine!"

"I don't know what you are trying to fasten upon me, for I am not in the least an adventurous spirit. Women are not like men."

Ralph slowly rose from his seat, and they walked together to the gate of the square. "No," he said; "women rarely boast of their courage; men do so with a certain frequency."

"Men have it to boast of!"

"Women have it too; you have a great deal."

"Enough to go home in a cab to Pratt's Hotel; but not more."

Ralph unlocked the gate, and after they had passed out he fastened it.

"We will find your cab," he said; and as they turned toward a neighboring street in which it seemed that this quest would be fruitful, he asked her again if he might not see her safely to the inn.

"By no means," she answered; "you are very tired; you must go home and go to bed."

The cab was found, and he helped her into it, standing a moment at the door.

"When people forget I am a sick man I am often annoyed," he said. "But it's worse when they remember it!"

❧ 16 ❧

Isabel had had no hidden motive in wishing her cousin not to take her home; it simply seemed to her that for some days past she had consumed an inordinate quantity of his time, and the independent spirit of the American girl who ends by regarding perpetual assistance as a sort of derogation to her sanity, had made her decide that for these few hours she must suffice to herself. She had moreover a great fondness for intervals of solitude, and since her arrival in England it had been but scantily gratified. It was a luxury she could always command at home, and she had missed it. That evening, however, an incident occurred which—had there been a critic to note it—would have taken all color from the theory that the love of solitude had caused her to dispense with Ralph's attendance. She was sitting, toward nine o'clock, in the dim illumination of Pratt's Hotel, trying with the aid of two tall candles to lose herself in a volume she had brought from Gardencourt, but succeeding only to the extent of reading other words on the page than those that were printed there—words that Ralph had spoken to her in the afternoon.

Suddenly the well-muffled knuckle of the waiter was applied to the door, which presently admitted him, bearing the card of a visitor. This card, duly considered, offered to Isabel's startled vision the name of Mr. Caspar Goodwood. She let the servant stand before her inquiringly for some instants, without signifying her wishes.

"Shall I show the gentleman up, ma'am?" he asked at last, with a slightly encouraging inflection.

Isabel hesitated still, and while she hesitated she glanced at the mirror.

"He may come in," she said at last; and waited for him with some emotion.

Caspar Goodwood came in and shook hands with her. He said nothing till the servant had left the room again, then he said—

"Why didn't you answer my letter?"

He spoke in a quick, full, slightly peremptory tone—the tone of a man whose questions were usually pointed, and who was capable of much insistence.

Isabel answered him by a question.

"How did you know I was here?"

"Miss Stackpole let me know," said Caspar Goodwood. "She told me that you would probably be at home alone this evening, and would be willing to see me."

"Where did she see you—to tell you that?"

"She didn't see me; she wrote to me."

Isabel was silent; neither of them had seated themselves; they stood there with a certain air of defiance, or at least of contention.

"Henrietta never told me that she was writing to you," Isabel said at last. "This is not kind of her."

"Is it so disagreeable to you to see me?" asked the young man.

"I didn't expect it. I don't like such surprises."

"But you knew I was in town; it was natural we should meet."

"Do you call this meeting? I hoped I should not see you. In so large a place as London it seemed to me very possible."

"Apparently it was disagreeable to you even to write to me," said Mr. Goodwood.

Isabel made no answer to this; the sense of Henrietta Stackpole's treachery, as she momentarily qualified it, was strong within her.

"Henrietta is not delicate!" she exclaimed with a certain bitterness. "It was a great liberty to take."

"I suppose I am not delicate either. The fault is mine as much as hers."

As Isabel looked at him it seemed to her that his jaw had never been more square. This might have displeased her; nevertheless she rejoined inconsequently—

"No, it is not your fault so much as hers. What you have done is very natural."

"It is indeed!" cried Caspar Goodwood, with a voluntary laugh. "And now that I have come, at any rate, may I not stay?"

"You may sit down, certainly."

And Isabel went back to her chair again, while her visitor took the first place that offered, in the manner of a man accustomed to pay little thought to the sort of chair he sat in.

"I have been hoping every day for an answer to my letter," he said. "You might have written me a few lines."

"It was not the trouble of writing that prevented me; I could as easily have written you four pages as one. But my silence was deliberate; I thought it best."

He sat with his eyes fixed on hers while she said this; then he lowered them and attached them to a spot in the carpet, as if he were making a strong effort to say nothing but what he ought to say. He was a strong man in the wrong, and he was acute enough to see that an uncompromising exhibition of his strength would only throw the falsity of his position into relief. Isabel was not incapable of finding it agreeable to have an advantage of position over a person of this quality, and though she was not a girl to flaunt her advantage in his face, she was woman enough to enjoy being able to say "You know you ought not to have written to me yourself!" and to say it with a certain air of triumph.

Caspar Goodwood raised his eyes to hers again; they wore an expression of ardent remonstrance. He had a strong sense of justice, and he was ready any day in the year—over and above this—to argue the question of his rights.

"You said you hoped never to hear from me again; I know that. But I never accepted the prohibition. I promised you that you should hear very soon."

"I did not say that I hoped never to hear from you," said Isabel.

"Not for five years, then; for ten years. It is the same thing."

"Do you find it so? It seems to me there is a great difference. I can imagine that at the end of ten years we might have a very pleasant correspondence. I shall have matured my epistolary style."

Isabel looked away while she spoke these words, for she knew they were of a much less earnest cast than the countenance of her listener. Her eyes, however, at last came back to him, just as he said, very irrelevantly—

"Are you enjoying your visit to your uncle?"

"Very much indeed." She hesitated, and then she broke out with even greater irrelevance, "What good do you expect to get by insisting?"

"The good of not losing you."

"You have no right to talk about losing what is not yours. And even from your own point of view," Isabel added, "you ought to know when to let one alone."

"I displease you very much," said Caspar Goodwood gloomily; not as if to provoke her to compassion for a man conscious of this blighting fact, but as if to set it well before himself, so that he might endeavor to act with his eyes upon it.

"Yes, you displease me very much, and the worst is that it is needless."

Isabel knew that his was not a soft nature, from which pinpricks would draw blood; and from the first of her acquaintance with him and of her having to defend herself against a certain air that he had of knowing better what was good for her than she knew herself, she had recognized the fact that perfect frankness was her best weapon. To attempt to spare his sensibility or to escape from him edgewise, as one might do from a man who had barred the way less sturdily—this, in dealing with Caspar Goodwood, who would take everything of every sort that one might give him, was wasted agility. It was not that he had not susceptibilities, but his passive surface, as well as his active, was large and firm, and he might always be trusted to dress his wounds himself. In measuring the effect of his suffering, one might always reflect that he had a sound constitution.

"I can't reconcile myself to that," he said.

There was a dangerous liberality about this; for Isabel felt that it was quite open to him to say that he had not always displeased her.

"I can't reconcile myself to it either, and it is not the state of things that ought to exist between us. If you would only try and banish me from your mind for a few months we should be on good terms again."

"I see. If I should cease to think of you for a few months I should find I could keep it up indefinitely."

"Indefinitely is more than I ask. It is more even than I should like."

"You know that what you ask is impossible," said the young man, taking his adjective for granted in a manner that Isabel found irritating.

"Are you not capable of making an effort?" she demanded. "You are strong for everything else; why shouldn't you be strong for that?"

"Because I am in love with you," said Caspar Goodwood simply. "If one is strong, one loves only the more strongly."

"There is a good deal in that;" and indeed our young lady felt the force of it. "Think of me or not, as you find most possible; only leave me alone."

"Until when?"

"Well, for a year or two."

"Which do you mean? Between one year and two there is a great difference."

"Call it two, then," said Isabel, wondering whether a little cynicism might not be effective.

"And what shall I gain by that?" Mr. Goodwood asked, giving no sign of wincing.

"You will have obliged me greatly."

"But what will be my reward?"

"Do you need a reward for an act of generosity?"

"Yes, when it involves a great sacrifice."

"There is no generosity without sacrifice. Men don't understand such things. If you make this sacrifice I shall admire you greatly."

"I don't care a straw for your admiration. Will you marry me? That is the question."

"Assuredly not, if I feel as I feel at present."

"Then I ask again, what I shall gain?"

"You will gain quite as much as by worrying me to death!"

Caspar Goodwood bent his eyes again and gazed for a while into the crown of his hat. A deep flush overspread his face, and Isabel could perceive that this dart at last had struck home. To see a strong man in pain had something terrible for her, and she immediately felt very sorry for her visitor.

"Why do you make me say such things to you?" she cried in a trembling voice. "I only want to be gentle—to be kind. It is not delightful to me to feel that people care for me, and yet to have to try and reason them out of it. I think others also ought to be considerate; we have each to judge for ourselves. I know you are considerate, as much as you can be; you have good reasons for what you do. But I don't want to marry. I shall probably never marry. I have a perfect right to feel that way, and it is no kindness to a woman to urge her—to persuade her against her will. If I give you pain I can only say I am very sorry. It is not my fault; I can't marry you simply to please you. I won't say that I shall always remain your friend, because when women say that, in these circumstances, it is supposed, I believe, to be a sort of mockery. But try me some day."

Caspar Goodwood, during this speech, had kept his eyes fixed upon the name of his hatter, and it was not until some time after she had ceased speaking that he raised them. When he did so, the sight of a certain rosy, lovely eagerness in Isabel's face threw some confusion into his attempt to analyze what she had said. "I will go home—I will go tomorrow—I will leave you alone," he murmured at last. "Only," he added in a louder tone—"I hate to lose sight of you!"

"Never fear. I will do no harm."

"You will marry someone else," said Caspar Goodwood.

"Do you think that is a generous charge?"

"Why not? Plenty of men will ask you."

"I told you just now that I don't wish to marry, and that I shall probably never do so."

"I know you did; but I don't believe it."

"Thank you very much. You appear to think I am attempting to deceive you; you say very delicate things."

"Why should I not say that? You have given me no promise that you will not marry."

"No, that is all that would be wanting!" cried Isabel, with a bitter laugh.

"You think you won't, but you will," her visitor went on, as if he were preparing himself for the worst.

"Very well, I will then. Have it as you please."

"I don't know, however," said Caspar Goodwood, "that my keeping you in sight would prevent it."

"Don't you indeed? I am, after all, very much afraid of you. Do you think I am so very easily pleased?" she asked suddenly, changing her tone.

"No, I don't; I shall try and console myself with that. But there are a certain number of very clever men in the world; if there were only one, it would be enough. You will be sure to take no one who is not."

"I don't need the aid of a clever man to teach me how to live," said Isabel. "I can find it out for myself."

"To live alone, do you mean? I wish that when you have found that out, you would teach me."

Isabel glanced at him a moment; then, with a quick smile—"Oh, *you* ought to marry!" she said.

Poor Caspar may be pardoned if for an instant this exclamation seemed to him to have the infernal note, and I cannot take upon myself to say that Isabel uttered it in obedience to an impulse strictly celestial. It was a fact, however, that it had always seemed to her that Caspar Goodwood, of all men, ought to enjoy the whole devotion of some tender woman. "God forgive you!" he murmured between his teeth, turning away.

Her exclamation had put her slightly in the wrong, and after a moment she felt the need to right herself. The easiest way to do it was to put her suitor in the wrong. "You do me great injustice—you say what you don't know!" she broke out. "I should not be an easy victim—I have proved it."

"Oh, to me, perfectly."

"I have proved it to others as well." And she paused a moment. "I refused a proposal of marriage last week—what they call a brilliant one."

"I am very glad to hear it," said the young man, gravely.

"It was a proposal that many girls would have accepted; it had everything to recommend it." Isabel had hesitated to tell this story, but now she had begun, the satisfaction of speaking it out and doing herself justice took possession of her. "I was offered a great position and a great fortune—by a person whom I like extremely."

Caspar gazed at her with great interest. "Is he an Englishman?"

"He is an English nobleman," said Isabel.

Mr. Goodwood received this announcement in silence; then, at last, he said—"I am glad he is disappointed."

"Well, then, as you have companions in misfortune, make the best of it."

"I don't call him a companion," said Caspar, grimly.

"Why not—since I declined his offer absolutely?"

"That doesn't make him my companion. Besides, he's an Englishman."

"And pray is not an Englishman a human being?" Isabel inquired.

"Oh, no; he's superhuman."

"You are angry," said the girl. "We have discussed this matter quite enough."

"Oh, yes, I am angry. I plead guilty to that!"

Isabel turned away from him, walked to the open window, and stood a moment looking into the dusky vacancy of the street, where a turbid gaslight alone represented social animation. For some time neither of these young persons spoke; Caspar lingered near the chimney-piece, with his eyes gloomily fixed upon our heroine. She had virtually requested him to withdraw—he knew that; but at the risk of making himself odious to her he kept his ground. She was far too dear to him to be easily forfeited, and he had sailed across the Atlantic to extract some pledge from her. Presently she left the window and stood before him again.

"You do me very little justice," she said—"after my telling you what I told you just now. I am sorry I told you—since it matters so little to you."

"Ah," cried the young man, "if you were thinking of *me* when you did it!" And then he paused, with the fear that she might contradict so happy a thought.

"I was thinking of you a little," said Isabel.

"A little? I don't understand. If the knowledge that I love you had any weight with you at all, it must have had a good deal."

Isabel shook her head impatiently, as if to carry off a blush. "I have refused a noble gentleman. Make the most of that."

"I thank you, then," said Caspar Goodwood, gravely. "I thank you immensely."

"And now you had better go home."

"May I not see you again?" he asked.

"I think it is better not. You will be sure to talk of this, and you see it leads to nothing."

"I promise you not to say a word that will annoy you."

Isabel reflected a little, and then she said—"I return in a day or two to my uncle's, and I can't propose to you to come there; it would be very inconsistent."

Caspar Goodwood, on his side, debated within himself. "You must do me justice too. I received an invitation to your uncle's more than a week ago, and I declined it."

"From whom was your invitation?" Isabel asked, surprised.

"From Mr. Ralph Touchett, whom I suppose to be your cousin. I declined it because I had not your authorization to accept it. The suggestion that Mr. Touchett should invite me appeared to have come from Miss Stackpole."

"It certainly did not come from me. Henrietta certainly goes very far," Isabel added.

"Don't be too hard on her—that touches me."

"No; if you declined, that was very proper of you, and I thank you for it." And Isabel gave a little shudder of dismay at the thought that Lord Warburton and Mr.

Goodwood might have met at Gardencourt: it would have been so awkward for Lord Warburton!

"When you leave your uncle, where are you going?" Caspar asked.

"I shall go abroad with my aunt—to Florence and other places."

The serenity of this announcement struck a chill to the young man's heart; he seemed to see her whirled away into circles from which he was inexorably excluded. Nevertheless he went on quickly with his questions. "And when shall you come back to America?"

"Perhaps not for a long time; I am very happy here."

"Do you mean to give up your country?"

"Don't be an infant."

"Well, you will be out of my sight indeed!" said Caspar Goodwood.

"I don't know," she answered, rather grandly. "The world strikes me as small."

"It is too large for me!" Caspar exclaimed, with a simplicity which our young lady might have found touching if her face had not been set against concessions.

This attitude was part of a system, a theory, that she had lately embraced, and to be thorough she said after a moment—"Don't think me unkind if I say that it's just that—being out of your sight—that I like. If you were in the same place as I, I should feel as if you were watching me, and I don't like that. I like my liberty too much. If there is a thing in the world that I am fond of," Isabel went on, with a slight recurrence of the grandeur that had shown itself a moment before—"it is my personal independence."

But whatever there was of grandeur in this speech moved Caspar Goodwood's admiration; there was nothing that displeased him in the sort of feeling it expressed. This feeling not only did no violence to his way of looking at the girl he wished to make his wife, but seemed a grace the more in so ardent a spirit. To his mind she had always had wings, and this was but the flutter of those stainless pinions. He was not afraid of having a wife with a certain largeness of movement; he was a man of long steps himself. Isabel's words, if they had been meant to shock him, failed of the mark, and only made him smile with the sense that here was common ground. "Who would wish less to curtail your liberty than I?" he asked. "What can give me greater pleasure than to see you perfectly independent—doing whatever you like? It is to make you independent that I want to marry you."

"That's a beautiful sophism," said the girl, with a smile more beautiful still.

"An unmarried woman—a girl of your age—is not independent. There are all sorts of things she can't do. She is hampered at every step."

"That's as she looks at the question," Isabel answered, with much spirit. "I am not in my first youth—I can do what I choose—I belong quite to the independent class. I have neither father nor mother; I am poor; I am of a serious disposition, and not pretty. I therefore am not bound to be timid and conventional; indeed I can't afford such luxuries. Besides, I try to judge things for myself; to judge wrong, I think, is more honorable than not to judge at all. I don't wish to be a mere sheep in the flock; I wish to choose my fate and know something of human affairs beyond what other people think it compatible with propriety to tell me." She paused a moment, but not long enough for her companion to reply. He was apparently on the point of doing so, when she went on—"Let me say this to you, Mr. Goodwood. You are so kind as to speak of being afraid of my marrying. If you should hear a rumor that I am on the point of doing so—girls are liable to have such things said about them—remember what I have told you about my love of liberty, and venture to doubt it."

There was something almost passionately positive in the tone in which Isabel gave him this advice, and he saw a shining candor in her eyes which helped him to believe her. On the whole he felt reassured, and you might have perceived it by the manner in which he said, quite eagerly—"You want simply to travel for two years? I am quite willing to wait two years, and you may do what you like in the interval. If that is all you want, pray say so. I don't want you to be conventional; do I strike you as conventional myself? Do you want to improve your mind? Your mind is quite good enough for me; but if it interests you to wander about a while and see different countries, I shall be delighted to help you, in any way in my power."

"You are very generous; that is nothing new to me. The best way to help me will be to put as many hundred miles of sea between us as possible."

"One would think you were going to commit a crime!" said Caspar Goodwood.

"Perhaps I am. I wish to be free even to do that, if the fancy takes me."

"Well then," he said, slowly, "I will go home." And he put out his hand, trying to look contented and confident.

Isabel's confidence in him, however, was greater than any he could feel in her. Not that he thought her capable of committing a crime; but, turn it over as he would, there was something ominous in the way she reserved her option. As Isabel took his hand, she felt a great respect for him; she knew how much he cared for her, and she thought him magnanimous. They stood so for a moment, looking at each other, united by a handclasp which was not merely passive on her side. "That's right," she said, very kindly, almost tenderly. "You will lose nothing by being a reasonable man."

"But I will come back, wherever you are, two years hence," he returned, with characteristic grimness.

We have seen that our young lady was inconsequent, and at this she suddenly changed her note. "Ah, remember, I promise nothing—absolutely nothing!" Then more softly, as if to help him to leave her, she added—"And remember, too, that I shall not be an easy victim!"

"You will get very sick of your independence."

"Perhaps I shall; it is even very probable. When that day comes I shall be very glad to see you."

She had laid her hand on the knob of the door that led into her room, and she waited a moment to see whether her visitor would not take his departure. But he appeared unable to move; there was still an immense unwillingness in his attitude—a deep remonstrance in his eyes.

"I must leave you now," said Isabel; and she opened the door, and passed into the other room.

This apartment was dark, but the darkness was tempered by a vague radiance sent up through the window from the court of the hotel, and Isabel could make out the masses of the furniture, the dim shining of the mirror, and the looming of the big four-posted bed. She stood still a moment, listening, and at last she heard Caspar Goodwood walk out of the sitting room and close the door behind him. She stood still a moment longer, and then, by an irresistible impulse, she dropped on her knees before her bed, and hid her face in her arms.

❧ 17 ❧

She was not praying; she was trembling—trembling all over. She was an excitable creature, and now she was much excited; but she wished to resist her excitement, and the attitude of prayer, which she kept for some time, seemed to help her to be still. She was extremely glad Caspar Goodwood was gone; there was something exhilarating in having got rid of him. As Isabel became conscious of this feeling she bowed her head a little lower; the feeling was there, throbbing in her heart; it was a part of her emotion; but it was a thing to be ashamed of—it was profane and out of place. It was not for some ten minutes that she rose from her knees, and when she came back to the sitting room she was still trembling a little. Her agitation had two causes; part of it was to be accounted for by her long discussion with Mr. Goodwood, but it might be feared that the rest was simply the enjoyment she found in the exercise of her power. She sat down in the same chair again, and took up her book, but without going through the form of opening the volume. She leaned back, with that low, soft, aspiring murmur with which she often expressed her gladness in accidents of which the brighter side was not superficially obvious, and gave herself up to the satisfaction of having refused two ardent suitors within a fortnight. That love of liberty of which she had given Caspar Goodwood so bold a sketch was as yet almost exclusively theoretic; she had not been able to indulge it on a large scale. But it seemed to her that she had done something; she had tasted of the delight, if not of battle, at least of victory; she had done what she preferred. In the midst of this agreeable sensation the image of Mr. Goodwood taking his sad walk homeward through the dingy town presented itself with a certain reproachful force; so that, as at the same moment the door of the room was opened, she rose quickly with an apprehension that he had come back. But it was only Henrietta Stackpole returning from her dinner.

Miss Stackpole immediately saw that something had happened to Isabel, and indeed the discovery demanded no great penetration. Henrietta went straight up to her friend, who received her without a greeting. Isabel's elation in having sent Caspar Goodwood back to America presupposed her being glad that he had come to see her; but at the same time she perfectly remembered that Henrietta had had no right to set a trap for her.

"Has he been here, dear?" Miss Stackpole inquired, softly.

Isabel turned away, and for some moments answered nothing.

"You acted very wrongly," she said at last.

"I acted for the best, dear. I only hope you acted as well."

"You are not the judge. I can't trust you," said Isabel.

This declaration was unflattering, but Henrietta was much too unselfish to heed the charge it conveyed; she cared only for what it intimated with regard to her friend.

"Isabel Archer," she declared, with equal abruptness and solemnity, "if you marry one of these people, I will never speak to you again!"

"Before making so terrible a threat, you had better wait till I am asked," Isabel replied. Never having said a word to Miss Stackpole about Lord Warburton's overtures, she had now no impulse whatever to justify herself to Henrietta by telling her that she had refused that nobleman.

"Oh, you'll be asked quick enough, once you get off on the continent. Annie Climber was asked three times in Italy—poor plain little Annie."

"Well, if Annie Climber was not captured, why should I be?"

"I don't believe Annie was pressed; but you'll be."

"That's a flattering conviction," said Isabel, with a laugh.

"I don't flatter you, Isabel, I tell you the truth!" cried her friend. "I hope you don't mean to tell me that you didn't give Mr. Goodwood some hope."

"I don't see why I should tell you anything; as I said to you just now, I can't trust you. But since you are so much interested in Mr. Goodwood, I won't conceal from you that he returns immediately to America."

"You don't mean to say you have sent him off?" Henrietta broke out in dismay.

"I asked him to leave me alone; and I ask you the same, Henrietta."

Miss Stackpole stood there with expanded eyes, and then she went to the mirror over the chimney-piece and took off her bonnet.

"I hope you have enjoyed your dinner," Isabel remarked, lightly, as she did so.

But Miss Stackpole was not to be diverted by frivolous propositions, nor bribed by the offer of autobiographic opportunities.

"Do you know where you are going, Isabel Archer?"

"Just now I am going to bed," said Isabel, with persistent frivolity.

"Do you know where you are drifting?" Henrietta went on, holding out her bonnet delicately.

"No, I haven't the least idea, and I find it very pleasant not to know. A swift carriage, of a dark night, rattling with four horses over roads that one can't see—that's my idea of happiness."

"Mr. Goodwood certainly didn't teach you to say such things as that—like the heroine of an immoral novel," said Miss Stackpole. "You are drifting to some great mistake."

Isabel was irritated by her friend's interference, but even in the midst of her irritation she tried to think what truth this declaration could represent. She could think of nothing that diverted her from saying—"You must be very fond of me, Henrietta, to be willing to be so disagreeable to me."

"I love you, Isabel," said Miss Stackpole, with feeling.

"Well, if you love me, let me alone. I asked that of Mr. Goodwood, and I must also ask it of you."

"Take care you are not let alone too much."

"That is what Mr. Goodwood said to me. I told him I must take the risks."

"You are a creature of risks—you make me shudder!" cried Henrietta. "When does Mr. Goodwood return to America?"

"I don't know—he didn't tell me."

"Perhaps you didn't inquire," said Henrietta, with the note of righteous irony.

"I gave him too little satisfaction to have the right to ask questions of him."

This assertion seemed to Miss Stackpole for a moment to bid defiance to comment; but at last she exclaimed—"Well, Isabel, if I didn't know you, I might think you were heartless!"

"Take care," said Isabel; "you are spoiling me."

"I am afraid I have done that already. I hope, at least," Miss Stackpole added, "that he may cross with Annie Climber!"

Isabel learned from her the next morning that she had determined not to return to Gardencourt (where old Mr. Touchett had promised her a renewed welcome), but to await in London the arrival of the invitation that Mr. Bantling had promised her from his sister, Lady Pensil. Miss Stackpole related very freely her conversation with Ralph Touchett's sociable friend, and declared to Isabel that she really believed she had now got hold of something that would lead to something. On the receipt of Lady Pensil's letter—Mr. Bantling had virtually guaranteed the arrival of this document—she would immediately depart for Bedfordshire, and if Isabel cared to look out for her impressions in the *Interviewer,* she would certainly find them. Henrietta was evidently going to see something of the inner life this time.

"Do you know where you are drifting, Henrietta Stackpole?" Isabel asked, imitating the tone in which her friend had spoken the night before.

"I am drifting to a big position—that of queen of American journalism. If my next letter isn't copied all over the West, I'll swallow my pen-wiper!"

She had arranged with her friend Miss Annie Climber, the young lady of the continental offers, that they should go together to make those purchases which were to constitute Miss Climber's farewell to a hemisphere in which she at least had been appreciated; and she presently repaired to Jermyn Street to pick up her companion. Shortly after her departure Ralph Touchett was announced, and as soon as he came in Isabel saw that he had something on his mind. He very soon took his cousin into his confidence. He had received a telegram from his mother, telling him that his father had had a sharp attack of his old malady, that she was much alarmed, and that she begged Ralph would instantly return to Gardencourt. On this occasion, at least, Mrs. Touchett's devotion to the electric wire had nothing incongruous.

"I have judged it best to see the great doctor, Sir Matthew Hope, first," Ralph said; "by great good luck he's in town. He is to see me at half-past twelve, and I shall make sure of his coming down to Gardencourt—which he will do the more readily as he has already seen my father several times, both there and in London. There is an express at two-forty-five, which I shall take, and you will come back with me, or remain here a few days longer, exactly as you prefer."

"I will go with you!" Isabel exclaimed. "I don't suppose I can be of any use to my uncle, but if he is ill I should like to be near him."

"I think you like him," said Ralph, with a certain shy pleasure in his eye. "You appreciate him, which all the world hasn't done. The quality is too fine."

"I think I love him," said Isabel, simply.

"That's very well. After his son, he is your greatest admirer."

Isabel welcomed this assurance, but she gave secretly a little sigh of relief at the thought that Mr. Touchett was one of those admirers who could not propose to marry her. This, however, was not what she said; she went on to inform Ralph that there were other reasons why she should not remain in London. She was tired of it and wished to leave it; and then Henrietta was going away—going to stay in Bedfordshire.

"In Bedfordshire?" Ralph exclaimed, with surprise.

"With Lady Pensil, the sister of Mr. Bantling, who has answered for an invitation."

Ralph was feeling anxious, but at this he broke into a laugh. Suddenly, however, he looked grave again. "Bantling is a man of courage. But if the invitation should get lost on the way?"

"I thought the British post-office was impeccable."

"The good Homer sometimes nods," said Ralph. "However," he went on, more brightly, "the good Bantling never does, and, whatever happens, he will take care of Henrietta."

Ralph went to keep his appointment with Sir Matthew Hope, and Isabel made her arrangements for quitting Pratt's Hotel. Her uncle's danger touched her nearly, and while she stood before her open trunk, looking about her vaguely for what she should put into it, the tears suddenly rushed into her eyes. It was perhaps for this reason that when Ralph came back at two o'clock to take her to the station she was not yet ready.

He found Miss Stackpole, however, in the sitting room, where she had just risen from the lunch table, and this lady immediately expressed her regret at his father's illness.

"He is a grand old man," she said; "he is faithful to the last. If it is really to be the last—excuse my alluding to it, but you must often have thought of the possibility—I am sorry that I shall not be at Gardencourt."

"You will amuse yourself much more in Bedfordshire."

"I shall be sorry to amuse myself at such a time," said Henrietta, with much propriety. But she immediately added—"I should like so to commemorate the closing scene."

"My father may live a long time," said Ralph, simply. Then, adverting to topics more cheerful, he interrogated Miss Stackpole as to her own future.

Now that Ralph was in trouble, she addressed him in a tone of larger allowance, and told him that she was much indebted to him for having made her acquainted with Mr. Bantling. "He has told me just the things I want to know," she said; "all the society items and all about the royal family. I can't make out that what he tells me about the royal family is much to their credit; but he says that's only my peculiar way of looking at it. Well, all I want is that he should give me the facts; I can put them together quick enough, once I've got them." And she added that Mr. Bantling had been so good as to promise to come and take her out in the afternoon.

"To take you where?" Ralph ventured to inquire.

"To Buckingham Palace. He is going to show me over it, so that I may get some idea how they live."

"Ah," said Ralph, "we leave you in good hands. The first thing we shall hear is that you are invited to Windsor Castle."

"If they ask me, I shall certainly go. Once I get started I am not afraid. But for all that," Henrietta added in a moment, "I am not satisfied; I am not satisfied about Isabel."

"What is her last misdemeanor?"

"Well, I have told you before, and I suppose there is no harm in my going on. I always finish a subject that I take up. Mr. Goodwood was here last night."

Ralph opened his eyes; he even blushed a little—his blush being the sign of an emotion somewhat acute. He remembered that Isabel, in separating from him in Winchester Square, had repudiated his suggestion that her motive in doing so was the expectation of a visitor at Pratt's Hotel, and it was a novel sensation to him to have to suspect her of duplicity. On the other hand, he quickly said to himself, what concern was it of his that she should have made an appointment with a lover? Had it not been thought graceful in every age that young ladies should make a mystery of such appointments? Ralph made Miss Stackpole a diplomatic answer. "I should have thought that, with the views you expressed to me the other day, that would satisfy you perfectly."

"That he should come to see her? That was very well, as far as it went. It was a little plot of mine; I let him know that we were in London, and when it had been arranged that I should spend the evening out, I just sent him a word—a word to the wise. I hoped he would find her alone; I won't pretend I didn't hope that you would be out of the way. He came to see her; but he might as well have stayed away."

"Isabel was cruel?" Ralph inquired, smiling, and relieved at learning that his cousin had not deceived him.

"I don't exactly know what passed between them. But she gave him no satisfaction—she sent him back to America."

"Poor Mr. Goodwood!" Ralph exclaimed.

"Her only idea seems to be to get rid of him," Henrietta went on.

"Poor Mr. Goodwood!" repeated Ralph. The exclamation, it must be confessed, was somewhat mechanical. It failed exactly to express his thoughts, which were taking another line.

"You don't say that as if you felt it; I don't believe you care."

"Ah," said Ralph, "you must remember that I don't know this interesting young man—that I have never seen him."

"Well, I shall see him, and I shall tell him not to give up. If I didn't believe Isabel would come round," said Miss Stackpole—"well, I'd give her up myself!"

❧ 18 ❧

It had occurred to Ralph that under the circumstances Isabel's parting with Miss Stackpole might be of a slightly embarrassed nature, and he went down to the door of the hotel in advance of his cousin, who after a slight delay followed, with the traces of an unaccepted remonstrance, as he thought, in her eye. The two made the journey to Gardencourt in almost unbroken silence, and the servant who met them at the station had no better news to give them of Mr. Touchett—a fact which caused Ralph to congratulate himself afresh on Sir Matthew Hope's having promised to come down in the five o'clock train and spend the night. Mrs. Touchett, he learned, on reaching home, had been constantly with the old man, and was with him at that moment; and this fact made Ralph say to himself that, after all, what his mother wanted was simply opportunity. The finest natures were those that shone on large occasions. Isabel went to her own room, noting, throughout the house, that perceptible hush which precedes a crisis. At the end of an hour, however, she came downstairs in search of her aunt, whom she wished to ask about Mr. Touchett. She went into the library, but Mrs. Touchett was not there, and as the weather, which had been damp and chill, was now altogether spoiled, it was not probable that she had gone for her usual walk in the grounds. Isabel was on the point of ringing to send an inquiry to her room, when her attention was taken by an unexpected sound—the sound of low music proceeding apparently from the drawing room. She knew that her aunt never touched the piano, and the musician was therefore probably Ralph, who played for his own amusement. That he should have resorted to this recreation at the present time, indicated apparently that his anxiety about his father had been relieved; so that Isabel took her way to the drawing room with much alertness. The drawing room at Gardencourt was an apartment of great distances, and as the piano was placed at the end of it furthest removed from the door at which Isabel entered, her arrival was not noticed by the person seated before the instrument. This person was neither Ralph nor his mother; it was a lady whom Isabel immediately saw to be a stranger to herself, although her back was presented to the door. This back—an ample and well-dressed one—Isabel contemplated for some moments in surprise. The lady was of course a visitor who had arrived during her absence, and who had not been mentioned by either of the servants—one of them her aunt's maid—of whom she had had speech since her return. Isabel had already learned, however, that the British domestic is not effusive, and she was particularly conscious of having been treated with dryness by her aunt's maid, whose offered assistance the young lady from Albany—versed, as young ladies are in Albany, in the very metaphysics of the toilet—had perhaps made too light of. The arrival of a visitor was far from disagreeable to Isabel; she had not yet divested herself of a youthful impression that each new acquaintance would exert some momentous influence upon her life. By the time she had made these reflections she became aware that the lady at the piano played remarkably well. She was playing something of Beethoven's—Isabel knew not what, but she recognized Beethoven—and she touched the piano softly and discreetly, but with evident skill. Her touch was that of an artist; Isabel sat down noiselessly on the nearest chair and waited till the end of the piece. When it was finished she felt a strong desire to thank the player, and rose from her seat to do so, while at the same time the lady at the piano turned quickly round, as if she had become aware of her presence.

"That is very beautiful, and your playing makes it more beautiful still," said Isabel, with all the young radiance with which she usually uttered a truthful rapture.

"You don't think I disturbed Mr. Touchett, then?" the musician answered, as sweetly as this compliment deserved. "The house is so large, and his room so far away, that I thought I might venture—especially as I played just—just *du bout des doigts.*"

"She is a Frenchwoman," Isabel said to herself; "she says that as if she were French." And this supposition made the stranger more interesting to our speculative heroine. "I hope my uncle is doing well," Isabel added. "I should think that to hear such lovely music as that would really make him feel better."

The lady gave a discriminating smile.

"I am afraid there are moments in life when even Beethoven has nothing to say to us. We must admit, however, that they are our worst moments."

"I am not in that state now," said Isabel. "On the contrary, I should be so glad if you would play something more."

"If it will give you pleasure—most willingly." And this obliging person took her place again, and struck a few chords, while Isabel sat down nearer the instrument. Suddenly the stranger stopped, with her hands on the keys, half-turning and looking over her shoulder at the girl. She was forty years old, and she was not pretty; but she had a delightful expression. "Excuse me," she said; "but are you the niece—the young American?"

"I am my aunt's niece," said Isabel, with naiveté.

The lady at the piano sat still a moment longer, looking over her shoulder with her charming smile.

"That's very well," she said, "we are compatriots."

And then she began to play.

"Ah, then she is not French," Isabel murmured; and as the opposite supposition had made her interesting, it might have seemed that this revelation would have diminished her effectiveness. But such was not the fact; for Isabel, as she listened to the music, found much stimulus to conjecture in the fact that an American should so strongly resemble a foreign woman.

Her companion played in the same manner as before, softly and solemnly, and while she played the shadows deepened in the room. The autumn twilight gathered in, and from her place Isabel could see the rain, which had now begun in earnest, washing the cold-looking lawn, and the wind shaking the great trees. At last, when the music had ceased, the lady got up, and, coming to her auditor, smiling, before Isabel had time to thank her again, said—

"I am very glad you have come back; I have heard a great deal about you."

Isabel thought her a very attractive person; but she nevertheless said, with a certain abruptness, in answer to this speech—

"From whom have you heard about me?"

The stranger hesitated a single moment, and then—

"From your uncle," she answered. "I have been here three days, and the first day he let me come and pay him a visit in his room. Then he talked constantly of you."

"As you didn't know me, that must have bored you."

"It made me want to know you. All the more that since then—your aunt being so much with Mr. Touchett—I have been quite alone, and have got rather tired of my own society. I have not chosen a good moment for my visit."

A servant had come in with lamps, and was presently followed by another, bearing the tea tray. On the appearance of this repast Mrs. Touchett had apparently been notified, for she now arrived and addressed herself to the teapot. Her greeting to her niece did not differ materially from her manner of raising the lid of this receptacle in order to glance at the contents: in neither act was it becoming to make a show of avidity. Questioned about her husband, she was unable to say that he was better; but the local doctor was with him, and much light was expected from this gentleman's consultation with Sir Matthew Hope.

"I suppose you two ladies have made acquaintance?" she said. "If you have not, I recommend you to do so; for so long as we continue—Ralph and I—to cluster about Mr. Touchett's bed, you are not likely to have much society but each other."

"I know nothing about you but that you are a great musician," Isabel said to the visitor.

"There is a good deal more than that to know," Mrs. Touchett affirmed, in her little dry tone.

"A very little of it, I am sure, will content Miss Archer!" the lady exclaimed, with a light laugh. "I am an old friend of your aunt's—I have lived much in Florence—I am Madame Merle."

She made this last announcement as if she were referring to a person of tolerably distinct identity.

For Isabel, however, it represented but little; she could only continue to feel that Madame Merle had a charming manner.

"She is not a foreigner, in spite of her name," said Mrs. Touchett. "She was born—I always forget where you were born."

"It is hardly worthwhile I should tell you, then."

"On the contrary," said Mrs. Touchett, who rarely missed a logical point; "if I remembered, your telling me would be quite superfluous."

Madame Merle glanced at Isabel with a fine, frank smile.

"I was born under the shadow of the national banner."

"She is too fond of mystery," said Mrs. Touchett; "that is her great fault."

"Ah," exclaimed Madame Merle, "I have great faults, but I don't think that is one of them; it certainly is not the greatest. I came into the world in the Brooklyn navy-yard. My father was a high officer in the United States navy, and had a post—a post of responsibility—in that establishment at the time. I suppose I ought to love the sea, but I hate it. That's why I don't return to America. I love the land; the great thing is to love something."

Isabel, as a dispassionate witness, had not been struck with the force of Mrs. Touchett's characterization of her visitor, who had an expressive, communicative, responsive face, by no means of the sort which, to Isabel's mind, suggested a secretive disposition. It was a face that told of a rich nature and of quick and liberal impulses, and though it had no regular beauty was in the highest degree agreeable to contemplate.

Madame Merle was a tall, fair, plump woman; everything in her person was round and replete, though without those accumulations which minister to indolence. Her features were thick, but there was a graceful harmony among them, and her complexion had a healthy clearness. She had a small gray eye, with a great deal of light in it—an eye incapable of dullness, and, according to some people, incapable of tears; and a wide, firm mouth, which, when she smiled, drew itself upward to the left side, in a manner that most people thought very odd, some very affected, and a few very graceful. Isabel inclined to range herself in the last category. Madame Merle had thick, fair hair, which was arranged with picturesque simplicity, and a large white hand, of a perfect shape—a shape so perfect that its owner, preferring to leave it unadorned, wore no rings. Isabel had taken her at first, as we have seen, for a Frenchwoman; but extended observation led her to say to herself that Madame Merle might be a German—a German of rank, a countess, a princess. Isabel would never have supposed that she had been born in Brooklyn—though she could doubtless not have justified her assumption that the air of distinction, possessed by Madame Merle in so eminent a degree, was inconsistent with such a birth. It was true that the national banner had floated immediately over the spot of the lady's nativity, and the breezy freedom of the stars and stripes might have shed an influence upon the attitude which she then and there took toward life. And yet Madame Merle had evidently nothing of the fluttered, flapping quality of a morsel of bunting in the wind; her deportment expressed the repose and confidence which come from a large experience. Experience, however, had not quenched her youth; it had simply made her sympathetic and supple. She was in a word a woman of ardent impulses, kept in admirable order. What an ideal combination! thought Isabel.

She made these reflections while the three ladies sat at their tea; but this ceremony was interrupted before long by the arrival of the great doctor from London, who had been immediately ushered into the drawing room. Mrs. Touchett took him off to the library, to confer with him in private; and then Madame Merle and Isabel parted, to meet again at dinner. The idea of seeing more of this interesting woman did much to mitigate Isabel's perception of the melancholy that now hung over Gardencourt.

When she came into the drawing room before dinner she found the place empty; but in the course of a moment Ralph arrived. His anxiety about his father had been lightened; Sir Matthew Hope's view of his condition was less somber than Ralph's had been. The doctor recommended that the nurse alone should remain with the old man for the next three or four hours; so that Ralph, his mother, and the great physician himself, were free to dine at table. Mrs. Touchett and Sir Matthew came in; Madame Merle was the last to appear.

Before she came, Isabel spoke of her to Ralph, who was standing before the fireplace.

"Pray who is Madame Merle?"

"The cleverest woman I know, not excepting yourself," said Ralph.

"I thought she seemed very pleasant."

"I was sure you would think her pleasant," said Ralph.

"Is that why you invited her?"

"I didn't invite her, and when we came back from London I didn't know she was here. No one invited her. She is a friend of my mother's, and just after you and I went to town, my mother got a note from her. She had arrived in England (she usually lives abroad, though she has first and last spent a good deal of time here), and she asked leave to come down for a few days. Madame Merle is a woman who can make such proposals with perfect confidence; she is so welcome wherever she goes. And with my mother there could be no question of hesitating; she is the one person in the world whom my mother very much admires. If she were not herself (which she after all much prefers), she would like to be Madame Merle. It would, indeed, be a great change."

"Well, she is very charming," said Isabel. "And she plays beautifully."

"She does everything beautifully. She is complete."

Isabel looked at her cousin a moment. "You don't like her."

"On the contrary, I was once in love with her."

"And she didn't care for you, and that's why you don't like her."

"How can we have discussed such things? M. Merle was then living."

"Is he dead now?"

"So she says."

"Don't you believe her?"

"Yes, because the statement agrees with the probabilities. The husband of Madame Merle would be likely to pass away."

Isabel gazed at her cousin again. "I don't know what you mean. You mean something—that you don't mean. What was M. Merle?"

"The husband of Madame."

"You are very odious. Has she any children?"

"Not the least little child—fortunately."

"Fortunately?"

"I mean fortunately for the child; she would be sure to spoil it."

Isabel was apparently on the point of assuring her cousin for the third time that he was odious; but the discussion was interrupted by the arrival of the lady who was the topic of it. She came rustling in quickly, apologizing for being late, fastening a bracelet, dressed in dark blue satin, which exposed a white bosom that was ineffectually covered by a curious silver necklace. Ralph offered her his arm with the exaggerated alertness of a man who was no longer a lover.

Even if this had still been his condition, however, Ralph had other things to think about. The great doctor spent the night at Gardencourt, and returning to London on the morrow, after another consultation with Mr. Touchett's own medical adviser, concurred in Ralph's desire that he should see the patient again on the day following. On the day following Sir Matthew Hope reappeared at Gardencourt, and on this occasion took a less encouraging view of the old man, who had grown worse in the twenty-four hours. His feebleness was extreme, and to his son, who constantly sat by his bedside, it often seemed that his end was at hand. The local doctor, who was a very sagacious man, and in whom Ralph had secretly more confidence than in his distinguished colleague, was constantly in attendance, and Sir Matthew Hope returned several times to Gardencourt. Mr. Touchett was much of the time unconscious; he slept a great deal; he rarely spoke. Isabel had a great desire to be useful to him, and was allowed to watch with him several times when his other attendants (of whom Mrs. Touchett was not the least regular) went to take rest. He never seemed to know her, and she always said to herself—"Suppose he should die while I am sitting here;" an idea which excited her and kept her awake. Once he opened his eyes for a while and fixed them upon her intelligently, but when she went to him, hoping he would recognize her, he closed them and relapsed into unconsciousness. The day after this, however, he revived for a longer time; but on this occasion Ralph was with him alone. The old man began to talk, much to his son's satisfaction, who assured him that they should presently have him sitting up.

"No, my boy," said Mr. Touchett, "not unless you bury me in a sitting posture, as some of the ancients—was it the ancients?—used to do."

"Ah, daddy, don't talk about that," Ralph murmured. "You must not deny that you are getting better."

"There will be no need of my denying it if you don't say so," the old man answered. "Why should we prevaricate, just at the last? We never prevaricated before. I have got to die some time, and it's better to die when one is sick than when one is well. I am very sick—as sick as I shall ever be. I hope you don't want to prove that I shall ever be worse than this? That would be too bad. You don't? Well then."

Having made this excellent point he became quiet, but the next time that Ralph was with him he again addressed himself to conversation. The nurse had gone to her supper and Ralph was alone with him, having just relieved Mrs. Touchett, who had been on guard since dinner. The room was lighted only by the flickering fire, which of late had become necessary, and Ralph's tall shadow was projected upon the wall and ceiling, with an outline constantly varying but always grotesque.

"Who is that with me—is it my son?" the old man asked.

"Yes, it's your son, daddy."

"And is there no one else?"

"No one else."

Mr. Touchett said nothing for a while; and then, "I want to talk a little," he went on.

"Won't it tire you?" Ralph inquired.

"It won't matter if it does. I shall have a long rest. I want to talk about you."

Ralph had drawn nearer to the bed; he sat leaning forward, with his hand on his father's. "You had better select a brighter topic," he said.

"You were always bright; I used to be proud of your brightness. I should like so much to think that you would do something."

"If you leave us," said Ralph, "I shall do nothing but miss you."

"That is just what I don't want; it's what I want to talk about. You must get a new interest."

"I don't want a new interest, daddy. I have more old ones than I know what to do with."

The old man lay there looking at his son; his face was the face of the dying, but his eyes were the eyes of Daniel Touchett. He seemed to be reckoning over Ralph's interests. "Of course you have got your mother," he said at last. "You will take care of her."

"My mother will always take care of herself," Ralph answered.

"Well," said his father, "perhaps as she grows older she will need a little help."

"I shall not see that. She will outlive me."

"Very likely she will; but that's no reason—" Mr. Touchett let his phrase die away in a helpless but not exactly querulous sigh, and remained silent again.

"Don't trouble yourself about us," said his son. "My mother and I get on very well together, you know."

"You get on by always being apart; that's not natural."

"If you leave us, we shall probably see more of each other."

"Well," the old man observed, with wandering irrelevance, "it cannot be said that my death will make much difference in your mother's life."

"It will probably make more than you think."

"Well, she'll have more money," said Mr. Touchett. "I have left her a good wife's portion, just as if she had been a good wife."

"She has been one, daddy, according to her own theory. She has never troubled you."

"Ah, some troubles are pleasant," Mr. Touchett murmured. "Those you have given me, for instance. But your mother has been less—less—what shall I call it? less out of the way since I have been ill. I presume she knows I have noticed it."

"I shall certainly tell her so; I am so glad you mention it."

"It won't make any difference to her; she doesn't do it to please me. She does it to please—to please—" And he lay a while, trying to think why she did it. "She does it to please herself. But that is not what I want to talk about," he added. "It's about you. You will be very well off."

"Yes," said Ralph, "I know that. But I hope you have not forgotten the talk we had a year ago—when I told you exactly what money I should need and begged you to make some good use of the rest."

"Yes, yes, I remember. I made a new will—in a few days. I suppose it was the first time such a thing had happened—a young man trying to get a will made against him."

"It is not against me," said Ralph. "It would be against me to have a large property to take care of. It is impossible for a man in my state of health to spend much money, and enough is as good as a feast."

"Well, you will have enough—and something over. There will be more than enough for one—there will be enough for two."

"That's too much," said Ralph.

"Ah, don't say that. The best thing you can do, when I am gone, will be to marry."

Ralph had foreseen what his father was coming to, and this suggestion was by no means novel. It had long been Mr. Touchett's most ingenious way of expressing the optimistic view of his son's health. Ralph had usually treated it humorously; but present circumstances made the humorous tone impossible. He simply fell back in his chair and returned his father's appealing gaze in silence.

"If I, with a wife who hasn't been very fond of me, have had a very happy life," said the old man, carrying his ingenuity further still, "what a life might you not have, if you should marry a person different from Mrs. Touchett. There are more different from her than there are like her."

Ralph still said nothing; and after a pause his father asked softly—"What do you think of your cousin?"

At this Ralph started, meeting the question with a rather fixed smile. "Do I understand you to propose that I should marry Isabel?"

"Well, that's what it comes to in the end. Don't you like her?"

"Yes, very much." And Ralph got up from his chair and wandered over to the fire. He stood before it an instant and then he stooped and stirred it, mechanically. "I like Isabel very much," he repeated.

"Well," said his father, "I know she likes you. She told me so."

"Did she remark that she would like to marry me?"

"No, but she can't have anything against you. And she is the most charming young lady I have ever seen. And she would be good to you. I have thought a great deal about it."

"So have I," said Ralph, coming back to the bedside again. "I don't mind telling you that."

"You *are* in love with her, then? I should think you would be. It's as if she came over on purpose."

"No, I am not in love with her; but I should be if—if certain things were different."

"Ah, things are always different from what they might be," said the old man. "If you wait for them to change, you will never do anything. I don't know whether you know," he went on; "but I suppose there is no harm in my alluding to it in such an hour as this: there was someone wanted to marry Isabel the other day, and she wouldn't have him."

"I know she refused Lord Warburton; he told me himself."

"Well, that proves that there is a chance for somebody else."

"Somebody else took his chance the other day in London—and got nothing by it."

"Was it you?" Mr. Touchett asked, eagerly.

"No, it was an older friend; a poor gentleman who came over from America to see about it."

"Well, I am sorry for him. But it only proves what I say—that the way is open to you."

"If it is, dear father, it is all the greater pity that I am unable to tread it. I haven't many convictions; but I have three or four that I hold strongly. One is that people, on the whole, had better not marry their cousins. Another is, that people in an advanced stage of pulmonary weakness had better not marry at all."

The old man raised his feeble hand and moved it to and fro a little before his face. "What do you mean by that? You look at things in a way that would make everything wrong. What sort of a cousin is a cousin that you have never seen for more than twenty years of her life? We are all each other's cousins, and if we stopped at that the human race would die out. It is just the same with your weak lungs. You are a great deal better than you used to be. All you want is to lead a natural life. It is a great deal more natural to marry a pretty young lady that you are in love with than it is to remain single on false principles."

"I am not in love with Isabel," said Ralph.

"You said just now that you would be if you didn't think it was wrong. I want to prove to you that it isn't wrong."

"It will only tire you, dear daddy," said Ralph, who marveled at his father's tenacity and at his finding strength to insist. "Then where shall we all be?"

"Where shall you be if I don't provide for you? You won't have anything to do with the bank, and you won't have me to take care of. You say you have got so many interests; but I can't make them out."

Ralph leaned back in his chair, with folded arms; his eyes were fixed for some time in meditation. At last, with the air of a man fairly mustering courage—"I take a great interest in my cousin," he said, "but not the sort of interest you desire. I shall not live many years; but I hope I shall live long enough to see what she does with herself. She is entirely independent of me; I can exercise very little influence upon her life. But I should like to do something for her."

"What should you like to do?"

"I should like to put a little wind in her sails."

"What do you mean by that?"

"I should like to put it into her power to do some of the things she wants. She wants to see the world, for instance. I should like to put money in her purse."

"Ah, I am glad you have thought of that," said the old man. "But I have thought of it too. I have left her a legacy—five thousand pounds."

"That is capital; it is very kind of you. But I should like to do a little more."

Something of that veiled acuteness with which it had been, on Daniel Touchett's part, the habit of a lifetime to listen to a financial proposition, still lingered in the face in which the invalid had not obliterated the man of business. "I shall be happy to consider it," he said, softly.

"Isabel is poor, then. My mother tells me that she has but a few hundred dollars a year. I should like to make her rich."

"What do you mean by rich?"

"I call people rich when they are able to gratify their imagination. Isabel has a great deal of imagination."

"So have you, my son," said Mr. Touchett, listening very attentively, but a little confusedly.

"You tell me I shall have money enough for two. What I want is that you should kindly relieve me of my superfluity and give it to Isabel. Divide my inheritance into two equal halves, and give the second half to her."

"To do what she likes with?"

"Absolutely what she likes."

"And without an equivalent?"

"What equivalent could there be?"

"The one I have already mentioned."

"Her marrying—someone or other? It's just to do away with anything of that sort that I make my suggestion. If she has an easy income she will never have to marry for a support. She wishes to be free, and your bequest will make her free."

"Well, you seem to have thought it out," said Mr. Touchett. "But I don't see why you appeal to me. The money will be yours, and you can easily give it to her yourself."

Ralph started a little. "Ah, dear father, I can't offer Isabel money!"

The old man gave a groan. "Don't tell me you are not in love with her! Do you want me to have the credit of it?"

"Entirely. I should like it simply to be a clause in your will, without the slightest reference to me."

"Do you want me to make a new will, then?"

"A few words will do it; you can attend to it the next time you feel a little lively."

"You must telegraph to Mr. Hilary, then. I will do nothing without my solicitor."

"You shall see Mr. Hilary tomorrow."

"He will think we have quarreled, you and I," said the old man.

"Very probably; I shall like him to think it," said Ralph, smiling; "and to carry out the idea, I give you notice that I shall be very sharp with you."

The humor of this appeared to touch his father; he lay a little while taking it in.

"I will do anything you like," he said at last; "but I'm not sure it's right. You say you want to put wind in her sails; but aren't you afraid of putting too much?"

"I should like to see her going before the breeze!" Ralph answered.

"You speak as if it were for your entertainment."

"So it is, a good deal."

"Well, I don't think I understand," said Mr. Touchett, with a sigh. "Young men are very different from what I was. When I cared for a girl—when I was young—I wanted to do more than look at her. You have scruples that I shouldn't have had, and you have ideas that I shouldn't have had either. You say that Isabel wants to be free, and that her being rich will keep her from marrying for money. Do you think that she is a girl to do that?"

"By no means. But she has less money than she has ever had before; her father gave her everything, because he used to spend his capital. She has nothing but the crumbs of that feast to live on, and she doesn't really know how meager they are—she has yet to learn it. My mother has told me all about it. Isabel will learn it when she is really thrown upon the world, and it would be very painful to me to think of her coming to the consciousness of a lot of wants that she should be unable to satisfy."

"I have left her five thousand pounds. She can satisfy a good many wants with that."

"She can indeed. But she would probably spend it in two or three years."

"You think she would be extravagant then?"

"Most certainly," said Ralph, smiling serenely.

Poor Mr. Touchett's acuteness was rapidly giving place to pure confusion. "It would merely be a question of time, then, her spending the larger sum?"

"No, at first I think she would plunge into that pretty freely; she would probably make over a part of it to each of her sisters. But after that she would come to her senses, remember that she had still a lifetime before her, and live within her means."

"Well, you *have* worked it out," said the old man, with a sigh. "You do take an interest in her, certainly."

"You can't consistently say I go too far. You wished me to go further."

"Well, I don't know," the old man answered. "I don't think I enter into your spirit. It seems to me immoral."

"Immoral, dear daddy?"

"Well, I don't know that it's right to make everything so easy for a person."

"It surely depends upon the person. When the person is good, your making things easy is all to the credit of virtue. To facilitate the execution of good impulses, what can be a nobler act?"

This was a little difficult to follow, and Mr. Touchett considered it for a while. At last he said—

"Isabel is a sweet young girl; but do you think she is as good as that?"

"She is as good as her best opportunities," said Ralph.

"Well," Mr. Touchett declared, "she ought to get a great many opportunities for sixty thousand pounds."

"I have no doubt she will."

"Of course I will do what you want," said the old man. "I only want to understand it a little."

"Well, dear daddy, don't you understand it now?" his son asked, caressingly. "If you don't, we won't take any more trouble about it; we will leave it alone."

Mr. Touchett lay silent a long time. Ralph supposed that he had given up the attempt to understand it. But at last he began again—

"Tell me this first. Doesn't it occur to you that a young lady with sixty thousand pounds may fall a victim to the fortune hunters?"

"She will hardly fall a victim to more than one."

"Well, one is too many."

"Decidedly. That's a risk, and it has entered into my calculation. I think it's appreciable, but I think it's small, and I am prepared to take it."

Poor Mr. Touchett's acuteness had passed into perplexity, and his perplexity now passed into admiration.

"Well, you *have* gone into it!" he exclaimed. "But I don't see what good you are to get of it."

Ralph leaned over his father's pillows and gently smoothed them; he was aware that their conversation had been prolonged to a dangerous point. "I shall get just the good that I said just now I wished to put into Isabel's reach—that of having gratified my imagination. But it's scandalous, the way I have taken advantage of you!"

❧ 19 ❧

As Mrs. Touchett had foretold, Isabel and Madame Merle were thrown much together during the illness of their host, and if they had not become intimate it would have been almost a breach of good manners. Their manners were of the best; but in addition to this they happened to please each other. It is perhaps too much to say that they swore an eternal friendship; but tacitly, at least, they called the future to witness. Isabel did so with a perfectly good conscience, although she would have hesitated to admit that she was intimate with her new friend in the sense which she privately attached to this term. She often wondered, indeed, whether she ever had been, or ever could be, intimate with anyone. She had an ideal of friendship, as well as of several other sentiments, and it did not seem to her in this case—it had not seemed to her in other cases—that the actual completely expressed it. But she often reminded herself that there were essential reasons why one's ideal could not become concrete. It was a thing to believe in, not to see—a matter of faith, not of experience. Experience, however, might supply us with very creditable imitations of it, and the part of wisdom was to make the best of these. Certainly, on the whole, Isabel had never encountered a more agreeable and interesting woman than Madame Merle; she had never met a woman who had less of that fault which is the principal obstacle to friendship—the air of reproducing the more tiresome parts of one's own personality. The gates of the girl's confidence were opened wider than they had ever been; she said things to Madame Merle that she had not yet said to anyone. Sometimes she took alarm at her candor; it was as if she had given to a comparative stranger the key to her cabinet of jewels. These spiritual gems were the only ones of any magnitude that Isabel possessed; but that was all the greater reason why they should be carefully guarded. Afterwards, however, the girl always said to herself that one should never regret a generous error, and that if Madame Merle had not the merits she attributed to her, so much the worse for Madame Merle. There was no doubt she had great merits— she was a charming, sympathetic, intelligent, cultivated woman. More than this (for it had not been Isabel's ill-fortune to go through life without meeting several persons of her own sex, of whom no less could fairly be said), she was rare, she was superior, she was preeminent. There are a great many amiable people in the world, and Madame Merle was far from being vulgarly good-natured and restlessly witty. She knew how to think—an accomplishment rare in women; and she had thought to very good purpose. Of course, too, she knew how to feel; Isabel could not have spent a week with her without being sure of that. This was, indeed, Madame Merle's great talent, her most perfect gift. Life had told upon her; she had felt it strongly, and it was part of the satisfaction that Isabel found in her society that when the girl talked of what she was pleased to call serious matters, her companion understood her so easily and quickly. Emotion, it is true, had become with her rather historic; she made no secret of the fact that the fountain of sentiment, thanks to having been rather violently tapped at one period, did not flow quite so freely as of yore. Her pleasure was now to judge rather than to feel; she freely admitted that of old she had been rather foolish, and now she pretended to be wise.

"I judge more than I used to," she said to Isabel; "but it seems to me that I have earned the right. One can't judge till one is forty; before that we are too eager, too hard, too cruel, and in addition too ignorant. I am sorry for you; it will be a long time before you are forty. But every gain is a loss of some kind; I often think that after forty one can't really feel. The freshness, the quickness have certainly gone. You will keep them longer than most people; it will be a great satisfaction to me to see you some years hence. I want to see what life makes of you. One thing is certain— it can't spoil you. It may pull you about horribly; but I defy it to break you up."

Isabel received this assurance as a young soldier, still panting from a slight skirmish in which he has come off with honor, might receive a pat on the shoulder from his colonel. Like such a recognition of merit, it seemed to come with authority. How could the lightest word do less, of a person who was prepared to say, of almost everything Isabel told her—"Oh, I have been in that, my dear; it passes, like everything else." Upon many of her interlocutors, Madame Merle might have produced an irritating effect; it was so difficult to surprise her. But Isabel, though by no means incapable of desiring to be effective, had not at present this motive. She was too sincere, too interested in her judicious companion. And then, moreover, Madame Merle never said such things in the tone of triumph or of boastfulness; they dropped from her like grave confessions.

A period of bad weather had settled down upon Gardencourt; the days grew shorter, and there was an end to the pretty tea-parties on the lawn. But Isabel had long indoor conversations with her fellow visitor, and in spite of the rain the two ladies often sallied forth for a walk, equipped with the defensive apparatus which the English climate and the English genius have between them brought to such perfection. Madame Merle was very appreciative; she liked almost everything, including the English rain. "There is always a little of it, and never too much at once," she said; "and it never wets you, and it always smells good." She declared that in England the pleasures of smell were great—that in this inimitable island there was a certain mixture of fog and beer and soot which, however odd it might sound, was the national aroma, and was most agreeable to the nostril; and she used to lift the sleeve of her British overcoat and bury her nose in it, to inhale the clear, fine odor of the wool. Poor Ralph Touchett, as soon as the autumn had begun to define itself, became almost a prisoner; in bad weather he was unable to step out of the house, and he used sometimes to stand at one of the windows, with his hands in his pockets, and, with a countenance half rueful, half critical, watch Isabel and Madame Merle as they walked down the avenue under a pair of umbrellas. The roads about Gardencourt were so firm, even in the worst weather, that the two ladies always came back with a healthy glow in their cheeks, looking at the soles of their neat, stout boots, and declaring that their walk had done them inexpressible good. Before lunch Madame Merle was always engaged; Isabel admired the invet-eracy with which she occupied herself. Our heroine had always passed for a person of resources and had taken a certain pride in being one; but she envied the talents, the accomplishments, the aptitudes, of Madame Merle. She found herself desiring to emulate them, and in this and other ways Madame Merle presented herself as a model. "I should like to be like that!" Isabel secretly exclaimed, more than once, as one of her friend's numerous facets suddenly caught the light, and before long she knew that she had learned a lesson from this exemplary woman. It took no very long time, indeed, for Isabel to feel that she was, as the phrase is, under an influ-ence. "What is the harm," she asked herself, "so long as it is a good one? The more one is under a good influence the better. The only thing is to see our steps as we take them—to understand them as we go. That I think I shall always do. I needn't be afraid of becoming too pliable; it is my fault that I am not pliable enough." It is said that imitation is the sincerest flattery; and if Isabel was tempted to reproduce in her deportment some of the most graceful features of that of her friend, it was not so much because she desired herself to shine as because she wished to hold up the lamp for Madame Merle. She liked her extremely; but she admired her even more than she liked her. She sometimes wondered what Henrietta Stackpole would say to her thinking so much of this brilliant fugitive from Brooklyn; and had a conviction that Henrietta would not approve of it. Henrietta would not like Madame Merle; for reasons that she could not have defined, this truth came home to Isabel. On the other hand she was equally sure that should the occasion offer, her new friend would accommodate herself perfectly to her old; Madame Merle was too humorous, too observant, not to do justice to Henrietta, and on becoming acquainted with her would probably give the measure of a tact which Miss Stackpole could not hope to emulate. She appeared to have, in her experience, a touchstone for everything, and somewhere in the capacious pocket of her genial memory she would find the key to Henrietta's virtues. "That is the great thing," Isabel reflected; "that is the supreme good fortune: to be in a better position for appreciating people than they are for appreciating you." And she added that this, when one considered it, was simply the essence of the aristocratic situation. In this light, if in none other, one should aim at the aristocratic situation.

I cannot enumerate all the links in the chain which led Isabel to think of Madame Merle's situation as aristocratic—a view of it never expressed in any reference made to it by that lady herself. She had known great things and great people, but she had never played a great part. She was one of the small ones of the earth; she had not been born to honors; she knew the world too well to be guilty of any fatuous illusions on the subject of her own place in it. She had known a good many of the fortunate few, and was perfectly aware of those points at which their fortune differed from hers. But if by her own measure she was nothing of a personage, she had yet, to Isabel's imagination, a sort of greatness. To be so graceful, so gracious, so wise, so good, and to make so light of it all—that was really to be a great lady; especially when one looked so much like one. If Madame Merle, however, made light of her advantages as regards the world, it was not because she had not, for her own entertainment, taken them, as I have intimated, as seriously as possible. Her natural talents, for instance; these she had zealously cultivated. After breakfast she wrote a succession of letters; her correspondence was a source of surprise to Isabel when they sometimes walked together to the village post-office, to deposit Madame Merle's contribution to the mail. She knew a multitude of people, and, as she told Isabel, something was always turning up to be written about. Of painting she was devotedly fond, and made no more of taking a sketch than of pulling off her gloves. At Gardencourt she was perpetually taking advantage of an hour's sunshine to go out with a camp-stool and a box of watercolors. That she was a brilliant musician we have already perceived, and it was evidence of the fact that when she seated herself at the piano, as she always did in the evening, her listeners resigned themselves without a murmur to losing the entertainment of her talk. Isabel, since she had known Madame Merle, felt ashamed of her own playing, which she now looked upon as meager and artless; and indeed, though she had been thought to play very well, the loss to society when, in taking her place upon the music stool, she turned her back to the room, was usually deemed greater than the gain. When Madame Merle was neither writing, nor painting, nor touching the piano, she was usually employed upon wonderful morsels of picturesque embroidery, cushions, curtains, decorations for the chimney-piece; a sort of work in which her bold, free invention was as remarkable as the agility of her needle. She was never idle, for when she was engaged in none of the ways I have mentioned, she was either reading (she appeared to Isabel to read everything important), or walking out, or playing patience with the cards, or talking with her fellow inmates. And with all this, she always had the social quality; she never was preoccupied, she never pressed too hard. She laid down her pastimes as easily as she took them up; she worked and talked at the same time, and she appeared to attach no importance to anything she did. She gave away her sketches and tapestries; she rose from the piano, or remained there, according to the convenience of her auditors, which she always unerringly divined. She was, in short, a most comfortable, profitable, agreeable person to live with. If for Isabel she had a fault, it was that she was not natural; by which the girl meant, not that she was affected or pretentious; for from these vulgar vices no woman could have been more exempt; but that her nature had been too much overlaid by custom and her angles too much smoothed. She had become too flexible, too supple; she was too finished, too civilized. She was, in a word, too perfectly the social animal that man and woman are supposed to have been intended to be; and she had rid herself of every remnant of that tonic wildness which we may assume to have belonged even to the most amiable persons in the ages before country-house life was the fashion. Isabel found it difficult to think of Madame Merle as an isolated figure; she existed only in her relations with her fellow mortals. Isabel often wondered what her relations might be with her own soul. She always ended, however, by feeling that having a charming surface does not necessarily prove that one is superficial; this was an illusion in which, in her youth, she had only just sufficiently escaped being nourished. Madame Merle was not superficial—not she. She was deep; and her nature spoke nonetheless in her behavior because it spoke a conventional language. "What is language at all but a convention?" said Isabel. "She has the good taste not to pretend, like some people I have met, to express herself by original signs."

"I am afraid you have suffered much," Isabel once found occasion to say to her, in response to some allusion that she had dropped.

"What makes you think that?" Madame Merle asked, with a picturesque smile. "I hope I have not the pose of a martyr."

"No; but you sometimes say things that I think people who have always been happy would not have found out."

"I have not always been happy," said Madame Merle, smiling still, but with a mock gravity, as if she were telling a child a secret. "What a wonderful thing!"

"A great many people give me the impression of never having felt anything very much," Isabel answered.

"It's very true; there are more iron pots, I think, than porcelain ones. But you may depend upon it that everyone has something; even the hardest iron pots have a little bruise, a little hole, somewhere. I flatter myself that I am rather stout porcelain; but if I must tell you the truth I have been chipped and cracked! I do very well for service yet, because I have been cleverly mended; and I try to remain in the cupboard—the quiet, dusky cupboard, where there is an odor of stale spices—as much as I can. But when I have to come out, and into a strong light, then, my dear, I am a horror!"

I know not whether it was on this occasion or some other, that when the conversation had taken the turn I have just indicated, she said to Isabel that some day she would relate her history. Isabel assured her that she should delight to listen to it, and reminded her more than once of this engagement. Madame Merle, however, appeared to desire a postponement, and at last frankly told the young girl that she must wait till they knew each other better. This would certainly happen; a long friendship lay before them. Isabel assented, but at the same time asked Madame Merle if she could not trust her—if she feared a betrayal of confidence.

"It is not that I am afraid of your repeating what I say," the elder lady answered; "I am afraid, on the contrary, of your taking it too much to yourself. You would judge me too harshly; you are of the cruel age." She preferred for the present to talk to Isabel about Isabel, and exhibited the greatest interest in our heroine's history, her sentiments, opinions, prospects. She made her chatter, and listened to her chatter with inexhaustible sympathy and good nature. In all this there was something flattering to the girl, who knew that Madame Merle knew a great many distinguished people, and had lived, as Mrs. Touchett said, in the best company in Europe. Isabel thought the better of herself for enjoying the favor of a person who had so large a field of comparison; and it was perhaps partly to gratify this sense of profiting by comparison that she often begged her friend to tell her about the people she knew. Madame Merle had been a dweller in many lands, and had social ties in a dozen different countries. "I don't pretend to be learned," she would say, "but I think I know my Europe;" and she spoke one day of going to Sweden to stay with an old friend, and another of going to Wallachia to follow up a new acquaintance. With England, where she had often stayed, she was thoroughly familiar; and for Isabel's benefit threw a great deal of light upon the customs of the country and the character of the people, who "after all," as she was fond of saying, were the finest people in the world.

"You must not think it strange, her staying in the house at such a time as this, when Mr. Touchett is passing away," Mrs. Touchett remarked to Isabel. "She is incapable of doing anything indiscreet; she is the best-bred woman I know. It's a favor to me that she stays; she is putting off a lot of visits at great houses," said Mrs. Touchett, who never forgot that when she herself was in England her social value sank two or three degrees in the scale. "She has her pick of places; she is not in want of a shelter. But I have asked her to stay because I wish you to know her. I think it will be a good thing for you. Serena Merle has no faults."

"If I didn't already like her very much that description might alarm me," Isabel said.

"She never does anything wrong. I have brought you out here, and I wish to do the best for you. Your sister Lily told me that she hoped I would give you plenty of opportunities. I give you one in securing Madame Merle. She is one of the most brilliant women in Europe."

"I like her better than I like your description of her," Isabel persisted in saying.

"Do you flatter yourself that you will find a fault in her? I hope you will let me know when you do."

"That will be cruel—to you," said Isabel.

"You needn't mind me. You never will find one."

"Perhaps not; but I think I shall not miss it."

"She is always up to the mark!" said Mrs. Touchett.

Isabel after this said to Madame Merle that she hoped she knew Mrs. Touchett believed she had not a fault.

"I am obliged to you, but I am afraid your aunt has no perception of spiritual things," Madame Merle answered.

"Do you mean by that that you have spiritual faults?"

"Ah no; I mean nothing so flat! I mean that having no faults, for your aunt, means that one is never late for dinner—that is, for *her* dinner. I was not late, by the way, the other day, when you came back from London; the clock was just at eight when I came into the drawing room; it was the rest of you that were before the time. It means that one answers a letter the day one gets it, and that when one comes to stay with her one doesn't bring too much luggage, and is careful not to be taken ill. For Mrs. Touchett those things constitute virtue; it's a blessing to be able to reduce it to its elements."

Madame Merle's conversation, it will be perceived, was enriched with bold, free touches of criticism, which, even when they had a restrictive effect, never struck Isabel as ill-natured. It never occurred to the girl, for instance, that Mrs. Touchett's accomplished guest was abusing her; and this for very good reasons. In the first place Isabel agreed with her; in the second Madame Merle implied that there was a great deal more to say; and in the third, to speak to one without ceremony of one's near relations was an agreeable sign of intimacy. These signs of intimacy multiplied as the days elapsed, and there was none of which Isabel was more sensible than of her companion's preference for making Miss Archer herself a topic. Though she alluded frequently to the incidents of her own life, she never lingered upon them; she was as little of an egotist as she was of a gossip.

"I am old, and stale, and faded," she said more than once; "I am of no more interest than last week's newspaper. You are young and fresh, and of today; you have the great thing—you have actuality. I once had it—we all have it for an hour. You, however, will have it for longer. Let us talk about you, then; you can say nothing that I shall not care to hear. It is a sign that I am growing old—that I like to talk with younger people. I think it's a very pretty compensation. If we can't have youth within us we can have it outside of us, and I really think we see it and feel it better that way. Of course we must be in sympathy with it—that I shall always be. I don't know that I shall ever be ill-natured with old people—I hope not; there are certainly some old people that I adore. But I shall never be ill-natured with the young; they touch me too much. I give you *carte blanche*, then; you can even be impertinent if you like; I shall let it pass. I talk as if I were a hundred years old, you say? Well, I am, if you please; I was born before the French Revolution. Ah, my dear *je viens de loin;* I belong to the old world. But it is not of that I wish to talk; I wish to talk about the new. You must tell me more about America; you never tell me enough. Here I have been since I was brought here as a helpless child, and it is ridiculous, or rather it's scandalous, how little I know about the land of my birth. There are a great many of us like that, over here; and I must say I think we are a wretched set of people. You should live in your own country; whatever it may be you have your natural place there. If we are not good Americans we are certainly poor Europeans; we have no natural place here. We are mere parasites, crawling over the surface; we haven't our feet in the soil. At least one can know it, and not have illusions. A woman, perhaps, can get on; a woman, it seems to me, has no natural place anywhere; wherever she finds herself she has to remain on the surface and, more or less, to crawl. You protest, my dear? you are horrified? you declare you will never crawl? It is very true that I don't see you crawling; you stand more upright than a good many poor creatures. Very good; on the whole, I don't think you will crawl. But the men, the Americans; *je vous demande un peu,* what do they make of it over here? I don't envy them, trying to arrange themselves. Look at poor Ralph Touchett; what sort of a figure do you call that? Fortunately he has got a consumption; I say fortunately, because it gives him something to do. His consumption is his career; it's a kind of position. You can say, 'Oh, Mr. Touchett, he takes care of his lungs, he knows a great deal about climates.' But without that, who would he be, what would he represent? 'Mr. Ralph Touchett, an American who lives in Europe.' That signifies absolutely nothing—it's impossible that anything should signify less.

'He is very cultivated,' they say; 'he has got a very pretty collection of old snuff-boxes.' The collection is all that is wanted to make it pitiful. I am tired of the sound of the word; I think it's grotesque. With the poor old father it's different; he has his identity, and it is rather a massive one. He represents a great financial house, and that, in our day, is as good as anything else. For an American, at any rate, that will do very well. But I persist in thinking your cousin is very lucky to have a chronic malady; so long as he doesn't die of it. It's much better than the snuff-boxes. If he were not ill, you say, he would do something?—he would take his father's place in the house. My poor child, I doubt it; I don't think he is at all fond of the house. However, you know him better than I, though I used to know him rather well, and he may have the benefit of the doubt. The worst case, I think, is a friend of mine, a countryman of ours, who lives in Italy (where he also was brought before he knew better), and who is one of the most delightful men I know. Some day you must know him. I will bring you together, and then you will see what I mean. He is Gilbert Osmond—he lives in Italy; that is all one can say about him. He is exceedingly clever, a man made to be distinguished; but, as I say, you exhaust the description when you say that he is Mr. Osmond, who lives in Italy. No career, no name, no position, no fortune, no past, no future, no anything. Oh yes, he paints, if you please—paints in watercolors, like me, only better than I. His painting is pretty bad; on the whole I am rather glad of that. Fortunately he is very indolent, so indolent that it amounts to a sort of position. He can say, 'Oh, I do nothing; I am too deadly lazy. You can do nothing today unless you get up at five o'clock in the morning.' In that way he becomes a sort of exception; you feel that he might do something if he would only rise early. He never speaks of his painting—to people at large; he is too clever for that. But he has a little girl—a dear little girl; he does speak of her. He is devoted to her, and if it were a career to be an excellent father he would be very distinguished. But I am afraid that is no better than the snuff-boxes; perhaps not even so good. Tell me what they do in America," pursued Madame Merle, who, it must be observed, parenthetically, did not deliver herself all at once of these reflections, which are presented in a cluster for the convenience of the reader. She talked of Florence, where Mr. Osmond lived, and where Mrs. Touchett occupied a medieval palace; she talked of Rome, where she herself had a little *pied-à-terre,* with some rather good old damask. She talked of places, of people, and even, as the phrase is, of "subjects"; and from time to time she talked of their kind old host and of the prospect of his recovery. From the first she had thought this prospect small, and Isabel had been struck with the positive, discriminating, competent way which she took of the measure of his remainder of life. One evening she announced definitely that he would not live.

"Sir Matthew Hope told me so, as plainly as was proper," she said; "standing there, near the fire, before dinner. He makes himself very agreeable, the great doctor. I don't mean that his saying that has anything to do with it. But he says such things with great tact. I had said to him that I felt ill at my ease, staying here at such a time; it seemed to me so indiscreet—it was not as if I could nurse. 'You must remain, you must remain,' he answered; 'your office will come later.' Was not that a very delicate way both of saying that poor Mr. Touchett would go, and that I might be of some use as a consoler? In fact, however, I shall not be of the slightest use. Your aunt will console herself; she, and she alone, knows just how much consolation she will require. It would be a very delicate matter for another person to undertake to administer the dose. With your cousin it will be different; he will miss his father sadly. But I should never presume to condole with Mr. Ralph; we are not on those terms."

Madame Merle had alluded more than once to some undefined incongruity in her relations with Ralph Touchett; so Isabel took this occasion of asking her if they were not good friends.

"Perfectly, but he doesn't like me."

"What have you done to him?"

"Nothing whatever. But one has no need of a reason for that."

"For not liking you? I think one has need of a very good reason."

"You are very kind. Be sure you have one ready for the day when you begin."

"Begin to dislike you? I shall never begin."

"I hope not; because if you do, you will never end. That is the way with your cousin; he doesn't get over it. It's an antipathy of nature—if I can call it that when it is all on his side. I have nothing whatever against him, and don't bear him the least little grudge for not doing me justice. Justice is all I want. However, one feels that he is a gentleman, and would never say anything underhand about one. *Cartes sur table*," Madame Merle subjoined in a moment, "I am not afraid of him."

"I hope not, indeed," said Isabel, who added something about his being the kindest fellow living. She remembered, however, that on her first asking him about Madame Merle he had answered her in a manner which this lady might have thought injurious without being explicit. There was something between them, Isabel said to herself, but she said nothing more than this. If it were something of importance, it should inspire respect; if it were not, it was not worth her curiosity. With all her love of knowledge, Isabel had a natural shrinking from raising curtains and looking into unlighted corners. The love of knowledge coexisted in her mind with a still tenderer love of ignorance.

But Madame Merle sometimes said things that startled her, made her raise her clear eyebrows at the time, and think of the words afterwards.

"I would give a great deal to be your age again," she broke out once, with a bitterness which, though diluted in her customary smile, was by no means disguised by it. "If I could only begin again—if I could have my life before me!"

"Your life is before you yet," Isabel answered gently, for she was vaguely awestruck.

"No; the best part is gone, and gone for nothing."

"Surely, not for nothing," said Isabel.

"Why not—what have I got? Neither husband, nor child, nor fortune, nor position, nor the traces of a beauty which I never had."

"You have friends, dear lady."

"I am not so sure!" cried Madame Merle.

"Ah, you are wrong. You have memories, talents——"

Madame Merle interrupted her.

"What have my talents brought me? Nothing but the need of using them still, to get through the hours, the years, to cheat myself with some pretence of action. As for my memories, the less said about them the better. You will be my friend till you find a better use for your friendship."

"It will be for you to see that I don't then," said Isabel.

"Yes; I would make an effort to keep you," Madame Merle rejoined, looking at her gravely. "When I say I should like to be your age," she went on, "I mean with your qualities—frank, generous, sincere, like you. In that case I should have made something better of my life."

"What should you have liked to do that you have not done?"

Madame Merle took a sheet of music—she was seated at the piano, and had abruptly wheeled about on the stool when she first spoke—and mechanically turned the leaves. At last she said—

"I am very ambitious!"

"And your ambitions have not been satisfied? They must have been great."

"They were great. I should make myself ridiculous by talking of them."

Isabel wondered what they could have been—whether Madame Merle had aspired to wear a crown. "I don't know what your idea of success may be, but you seem to me to have been successful. To me, indeed, you are an image of success."

Madame Merle tossed away the music with a smile.

"What is *your* idea of success?"

"You evidently think it must be very tame," said Isabel. "It is to see some dream of one's youth come true."

"Ah," Madame Merle exclaimed, "that I have never seen! But my dreams were so great—so preposterous. Heaven forgive me, I am dreaming now." And she turned back to the piano and began to play with energy.

On the morrow she said to Isabel that her definition of success had been very pretty, but frightfully sad. Measured in that way, who had succeeded? The dreams of one's youth, why they were enchanting, they were divine! Who had ever seen such things come to pass?

"I myself—a few of them," Isabel ventured to answer.

"Already? They must have been dreams of yesterday."

"I began to dream very young," said Isabel, smiling.

"Ah, if you mean the aspirations of your childhood—that of having a pink sash and a doll that could close her eyes."

"No, I don't mean that."

"Or a young man with a moustache going down on his knees to you."

"No, nor that either," Isabel declared, blushing.

Madame Merle gave a glance at her blush which caused it to deepen.

"I suspect that is what you do mean. We have all had the young man with the moustache. He is the inevitable young man; he doesn't count."

Isabel was silent for a moment, and then, with extreme and characteristic inconsequence—

"Why shouldn't he count? There are young men and young men."

"And yours was a paragon—is that what you mean?" cried her friend with a laugh. "If you have had the identical young man you dreamed of, then that was success, and I congratulate you. Only, in that case, why didn't you fly with him to his castle in the Apennines?"

"He has no castle in the Apennines."

"What has he? An ugly brick house in Fortieth Street? Don't tell me that; I refuse to recognize that as an ideal."

"I don't care anything about his house," said Isabel.

"That is very crude of you. When you have lived as long as I, you will see that every human being has his shell, and that you must take the shell into account. By the shell I mean the whole envelope of circumstances. There is no such thing as an isolated man or woman; we are each of us made up of a cluster of appurtenances. What do you call one's self? Where does it begin? where does it end? It overflows into everything that belongs to us—and then it flows back again. I know that a large part of myself is in the dresses I choose to wear. I have a great respect for *things!* One's self—for other people—is one's expression of one's self; and one's house, one's clothes, the book one reads, the company one keeps—these things are all expressive."

This was very metaphysical; not more so, however, than several observations Madame Merle had already made. Isabel was fond of metaphysics, but she was unable to accompany her friend into this bold analysis of the human personality.

"I don't agree with you," she said. "I think just the other way. I don't know whether I succeed in expressing myself, but I know that nothing else expresses me. Nothing that belongs to me is any measure of me; on the contrary, it's a limit, a barrier, and a perfectly arbitrary one. Certainly, the clothes which, as you say, I choose to wear, don't express me; and heaven forbid they should!"

"You dress very well," interposed Madame Merle, skillfully.

"Possibly; but I don't care to be judged by that. My clothes may express the dress-maker, but they don't express me. To begin with, it's not my choice that I wear them; they are imposed upon me by society."

"Should you prefer to go without them?" Madame Merle inquired, in a tone which virtually terminated the discussion.

I am bound to confess, though it may cast some discredit upon the sketch I have given of the youthful loyalty which our heroine practiced toward this accomplished woman, that Isabel had said nothing whatever to her about Lord Warburton, and had been equally reticent on the subject of Caspar Goodwood. Isabel had not con-cealed from her, however, that she had had opportunities of marrying, and had even let her know that they were of a highly advantageous kind. Lord Warburton had left Lockleigh, and was gone to Scotland, taking his sisters with him; and though he had written to Ralph more than once, to ask about Mr. Touchett's health, the girl was not liable to the embarrassment of such inquiries as, had he still been in the neigh-borhood, he would probably have felt bound to make in person. He had admirable self-control, but she felt sure that if he had come to Gardencourt he would have seen Madame Merle, and that if he had seen her he would have liked her, and betrayed to her that he was in love with her young friend.

It so happened that during Madame Merle's previous visits to Gardencourt—each of them much shorter than the present one—he had either not been at Lock-leigh or had not called at Mr. Touchett's. Therefore, though she knew him by name as the great man of that county, she had no cause to suspect him of being a suitor of Mrs. Touchett's freshly imported niece.

"You have plenty of time," she had said to Isabel, in return for the mutilated con-fidences which Isabel made her, and which did not pretend to be perfect, though we have seen that at moments the girl had compunctions at having said so much. "I am glad you have done nothing yet—that you have it still to do. It is a very good thing for a girl to have refused a few good offers—so long, of course, as they are not the best she is likely to have. Excuse me if my tone seems horribly worldly; one must take that view sometimes. Only don't keep on refusing for the sake of refus-ing. It's a pleasant exercise of power; but accepting is after all an exercise of power as well. There is always the danger of refusing once too often. It was not the one I fell into—I didn't refuse often enough. You are an exquisite creature, and I should like to see you married to a prime minister. But speaking strictly, you know you are not what is technically called a *parti*. You are extremely good-looking, and extremely clever; in yourself you are quite exceptional. You appear to have the vaguest ideas about your earthly possessions; but from what I can make out, you are not embarrassed with an income. I wish you had a little money."

"I wish I had!" said Isabel, simply, apparently forgetting for the moment that her poverty had been a venial fault for two gallant gentlemen.

In spite of Sir Matthew Hope's benevolent recommendation, Madame Merle did not remain to the end, as the issue of poor Mr. Touchett's malady had now come frankly to be designated. She was under pledges to other people which had at last to be redeemed, and she left Gardencourt with the understanding that she should in any event see Mrs. Touchett there again, or in town, before quitting England. Her parting with Isabel was even more like the beginning of a friendship than their meeting had been.

"I am going to six places in succession," she said, "but I shall see no one I like so well as you. They will all be old friends, however; one doesn't make new friends at my age. I have made a great exception for you. You must remember that, and you must think well of me. You must reward me by believing in me."

By way of answer, Isabel kissed her, and though some women kiss with facility, there are kisses and kisses, and this embrace was satisfactory to Madame Merle.

Isabel, after this, was much alone; she saw her aunt and cousin only at meals, and discovered that of the hours that Mrs. Touchett was invisible, only a minor portion was now devoted to nursing her husband. She spent the rest in her own apartments, to which access was not allowed even to her niece, in mysterious and inscrutable exercises. At table she was grave and silent; but her solemnity was not an attitude—Isabel could see that it was a conviction. She wondered whether her aunt repented of having taken her own way so much; but there was no visible evidence of this—no tears, no sighs, no exaggeration of a zeal which had always deemed itself sufficient. Mrs. Touchett seemed simply to feel the need of thinking things over and summing them up; she had a little moral account-book—with columns unerringly ruled, and a sharp steel clasp—which she kept with exemplary neatness.

"If I had foreseen this I would not have proposed your coming abroad now," she said to Isabel after Madame Merle had left the house. "I would have waited and sent for you next year."

Her remarks had usually a practical ring.

"So that perhaps I should never have known my uncle? It's a great happiness to me to have come now."

"That's very well. But it was not that you might know your uncle that I brought you to Europe." A perfectly veracious speech; but, as Isabel thought, not as perfectly timed.

She had leisure to think of this and other matters. She took a solitary walk every day, and spent much time in turning over the books in the library. Among the subjects that engaged her attention were the adventures of her friend Miss Stackpole, with whom she was in regular correspondence. Isabel liked her friend's private epistolary style better than her public; that is, she thought her public letters would have been excellent if they had not been printed. Henrietta's career, however, was not so successful as might have been wished even in the interest of her private felicity; that view of the inner life of Great Britain which she was so eager to take appeared to dance before her like an *ignis fatuus*. The invitation from Lady Pensil, for mysterious reasons, had never arrived; and poor Mr. Bantling himself, with all his friendly ingenuity, had been unable to explain so grave a dereliction on the part of a missive that had obviously been sent. Mr. Bantling, however, had evidently taken Henrietta's affairs much to heart, and believed that he owed her a set-off to this illusory visit to Bedfordshire. "He says he should think I would go to the Continent," Henrietta wrote; "and as he thinks of going there himself, I suppose his advice is sincere. He wants to know why I don't take a view of French life; and it is a fact that I want very much to see the new Republic. Mr. Bantling doesn't care much about the Republic, but he thinks of going over to Paris anyway. I must say he is quite as attentive as I could wish, and at any rate I shall have seen one polite Englishman. I keep telling Mr. Bantling that he ought to have been an American; and you ought to see how it pleases him. Whenever I say so, he always breaks out with the same exclamation—'Ah, but really, come now!' " A few days later she wrote that she had decided to go to Paris at the end of the week, and that Mr. Bantling had promised to see her off—perhaps even he would go as far as Dover with her. She would wait in Paris till Isabel should arrive, Henrietta added; speaking quite as if Isabel were to start on her Continental journey alone, and making no allusion to Mrs. Touchett. Bearing in mind his interest in their late companion, our heroine communicated several passages from Miss Stackpole's letters to Ralph, who followed with an emotion akin to suspense the career of the correspondent of the *Interviewer.*

"It seems to me that she is doing very well," he said, "going over to Paris with an ex-guardsman! If she wants something to write about, she has only to describe that episode."

"It is not conventional, certainly," Isabel answered; "but if you mean that—as far as Henrietta is concerned—it is not perfectly innocent, you are very much mistaken. You will never understand Henrietta."

"Excuse me; I understand her perfectly. I didn't at all at first; but now I have got the point of view. I am afraid, however, that Bantling has not; he may have some surprises. Oh, I understand Henrietta as well as if I had made her!"

Isabel was by no means sure of this; but she abstained from expressing further doubt, for she was disposed in these days to extend a great charity to her cousin. One afternoon, less than a week after Madame Merle's departure, she was seated in the library with a volume to which her attention was not fastened. She had placed herself in a deep window-bench, from which she looked out into the dull, damp park; and as the library stood at right angles to the entrance front of the house, she could see the doctor's dog-cart, which had been waiting for the last two hours before the door. She was struck with the doctor's remaining so long; but at last she saw him appear in the portico, stand a moment, slowly drawing on his gloves and looking at the knees of his horse, and then get into the vehicle and drive away. Isabel kept her place for half-an-hour; there was a great stillness in the house. It was so great that when she at last heard a soft, slow step on the deep carpet of the room, she was almost startled by the sound. She turned quickly away from the window, and saw Ralph Touchett standing there, with his hands still in his pockets, but with a face absolutely void of its usual latent smile. She got up, and her movement and glance were a question.

"It's all over," said Ralph.

"Do you mean that my uncle——?" And Isabel stopped.

"My father died an hour ago."

"Ah, my poor Ralph!" the girl murmured, putting out her hand to him.

❧ 20 ❧

Some fortnight after this incident Madame Merle drove up in a hansom cab to the house in Winchester Square. As she descended from her vehicle she observed, suspended between the dining room windows, a large, neat, wooden tablet, on whose fresh black ground were inscribed in white paint the words—"This noble freehold mansion to be sold;" with the name of the agent to whom application should be made. "They certainly lose no time," said the visitor, as, after sounding the big brass knocker, she waited to be admitted; "it's a practical country!" And within the house, as she ascended to the drawing room, she perceived numerous signs of abdication; pictures removed from the walls and placed upon sofas, windows undraped and floors laid bare. Mrs. Touchett presently received her, and intimated in a few words that condolences might be taken for granted.

"I know what you are going to say—he was a very good man. But I know it better than anyone, because I gave him more chance to show it. In that I think I was a good wife." Mrs. Touchett added that at the end her husband apparently recognized this fact. "He has treated me liberally," she said; "I won't say more liberally than I expected, because I didn't expect. You know that as a general thing I don't expect. But he chose, I presume, to recognise the fact that though I lived much abroad, and mingled—you may say freely—in foreign life, I never exhibited the smallest preference for anyone else."

"For anyone but yourself," Madame Merle mentally observed; but the reflection was perfectly inaudible.

"I never sacrificed my husband to another," Mrs. Touchett continued, with her stout curtness.

"Oh no," thought Madame Merle; "you never did anything for another!"

There was a certain cynicism in these mute comments which demands an explanation; the more so as they are not in accord either with the view—somewhat superficial perhaps—that we have hitherto enjoyed of Madame Merle's character, or with the literal facts of Mrs. Touchett's history; the more so, too, as Madame Merle had a well-founded conviction that her friend's last remark was not in the least to be construed as a side-thrust at herself. The truth is, that the moment she had crossed the threshold she received a subtle impression that Mr. Touchett's death had had consequences, and that these consequences had been profitable to a little circle of persons among whom she was not numbered. Of course it was an event which would naturally have consequences; her imagination had more than once rested upon this fact during her stay at Gardencourt. But it had been one thing to foresee it mentally, and it was another to behold it actually. The idea of a distribution of property—she would almost have said of spoils—just now pressed upon her senses and irritated her with a sense of exclusion. I am far from wishing to say that Madame Merle was one of the hungry ones of the world; but we have already perceived that she had desires which had never been satisfied. If she had been questioned, she would of course have admitted—with a most becoming smile—that she had not the faintest claim to a share in Mr. Touchett's relics. "There was never anything in the world between us," she would have said. "There was never that, poor man!"—with a fillip of her thumb and her third finger. I hasten to add, moreover, that if her private attitude at the present moment was somewhat incongruously invidious, she was very careful not to betray herself. She had, after all, as much sympathy for Mrs. Touchett's gains as for her losses.

"He has left me this house," the newly-made widow said; "but of course I shall not live in it; I have a much better house in Florence. The will was opened only three days since, but I have already offered the house for sale. I have also a share in the bank; but I don't yet understand whether I am obliged to leave it there. If not, I shall certainly take it out. Ralph, of course, has Gardencourt; but I am not sure that he will have means to keep up the place. He is of course left very well off, but his father has given away an immense deal of money; there are bequests to a string of third cousins in Vermont. Ralph, however, is very fond of Gardencourt, and would be quite capable of living there—in summer—with a maid-of-all-work and a gardener's boy. There is one remarkable clause in my husband's will," Mrs. Touchett added. "He has left my niece a fortune."

"A fortune!" Madame Merle repeated, softly.

"Isabel steps into something like seventy thousand pounds."

Madame Merle's hands were clasped in her lap; at this she raised them, still clasped, and held them a moment against her bosom, while her eyes, a little dilated, fixed themselves on those of her friend. "Ah," she cried, "the clever creature!"

Mrs. Touchett gave her a quick look. "What do you mean by that?"

For an instant Madame Merle's color rose, and she dropped her eyes. "It certainly is clever to achieve such results—without an effort!"

"There certainly was no effort; don't call it an achievement."

Madame Merle was rarely guilty of the awkwardness of retracting what she had said; her wisdom was shown rather in maintaining it and placing it in a favorable light. "My dear friend, Isabel would certainly not have had seventy thousand pounds left her if she had not been the most charming girl in the world. Her charm includes great cleverness."

"She never dreamed, I am sure, of my husband's doing anything for her; and I never dreamed of it either, for he never spoke to me of his intention," Mrs. Touchett said. "She had no claim upon him whatever; it was no great recommendation to him that she was my niece. Whatever she achieved she achieved unconsciously."

"Ah," rejoined Madame Merle, "those are the greatest strokes!"

Mrs. Touchett gave a shrug. "The girl is fortunate; I don't deny that. But for the present she is simply stupefied."

"Do you mean that she doesn't know what to do with the money?"

"That, I think, she has hardly considered. She doesn't know what to think about the matter at all. It has been as if a big gun were suddenly fired off behind her; she is feeling herself, to see if she be hurt. It is but three days since she received a visit from the principal executor who came in person, very gallantly, to notify her. He told me afterwards that when he had made his little speech she suddenly burst into tears. The money is to remain in the bank, and she is to draw the interest."

Madame Merle shook her head, with a wise, and now quite benignant, smile. "After she has done that two or three times she will get used to it." Then after a silence—"What does your son think of it?" she abruptly asked.

"He left England just before it came out—used up by his fatigue and anxiety, and hurrying off to the south. He is on his way to the Riviera, and I have not yet heard from him. But it is not likely he will ever object to anything done by his father."

"Didn't you say his own share had been cut down?"

"Only at his wish. I know that he urged his father to do something for the people in America. He is not in the least addicted to looking after number one."

"It depends upon whom he regards as number one!" said Madame Merle. And she remained thoughtful a moment, with her eyes bent upon the floor. "Am I not to see your happy niece?" she asked at last, looking up.

"You may see her; but you will not be struck with her being happy. She has looked as solemn, these three days, as a Cimabue Madonna!" And Mrs. Touchett rang for a servant.

Isabel came in shortly after the footman had been sent to call her; and Madame Merle thought, as she appeared, that Mrs. Touchett's comparison had its force. The girl was pale and grave—an effect not mitigated by her deeper mourning; but the smile of her brightest moments came into her face as she saw Madame Merle, who went forward, laid her hand on our heroine's shoulder, and after looking at her a moment, kissed her as if she were returning the kiss that she had received from Isabel at Gardencourt. This was the only allusion that Madame Merle, in her great good taste, made for the present to her young friend's inheritance.

Mrs. Touchett did not remain in London until she had sold her house. After selecting from among its furniture those objects which she wished to transport to her Florentine residence, she left the rest of its contents to be disposed of by the auctioneer, and took her departure for the Continent. She was, of course, accompanied on this journey by her niece, who now had plenty of leisure to contemplate the windfall on which Madame Merle had covertly congratulated her. Isabel thought of it very often and looked at it in a dozen different lights; but we shall not at present attempt to enter into her meditations or to explain why it was that some of them were of a rather pessimistic cast. The pessimism of this young lady was transient; she ultimately made up her mind that to be rich was a virtue, because it was to be able to *do,* and to do was sweet. It was the contrary of weakness. To be weak was, for a young lady, rather graceful, but, after all, as Isabel said to herself, there was a larger grace than that. Just now, it is true, there was not much to do— once she had sent off a cheque to Lily and another to poor Edith; but she was thankful for the quiet months which her mourning robes and her aunt's fresh widowhood compelled the two ladies to spend. The acquisition of power made her serious; she scrutinized her power with a kind of tender ferocity, but she was not eager to exercise it. She began to do so indeed during a stay of some weeks which she presently made with her aunt in Paris, but in ways that will probably be thought rather vulgar. They were the ways that most naturally presented themselves in a city in which the shops are the admiration of the world, especially under the guidance of Mrs. Touchett, who took a rigidly practical view of the transformation of her niece from a poor girl to a rich one. "Now that you are a young woman of fortune you must know how to play the part—I mean to play it well," she said to Isabel, once for all; and she added that the girl's first duty was to have everything handsome. "You don't know how to take care of your things, but you must learn," she went on; this was Isabel's second duty. Isabel submitted, but for the present her imagination was not kindled; she longed for opportunities, but these were not the opportunities she meant.

Mrs. Touchett rarely changed her plans, and having intended before her husband's death to spend a part of the winter in Paris she saw no reason to deprive herself—still less to deprive her companion—of this advantage. Though they would live in great retirement, she might still present her niece, informally, to the little circle of her fellow-countrymen dwelling upon the skirts of the Champs Elysées. With many of these amiable colonists Mrs. Touchett was intimate; she shared their expatriation, their convictions, their pastimes, their ennui. Isabel saw them come with a good deal of assiduity to her aunt's hotel, and judged them with a trenchancy which is doubtless to be accounted for by the temporary exaltation of her sense of human duty. She made up her mind that their manner of life was superficial, and incurred some disfavor by expressing this view on bright Sunday afternoons, when the American absentees were engaged in calling upon each other. Though her listeners were the most good-natured people in the world, two or three of them thought her cleverness, which was generally admitted, only a dangerous variation of impertinence.

"You all live here this way, but what does it all lead to?" she was pleased to ask. "It doesn't seem to lead to anything, and I should think you would get very tired of it."

Mrs. Touchett thought the question worthy of Henrietta Stackpole. The two ladies had found Henrietta in Paris, and Isabel constantly saw her; so that Mrs. Touchett had some reason for saying to herself that if her niece were not clever enough to originate almost anything, she might be suspected of having borrowed that style of remark from her journalistic friend. The first occasion on which Isabel had spoken was that of a visit paid by the two ladies to Mrs. Luce, an old friend of Mrs. Touchett's, and the only person in Paris she now went to see. Mrs. Luce had been living in Paris since the days of Louis Philippe; she used to say jocosely that she was one of the generation of 1830—a joke of which the point was not always taken. When it failed Mrs. Luce used always to explain—"Oh yes, I am one of the romantics;" her French had never become very perfect. She was always at home on Sunday afternoons, and surrounded by sympathetic compatriots, usually the same. In fact she was at home at all times, and led in her well-cushioned little corner of the brilliant city as quiet and domestic a life as she might have led in her native Baltimore. The existence of Mr. Luce, her worthy husband, was somewhat more inscrutable. Superficially indeed, there was no mystery about it; the mystery lay deeper, and resided in the wonder of his supporting existence at all. He was the most unoccupied man in Europe, for he not only had no duties, but he had no pleasures. Habits certainly he had, but they were few in number, and had been worn threadbare by forty years of use. Mr. Luce was a tall, lean, grizzled, well-brushed gentleman, who wore a gold eye-glass and carried his hat a little too much on the back of his head. He went every day to the American banker's, where there was a post-office which was almost as sociable and colloquial an institution as that of an American country town. He passed an hour (in fine weather) in a chair in the Champs Elysées, and he dined uncommonly well at his own table, seated above a waxed floor, which it was Mrs. Luce's happiness to believe had a finer polish than any other in Paris. Occasionally he dined with a friend or two at the Café Anglais, where his talent for ordering a dinner was a source of felicity to his companions and an object of admiration even to the headwaiter of the establishment. These were his only known avocations, but they had beguiled his hours for upwards of half a century, and they doubtless justified his frequent declaration that there was no place like Paris. In no other place, on these terms, could Mr. Luce flatter himself that he was enjoying life. There was nothing like Paris, but it must be confessed that Mr. Luce thought less highly of the French capital than in earlier days. In the list of his occupations his political reveries should not be omitted, for they were doubtless the animating principle of many hours that superficially seemed vacant. Like many of his fellow colonists, Mr. Luce was a high—or rather a deep—conservative, and gave no countenance to the government recently established in France. He had no faith in its duration, and would assure you from year to year that its end was close at hand. "They want to be kept down, sir, to be kept down; nothing but the strong hand—the iron heel—will do for them," he would frequently say of the French people; and his ideal of a fine government was that of the lately abolished Empire. "Paris is much less attractive than in the days of the Emperor; he knew how to make a city pleasant," Mr. Luce had often remarked to Mrs. Touchett, who was quite of his own way of thinking, and wished to know what one had crossed that odious Atlantic for but to get away from republics.

"Why, madam, sitting in the Champs Elysées, opposite to the Palace of Industry, I have seen the court carriages from the Tuileries pass up and down as many as seven times a day. I remember one occasion when they went as high as nine times. What do you see now? It's no use talking, the style's all gone. Napoleon knew what the French people want, and there'll be a cloud over Paris till they get the Empire back again."

Among Mrs. Luce's visitors on Sunday afternoons was a young man with whom Isabel had had a good deal of conversation, and whom she found full of valuable knowledge. Mr. Edward Rosier—Ned Rosier, as he was called—was a native of New York, and had been brought up in Paris, living there under the eye of his father, who, as it happened, had been an old and intimate friend of the late Mr. Archer. Edward Rosier remembered Isabel as a little girl; it had been his father who came to the rescue of the little Archers at the inn at Neufchâtel (he was traveling that way with the boy, and stopped at the hotel by chance), after their *bonne* had gone off with the Russian prince and when Mr. Archer's whereabouts remained for some days a mystery. Isabel remembered perfectly the neat little male child, whose hair smelt of a delicious cosmetic, and who had a *bonne* of his own, warranted to lose sight of him under no provocation. Isabel took a walk with the pair beside the lake, and thought little Edward as pretty as an angel—a comparison by no means conventional in her mind, for she had a very definite conception of a type of features which she supposed to be angelic, and which her new friend perfectly illustrated. A small pink face, surmounted by a blue velvet bonnet and set off by a stiff embroidered collar, became the countenance of her childish dreams; and she firmly believed for some time afterwards that the heavenly hosts conversed among themselves in a queer little dialect of French-English, expressing the properest sentiments, as when Edward told her that he was "defended" by his *bonne* to go near the edge of the lake, and that one must always obey to one's *bonne*. Ned Rosier's English had improved; at least it exhibited in a less degree the French variation. His father was dead and his *bonne* was dismissed, but the young man still conformed to the spirit of their teaching—he never went to the edge of the lake. There was still something agreeable to the nostril about him, and something not offensive to nobler organs. He was a very gentle and gracious youth, with what are called cultivated tastes—an acquaintance with old china, with good wine, with the bindings of books, with the *Almanach de Gotha*, with the best shops, the best hotels, the hours of railway trains. He could order a dinner almost as well as Mr. Luce, and it was probable that as his experience accumulated he would be a worthy successor to that gentleman, whose rather grim politics he also advocated, in a soft and innocent voice. He had some charming rooms in Paris, decorated with old Spanish altarlace, the envy of his female friends, who declared that his chimney-piece was better draped than many a duchess. He usually, however, spent a part of every winter at Pau, and had once passed a couple of months in the United States.

He took a great interest in Isabel, and remembered perfectly the walk at Neufchâtel, when she would persist in going so near the edge. He seemed to recognize this same tendency in the subversive inquiry that I quoted a moment ago, and set himself to answer our heroine's question with greater urbanity than it perhaps deserved. "What does it lead to, Miss Archer? Why Paris leads everywhere. You can't go anywhere unless you come here first. Everyone that comes to Europe has got to pass through. You don't mean it in that sense so much? You mean what good it does you? Well, how can you penetrate futurity? How can you tell what lies ahead? If it's a pleasant road I don't care where it leads. I like the road, Miss Archer; I like the dear old asphalte. You can't get tired of it—you can't if you try. You think you would, but you wouldn't; there's always something new and fresh. Take the Hôtel Drouot, now; they sometimes have three and four sales a week. Where can you get such things as you can here? In spite of all they say, I maintain they are cheaper too, if you know the right places. I know plenty of places, but I keep them to myself. I'll tell you, if you like, as a particular favor; only you must not tell anyone else. Don't you go anywhere without asking me first; I want you to promise me that. As a general thing avoid the Boulevards; there is very little to be done on the Boulevards. Speaking conscientiously—*sans blague*—I don't believe anyone knows Paris better than I. You and Mrs. Touchett must come and breakfast with me some day, and I'll show you my things; *je ne vous dis que ça!* There has been a great deal of talk about London of late; it's the fashion to cry up London. But there is nothing in it—you can't do anything in London. No Louis Quinze—nothing of the First Empire; nothing but their eternal Queen Anne. It's good for one's bedroom, Queen Anne—for one's washing-room; but it isn't proper for a *salon.* Do I spend my life at the auctioneer's?" Mr. Rosier pursued, in answer to another question of Isabel's. "Oh, no; I haven't the means. I wish I had. You think I'm a mere trifler; I can tell by the expression of your face—you have got a wonderfully expressive face. I hope you don't mind my saying that; I mean it as a kind of warning. You think I ought to do something, and so do I, so long as you leave it vague. But when you come to the point, you see you have to stop. I can't go home and be a shopkeeper. You think I am very well fitted? Ah, Miss Archer, you overrate me. I can buy very well, but I can't sell; you should see when I sometimes try to get rid of my things. It takes much more ability to make other people buy than to buy yourself. When I think how clever they must be, the people who make *me* buy! Ah, no; I couldn't be a shopkeeper. I can't be a doctor, it's a repulsive business. I can't be a clergyman, I haven't got convictions. And then I can't pronounce the names right in the Bible. They are very difficult, in the Old Testament particularly. I can't be a lawyer; I don't understand—how do you call it?—the American *procédure.* Is there anything else? There is nothing for a gentleman to do in America. I should like to be a diplomatist; but American diplomacy—that is not for gentlemen either. I am sure if you had seen the last min—"

Henrietta Stackpole, who was often with her friend when Mr. Rosier, coming to pay his compliments, late in the afternoon, expressed himself after the fashion I have sketched, usually interrupted the young man at this point and read him a lecture on the duties of the American citizen. She thought him most unnatural; he was worse than Mr. Ralph Touchett. Henrietta, however, was at this time more than ever addicted to fine criticism, for her conscience had been freshly alarmed as regards Isabel. She had not congratulated this young lady on her accession of fortune, and begged to be excused from doing so.

"If Mr. Touchett had consulted me about leaving you the money," she frankly said, "I would have said to him, 'Never!'"

"I see," Isabel had answered. "You think it will prove a curse in disguise. Perhaps it will."

"Leave it to someone you care less for—that's what I should have said."

"To yourself, for instance?" Isabel suggested, jocosely. And then—"Do you really believe it will ruin me?" she asked, in quite another tone.

"I hope it won't ruin you; but it will certainly confirm your dangerous tendencies."

"Do you mean the love of luxury—of extravagance?"

"No, no," said Henrietta; "I mean your moral tendencies. I approve of luxury; I think we ought to be as elegant as possible. Look at the luxury of our western cities; I have seen nothing over here to compare with it. I hope you will never become sensual; but I am not afraid of that. The peril for you is that you live too much in the world of your own dreams—you are not enough in contact with reality—with the toiling, striving, suffering, I may even say sinning, world that surrounds you. You are too fastidious; you have too many graceful illusions. Your newly acquired thousands will shut you up more and more to the society of a few selfish and heartless people, who will be interested in keeping up those illusions."

Isabel's eyes expanded as she gazed upon this vivid but dusky picture of her future. "What are my illusions?" she asked. "I try so hard not to have any."

"Well," said Henrietta, "you think that you can lead a romantic life, that you can live by pleasing yourself and pleasing others. You will find you are mistaken. Whatever life you lead, you must put your soul into it—to make any sort of success of it; and from the moment you do that it ceases to be romance, I assure you; it becomes reality! And you can't always please yourself; you must sometimes please other people. That, I admit, you are very ready to do; but there is another thing that is still more important—you must often *dis*please others. You must always be ready for that—you must never shrink from it. That doesn't suit you at all—you are too fond of admiration, you like to be thought well of. You think we can escape disagreeable duties by taking romantic views—that is your great illusion, my dear. But we can't. You must be prepared on many occasions in life to please no one at all—not even yourself."

Isabel shook her head sadly; she looked troubled and frightened. "This, for you, Henrietta," she said, "must be one of those occasions!"

It was certainly true that Miss Stackpole, during her visit to Paris, which had been professionally more remunerative than her English sojourn, had not been living in the world of dreams. Mr. Bantling, who had now returned to England, was her companion for the first four weeks of her stay; and about Mr. Bantling there was nothing dreamy. Isabel learned from her friend that the two had led a life of great intimacy, and that this had been a peculiar advantage to Henrietta, owing to the gentleman's remarkable knowledge of Paris. He had explained everything, shown her everything, been her constant guide and interpreter. They had breakfasted together, dined together, gone to the theater together, supped together, really in a manner quite lived together. He was a true friend, Henrietta more than once assured our heroine; and she had never supposed that she could like any Englishman so well. Isabel could not have told you why, but she found something that ministered to mirth in the alliance the correspondent of the *Interviewer* had struck with Lady Pensil's brother; and her amusement subsisted in the face of the fact that she thought it a credit to each of them. Isabel could not rid herself of a suspicion that they were playing, somehow, at cross-purposes—that the simplicity of each of them had been entrapped. But this simplicity was nonetheless honorable on either side; it was as graceful on Henrietta's part to believe that Mr. Bantling took an interest in the diffusion of lively journalism, and in consolidating the position of lady correspondents, as it was on the part of her companion to suppose that the cause of the *Interviewer*—a periodical of which he never formed a very definite conception—was, if subtly analyzed (a task to which Mr. Bantling felt himself quite equal), but the cause of Miss Stackpole's coquetry. Each of these harmless confederates supplied at any rate a want of which the other was somewhat eagerly conscious. Mr. Bantling, who was of a rather slow and discursive habit, relished a prompt, keen, positive woman, who charmed him with the spectacle of a brilliant eye and a kind of bandbox neatness, and who kindled a perception of raciness in a mind to which the usual fare of life seemed unsalted. Henrietta, on the other hand, enjoyed the society of a fresh-looking, professionless gentleman, whose leisured state, though generally indefensible, was a decided advantage to Miss Stackpole, and who was furnished with an easy, traditional, though by no means exhaustive, answer to almost any social or practical question that could come up. She often found Mr. Bantling's answers very convenient, and in the press of catching the American post would make use of them in her correspondence. It was to be feared that she was indeed drifting toward those mysterious shallows as to which Isabel, wishing for a good-humored retort, had warned her. There might be danger in store for Isabel; but it was scarcely to be hoped that Miss Stackpole, on her side, would find permanent safety in the adoption of second-hand views. Isabel continued to warn her, good-humoredly; Lady Pensil's obliging brother was sometimes, on our heroine's lips, an object of irreverent and facetious allusion. Nothing, however, could exceed Henrietta's amiability on this point; she used to abound in the sense of Isabel's irony, and to enumerate with elation the hours she had spent with the good Mr. Bantling. Then, a few moments later, she would forget that they had been talking jocosely, and would mention with impulsive earnestness some expedition she had made in the company of the gallant ex-guardsman. She would say—"Oh, I know all about Versailles; I went there with Mr. Bantling. I was bound to see it thoroughly—I warned him when we went out there that I was thorough; so we spent three days at the hotel and wandered all over the place. It was lovely weather—a kind of Indian summer, only not so good. We just lived in that park. Oh yes; you can't tell me anything about Versailles." Henrietta appeared to have made arrangements to meet Mr. Bantling in the spring, in Italy.

❧ 21 ❧

Mrs. Touchett, before arriving in Paris, had fixed the day for her departure; and by the middle of February she had begun to travel southward. She did not go directly to Florence, but interrupted her journey to pay a visit to her son, who at San Remo, on the Italian shore of the Mediterranean, had been spending a dull, bright winter, under a white umbrella. Isabel went with her aunt, as a matter of course, though Mrs. Touchett, with her usual homely logic, had laid before her a pair of alternatives.

"Now, of course, you are completely your own mistress," she said. "Excuse me; I don't mean that you were not so before. But you are on a different footing—property erects a kind of barrier. You can do a great many things if you are rich, which would be severely criticized if you were poor. You can go and come, you can travel alone, you can have your own establishment: I mean of course if you will take a companion—some decayed gentlewoman with a darned cashmere and dyed hair, who paints on velvet. You don't think you would like that? Of course you can do as you please; I only want you to understand that you are at liberty. You might take Miss Stackpole as your *dame de compagnie;* she would keep people off very well. I think, however, that it is a great deal better you should remain with me, in spite of there being no obligation. It's better for several reasons, quite apart from your liking it. I shouldn't think you would like it, but I recommend you to make the sacrifice. Of course, whatever novelty there may have been at first in my society has quite passed away, and you see me as I am—a dull, obstinate, narrow-minded old woman."

"I don't think you are at all dull," Isabel had replied to this.

"But you do think I am obstinate and narrow-minded? I told you so!" said Mrs. Touchett, with much elation at being justified.

Isabel remained for the present with her aunt, because, in spite of eccentric impulses, she had a great regard for what was usually deemed decent, and a young gentlewoman without visible relations had always struck her as a flower without foliage. It was true that Mrs. Touchett's conversation had never again appeared so brilliant as that first afternoon in Albany, when she sat in her damp waterproof and sketched the opportunities that Europe would offer to a young person of taste. This, however, was in a great measure the girl's own fault; she had got a glimpse of her aunt's experience, and her imagination constantly anticipated the judgments and emotions of a woman who had very little of the same faculty. Apart from this, Mrs. Touchett had a great merit; she was as honest as a pair of compasses. There was a comfort in her stiffness and firmness; you knew exactly where to find her, and were never liable to chance encounters with her. On her own ground she was always to be found; but she was never over-inquisitive as regards the territory of her neighbor. Isabel came at last to have a kind of undemonstrable pity for her; there seemed something so dreary in the condition of a person whose nature had, as it were, so little surface—offered so limited a face to the accretions of human contact. Nothing tender, nothing sympathetic, had ever had a chance to fasten upon it—no windsown blossom, no familiar moss. Her passive extent, in other words, was about that of a knife-edge. Isabel had reason to believe, however, that as she advanced in life she grew more disposed to confer those sentimental favors which she was still unable to accept—to sacrifice consistency to considerations of that inferior order for which the excuse must be found in the particular case. It was not to the credit of her absolute rectitude that she should have gone the longest way round to Florence, in order to spend a few weeks with her invalid son; for in former years it had been one of her most definite convictions that when Ralph wished to see her he was at liberty to remember that the Palazzo Crescentini contained a spacious apartment which was known as the room of the signorino.

"I want to ask you something," Isabel said to this young man, the day after her arrival at San Remo—"something that I have thought more than once of asking you by letter, but that I have hesitated on the whole to write about. Face to face, nevertheless, my question seems easy enough. Did you know that your father intended to leave me so much money?"

Ralph stretched his legs a little further than usual, and gazed a little more fixedly at the Mediterranean. "What does it matter, my dear Isabel, whether I knew? My father was very obstinate."

"So," said the girl, "you did know."

"Yes; he told me. We even talked it over a little."

"What did he do it for?" asked Isabel, abruptly.

"Why, as a kind of souvenir."

"He liked me too much," said Isabel.

"That's a way we all have."

"If I believed that, I should be very unhappy. Fortunately I don't believe it. I want to be treated with justice; I want nothing but that."

"Very good. But you must remember that justice to a lovely being is after all a florid sort of sentiment."

"I am not a lovely being. How can you say that, at the very moment when I am asking such odious questions? I must seem to you delicate."

"You seem to me troubled," said Ralph.

"I am troubled."

"About what?"

For a moment she answered nothing; then she broke out—

"Do you think it good for me suddenly to be made so rich? Henrietta doesn't."

"Oh, hang Henrietta!" said Ralph, coarsely. "If you ask me, I am delighted at it."

"Is that why your father did it—for your amusement?"

"I differ with Miss Stackpole," Ralph said, more gravely. "I think it's very good for you to have means."

Isabel looked at him a moment with serious eyes. "I wonder whether you know what is good for me—or whether you care."

"If I know, depend upon it I care. Shall I tell you what it is? Not to torment yourself."

"Not to torment you, I suppose you mean."

"You can't do that; I am proof. Take things more easily. Don't ask yourself so much whether this or that is good for you. Don't question your conscience so much—it will get out of tune, like a strummed piano. Keep it for great occasions. Don't try so much to form your character—it's like trying to pull open a rosebud. Live as you like best, and your character will form itself. Most things are good for you; the exceptions are very rare, and a comfortable income is not one of them." Ralph paused, smiling; Isabel had listened quickly. "You have too much conscience," Ralph added. "It's out of all reason, the number of things you think wrong. Spread your wings; rise above the ground. It's never wrong to do that."

She had listened eagerly, as I say; and it was her nature to understand quickly.

"I wonder if you appreciate what you say. If you do, you take a great responsibility."

"You frighten me a little, but I think I am right," said Ralph, continuing to smile.

"All the same, what you say is very true," Isabel went on. "You could say nothing more true. I am absorbed in myself—I look at life too much as a doctor's prescription. Why, indeed, should we perpetually be thinking whether things are good for us, as if we were patients lying in a hospital? Why should I be so afraid of not doing right? As if it mattered to the world whether I do right or wrong!"

"You are a capital person to advise," said Ralph; "you take the wind out of *my* sails!"

She looked at him as if she had not heard him—though she was following out the train of reflection which he himself had kindled. "I try to care more about the world than about myself—but I always come back to myself. It's because I am afraid." She stopped; her voice had trembled a little. "Yes, I am afraid; I can't tell you. A large fortune means freedom, and I am afraid of that. It's such a fine thing, and one should make such a good use of it. If one shouldn't, one would be ashamed. And one must always be thinking—it's a constant effort. I am not sure that it's not a greater happiness to be powerless."

"For weak people I have no doubt it's a greater happiness. For weak people the effort not to be contemptible must be great."

"And how do you know I am not weak?" Isabel asked.

"Ah," Ralph answered, with a blush which the girl noticed, "if you are, I am awfully sold!"

The charm of the Mediterranean coast only deepened for our heroine on acquaintance; for it was the threshold of Italy—the gate of admirations. Italy, as yet imperfectly seen and felt, stretched before her as a land of promise, a land in which a love of the beautiful might be comforted by endless knowledge. Whenever she strolled upon the shore with her cousin—and she was the companion of his daily walk—she looked a while across the sea, with longing eyes, to where she knew that Genoa lay. She was glad to pause, however, on the edge of this larger knowledge; the stillness of these soft weeks seemed good to her. They were a peaceful interlude in a career which she had little warrant as yet for regarding as agitated, but which nevertheless she was constantly picturing to herself by the light of her hopes, her fears, her fancies, her ambitions, her predilections, and which reflected these subjective accidents in a manner sufficiently dramatic. Madame Merle had predicted to Mrs. Touchett that after Isabel had put her hand into her pocket half-a-dozen times she would be reconciled to the idea that it had been filled by a munificent uncle; and the event justified, as it had so often justified before, Madame Merle's perspicacity. Ralph Touchett had praised his cousin for being morally inflammable; that is, for being quick to take a hint that was meant as good advice. His advice had perhaps helped the matter; at any rate before she left San Remo she had grown used to feeling rich. The consciousness found a place in rather a dense little group of ideas that she had about her herself, and often it was by no means the least agreeable. It was a perpetual implication of good intentions. She lost herself in a maze of visions; the fine things a rich, independent, generous girl, who took a large, human view of her opportunities and obligations, might do, were really innumerable. Her fortune therefore became to her mind a part of her better self; it gave her importance, gave her even, to her own imagination, a certain ideal beauty. What it did for her in the imagination of others is another affair, and on this point we must also touch in time. The visions I have just spoken of were intermingled with other reveries. Isabel liked better to think of the future than of the past; but at times, as she listened to the murmur of the Mediterranean waves, her glance took a backward flight. It rested upon two figures which, in spite of increasing distance, were still sufficiently salient; they were recognizable without difficulty as those of Caspar Goodwood and Lord Warburton. It was strange how quickly these gentlemen had fallen into the background of our young lady's life. It was in her disposition at all times to lose faith in the reality of absent things; she could summon back her faith, in case of need, with an effort, but the effort was often painful, even when the reality had been pleasant. The past was apt to look dead, and its revival to wear the supernatural aspect of a resurrection. Isabel moreover was not prone to take for granted that she herself lived in the mind of others—she had not the fatuity to believe that she left indelible traces. She was capable of being wounded by the discovery that she had been forgotten; and yet, of all liberties, the one she herself found sweetest was the liberty to forget. She had not given her last shilling, sentimentally speaking, either to Caspar Goodwood or to Lord Warburton, and yet she did not regard them as appreciably in her debt. She had, of course, reminded herself that she was to hear from Mr. Goodwood again; but this was not to be for another year and a half, and in that time a great many things might happen. Isabel did not say to herself that her American suitor might find some other girl more comfortable to woo; because, though it was certain that many other girls would prove so, she had not the smallest belief that this merit would attract him. But she reflected that she herself might change her humor—might weary of those things that were not Caspar (and there were so many things that were not Caspar!), and might find satisfaction in the very qualities which struck her today as his limitations. It was conceivable that his limitations should some day prove a sort of blessing in disguise—a clear and quiet harbor, inclosed by a fine granite breakwater. But that day could only come in its order, and she could not wait for it with folded hands. That Lord Warburton should continue to cherish her image seemed to her more than modesty should not only expect, but even desire. She had so definitely undertaken to forget him, as a lover, that a corresponding effort on his own part would be eminently proper. This was not, as it may seem, merely a theory tinged with sarcasm. Isabel really believed that his lordship would, in the usual phrase, get over it. He had been deeply smitten—this she believed, and she was still capable of deriving pleasure from the belief; but it was absurd that a man so completely absolved from fidelity should stiffen himself in an attitude it would be more graceful to discontinue. Englishmen liked to be comfortable, said Isabel, and there could be little comfort for Lord Warburton, in the long run, in thinking of a self-sufficient American girl who had been but a casual acquaintance. Isabel flattered herself that should she hear, from one day to another, that he had married some young lady of his own country who had done more to deserve him, she should receive the news without an impulse of jealousy. It would have proved that he believed she was firm—which was what she wished to seem to him; and this was grateful to her pride.

❧ 22 ❧

O
n one of the first days of May, some six months after old Mr. Touchett's
death, a picturesque little group was gathered in one of the many rooms
of an ancient villa which stood on the summit of an olive-muffled hill, outside of the Roman gate of Florence. The villa was a long, rather blank-looking structure, with the far-projecting roof which Tuscany loves, and which, on the hills that
encircle Florence, when looked at from a distance, makes so harmonious a rectan-
gle with the straight, dark, definite cypresses that usually rise, in groups of three or
four, beside it. The house had a front upon a little grassy, empty, rural piazza which
occupied a part of the hilltop; and this front, pierced with a few windows in irregular relations and furnished with a stone bench which ran along the base of the
structure and usually afforded a lounging-place to one or two persons wearing more
or less of that air of undervalued merit which in Italy, for some reason or other,
always gracefully invests anyone who confidently assumes a perfectly passive attitude—this ancient, solid, weather-worn, yet imposing front, had a somewhat
incommunicative character. It was the mask of the house; it was not its face. It had
heavy lids, but no eyes; the house in reality looked another way—looked off behind,
into splendid openness and the range of the afternoon light. In that quarter the
villa overhung the slope of its hill and the long valley of the Arno, hazy with Italian
color. It had a narrow garden, in the manner of a terrace, productive chiefly of tan-
gles of wild roses and old stone benches, mossy and sun-warmed. The parapet of
the terrace was just the height to lean upon, and beneath it the ground declined
into the vagueness of olive-crops and vineyards. It is not, however, with the outside
of the place that we are concerned; on this bright morning of ripened spring its tenants had reason to prefer the shady side of the wall. The windows of the ground
floor, as you saw them from the piazza, were, in their noble proportions, extremely
architectural; but their function seemed to be less to offer communication with the
world than to defy the world to look in. They were massively cross-barred and
placed at such a height that curiosity, even on tip-toe, expired before it reached
them. In an apartment lighted by a row of three of these obstructive apertures—
one of the several distinct apartments into which the villa was divided, and which
were mainly occupied by foreigners of conflicting nationality long resident in Flo-

rence—a gentleman was seated, in company with a young girl and two good sisters from a religious house. The room was, however, much less gloomy than my indications may have represented, for it had a wide, high door, which now stood open into the tangled garden behind; and the tall iron lattices admitted on occasion more than enough of the Italian sunshine. The place, moreover, was almost luxuriously comfortable; it told of habitation being practiced as a fine art. It contained a variety of those faded hangings of damask and tapestry, those chests and cabinets of carved and time-polished oak, those primitive specimens of pictorial art in frames pedantically rusty, those perverse looking relics of medieval brass and pottery, of which Italy has long been the not quite exhausted storehouse. These things were intermingled with articles of modern furniture, in which liberal concession had been made to cultivated sensibilities; it was to be noticed that all the chairs were deep and well padded, and that much space was occupied by a writing-table of which the ingenious perfection bore the stamp of London and the nineteenth century. There were books in profusion, and magazines and newspapers, and a few small modern pictures, chiefly in watercolor. One of these productions stood on a drawing room easel, before which, at the moment when we begin to be concerned with her, the young girl I have mentioned had placed herself. She was looking at the picture in silence.

Silence—absolute silence—had not fallen upon her companions; but their conversation had an appearance of embarrassed continuity. The two good sisters had not settled themselves in their respective chairs; their attitude was noticeably provisional, and they evidently wished to emphasize the transitory character of their presence. They were plain, comfortable, mild-faced women, with a kind of businesslike modesty, to which the impersonal aspect of their stiffened linen and inexpressive serge gave an advantage. One of them, a person of a certain age, in spectacles, with a fresh complexion and a full cheek, had a more discriminating manner than her colleague, and had evidently the responsibility of their errand, which apparently related to the young girl. This young lady wore her hat—a coiffure of extreme simplicity, which was not at variance with a plain muslin gown, too short for the wearer, though it must already have been "let out." The gentleman who might have been supposed to be entertaining the two nuns was perhaps conscious of the difficulties of his function; to entertain a nun is, in fact, a sufficiently delicate operation. At the same time he was plainly much interested in his youthful companion, and while she turned her back to him his eyes rested gravely upon her slim, small figure. He was a man of forty, with a well-shaped head, upon which the hair, still dense, but prematurely grizzled, had been cropped close. He had a thin, delicate, sharply-cut face, of which the only fault was that it looked too pointed; an appearance to which the shape of his beard contributed not a little. This beard, cut in the manner of the portraits of the sixteenth century and surmounted by a fair moustache, of which the ends had a picturesque upward flourish, gave its wearer a somewhat foreign, traditionary look, and suggested that he was a gentleman who studied effect. His luminous intelligent eye, an eye which expressed both softness and keenness—the nature of the observer as well as of the dreamer—would have assured you, however, that he studied it only within well-chosen limits, and that insofar as he sought it he found it. You would have been much at a loss to determine his nationality; he had none of the superficial signs that usually render the answer to this question an insipidly easy one. If he had English blood in his veins, it had probably received some French or Italian com-mixture; he was one of those persons who, in the matter of race, may, as the phrase is, pass for anything. He had a light, lean, lazy-looking figure, and was apparently neither tall nor short. He was dressed as a man dressed who takes little trouble about it.

"Well, my dear, what do you think of it?" he asked of the young girl. He used the Italian tongue, and used it with perfect ease; but this would not have convinced you that he was an Italian.

The girl turned her head a little to one side and the other.

"It is very pretty, papa. Did you make it yourself?"

"Yes, my child; I made it. Don't you think I am clever?"

"Yes, papa, very clever; I also have learned to make pictures." And she turned round and showed a small, fair face, of which the natural and usual expression seemed to be a smile of perfect sweetness.

"You should have brought me a specimen of your powers."

"I have brought a great many; they are in my trunk," said the child.

"She draws very—very carefully," the elder of the nuns remarked, speaking in French.

"I am glad to hear it. Is it you who have instructed her?"

"Happily, no," said the good sister, blushing a little. "*Ce n'est pas ma partie.* I teach nothing; I leave that to those who are wiser. We have an excellent drawing-master, Mr.—Mr.—what is his name?" she asked of her companion.

Her companion looked about at the carpet.

"It's a German name," she said in Italian, as if it needed to be translated.

"Yes," the other went on, "he is a German, and we have had him for many years."

The young girl, who was not heeding the conversation, had wandered away to the open door of the large room, and stood looking into the garden.

"And you, my sister, are French," said the gentleman.

"Yes, sir," the woman replied, gently. "I speak to the pupils in my own language. I know no other. But we have sisters of other countries—English, German, Irish. They all speak their own tongue."

The gentleman gave a smile.

"Has my daughter been under the care of one of the Irish ladies?" And then, as he saw that his visitors suspected a joke, but failed to understand it—"You are very complete," he said, instantly.

"Oh, yes, we are complete. We have everything, and everything is of the best."

"We have gymnastics," the Italian sister ventured to remark. "But not dangerous."

"I hope not. Is that your branch?" A question which provoked much candid hilarity on the part of the two ladies; on the subsidence of which their entertainer, glancing at his daughter, remarked that she had grown.

"Yes, but I think she has finished. She will remain little," said the French sister.

"I am not sorry. I like little women," the gentleman declared, frankly. "But I know no particular reason why my child should be short."

The nun gave a temperate shrug, as if to intimate that such things might be beyond our knowledge.

"She is in very good health; that is the best thing."

"Yes, she looks well." And the young girl's father watched her a moment. "What do you see in the garden?" he asked, in French.

"I see many flowers," she replied, in a sweet, small voice, and with a French accent as good as his own.

"Yes, but not many good ones. However, such as they are, go out and gather some for *ces dames.*"

The child turned to him, with her smile brightened by pleasure. "May I, truly?" she asked.

"Ah, when I tell you," said her father.

The girl glanced at the elder of the nuns.

"May I, truly, *ma mère?*"

"Obey monsieur your father, my child," said the sister, blushing again.

The child, satisfied with this authorization, descended from the threshold, and was presently lost to sight.

"You don't spoil them," said her father, smiling.

"For everything they must ask leave. That is our system. Leave is freely granted, but they must ask it."

"Oh, I don't quarrel with your system; I have no doubt it is a very good one. I sent you my daughter to see what you would make of her. I had faith."

"One must have faith," the sister blandly rejoined, gazing through her spectacles.

"Well, has my faith been rewarded? What have you made of her?"

The sister dropped her eyes a moment.

"A good Christian, monsieur."

Her host dropped his eyes as well; but it was probable that the movement had in each case a different spring.

"Yes," he said in a moment, "and what else?"

He watched the lady from the convent, probably thinking that she would say that a good Christian was everything.

But for all her simplicity, she was not so crude as that. "A charming young lady—a real little woman—a daughter in whom you will have nothing but contentment."

"She seems to me very nice," said the father. "She is very pretty."

"She is perfect. She has no faults."

"She never had any as a child, and I am glad you have given her none."

"We love her too much," said the spectacled sister, with dignity. "And as for faults, how can we give what we have not? *Le couvent n'est pas comme le monde, monsieur.* She is our child, as you may say. We have had her since she was so small."

"Of all those we shall lose this year she is the one we shall miss most," the younger woman murmured, deferentially.

"Ah, yes, we shall talk long of her," said the other. "We shall hold her up to the new ones."

And at this the good sister appeared to find her spectacles dim; while her companion, after fumbling a moment, presently drew forth a pocket-handkerchief of durable texture.

"It is not certain that you will lose her; nothing is settled yet," the host rejoined, quickly; not as if to anticipate their tears, but in the tone of a man saying what was most agreeable to himself.

"We should be very happy to believe that. Fifteen is very young to leave us."

"Oh," exclaimed the gentleman, with more vivacity than he had yet used, "it is not I who wish to take her away. I wish you could keep her always!"

"Ah, monsieur," said the elder sister, smiling and getting up, "good as she is, she is made for the world. *Le monde y gagnera.*"

"If all the good people were hidden away in convents, how would the world get on?" her companion softly inquired, rising also.

This was a question of a wider bearing than the good woman apparently supposed; and the lady in spectacles took a harmonizing view by saying comfortably—

"Fortunately there are good people everywhere."

"If you are going there will be two less here," her host remarked, gallantly.

For this extravagant sally his simple visitors had no answer, and they simply looked at each other in decent deprecation; but their confusion was speedily covered by the return of the young girl, with two large bunches of roses—one of them all white, the other red.

"I give you your choice, mamman Catherine," said the child. "It is only the color that is different, mamman Justine; there are just as many roses in one bunch as another."

The two sisters turned to each other, smiling and hesitating, with—"Which will you take?" and "No, it's for you to choose."

"I will take the red," said mother Catherine, in the spectacles. "I am so red myself. They will comfort us on our way back to Rome."

"Ah, they won't last," cried the young girl. "I wish I could give you something that would last!"

"You have given us a good memory of yourself, my daughter. That will last!"

"I wish nuns could wear pretty things. I would give you my blue beads," the child went on.

"And do you go back to Rome tonight?" her father asked.

"Yes, we take the train again. We have so much to do *làbas*."

"Are you not tired?"

"We are never tired."

"Ah, my sister, sometimes," murmured the junior votaress.

"Not today, at any rate. We have rested too well here. *Que Dieu vous garde, ma fille.*"

Their host, while they exchanged kisses with his daughter, went forward to open the door through which they were to pass; but as he did so he gave a slight exclamation, and stood looking beyond. The door opened into a vaulted ante-chamber, as high as a chapel, and paved with red tiles; and into this antechamber a lady had just been admitted by a servant, a lad in shabby livery, who was now ushering her toward the apartment in which our friends were grouped. The gentleman at the door, after dropping his exclamation, remained silent; in silence, too, the lady advanced. He gave her no further audible greeting, and offered her no hand, but stood aside to let her pass into the drawing room. At the threshold she hesitated.

"Is there anyone?" she asked.

"Someone you may see."

She went in, and found herself confronted with the two nuns and their pupil, who was coming forward between them, with a hand in the arm of each. At the sight of the new visitor they all paused, and the lady, who had stopped too, stood looking at them. The young girl gave a little soft cry—

"Ah, Madame Merle!"

The visitor had been slightly startled; but her manner the next instant was none the less gracious.

"Yes, it's Madame Merle, come to welcome you home."

And she held out two hands to the girl, who immediately came up to her, presenting her forehead to be kissed. Madame Merle saluted this portion of her charming little person, and then stood smiling at the two nuns. They acknowledged her smile with a decent obeisance, but permitted themselves no direct scrutiny of this imposing, brilliant woman, who seemed to bring in with her something of the radiance of the outer world.

"These ladies have brought my daughter home, and now they return to the convent," the gentleman explained.

"Ah, you go back to Rome? I have lately come from there. It is very lovely now," said Madame Merle.

The good sisters, standing with their hands folded into their sleeves, accepted this statement uncritically; and the master of the house asked Madame Merle how long it was since she had left Rome.

"She came to see me at the convent," said the young girl, before her father's visitors had time to reply.

"I have been more than once, Pansy," Madame Merle answered. "Am I not your great friend in Rome?"

"I remember the last time best," said Pansy, "because you told me I should leave the place."

"Did you tell her that?" the child's father asked.

"I hardly remember. I told her what I thought would please her. I have been in Florence a week. I hoped you would come and see me."

"I should have done so if I had known you were here. One doesn't know such things by inspiration—though I suppose one ought. You had better sit down."

These two speeches were made in a peculiar tone of voice—a tone half-lowered, and carefully quiet, but as from habit rather than from any definite need.

Madame Merle looked about her, choosing her seat.

"You are going to the door with these women? Let me of course not interrupt the ceremony. *Je vous salue, mesdames,*" she added, in French, to the nuns, as if to dismiss them.

"This lady is a great friend of ours; you will have seen her at the convent," said the host. "We have much faith in her judgment, and she will help me to decide whether my daughter shall return to you at the end of the holidays."

"I hope you will decide in our favor, madam," the sister in spectacles ventured to remark.

"That is Mr. Osmond's pleasantry; I decide nothing," said Madame Merle, smiling still. "I believe you have a very good school, but Miss Osmond's friends must remember that she is meant for the world."

"That is what I have told monsieur," sister Catherine answered. "It is precisely to fit her for the world," she murmured, glancing at Pansy, who stood at a little distance, looking at Madame Merle's elegant apparel.

"Do you hear that, Pansy? You are meant for the world," said Pansy's father.

The child gazed at him an instant with her pure young eyes.

"Am I not meant for you, papa?" she asked.

Papa gave a quick, light laugh.

"That doesn't prevent it! I am of the world, Pansy."

"Kindly permit us to retire," said sister Catherine. "Be good, in any case, my daughter."

"I shall certainly come back and see you," Pansy declared, recommencing her embraces, which were presently interrupted by Madame Merle.

"Stay with me, my child," she said, "while your father takes the good ladies to the door."

Pansy stared, disappointed, but not protesting. She was evidently impregnated with the idea of submission, which was due to anyone who took the tone of authority; and she was a passive spectator of the operation of her fate.

"May I not see mamman Catherine get into the carriage?" she asked very gently.

"It would please me better if you would remain with me," said Madame Merle, while Mr. Osmond and his companions, who had bowed low again to the other visitor, passed into the antechamber.

"Oh yes, I will stay," Pansy answered; and she stood near Madame Merle, surrendering her little hand, which this lady took. She stared out of the window; her eyes had filled with tears.

"I am glad they have taught you to obey," said Madame Merle. "That is what little girls should do."

"Oh yes, I obey very well," said Pansy, with soft eagerness, almost with boastfulness, as if she had been speaking of her piano playing. And then she gave a faint, just audible sigh.

Madame Merle, holding her hand, drew it across her own fine palm and looked at it. The gaze was critical, but it found nothing to deprecate; the child's small hand was delicate and fair.

"I hope they always see that you wear gloves," she said in a moment. "Little girls usually dislike them."

"I used to dislike them, but I like them now," the child answered.

"Very good, I will make you a present of a dozen."

"I thank you very much. What colors will they be?" Pansy demanded, with interest.

Madame Merle meditated a moment.

"Useful colors."

"But will they be pretty?"

"Are you fond of pretty things?"

"Yes; but—but not too fond," said Pansy, with a trace of asceticism.

"Well, they will not be too pretty," Madame Merle answered, with a laugh. She took the child's other hand, and drew her nearer; and then, looking at her a moment—"Shall you miss mother Catherine?"

"Yes—when I think of her."

"Try, then, not to think of her. Perhaps some day," added Madame Merle, "you will have another mother."

"I don't think that is necessary," Pansy said, repeating her little soft, conciliatory sigh. "I had more than thirty mothers at the convent."

Her father's step sounded again in the antechamber, and Madame Merle got up, releasing the child. Mr. Osmond came in and closed the door; then, without looking at Madame Merle, he pushed one or two chairs back into their places.

His visitor waited a moment for him to speak, watching him as he moved about. Then at last she said—"I hoped you would have come to Rome. I thought it possible you would have come to fetch Pansy away."

"That was a natural supposition; but I am afraid it is not the first time I have acted in defiance of your calculations."

"Yes," said Madame Merle, "I think you are very perverse."

Mr. Osmond busied himself for a moment in the room—there was plenty of space in it to move about—in the fashion of a man mechanically seeking pretexts for not giving an attention which may be embarrassing. Presently, however, he had exhausted his pretexts; there was nothing left for him—unless he took up a book— but to stand with his hands behind him, looking at Pansy. "Why didn't you come and see the last of mamman Catherine?" he asked of her abruptly, in French.

Pansy hesitated a moment, glancing at Madame Merle. "I asked her to stay with me," said this lady, who had seated herself again in another place.

"Ah, that was better," said Osmond. Then, at last, he dropped into a chair, and sat looking at Madame Merle; leaning forward a little, with his elbows on the edge of the arms and his hands interlocked.

"She is going to give me some gloves," said Pansy.

"You needn't tell that to everyone, my dear," Madame Merle observed.

"You are very kind to her," said Osmond. "She is supposed to have everything she needs."

"I should think she had had enough of the nuns."

"If we are going to discuss that matter, she had better go out of the room."

"Let her stay," said Madame Merle. "We will talk of something else."

"If you like, I won't listen," Pansy suggested, with an appearance of candor which imposed conviction.

"You may listen, charming child, because you won't understand," her father replied. The child sat down deferentially, near the open door, within sight of the garden, into which she directed her innocent, wistful eyes; and Mr. Osmond went on, irrelevantly, addressing himself to his other companion. "You are looking particularly well."

"I think I always look the same," said Madame Merle.

"You always *are* the same. You don't vary. You are a wonderful woman."

"Yes, I think I am."

"You sometimes change your mind, however. You told me on your return from England that you would not leave Rome again for the present."

"I am pleased that you remember so well what I say. That was my intention. But I have come to Florence to meet some friends who have lately arrived, and as to whose movements I was at that time uncertain."

"That reason is characteristic. You are always doing something for your friends."

Madame Merle looked straight at her interlocutor, smiling. "It is less characteristic than your comment upon it—which is perfectly insincere. I don't, however, make a crime of that," she added, "because if you don't believe what you say there is no reason why you should. I don't ruin myself for my friends; I don't deserve your praise. I care greatly for myself."

"Exactly; but yourself includes so many other selves—so much of everything. I never knew a person whose life touched so many other lives."

"What do you call one's life?" asked Madame Merle. "One's appearance, one's movements, one's engagements, one's society?"

"I call your life—your ambitions," said Osmond.

Madame Merle looked a moment at Pansy. "I wonder whether she understands that," she murmured.

"You see she can't stay with us!" And Pansy's father gave a rather joyless smile. "Go into the garden, *ma bonne,* and pluck a flower or two for Madame Merle," he went on, in French.

"That's just what I wanted to do," Pansy exclaimed, rising with promptness and noiselessly departing. Her father followed her to the open door, stood a moment watching her, and then came back, but remained standing, or rather strolling to and fro, as if to cultivate a sense of freedom which in another attitude might be wanting.

"My ambitions are principally for you," said Madame Merle, looking up at him with a certain nobleness of expression.

"That comes back to what I say. I am part of your life—I and a thousand others. You are not selfish—I can't admit that. If you were selfish, what should I be? What epithet would properly describe me?"

"You are indolent. For me that is your worst fault."

"I am afraid it is really my best."

"You don't care," said Madame Merle, gravely.

"No; I don't think I care much. What sort of a fault do you call that? My indolence, at any rate, was one of the reasons I didn't go to Rome. But it was only one of them."

"It is not of importance—to me at least—that you didn't go; though I should have been glad to see you. I am glad that you are not in Rome now—which you might be, would probably be, if you had gone there a month ago. There is something I should like you to do at present in Florence."

"Please remember my indolence," said Osmond.

"I will remember it; but I beg you to forget it. In that way you will have both the virtue and the reward. This is not a great labor, and it may prove a great pleasure. How long is it since you made a new acquaintance?"

"I don't think I have made any since I made yours."

"It is time you should make another, then. There is a friend of mine I want you to know."

Mr. Osmond, in his walk, had gone back to the open door again, and was looking at his daughter, as she moved about in the intense sunshine. "What good will it do me?" he asked, with a sort of genial crudity.

Madame Merle reflected a moment. "It will amuse you." There was nothing crude in this rejoinder; it had been thoroughly well considered.

"If you say that, I believe it," said Osmond, coming toward her. "There are some points in which my confidence in you is complete. I am perfectly aware, for instance, that you know good society from bad."

"Society is all bad."

"Excuse me. That isn't a common sort of wisdom. You have gained it in the right way—experimentally; you have compared an immense number of people with each other."

"Well, I invite you to profit by my knowledge."

"To profit? Are you very sure that I shall?"

"It's what I hope. It will depend upon yourself. If I could only induce you to make an effort!"

"Ah, there you are! I knew something tiresome was coming. What in the world—that is likely to turn up here—is worth an effort?"

Madame Merle flushed a little, and her eye betrayed vexation. "Don't be foolish, Osmond. There is no one knows better than you that there are many things worth an effort."

"Many things, I admit. But they are none of them probable things."

"It is the effort that makes them probable," said Madame Merle.

"There's something in that. Who is your friend?"

"The person I came to Florence to see. She is a niece of Mrs. Touchett, whom you will not have forgotten."

"A niece? The word niece suggests youth. I see what you are coming to."

"Yes, she is young—twenty-two years old. She is a great friend of mine. I met her for the first time in England, several months ago, and we took a great fancy to each other. I like her immensely, and I do what I don't do every day—I admire her. You will do the same."

"Not if I can help it."

"Precisely. But you won't be able to help it."

"Is she beautiful, clever, rich, splendid, universally intelligent and unprecedent-edly virtuous? It is only on those conditions that I care to make her acquaintance. You know I asked you some time ago never to speak to me of anyone who should not correspond to that description. I know plenty of dingy people; I don't want to know any more."

"Miss Archer is not dingy; she's as bright as the morning. She corresponds to your description; it is for that I wish you to know her. She fills all your requirements."

"More or less, of course."

"No; quite literally. She is beautiful, accomplished, generous, and for an American, well-born. She is also very clever and very amiable, and she has a handsome fortune."

Mr. Osmond listened to this in silence, appearing to turn it over in his mind, with his eyes on his informant. "What do you want to do with her?" he asked, at last.

"What you see. Put her in your way."

"Isn't she meant for something better than that?"

"I don't pretend to know what people are meant for," said Madame Merle. "I only know what I can do with them."

"I am sorry for Miss Archer!" Osmond declared.

Madame Merle got up. "If that is a beginning of interest in her, I take note of it."

The two stood there, face to face; she settled her mantilla, looking down at it as she did so.

"You are looking very well," Osmond repeated, still more irrelevantly than before. "You have got some idea. You are never as well as when you have got an idea; they are always becoming to you."

In the manner of these two persons, on first meeting on any occasion, and especially when they met in the presence of others, there was something indirect and circumspect, which showed itself in glance and tone. They approached each other obliquely, as it were, and they addressed each other by implication. The effect of each appeared to be to intensify to an embarrassing degree the self-consciousness of the other. Madame Merle of course carried off such embarrassments better than her friend; but even Madame Merle had not on this occasion the manner she would have liked to have—the perfect self-possession she would have wished to exhibit to her host. The point I wish to make is, however, that at a certain moment the obstruction, whatever it was, always leveled itself, and left them more closely face to face than either of them ever was with anyone else. This was what had happened now. They stood there, knowing each other well, and each of them on the whole willing to accept the satisfaction of knowing, as a compensation for the inconvenience—whatever it might be—of being known.

"I wish very much you were not so heartless," said Madame Merle, quietly. "It has always been against you, and it will be against you now."

"I am not so heartless as you think. Every now and then something touches me—as for instance your saying just now that your ambitions are for me. I don't understand it; I don't see how or why they should be. But it touches me, all the same."

"You will probably understand it even less as time goes on. There are some things you will never understand. There is no particular need that you should."

"You, after all, are the most remarkable woman," said Osmond. "You have more in you than almost anyone. I don't see why you think Mrs. Touchett's niece should matter very much to me, when—when—" and he paused a moment.

"When I myself have mattered so little?"

"That of course is not what I meant to say. When I have known and appreciated such a woman as you."

"Isabel Archer is better than I," said Madame Merle.

Her companion gave a laugh. "How little you must think of her to say that!"

"Do you suppose I am capable of jealousy? Please answer me that."

"With regard to me? No; on the whole I don't."

"Come and see me, then, two days hence. I am staying at Mrs. Touchett's—the Palazzo Crescentini—and the girl will be there."

"Why didn't you ask me that at first, simply, without speaking of the girl?" said Osmond. "You could have had her there at any rate."

Madame Merle looked at him in the manner of a woman whom no question that he could ask would find unprepared. "Do you wish to know why? Because I have spoken of you to her."

Osmond frowned and turned away. "I would rather not know that." Then, in a moment, he pointed out the easel supporting the little watercolor drawing. "Have you seen that—my last?"

Madame Merle drew near and looked at it a moment. "Is it the Venetian Alps—one of your last year's sketches?"

"Yes—but how you guess everything!"

Madame Merle looked for a moment longer; then she turned away. "You know I don't care for your drawings."

"I know it, yet I am always surprised at it. They are really so much better than most people's."

"That may very well be. But as the only thing you do, it's so little. I should have liked you to do so many other things: those were my ambitions."

"Yes; you have told me many times—things that were impossible."

"Things that were impossible," said Madame Merle. And then, in quite a different tone—"In itself your little picture is very good." She looked about the room—at the old cabinets, the pictures, the tapestries, the surfaces of faded silk. "Your rooms, at least, are perfect," she went on. "I am struck with that afresh, whenever I come back; I know none better anywhere. You understand this sort of thing as no one else does."

"I am very sick of it," said Osmond.

"You must let Miss Archer come and see all this. I have told her about it."

"I don't object to showing my things—when people are not idiots."

"You do it delightfully. As a cicerone in your own museum you appear to particular advantage."

Mr. Osmond, in return for this compliment, simply turned upon his companion an eye expressive of perfect clairvoyance.

"Did you say she was rich?" he asked in a moment.

"She has seventy thousand pounds."

"En écus bien comptés?"

"There is no doubt whatever about her fortune. I have seen it, as I may say."

"Satisfactory woman!—I mean you. And if I go to see her, shall I see the mother?"

"The mother? She has none—nor father either."

"The aunt then; whom did you say?—Mrs. Touchett."

"I can easily keep her out of the way."

"I don't object to her," said Osmond; "I rather like Mrs. Touchett. She has a sort of old-fashioned character that is passing away—a vivid identity. But that long jackanapes, the son—is he about the place?"

"He is there, but he won't trouble you."

"He's an awful ass."

"I think you are mistaken. He is a very clever man. But he is not fond of being about when I am there, because he doesn't like me."

"What could be more asinine than that? Did you say that she was pretty?" Osmond went on.

"Yes; but I won't say it again, lest you should be disappointed. Come and make a beginning; that is all I ask of you."

"A beginning of what?"

Madame Merle was silent a moment. "I want you of course to marry her."

"The beginning of the end! Well, I will see for myself. Have you told her that?"

"For what do you take me? She is a very delicate piece of machinery."

"Really," said Osmond, after some meditation, "I don't understand your ambitions."

"I think you will understand this one after you have seen Miss Archer. Suspend your judgment till then." Madame Merle, as she spoke, had drawn near the open door of the garden, where she stood a moment, looking out. "Pansy has grown pretty," she presently added.

"So it seemed to me."

"But she has had enough of the convent."

"I don't know," said Osmond. "I like what they have made of her. It's very charming."

"That's not the convent. It's the child's nature."

"It's the combination, I think. She's as pure as a pearl."

"Why doesn't she come back with my flowers, then?" Madame Merle asked. "She is not in a hurry."

"We will go and get them," said her companion.

"She doesn't like me," murmured Madame Merle, as she raised her parasol, and they passed into the garden.

❧ 23 ❧

Madame Merle, who had come to Florence on Mrs. Touchett's arrival at the invitation of this lady—Mrs. Touchett offering her for a month the hospitality of the Palazzo Crescentini—the judicious Madame Merle spoke to Isabel afresh about Gilbert Osmond, and expressed the wish that she should know him; but made no such point of the matter as we have seen her do in recommending the girl herself to Mr. Osmond's attention. The reason of this was perhaps that Isabel offered no resistance whatever to Madame Merle's proposal. In Italy, as in England, the lady had a multitude of friends, both among the natives of the country and its heterogeneous visitors. She had mentioned to Isabel most of the people the girl would find it well to know—of course, she said, Isabel could know whomever she would—and she had placed Mr. Osmond near the top of the list. He was an old friend of her own; she had known him these ten years; he was one of the cleverest and most agreeable men it was possible to meet. He was altogether above the respectable average; quite another affair. He was not perfect—far from it; the effect he produced depended a good deal on the state of his nerves and his spirits. If he were not in the right mood he could be very unsatisfactory—like most people, after all; but when he chose to exert himself no man could do it to better purpose. He had his peculiarities—which indeed Isabel would find to be the case with all the men really worth knowing—and he did not cause his light to shine equally for all persons. Madame Merle, however, thought she could undertake that for Isabel he would be brilliant. He was easily bored—too easily, and dull people always put him out; but a quick and cultivated girl like Isabel would give him a stimulus which was too absent from his life. At any rate, he was a person to know. One should not attempt to live in Italy without making a friend of Gilbert Osmond, who knew more about the country than anyone except two or three German professors. And if they had more knowledge than he, he had infinitely more taste; he had a taste which was quite by itself. Isabel remembered that her friend had spoken of him during their multifarious colloquies at Gardencourt, and wondered a little what was the nature of the tie that united them. She was inclined to imagine that Madame Merle's ties were peculiar, and such a possibility was a part of the interest created by this suggestive woman. As regards her relations with Mr. Osmond, however, Madame Merle hinted at nothing but a long-established and tranquil friendship. Isabel said that she should be happy to know a person who had enjoyed her friend's confidence for so many years. "You ought to see a great many men," Madame Merle remarked; "you ought to see as many as possible, so as to get used to them."

"Used to them?" Isabel repeated, with that exceedingly serious gaze which sometimes seemed to proclaim that she was deficient in a sense of humor—an intimation which at other moments she effectively refuted. "I am not afraid of them!"

"Used to them, I mean, so as to despise them. That's what one comes to with most of them. You will pick out, for your society, the few whom you don't despise."

This remark had a bitterness which Madame Merle did not often allow herself to betray; but Isabel was not alarmed by it, for she had never supposed that, as one saw more of the world, the sentiment of respect became the most active of one's emotions. This sentiment was excited, however, by the beautiful city of Florence, which pleased her not less than Madame Merle had promised; and if her unassisted perception had not been able to gauge its charms, she had clever companions to call attention to latent merits. She was in no want, indeed, of aesthetic illumination, for Ralph found it a pleasure which renewed his own earlier sensations, to act as cicerone to his eager young kinswoman. Madame Merle remained at home; she had seen the treasures of Florence so often, and she had always something to do. But she talked of all things with remarkable vividness of memory—she remembered the right-hand angle in the large Perugino, and the position of the hands of the Saint Elizabeth in the picture next to it; and had her own opinions as to the character of many famous works of art, differing often from Ralph with great sharpness, and defending her interpretations with as much ingenuity as good-humor. Isabel listened to the discussions which took place between the two, with a sense that she might derive much benefit from them and that they were among the advantages which—for instance—she could not have enjoyed in Albany. In the clear May mornings, before the formal breakfast—this repast at Mrs. Touchett's was served at twelve o'clock—Isabel wandered about with her cousin through the narrow and somber Florentine streets, resting a while in the thicker dusk of some historic church, or the vaulted chambers of some dispeopled convent. She went to

the galleries and palaces; she looked at the pictures and statues which had hitherto been great names to her, and exchanged for a knowledge which was sometimes
a limitation, a presentiment which proved usually to have been a blank. She performed all those acts of mental prostration in which, on a first visit to Italy, youth
and enthusiasm so freely indulge; she felt her heart beat in the presence of immortal genius, and knew the sweetness of rising tears in eyes to which faded fresco and
darkened marble grew dim. But the return, every day, was even pleasanter than the
going forth; the return into the wide, monumental court of the great house in which
Mrs. Touchett, many years before, had established herself, and into the high, cool
rooms where carven rafters and pompous frescoes of the sixteenth century looked
down upon the familiar commodities of the nineteenth. Mrs. Touchett inhabited an
historic building in a narrow street whose very name recalled the strife of medieval
factions; and found compensation for the darkness of her frontage in the modic-
ity of her rent and the brightness of a garden in which nature itself looked as
archaic as the rugged architecture of the palace and which illumined the rooms
that were in regular use. Isabel found that to live in such a place might be a source
of happiness—almost of excitement. At first it had struck her as a sort of prison;
but very soon its prison-like quality became a merit, for she discovered that it contained other prisoners than the members of her aunt's household. The spirit of the
past was shut up there, like a refugee from the outer world; it lurked in lonely corners, and, at night, haunted even the rooms in which Mrs. Touchett diffused her
matter-of-fact influence. Isabel used to hear vague echoes and strange reverbera-
tions; she had a sense of the hovering of unseen figures, of the flitting of ghosts.
Often she paused, listening, half-startled, half-disappointed, on the great cold
stone staircase.
    Gilbert Osmond came to see Madame Merle, who presented him to the young
lady seated almost out of sight at the other end of the room. Isabel, on this occasion, took little share in the conversation; she scarcely even smiled when the others turned to her appealingly; but sat there as an impartial auditor of their brilliant
discourse. Mrs. Touchett was not present, and these two had it their own way. They
talked extremely well; it struck Isabel almost as a dramatic entertainment,
rehearsed in advance. Madame Merle referred everything to her, but the girl
answered nothing, though she knew that this attitude would make Mr. Osmond
think she was one of those dull people who bored him. It was the worse, too, that
Madame Merle would have told him she was almost as much above the merely
respectable average as he himself, and that she was putting her friend dreadfully in
the wrong. But this was no matter, for once; even if more had depended on it, Isabel
could not have made an attempt to shine. There was something in Mr. Osmond that
arrested her and held her in suspense—made it seem more important that she
should get an impression of him than that she should produce one herself. Besides,

Isabel had little skill in producing an impression which she knew to be expected; nothing could be more charming, in general, than to seem dazzling; but she had a perverse unwillingness to perform by arrangement. Mr. Osmond, to do him justice, had a well-bred air of expecting nothing; he was a quiet gentleman, with a colorless manner, who said elaborate things with a great deal of simplicity. Isabel, however, privately perceived that if he did not expect he observed; she was very sure he was sensitive. His face, his head was sensitive; he was not handsome, but he was fine, as fine as one of the drawings in the long gallery above the bridge, at the Uffizi. Mr. Osmond was very delicate; the tone of his voice alone would have proved it. It was the visitor's delicacy that made her abstain from interference. His talk was like the tinkling of glass, and if she had put out her finger she might have changed the pitch and spoiled the concert. Before he went he made an appeal to her.

"Madame Merle says she will come up to my hilltop some day next week and drink tea in my garden. It would give me much pleasure if you would come with her. It's thought rather pretty—there's what they call a general view. My daughter, too, would be so glad—or rather, for she is too young to have strong emotions, I should be so glad—so very glad." And Mr. Osmond paused a moment, with a slight air of embarrassment, leaving his sentence unfinished. "I should be so happy if you could know my daughter," he went on, a moment afterwards.

Isabel answered that she should be delighted to see Miss Osmond, and that if Madame Merle would show her the way to the hilltop she should be very grateful. Upon this assurance the visitor took his leave; after which Isabel fully expected that her friend would scold her for having been so stupid. But to her surprise, Madame Merle, who indeed never fell into the matter-of-course, said to her in a few moments—

"You were charming, my dear; you were just as one would have wished you. You are never disappointing."

A rebuke might possibly have been irritating, though it is much more probable that Isabel would have taken it in good part; but, strange to say, the words that Madame Merle actually used caused her the first feeling of displeasure she had known this lady to excite. "That is more than I intended," she answered, coldly. "I am under no obligation that I know of to charm Mr. Osmond."

Madame Merle colored a moment; but we know it was not her habit to retract. "My dear child, I didn't speak for him, poor man; I spoke for yourself. It is not of course a question as to his liking you; it matters little whether he likes you or not! But I thought you liked him."

"I did," said Isabel, honestly. "But I don't see what that matters, either."

"Everything that concerns you matters to me," Madame Merle returned, with a sort of noble gentleness, "especially when at the same time another old friend is concerned."

Whatever Isabel's obligations may have been to Mr. Osmond, it must be admitted that she found them sufficient to lead her to ask Ralph sundry questions about him. She thought Ralph's judgments cynical, but she flattered herself that she had learned to make allowance for that.

"Do I know him?" said her cousin. "Oh, yes, I know him; not well, but on the whole enough. I have never cultivated his society, and he apparently has never found mine indispensable to his happiness. Who is he—what is he? He is a mysterious American, who has been living these twenty years, or more, in Italy. Why do I call him mysterious? Only as a cover for my ignorance; I don't know his antecedents, his family, his origin. For all I know, he may be a prince in disguise; he rather looks like one, by the way—like a prince who has abdicated in a fit of magnanimity, and has been in a state of disgust ever since. He used to live in Rome; but of late years he has taken up his abode in Florence; I remember hearing him say once that Rome has grown vulgar. He has a great dread of vulgarity; that's his special line; he hasn't any other that I know of. He lives on his income, which I suspect of not being vulgarly large. He's a poor gentleman—that's what he calls himself. He married young and lost his wife, and I believe he has a daughter. He also has a sister, who is married to some little Count or other, of these parts; I remember meeting her of old. She is nicer than he, I should think, but rather wicked. I remember there used to be some stories about her. I don't think I recommend you to know her. But why don't you ask Madame Merle about these people? She knows them all much better than I."

"I ask you because I want your opinion as well as hers," said Isabel.

"A fig for my opinion! If you fall in love with Mr. Osmond, what will you care for that?"

"Not much, probably. But meanwhile it has a certain importance. The more information one has about a person the better."

"I don't agree to that. We know too much about people in these days; we hear too much. Our ears, our minds, our mouths, are stuffed with personalities. Don't mind anything that anyone tells you about anyone else. Judge everyone and everything for yourself."

"That's what I try to do," said Isabel; "but when you do that people call you conceited."

"You are not to mind them—that's precisely my argument; not to mind what they say about yourself anymore than what they say about your friend or your enemy."

Isabel was silent a moment. "I think you are right; but there are some things I can't help minding; for instance, when my friend is attacked, or when I myself am praised."

"Of course you are always at liberty to judge the critic. Judge people as critics, however," Ralph added, "and you will condemn them all!"

"I shall see Mr. Osmond for myself," said Isabel. "I have promised to pay him a visit."

"To pay him a visit?"

"To go and see his view, his pictures, his daughter—I don't know exactly what. Madame Merle is to take me; she tells me a great many ladies call upon him."

"Ah, with Madame Merle you may go anywhere, *de confiance*," said Ralph. "She knows none but the best people."

Isabel said no more about Mr. Osmond, but she presently remarked to her cousin that she was not satisfied with his tone about Madame Merle. "It seems to me that you insinuate things about her. I don't know what you mean, but if you have any grounds for disliking her, I think you should either mention them frankly or else say nothing at all."

Ralph, however, resented this charge with more apparent earnestness than he commonly used. "I speak of Madame Merle exactly as I speak to her: with an even exaggerated respect."

"Exaggerated, precisely. That is what I complain of."

"I do so because Madame Merle's merits are exaggerated."

"By whom, pray? By me? If so, I do her a poor service."

"No, no; by herself."

"Ah, I protest!" Isabel cried with fervor. "If ever there was a woman who made small claims—"

"You put your finger on it," Ralph interrupted. "Her modesty is exaggerated. She has no business with small claims—she has a perfect right to make large ones."

"Her merits are large, then. You contradict yourself."

"Her merits are immense," said Ralph. "She is perfect; she is the only woman I know who has but that one little fault."

Isabel turned away with impatience. "I don't understand you; you are too paradoxical for my plain mind."

"Let me explain. When I say she exaggerates, I don't mean it in the vulgar sense—that she boasts, overstates, gives too fine an account of herself. I mean literally that she pushes the search for perfection too far—that her merits are in themselves overstrained. She is too good, too kind, too clever, too learned, too accomplished, too everything. She is too complete, in a word. I confess to you that she acts a little on my nerves, and that I feel about her a good deal as that intensely human Athenian felt about Aristides the Just."

Isabel looked hard at her cousin; but the mocking spirit, if it lurked in his words, failed on this occasion to peep from his eye. "Do you wish Madame Merle to be banished?" she inquired.

"By no means. She is much too good company. I delight in Madame Merle," said Ralph Touchett, simply.

"You are very odious, sir!" Isabel exclaimed. And then she asked him if he knew anything that was not to the honor of her brilliant friend.

"Nothing whatever. Don't you see that is just what I mean? Upon the character of everyone else you may find some little black speck; if I were to take half-an-hour to it, some day, I have no doubt I should be able to find one on yours. For my own, of course, I am spotted like a leopard. But on Madame Merle's nothing, nothing, nothing!"

"That is just what I think!" said Isabel, with a toss of her head. "That is why I like her so much."

"She is a capital person for you to know. Since you wish to see the world you couldn't have a better guide."

"I suppose you mean by that that she is worldly?"

"Worldly? No," said Ralph, "she is the world itself!"

It had certainly not, as Isabel for the moment took it into her head to believe, been a refinement of malice in him to say that he delighted in Madame Merle. Ralph Touchett took his entertainment wherever he could find it, and he would not have forgiven himself if he had not been able to find a great deal in the society of a woman in whom the social virtues existed in polished perfection. There are deep-lying sympathies and antipathies; and it may have been that in spite of the intellectual justice he rendered her, her absence from his mother's house would not have made life seem barren. But Ralph Touchett had learned to appreciate, and there could be no better field for such a talent than the table-talk of Madame Merle. He talked with her largely, treated her with conspicuous civility, occupied himself with her and let her alone, with an opportuneness which she herself could not have surpassed. There were moments when he felt almost sorry for her; and these, oddly enough, were the moments when his kindness was least demonstrative. He was sure that she had been richly ambitious, and that what she had visibly accomplished was far below her ambition. She had got herself into perfect training, but she had won none of the prizes. She was always plain Madame Merle, the widow of a Swiss *négociant,* with a small income and a large acquaintance, who stayed with people a great deal, and was universally liked. The contrast between this position and any one of some half-dozen others which he vividly imagined her to have had her eyes upon at various moments, had an element of the tragical. His mother thought he got on beautifully with their pliable guest; to Mrs. Touchett's sense two people who dealt so largely in factitious theories of conduct would have much in common. He had given a great deal of consideration to Isabel's intimacy with Madame Merle—having long since made up his mind that he could not, without opposition, keep his cousin to himself; and he regarded it on the whole with philosophic tolerance. He believed it would take care of itself; it would not last forever. Neither of these two superior persons knew the other as well as she supposed, and when each of them had made certain discoveries, there would be, if not a rupture, at least a relaxation. Meanwhile he was quite willing to admit that the conversation of the elder lady was an advantage to the younger, who had a great deal to learn, and would doubtless learn it better from Madame Merle than from some other instructors of the young. It was not probable that Isabel would be injured.

❦ 24 ❦

It would certainly have been hard to see what injury could arise to her from the visit she presently paid to Mr. Osmond's hilltop. Nothing could have been more charming than this occasion—a soft afternoon in May, in the full maturity of the Italian spring. The two ladies drove out of the Roman Gate, beneath the enormous blank superstructure which crowns the fine clear arch of that portal and makes it nakedly impressive, and wound between high-walled lanes, into which the wealth of blossoming orchards overdrooped and flung a perfume, until they reached the small superurban piazza, of crooked shape, of which the long brown wall of the villa occupied in part by Mr. Osmond, formed the principal, or at least the most imposing, side. Isabel went with her friend through a wide, high court, where a clear shadow rested below, and a pair of light-arched galleries, facing each other above, caught the upper sunshine upon their slim columns and the flowering plants in which they were dressed. There was something rather severe about the place; it looked somehow as if, once you were in, it would not be easy to get out. For Isabel, however, there was of course as yet no thought of getting out, but only of advancing. Mr. Osmond met her in the cold antechamber—it was cold even in the month of May—and ushered her, with her companion, into the apartment to which we have already been introduced. Madame Merle was in front, and while Isabel lingered a little, talking with Mr. Osmond, she went forward, familiarly, and greeted two persons who were seated in the drawing room. One of these was little Pansy, on whom she bestowed a kiss; the other was a lady whom Mr. Osmond presented to Isabel as his sister, the Countess Gemini. "And that is my little girl," he said, "who has just come out of a convent."

Pansy had on a scanty white dress, and her fair hair was neatly arranged in a net; she wore a pair of slippers, tied, sandal-fashion, about her ankles. She made Isabel a little conventional curtsey, and then came to be kissed. The Countess Gemini simply nodded, without getting up; Isabel could see that she was a woman of fashion.

She was thin and dark, and not at all pretty, having features that suggested some tropical bird—a long beak-like nose, a small, quickly-moving eye, and a mouth and chin that receded extremely. Her face, however, thanks to a very human and feminine expression, was by no means disagreeable, and, as regards her appearance, it was evident that she understood herself and made the most of her points. The soft brilliancy of her toilet had the look of shimmering plumage, and her attitudes were light and sudden, like those of a creature that perched upon twigs. She had a great deal of manner; Isabel, who had never known anyone with so much manner, immediately classified the Countess Gemini as the most affected of women. She remembered that Ralph had not recommended her as an acquaintance; but she was ready to acknowledge that on a casual view the Countess presented no appearance of wickedness. Nothing could have been kinder or more innocent than her greeting to Isabel.

"You will believe that I am glad to see you when I tell you that it is only because I knew you were to be here that I came myself. I don't come and see my brother— I make him come and see me. This hill of his is impossible—I don't see what possesses him. Really, Osmond, you will be the ruin of my horses some day; and if they receive an injury you will have to give me another pair. I heard them panting today; I assure you I did. It is very disagreeable to hear one's horses panting when one is sitting in the carriage; it sounds, too, as if they were not what they should be. But I have always had good horses; whatever else I may have lacked, I have always managed that. My husband doesn't know much, but I think he does know a horse. In general the Italians don't, but my husband goes in, according to his poor light, for everything English. My horses are English—so it is all the greater pity they should be ruined. I must tell you," she went on, directly addressing Isabel, "that Osmond doesn't often invite me; I don't think he likes to have me. It was quite my own idea, coming today. I like to see new people, and I am sure you are very new. But don't sit there; that chair is not what it looks. There are some very good seats here, but there are also some horrors."

These remarks were delivered with a variety of little jerks and glances, in a tone which, although it expressed a high degree of good nature, was rather shrill than sweet.

"I don't like to have you, my dear?" said her brother. "I am sure you are invaluable."

"I don't see any horrors anywhere," Isabel declared, looking about her. "Everything here seems to me very beautiful."

"I have got a few good things," Mr. Osmond murmured; "indeed I have nothing very bad. But I have not what I should have liked."

He stood there a little awkwardly, smiling and glancing about; his manner was an odd mixture of the indifferent and the expressive. He seemed to intimate that nothing was of much consequence. Isabel made a rapid induction: perfect simplicity was not the badge of his family. Even the little girl from the convent, who, in her prim white dress, with her small submissive face and her hands locked before her, stood there as if she were about to partake of her first communion—even Mr. Osmond's diminutive daughter had a kind of finish which was not entirely artless.

"You would have liked a few things from the Uffizi and the Pitti—that's what you would have liked," said Madame Merle.

"Poor Osmond, with his old curtains and crucifixes!" the Countess Gemini exclaimed; she appeared to call her brother only by his family name. Her ejaculation had no particular object; she smiled at Isabel as she made it, and looked at her from head to foot.

Her brother had not heard her; he seemed to be thinking what he could say to Isabel. "Won't you have some tea?—you must be very tired," he at last bethought himself of remarking.

"No, indeed, I am not tired; what have I done to tire me?" Isabel felt a certain need of being very direct, of pretending to nothing; there was something in the air, in her general impression of things—she could hardly have said what it was—that deprived her of all disposition to put herself forward. The place, the occasion, the combination of people, signified more than lay on the surface; she would try to understand—she would not simply utter graceful platitudes. Poor Isabel was perhaps not aware that many women would have uttered graceful platitudes to cover the working of their observation. It must be confessed that her pride was a trifle alarmed. A man whom she had heard spoken of in terms that excited interest, and who was evidently capable of distinguishing himself, had invited her, a young lady not lavish of her favors, to come to his house. Now that she had done so, the burden of the entertainment rested naturally upon himself. Isabel was not rendered less observant, and for the moment, I am afraid, she was not rendered more indulgent, by perceiving that Mr. Osmond carried his burden less complacently than might have been expected. "What a fool I was to have invited these women here!" she could fancy his exclaiming to himself.

"You will be tired when you go home, if he shows you all his *bibelots* and gives you a lecture on each," said the Countess Gemini.

"I am not afraid of that; but if I am tired, I shall at least have learned something."

"Very little, I suspect. But my sister is dreadfully afraid of learning anything," said Mr. Osmond.

"Oh, I confess to that; I don't want to know anything more—I know too much already. The more you know, the more unhappy you are."

"You should not undervalue knowledge before Pansy, who has not finished her education," Madame Merle interposed, with a smile.

"Pansy will never know any harm," said the child's father. "Pansy is a little convent-flower."

"Oh, the convents, the convents!" cried the Countess, with a sharp laugh. "Speak to me of the convents. You may learn anything there; I am a convent-flower myself. I don't pretend to be good, but the nuns do. Don't you see what I mean?" she went on, appealing to Isabel.

Isabel was not sure that she saw, and she answered that she was very bad at following arguments. The Countess then declared that she herself detested arguments, but that this was her brother's taste—he would always discuss. "For me," she said, "one should like a thing or one shouldn't; one can't like everything, of course. But one shouldn't attempt to reason it out—you never know where it may lead you. There are some very good feelings that may have bad reasons; don't you know? And then there are very bad feelings, sometimes, that have good reasons. Don't you see what I mean? I don't care anything about reasons, but I know what I like."

"Ah, that's the great thing," said Isabel, smiling, but suspecting that her acquaintance with this lightly. flitting personage would not lead to intellectual repose. If the Countess objected to argument, Isabel at this moment had as little taste for it, and she put out her hand to Pansy with a pleasant sense that such a gesture committed her to nothing that would admit of a divergence of views. Gilbert Osmond apparently took a rather hopeless view of his sister's tone, and he turned the conversation to another topic. He presently sat down on the other side of his daughter, who had taken Isabel's hand for a moment; but he ended by drawing her out of her chair, and making her stand between his knees, leaning against him while he passed his arm round her little waist. The child fixed her eyes on Isabel with a still, disinterested gaze, which seemed void of an intention, but conscious of an attraction. Mr. Osmond talked of many things; Madame Merle had said he could be agreeable when he chose, and today, after a little, he appeared not only to have chosen, but to have determined. Madame Merle and the Countess Gemini sat a little apart, conversing in the effortless manner of persons who knew each other well enough to take their ease; every now and then Isabel heard the Countess say something extravagant. Mr. Osmond talked of Florence, of Italy, of the pleasure of living in that country, and of the abatements to such pleasure. There were both satisfactions and drawbacks; the drawbacks were pretty numerous; strangers were too apt to see Italy in rose-color. On the whole it was better than other countries, if one was content to lead a quiet life and take things as they came. It was very dull sometimes, but there were advantages in living in the country which contained the most beauty. There were certain impressions that one could get only in Italy. There were others that one never got there, and one got some that were very bad. But from time to time one got a delightful one, which made up for everything. He was inclined to think that Italy had spoiled a great many people; he was even fatuous enough to believe at times that he himself might have been a better man if he had spent less of his life there. It made people idle and dilettantish, and second-rate; there was nothing tonic in an Italian life. One was out of the current; one was not *dans le mouvement,* as the French said; one was too far from Paris and London. "We are gloriously provincial, I assure you," said Mr. Osmond, "and I am perfectly aware that I myself am as rusty as a key that has no lock to fit it. It polishes me up a little to talk with you—not that I venture to pretend I can turn that very complicated lock I suspect your intellect of being! But you will be going away before I have seen you three times, and I shall perhaps never see you after that. That's what it is to live in a country that people come to. When they are disagreeable it is bad enough; when they are agreeable it is still worse. As soon as you find you like them they are off again! I have been deceived too often; I have ceased to form attachments; to permit myself to feel attractions. You mean to stay—to settle? That would be really comfortable. Ah yes, your aunt is a sort of guarantee; I believe she may be depended upon. Oh, she's an old Florentine; I mean literally an old one; not a modern outsider. She is a contemporary of the Medici; she must have been present at the burning of Savonarola, and I am not sure she didn't throw a handful of chips into the flame. Her face is very much like some faces in the early pictures; little, dry, definite faces, that must have had a good deal of expression, but almost always the same one. Indeed, I can show you her portrait in a fresco of Ghirlandaio's. I hope you don't object to my speaking that way of your aunt, eh? I have an idea you don't. Perhaps you think that's even worse. I assure you there is no want of respect in it, to either of you. You know I'm a particular admirer of Mrs. Touchett."

While Isabel's host exerted himself to entertain her in this somewhat confidential fashion, she looked occasionally at Madame Merle, who met her eyes with an inattentive smile in which, on this occasion, there was no infelicitous intimation that our heroine appeared to advantage. Madame Merle eventually proposed to the Countess Gemini that they should go into the garden, and the Countess, rising and shaking out her soft plumage, began to rustle toward the door.

"Poor Miss Archer!" she exclaimed, surveying the other group with expressive compassion. "She has been brought quite into the family."

"Miss Archer can certainly have nothing but sympathy for a family to which you belong," Mr. Osmond answered, with a laugh which, though it had something of a mocking ring, was not ill-natured.

"I don't know what you mean by that! I am sure she will see no harm in me but what you tell her. I am better than he says, Miss Archer," the Countess went on. "I am only rather light. Is that all he has said? Ah then, you keep him in good humor. Has he opened on one of his favorite subjects? I give you notice that there are two or three that he treats *à fond.* In that case you had better take off your bonnet."

"I don't think I know what Mr. Osmond's favorite subjects are," said Isabel, who had risen to her feet.

The Countess assumed, for an instant, an attitude of intense meditation; pressing one of her hands, with the fingertips gathered together, to her forehead.

"I'll tell you in a moment," she answered. "One is Machiavelli, the other is Vittoria Colonna, the next is Metastasio."

"Ah, with me," said Madame Merle, passing her arm into the Countess Gemini's, as if to guide her course to the garden, "Mr. Osmond is never so historical."

"Oh you," the Countess answered as they moved away, "you yourself are Machiavelli—you yourself are Vittoria Colonna!"

"We shall hear next that poor Madame Merle is Metastasio!" Gilbert Osmond murmured, with a little melancholy smile.

Isabel had got up, on the assumption that they too were to go into the garden; but Mr. Osmond stood there, with no apparent inclination to leave the room, with his hands in the pockets of his jacket, and his daughter, who had now locked her arm into one of his own, clinging to him and looking up, while her eyes moved from his own face to Isabel's. Isabel waited, with a certain unuttered contentedness, to have her movements directed; she liked Mr. Osmond's talk, his company; she felt that she was being entertained. Through the open doors of the great room she saw Madame Merle and the Countess stroll across the deep grass of the garden; then she turned, and her eyes wandered over the things that were scattered about her. The understanding had been that her host should show her his treasures; his pictures and cabinets all looked like treasures. Isabel, after a moment, went toward one of the pictures to see it better; but just as she had done so Mr. Osmond said to her abruptly—

"Miss Archer, what do you think of my sister?"

Isabel turned, with a good deal of surprise.

"Ah, don't ask me that—I have seen your sister too little."

"Yes, you have seen her very little; but you must have observed that there is not a great deal of her to see. What do you think of our family tone?" Osmond went on, smiling. "I should like to know how it strikes a fresh, unprejudiced mind. I know what you are going to say—you have had too little observation of it. Of course this is only a glimpse. But just take notice, in future, if you have a chance. I sometimes think we have got into a rather bad way, living off here among things and people not our own, without responsibilities or attachments, with nothing to hold us together or keep us up; marrying foreigners, forming artificial tastes, playing tricks with our natural mission. Let me add, though, that I say that much more for myself than for my sister. She's a very good woman—better than she seems. She is rather unhappy, and as she is not of a very serious disposition, she doesn't tend to show it tragically; she shows it comically instead. She has got a nasty husband, though I am not sure she makes the best of him. Of course, however, a nasty husband is an awkward thing. Madame Merle gives her excellent advice, but it's a good deal like giving a child a dictionary to learn a language with. He can look out the words, but he can't put them together. My sister needs a grammar, but unfortunately she is not grammatical. Excuse my troubling you with these details; my sister was very right in saying that you have been taken into the family. Let me take down that picture; you want more light."

He took down the picture, carried it toward the window, related some curious facts about it. She looked at the other works of art, and he gave her such further information as might appear to be most acceptable to a young lady making a call on a summer afternoon. His pictures, his carvings and tapestries were interesting; but after a while Isabel became conscious that the owner was more interesting still. He resembled no one she had ever seen; most of the people she knew might be divided into groups of half-a-dozen specimens. There were one or two exceptions to this; she could think, for instance, of no group that would contain her Aunt Lydia. There were other people who were, relatively speaking, original—original, as one might say, by courtesy—such as Mr. Goodwood, as her cousin Ralph, as Henrietta Stackpole, as Lord Warburton, as Madame Merle. But in essentials, when one came to look at them, these individuals belonged to types which were already present to her mind. Her mind contained no class which offered a natural place to Mr. Osmond—he was a specimen apart. Isabel did not say all these things to herself at the time; but she felt them, and afterwards they became distinct. For the moment she only said to herself that Mr. Osmond had the interest of rareness. It was not so much what he said and did, but rather what he withheld, that distinguished him; he indulged in no striking deflections from common usage; he was an original without being an eccentric. Isabel had never met a person of so fine a grain. The peculiarity was physical, to begin with, and it extended to his immaterial part. His dense, delicate hair, his overdrawn, retouched features, his clear complexion, ripe without being coarse, the very evenness of the growth of his beard, and that light, smooth, slenderness of structure which made the movement of a single one of his fingers produce the effect of an expressive gesture—these personal points struck our observant young lady as the signs of an unusual sensibility. He was certainly fastidious and critical; he was probably irritable. His sensibility had governed him—possibly governed him too much; it had made him impatient of vulgar troubles and had led him to live by himself, in a serene, impersonal way, thinking about art and beauty and history. He had consulted his taste in everything—his taste alone, perhaps; that was what made him so different from everyone else. Ralph had something of this same quality, this appearance of thinking that life was a matter of connoisseurship; but in Ralph it was an anomaly, a kind of humorous excrescence, whereas in Mr. Osmond it was the key-note, and everything was in harmony with it. Isabel was certainly far from understanding him completely; his meaning was not at all times obvious. It was hard to see what he meant, for instance, by saying that he was gloriously provincial—which was so exactly the opposite of what she had supposed. Was it a harmless paradox, intended to puzzle her? or was it the last refinement of high culture? Isabel trusted that she should learn in time; it would be very interesting to learn. If Mr. Osmond were provincial, pray what were the characteristics of the capital? Isabel could ask herself this question, in spite of having perceived that her host was a shy personage; for such shyness as his—the shyness of ticklish nerves and fine perceptions—was perfectly consistent with the best breeding. Indeed, it was almost a proof of superior qualities. Mr. Osmond was not a man of easy assurance, who chatted and gossiped with the fluency of a superficial nature; he was critical of himself as well as of others, and exacting a good deal of others (to think them agreeable), he probably took a rather ironical view of what he himself offered: a proof, into the bargain, that he was not grossly conceited. If he had not been shy, he would not have made that gradual, subtle, successful effort to overcome his shyness, to which Isabel felt that she owed both what pleased and what puzzled her in his conversation today. He suddenly asked her what she thought of the Countess Gemini—that was doubtless a proof that he was interested in her feelings; it could scarcely be as a help to knowledge of his own sister. That he should be so interested showed an inquiring mind; but it was a little singular that he should sacrifice his fraternal feeling to his curiosity. This was the most eccentric thing he had done.

There were two other rooms, beyond the one in which she had been received, equally full of picturesque objects, and in these apartments Isabel spent a quarter of an hour. Everything was very curious and valuable, and Mr. Osmond continued to be the kindest of ciceroni, as he led her from one fine piece to another, still holding his little girl by the hand. His kindness almost surprised our young lady, who wondered why he should take so much trouble for her; and she was oppressed at last with the accumulation of beauty and knowledge to which she found herself introduced. There was enough for the present; she had ceased to attend to what he said; she listened to him with attentive eyes, but she was not thinking of what he told her. He probably thought she was cleverer than she was; Madame Merle would have told him so; which was a pity, because in the end he would be sure to find out, and then perhaps even her real cleverness would not reconcile him to his mistake. A part of Isabel's fatigue came from the effort to appear as intelligent as she believed Madame Merle had described her, and from the fear (very unusual with her) of exposing—not her ignorance; for that she cared comparatively little—but her possible grossness of perception. It would have annoyed her to express a liking for something which her host, in his superior enlightenment, would think she ought not to like; or to pass by something at which the truly initiated mind would arrest itself. She was very careful, therefore, as to what she said, as to what she noticed or failed to notice—more careful than she had ever been before.

They came back into the first of the rooms, where the tea had been served; but as the two other ladies were still on the terrace, and as Isabel had not yet been made acquainted with the view, which constituted the paramount distinction of the place, Mr. Osmond directed her steps into the garden without more delay. Madame Merle and the Countess had had chairs brought out, and as the afternoon was lovely, the Countess proposed they should take their tea in the open air. Pansy, therefore, was sent to bid the servant bring out the tray. The sun had got low, the golden light took a deeper tone, and on the mountains and the plain that stretched beneath them, the masses of purple shadow seemed to glow as richly as the places that were still exposed. The scene had an extraordinary charm. The air was almost solemnly still, and the large expanse of the landscape, with its gardenlike culture and nobleness of outline, its teeming valley and delicately fretted hills, its peculiarly human-looking touches of habitation, lay there in splendid harmony and classic grace.

"You seem so well pleased that I think you can be trusted to come back," Mr. Osmond said, as he led his companion to one of the angles of the terrace.

"I shall certainly come back," Isabel answered, "in spite of what you say about its being bad to live in Italy. What was that you said about one's natural mission? I wonder if I should forsake my natural mission if I were to settle in Florence."

"A woman's natural mission is to be where she is most appreciated."

"The point is to find out where that is."

"Very true—a woman often wastes a great deal of time in the inquiry. People ought to make it very plain to her."

"Such a matter would have to be made very plain to me," said Isabel, smiling.

"I am glad, at any rate, to hear you talk of settling. Madame Merle had given me an idea that you were of a rather roving disposition. I thought she spoke of your having some plan of going round the world."

"I am rather ashamed of my plans; I make a new one every day."

"I don't see why you should be ashamed; it's the greatest of pleasures."

"It seems frivolous, I think," said Isabel. "One ought to choose something very deliberately, and be faithful to that."

"By that rule, then, I have not been frivolous."

"Have you never made plans?"

"Yes, I made one years ago, and I am acting on it today."

"It must have been a very pleasant one," said Isabel.

"It was very simple. It was to be as quiet as possible."

"As quiet?" the girl repeated.

"Not to worry—not to strive nor struggle. To resign myself. To be content with a little." He uttered these sentences slowly, with little pauses between, and his intelligent eyes were fixed upon Isabel's with the conscious look of a man who has brought himself to confess something.

"Do you call that simple?" Isabel asked, with a gentle laugh.

"Yes, because it's negative."

"Has your life been negative?"

"Call it affirmative if you like. Only it has affirmed my indifference. Mind you, not my natural indifference—I had none. But my studied, my willful renunciation."

Isabel scarcely understood him; it seemed a question whether he were joking or not. Why should a man who struck her as having a great fund of reserve suddenly bring himself to be so confidential? This was his affair, however, and his confidences were interesting. "I don't see why you should have renounced," she said in a moment.

"Because I could do nothing. I had no prospects, I was poor, and I was not a man of genius. I had no talents even; I took my measure early in life. I was simply the most fastidious young gentleman living. There were two or three people in the world I envied—the Emperor of Russia, for instance, and the Sultan of Turkey! There were even moments when I envied the Pope of Rome—for the consideration he enjoys. I should have been delighted to be considered to that extent; but since that couldn't be, I didn't care for anything less, and I made up my mind not to go in for honors. A gentleman can always consider himself, and fortunately, I was a gentleman. I could do nothing in Italy—I couldn't even be an Italian patriot. To do that, I should have had to go out of the country; and I was too fond of it to leave it. So I have passed a great many years here, on that quiet plan I spoke of. I have not been at all unhappy. I don't mean to say I have cared for nothing; but the things I have cared for have been definite—limited. The events of my life have been absolutely unperceived by anyone save myself; getting an old silver crucifix at a bargain (I have never bought anything dear, of course), or discovering, as I once did, a sketch by Correggio on a panel daubed over by some inspired idiot!"

This would have been rather a dry account of Mr. Osmond's career if Isabel had fully believed it; but her imagination supplied the human element which she was sure had not been wanting. His life had been mingled with other lives more than he admitted; of course she could not expect him to enter into this. For the present she abstained from provoking further revelations; to intimate that he had not told her everything would be more familiar and less considerate than she now desired to be. He had certainly told her quite enough. It was her present inclination, however, to express considerable sympathy for the success with which he had preserved his independence. "That's a very pleasant life," she said, "to renounce everything but Correggio!"

"Oh, I have been very happy; don't imagine me to suggest for a moment that I have not. It's one's own fault if one is not happy."

"Have you lived here always?"

"No, not always. I lived a long time at Naples, and many years in Rome. But I have been here a good while. Perhaps I shall have to change, however; to do something else. I have no longer myself to think of. My daughter is growing up, and it is very possible she may not care so much for the Correggios and crucifixes as I. I shall have to do what is best for her."

"Yes, do that," said Isabel. "She is such a dear little girl."

"Ah," cried Gilbert Osmond, with feeling, "she is a little saint of heaven! She is my great happiness!"

❧ 25 ❧

While this sufficiently intimate colloquy (prolonged for some time after we cease to follow it) was going on, Madame Merle and her companion, breaking a silence of some duration, had begun to exchange remarks. They were sitting in an attitude of unexpressed expectancy; an attitude especially marked on the part of the Countess Gemini, who, being of a more nervous temperament than Madame Merle, practised with less success the art of disguising impatience. What these ladies were waiting for would not have been apparent, and was perhaps not very definite to their own minds. Madame Merle waited for Osmond to release their young friend from her *tête-à-tête,* and the Countess waited because Madame Merle did. The Countess, moreover, by waiting, found the time ripe for saying something discordant; a necessity of which she had been conscious for the last twenty minutes. Her brother wandered with Isabel to the end of the garden, and she followed the pair for a while with her eyes.

"My dear," she then observed to Madame Merle, "you will excuse me if I don't congratulate you!"

"Very willingly; for I don't in the least know why you should."

"Haven't you a little plan that you think rather well of?" And the Countess nodded towards the retreating couple.

Madame Merle's eyes took the same direction; then she looked serenely at her neighbor. "You know I never understand you very well," she answered, smiling.

"No one can understand better than you when you wish. I see that, just now, you don't wish to."

"You say things to me that no one else does," said Madame Merle, gravely, but without bitterness.

"You mean things you don't like? Doesn't Osmond sometimes say such things?"

"What your brother says has a point."

"Yes, a very sharp one sometimes. If you mean that I am not so clever as he, you must not think I shall suffer from your saying it. But it will be much better that you should understand me."

"Why so?" asked Madame Merle; "what difference will it make?"

"If I don't approve of your plan, you ought to know it in order to appreciate the danger of my interfering with it."

Madame Merle looked as if she were ready to admit that there might be something in this; but in a moment she said quietly—"You think me more calculating than I am."

"It's not your calculating that I think ill of; it's your calculating wrong. You have done so in this case."

"You must have made extensive calculations yourself to discover it."

"No, I have not had time for that. I have seen the girl but this once," said the Countess, "and the conviction has suddenly come to me. I like her very much."

"So do I," Madame Merle declared.

"You have a strange way of showing it."

"Surely—I have given her the advantage of making your acquaintance."

"That, indeed," cried the Countess, with a laugh, "is perhaps the best thing that could happen to her!"

Madame Merle said nothing for some time. The Countess's manner was impertinent, but she did not suffer this to discompose her; and with her eyes upon the violet slope of Monte Morello she gave herself up to reflection.

"My dear lady," she said at last, "I advise you not to agitate yourself. The matter you allude to concerns three persons much stronger of purpose than yourself."

"Three persons? You and Osmond, of course. But is Miss Archer also very strong of purpose?"

"Quite as much so as we."

"Ah then," said the Countess radiantly, "if I convince her it's her interest to resist you, she will do so successfully!"

"Resist us? Why do you express yourself so coarsely? She is not to be subjected to force."

"I am not sure of that. You are capable of anything, you and Osmond. I don't mean Osmond by himself, and I don't mean you by yourself. But together you are dangerous—like some chemical combination."

"You had better leave us alone, then," said Madame Merle, smiling.

"I don't mean to touch you—but I shall talk to that girl."

"My poor Amy," Madame Merle murmured, "I don't see what has got into your head."

"I take an interest in her—that is what has got into my head. I like her."

Madame Merle hesitated a moment. "I don't think she likes you."

The Countess's bright little eyes expanded, and her face was set in a grimace. "Ah, you *are* dangerous," she cried, "even by yourself!"

"If you want her to like you, don't abuse your brother to her," said Madame Merle.

"I don't suppose you pretend she has fallen in love with him—in two interviews."

Madame Merle looked a moment at Isabel and at the master of the house. He was leaning against the parapet, facing her, with his arms folded; and she, at present, though she had her face turned to the opposite prospect, was evidently not scrutinizing it. As Madame Merle watched her she lowered her eyes; she was listening, possibly with a certain embarrassment, while she pressed the point of her parasol into the path. Madame Merle rose from her chair. "Yes, I think so!" she said.

The shabby footboy, summoned by Pansy, had come out with a small table, which he placed upon the grass, and then had gone back and fetched the tea tray; after which he again disappeared, to return with a couple of chairs. Pansy had watched these proceedings with the deepest interest, standing with her small hands folded together upon the front of her scanty frock; but she had not presumed to offer assistance to the servant. When the tea table had been arranged, however, she gently approached her aunt.

"Do you think papa would object to my making the tea?"

The Countess looked at her with a deliberately critical gaze, and without answering her question. "My poor niece," she said, "is that your best frock?"

"Ah no," Pansy answered, "it's just a little toilet for common occasions."

"Do you call it a common occasion when I come to see you?—to say nothing of Madame Merle and the pretty lady yonder."

Pansy reflected a moment, looking gravely from one of the persons mentioned to the other. Then her face broke into its perfect smile. "I have a pretty dress, but even that one is very simple. Why should I expose it beside your beautiful things?"

"Because it's the prettiest you have; for me you must always wear the prettiest. Please put it on the next time. It seems to me they don't dress you so well as they might."

The child stroked down her antiquated skirt, sparingly. "It's a good little dress to make tea—don't you think? Do you not believe papa would allow me?"

"Impossible for me to say, my child," said the Countess. "For me, your father's ideas are unfathomable. Madame Merle understands them better; ask her."

Madame Merle smiled with her usual geniality. "It's a weighty question—let me think. It seems to me it would please your father to see a careful little daughter making his tea. It's the proper duty of the daughter of the house—when she grows up."

"So it seems to me, Madame Merle!" Pansy cried. "You shall see how well I will make it. A spoonful for each." And she began to busy herself at the table.

"Two spoonfuls for me," said the Countess, who, with Madame Merle, remained for some moments watching her. "Listen to me, Pansy," the Countess resumed at last. "I should like to know what you think of your visitor."

"Ah, she is not mine—she is papa's," said Pansy.

"Miss Archer came to see you as well," Madame Merle remarked.

"I am very happy to hear that. She has been very polite to me."

"Do you like her, then?" the Countess asked.

"She is charming—charming," said Pansy, in her little neat, conversational tone. "She pleases me exceedingly."

"And you think she pleases your father?"

"Ah, really, Countess," murmured Madame Merle, dissuasively. "Go and call them to tea," she went on, to the child.

"You will see if they don't like it!" Pansy declared; and went off to summon the others, who were still lingering at the end of the terrace.

"If Miss Archer is to become her mother it is surely interesting to know whether the child likes her," said the Countess.

"If your brother marries again it won't be for Pansy's sake," Madame Merle replied. "She will soon be sixteen, and after that she will begin to need a husband rather than a stepmother."

"And will you provide the husband as well?"

"I shall certainly take an interest in her marrying well. I imagine you will do the same."

"Indeed I shan't!" cried the Countess. "Why should I, of all women, set such a price on a husband?"

"You didn't marry well; that's what I am speaking of. When I say a husband, I mean a good one."

"There are no good ones. Osmond won't be a good one."

Madame Merle closed her eyes a moment. "You are irritated just now; I don't know why," she said, presently. "I don't think you will really object either to your brother, or to your niece's, marrying, when the time comes for them to do so; and as regards Pansy, I am confident that we shall some day have the pleasure of looking for a husband for her together. Your large acquaintance will be a great help."

"Yes, I am irritated," the Countess answered. "You often irritate me. Your own coolness is fabulous; you are a strange woman."

"It is much better that we should always act together," Madame Merle went on.

"Do you mean that as a threat?" asked the Countess, rising.

Madame Merle shook her head, with a smile of sadness. "No indeed, you have not my coolness!"

Isabel and Mr. Osmond were now coming toward them, and Isabel had taken Pansy by the hand.

"Do you pretend to believe he would make her happy?" the Countess demanded.

"If he should marry Miss Archer I suppose he would behave like a gentleman."

The Countess jerked herself into a succession of attitudes. "Do you mean as most gentlemen behave? That would be much to be thankful for! Of course Osmond's a gentleman; his own sister needn't be reminded of that. But does he think he can marry any girl he happens to pick out? Osmond's a gentleman, of course; but I must say I have never, no never, seen any one of Osmond's pretensions! What they are all based upon is more than I can say. I am his own sister; I might be supposed to know. Who is he, if you please? What has he ever done? If there had been anything particularly grand in his origin—if he were made of some superior clay—I suppose I should have got some inkling of it. If there had been any great honors or splendors in the family, I should certainly have made the most of them; they would have been quite in my line. But there is nothing, nothing, nothing. One's parents were charming people of course; but so were yours, I have no doubt. Everyone is a charming person, nowadays. Even I am a charming person; don't laugh, it has literally been said. As for Osmond, he has always appeared to believe that he is descended from the gods."

"You may say what you please," said Madame Merle, who had listened to this quick outbreak nonetheless attentively, we may believe, because her eye wandered away from the speaker, and her hands busied themselves with adjusting the knots of ribbon on her dress. "You Osmonds are a fine race—your blood must flow from some very pure source. Your brother, like an intelligent man, has had the conviction of it, if he has not had the proofs. You are modest about it, but you yourself are extremely distinguished. What do you say about your niece? The child's a little duchess. Nevertheless," Madame Merle added, "it will not be an easy matter for Osmond to marry Miss Archer. But he can try."

"I hope she will refuse him. It will take him down a little."

"We must not forget that he is one of the cleverest of men."

"I have heard you say that before; but I haven't yet discovered what he has done."

"What he has done? He has done nothing that has had to be undone. And he has known how to wait."

"To wait for Miss Archer's money? How much of it is there?"

"That's not what I mean," said Madame Merle. "Miss Archer has seventy thousand pounds."

"Well, it is a pity she is so nice," the Countess declared. "To be sacrificed, any girl would do. She needn't be superior."

"If she were not superior, your brother would never look at her. He must have the best."

"Yes," rejoined the Countess, as they went forward a little to meet the others, "he is very hard to please. That makes me fear for her happiness!"

❧ 26 ❧

Gilbert Osmond came to see Isabel again; that is, he came to the Palazzo Crescentini. He had other friends there as well; and to Mrs. Touchett and Madame Merle he was always impartially civil; but the former of these ladies noted the fact that in the course of a fortnight he called five times, and compared it with another fact that she found no difficulty in remembering. Two visits a year had hitherto constituted his regular tribute to Mrs. Touchett's charms, and she had never observed that he selected for such visits those moments, of almost periodical recurrence, when Madame Merle was under her roof. It was not for Madame Merle that he came; these two were old friends, and he never put himself out for her. He was not fond of Ralph—Ralph had told her so—and it was not supposable that Mr. Osmond had suddenly taken a fancy to her son. Ralph was imperturbable—Ralph had a kind of loose-fitting urbanity that wrapped him about like an ill-made overcoat, but of which he never divested himself; he thought Mr. Osmond very good company, and would have been willing at any time to take the hospitable view of his idiosyncracies. But he did not flatter himself that the desire to repair a past injustice was the motive of their visitor's calls; he read the situation more clearly. Isabel was the attraction, and in all conscience a sufficient one. Osmond was a critic, a student of the exquisite, and it was natural he should admire an admirable person. So when his mother said to him that it was very plain what Mr. Osmond was thinking of, Ralph replied that he was quite of her opinion. Mrs. Touchett had always liked Mr. Osmond; she thought him so much of a gentleman. As he had never been an importunate visitor he had had no chance to be offensive, and he was recommended to Mrs. Touchett by his appearance of being as well able to do without her as she was to do without him—a quality that always excited her esteem. It gave her no satisfaction, however, to think that he had taken it into his head to marry her niece. Such an alliance, on Isabel's part, would have an air of almost morbid perversity. Mrs. Touchett easily remembered that the girl had refused an English peer; and that a young lady for whom Lord Warburton had not been up to the mark should content herself with an obscure American dilettante, a middle-aged widower with an overgrown daughter and an income of nothing—this answered to nothing in Mrs. Touchett's conception of success. She took, it will be observed, not the sentimental, but the political, view of matrimony—a view which has always had much to recommend it. "I trust she won't have the folly to listen to him," she said to her son; to which Ralph replied that Isabel's listening was one thing and her answering quite another. He knew that she had listened to others, but that she had made them listen to her in return; and he found much entertainment in the idea that, in these few months that he had known her, he should see a third suitor at her gate. She had wanted to see life, and fortune was serving her to her taste; a succession of gentlemen going down on their knees to her was by itself a respectable chapter of experience. Ralph looked forward to a fourth and a fifth *soupirant;* he had no conviction that she would stop at a third. She would keep the gate ajar and open a parley; she would certainly not allow number three to come in. He expressed this view, somewhat after this fashion, to his mother, who looked at him as if he had been dancing a jig. He had such a fanciful, pictorial way of saying things that he might as well address her in the deaf-mute's alphabet.

"I don't think I know what you mean," she said; "you use too many metaphors; I could never understand allegories. The two words in the language I most respect are Yes and No. If Isabel wants to marry Mr. Osmond, she will do so in spite of all your similes. Let her alone to find a favorable comparison for anything she undertakes. I know very little about the young man in America; I don't think she spends much of her time in thinking of him, and I suspect he has got tired of waiting for her. There is nothing in life to prevent her marrying Mr. Osmond, if she only looks at him in a certain way. That is all very well; no one approves more than I of one's pleasing one's self. But she takes her pleasure in such odd things; she is capable of marrying Mr. Osmond for his opinions. She wants to be disinterested: as if she were the only person who is in danger of not being so! Will he be so disinterested when he has the spending of her money? That was her idea before your father's death, and it has acquired new charms for her since. She ought to marry someone of whose disinterestedness she should be sure, herself; and there would be no such proof of that as his having a fortune of his own."

"My dear mother, I am not afraid," Ralph answered. "She is making fools of us all. She will please herself, of course; but she will do so by studying human nature and retaining her liberty. She has started on an exploring expedition, and I don't think she will change her course, at the outset, at a signal from Gilbert Osmond. She may have slackened speed for an hour, but before we know it she will be steaming away again. Excuse another metaphor."

Mrs. Touchett excused it perhaps, but she was not so much reassured as to withhold from Madame Merle the expression of her fears. "You who know everything," she said, "you must know this: whether that man is making love to my niece."

Madame Merle opened her expressive eyes, and with a brilliant smile—"Heaven help us," she exclaimed, "that's an idea!"

"Has it never occurred to you?"

"You make me feel like a fool—but I confess it hasn't. I wonder," added Madame Merle, "whether it has occurred to her."

"I think I will ask her," said Mrs. Touchett.

Madame Merle reflected a moment. "Don't put it into her head. The thing would be to ask Mr. Osmond."

"I can't do that," said Mrs. Touchett; "it's none of my business."

"I will ask him myself," Madame Merle declared, bravely.

"It's none of yours, either."

"That's precisely why I can afford to ask him; it is so much less my business than anyone's else, that in me the question will not seem to him embarrassing."

"Pray let me know on the first day, then," said Mrs. Touchett. "If I can't speak to him, at least I can speak to her."

"Don't be too quick with her; don't inflame her imagination."

"I never did anything to anyone's imagination. But I am always sure she will do something I don't like."

"You wouldn't like this," Madame Merle observed, without the point of interrogation.

"Why should I, pray? Mr. Osmond has nothing to offer."

Again Madame Merle was silent, while her thoughtful smile drew up her mouth more than usual toward the left corner. "Let us distinguish. Gilbert Osmond is certainly not the first comer. He is a man who under favorable circumstances might very well make an impression. He has made an impression, to my knowledge, more than once."

"Don't tell me about his love-affairs; they are nothing to me!" Mrs. Touchett cried. "What you say is precisely why I wish he would cease his visits. He has nothing in the world that I know of but a dozen or two of early masters and a grown-up daughter."

"The early masters are worth a good deal of money," said Madame Merle, "and the daughter is a very young and very harmless person."

"In other words, she is an insipid schoolgirl. Is that what you mean? Having no fortune, she can't hope to marry, as they marry here; so that Isabel will have to furnish her either with a maintenance or with a dowry."

"Isabel probably would not object to being kind to her. I think she likes the child."

"Another reason for Mr. Osmond stopping at home! Otherwise, a week hence, we shall have Isabel arriving at the conviction that her mission in life is to prove that a stepmother may sacrifice herself—and that, to prove it, she must first become one."

"She would make a charming stepmother," said Madame Merle, smiling; "but I quite agree with you that she had better not decide upon her mission too hastily. Changing one's mission is often awkward! I will investigate and report to you."

All this went on quite over Isabel's head; she had no suspicion that her relations with Mr. Osmond were being discussed. Madame Merle had said nothing to put her on her guard; she alluded no more pointedly to Mr. Osmond than to the other gentlemen of Florence, native and foreign, who came in considerable numbers to pay their respects to Miss Archer's aunt. Isabel thought him very pleasant; she liked to think of him. She had carried away an image from her visit to his hilltop which her subsequent knowledge of him did nothing to efface and which happened to take her fancy particularly—the image of a quiet, clever, sensitive, distinguished man, strolling on a moss-grown terrace above the sweet Val d'Arno, and holding by the hand a little girl whose sympathetic docility gave a new aspect to childhood. The picture was not brilliant, but she liked its lowness of tone, and the atmosphere of summer twilight that pervaded it. It seemed to tell a story—a story of the sort that touched her most easily; to speak of a serious choice, a choice between things of a shallow, and things of a deep, interest; of a lonely, studious life in a lovely land; of an old sorrow that sometimes ached today; a feeling of pride that was perhaps exaggerated, but that had an element of nobleness; a care for beauty and perfection so natural and so cultivated together, that it had been the main occupation of a lifetime of which the arid places were watered with the sweet sense of a quaint, half-anxious, half-helpless fatherhood. At the Palazzo Crescentini Mr. Osmond's manner remained the same; shy at first, and full of the effort (visible only to a sympathetic eye) to overcome this disadvantage; an effort which usually resulted in a great deal of easy, lively, very positive, rather aggressive, and always effective, talk. Mr. Osmond's talk was not injured by the indication of an eagerness to shine; Isabel found no difficulty in believing that a person was sincere who had so many of the signs of strong conviction—as, for instance, an explicit and graceful appreciation of anything that might be said on his own side, said perhaps by Miss Archer in particular. What continued to please this young lady was his extraordinary subtlety. There was such a fine intellectual intention in what he said, and the movement of his wit was like that of a quick-flashing blade. One day he brought his little daughter with him, and Isabel was delighted to renew acquaintance with the child, who, as she presented her forehead to be kissed by every member of the circle, reminded her vividly of an *ingénue* in a French play. Isabel had never seen a young girl of this pattern; American girls were very different—different too were the daughters of England. This young lady was so neat, so complete in her manner; and yet in character, as one could see, so innocent and infantine. She sat on the sofa, by Isabel; she wore a small grenadine mantle and a pair of the useful gloves that Madame Merle had given her—little gray gloves, with a single button. She was like a sheet of blank paper—the ideal *jeune fille* of foreign fiction. Isabel hoped that so fair and smooth a page would be covered with an edifying text.

The Countess Gemini also came to call upon her, but the Countess was quite another affair. She was by no means a blank sheet; she had been written over in a variety of hands, and Mrs. Touchett, who felt by no means honored by her visit, declared that a number of unmistakable blots were to be seen upon her surface. The Countess Gemini was indeed the occasion of a slight discussion between the mistress of the house and the visitor from Rome, in which Madame Merle (who was not such a fool as to irritate people by always agreeing with them) availed herself humorously of that large license of dissent which her hostess permitted as freely as she practiced it. Mrs. Touchett had pronounced it a piece of audacity that the Countess Gemini should have presented herself at this time of day at the door of a house in which she was esteemed so little as she must long have known herself to be at the Palazzo Crescentini. Isabel had been made acquainted with the estimate which prevailed under this roof; it represented Mr. Osmond's sister as a kind of flighty reprobate. She had been married by her mother—a heartless feather-head like herself, with an appreciation of foreign titles which the daughter, to do her justice, had probably by this time thrown off—to an Italian nobleman who had perhaps given her some excuse for attempting to quench the consciousness of neglect. The Countess, however, had consoled herself too well, and it was notorious in Florence that she had consoled others also. Mrs. Touchett had never consented to receive her, though the Countess had made overtures of old. Florence was not an austere city; but, as Mrs. Touchett said, she had to draw the line somewhere.

Madame Merle defended the unhappy lady with a great deal of zeal and wit. She could not see why Mrs. Touchett should make a scapegoat of that poor Countess, who had really done no harm, who had only done good in the wrong way. One must certainly draw the line, but while one was about it one should draw it straight; it was a very crooked chalk-mark that would exclude the Countess Gemini. In that case Mrs. Touchett had better shut up her house; this perhaps would be the best course so long as she remained in Florence. One must be fair and not make arbitrary differences; the Countess had doubtless been imprudent; she had not been so clever as other women. She was a good creature, not clever at all; but since when had that been a ground of exclusion from the best society? It was a long time since one had heard anything about her, and there could be no better proof of her having renounced the error of her ways than her desire to become a member of Mrs. Touchett's circle. Isabel could contribute nothing to this interesting dispute, not even a patient attention; she contented herself with having given a friendly welcome to the Countess Gemini, who, whatever her defects, had at least the merit of being Mr. Osmond's sister. As she liked the brother, Isabel thought it proper to try and like the sister; in spite of the growing perplexity of things she was still perfectly capable of these rather primitive sequences of feeling. She had not received the happiest impression of the Countess on meeting her at the villa, but she was thankful for an opportunity to repair this accident. Had not Mr. Osmond declared that she was a good woman? To have proceeded from Gilbert Osmond, this was rather a rough statement; but Madame Merle bestowed upon it a certain improving polish. She told Isabel more about the poor Countess than Mr. Osmond had done, and related the history of her marriage and its consequences. The Count was a member of an ancient Tuscan family, but so poor that he had been glad to accept Amy Osmond, in spite of her being no beauty, with the modest dowry her mother was able to offer— a sum about equivalent to that which had already formed her brother's share of their patrimony. Count Gemini, since then, however, had inherited money, and now they were well enough off, as Italians went, though Amy was horribly extravagant. The Count was a low-lived brute; he had given his wife every excuse. She had no children; she had lost three within a year of their birth. Her mother, who had pretensions to "culture," wrote descriptive poems, and corresponded on Italian subjects with the English weekly journals—her mother had died three years after the Countess's marriage, the father having died long before. One could see this in Gilbert Osmond, Madame Merle thought—see that he had been brought up by a woman; though, to do him justice, one would suppose it had been by a more sensible woman than the American Corinne, as Mrs. Osmond liked to be called. She had brought her children to Italy after her husband's death, and Mrs. Touchett remembered her during the years that followed her arrival. She thought her a horrible snob; but this was an irregularity of judgment on Mrs. Touchett's part, for she, like Mrs. Osmond, approved of political marriages. The Countess was very good company, and not such a fool as she seemed; one got on with her perfectly if one observed a single simple condition—that of not believing a word she said. Madame Merle had always made the best of her for her brother's sake; he always appreciated any kindness shown to Amy, because (if it had to be confessed for him) he was rather ashamed of her. Naturally, he couldn't like her style, her loudness, her want of repose. She displeased him; she acted on his nerves; she was not *his* sort of woman. What was his sort of woman? Oh, the opposite of the Countess, a woman who should always speak the truth. Isabel was unable to estimate the number of fibs her visitor had told her; the Countess indeed had given her an impression of rather silly sincerity. She had talked almost exclusively about herself; how much she should like to know Miss Archer; how thankful she should be for a real friend; how nasty the people in Florence were; how tired she was of the place; how much she should like to live somewhere else—in Paris, or London, or St. Petersburg; how impossible it was to get anything nice to wear in Italy, except a little old lace; how dear the world was growing everywhere; what a life of suffering and privation she had led. Madame Merle listened with interest to Isabel's account of her conversation with this plaintive butterfly; but she had not needed it to feel exempt from anxiety. On the whole, she was not afraid of the Countess, and she could afford to do what was altogether best—not to appear so.

Isabel had another visitor, whom it was not, even behind her back, so easy a matter to patronize. Henrietta Stackpole, who had left Paris after Mrs. Touchett's departure for San Remo and had worked her way down, as she said, through the cities of North Italy, arrived in Florence about the middle of May. Madame Merle surveyed her with a single glance, comprehended her, and, after a moment's concentrated reflection, determined to like her. She determined, indeed, to delight in her. To like her was impossible; but the intenser sentiment might be managed. Madame Merle managed it beautifully, and Isabel felt that in foreseeing this event she had done justice to her friend's breadth of mind. Henrietta's arrival had been announced by Mr. Bantling, who, coming down from Nice while she was at Venice, and expecting to find her in Florence, which she had not yet reached, came to the Palazzo Crescentini to express his disappointment. Henrietta's own advent occurred two days later, and produced in Mr. Bantling an emotion amply accounted for by the fact that he had not seen her since the termination of the episode at Versailles. The humorous view of his situation was generally taken, but it was openly expressed only by Ralph Touchett, who, in the privacy of his own apartment, when Bantling smoked a cigar there, indulged in Heaven knows what genial pleasantries on the subject of the incisive Miss Stackpole and her British ally. This gentleman took the joke in perfectly good part, and artlessly confessed that he regarded the affair as an intellectual flirtation. He liked Miss Stackpole extremely; he thought she had a wonderful head on her shoulders, and found great comfort in the society of a woman who was not perpetually thinking about what would be said and how it would look. Miss Stackpole never cared how it looked, and if she didn't care, pray why should he? But his curiosity had been roused; he wanted awfully to see whether she ever would care. He was prepared to go as far as she—he did not see why he should stop first.

Henrietta showed no signs of stopping at all. Her prospects, as we know, had brightened upon her leaving England, and she was now in the full enjoyment of her copious resources. She had indeed been obliged to sacrifice her hopes with regard to the inner life; the social question, on the continent, bristled with difficulties even more numerous than those she had encountered in England. But on the continent there was the outer life, which was palpable and visible at every turn, and more easily convertible to literary uses than the customs of those opaque islanders. Out of doors, in foreign lands, as Miss Stackpole ingeniously remarked, one seemed to see the right side of the tapestry; out of doors, in England, one seemed to see the wrong side, which gave one no notion of the figure. It is mortifying to be obliged to confess it, but Henrietta, despairing of more occult things, was now paying much attention to the outer life. She had been studying it for two months at Venice, from which city she sent to the *Interviewer* a conscientious account of the gondolas, the Piazza, the Bridge of Sighs, the pigeons and the young boatman who chanted Tasso.

The *Interviewer* was perhaps disappointed, but Henrietta was at least seeing Europe. Her present purpose was to get down to Rome before the malaria should come on—she apparently supposed that it began on a fixed day; and with this design she was to spend at present but few days in Florence. Mr. Bantling was to go with her to Rome, and she pointed out to Isabel that as he had been there before, as he was a military man, and as he had had a classical education—he was brought up at Eton, where they study nothing but Latin, said Miss Stackpole—he would be a most useful companion in the city of the Caesars. At this juncture Ralph had the happy idea of proposing to Isabel that she also, under his own escort, should make a pilgrimage to Rome. She expected to pass a portion of the next winter there—that was very well; but meantime there was no harm in surveying the field. There were ten days left of the beautiful month of May—the most precious month of all to the true Rome-lover. Isabel would become a Rome-lover; that was a foregone conclusion. She was provided with a well-tested companion of her own sex, whose society, thanks to the fact that she had other calls upon her sympathy, would probably not be oppressive. Madame Merle would remain with Mrs. Touchett; she had left Rome for the summer and would not care to return. This lady professed herself delighted to be left at peace in Florence; she had locked up her apartment and sent her cook home to Palestrina. She urged Isabel, however, to assent to Ralph's proposal, and assured her that a good introduction to Rome was not a thing to be despised. Isabel, in truth, needed no urging, and the party of four arranged its little journey. Mrs. Touchett, on this occasion, had resigned herself to the absence of a duenna; we have seen that she now inclined to the belief that her niece should stand alone.

Isabel saw Gilbert Osmond before she started, and mentioned her intention to him.

"I should like to be in Rome with you," he said; "I should like to see you there."

She hesitated a moment.

"You might come, then."

"But you'll have a lot of people with you."

"Ah," Isabel admitted, "of course I shall not be alone."

For a moment he said nothing more.

"You'll like it," he went on, at last. "They have spoiled it, but you'll like it."

"Ought I to dislike it, because it's spoiled?" she asked.

"No, I think not. It has been spoiled so often. If I were to go, what should I do with my little girl?"

"Can't you leave her at the villa?"

"I don't know that I like that—though there is a very good old woman who looks after her. I can't afford a governess."

"Bring her with you, then," said Isabel, smiling.

Mr. Osmond looked grave.

"She has been in Rome all winter, at her convent; and she is too young to make journeys of pleasure."

"You don't like bringing her forward?" Isabel suggested.

"No, I think young girls should be kept out of the world."

"I was brought up on a different system."

"You? Oh, with you it succeeded, because you—you were exceptional."

"I don't see why," said Isabel, who, however, was not sure there was not some truth in the speech.

Mr. Osmond did not explain; he simply went on. "If I thought it would make her resemble you to join a social group in Rome, I would take her there tomorrow."

"Don't make her resemble me," said Isabel; "keep her like herself."

"I might send her to my sister," Mr. Osmond suggested. He had almost the air of asking advice; he seemed to like to talk over his domestic matters with Isabel.

"Yes," said the girl; "I think that would not do much toward making her resemble me!"

After she had left Florence, Gilbert Osmond met Madame Merle at the Countess Gemini's. There were other people present; the Countess's drawing room was usually well filled, and the talk had been general; but after a while Osmond left his place and came and sat on an ottoman half-behind, half-beside, Madame Merle's chair.

"She wants me to go to Rome with her," he announced, in a low voice.

"To go with her?"

"To be there while she is there. She proposed it."

"I suppose you mean that you proposed it, and that she assented."

"Of course I gave her a chance. But she is encouraging—she is very encouraging."

"I am glad to hear it—but don't cry victory too soon. Of course you will go to Rome."

"Ah," said Osmond, "it makes one work, this idea of yours!"

"Don't pretend you don't enjoy it—you are very ungrateful. You have not been so well occupied these many years."

"The way you take it is beautiful," said Osmond. "I ought to be grateful for that."

"Not too much so, however," Madame Merle answered. She talked with her usual smile, leaning back in her chair, and looking round the room. "You have made a very good impression, and I have seen for myself that you have received one. You have not come to Mrs. Touchett's seven times to oblige me."

"The girl is not disagreeable," Osmond quietly remarked.

Madame Merle dropped her eye on him a moment, during which her lips closed with a certain firmness.

"Is that all you can find to say about that fine creature?"

"All? Isn't it enough? Of how many people have you heard me say more?"

She made no answer to this, but still presented her conversational smile to the room.

"You're unfathomable," she murmured at last. "I am frightened at the abyss into which I shall have dropped her!"

Osmond gave a laugh.

"You can't draw back—you have gone too far."

"Very good; but you must do the rest yourself."

"I shall do it," said Osmond.

Madame Merle remained silent, and he changed his place again; but when she rose to go he also took leave. Mrs. Touchett's victoria was awaiting her in the court, and after he had helped Madame Merle into it he stood there detaining her.

"You are very indiscreet," she said, rather wearily; "you should not have moved when I did."

He had taken off his hat; he passed his hand over his forehead.

"I always forget; I am out of the habit."

"You are quite unfathomable," she repeated, glancing up at the windows of the house; a modern structure in the new part of the town.

He paid no heed to this remark, but said to Madame Merle, with a considerable appearance of earnestness—

"She is really very charming; I have scarcely known anyone more graceful."

"I like to hear you say that. The better you like her, the better for me."

"I like her very much. She is all you said, and into the bargain she is capable of great devotion. She has only one fault."

"What is that?"

"She has too many ideas."

"I warned you she was clever."

"Fortunately they are very bad ones," said Osmond.

"Why is that fortunate?"

"*Dame,* if they must be sacrificed!"

Madame Merle leaned back, looking straight before her; then she spoke to the coachman. But Osmond again detained her.

"If I go to Rome, what shall I do with Pansy?"

"I will go and see her," said Madame Merle.

❦ 27 ❦

I shall not undertake to give an account of Isabel's impressions of Rome, to analyze her feelings as she trod the ancient pavement of the Forum, or to number her pulsations as she crossed the threshold of St. Peter's. It is enough to say that her perception of the endless interest of the place was such as might have been expected in a young woman of her intelligence and culture. She had always been fond of history, and here was history in the stones of the street and the atoms of the sunshine. She had an imagination that kindled at the mention of great deeds, and wherever she turned some great deed had been acted. These things excited her, but she was quietly excited. It seemed to her companions that she spoke less than usual, and Ralph Touchett, when he appeared to be looking listlessly and awkwardly over her head, was really dropping an eye of observation upon her. To her own knowledge she was very happy; she would even have been willing to believe that these were to be on the whole the happiest hours of her life. The sense of the mighty human past was heavy upon her, but it was interfused in the strangest, suddenest, most capricious way, with the fresh, cool breath of the future. Her feelings were so mingled that she scarcely knew whither any of them would lead her, and she went about in a kind of repressed ecstasy of contemplation, seeing often in the things she looked at a great deal more than was there, and yet not seeing many of the items enumerated in "Murray." Rome, as Ralph said, was in capital condition. The herd of reechoing tourists had departed, and most of the solemn places had relapsed into solemnity. The sky was a blaze of blue, and the plash of the fountains, in their mossy niches, had lost its chill and doubled its music. On the corners of the warm, bright streets one stumbled upon bundles of flowers.

Our friends had gone one afternoon—it was the third of their stay—to look at the latest excavations in the Forum; these labors having been for some time previous largely extended. They had gone down from the modern street to the level of the Sacred Way, along which they wandered with a reverence of step which was not the same on the part of each. Henrietta Stackpole was struck with the fact that ancient Rome had been paved a good deal like New York, and even found an analogy between the deep chariot-ruts which are traceable in the antique street, and the iron grooves which mark the course of the American horse-car. The sun had begun to sink, the air was filled with a golden haze, and the long shadows of broken column and formless pedestal were thrown across the field of ruin. Henrietta wandered away with Mr. Bantling, in whose Latin reminiscences she was apparently much engrossed, and Ralph addressed such elucidations as he was prepared to offer, to the attentive ear of our heroine. One of the humble archaeologists who hover about the place had put himself at the disposal of the two, and repeated his lesson with a fluency which the decline of the season had done nothing to impair. A process of digging was going on in a remote corner of the Forum, and he presently remarked that if it should please the *signori* to go and watch it a little, they might see something interesting. The proposal commended itself more to Ralph than to Isabel, who was weary with much wandering; so that she charged her companion to satisfy his curiosity while she patiently awaited his return. The hour and the place were much to her taste, and she should enjoy being alone. Ralph accordingly went off with the cicerone, while Isabel sat down on a prostrate column, near the foundations of the Capitol. She desired a quarter of an hour's solitude, but she was not long to enjoy it. Keen as was her interest in the rugged relics of the Roman past that lay scattered around her, and in which the corrosion of centuries had still left so much of individual life, her thoughts, after resting a while on these things, had wandered, by a concatenation of stages it might require some subtlety to trace, to regions and objects more contemporaneous. From the Roman past to Isabel Archer's future was a long stride, but her imagination had taken it in a single flight, and now hovered in slow circles over the nearer and richer field. She was so absorbed in her thoughts, as she bent her eyes upon a row of cracked but not dislocated slabs covering the ground at her feet, that she had not heard the sound of approaching footsteps before a shadow was thrown across the line of her vision. She looked up and saw a gentleman—a gentleman who was not Ralph come back to say that the excavations were a bore. This personage was startled as she was startled; he stood there, smiling a little, blushing a good deal, and raising his hat.

"Lord Warburton!" Isabel exclaimed, getting up.

"I had no idea it was you," he said. "I turned that corner and came upon you."

Isabel looked about her.

"I am alone, but my companions have just left me. My cousin is gone to look at the digging over there."

"Ah yes; I see." And Lord Warburton's eyes wandered vaguely in the direction Isabel had indicated. He stood firmly before her; he had stopped smiling; he folded his arms with a kind of deliberation. "Don't let me disturb you," he went on, looking at her dejected pillar. "I am afraid you are tired."

"Yes, I am rather tired." She hesitated a moment, and then she sat down. "But don't let me interrupt you," she added.

"Oh dear, I am quite alone, I have nothing on earth to do. I had no idea you were in Rome. I have just come from the East. I am only passing through."

"You have been making a long journey," said Isabel, who had learned from Ralph that Lord Warburton was absent from England.

"Yes, I came abroad for six months—soon after I saw you last. I have been in Turkey and Asia Minor; I came the other day from Athens." He spoke with visible embarrassment; this unexpected meeting caused him an emotion he was unable to conceal. He looked at Isabel a moment, and then he said, abruptly—"Do you wish me to leave you, or will you let me stay a little?"

She looked up at him, gently. "I don't wish you to leave me, Lord Warburton; I am very glad to see you."

"Thank you for saying that. May I sit down?"

The fluted shaft on which Isabel had taken her seat would have afforded a resting-place to several persons, and there was plenty of room even for a highly-developed Englishman. This fine specimen of that great class seated himself near our young lady, and in the course of five minutes he had asked her several questions, taken rather at random, and of which, as he asked some of them twice over, he apparently did not always heed the answer; had given her, too, some information about himself which was not wasted upon her calmer feminine sense. Lord Warburton, though he tried hard to seem easy, was agitated; he repeated more than once that he had not expected to meet her, and it was evident that the encounter touched him in a way that would have made preparation advisable. He had abrupt alternations of gaiety and gravity; he appeared at one moment to seek his neighbor's eye and at the next to avoid it. He was splendidly sunburnt; even his multitudinous beard seemed to have been burnished by the fire of Asia. He was dressed in the loose-fitting, heterogeneous garments in which the English traveler in foreign lands is wont to consult his comfort and affirm his nationality; and with his clear gray eye, his bronzed complexion, fresh beneath its brownness, his manly figure, his modest manner, and his general air of being a gentleman and an explorer, he was such a representative of the British race as need not in any clime have been disavowed by those who have a kindness for it. Isabel noted these things, and was glad she had always liked Lord Warburton. He was evidently as likeable as before, and the tone of his voice, which she had formerly thought delightful, was as good as an assurance that he would never change for the worse. They talked about the matters that were naturally in order; her uncle's death, Ralph's state of health, the way she had passed her winter, her visit to Rome, her return to Florence, her plans for the summer, the hotel she was staying at; and then Lord Warburton's own adventures, movements, intentions, impressions and present domicile. At last there was a silence, and she knew what he was thinking of. His eyes were fixed on the ground; but at last he raised them and said gravely—"I have written to you several times."

"Written to me? I have never got your letters."

"I never sent them. I burned them up."

"Ah," said Isabel with a laugh, "it was better that you should do that than I!"

"I thought you wouldn't care about them," he went on, with a simplicity that might have touched her. "It seemed to me that after all I had no right to trouble you with letters."

"I should have been very glad to have news of you. You know that I hoped that—that—" Isabel stopped; it seemed to her there would be a certain flatness in the utterance of her thought.

"I know what you are going to say. You hoped we should always remain good friends." This formula, as Lord Warburton uttered it, was certainly flat enough; but then he was interested in making it appear so.

Isabel found herself reduced simply to saying—"Please don't talk of all that;" a speech which hardly seemed to her an improvement on the other.

"It's a small consolation to allow me!" Lord Warburton exclaimed, with force.

"I can't pretend to console you," said the girl, who, as she sat there, found it good to think that she had given him the answer that had satisfied him so little six months before. He was pleasant, he was powerful, he was gallant, there was no better man than he. But her answer remained.

"It's very well you don't try to console me; it would not be in your power," she heard him say, through the medium of her quickened reflections.

"I hoped we should meet again, because I had no fear you would attempt to make me feel I had wronged you. But when you do that—the pain is greater than the pleasure." And Isabel got up, looking for her companions.

"I don't want to make you feel that; of course I can't say that. I only just want you to know one or two things, in fairness to myself as it were. I won't return to the subject again. I felt very strongly what I expressed to you last year; I couldn't think of anything else. I tried to forget—energetically, systematically. I tried to take an interest in someone else. I tell you this because I want you to know I did my duty. I didn't succeed. It was for the same purpose I went abroad—as far away as possible. They say traveling distracts the mind; but it didn't distract mine. I have thought of you perpetually, ever since I last saw you. I am exactly the same. I love you just as much, and everything I said to you then is just as true. However, I don't mean to trouble you now; it's only for a moment. I may add that when I came upon you a moment since, without the smallest idea of seeing you, I was in the very act of wishing I knew where you were."

He had recovered his self-control, as I say, and while he spoke it became complete. He spoke plainly and simply, in a low tone of voice, in a matter-of-fact way. There might have been something impressive, even to a woman of less imagination than the one he addressed, in hearing this brilliant, brave-looking gentleman express himself so modestly and reasonably.

"I have often thought of you, Lord Warburton," Isabel answered. "You may be sure I shall always do that." And then she added, with a smile—"There is no harm in that, on either side."

They walked along together, and she asked kindly about his sisters and requested him to let them know she had done so. He said nothing more about his own feelings, but returned to those more objective topics they had already touched upon. Presently he asked her when she was to leave Rome, and on her mentioning the limit of her stay, declared he was glad it was still so distant.

"Why do you say that, if you yourself are only passing through?" she inquired, with some anxiety.

"Ah, when I said I was passing through, I didn't mean that one would treat Rome as if it were Clapham Junction. To pass through Rome is to stop a week or two."

"Say frankly that you mean to stay as long as I do!"

Lord Warburton looked at her a moment, with an uncomfortable smile. "You won't like that. You are afraid you will see too much of me."

"It doesn't matter what I like. I certainly can't expect you to leave this delightful place on my account. But I confess I am afraid of you."

"Afraid I will begin again? I promise to be very careful."

They had gradually stopped, and they stood a moment face to face. "Poor Lord Warburton!" said Isabel, with a melancholy smile.

"Poor Lord Warburton, indeed! But I will be careful."

"You may be unhappy, but you shall not make me so. That I can't allow."

"If I believed I could make you unhappy, I think I should try it." At this she walked in advance, and he also proceeded. "I will never say a word to displease you," he promised, very gently.

"Very good. If you do, our friendship's at an end."

"Perhaps some day—after a while—you will give me leave," he suggested.

"Give you leave—to make me unhappy?"

He hesitated. "To tell you again—" But he checked himself. "I will be silent," he said; "silent always."

Ralph Touchett had been joined, in his visit to the excavation, by Miss Stackpole and her attendant, and these three now emerged from among the mounds of earth and stone collected round the aperture, and came into sight of Isabel and her companion. Ralph Touchett gave signs of greeting to Lord Warburton, and Henrietta exclaimed in a high voice, "Gracious, there's that lord!" Ralph and his friend met each other with undemonstrative cordiality, and Miss Stackpole rested her large intellectual gaze upon the sunburnt traveler.

"I don't suppose you remember me, sir," she soon remarked.

"Indeed I do remember you," said Lord Warburton. "I asked you to come and see me, and you never came."

"I don't go everywhere I am asked," Miss Stackpole answered, coldly.

"Ah, well, I won't ask you again," said the master of Lockleigh, good-humoredly.

"If you do I will go; so be sure!"

Lord Warburton, for all his good-humor, seemed sure enough. Mr. Bantling had stood by, without claiming a recognition, but he now took occasion to nod to his lordship, who answered him with a friendly "Oh, you here, Bantling?" and a hand-shake.

"Well," said Henrietta, "I didn't know you knew him!"

"I guess you don't know everyone I know," Mr. Bantling rejoined, facetiously.

"I thought that when an Englishman knew a lord he always told you."

"Ah, I am afraid Bantling was ashamed of me," said Lord Warburton, laughing. Isabel was glad to hear him laugh; she gave a little sigh of relief as they took their way homeward.

The next day was Sunday; she spent her morning writing two long letters—one to her sister Lily, the other to Madame Merle; but in neither of these epistles did she mention the fact that a rejected suitor had threatened her with another appeal. Of a Sunday afternoon all good Romans (and the best Romans are often the northern barbarians) follow the custom of going to hear vespers at St. Peter's; and it had been agreed among our friends that they would drive together to the great church. After lunch, an hour before the carriage came, Lord Warburton presented himself at the Hôtel de Paris and paid a visit to the two ladies, Ralph Touchett and Mr. Bantling having gone out together. The visitor seemed to have wished to give Isabel an example of his intention to keep the promise he had made her the evening before; he was both discreet and frank; he made not even a tacit appeal, but left it for her to judge what a mere good friend he could be. He talked about his travels, about Persia, about Turkey, and when Miss Stackpole asked him whether it would "pay" for her to visit those countries, assured her that they offered a great field to female enterprise. Isabel did him justice, but she wondered what his purpose was, and what he expected to gain even by behaving heroically. If he expected to melt her by showing what a good fellow he was, he might spare himself the trouble. She knew already he was a good fellow, and nothing he could do would add to this conviction. Moreover, his being in Rome at all made her vaguely uneasy. Nevertheless, when on bringing his call to a close, he said that he too should be at St. Peter's and should look out for Isabel and her friends, she was obliged to reply that it would be a pleasure to see him again.

In the church, as she strolled over its tesselated acres, he was the first person she encountered. She had not been one of the superior tourists who are "disappointed" in St. Peter's and find it smaller than its fame; the first time she passed beneath the huge leathern curtain that strains and bangs at the entrance—the first time she found herself beneath the far-arching dome and saw the light drizzle down through the air thickened with incense and with the reflections of marble and gilt, of mosaic and bronze, her conception of greatness received an extension. After this it never lacked space to soar. She gazed and wondered, like a child or a peasant, and paid her silent tribute to visible grandeur. Lord Warburton walked beside her and talked of Saint Sophia of Constantinople; she was afraid that he would end by calling attention to his exemplary conduct. The service had not yet begun, but at St. Peter's there is much to observe, and as there is something almost profane in the vastness of the place, which seems meant as much for physical as for spiritual exercise, the different figures and groups, the mingled worshippers and spectators, may follow their various intentions without mutual scandal. In that splendid immensity individual indiscretion carries but a short distance. Isabel and her companions, however, were guilty of none; for though Henrietta was obliged to declare that Michael Angelo's dome suffered by comparison with that of the Capitol at Washington, she addressed her protest chiefly to Mr. Bantling's ear, and reserved it, in its more accentuated form, for the columns of the *Interviewer.* Isabel made the circuit of the church with Lord Warburton, and as they drew near the choir on the left of the entrance the voices of the Pope's singers were borne toward them over the heads of the large number of persons clustered outside the doors. They paused a while on the skirts of this crowd, composed in equal measure of Roman cockneys and inquisitive strangers, and while they stood there the sacred concert went forward. Ralph, with Henrietta and Mr. Bantling, was apparently within, where Isabel, above the heads of the dense group in front of her, saw the afternoon light, silvered by clouds of incense that seemed to mingle with the splendid chant, sloping through the embossed recesses of high windows. After a while the singing stopped, and then Lord Warburton seemed disposed to turn away again. Isabel for a moment did the same; whereupon she found herself confronted with Gilbert Osmond, who appeared to have been standing at a short distance behind her. He now approached, with a formal salutation.

"So you decided to come?" she said, putting out her hand.

"Yes, I came last night, and called this afternoon at your hotel. They told me you had come here, and I looked about for you."

"The others are inside," said Isabel.

"I didn't come for the others," Gilbert Osmond murmured, smiling.

She turned away; Lord Warburton was looking at them; perhaps he had heard this. Suddenly she remembered that it was just what he had said to her the morning he came to Gardencourt to ask her to marry him. Mr. Osmond's words had brought the color to her cheek, and this reminiscence had not the effect of dispelling it. Isabel sought refuge from her slight agitation in mentioning to each gentleman the name of the other, and fortunately at this moment Mr. Bantling made his way out of the choir, cleaving the crowd with British valor, and followed by Miss

Stackpole and Ralph Touchett. I say fortunately, but this is perhaps a superficial view of the matter; for on perceiving the gentleman from Florence, Ralph Touchett exhibited symptoms of surprise which might not perhaps have seemed flattering to Mr. Osmond. It must be added, however, that these manifestations were momentary, and Ralph was presently able to say to his cousin, with due jocularity, that she would soon have all her friends about her. His greeting to Mr. Osmond was apparently frank; that is, the two men shook hands and looked at each other. Miss Stackpole had met the newcomer in Florence, but she had already found occasion to say to Isabel that she liked him no better than her other admirers—than Mr. Touchett, Lord Warburton, and little Mr. Rosier in Paris. "I don't know what it is in you," she had been pleased to remark, "but for a nice girl you do attract the most unpleasant people. Mr. Goodwood is the only one I have any respect for, and he's just the one you don't appreciate."

"What's your opinion of St. Peter's?" Mr. Osmond asked of Isabel.

"It's very large and very bright," said the girl.

"It's too large; it makes one feel like an atom."

"Is not that the right way to feel—in a church?" Isabel asked, with a faint but interested smile.

"I suppose it's the right way to feel everywhere, when one *is* nobody. But I like it in a church as little as anywhere else."

"You ought indeed to be a Pope!" Isabel exclaimed, remembering something he had said to her in Florence.

"Ah, I should have enjoyed that!" said Gilbert Osmond.

Lord Warburton meanwhile had joined Ralph Touchett, and the two strolled away together.

"Who is the gentleman speaking to Miss Archer?" his lordship inquired.

"His name is Gilbert Osmond—he lives in Florence," Ralph said.

"What is he besides?"

"Nothing at all. Oh yes, he is an American; but one forgets that; he is so little of one."

"Has he known Miss Archer long?"

"No, about a fortnight."

"Does she like him?"

"Yes, I think she does."

"Is he a good fellow?"

Ralph hesitated a moment. "No, he's not," he said, at last.

"Why then does she like him?" pursued Lord Warburton, with noble naiveté.

"Because she's a woman."

Lord Warburton was silent a moment. "There are other men who *are* good fellows," he presently said, "and them—and them—"

"And them she likes also!" Ralph interrupted, smiling.

"Oh, if you mean she likes him in that way!" And Lord Warburton turned round again. As far as he was concerned, however, the party was broken up. Isabel remained in conversation with the gentleman from Florence till they left the church, and her English lover consoled himself by lending such attention as he might to the strains which continued to proceed from the choir.

<h1 style="text-align:center">❧ 28 ❧</h1>

On the morrow, in the evening, Lord Warburton went again to see his friends at their hotel, and at this establishment he learned that they had gone to the opera. He drove to the opera, with the idea of paying them a visit in their box, in accordance with the time-honored Italian custom; and after he had obtained his admittance—it was one of the secondary theaters—looked about the large, bare, ill-lighted house. An act had just terminated, and he was at liberty to pursue his quest. After scanning two or three tiers of boxes, he perceived in one of the largest of these receptacles a lady whom he easily recognized. Miss Archer was seated facing the stage, and partly screened by the curtain of the box; and beside her, leaning back in his chair, was Gilbert Osmond. They appeared to have the place to themselves, and Warburton supposed that their companions had taken advantage of the *entracte* to enjoy the relative coolness of the lobby. He stood a while watching the interesting pair in the box, and asking himself whether he should go up and interrupt their harmonious colloquy. At last it became apparent that Isabel had seen him, and this accident determined him. He took his way to the upper regions, and on the staircase he met Ralph Touchett, slowly descending, with his hat in the attitude of ennui and his hands where they usually were.

"I saw you below a moment since, and was going down to you. I feel lonely and want company," Ralph remarked.

"You have some that is very good that you have deserted."

"Do you mean my cousin? Oh, she has got a visitor and doesn't want me. Then Miss Stackpole and Bantling have gone out to a café to eat an ice—Miss Stackpole delights in an ice. I didn't think they wanted me either. The opera is very bad; the women look like laundresses and sing like peacocks. I feel very low."

"You had better go home," Lord Warburton said, without affectation.

"And leave my young lady in this sad place? Ah no, I must watch over her."

"She seems to have plenty of friends."

"Yes, that's why I must watch," said Ralph, with the same low-voiced mock-melancholy.

"If she doesn't want you, it's probable she doesn't want me."

"No, you are different. Go to the box and stay there while I walk about."

Lord Warburton went to the box, where he received a very gracious welcome from the more attractive of its occupants. He exchanged greetings with Mr. Osmond, to whom he had been introduced the day before, and who, after he came in, sat very quietly, scarcely mingling in the somewhat disjointed talk in which Lord Warburton engaged with Isabel. It seemed to the latter gentleman that Miss Archer was very pretty; he even thought she looked excited; as she was, however, at all times a keenly-glancing, quickly-moving completely animated young woman, he may have been mistaken on this point. Her talk with him betrayed little agitation; it expressed a kindness so ingenious and deliberate as to indicate that she was in undisturbed possession of her faculties. Poor Lord Warburton had moments of bewilderment. She had discouraged him, formally, as much as a woman could; what business had she then to have such soft, reassuring tones in her voice? The others came back; the bare, familiar, trivial opera began again. The box was large, and there was room for Lord Warburton to remain if he would sit a little behind, in the dark. He did so for half-an-hour, while Mr. Osmond sat in front, leaning forward, with his elbows on his knees, just behind Isabel. Lord Warburton heard nothing, and from his gloomy corner saw nothing but the clear profile of this young lady, defined against the dim illumination of the house. When there was another interval no one moved. Mr. Osmond talked to Isabel, and Lord Warburton remained in his corner. He did so but for a short time, however; after which he got up and bade good-night to the ladies. Isabel said nothing to detain him, and then he was puzzled again. Why had she so sweet a voice—such a friendly accent? He was angry with himself for being puzzled, and then angry for being angry. Verdi's music did little to comfort him, and he left the theater and walked homeward, without knowing his way, through the tortuous, tragical streets of Rome, where heavier sorrows than his had been carried under the stars.

"What is the character of that gentleman?" Osmond asked of Isabel, after the visitor had gone.

"Irreproachable—don't you see it?"

"He owns about half England; that's his character," Henrietta remarked. "That's what they call a free country!"

"Ah, he is a great proprietor? Happy man!" said Gilbert Osmond.

"Do you call that happiness—the ownership of human beings?" cried Miss Stackpole. "He owns his tenants, and he has thousands of them. It is pleasant to own something, but inanimate objects are enough for me. I don't insist on flesh and blood, and minds and consciences."

"It seems to me you own a human being or two," Mr. Bantling suggested jocosely. "I wonder if Warburton orders his tenants about as you do me."

"Lord Warburton is a great radical," Isabel said. "He has very advanced opinions."

"He has very advanced stone walls. His park is inclosed by a gigantic iron fence, some thirty miles round," Henrietta announced, for the information of Mr. Osmond. "I should like him to converse with a few of our Boston radicals."

"Don't they approve of iron fences?" asked Mr. Bantling.

"Only to shut up wicked conservatives. I always feel as if I were talking to you over a fence!"

"Do you know him well, this unreformed reformer?" Osmond went on, questioning Isabel.

"Well enough."

"Do you like him?"

"Very much."

"Is he a man of ability?"

"Of excellent ability, and as good as he looks."

"As good as he is good-looking do you mean? He is very good-looking. How detestably fortunate! to be a great English magnate, to be clever and handsome into the bargain, and, by way of finishing off, to enjoy your favor! That's a man I could envy."

Isabel gave a serious smile.

"You seem to me to be always envying someone. Yesterday it was the Pope; today it's poor Lord Warburton."

"My envy is not dangerous; it is very platonic. Why do you call him poor?"

"Women usually pity men after they have hurt them; that is their great way of showing kindness," said Ralph, joining in the conversation for the first time, with a cynicism so transparently ingenious as to be virtually innocent.

"Pray, have I hurt Lord Warburton?" Isabel asked, raising her eyebrows, as if the idea were perfectly novel.

"It serves him right if you have," said Henrietta, while the curtain rose for the ballet.

Isabel saw no more of her attributive victim for the next twenty-four hours, but on the second day after the visit to the opera she encountered him in the gallery of the Capitol, where he was standing before the lion of the collection, the statue of the Dying Gladiator. She had come in with her companions, among whom, on this occasion again, Gilbert Osmond was numbered, and the party, having ascended the staircase, entered the first and finest of the rooms. Lord Warburton spoke to her with all his usual geniality, but said in a moment that he was leaving the gallery.

"And I am leaving Rome," he added. "I should bid you goodbye."

I shall not undertake to explain why, but Isabel was sorry to hear it. It was, perhaps, because she had ceased to be afraid of his renewing his suit; she was thinking of something else. She was on the point of saying she was sorry, but she checked herself and simply wished him a happy journey.

He looked at her with a somewhat heavy eye.

"I am afraid you think me rather inconsistent," he said. "I told you the other day that I wanted so much to stay a while."

"Oh no; you could easily change your mind."

"That's what I have done."

"*Bon voyage,* then."

"You're in a great hurry to get rid of me," said his lordship, rather dismally.

"Not in the least. But I hate partings."

"You don't care what I do," he went on pitifully.

Isabel looked at him for a moment.

"Ah," she said, "you are not keeping your promise!"

He colored like a boy of fifteen.

"If I am not, then it's because I can't; and that's why I am going."

"Goodbye, then."

"Goodbye." He lingered still, however. "When shall I see you again?"

Isabel hesitated, and then, as if she had had a happy inspiration—"Some day after you are married."

"That will never be. It will be after you are."

"That will do as well," said Isabel, smiling.

"Yes, quite as well. Goodbye."

They shook hands, and he left her alone in the beautiful room, among the shining antique marbles. She sat down in the middle of the circle of statues, looking at them vaguely, resting her eyes on their beautiful blank faces; listening, as it were, to their eternal silence. It is impossible, in Rome at least, to look long at a great company of Greek sculptures without feeling the effect of their noble quietude. It soothes and moderates the spirit, it purifies the imagination. I say in Rome especially, because the Roman air is an exquisite medium for such impressions. The golden sunshine mingles with them, the great stillness of the past, so vivid yet, though it is nothing but a void full of names, seems to throw a solemn spell upon them. The blinds were partly closed in the windows of the Capitol, and a clear, warm shadow rested on the figures and made them more perfectly human. Isabel sat there a long time, under the charm of their motionless grace, seeing life between their gazing eyelids and purpose in their marble lips. The dark red walls of the room threw them into relief; the polished marble floor reflected their beauty. She had seen them all before, but her enjoyment repeated itself, and it was all the greater because she was glad, for the time, to be alone. At the last her thoughts wandered away from them, solicited by images of a vitality more complete. An occasional tourist came into the room, stopped and stared a moment at the Dying Gladiator, and then passed out of the other door, creaking over the smooth pavement. At the end of half-an-hour Gilbert Osmond reappeared, apparently in advance of his companions. He strolled toward her slowly, with his hands behind him, and with his usual bright, inquiring, yet not appealing smile.

"I am surprised to find you alone," he said. "I thought you had company."

"So I have—the best." And Isabel glanced at the circle of sculpture.

"Do you call this better company than an English peer?"

"Ah, my English peer left me some time ago," said Isabel, getting up. She spoke, with intention, a little dryly.

Mr. Osmond noted her dryness, but it did not prevent him from giving a laugh.

"I am afraid that what I heard the other evening is true; you are rather cruel to that nobleman."

Isabel looked a moment at the vanquished Gladiator.

"It is not true. I am scrupulously kind."

"That's exactly what I mean!" Gilbert Osmond exclaimed, so humorously that his joke needs to be explained.

We knew that he was fond of originals, of rarities, of the superior, the exquisite; and now that he had seen Lord Warburton, whom he thought a very fine example of his race and order, he perceived a new attraction in the idea of taking to himself a young lady who had qualified herself to figure in his collection of choice objects by rejecting the splendid offer of a British aristocrat. Gilbert Osmond had a high appreciation of the British aristocracy—he had never forgiven Providence for not making him an English duke—and could measure the unexpectedness of this conduct. It would be proper that the woman he should marry should have done something of that sort.

❦ 29 ❦

Ralph Touchett, for reasons best known to himself, had seen fit to say that Gilbert Osmond was not a good fellow; but this assertion was not borne out by the gentleman's conduct during the rest of the visit to Rome. He spent a portion of each day with Isabel and her companions, and gave every indication of being an easy man to live with. It was impossible not to feel that he had excellent points, and indeed this is perhaps why Ralph Touchett made his want of good fellowship a reproach to him. Even Ralph was obliged to admit that just now he was a delightful companion. His good humor was imperturbable, his knowledge universal, his manners were the gentlest in the world. His spirits were not visibly high; it was difficult to think of Gilbert Osmond as boisterous; he had a mortal dislike to loudness or eagerness. He thought Miss Archer sometimes too eager, too pronounced. It was a pity she had that fault; because if she had not had it she would really have had none; she would have been as bright and soft as an April cloud. If Osmond was not loud, however, he was deep, and during these closing days of the Roman May he had a gaiety that matched with slow irregular walks under the pines of the Villa Borghese, among the small sweet meadow flowers and the mossy marbles. He was pleased with everything; he had never before been pleased with so many things at once. Old impressions, old enjoyments, renewed themselves; one evening, going home to his room at the inn, he wrote down a little sonnet to which he prefixed the title of "Rome Revisited." A day or two later he showed this piece of correct and ingenious verse to Isabel, explaining to her that it was an Italian fashion to commemorate the pleasant occasions of life by a tribute to the muse. In general Osmond took his pleasures singly; he was usually disgusted with something that seemed to him ugly or offensive; his mind was rarely visited with moods of comprehensive satisfaction. But at present he was happy—happier than he had perhaps ever been in his life; and the feeling had a large foundation. This was simply the sense of success—the most agreeable emotion of the human heart. Osmond had never had too much of it; in this respect he had never been spoiled; as he knew perfectly well and often reminded himself. "Ah no, I have not been spoiled; certainly I have not been spoiled," he used to repeat to himself. "If I do succeed before I die, I shall have earned it well." Absolutely void of success his career had not been; a very moderate amount of reflection would have assured him of this. But his triumphs were, some of them, now, too old; others had been too easy. The present one had been less difficult than might have been expected; but it had been easy—that is, it had been rapid—only because he had made an altogether exceptional effort, a greater effort than he had believed it was in him to make. The desire to succeed greatly—in something or other—had been the dream of his youth; but as the years went on, the conditions attached to success became so various and repulsive that the idea of making an effort gradually lost its charm. It was not dead, however; it only slept; it revived after he had made the acquaintance of Isabel Archer. Osmond had felt that any enterprise in which the chance of failure was at all considerable would never have an attraction for him; to fail would have been unspeakably odious, would have left an ineffaceable stain upon his life. Success was to seem in advance definitely certain—certain, that is, on this one condition, that the effort should be an agreeable one to make. That of exciting an interest on the part of Isabel Archer corresponded to this description, for the girl had pleased him from the first of his seeing her. We have seen that she thought him "fine"; and Gilbert Osmond returned the compliment. We have also seen (or heard) that he had a great dread of vulgarity, and on this score his mind was at rest with regard to our young lady. He was not afraid that she would disgust him or irritate him; he had no fear that she would even, in the more special sense of the word, displease him. If she was too eager, she could be taught to be less so; that was a fault which diminished with growing knowledge. She might defy him, she might anger him; this was another matter from displeasing him, and on the whole a less serious one. If a woman were ungraceful and common, her whole quality was vitiated, and one could take no precautions against that; one's own delicacy would avail little. If, however, she were only willful and high-tempered, the defect might be managed with comparative ease; for had one not a will of one's own that one had been keeping for years in the best condition— as pure and keen as a sword protected by its sheath?

Though I have tried to speak with extreme discretion, the reader may have gathered a suspicion that Gilbert Osmond was not untainted by selfishness. This is rather a coarse imputation to put upon a man of his refinement; and it behooves us at all times to remember the familiar proverb about those who live in glass houses. If Mr. Osmond was more selfish than most of his fellows, the fact will still establish itself. Lest it should fail to do so, I must decline to commit myself to an accusation so gross; the more especially as several of the items of our story would seem to point the other way. It is well known that there are few indications of selfishness more conclusive (on the part of a gentleman at least) than the preference for a single life. Gilbert Osmond, after having tasted of matrimony, had spent a succession of years in the full enjoyment of recovered singleness. He was familiar with the simplicity of purpose, the lonely liberties, of bachelorhood. He had reached that period of life when it is supposed to be doubly difficult to renounce these liberties, endeared as they are by long association; and yet he was prepared to make the generous sacrifice. It would seem that this might fairly be set down to the credit of the noblest of our qualities—the faculty of self-devotion. Certain it is that Osmond's desire to marry had been deep and distinct. It had not been notorious; he had not gone about asking people whether they knew a nice girl with a little money. Money was an object; but this was not his manner of proceeding, and no one knew—or even greatly cared—whether he wished to marry or not. Madame Merle knew—that we have already perceived. It was not that he had told her; on the whole he would not have cared to tell her. But there were things of which she had no need to be told— things as to which she had a sort of creative intuition. She had recognized a truth that was nonetheless pertinent for being very subtle: the truth that there was something very imperfect in Osmond's situation as it stood. He was a failure, of course; that was an old story; to Madame Merle's perception he would always be a failure.

But there were degrees of ineffectiveness, and there was no need of taking one of the highest. Success, for Gilbert Osmond, would be to make himself felt; that was the only success to which he could now pretend. It is not a kind of distinction that is officially recognized—unless indeed the operation be performed upon multitudes of men. Osmond's line would be to impress himself not largely but deeply; a distinction of the most private sort. A single character might offer the whole measure of it; the clear and sensitive nature of a generous girl would make space for the record. The record of course would be complete if the young lady should have a fortune, and Madame Merle would have taken no pains to make Mr. Osmond acquainted with Mrs. Touchett's niece if Isabel had been as scantily dowered as when first she met her. He had waited all these years because he wanted only the best, and a portionless bride naturally would not have been the best. He had waited so long in vain that he finally almost lost his interest in the subject—not having kept it up by venturesome experiments. It had become improbable that the best was now to be had, and if he wished to make himself felt, there was soft and supple little Pansy, who would evidently respond to the slightest pressure. When at last the best did present itself Osmond recognized it like a gentleman. There was therefore no incongruity in his wishing to marry—it was his own idea of success, as well as that which Madame Merle, with her old-time interest in his affairs, entertained for him. Let it not, however, be supposed that he was guilty of the error of believing that Isabel's character was of that passive sort which offers a free field for domination. He was sure that she would constantly act—act in the sense of enthusiastic concession.

Shortly before the time which had been fixed in advance for her return to Florence, this young lady received from Mrs. Touchett a telegram which ran as follows:—"Leave Florence 4th June, Bellaggio, and take you if you have not other views. But can't wait if you dawdle in Rome." The dawdling in Rome was very pleasant, but Isabel had no other views, and she wrote to her aunt that she would immediately join her. She told Gilbert Osmond that she had done so, and he replied that, spending many of his summers as well as his winters in Italy, he himself would loiter a little longer among the Seven Hills. He should not return to Florence for ten days more, and in that time she would have started for Bellaggio. It might be long, in this case, before he should see her again. This conversation took place in the large decorated sitting room which our friends occupied at the hotel; it was late in the evening, and Ralph Touchett was to take his cousin back to Florence on the morrow. Osmond had found the girl alone; Miss Stackpole had contracted a friendship with a delightful American family on the fourth floor, and had mounted the interminable staircase to pay them a visit. Miss Stackpole contracted friendships, in traveling, with great freedom, and had formed several in railway carriages, which were among her most valued ties. Ralph was making arrangements for the morrow's journey, and Isabel sat alone in a wilderness of yellow upholstery. The chairs and sofas were orange; the walls and windows were draped in purple and gilt. The mirrors, the pictures, had great flamboyant frames; the ceiling was deeply vaulted and painted over with naked muses and cherubs. To Osmond the place was painfully ugly; the false colors, the sham splendor, made him suffer. Isabel had taken in hand a volume of Ampère, presented, on their arrival in Rome, by Ralph; but though she held it in her lap with her finger vaguely kept in the place, she was not impatient to go on with her reading. A lamp covered with a drooping veil of pink tissue-paper burned on the table beside her, and diffused a strange pale rosiness over the scene.

"You say you will come back; but who knows?" Gilbert Osmond said. "I think you are much more likely to start on your voyage round the world. You are under no obligation to come back; you can do exactly what you choose; you can roam through space."

"Well, Italy is a part of space," Isabel answered; "I can take it on the way."

"On the way round the world? No, don't do that. Don't put us into a parenthesis—give us a chapter to ourselves. I don't want to see you on your travels. I would rather see you when they are over. I should like to see you when you are tired and satiated," Osmond added, in a moment. "I shall prefer you in that state."

Isabel, with her eyes bent down, fingered the pages of M. Ampère a little.

"You turn things into ridicule without seeming to do it, though not, I think, without intending it," she said at last. "You have no respect for my travels—you think them ridiculous."

"Where do you find that?"

Isabel went on in the same tone, fretting the edge of her book with the paper-knife.

"You see my ignorance, my blunders, the way I wander about as if the world belonged to me, simply because—because it has been put into my power to do so. You don't think a woman ought to do that. You think it bold and ungraceful."

"I think it beautiful," said Osmond. "You know my opinions—I have treated you to enough of them. Don't you remember my telling you that one ought to make one's life a work of art? You looked rather shocked at first; but then I told you that it was exactly what you seemed to me to be trying to do with your own life."

Isabel looked up from her book.

"What you despise most in the world is bad art."

"Possibly. But yours seems to me very good."

"If I were to go to Japan next winter, you would laugh at me," Isabel continued.

Osmond gave a smile—a keen one, but not a laugh, for the tone of their conversation was not jocular. Isabel was almost tremulously serious; he had seen her so before.

"You have an imagination that startles one!"

"That is exactly what I say. You think such an idea absurd."

"I would give my little finger to go to Japan; it is one of the countries I want most to see. Can't you believe that, with my taste for old lacquer?"

"I haven't a taste for old lacquer to excuse me," said Isabel.

"You have a better excuse—the means of going. You are quite wrong in your theory that I laugh at you. I don't know what put it into your head."

"It wouldn't be remarkable if you did think it ridiculous that I should have the means to travel, when you have not; for you know everything, and I know nothing."

"The more reason why you should travel and learn," said Osmond, smiling. "Besides," he added, more gravely, "I don't know everything."

Isabel was not struck with the oddity of his saying this gravely; she was thinking that the pleasantest incident of her life—so it pleased her to qualify her little visit to Rome—was coming to an end. That most of the interest of this episode had been owing to Mr. Osmond—this reflection she was not just now at pains to make; she had already done the point abundant justice. But she said to herself that if there were a danger that they should not meet again, perhaps after all it would be as well. Happy things do not repeat themselves, and these few days had been interfused with the element of success. She might come back to Italy and find him different—this strange man who pleased her just as he was; and it would be better not to come than run the risk of that. But if she was not to come, the greater was the pity that this happy week was over; for a moment she felt her heart throb with a kind of delicious pain. The sensation kept her silent, and Gilbert Osmond was silent too; he was looking at her.

"Go everywhere," he said at last, in a low, kind voice; "do everything; get everything out of life. Be happy—be triumphant."

"What do you mean by being triumphant?"

"Doing what you like."

"To triumph, then, it seems to me, is to fail! Doing what we like is often very tiresome."

"Exactly," said Osmond, with his quick responsiveness. "As I intimated just now, you will be tired some day." He paused a moment, and then he went on: "I don't know whether I had better not wait till then for something I wish to say to you."

"Ah, I can't advise you without knowing what it is. But I am horrid when I am tired," Isabel added, with due inconsequence.

"I don't believe that. You are angry, sometimes—that I can believe, though I have never seen it. But I am sure you are never disagreeable."

"Not even when I lose my temper?"

"You don't lose it—you find it, and that must be beautiful." Osmond spoke very simply—almost solemnly. "There must be something very noble about that."

"If I could only find it now!" the girl exclaimed, laughing, yet frowning.

"I am not afraid; I should fold my arms and admire you. I am speaking very seriously." He was leaning forward, with a hand on each knee; for some moments he bent his eyes on the floor. "What I wish to say to you," he went on at last, looking up, "is that I find I am in love with you."

Isabel instantly rose from her chair.

"Ah, keep that till I am tired!" she murmured.

"Tired of hearing it from others?" And Osmond sat there, looking up at her. "No, you may heed it now, or never, as you please. But, after all, I must say it now."

She had turned away, but in the movement she had stopped herself and dropped her gaze upon him. The two remained a moment in this situation, exchanging a long look—the large, conscious look of the critical hours of life. Then he got up and came near her, deeply respectful, as if he were afraid he had been too familiar.

"I am thoroughly in love with you."

He repeated the announcement in a tone of almost impersonal discretion; like a man who expected very little from it, but spoke for his own relief.

The tears came into Isabel's eyes—they were caused by an intenser throb of that pleasant pain I spoke of a moment ago. There was an immense sweetness in the words he had uttered; but, morally speaking, she retreated before them—facing him still—as she had retreated in two or three cases that we know of in which the same words had been spoken.

"Oh, don't say that, please," she answered at last, in a tone of entreaty which had nothing of conventional modesty, but which expressed the dread of having, in this case too, to choose and decide. What made her dread great was precisely the force which, as it would seem, ought to have banished all dread—the consciousness of what was in her own heart. It was terrible to have to surrender herself to that.

"I haven't the idea that it will matter much to you," said Osmond. "I have too little to offer you. What I have—it's enough for me; but it's not enough for you. I have neither fortune, nor fame, nor extrinsic advantages of any kind. So I offer nothing. I only tell you because I think it can't offend you, and some day or other it may give you pleasure. It gives me pleasure, I assure you," he went on, standing there before her, bending forward a little, turning his hat, which he had taken up, slowly round, with a movement which had all the decent tremor of awkwardness and none of its oddity, and presenting to her his keen, expressive, emphatic face. "It gives me no pain, because it is perfectly simple. For me you will always be the most important woman in the world."

Isabel looked at herself in this character—looked intently, and thought that she filled it with a certain grace. But what she said was not an expression of this complacency. "You don't offend me; but you ought to remember that, without being offended, one may be incommoded, troubled." "Incommoded": she heard herself saying that, and thought it a ridiculous word. But it was the word that came to her.

"I remember, perfectly. Of course you are surprised and startled. But if it is nothing but that, it will pass away. And it will perhaps leave something that I may not be ashamed of."

"I don't know what it may leave. You see at all events that I am not overwhelmed," said Isabel, with rather a pale smile. "I am not too troubled to think. And I think that I am glad we are separating—that I leave Rome tomorrow."

"Of course I don't agree with you there."

"I don't know you," said Isabel, abruptly; and then she colored, as she heard herself saying what she had said almost a year before to Lord Warburton.

"If you were not going away you would know me better."

"I shall do that some other time."

"I hope so. I am very easy to know."

"No, no," said the girl, with a flash of bright eagerness; "there you are not sincere. You are not easy to know; no one could be less so."

"Well," Osmond answered, with a laugh, "I said that because I know myself. That may be a boast, but I do."

"Very likely; but you are very wise."

"So are you, Miss Archer!" Osmond exclaimed.

"I don't feel so just now. Still, I am wise enough to think you had better go. Good night."

"God bless you!" said Gilbert Osmond, taking the hand which she failed to surrender to him. And then in a moment he added, "If we meet again, you will find me as you leave me. If we don't, I shall be so, all the same."

"Thank you very much. Goodbye."

There was something quietly firm about Isabel's visitor; he might go of his own movement, but he would not be dismissed. "There is one thing more," he said. "I haven't asked anything of you—not even a thought in the future; you must do me that justice. But there is a little service I should like to ask. I shall not return home for several days; Rome is delightful, and it is a good place for a man in my state of mind. Oh, I know you are sorry to leave it; but you are right to do what your aunt wishes."

"She doesn't even wish it!" Isabel broke out, strangely.

Osmond for a moment was apparently on the point of saying something that would match these words. But he changed his mind, and rejoined, simply—"Ah well, it's proper you should go with her, all the same. Do everything that's proper; I go in for that. Excuse my being so patronising. You say you don't know me; but when you do you will discover what a worship I have for propriety."

"You are not conventional?" said Isabel, very gravely.

"I like the way you utter that word! No, I am not conventional: I am convention itself. You don't understand that?" And Osmond paused a moment, smiling. "I should like to explain it." Then, with a sudden, quick, bright naturalness—"Do come back again!" he cried. "There are so many things we might talk about."

Isabel stood there with lowered eyes. "What service did you speak of just now?"

"Go and see my little daughter before you leave Florence. She is alone at the villa; I decided not to send her to my sister, who hasn't my ideas. Tell her she must love her poor father very much," said Gilbert Osmond, gently.

"It will be a great pleasure to me to go," Isabel answered. "I will tell her what you say. Once more, goodbye."

On this he took a rapid, respectful leave. When he had gone, she stood a moment, looking about her, and then she seated herself, slowly, with an air of deliberation. She sat there till her companions came back, with folded hands, gazing at the ugly carpet. Her agitation—for it had not diminished—was very still, very deep. That which had happened was something that for a week past her imagination had been going forward to meet; but here, when it came, she stopped—her imagination halted. The working of this young lady's spirit was strange, and I can only give it to you as I see it, not hoping to make it seem altogether natural. Her imagination stopped, as I say; there was a last vague space it could not cross—a dusky, uncertain tract which looked ambiguous, and even slightly treacherous, like a moorland seen in the winter twilight. But she was to cross it yet.

❧ 30 ❧

Under her cousin's escort Isabel returned on the morrow to Florence, and Ralph Touchett, though usually he was not fond of railway journeys, thought very well of the successive hours passed in the train which hurried his companion away from the city now distinguished by Gilbert Osmond's preference—hours that were to form the first stage in a still larger scheme of travel. Miss Stackpole had remained behind; she was planning a little trip to Naples, to be executed with Mr. Bantling's assistance. Isabel was to have but three days in Florence before the 4th of June, the date of Mrs. Touchett's departure, and she determined to devote the last of these to her promise to go and see Pansy Osmond. Her plan, however, seemed for a moment likely to modify itself, in deference to a plan of Madame Merle's. This lady was still at Casa Touchett; but she too was on the point of leaving Florence, her next station being an ancient castle in the mountains of Tuscany, the residence of a noble family of that country, whose acquaintance (she had known them, as she said, "forever") seemed to Isabel, in the light of certain photographs of their immense crenellated dwelling which her friend was able to show her, a precious privilege.

She mentioned to Madame Merle that Mr. Osmond had asked her to call upon his daughter; she did not mention to her that he had also made her a declaration of love.

"*Ah, comme cela se trouve!*" the elder lady exclaimed. "I myself have been thinking it would be a kindness to take a look at the child before I go into the country."

"We can go together, then," said Isabel, reasonably. I say "reasonably," because the proposal was not uttered in the spirit of enthusiasm. She had prefigured her visit as made in solitude; she should like it better so. Nevertheless, to her great consideration for Madame Merle she was prepared to sacrifice this mystic sentiment.

Her friend meditated, with her usual suggestive smile. "After all," she presently said, "why should we both go; having, each of us, so much to do during these last hours?"

"Very good; I can easily go alone."

"I don't know about your going alone—to the house of a handsome bachelor. He has been married—but so long ago!"

Isabel stared. "When Mr. Osmond is away, what does it matter?"

"They don't know he is away, you see."

"They? Whom do you mean?"

"Everyone. But perhaps it doesn't matter."

"If you were going, why shouldn't I?" Isabel asked.

"Because I am an old frump, and you are a beautiful young woman."

"Granting all that, you have not promised."

"How much you think of your promises!" said Madame Merle, with a smile of genial mockery.

"I think a great deal of my promises. Does that surprise you?"

"You are right," Madame Merle reflected audibly. "I really think you wish to be kind to the child."

"I wish very much to be kind to her."

"Go and see her, then; no one will be the wiser. And tell her I would have come if you had not.—Or rather," Madame Merle added—"don't tell her; she won't care."

As Isabel drove, in the publicity of an open vehicle, along the charming winding way which led to Mr. Osmond's hilltop, she wondered what Madame Merle had meant by no one being the wiser. Once in a while, at large intervals, this lady, in whose discretion, as a general thing, there was something almost brilliant, dropped a remark of ambiguous quality, struck a note that sounded false. What cared Isabel Archer for the vulgar judgments of obscure people? and did Madame Merle suppose that she was capable of doing a deed in secret? Of course not—she must have meant something else—something which in the press of the hours that preceded her departure she had not had time to explain. Isabel would return to this some day; there were certain things as to which she liked to be clear. She heard Pansy strumming at the piano in another apartment, as she herself was ushered into Mr. Osmond's drawing room; the little girl was "practicing," and Isabel was pleased to think that she performed this duty faithfully. Presently Pansy came in, smoothing down her frock, and did the honors of her father's house with the wide-eyed conscientiousness of a sensitive child. Isabel sat there for half-an-hour, and Pansy entertained her like a little lady—not chattering, but conversing, and showing the same courteous interest in Isabel's affairs that Isabel was so good as to take in hers. Isabel wondered at her; as I have said before, she had never seen a child like that. How well she had been taught, said our keen young lady, how prettily she had been directed and fashioned; and yet how simple, how natural, how innocent she has been kept! Isabel was fond of psychological problems, and it had pleased her, up to this time, to be in doubt as to whether Miss Pansy were not all-knowing. Was her infantine serenity but the perfection of self-consciousness? Was it put on to please her father's visitor, or was it the direct expression of a little neat, orderly character? The hour that Isabel spent in Mr. Osmond's beautiful empty, dusky rooms—the windows had been half-darkened, to keep out the heat, and here and there, through an easy crevice, the splendid summer day peeped in, lighting a gleam of faded color or tarnished gilt in the rich-looking gloom—Isabel's interview with the daughter of the house, I say, effectually settled this question. Pansy was really a blank page, a pure white surface; she was not clever enough for precocious coquetries. She was not clever; Isabel could see that; she only had nice feelings. There was something touching about her; Isabel had felt it before; she would be an easy victim of fate. She would have no will, no power to resist, no sense of her own importance; only an exquisite taste, and an appreciation, equally exquisite, of such affection as might be bestowed upon her. She would easily be mystified, easily crushed; her force would be solely in her power to cling. She moved about the place with Isabel, who had asked leave to walk through the other rooms again, where Pansy gave her judgment on several works of art. She talked about her prospects, her occupations, her father's intentions; she was not egotistical, but she felt the propriety of giving Isabel the information that so observant a visitor would naturally expect.

"Please tell me," she said, "did papa, in Rome, go to see Madame Catherine? He told me he would if he had time. Perhaps he had not time. Papa likes a great deal of time. He wished to speak about my education; it isn't finished yet, you know. I don't know what they can do with me more; but it appears it is far from finished. Papa told me one day he thought he would finish it himself; for the last year or two, at the convent, the masters that teach the tall girls are so very dear. Papa is not rich, and I should be very sorry if he were to pay much money for me, because I don't think I am worth it. I don't learn quickly enough, and I have got no memory. For what I am told, yes—especially when it is pleasant; but not for what I learn in a book. There was a young girl, who was my best friend, and they took her away from the convent when she was fourteen, to make—how do you say it in English?— to make a *dot*. You don't say it in English? I hope it isn't wrong; I only mean they wished to keep the money, to marry her. I don't know whether it is for that that papa wishes to keep the money, to marry me. It costs so much to marry!" Pansy went on, with a sigh; "I think papa might make that economy. At any rate I am too young to think about it yet, and I don't care for any gentleman; I mean for any but him. If he were not my papa I should like to marry him; I would rather be his daughter than the wife of—of some strange person. I miss him very much, but not so much as you might think, for I have been so much away from him. Papa has always been principally for holidays. I miss Madame Catherine almost more; but you must not tell him that. You shall not see him again? I am very sorry for that. Of everyone who comes here I like you the best. That is not a great compliment, for there are not many people. It was very kind of you to come today—so far from your house; for I am as yet only a child. Oh, yes, I have only the occupations of a child. When did you give them up, the occupations of a child? I should like to know how old you are, but I don't know whether it is right to ask. At the convent they told us that we must never ask the age. I don't like to do anything that is not expected; it looks as if one had not been properly taught. I myself—I should never like to be taken by surprise. Papa left directions for everything. I go to bed very early. When the sun goes off that side I go into the garden. Papa left strict orders that I was not to get scorched. I always enjoy the view; the mountains are so graceful. In Rome, from the convent, we saw nothing but roofs and bell-towers. I practice three hours. I do not play very well. You play yourself? I wish very much that you would play something for me; papa wishes very much that I should hear good music. Madame Merle has played for me several times; that is what I like best about Madame Merle; she has great facility. I shall never have facility. And I have no voice—just a little thread."

Isabel gratified this respectful wish, drew off her gloves, and sat down to the piano, while Pansy, standing beside her, watched her white hands move quickly over the keys. When she stopped, she kissed the child goodbye, and held her a moment, looking at her.

"Be a good child," she said; "give pleasure to your father."

"I think that is what I live for," Pansy answered. "He has not much pleasure; he is rather a sad man."

Isabel listened to this assertion with an interest which she felt it to be almost a torment that she was obliged to conceal from the child. It was her pride that obliged her, and a certain sense of decency; there were still other things in her head which she felt a strong impulse, instantly checked, to say to Pansy about her father; there were things it would have given her pleasure to hear the child, to make the child, say. But she no sooner became conscious of these things than her imagination was hushed with horror at the idea of taking advantage of the little girl—it was of this she would have accused herself—and of leaving an audible trace of her emotion behind. She had come—she had come; but she had stayed only an hour! She rose quickly from the music stool; even then, however, she lingered a moment, still holding her small companion, drawing the child's little tender person closer, and looking down at her. She was obliged to confess it to herself—she would have taken a passionate pleasure in talking about Gilbert Osmond to this innocent, diminutive creature who was near to him. But she said not another word; she only kissed Pansy once more. They went together through the vestibule, to the door which opened into the court; and there Pansy stopped, looking rather wistfully beyond.

"I may go no further," she said. "I have promised papa not to go out of this door."

"You are right to obey him; he will never ask you anything unreasonable."

"I shall always obey him. But when will you come again?"

"Not for a long time, I am afraid."

"As soon as you can, I hope. I am only a little girl," said Pansy, "but I shall always expect you."

And the small figure stood in the high, dark doorway, watching Isabel cross the clear, gray court, and disappear into the brightness beyond the big *portone*, which gave a wider gleam as it opened.

❧ 31 ❧

Isabel came back to Florence, but only after several months; an interval sufficiently replete with incident. It is not, however, during this interval that we are closely concerned with her; our attention is engaged again on a certain day in the late springtime, shortly after her return to the Palazzo Crescentini, and a year from the date of the incidents I have just narrated. She was alone on this occasion, in one of the smaller of the numerous rooms devoted by Mrs. Touchett to social uses, and there was that in her expression and attitude which would have suggested that she was expecting a visitor. The tall window was open, and though its green shutters were partly drawn, the bright air of the garden had come in through a broad interstice and filled the room with warmth and perfume. Our young lady stood for some time at the window, with her hands clasped behind her, gazing into the brilliant aperture in the manner of a person relapsing into reverie. She was pre-occupied; she was too restless to sit down, to work, to read. It was evidently not her design, however, to catch a glimpse of her visitor before he should pass into the house; for the entrance to the palace was not through the garden, in which stillness and privacy always reigned. She was endeavoring rather to anticipate his arrival by a process of conjecture, and to judge by the expression of her face this attempt gave her plenty to do. She was extremely grave; not sad exactly, but deeply serious. The lapse of a year may doubtless account for a considerable increase of gravity; though this will depend a good deal upon the manner in which the year has been spent. Isabel had spent hers in seeing the world; she had moved about; she had traveled; she had exerted herself with an almost passionate activity. She was now, to her own sense, a very different person from the frivolous young woman from Albany who had begun to see Europe upon the lawn at Gardencourt a couple of years before. She flattered herself that she had gathered a rich experience, that she knew a great deal more of life than this light-minded creature had even suspected. If her thoughts just now had inclined themselves to retrospect, instead of fluttering their wings nervously about the present, they would have evoked a multitude of interest-ing pictures. These pictures would have been both landscapes and figure-pieces; the latter, however, would have been the more numerous. With several of the fig-ures concerned in these combinations we are already acquainted. There would be, for instance, the conciliatory Lily, our heroine's sister and Edmund Ludlow's wife, who came out from New York to spend five months with Isabel. She left her hus-band behind her, but she brought her children, to whom Isabel now played with equal munificence and tenderness the part of maiden-aunt. Mr. Ludlow, toward the last, had been able to snatch a few weeks from his forensic triumphs, and, crossing the ocean with extreme rapidity, spent a month with the two ladies in Paris, before taking his wife home. The little Ludlows had not yet, even from the American point of view, reached the proper tourist age; so that while her sister was with her, Isabel confined her movements to a narrow circle. Lily and the babies had joined her in Switzerland in the month of July, and they had spent a summer of fine weather in an Alpine valley where the flowers were thick in the meadows, and the shade of great chestnuts made a resting place in such upward wanderings as might be undertaken by ladies and children on warm afternoons. Afterwards they had come to Paris, a city beloved by Lily, but less appreciated by Isabel, who in those days was constantly thinking of Rome. Mrs. Ludlow enjoyed Paris, but she was nevertheless somewhat disappointed and puzzled; and after her husband had joined her she was in addition a good deal depressed at not being able to induce him to enter into these somewhat subtle and complex emotions. They all had Isabel for their object; but Edmund Ludlow, as he had always done before, declined to be surprised, or distressed, or mystified, or elated, at anything his sister-in-law might have done or have failed to do. Mrs. Ludlow's feelings were various. At one moment she thought it would be so natural for Isabel to come home and take a house in New York—the Rossiters', for instance, which had an elegant conservatory, and was just round the corner from her own; at another she could not conceal her surprise at the girl's not marrying some gentleman of rank in one of the foreign countries. On the whole, as I have said, she was rather disappointed. She had taken more satisfaction in Isabel's accession of fortune than if the money had been left to herself; it had seemed to her to offer just the proper setting for her sister's slender but eminent figure. Isabel had developed less, however, than Lily had thought likely—development, to Lily's understanding, being somehow mysteriously connected with morning-calls and evening-parties. Intellectually, doubtless, she had made immense strides; but she appeared to have achieved few of those social conquests of which Mrs. Ludlow had expected to admire the trophies. Lily's conception of such achievements was extremely vague; but this was exactly what she had expected of Isabel—to give it form and body. Isabel could have done as well as she had done in New York; and Mrs. Ludlow appealed to her husband to know whether there was any privilege that she enjoyed in Europe which the society of that city might not offer her. We know, ourselves, that Isabel had made conquests—whether inferior or not to those she might have effected in her native land, it would be a delicate matter to decide; and it is not altogether with a feeling of complacency that I again mention that she had not made these honorable victories public. She had not told her sister the history of Lord Warburton, nor had she given her a hint of Mr. Osmond's state of mind; and she had no better reason for her silence than that she didn't wish to speak. It entertained her more to say nothing, and she had no idea of asking poor Lily's advice. But Lily knew nothing of these rich mysteries, and it is no wonder, therefore, that she pronounced her sister's career in Europe rather dull—an impression confirmed by the fact that Isabel's silence about Mr. Osmond, for instance, was in direct proportion to the frequency with which he occupied her thoughts. As this happened very often, it sometimes appeared to Mrs. Ludlow that her sister was really losing her gaiety. So very strange a result of so exhilarating an incident as inheriting a fortune was of course perplexing to the cheerful Lily; it added to her general sense that Isabel was not at all like other people.

Isabel's gaiety, however—superficially speaking, at least—exhibited itself rather more after her sister had gone home. She could imagine something more poetic than spending the winter in Paris—Paris was like smart, neat prose—and her frequent correspondence with Madame Merle did much to stimulate such fancies. She had never had a keener sense of freedom, of the absolute boldness and wantonness of liberty, than when she turned away from the platform at the Euston station, on one of the latter days of November, after the departure of the train which was to convey poor Lily, her husband, and her children, to their ship at Liverpool. It had been good for her to have them with her; she was very conscious of that; she was very observant, as we know, of what was good for her, and her effort was constantly to find something that was good enough. To profit by the present advantage till the latest moment, she had made the journey from Paris with the unenvied travelers. She would have accompanied them to Liverpool as well, only Edmund Ludlow had asked her, as a favor, not to do so; it made Lily so fidgety, and she asked such impossible questions. Isabel watched the train move away; she kissed her hand to the elder of her small nephews, a demonstrative child who leaned dangerously far out of the window of the carriage and made separation an occasion of violent hilarity, and then she walked back into the foggy London street. The world lay before her—she could do whatever she chose. There was something exciting in the feeling, but for the present her choice was tolerably discreet; she chose simply to walk back from Euston Square to her hotel. The early dusk of a November afternoon had already closed in; the street lamps, in the thick, brown air, looked weak and red; our young lady was unattended, and Euston Square was a long way from Piccadilly. But Isabel performed the journey with a positive enjoyment of its dangers, and lost her way almost on purpose, in order to get more sensations, so that she was disappointed when an obliging policeman easily set her right again. She was so fond of the spectacle of human life that she enjoyed even the aspect of gathering dusk in the London streets—the moving crowds, the hurrying cabs, the lighted shops, the flaring stalls, the dark, shining dampness of everything. That evening, at her hotel, she wrote to Madame Merle that she should start in a day or two for Rome. She made her way down to Rome without touching at Florence— having gone first to Venice and then proceeded southward by Ancona. She accomplished this journey without other assistance than that of her servant, for her natural protectors were not now on the ground. Ralph Touchett was spending the winter at Corfu, and Miss Stackpole, in the September previous, had been recalled to America by a telegram from the *Interviewer*. This journal offered its brilliant correspondent a fresher field for her talents than the mouldering cities of Europe, and Henrietta was cheered on her way by a promise from Mr. Bantling that he would soon come over and see her. Isabel wrote to Mrs. Touchett to apologize for not coming just then to Florence, and her aunt replied characteristically enough. Apologies, Mrs. Touchett intimated, were of no more use than soap-bubbles, and she herself never dealt in such articles. One either did the thing or one didn't, and what one would have done belonged to the sphere of the irrelevant, like the idea of a future life or of the origin of things. Her letter was frank, but (a rare case with Mrs. Touchett) it was not so frank as it seemed. She easily forgave her niece for not stopping at Florence, because she thought it was a sign that there was nothing going on with Gilbert Osmond. She watched, of course, to see whether Mr. Osmond would now go to Rome, and took some comfort in learning that he was not guilty of an absence. Isabel, on her side, had not been a fortnight in Rome before she proposed to Madame Merle that they should make a little pilgrimage to the East. Madame Merle remarked that her friend was restless, but she added that she herself had always been consumed with the desire to visit Athens and Constantinople. The two ladies accordingly embarked on this expedition, and spent three months in Greece, in Turkey, in Egypt. Isabel found much to interest her in these countries, though Madame Merle continued to remark that even among the most classic sites, the scenes most calculated to suggest repose and reflection, her restlessness prevailed. Isabel traveled rapidly, eagerly, audaciously; she was like a thirsty person draining cup after cup. Madame Merle, for the present, was a most efficient duenna. It was on Isabel's invitation she had come, and she imparted all necessary dignity to the girl's uncountenanced condition. She played her part with the sagacity that might have been expected of her; she effaced herself, she accepted the position of a companion whose expenses were profusely paid. The situation, however, had no hardships, and people who met this graceful pair on their travels would not have been able to tell you which was the patroness and which the client. To say that Madame Merle improved on acquaintance would misrepresent the impression she made upon Isabel, who had thought her from the first a perfectly enlightened woman. At the end of an intimacy of three months Isabel felt that she knew her better; her character had revealed itself, and Madame Merle had also at last redeemed her promise of relating her history from her own point of view—a consummation the more desirable as Isabel had already heard it related from the point of view of others. This history was so sad a one (insofar as it concerned the late M. Merle, an adventurer of the lowest class, who had taken advantage, years before, of her youth, and of an inexperience in which doubtless those who knew her only now would find it difficult to believe); it abounded so in startling and lamentable incidents, that Isabel wondered the poor lady had kept so much of her freshness, her interest in life. Into this freshness of Madame Merle's she obtained a considerable insight; she saw that it was, after all, a tolerably artificial bloom. Isabel liked her as much as ever, but there was a certain corner of the curtain that never was lifted; it was as if Madame Merle had remained after all a foreigner. She had once said that she came from a distance, that she belonged to the old world, and Isabel never lost the impression that she was the product of a different clime from her own, that she had grown up under other stars. Isabel believed that at bottom she had a different morality. Of course the morality of civilized persons has always much in common; but Isabel suspected that her friend had esoteric views. She believed, with the presumption of youth, that a morality which differed from her own must be inferior to it; and this conviction was an aid to detecting an occasional flash of cruelty, an occasional lapse from candor, in the conversation of a woman who had raised delicate kindness to an art, and whose nature was too large for the narrow ways of deception. Her conception of human motives was different from Isabel's, and there were several in her list of which our heroine had not even heard. She had not heard of everything, that was very plain; and there were evidently things in the world of which it was not advantageous to hear. Once or twice Isabel had a sort of fright, but the reader will be amused at the cause of it. Madame Merle, as we know, comprehended, responded, sympathized, with wonderful readiness; yet it had nevertheless happened that her young friend mentally exclaimed— "Heaven forgive her, she doesn't understand me!" Absurd as it may seem, this discovery operated as a shock; it left Isabel with a vague horror, in which there was even an element of foreboding. The horror of course subsided, in the light of some sudden proof of Madame Merle's remarkable intelligence; but it left a sort of high watermark in the development of this delightful intimacy. Madame Merle had once said that, in her belief, when a friendship ceased to grow, it immediately began to decline—there was no point of equilibrium between liking a person more and liking him less. A stationary affection, in other words, was impossible—it must move one way or the other. Without estimating the value of this doctrine, I may say that if Isabel's imagination, which had hitherto been so actively engaged on her friend's behalf, began at last to languish, she enjoyed her society not a particle less than before. If their friendship had declined, it had declined to a very comfortable level. The truth is that in these days the girl had other uses for her imagination, which was better occupied than it had ever been. I do not allude to the impulse it received as she gazed at the Pyramids in the course of an excursion from Cairo, or as she stood among the broken columns of the Acropolis and fixed her eyes upon the point designated to her as the Strait of Salamis; deep and memorable as these emotions had been. She came back by the last of March from Egypt and Greece, and made another stay in Rome. A few days after her arrival Gilbert Osmond came down from Florence, and remained three weeks, during which the fact of her being with his old friend, Madame Merle, in whose house she had gone to lodge, made it virtually inevitable that he should see her every day. When the last of April came she wrote to Mrs. Touchett that she should now be very happy to accept an invitation given long before, and went to pay a visit at the Palazzo Crescentini, Madame Merle on this occasion remaining in Rome. Isabel found her aunt alone; her cousin was still at Corfu. Ralph, however, was expected in Florence from day to day, and Isabel, who had not seen him for upwards of a year, was prepared to give him the most affectionate welcome.

❧ 32 ❧

It was not of him, nevertheless, that she was thinking while she stood at the window, where we found her a while ago, and it was not of any of the matters that I have just rapidly sketched. She was not thinking of the past, but of the future; of the immediate, impending hour. She had reason to expect a scene, and she was not fond of scenes. She was not asking herself what she should say to her visitor; this question had already been answered. What he would say to her—that was the interesting speculation. It could be nothing agreeable; Isabel was convinced of this, and the conviction had something to do with her being rather paler than usual. For the rest, however, she wore her natural brightness of aspect; even deep grief, with this vivid young lady, would have had a certain soft effulgence. She had laid aside her mourning, but she was still very simply dressed, and as she felt a good deal older than she had done a year before, it is probable that to a certain extent she looked so. She was not left indefinitely to her apprehensions, for the servant at last came in and presented her a card.

"Let the gentleman come in," said Isabel, who continued to gaze out of the window after the footman had retired. It was only when she had heard the door close behind the person who presently entered that she looked round.

Caspar Goodwood stood there—stood and received a moment, from head to foot, the bright, dry gaze with which she rather withheld than offered a greeting. Whether on his side Mr. Goodwood felt himself older than on the first occasion of our meeting him, is a point which we shall perhaps presently ascertain; let me say meanwhile that to Isabel's critical glance he showed nothing of the injury of time. Straight, strong, and fresh, there was nothing in his appearance that spoke positively either of youth or of age; he looked too deliberate, too serious to be young, and too eager, too active to be old. Old he would never be, and this would serve as a compensation for his never having known the age of chubbiness. Isabel perceived that his jaw had quite the same voluntary look that it had worn in earlier days; but she was prepared to admit that such a moment as the present was not a time for relaxation. He had the air of a man who had traveled hard; he said nothing at first, as if he had been out of breath. This gave Isabel time to make a reflection. "Poor fellow," she mentally murmured, "what great things he is capable of, and what a pity that he should waste his splendid force! What a pity, too, that one can't satisfy everybody!" It gave her time to do more—to say at the end of a minute,

"I can't tell you how I hoped that you wouldn't come."

"I have no doubt of that." And Caspar Goodwood looked about him for a seat. Not only had he come, but he meant to stay a little.

"You must be very tired," said Isabel, seating herself, generously, as she thought, to give him his opportunity.

"No, I am not at all tired. Did you ever know me to be tired?"

"Never; I wish I had. When did you arrive here?"

"Last night, very late; in a kind of snail-train they call the express. These Italian trains go at about the rate of an American funeral."

"That is in keeping—you must have felt as if you were coming to a funeral," Isabel said, forcing a smile, in order to offer such encouragement as she might to an easy treatment of their situation. She had reasoned out the matter elaborately; she had made it perfectly clear that she broke no faith, that she falsified no contract; but for all this she was afraid of him. She was ashamed of her fear; but she was devoutly thankful there was nothing else to be ashamed of. He looked at her with his stiff persistency—a persistency in which there was almost a want of tact; especially as there was a dull dark beam in his eye which rested on her almost like a physical weight.

"No, I didn't feel that; because I couldn't think of you as dead. I wish I could!" said Caspar Goodwood, plainly.

"I thank you immensely."

"I would rather think of you as dead than as married to another man."

"That is very selfish of you!" Isabel cried, with the ardor of a real conviction. "If you are not happy yourself, others have a right to be."

"Very likely it is selfish; but I don't in the least mind your saying so. I don't mind anything you can say now—I don't feel it. The cruelest things you could think of would be mere pinpricks. After what you have done I shall never feel anything. I mean anything but that. That I shall feel all my life."

Mr. Goodwood made these detached assertions with a sort of dry deliberateness, in his hard, slow American tone, which flung no atmospheric color over propositions intrinsically crude. The tone made Isabel angry rather than touched her; but her anger perhaps was fortunate, inasmuch as it gave her a further reason for controlling herself. It was under the pressure of this control that she said, after a little, irrelevantly, by way of answer to Mr. Goodwood's speech—"When did you leave New York?"

He threw up his head a moment, as if he were calculating. "Seventeen days ago."

"You must have traveled fast in spite of your slow trains."

"I came as fast as I could. I would have come five days ago if I had been able."

"It wouldn't have made any difference, Mr. Goodwood," said Isabel, smiling.

"Not to you—no. But to me."

"You gain nothing that I see."

"That is for me to judge!"

"Of course. To me it seems that you only torment yourself." And then, to change the subject, Isabel asked him if he had seen Henrietta Stackpole.

He looked as if he had not come from Boston to Florence to talk about Henrietta Stackpole; but he answered distinctly enough, that this young lady had come to see him just before he left America.

"She came to see you?"

"Yes, she was in Boston, and she called at my office. It was the day I had got your letter."

"Did you tell her?" Isabel asked, with a certain anxiety.

"Oh no," said Caspar Goodwood, simply; "I didn't want to. She will hear it soon enough; she hears everything."

"I shall write to her; and then she will write to me and scold me," Isabel declared, trying to smile again.

Caspar, however, remained sternly grave. "I guess she'll come out," he said.

"On purpose to scold me?"

"I don't know. She seemed to think she had not seen Europe thoroughly."

"I am glad you tell me that," Isabel said. "I must prepare for her."

Mr. Goodwood fixed his eyes for a moment on the floor; then at last, raising them—"Does she know Mr. Osmond?" he asked.

"A little. And she doesn't like him. But of course I don't marry to please Henrietta," Isabel added.

It would have been better for poor Caspar if she had tried a little more to gratify Miss Stackpole; but he did not say so; he only asked, presently, when her marriage would take place.

"I don't know yet. I can only say it will be soon. I have told no one but yourself and one other person—an old friend of Mr. Osmond's."

"Is it a marriage your friends won't like?" Caspar Goodwood asked.

"I really haven't an idea. As I say, I don't marry for my friends."

He went on, making no exclamation, no comment, only asking questions.

"What is Mr. Osmond?"

"What is he? Nothing at all but a very good man. He is not in business," said Isabel. "He is not rich; he is not known for anything in particular."

She disliked Mr. Goodwood's questions, but she said to herself that she owed it to him to satisfy him as far as possible.

The satisfaction poor Caspar exhibited was certainly small; he sat very upright, gazing at her.

"Where does he come from?" he went on.

"From nowhere. He has spent most of his life in Italy."

"You said in your letter that he was an American. Hasn't he a native place?"

"Yes, but he has forgotten it. He left it as a small boy."

"Has he never gone back?"

"Why should he go back?" Isabel asked, flushing a little, and defensively. "He has no profession."

"He might have gone back for his pleasure. Doesn't he like the United States?"

"He doesn't know them. Then he is very simple—he contents himself with Italy."

"With Italy and with you," said Mr. Goodwood, with gloomy plainness, and no appearance of trying to make an epigram. "What has he ever done?" he added, abruptly.

"That I should marry him? Nothing at all," Isabel replied, with a smile that had gradually become a trifle defiant. "If he had done great things would you forgive me any better? Give me up, Mr. Goodwood; I am marrying a nonentity. Don't try to take an interest in him; you can't."

"I can't appreciate him; that's what you mean. And you don't mean in the least that he is a nonentity. You think he is a great man, though no one else thinks so."

Isabel's color deepened; she thought this very clever of her companion, and it was certainly a proof of the clairvoyance of such a feeling as his.

"Why do you always come back to what others think? I can't discuss Mr. Osmond with you."

"Of course not," said Caspar, reasonably.

And he sat there with his air of stiff helplessness, as if not only this were true, but there were nothing else that they might discuss.

"You see how little you gain," Isabel broke out—"how little comfort or satisfaction I can give you."

"I didn't expect you to give me much."

"I don't understand, then, why you came."

"I came because I wanted to see you once more—as you are."

"I appreciate that; but if you had waited a while, sooner or later we should have been sure to meet, and our meeting would have been pleasanter for each of us than this."

"Waited till after you are married? That is just what I didn't want to do. You will be different then."

"Not very. I shall still be a great friend of yours. You will see."

"That will make it all the worse," said Mr. Goodwood, grimly.

"Ah, you are unaccommodating! I can't promise to dislike you, in order to help you to resign yourself."

"I shouldn't care if you did!"

Isabel got up, with a movement of repressed impatience, and walked to the window, where she remained a moment, looking out. When she turned round, her visitor was still motionless in his place. She came toward him again and stopped, resting her hand on the back of the chair she had just quitted.

"Do you mean you came simply to look at me? That's better for you, perhaps, than for me."

"I wished to hear the sound of your voice," said Caspar.

"You have heard it, and you see it says nothing very sweet."

"It gives me pleasure, all the same."

And with this he got up.

She had felt pain and displeasure when she received that morning the note in which he told her that he was in Florence, and, with her permission, would come within an hour to see her. She had been vexed and distressed, though she had sent back word by his messenger that he might come when he would. She had not been better pleased when she saw him; his being there at all was so full of implication. It implied things she could never assent to—rights, reproaches, remonstrance, rebuke, the expectation of making her change her purpose. These things, however, if implied, had not been expressed; and now our young lady, strangely enough, began to resent her visitor's remarkable self-control. There was a dumb misery about him which irritated her; there was a manly staying of his hand which made her heart beat faster. She felt her agitation rising, and she said to herself that she was as angry as a woman who had been in the wrong. She was not in the wrong; she had fortunately not that bitterness to swallow; but, all the same, she wished he would denounce her a little. She had wished his visit would be short; it had no purpose, no propriety; yet now that he seemed to be turning away, she felt a sudden horror of his leaving her without uttering a word that would give her an opportunity to defend herself more than she had done in writing to him a month before, in a few carefully chosen words, to announce her engagement. If she were not in the wrong, however, why should she desire to defend herself? It was an excess of generosity on Isabel's part to desire that Mr. Goodwood should be angry.

If he had not held himself hard it might have made him so to hear the tone in which she suddenly exclaimed, as if she were accusing him of having accused her.

"I have not deceived you! I was perfectly free!"

"Yes, I know that," said Caspar.

"I gave you full warning that I would do as I chose."

"You said you would probably never marry, and you said it so positively that I pretty well believed it."

Isabel was silent an instant.

"No one can be more surprised than myself at my present intention."

"You told me that if I heard you were engaged, I was not to believe it," Caspar went on. "I heard it twenty days ago from yourself, but I remembered what you had said. I thought there might be some mistake, and that is partly why I came."

"If you wish me to repeat it by word of mouth, that is soon done. There is no mistake at all."

"I saw that as soon as I came into the room."

"What good would it do you that I shouldn't marry?" Isabel asked, with a certain fierceness.

"I should like it better than this."

"You are very selfish, as I said before."

"I know that. I am selfish as iron."

"Even iron sometimes melts. If you will be reasonable I will see you again."

"Don't you call me reasonable now?"

"I don't know what to say to you," she answered, with sudden humility.

"I sha'n't trouble you for a long time," the young man went on. He made a step toward the door, but he stopped. "Another reason why I came was that I wanted to hear what you would say in explanation of your having changed your mind."

Isabel's humbleness as suddenly deserted her.

"In explanation? Do you think I am bound to explain?"

Caspar gave her one of his long dumb looks.

"You were very positive. I did believe it."

"So did I. Do you think I could explain if I would?"

"No, I suppose not. Well," he added, "I have done what I wished. I have seen you."

"How little you make of these terrible journeys," Isabel murmured.

"If you are afraid I am tired, you may be at your ease about that." He turned away, this time in earnest, and no handshake, no sign of parting, was exchanged between them. At the door he stopped, with his hand on the knob. "I shall leave Florence tomorrow," he said.

"I am delighted to hear it!" she answered, passionately. And he went out. Five minutes after he had gone she burst into tears.

❦ 33 ❦

Her fit of weeping, however, was of brief duration, and the signs of it had vanished when, an hour later, she broke the news to her aunt. I use this expression because she had been sure Mrs. Touchett would not be pleased; Isabel had only waited to tell her till she had seen Mr. Goodwood. She had an odd impression that it would not be honorable to make the fact public before she should have heard what Mr. Goodwood would say about it. He had said rather less than she expected, and she now had a somewhat angry sense of having lost time. But she would lose no more; she waited till Mrs. Touchett came into the drawing room before the mid-day breakfast, and then she said to her—

"Aunt Lydia, I have something to tell you."

Mrs. Touchett gave a little jump and looked at the girl almost fiercely.

"You needn't tell me; I know what it is."

"I don't know how you know."

"The same way that I know when the window is open—by feeling a draught. You are going to marry that man."

"What man do you mean?" Isabel inquired, with great dignity.

"Madame Merle's friend—Mr. Osmond."

"I don't know why you call him Madame Merle's friend. Is that the principal thing he is known by?"

"If he is not her friend he ought to be—after what she has done for him!" cried Mrs. Touchett. "I shouldn't have expected it of her; I am disappointed."

"If you mean that Madame Merle has had anything to do with my engagement you are greatly mistaken," Isabel declared, with a sort of ardent coldness.

"You mean that your attractions were sufficient, without the gentleman being urged? You are quite right. They are immense, your attractions, and he would never have presumed to think of you if she had not put him up to it. He has a very good opinion of himself, but he was not a man to take trouble. Madame Merle took the trouble for him."

"He has taken a great deal for himself!" cried Isabel, with a voluntary laugh.

Mrs. Touchett gave a sharp nod.

"I think he must, after all, to have made you like him."

"I thought you liked him yourself."

"I did, and that is why I am angry with him."

"Be angry with me, not with him," said the girl.

"Oh, I am always angry with you; that's no satisfaction! Was it for this that you refused Lord Warburton?"

"Please don't go back to that. Why shouldn't I like Mr. Osmond, since you did?"

"I never wanted to marry him; there is nothing of him."

"Then he can't hurt me," said Isabel.

"Do you think you are going to be happy? No one is happy."

"I shall set the fashion then. What does one marry for?"

"What you will marry for, heaven only knows. People usually marry as they go into partnership—to set up a house. But in your partnership you will bring everything."

"Is it that Mr. Osmond is not rich? Is that what you are talking about?" Isabel asked.

"He has no money; he has no name; he has no importance. I value such things and I have the courage to say it; I think they are very precious. Many other people think the same, and they show it. But they give some other reason!"

Isabel hesitated a little.

"I think I value everything that is valuable. I care very much for money, and that is why I wish Mr. Osmond to have some."

"Give it to him, then; but marry someone else."

"His name is good enough for me," the girl went on. "It's a very pretty name. Have I such a fine one myself?"

"All the more reason you should improve on it. There are only a dozen American names. Do you marry him out of charity?"

"It was my duty to tell you, Aunt Lydia, but I don't think it is my duty to explain to you. Even if it were, I shouldn't be able. So please don't remonstrate; in talking about it you have me at a disadvantage. I can't talk about it."

"I don't remonstrate, I simply answer you; I must give some sign of intelligence. I saw it coming, and I said nothing. I never meddle."

"You never do, and I am greatly obliged to you. You have been very considerate."

"It was not considerate—it was convenient," said Mrs. Touchett. "But I shall talk to Madame Merle."

"I don't see why you keep bringing her in. She has been a very good friend to me."

"Possibly; but she has been a poor one to me."

"What has she done to you?"

"She has deceived me. She had as good as promised me to prevent your engagement."

"She couldn't have prevented it."

"She can do anything; that is what I have always liked her for. I knew she could play any part; but I understood that she played them one by one. I didn't understand that she would play two at the same time."

"I don't know what part she may have played to you," Isabel said; "that is between yourselves. To me she has been honest, and kind, and devoted."

"Devoted, of course; she wished you to marry her candidate. She told me that she was watching you only in order to interpose."

"She said that to please you," the girl answered; conscious, however, of the inadequacy of the explanation.

"To please me by deceiving me? She knows me better. Am I pleased today?"

"I don't think you are ever much pleased," Isabel was obliged to reply. "If Madame Merle knew you would learn the truth, what had she to gain by insincerity?"

"She gained time, as you see. While I waited for her to interfere you were marching away, and she was really beating the drum."

"That is very well. But by your own admission you saw I was marching, and even if she had given the alarm you would not have tried to stop me."

"No, but someone else would."

"Whom do you mean?" Isabel asked, looking very hard at her aunt.

Mrs. Touchett's little bright eyes, active as they usually were, sustained her gaze rather than returned it.

"Would you have listened to Ralph?"

"Not if he had abused Mr. Osmond."

"Ralph doesn't abuse people; you know that perfectly. He cares very much for you."

"I know he does," said Isabel; "and I shall feel the value of it now, for he knows that whatever I do I do with reason."

"He never believed you would do this. I told him you were capable of it, and he argued the other way."

"He did it for the sake of argument," said Isabel, smiling. "You don't accuse him of having deceived you; why should you accuse Madame Merle?"

"He never pretended he would prevent it."

"I am glad of that!" cried the girl, gaily. "I wish very much," she presently added, "that when he comes you would tell him first of my engagement."

"Of course I will mention it," said Mrs. Touchett. "I will say nothing more to you about it, but I give you notice I will talk to others."

"That's as you please. I only meant that it is rather better the announcement should come from you than from me."

"I quite agree with you; it is much more proper!"

And on this the two ladies went to breakfast, where Mrs. Touchett was as good as her word, and made no allusion to Gilbert Osmond. After an interval of silence, however, she asked her companion from whom she had received a visit an hour before.

"From an old friend—an American gentleman," Isabel said, with a color in her cheek.

"An American, of course. It is only an American that calls at ten o'clock in the morning."

"It was half-past ten; he was in a great hurry; he goes away this evening."

"Couldn't he have come yesterday, at the usual time?"

"He only arrived last night."

"He spends but twenty-four hours in Florence?" Mrs. Touchett cried. "He's an American truly."

"He is indeed," said Isabel, thinking with a perverse admiration of what Caspar Goodwood had done for her.

Two days afterward Ralph arrived; but though Isabel was sure that Mrs. Touchett had lost no time in telling him the news, he betrayed at first no knowledge of the great fact. Their first talk was naturally about his health; Isabel had many questions to ask about Corfu. She had been shocked by his appearance when he came into the room; she had forgotten how ill he looked. In spite of Corfu, he looked very ill today, and Isabel wondered whether he were really worse or whether she was simply disaccustomed to living with an invalid. Poor Ralph grew no handsomer as he advanced in life, and the now apparently complete loss of his health had done little to mitigate the natural oddity of his person. His face wore its pleasant perpetual smile, which perhaps suggested wit rather than achieved it; his thin whisker languished upon a lean cheek; the exorbitant curve of his nose defined itself more sharply. Lean he was altogether; lean and long and loose-jointed; an accidental cohesion of relaxed angles. His brown velvet jacket had become perennial; his hands had fixed themselves in his pockets; he shambled, and stumbled, and shuffled, in a manner that denoted great physical helplessness. It was perhaps this whimsical gait that helped to mark his character more than ever as that of the humorous invalid—the invalid for whom even his own disabilities are part of the general joke. They might well indeed with Ralph have been the chief cause of the want of seriousness with which he appeared to regard a world in which the reason for his own presence was past finding out. Isabel had grown fond of his ugliness; his awkwardness had become dear to her. These things were endeared by association; they struck her as the conditions of his being so charming. Ralph was so charming that her sense of his being ill had hitherto had a sort of comfort in it; the state of his health had seemed not a limitation, but a kind of intellectual advantage; it absolved him from all professional and official emotions and left him the luxury of being simply personal. This personality of Ralph's was delightful; it had none of the staleness of disease; it was always easy and fresh and genial. Such had been the girl's impression of her cousin; and when she had pitied him it was only on reflection. As she reflected a good deal she had given him a certain amount of compassion; but Isabel always had a dread of wasting compassion—a precious article, worth more to the giver than to anyone else. Now, however, it took no great ingenuity to discover that poor Ralph's tenure of life was less elastic than it should be. He was a dear, bright, generous fellow; he had all the illumination of wisdom and none of its pedantry, and yet he was dying. Isabel said to herself that life was certainly hard for some people, and she felt a delicate glow of shame as she thought how easy it now promised to become for herself. She was prepared to learn that Ralph was not pleased with her engagement; but she was not prepared, in spite of her affection for her cousin, to let this fact spoil the situation. She was not even prepared— or so she thought—to resent his want of sympathy; for it would be his privilege—it would be indeed his natural line—to find fault with any step she might take toward marriage. One's cousin always pretended to hate one's husband; that was traditional, classical; it was a part of one's cousin's always pretending to adore one.

Ralph was nothing if not critical; and though she would certainly, other things being equal, have been as glad to marry to please Ralph as to please anyone, it would be absurd to think it important that her choice should square with his views. What were his views, after all? He had pretended to think she had better marry Lord Warburton; but this was only because she had refused that excellent man. If she had accepted him Ralph would certainly have taken another tone; he always took the opposite one. You could criticize any marriage; it was the essence of a marriage to be open to criticism. How well she herself, if she would only give her mind to it, might criticize this union of her own! She had other employment, however, and Ralph was welcome to relieve her of the care. Isabel was prepared to be wonderfully good-humored.

He must have seen that, and this made it the more odd that he should say nothing. After three days had elapsed without his speaking, Isabel became impatient; dislike it as he would, he might at least go through the form. We who know more about poor Ralph than his cousin, may easily believe that during the hours that followed his arrival at the Palazzo Crescentini, he had privately gone through many forms. His mother had literally greeted him with the great news, which was even more sensibly chilling than Mrs. Touchett's maternal kiss. Ralph was shocked and humiliated; his calculations had been false, and his cousin was lost. He drifted about the house like a rudderless vessel in a rocky stream, or sat in the garden of the palace in a great cane chair, with his long legs extended, his head thrown back, and his hat pulled over his eyes. He felt cold about the heart; he had never liked anything less. What could he do, what could he say? If Isabel were irreclaimable, could he pretend to like it? To attempt to reclaim her was permissible only if the attempt should succeed. To try to persuade her that the man to whom she had pledged her faith was a humbug would be decently discreet only in the event of her being persuaded. Otherwise he should simply have damned himself. It cost him an equal effort to speak his thought and to dissemble; he could neither assent with sincerity nor protest with hope. Meanwhile he knew—or rather he supposed—that the affianced pair were daily renewing their mutual vows. Osmond, at this moment, showed himself little at the Palazzo Crescentini; but Isabel met him every day elsewhere, as she was free to do after their engagement had been made public. She had taken a carriage by the month, so as not to be indebted to her aunt for the means of pursuing a course of which Mrs. Touchett disapproved, and she drove in the morning to the Cascine. This suburban wilderness, during the early hours, was void of all intruders, and our young lady, joined by her lover in its quietest part, strolled with him a while in the gray Italian shade and listened to the nightingales.

❧34❧

One morning, on her return from her drive, some half-hour before luncheon, she quitted her vehicle in the court of the palace, and instead of ascending the great staircase, crossed the court, passed beneath another archway, and entered the garden. A sweeter spot, at this moment, could not have been imagined. The stillness of noontide hung over it; the warm shade was motionless, and the hot light made it pleasant. Ralph was sitting there in the clear gloom, at the base of a statue of Terpsichore—a dancing nymph with taper fingers and inflated draperies, in the manner of Bernini; the extreme relaxation of his attitude suggested at first to Isabel that he was asleep. Her light footstep on the grass had not roused him, and before turning away she stood for a moment looking at him. During this instant he opened his eyes; upon which she sat down on a rustic chair that matched with his own. Though in her irritation she had accused him of indifference, she was not blind to the fact that he was visibly preoccupied. But she had attributed his long reveries partly to the languor of his increased weakness, partly to his being troubled about certain arrangements he had made as to the property inherited from his father—arrangements of which Mrs. Touchett disapproved, and which, as she had told Isabel, now encountered opposition from the other partners in the bank. He ought to have gone to England, his mother said, instead of coming to Florence; he had not been there for months, and he took no more interest in the bank than in the state of Patagonia.

"I am sorry I waked you," Isabel said; "you look tired."

"I feel tired. But I was not asleep. I was thinking of you."

"Are you tired of that?"

"Very much so. It leads to nothing. The road is long and I never arrive."

"What do you wish to arrive at?" Isabel said, closing her parasol.

"At the point of expressing to myself properly what I think of your engagement."

"Don't think too much of it," said Isabel, lightly.

"Do you mean that it's none of my business?"

"Beyond a certain point, yes."

"That's the point I wish to fix. I had an idea that you have found me wanting in good manners; I have never congratulated you."

"Of course I have noticed that; I wondered why you were silent."

"There have been a good many reasons; I will tell you now," said Ralph.

He pulled off his hat and laid it on the ground; then he sat looking at her. He leaned back, with his head against the marble pedestal of Terpsichore, his arms dropped on either side of him, his hands laid upon the sides of his wide chair. He looked awkward, uncomfortable; he hesitated for a long time. Isabel said nothing; when people were embarrassed she was usually sorry for them; but she was determined not to help Ralph to utter a word that should not be to the honor of her ingenious purpose.

"I think I have hardly got over my surprise," he said at last. "You were the last person I expected to see caught."

"I don't know why you call it caught."

"Because you are going to be put into a cage."

"If I like my cage, that needn't trouble you," said Isabel.

"That's what I wonder at; that's what I have been thinking of."

"If you have been thinking, you may imagine how I have thought! I am satisfied that I am doing well."

"You must have changed immensely. A year ago you valued your liberty beyond everything. You wanted only to see life."

"I have seen it," said Isabel. "It doesn't seem to me so charming."

"I don't pretend it is; only I had an idea that you took a genial view of it and wanted to survey the whole field."

"I have seen that one can't do that. One must choose a corner and cultivate that."

"That's what I think. And one must choose a good corner. I had no idea, all winter, while I read your delightful letters, that you were choosing. You said nothing about it, and your silence put me off my guard."

"It was not a matter I was likely to write to you about. Besides, I knew nothing of the future. It has all come lately. If you had been on your guard, however," Isabel asked, "what would you have done?"

"I should have said—'Wait a little longer.' "

"Wait for what?"

"Well, for a little more light," said Ralph, with a rather absurd smile, while his hands found their way into his pockets.

"Where should my light have come from? From you?"

"I might have struck a spark or two!"

Isabel had drawn off her gloves; she smoothed them out as they lay upon her knee. The gentleness of this movement was accidental, for her expression was not conciliatory.

"You are beating about the bush, Ralph. You wish to say that you don't like Mr. Osmond, and yet you are afraid."

"I am afraid of you, not of him. If you marry him it won't be a nice thing to have said."

"*If* I marry him! Have you had any expectation of dissuading me?"

"Of course that seems to you too fatuous."

"No," said Isabel, after a little; "it seems to me touching."

"That's the same thing. It makes me so ridiculous that you pity me."

Isabel stroked out her long gloves again.

"I know you have a great affection for me. I can't get rid of that."

"For heaven's sake don't try. Keep that well in sight. It will convince you how intensely I want you to do well."

"And how little you trust me!"

There was a moment's silence; the warm noontide seemed to listen.

"I trust you, but I don't trust him," said Ralph.

Isabel raised her eyes and gave him a wide, deep look.

"You have said it now; you will suffer for it."

"Not if you are just."

"I am very just," said Isabel. "What better proof of it can there be than that I am not angry with you? I don't know what is the matter with me, but I am not. I was when you began, but it has passed away. Perhaps I ought to be angry, but Mr. Osmond wouldn't think so. He wants me to know everything; that's what I like him for. You have nothing to gain, I know that. I have never been so nice to you, as a girl, that you should have much reason for wishing me to remain one. You give very good advice; you have often done so. No, I am very quiet; I have always believed in your wisdom," Isabel went on, boasting of her quietness, yet speaking with a kind of contained exaltation. It was her passionate desire to be just; it touched Ralph to the heart, affected him like a caress from a creature he had injured. He wished to interrupt, to reassure her; for a moment he was absurdly inconsistent; he would have retracted what he had said. But she gave him no chance; she went on, having caught a glimpse, as she thought, of the heroic line, and desiring to advance in that direction. "I see you have got some idea; I should like very much to hear it. I am sure it's disinterested; I feel that. It seems a strange thing to argue about, and of course I ought to tell you definitely that if you expect to dissuade me you may give it up. You will not move me at all; it is too late. As you say, I am caught. Certainly it won't be pleasant for you to remember this, but your pain will be in your own thoughts. I shall never reproach you."

"I don't think you ever will," said Ralph. "It is not in the least the sort of marriage I thought you would make."

"What sort of marriage was that, pray?"

"Well, I can hardly say. I hadn't exactly a positive view of it, but I had a negative. I didn't think you would marry a man like Mr. Osmond."

"What do you know against him? You know him scarcely at all."

"Yes," Ralph said, "I know him very little, and I know nothing against him. But all the same I can't help feeling that you are running a risk."

"Marriage is always a risk, and his risk is as great as mine."

"That's his affair! If he is afraid, let him recede; I wish he would."

Isabel leaned back in her chair, folded her arms, and gazed a while at her cousin. "I don't think I understand you," she said at last, coldly. "I don't know what you are talking about."

"I thought you would marry a man of more importance."

Cold, I say, her tone had been, but at this a color like a flame leaped into her face. "Of more importance to whom? It seems to me enough that one's husband should be important to one's self!"

Ralph blushed as well; his attitude embarrassed him. Physically speaking, he proceeded to change it; he straightened himself, then leaned forward, resting a hand on each knee. He fixed his eyes on the ground; he had an air of the most respectful deliberation.

"I will tell you in a moment what I mean," he presently said. He felt agitated, intensely eager; now that he had opened the discussion he wished to discharge his mind. But he wished also to be superlatively gentle.

Isabel waited a little, and then she went on, with majesty.

"In everything that makes one care for people, Mr. Osmond is preeminent. There may be nobler natures, but I have never had the pleasure of meeting one. Mr. Osmond is the best I know; he is important enough for me."

"I had a sort of vision of your future," Ralph said, without answering this; "I amused myself with planning out a kind of destiny for you. There was to be nothing of this sort in it. You were not to come down so easily, so soon."

"To come down? What strange expressions you use! Is that your description of my marriage?"

"It expresses my idea of it. You seemed to me to be soaring far up in the blue— to be sailing in the bright light, over the heads of men. Suddenly someone tosses up a faded rosebud—a missile that should never have reached you—and down you drop to the ground. It hurts me," said Ralph, audaciously, "as if I had fallen myself!"

The look of pain and bewilderment deepened in his companion's face.

"I don't understand you in the least," she repeated. "You say you amused yourself with planning out my future—I don't understand that. Don't amuse yourself too much, or I shall think you are doing it at my expense."

Ralph shook his head.

"I am not afraid of your not believing that I have had great ideas for you."

"What do you mean by my soaring and sailing?" the girl asked. "I have never moved on a higher line than I am moving on now. There is nothing higher for a girl than to marry a—a person she likes," said poor Isabel, wandering into the didactic.

"It's your liking the person we speak of that I venture to criticize, my dear Isabel! I should have said that the man for you would have been a more active, larger, freer sort of nature." Ralph hesitated a moment, then he added, "I can't get over the belief that there's something small in Osmond."

He had uttered these last words with a tremor of the voice; he was afraid that she would flash out again. But to his surprise she was quiet; she had the air of considering.

"Something small?" she said reflectively.

"I think he's narrow, selfish. He takes himself so seriously!"

"He has a great respect for himself; I don't blame him for that," said Isabel. "It's the proper way to respect others."

Ralph for a moment felt almost reassured by her reasonable tone.

"Yes, but everything is relative; one ought to feel one's relations. I don't think Mr. Osmond does that."

"I have chiefly to do with the relation in which he stands to me. In that he is excellent."

"He is the incarnation of taste," Ralph went on, thinking hard how he could best express Gilbert Osmond's sinister attributes without putting himself in the wrong by seeming to describe him coarsely. He wished to describe him impersonally, scientifically. "He judges and measures, approves and condemns, altogether by that."

"It is a happy thing then that his tastes should be exquisite."

"It is exquisite, indeed, since it has led him to select you as his wife. But have you ever seen an exquisite taste ruffled?"

"I hope it may never be my fortune to fail to gratify my husband's."

At these words a sudden passion leaped to Ralph's lips. "Ah, that's willful, that's unworthy of you!" he cried. "You were not meant to be measured in that way—you were meant for something better than to keep guard over the sensibilities of a sterile dilettante!"

Isabel rose quickly and Ralph did the same, so that they stood for a moment looking at each other as if he had flung down a defiance or an insult.

"You go too far," she murmured.

"I have said what I had on my mind—and I have said it because I love you!"

Isabel turned pale: was he too on that tiresome list? She had a sudden wish to strike him off. "Ah then, you are not disinterested!"

"I love you, but I love without hope," said Ralph, quickly, forcing a smile, and feeling that in that last declaration he had expressed more than he intended.

Isabel moved away and stood looking into the sunny stillness of the garden; but after a little she turned back to him. "I am afraid your talk, then, is the wildness of despair. I don't understand it—but it doesn't matter. I am not arguing with you; it is impossible that I should; I have only tried to listen to you. I am much obliged to you for attempting to explain," she said gently, as if the anger with which she had just sprung up had already subsided. "It is very good of you to try to warn me, if you are really alarmed. But I won't promise to think of what you have said; I shall forget it as soon as possible. Try and forget it yourself; you have done your duty, and no man can do more. I can't explain to you what I feel, what I believe, and I wouldn't if I could." She paused a moment, and then she went on, with an inconsequence that Ralph observed even in the midst of his eagerness to discover some symptom of concession. "I can't enter into your idea of Mr. Osmond; I can't do it justice, because I see him in quite another way. He is not important—no, he is not important; he is a man to whom importance is supremely indifferent. If that is what you mean when you call him 'small,' then he is as small as you please. I call that large—it's the largest thing I know. I won't pretend to argue with you about a person I am going to marry," Isabel repeated. "I am not in the least concerned to defend Mr. Osmond; he is not so weak as to need my defence. I should think it would seem strange, even to yourself, that I should talk of him so quietly and coldly, as if he were anyone else. I would not talk of him at all, to anyone but you; and you, after what you have said— I may just answer you once for all. Pray, would you wish me to make a mercenary marriage—what they call a marriage of ambition? I have only one ambition—to be free to follow out a good feeling. I had others once; but they have passed away. Do you complain of Mr. Osmond because he is not rich? That is just what I like him for. I have fortunately money enough; I have never felt so thankful for it as today. There have been moments when I should like to go and kneel down by your father's grave; he did perhaps a better thing than he knew when he put it into my power to marry a poor man—a man who has borne his poverty with such dignity, with such indifference. Mr. Osmond has never scrambled nor struggled—he has cared for no worldly prize. If that is to be narrow, if that is to be selfish, then it's very well. I am not frightened by such words, I am not even displeased; I am only sorry that you should make a mistake. Others might have done so, but I am surprised that you should. You might know a gentleman when you see one—you might know a fine mind. Mr. Osmond makes no mistakes! He knows everything, he understands everything, he has the kindest, gentlest, highest spirit. You have got hold of some false idea; it's a pity, but I can't help it; it regards you more than me." Isabel paused a moment, looking at her cousin with an eye illuminated by a sentiment which contradicted the careful calmness of her manner—a mingled sentiment, to which the angry pain excited by his words and the wounded pride of having needed to justify a choice of which she felt only the nobleness and purity, equally contributed. Though she paused, Ralph said nothing; he saw she had more to say. She was superb, but she was eager; she was indifferent, but she was secretly trembling. "What sort of a person should you have liked me to marry?" she asked, suddenly. "You talk about one's soaring and sailing, but if one marries at all one touches the earth. One has human feelings and needs, one has a heart in one's bosom, and one must marry a particular individual. Your mother has never forgiven me for not having come to a better understanding with Lord Warburton, and she is horrified at my contenting myself with a person who has none of Lord Warburton's great advantages—no property, no title, no honors, no houses, nor lands, nor position, nor reputation, nor brilliant belongings of any sort. It is the total absence of all these things that pleases me. Mr. Osmond is simply a man—he is not a proprietor!"

Ralph had listened with great attention, as if everything she said merited deep consideration; but in reality he was only half thinking of the things she said, he was for the rest simply accommodating himself to the weight of his total impression— the impression of her passionate good faith. She was wrong, but she believed; she was deluded, but she was consistent. It was wonderfully characteristic of her that she had invented a fine theory about Gilbert Osmond, and loved him, not for what he really possessed, but for his very poverties dressed out as honors. Ralph remembered what he had said to his father about wishing to put it into Isabel's power to gratify her imagination. He had done so, and the girl had taken full advantage of the privilege. Poor Ralph felt sick; he felt ashamed. Isabel had uttered her last words with a low solemnity of conviction which virtually terminated the discussion, and she closed it formally by turning away and walking back to the house. Ralph walked beside her, and they passed into the court together and reached the big staircase. Here Ralph stopped, and Isabel paused, turning on him a face full of a deep elation at his opposition having made her own conception of her conduct more clear to her.

"Shall you not come up to breakfast?" she asked.

"No; I want no breakfast, I am not hungry."

"You ought to eat," said the girl; "you live on air."

"I do, very much, and I shall go back into the garden and take another mouthful of it. I came thus far simply to say this. I said to you last year that if you were to get into trouble I should feel terribly sold. That's how I feel today."

"Do you think I am in trouble?"

"One is in trouble when one is in error."

"Very well," said Isabel; "I shall never complain of my trouble to you!" And she moved up the staircase.

Ralph, standing there with his hands in his pockets, followed her with his eyes; then the lurking chill of the high-walled court struck him and made him shiver, so that he returned to the garden, to breakfast on the Florentine sunshine.

❧ 35 ❧

Isabel, when she strolled in the Cascine with her lover, felt no impulse to tell him that he was not thought well of at the Palazzo Crescentini. The discreet opposition offered to her marriage by her aunt and her cousin made on the whole little impression upon her; the moral of it was simply that they disliked Gilbert Osmond. This dislike was not alarming to Isabel; she scarcely even regretted it; for it served mainly to throw into higher relief the fact, in every way so honorable, that she married to please herself. One did other things to please other people; one did this for a more personal satisfaction; and Isabel's satisfaction was confirmed by her lover's admirable good conduct. Gilbert Osmond was in love, and he had never deserved less than during these still, bright days, each of them numbered, which preceded the fulfillment of his hopes, the harsh criticism passed upon him by Ralph Touchett. The chief impression produced upon Isabel's mind by this criticism was that the passion of love separated its victim terribly from everyone but the loved object. She felt herself disjoined from everyone she had ever known before—from her two sisters, who wrote to express a dutiful hope that she would be happy, and a surprise, somewhat more vague, at her not having chosen a consort who was the hero of a richer accumulation of anecdote; from Henrietta, who, she was sure, would come out, too late, on purpose to remonstrate; from Lord Warburton, who would certainly console himself, and from Caspar Goodwood, who perhaps would not; from her aunt, who had cold, shallow ideas about marriage, for which she was not sorry to manifest her contempt; and from Ralph, whose talk about having great views for her was surely but a whimsical cover for a personal disappointment. Ralph apparently wished her not to marry at all—that was what it really meant—because he was amused with the spectacle of her adventures as a single woman. His disappointment made him say angry things about the man she had preferred even to him: Isabel flattered herself that she believed Ralph had been angry. It was the more easy for her to believe this, because, as I say, she thought on the whole but little about it, and accepted as an incident of her lot the idea that to prefer Gilbert Osmond as she preferred him was perforce to break all other ties. She tasted of the sweets of this preference, and they made her feel that there was after all something very invidious in being in love; much as the sentiment was theoretically approved of. It was the tragical side of happiness; one's right was always made of the wrong of someone else. Gilbert Osmond was not demonstrative; the consciousness of success, which must now have flamed high within him, emitted very little smoke for so brilliant a blaze. Contentment, on his part, never took a vulgar form; excitement, in the most self-conscious of men, was a kind of ecstasy of self-control. This disposition, however, made him an admirable lover; it gave him a constant view of the amorous character. He never forgot himself, as I say; and so he never forgot to be graceful and tender, to wear the appearance of devoted intention. He was immensely pleased with his young lady; Madame Merle had made him a present of incalculable value. What could be a finer thing to live with than a high spirit attuned to softness? For would not the softness be all for one's self, and the strenuousness for society, which admired the air of superiority? What could be a happier gift in a companion than a quick, fanciful mind, which saved one repetitions, and reflected one's thought upon a scintillating surface? Osmond disliked to see his thought reproduced literally—that made it look stale and stupid; he preferred it to be brightened in the reproduction. His egotism, if egotism it was, had never taken the crude form of wishing for a dull wife; this lady's intelligence was to be a silver plate, not an earthen one—a plate that he might heap up with ripe fruits, to which it would give a decorative value, so that conversation might become a sort of perpetual dessert. He found the silvery quality in perfection in Isabel; he could tap her imagination with his knuckle and make it ring. He knew perfectly, though he had not been told, that the union found little favor among the girl's relations; but he had always treated her so completely as an independent person that it hardly seemed necessary to express regret for the attitude of her family. Nevertheless, one morning, he made an abrupt allusion to it.

"It's the difference in our fortune they don't like," he said. "They think I am in love with your money."

"Are you speaking of my aunt—of my cousin?" Isabel asked. "How do you know what they think?"

"You have not told me that they are pleased, and when I wrote to Mrs. Touchett the other day she never answered my note. If they had been delighted I should have learnt it, and the fact of my being poor and you rich is the most obvious explanation of their want of delight. But, of course, when a poor man marries a rich girl he must be prepared for imputations. I don't mind them; I only care for one thing—your thinking it's all right. I don't care what others think. I have never cared much, and why should I begin today, when I have taken to myself a compensation for everything? I won't pretend that I am sorry you are rich; I am delighted. I delight in everything that is yours—whether it be money or virtue. Money is a great advantage. It seems to me, however, that I have sufficiently proved that I can get on without it; I never in my life tried to earn a penny, and I ought to be less subject to suspicion than most people. I suppose it is their business to suspect—that of your own family; it's proper on the whole they should. They will like me better some day; so will you, for that matter. Meanwhile my business is not to bother, but simply to be thankful for life and love. It has made me better, loving you," he said on another occasion; "it has made me wiser, and easier, and brighter. I used to want a great many things before, and to be angry that I didn't have them. Theoretically, I was satisfied, as I once told you. I flattered myself that I had limited my wants. But I was subject to irritation; I used to have morbid, sterile, hateful fits of hunger, of desire. Now I am really satisfied, because I can't think of anything better. It is just as when one has been trying to spell out a book in the twilight, and suddenly the lamp comes in. I had been putting out my eyes over the book of life, and finding nothing to reward me for my pains; but now that I can read it properly I see that it's a delightful story. My dear girl, I can't tell you how life seems to stretch there before us—what a long summer afternoon awaits us. It's the latter half of an Italian day—with a golden haze, and the shadows just lengthening, and that divine delicacy in the light, the air, the landscape, which I have loved all my life, and which you love today. Upon my word, I don't see why we shouldn't get on. We have got what we like—to say nothing of having each other. We have the faculty of admiration, and several excellent beliefs. We are not stupid, we are not heavy, we are not under bonds to any dull limitations. You are very fresh, and I am well-seasoned. We have got my poor child to amuse us; we will try and make up some little life for her. It is all soft and mellow—it has the Italian coloring."

They made a good many plans, but they left themselves also a good deal of latitude; it was a matter of course, however, that they should live for the present in Italy. It was in Italy that they had met, Italy had been a party to their first impressions of each other, and Italy should be a party to their happiness. Osmond had the attachment of old acquaintance, and Isabel the stimulus of new, which seemed to assure her a future of beautiful hours. The desire for unlimited expansion had been succeeded in her mind by the sense that life was vacant without some private duty which gathered one's energies to a point. She told Ralph that she had "seen life" in a year or two, and that she was already tired, not of life, but of observation. What had become of all her ardors, her aspirations, her theories, her high estimate of her independence, and her incipient conviction that she should never marry? These things had been absorbed in a more primitive sentiment—a sentiment which answered all questions, satisfied all needs, solved all difficulties. It simplified the future at a stroke, it came down from above, like the light of the stars, and it needed no explanation. There was explanation enough in the fact that he was her lover, her own, and that she was able to be of use to him. She could marry him with a kind of pride; she was not only taking, but giving.

He brought Pansy with him two or three times to the Cascine—Pansy who was very little taller than a year before, and not much older. That she would always be a child was the conviction expressed by her father, who held her by the hand when she was in her sixteenth year, and told her to go and play while he sat down a while with the pretty lady. Pansy wore a short dress and a long coat; her hat always seemed too big for her. She amused herself with walking off, with quick, short steps, to the end of the alley, and then walking back with a smile that seemed an appeal for approbation. Isabel gave her approbation in abundance, and it was of that demonstrated personal kind which the child's affectionate nature craved. She watched her development with a kind of amused suspense; Pansy had already become a little daughter. She was treated so completely as a child that Osmond had not yet explained to her the new relation in which he stood to the elegant Miss Archer. "She doesn't know," he said to Isabel; "she doesn't suspect; she thinks it perfectly natural that you and I should come and walk here together, simply as good friends. There seems to me something enchantingly innocent in that; it's the way I like her to be. No, I am not a failure, as I used to think; I have succeeded in two things. I am to marry the woman I adore, and I have brought up my child as I wished, in the old way."

He was very fond, in all things, of the "old way;" that had struck Isabel as an element in the refinement of his character.

"It seems to me you will not know whether you have succeeded until you have told her," she said. "You must see how she takes your news. She may be horrified—she may be jealous."

"I am not afraid of that; she is too fond of you on her own account. I should like to leave her in the dark a little longer—to see if it will come into her head that if we are not engaged we ought to be."

Isabel was impressed by Osmond's aesthetic relish of Pansy's innocence—her own appreciation of it being more moral. She was perhaps not the less pleased when he told her a few days later that he had broken the news to his daughter, who made such a pretty little speech. "Oh, then I shall have a sister!" She was neither surprised nor alarmed; she had not cried, as he expected.

"Perhaps she had guessed it," said Isabel.

"Don't say that; I should be disgusted if I believed that. I thought it would be just a little shock; but the way she took it proves that her good manners are paramount. That is also what I wished. You shall see for yourself; tomorrow she shall make you her congratulations in person."

The meeting, on the morrow, took place at the Countess Gemini's, whither Pansy had been conducted by her father, who knew that Isabel was to come in the afternoon to return a visit made her by the Countess on learning that they were to become sisters-in-law. Calling at Casa Touchett, the visitor had not found Isabel at home; but after our young lady had been ushered into the Countess's drawing room, Pansy came in to say that her aunt would presently appear. Pansy was spending the day with her aunt, who thought she was of an age when she should begin to learn how to carry herself in company. It was Isabel's view that the little girl might have given lessons in deportment to the elder lady, and nothing could have justified this conviction more than the manner in which Pansy acquitted herself while they waited together for the Countess. Her father's decision, the year before, had finally been to send her back to the convent to receive the last graces, and Madame Catherine had evidently carried out her theory that Pansy was to be fitted for the great world.

"Papa has told me that you have kindly consented to marry him," said the good woman's pupil. "It is very delightful; I think you will suit very well."

"You think I shall suit you?"

"You will suit me beautifully; but what I mean is that you and papa will suit each other. You are both so quiet and so serious. You are not so quiet as he—or even as Madame Merle; but you are more quiet than many others. He should not, for instance, have a wife like my aunt. She is always moving; today especially; you will see when she comes in. They told us at the convent it was wrong to judge our elders, but I suppose there is no harm if we judge them favorably. You will be a delightful companion for papa."

"For you too, I hope," Isabel said.

"I speak first of him on purpose. I have told you already what I myself think of you; I liked you from the first. I admire you so much that I think it will be a great good fortune to have you always before me. You will be my model; I shall try to imitate you—though I am afraid it will be very feeble. I am very glad for papa—he needed something more than me. Without you, I don't see how he could have got it. You will be my stepmother; but we must not use that word. You don't look at all like the word; it is somehow so ugly. They are always said to be cruel; but I think you will never be cruel. I am not afraid."

"My good little Pansy," said Isabel, gently, "I shall be very kind to you."

"Very well then; I have nothing to fear," the child declared, lightly.

Her description of her aunt had not been incorrect; the Countess Gemini was less than ever in a state of repose. She entered the room with a great deal of expression, and kissed Isabel, first on her lips, and then on each cheek, in the short, quick manner of a bird drinking. She made Isabel sit down on the sofa beside her, and looking at our heroine with a variety of turns of the head, delivered herself of a hundred remarks, from which I offer the reader but a brief selection.

"If you expect me to congratulate you, I must beg you to excuse me. I don't suppose you care whether I do or not; I believe you are very proud. But I care myself whether I tell fibs or not; I never tell them unless there is something to be gained. I don't see what there is to be gained with you—especially as you would not believe me. I don't make phrases—I never made a phrase in my life. My fibs are always very crude. I am very glad, for my own sake, that you are going to marry Osmond; but I won't pretend I am glad for yours. You are very remarkable—you know that's what people call you; you are an heiress, and very good-looking and clever, very original; so it's a good thing to have you in the family. Our family is very good, you know; Osmond will have told you that; and my mother was rather distinguished—she was called the American Corinne. But we are rather fallen, I think, and perhaps you will pick us up. I have great confidence in you; there are ever so many things I want to talk to you about. I never congratulate any girl on marrying; I think it's the worst thing she can do. I suppose Pansy oughtn't to hear all this; but that's what she has come to me for—to acquire the tone of society. There is no harm in her knowing that it isn't such a blessing to get married. When first I got an idea that my brother had designs upon you, I thought of writing to you, to recommend you, in the strongest terms, not to listen to him. Then I thought it would be disloyal, and I hate anything of that kind. Besides, as I say, I was enchanted, for myself; and after all, I am very selfish. By the way, you won't respect me, and we shall never be intimate. I should like it, but you won't. Some day, all the same, we shall be better friends than you will believe at first. My husband will come and see you, though, as you probably know, he is on no sort of terms with Osmond. He is very fond of going to see pretty women, but I am not afraid of you. In the first place, I don't care what he does. In the second, you won't care a straw for him; you will take his measure at a glance. Some day I will tell you all about him. Do you think my niece ought to go out of the room? Pansy, go and practice a little in my boudoir."

"Let her stay, please," said Isabel. "I would rather hear nothing that Pansy may not!"

❧ 36 ❧

One afternoon, toward dusk, in the autumn of 1876, a young man of pleasing appearance rang at the door of a small apartment on the third floor of an old Roman house. On its being opened he inquired for Madame Merle, whereupon the servant, a neat, plain woman, with a French face and a lady's maid's manner, ushered him into a diminutive drawing room and requested the favor of his name.

"Mr. Edward Rosier," said the young man, who sat down to wait till his hostess should appear.

The reader will perhaps not have forgotten that Mr. Rosier was an ornament of the American circle in Paris, but it may also be remembered that he sometimes vanished from its horizon. He had spent a portion of several winters at Pau, and as he was a gentleman of tolerably inveterate habits he might have continued for years to pay his annual visit to this charming resort. In the summer of 1876, however, an incident befell him which changed the current, not only of his thoughts, but of his proceedings. He passed a month in the Upper Engadine, and encountered at St. Moritz a charming young girl. For this young lady he conceived a peculiar admiration; she was exactly the household angel he had long been looking for. He was never precipitate; he was nothing if not discreet; so he forbore for the present to declare his passion; but it seemed to him when they parted—the young lady to go down into Italy, and her admirer to proceed to Geneva, where he was under bonds to join some friends—that he should be very unhappy if he were not to see her again. The simplest way to do so was to go in the autumn to Rome, where Miss Osmond was domiciled with her family. Rosier started on his pilgrimage to the Italian capital and reached it on the first of November. It was a pleasant thing to do; but for the young man there was a strain of the heroic in the enterprise. He was nervous about the fever, and November, after all, was rather early in the season. Fortune, however, favors the brave; and Mr. Rosier, who took three grains of quinine every day, had at the end of a month no cause to deplore his temerity. He had made to a certain extent good use of his time; that is, he had perceived that Miss Pansy Osmond had not a flaw in her composition. She was admirably finished—she was in excellent style. He thought of her in amorous meditation a good deal as he might have thought of a Dresden-china shepherdess. Miss Osmond, indeed, in the bloom of her juvenility, had a touch of the rococo, which Rosier, whose taste was predominantly for that manner, could not fail to appreciate. That he esteemed the productions of comparatively frivolous periods would have been apparent from the attention he bestowed upon Madame Merle's drawing room, which, although furnished with specimens of every style, was especially rich in articles of the last two centuries. He had immediately put a glass into one eye and looked round; and then—"By Jove! she has some jolly good things!" he had murmured to himself. The room was small, and densely filled with furniture; it gave an impression of faded silk and little statuettes which might totter if one moved. Rosier got up and wandered about with his careful tread, bending over the tables charged with knickknacks and the cushions embossed with princely arms. When Madame Merle came in she found him standing before the fireplace, with his nose very close to the great lace flounce attached to the damask cover of the mantel. He had lifted it delicately, as if he were smelling it.

"It's old Venetian," she said; "it's rather good."

"It's too good for this; you ought to wear it."

"They tell me you have some better in Paris, in the same situation."

"Ah, but I can't wear mine," said Rosier, smiling.

"I don't see why you shouldn't! I have better lace than that to wear."

Rosier's eyes wandered, lingeringly, round the room again.

"You have some very good things."

"Yes, but I hate them."

"Do you want to get rid of them?" the young man asked quickly.

"No, it's good to have something to hate; one works it off."

"I love my things," said Rosier, as he sat there smiling. "But it's not about them—nor about yours, that I came to talk to you." He paused a moment, and then, with greater softness—"I care more for Miss Osmond than for all the *bibelots* in Europe!"

Madame Merle started a little.

"Did you come to tell me that?"

"I came to ask your advice."

She looked at him with a little frown, stroking her chin.

"A man in love, you know, doesn't ask advice."

"Why not, if he is in a difficult position? That's often the case with a man in love. I have been in love before, and I know. But never so much as this time—really, never so much. I should like particularly to know what you think of my prospects. I'm afraid Mr. Osmond doesn't think me a phoenix."

"Do you wish me to intercede?" Madame Merle asked, with her fine arms folded, and her mouth drawn up to the left.

"If you could say a good word for me, I should be greatly obliged. There will be no use in my troubling Miss Osmond unless I have good reason to believe her father will consent."

"You are very considerate; that's in your favor. But you assume, in rather an off-hand way, that I think you a prize."

"You have been very kind to me," said the young man. "That's why I came."

"I am always kind to people who have good *bibelots*; there is no telling what one may get by it."

And the left-hand corner of Madame Merle's mouth gave expression to the joke.

Edward Rosier stared and blushed; his correct features were suffused with disappointment.

"Ah, I thought you liked me for myself!"

"I like you very much; but, if you please, we won't analyze. Excuse me if I seem patronising; but I think you a perfect little gentleman. I must tell you, however, that I have not the marrying of Pansy Osmond."

"I didn't suppose that. But you have seemed to me intimate with her family, and I thought you might have influence."

Madame Merle was silent a moment.

"Whom do you call her family?"

"Why, her father; and—how do you say it in English?—her *belle-mère.*"

"Mr. Osmond is her father, certainly; but his wife can scarcely be termed a member of her family. Mrs. Osmond has nothing to do with marrying her."

"I am sorry for that," said Rosier, with an amiable sigh. "I think Mrs. Osmond would favor me."

"Very likely—if her husband does not."

Edward Rosier raised his eyebrows.

"Does she take the opposite line from him?"

"In everything. They think very differently."

"Well," said Rosier, "I am sorry for that; but it's none of my business. She is very fond of Pansy."

"Yes, she is very fond of Pansy."

"And Pansy has a great affection for her. She has told me that she loves her as if she were her own mother."

"You must, after all, have had some very intimate talk with the poor child," said Madame Merle. "Have you declared your sentiments?"

"Never!" cried Rosier, lifting his neatly-gloved hand. "Never, until I have assured myself of those of the parents."

"You always wait for that? You have excellent principles; your conduct is most estimable."

"I think you are laughing at me," poor Rosier murmured, dropping back in his chair, and feeling his small moustache. "I didn't expect that of you, Madame Merle."

She shook her head calmly, like a person who saw things clearly.

"You don't do me justice. I think your conduct is in excellent taste and the best you could adopt. Yes, that's what I think."

"I wouldn't agitate her—only to agitate her; I love her too much for that," said Ned Rosier.

"I am glad, after all, that you have told me," Madame Merle went on. "Leave it to me a little; I think I can help you."

"I said you were the person to come to!" cried the young man, with an ingenuous radiance in his face.

"You were very clever," Madame Merle returned, more drily. "When I say I can help you, I mean once assuming that your cause is good. Let us think a little whether it is."

"I'm a dear little fellow," said Rosier, earnestly. "I won't say I have no faults, but I will say I have no vices."

"All that is negative. What is the positive side? What have you got besides your Spanish lace and your Dresden teacups?"

"I have got a comfortable little fortune—about forty thousand francs a year. With the talent that I have for arranging, we can live beautifully on such an income."

"Beautifully, no. Sufficiently, yes. Even that depends on where you live."

"Well, in Paris. I would undertake it in Paris."

Madame Merle's mouth rose to the left.

"It wouldn't be splendid; you would have to make use of the teacups, and they would get broken."

"We don't want to be splendid. If Miss Osmond should have everything pretty, it would be enough. When one is as pretty as she, one can afford to be simple. She ought never to wear anything but muslin," said Rosier, reflectively.

"She would be much obliged to you for that theory."

"It's the correct one, I assure you; and I am sure she would enter into it. She understands all that; that's why I love her."

"She is a very good little girl, and extremely graceful. But her father, to the best of my belief, can give her nothing."

Rosier hesitated a moment.

"I don't in the least desire that he should. But I may remark, all the same, that he lives like a rich man."

"The money is his wife's; she brought him a fortune."

"Mrs. Osmond, then, is very fond of her step-daughter; she may do something."

"For a love-sick swain you have your eyes about you!" Madame Merle exclaimed, with a laugh.

"I esteem a *dot* very much. I can do without it, but I esteem it."

"Mrs. Osmond," Madame Merle went on, "will probably prefer to keep her money for her own children."

"Her own children? Surely she has none."

"She may have yet. She had a poor little boy, who died two years ago, six months after his birth. Others, therefore, may come."

"I hope they will, if it will make her happy. She is a splendid woman."

Madame Merle was silent a moment.

"Ah, about her there is much to be said. Splendid as you like! We have not exactly made out that you are a *parti*. The absence of vices is hardly a source of income."

"Excuse me, I think it may be," said Rosier, with his persuasive smile.

"You'll be a touching couple, living on your innocence!"

"I think you underrate me."

"You are not so innocent as that? Seriously," said Madame Merle, "of course forty thousand francs a year and a nice character are a combination to be considered. I don't say it's to be jumped at; but there might be a worse offer. Mr. Osmond will probably incline to believe he can do better."

"He can do so, perhaps; but what can his daughter do? She can't do better than marry the man she loves. For she does, you know," Rosier added, eagerly.

"She does—I know it."

"Ah," cried the young man, "I said you were the person to come to."

"But I don't know how you know it, if you haven't asked her," Madame Merle went on.

"In such a case there is no need of asking and telling; as you say, we are an innocent couple. How did *you* know it?"

"I who am not innocent? By being very crafty. Leave it to me; I will find out for you."

Rosier got up, and stood smoothing his hat.

"You say that rather coldly. Don't simply find out how it is, but try to make it as it should be."

"I will do my best. I will try to make the most of your advantages."

"Thank you so very much. Meanwhile, I will say a word to Mrs. Osmond."

"*Gardez-vous en bien!*" And Madame Merle rose, rapidly. "Don't set her going, or you'll spoil everything."

Rosier gazed into his hat; he wondered whether his hostess had been after all the right person to come to.

"I don't think I understand you. I am an old friend of Mrs. Osmond, and I think she would like me to succeed."

"Be an old friend as much as you like; the more old friends she has the better, for she doesn't get on very well with some of her new. But don't for the present try to make her take up the cudgels for you. Her husband may have other views, and, as a person who wishes her well, I advise you not to multiply points of difference between them."

Poor Rosier's face assumed an expression of alarm; a suit for the hand of Pansy Osmond was even a more complicated business than his taste for proper transitions had allowed. But the extreme good sense which he concealed under a surface suggesting sprigged porcelain, came to his assistance.

"I don't see that I am bound to consider Mr. Osmond so much!" he exclaimed.

"No, but you should consider her. You say you are an old friend. Would you make her suffer?"

"Not for the world."

"Then be very careful, and let the matter alone until I have taken a few soundings."

"Let the matter alone, dear Madame Merle? Remember that I am in love."

"Oh, you won't burn up. Why did you come to me, if you are not to heed what I say?"

"You are very kind; I will be very good," the young man promised. "But I am afraid Mr. Osmond is rather difficult," he added, in his mild voice, as he went to the door.

Madame Merle gave a light laugh.

"It has been said before. But his wife is not easy either."

"Ah, she's a splendid woman!" Ned Rosier repeated, passing out.

He resolved that his conduct should be worthy of a young man who was already a model of discretion; but he saw nothing in any pledge he had given Madame Merle that made it improper he should keep himself in spirits by an occasional visit to Miss Osmond's home. He reflected constantly on what Madame Merle had said to him, and turned over in his mind the impression of her somewhat peculiar manner. He had gone to her *de confiance*, as they said in Paris; but it was possible that he had been precipitate. He found difficulty in thinking of himself as rash—he had incurred this reproach so rarely; but it certainly was true that he had known Madame Merle only for the last month, and that his thinking her a delightful woman was not, when one came to look into it, a reason for assuming that she would be eager to push Pansy Osmond into his arms—gracefully arranged as these members might be to receive her. Beyond this, Madame Merle had been very gracious to him, and she was a person of consideration among the girl's people, where she had a rather striking appearance (Rosier had more than once wondered how she managed it), of being intimate without being familiar. But possibly he had exaggerated these advantages. There was no particular reason why she should take trouble for him; a charming woman was charming to everyone, and Rosier felt rather like a fool when he thought of his appealing to Madame Merle on the ground that she had distinguished him. Very likely—though she had appeared to say it in joke—she was really only thinking of his *bibelots*. Had it come into her head that he might offer her two or three of the gems of his collection? If she would only help him to marry Miss Osmond, he would present her with his whole museum. He could hardly say so to her outright; it would seem too gross a bribe. But he should like her to believe it.

It was with these thoughts that he went again to Mrs. Osmond's, Mrs. Osmond having an "evening"—she had taken the Thursday of each week—when his presence could be accounted for on general principles of civility. The object of Mr. Rosier's well-regulated affection dwelt in a high house in the very heart of Rome; a dark and massive structure, overlooking a sunny *piazzetta* in the neighborhood of the Farnese Palace. In a palace, too, little Pansy lived—a palace in Roman parlance, but a dungeon to poor Rosier's apprehensive mind. It seemed to him of evil omen that the young lady he wished to marry, and whose fastidious father he doubted of his ability to conciliate, should be immured in a kind of domestic fortress, which bore a stern old Roman name, which smelt of historic deeds, of crime and craft and violence, which was mentioned in "Murray" and visited by tourists who looked disappointed and depressed, and which had frescoes by Caravaggio in the *piano nobile* and a row of mutilated statues and dusty urns in the wide, nobly-arched loggia overlooking the damp court where a fountain gushed out of a mossy niche. In a less preoccupied frame of mind he could have done justice to the Palazzo Roccanera; he could have entered into the sentiment of Mrs. Osmond, who had once told him that on settling themselves in Rome she and her husband chose this habitation for the love of local color. It had local color enough, and though he knew less about architecture than about Limoges enamel, he could see that the proportions of the windows, and even the details of the cornice, had quite the grand air. But Rosier was haunted by the conviction that at picturesque periods young girls had been shut up there to keep them from their true loves, and, under the threat of being thrown into convents, had been forced into unholy marriages. There was one point, however, to which he always did justice when once he found himself in Mrs. Osmond's warm, rich-looking reception rooms, which were on the second floor. He acknowledged that these people were very strong in *bibelots*. It was a taste of Osmond's own—not at all of hers; this she had told him the first time he came to the house, when, after asking himself for a quarter of an hour whether they had better things than he, he was obliged to admit that they had, very much, and vanquished his envy, as a gentleman should, to the point of expressing to his hostess his pure admiration of her treasures. He learned from Mrs. Osmond that her husband had made a large collection before their marriage, and that, though he had obtained a number of fine pieces within the last three years, he had got his best things at a time when he had not the advantage of her advice. Rosier interpreted this information according to principles of his own. For "advice" read "money," he said to himself; and the fact that Gilbert Osmond had landed his great prizes during his impecunious season, confirmed his most cherished doctrine—the doctrine that a collector may freely be poor if he be only patient. In general, when Rosier presented himself on a Thursday evening, his first glance was bestowed upon the walls of the room; there were three or four objects that his eyes really yearned for. But after his talk with Madame Merle he felt the extreme seriousness of his position; and now, when he came in, he looked about for the daughter of the house with such eagerness as might be permitted to a gentleman who always crossed a threshold with an optimistic smile.

❧ 37 ❧

Pansy was not in the first of the rooms, a large apartment with a concave ceiling and walls covered with old red damask; it was here that Mrs. Osmond usually sat—though she was not in her usually customary place tonight—and that a circle of more especial intimates gathered about the fire. The room was warm, with a sort of subdued brightness; it contained the larger things, and—almost always—an odor of flowers. Pansy on this occasion was presumably in the chamber beyond, the resort of younger visitors, where tea was served. Osmond stood before the chimney, leaning back, with his hands behind him; he had one foot up and was warming the sole. Half-a-dozen people, scattered near him, were talking together; but he was not in the conversation; his eyes were fixed, abstractedly. Rosier, coming in unannounced, failed to attract his attention; but the young man, who was very punctilious, though he was even exceptionally conscious that it was the wife, not the husband, he had come to see, went up to shake hands with him. Osmond put out his left hand, without changing his attitude.

"How d'ye do? My wife's somewhere about."

"Never fear; I shall find her," said Rosier, cheerfully.

Osmond stood looking at him; he had never before felt the keenness of this gentleman's eyes. "Madame Merle has told him, and he doesn't like it," Rosier said to himself. He had hoped Madame Merle would be there; but she was not within sight; perhaps she was in one of the other rooms, or would come later. He had never especially delighted in Gilbert Osmond; he had a fancy that he gave himself airs. But Rosier was not quickly resentful, and where politeness was concerned he had an inveterate wish to be in the right. He looked round him, smiling, and then, in a moment, he said—

"I saw a jolly good piece of Capo di Monte today."

Osmond answered nothing at first; but presently, while he warmed his boot-sole, "I don't care a fig for Capo di Monte!" he returned.

"I hope you are not losing your interest?"

"In old pots and plates? Yes, I am losing my interest."

Rosier for a moment forgot the delicacy of his position.

"You are not thinking of parting with a—a piece or two?"

"No, I am not thinking of parting with anything at all, Mr. Rosier," said Osmond, with his eyes still on the eyes of his visitor.

"Ah, you want to keep, but not to add," Rosier remarked, brightly.

"Exactly. I have nothing that I wish to match."

Poor Rosier was aware that he had blushed, and he was distressed at his want of assurance. "Ah, well, I have!" was all that he could murmur; and he knew that his murmur was partly lost as he turned away. He took his course to the adjoining room, and met Mrs. Osmond coming out of the deep doorway. She was dressed in black velvet; she looked brilliant and noble. We know what Mr. Rosier thought of her, and the terms in which, to Madame Merle, he had expressed his admiration. Like his appreciation of her dear little step-daughter, it was based partly on his fine sense of the plastic; but also on a relish for a more impalpable sort of merit—that merit of a bright spirit, which Rosier's devotion to brittle wares had not made him cease to regard as a quality. Mrs. Osmond, at present, might well have gratified such tastes. The years had touched her only to enrich her; the flower of her youth had not faded, it only hung more quietly on its stem. She had lost something of that quick eagerness to which her husband had privately taken exception—she had more the air of being able to wait. Now, at all events, framed in the gilded doorway, she struck our young man as the picture of a gracious lady.

"You see I am very regular," he said. "But who should be if I am not?"

"Yes, I have known you longer than anyone here. But we must not indulge in tender reminiscences. I want to introduce you to a young lady."

"Ah, please, what young lady?" Rosier was immensely obliging; but this was not what he had come for.

"She sits there by the fire in pink, and has no one to speak to."

Rosier hesitated a moment.

"Can't Mr. Osmond speak to her? He is within six feet of her."

Mrs. Osmond also hesitated.

"She is not very lively, and he doesn't like dull people."

"But she is good enough for me? Ah now, that is hard."

"I only mean that you have ideas for two. And then you are so obliging."

"So is your husband."

"No, he is not—to me." And Mrs. Osmond smiled vaguely.

"That's a sign he should be doubly so to other women."

"So I tell him," said Mrs. Osmond, still smiling.

"You see I want some tea," Rosier went on, looking wistfully beyond.

"That's perfect. Go and give some to my young lady."

"Very good; but after that I will abandon her to her fate. The simple truth is that I am dying to have a little talk with Miss Osmond."

"Ah," said Isabel, turning away, "I can't help you there!"

Five minutes later, while he handed a teacup to the young lady in pink, whom he had conducted into the other room, he wondered whether, in making to Mrs. Osmond the profession I have just quoted, he had broken the spirit of his promise to Madame Merle. Such a question was capable of occupying this young man's mind for a considerable time. At last, however, he became—comparatively speaking—reckless, and cared little what promises he might break. The fate to which he had threatened to abandon the young lady in pink proved to be none so terrible; for Pansy Osmond, who had given him the tea for his companion—Pansy was as fond as ever of making tea—presently came and talked to her. Into this mild colloquy Edward Rosier entered little; he sat by moodily, watching his small sweetheart. If we look at her now through his eyes, we shall at first not see much to remind us of the obedient little girl who, at Florence, three years before, was sent to walk short distances in the Cascine while her father and Miss Archer talked together of matters sacred to elder people. But after a moment we shall perceive that if at nineteen Pansy has become a young lady, she does not really fill out the part; that if she has grown very pretty, she lacks in a deplorable degree the quality known and esteemed in the appearance of females as style; and that if she is dressed with great freshness, she wears her smart attire with an undisguised appearance of saving it—very much as if it were lent her for the occasion. Edward Rosier, it would seem, would have been just the man to note these defects; and in point of fact there was not a quality of this young lady, of any sort, that he had not noted. Only he called her qualities by names of his own—some of which indeed were happy enough. "No, she is unique—she is absolutely unique," he used to say to himself; and you may be sure that not for an instant would he have admitted to you that she was wanting in style. Style? Why, she had the style of a little princess; if you couldn't see it you had no eye. It was not modern, it was not conscious, it would produce no impression in Broadway; the small, serious damsel, in her stiff little dress, only looked like an Infanta of Velasquez. This was enough for Edward Rosier, who thought her delightfully old-fashioned. Her anxious eyes, her charming lips, her slip of a figure, were as touching as a childish prayer. He had now an acute desire to know just to what point she liked him—a desire which made him fidget as he sat in his chair. It made him feel hot, so that he had to pat his forehead with his handkerchief; he had never been so uncomfortable. She was such a perfect *jeune fille;* and one couldn't make of a *jeune fille* the inquiry necessary for throwing light on such a point. A *jeune fille* was what Rosier had always dreamed of—a *jeune fille* who should yet not be French, for he had felt that this nationality would complicate the question. He was sure that Pansy had never looked at a newspaper, and that, in the way of novels, if she had read Sir Walter Scott it was the very most. An American *jeune fille;* what would be better than that? She would be frank and gay, and yet would not have walked alone, nor have received letters from men, nor have been taken to the theater to see the comedy of manners. Rosier could not deny that, as the matter stood, it would be a breach of hospitality to appeal directly to this unsophisticated creature; but he was now in imminent danger of asking himself whether hospitality were the most sacred thing in the world. Was not the sentiment that he entertained for Miss Osmond of infinitely greater importance? Of greater importance to him—yes; but not probably to the master of the house. There was one comfort; even if this gentleman had been placed on his guard by Madame Merle, he would not have extended the warning to Pansy; it would not have been part of his policy to let her know that a prepossessing young man was in love with her. But he *was* in love with her, the prepossessing young man; and all these restrictions of circumstance had ended by irritating him. What had Gilbert Osmond meant by giving him two fingers of his left hand? If Osmond was rude, surely he himself might be bold. He felt extremely bold after the dull girl in pink had responded to the call of her mother, who came in to say, with a significant simper at Rosier, that she must carry her off to other triumphs. The mother and daughter departed together, and now it depended only upon him that he should be virtually alone with Pansy. He had never been alone with her before; he had never been alone with a *jeune fille*. It was a great moment; poor Rosier began to pat his forehead again. There was another room, beyond the one in which they stood—a small room which had been thrown open and lighted, but, the company not being numerous, had remained empty all the evening. It was empty yet; it was upholstered in pale yellow; there were several lamps; through the open door it looked very pretty. Rosier stood a moment, gazing through this aperture; he was afraid that Pansy would run away, and felt almost capable of stretching out a hand to detain her. But she lingered where the young lady in pink had left them, making no motion to join a knot of visitors on the other side of the room. For a moment it occurred to him that she was frightened—too frightened perhaps to move; but a glance assured him that she was not, and then he reflected that she was too innocent, indeed, for that. After a moment's supreme hesitation he asked her whether he might go and look at the yellow room, which seemed so attractive yet so virginal. He had been there already with Osmond, to inspect the furniture, which was of the First French Empire, and especially to admire the clock (which he did not really admire), an immense classic structure of that period. He therefore felt that he had now begun to maneuver.

"Certainly, you may go," said Pansy; "and if you like, I will show you." She was not in the least frightened.

"That's just what I hoped you would say; you are so very kind," Rosier murmured.

They went in together; Rosier really thought the room very ugly, and it seemed cold. The same idea appeared to have struck Pansy.

"It's not for winter evenings; it's more for summer," she said. "It's papa's taste; he has so much."

He had a good deal, Rosier thought; but some of it was bad. He looked about him; he hardly knew what to say in such a situation. "Doesn't Mrs. Osmond care how her rooms are done? Has she no taste?" he asked.

"Oh yes, a great deal; but it's more for literature," said Pansy—"and for conversation. But papa cares also for those things: I think he knows everything."

Rosier was silent a moment. "There is one thing I am sure he knows!" he broke out presently. "He knows that when I come here it is, with all respect to him, with all respect to Mrs. Osmond, who is so charming—it is really," said the young man, "to see you!"

"To see me?" asked Pansy, raising her vaguely troubled eyes.

"To see you; that's what I come for," Rosier repeated, feeling the intoxication of a rupture with authority. Pansy stood looking at him, simply, intently, openly; a blush was not needed to make her face more modest.

"I thought it was for that," she said.

"And it was not disagreeable to you?"

"I couldn't tell; I didn't know. You never told me," said Pansy.

"I was afraid of offending you."

"You don't offend me," the young girl murmured, smiling as if an angel had kissed her.

"You like me then, Pansy?" Rosier asked, very gently, feeling very happy.

"Yes—I like you."

They had walked to the chimney-piece, where the big cold Empire clock was perched; they were well within the room, and beyond observation from without. The tone in which she had said these four words seemed to him the very breath of nature, and his only answer could be to take her hand and hold it a moment. Then he raised it to his lips. She submitted, still with her pure, trusting smile, in which there was something ineffably passive. She liked him—she had liked him all the while; now anything might happen! She was ready—she had been ready always, waiting for him to speak. If he had not spoken she would have waited forever; but when the word came she dropped like the peach from the shaken tree. Rosier felt that if he should draw her toward him and hold her to his heart, she would submit without a murmur, she would rest there without a question. It was true that this would be a rash experiment in a yellow Empire *salottino*. She had known it was for her he came; and yet like what a perfect little lady she had carried it off!

"You are very dear to me," he murmured, trying to believe that there was after all such a thing as hospitality.

She looked a moment at her hand, where he had kissed it. "Did you say that papa knows?"

"You told me just now he knows everything."

"I think you must make sure," said Pansy.

"Ah, my dear, when once I am sure of you!" Rosier murmured in her ear, while she turned back to the other rooms with a little air of consistency which seemed to imply that their appeal should be immediate.

The other rooms meanwhile had become conscious of the arrival of Madame Merle, who, wherever she went, produced an impression when she entered. How she did it the most attentive spectator could not have told you; for she neither spoke loud, nor laughed profusely, nor moved rapidly, nor dressed with splendor, nor appealed in any appreciable manner to the audience. Large, fair, smiling, serene, there was something in her very tranquility that diffused itself, and when people looked round it was because of a sudden quiet. On this occasion she had done the quietest thing she could do; after embracing Mrs. Osmond, which was more striking, she had sat down on a small sofa to commune with the master of the house. There was a brief exchange of commonplaces between these two—they always paid, in public, a certain formal tribute to the commonplace—and then Madame Merle, whose eyes had been wandering, asked if little Mr. Rosier had come this evening.

"He came nearly an hour ago—but he has disappeared," Osmond said.

"And where is Pansy?"

"In the other room. There are several people there."

"He is probably among them," said Madame Merle.

"Do you wish to see him?" Osmond asked, in a provokingly pointless tone.

Madame Merle looked at him a moment; she knew his tones, to the eighth of a note. "Yes, I should like to say to him that I have told you what he wants, and that it interests you but feebly."

"Don't tell him that, he will try to interest me more—which is exactly what I don't want. Tell him I hate his proposal."

"But you don't hate it."

"It doesn't signify: I don't love it. I let him see that, myself, this evening; I was rude to him on purpose. That sort of thing is a great bore. There is no hurry."

"I will tell him that you will take time and think it over."

"No, don't do that. He will hang on."

"If I discourage him he will do the same."

"Yes, but in the one case he will try and talk and explain; which would be exceedingly tiresome. In the other he will probably hold his tongue and go in for some deeper game. That will leave me quiet. I hate talking with a donkey."

"Is that what you call poor Mr. Rosier?"

"Oh, he's enervating, with his eternal majolica."

Madame Merle dropped her eyes, with a faint smile. "He's a gentleman, he has a charming temper; and, after all, an income of forty thousand francs—"

"It's misery—genteel misery," Osmond broke in. "It's not what I have dreamed of for Pansy."

"Very good, then. He has promised me not to speak to her."

"Do you believe him?" Osmond asked, absent-mindedly.

"Perfectly. Pansy has thought a great deal about him; but I don't suppose you think that matters."

"I don't think it matters at all; but neither do I believe she has thought about him."

"That opinion is more convenient," said Madame Merle, quietly.

"Has she told you that she is in love with him?"

"For what do you take her? And for what do you take me?" Madame Merle added in a moment.

Osmond had raised his foot and was resting his slim ankle on the other knee; he clasped his ankle in his hand, familiarly, and gazed a while before him. "This kind of thing doesn't find me unprepared. It's what I educated her for. It was all for this—that when such a case should come up she should do what I prefer."

"I am not afraid that she will not do it."

"Well then, where is the hitch?"

"I don't see any. But all the same, I recommend you not to get rid of Mr. Rosier. Keep him on hand, he may be useful."

"I can't keep him. Do it yourself."

"Very good; I will put him into a corner and allow him so much a day." Madame Merle had, for the most part, while they talked, been glancing about her; it was her habit, in this situation, just as it was her habit to interpose a good many blank-looking pauses. A long pause followed the last words I have quoted; and before it was broken again, she saw Pansy come out of the adjoining room, followed by Edward Rosier. Pansy advanced a few steps and then stopped and stood looking at Madame Merle and at her father.

"He has spoken to her," Madame Merle said, simply, to Osmond.

Her companion never turned his head. "So much for your belief in his promises. He ought to be horsewhipped."

"He intends to confess, poor little man!"

Osmond got up; he had now taken a sharp look at his daughter. "It doesn't matter," he murmured, turning away.

Pansy after a moment came up to Madame Merle with her little manner of unfamiliar politeness. This lady's reception of her was not more intimate; she simply, as she rose from the sofa, gave her a friendly smile.

"You are very late," said the young girl, gently.

"My dear child, I am never later than I intend to be."

Madame Merle had not got up to be gracious to Pansy; she moved toward Edward Rosier. He came to meet her, and, very quickly, as if to get it off his mind—"I have spoken to her!" he whispered.

"I know it, Mr. Rosier."

"Did she tell you?"

"Yes, she told me. Behave properly for the rest of the evening, and come and see me tomorrow at a quarter past five."

She was severe, and in the manner in which she turned her back to him there was a degree of contempt which caused him to mutter a decent imprecation.

He had no intention of speaking to Osmond; it was neither the time nor the place. But he instinctively wandered toward Isabel, who sat talking with an old lady. He sat down on the other side of her; the old lady was an Italian, and Rosier took for granted that she understood no English.

"You said just now you wouldn't help me," he began, to Mrs. Osmond. "Perhaps you will feel differently when you know—when you know—"

He hesitated a little.

"When I know what?" Isabel asked, gently.

"That she is all right."

"What do you mean by that?"

"Well, that we have come to an understanding."

"She is all wrong," said Isabel. "It won't do."

Poor Rosier gazed at her half-pleadingly, half-angrily; a sudden flush testified to his sense of injury.

"I have never been treated so," he said. "What is there against me, after all? That is not the way I am usually considered. I could have married twenty times."

"It's a pity you didn't. I don't mean twenty times, but once, comfortably," Isabel added, smiling kindly. "You are not rich enough for Pansy."

"She doesn't care a straw for one's money."

"No, but her father does."

"Ah yes, he has proved that!" cried the young man.

Isabel got up, turning away from him, leaving her old lady, without saying anything; and he occupied himself for the next ten minutes in pretending to look at Gilbert Osmond's collection of miniatures, which were neatly arranged on a series of small velvet screens. But he looked without seeing; his cheek burned; he was too full of his sense of injury. It was certain that he had never been treated that way before; he was not used to being thought not good enough. He knew how good he was, and if such a fallacy had not been so pernicious, he could have laughed at it. He looked about again for Pansy, but she had disappeared, and his main desire was now to get out of the house. Before doing so he spoke to Isabel again; it was not agreeable to him to reflect that he had just said a rude thing to her—the only point that would now justify a low view of him.

"I spoke of Mr. Osmond as I shouldn't have done, a while ago," he said. "But you must remember my situation."

"I don't remember what you said," she answered, coldly.

"Ah, you are offended, and now you will never help me."

She was silent an instant, and then, with a change of tone—

"It's not that I won't; I simply can't!" Her manner was almost passionate.

"If you could—just a little," said Rosier, "I would never again speak of your husband save as an angel."

"The inducement is great," said Isabel gravely—inscrutably, as he afterwards, to himself, called it; and she gave him, straight in the eyes, a look which was also inscrutable. It made him remember, somehow, that he had known her as a child; and yet it was keener than he liked, and he took himself off.

❧ 38 ❧

He went to see Madame Merle on the morrow, and to his surprise she let him off rather easily. But she made him promise that he would stop there until something should have been decided. Mr. Osmond had had higher expectations; it was very true that as he had no intention of giving his daughter a portion, such expectations were open to criticism, or even, if one would, to ridicule. But she would advise Mr. Rosier not to take that tone; if he would possess his soul in patience he might arrive at his felicity. Mr. Osmond was not favorable to his suit, but it would not be a miracle if he should gradually come round. Pansy would never defy her father, he might depend upon that, so nothing was to be gained by precipitation. Mr. Osmond needed to accustom his mind to an offer of a sort that he had not hitherto entertained, and this result must come of itself—it was useless to try to force it. Rosier remarked that his own situation would be in the meanwhile the most uncomfortable in the world, and Madame Merle assured him that she felt for him. But, as she justly declared, one couldn't have everything one wanted; she had learned that lesson for herself. There would be no use in his writing to Gilbert Osmond, who had charged her to tell him as much. He wished the matter dropped for a few weeks, and would himself write when he should have anything to communicate which it would please Mr. Rosier to hear. .

"He doesn't like your having spoken to Pansy. Ah, he doesn't like it at all," said Madame Merle.

"I am perfectly willing to give him a chance to tell me so!"

"If you do that he will tell you more than you care to hear. Go to the house, for the next month, as little as possible, and leave the rest to me."

"As little as possible? Who is to measure that?"

"Let me measure it. Go on Thursday evenings with the rest of the world; but don't go at all at odd times, and don't fret about Pansy. I will see that she understands everything. She's a calm little nature; she will take it quietly."

Edward Rosier fretted about Pansy a good deal, but he did as he was advised, and waited for another Thursday evening before returning to the Palazzo Roccanera. There had been a party at dinner, so that although he went early the company was already tolerably numerous. Osmond, as usual, was in the first room, near the fire, staring straight at the door, so that, not to be distinctly uncivil, Rosier had to go and speak to him.

"I am glad that you can take a hint," Pansy's father said, slightly closing his keen, conscious eye.

"I take no hints. But I took a message, as I supposed it to be."

"You took it? Where did you take it?"

It seemed to poor Rosier that he was being insulted, and he waited a moment, asking himself how much a true lover ought to submit to.

"Madame Merle gave me, as I understood it, a message from you—to the effect that you declined to give me the opportunity I desire—the opportunity to explain my wishes to you."

Rosier flattered himself that he spoke rather sternly.

"I don't see what Madame Merle has to do with it. Why did you apply to Madame Merle?"

"I asked her for an opinion—for nothing more. I did so because she had seemed to me to know you very well."

"She doesn't know me so well as she thinks," said Osmond.

"I am sorry for that, because she has given me some little ground for hope."

Osmond stared into the fire for a moment.

"I set a great price on my daughter."

"You can't set a higher one than I do. Don't I prove it by wishing to marry her?"

"I wish to marry her very well," Osmond went on, with a dry impertinence which, in another mood, poor Rosier would have admired.

"Of course I pretend that she would marry well in marrying me. She couldn't marry a man who loves her more; or whom, I may venture to add, she loves more."

"I am not bound to accept your theories as to whom my daughter loves," Osmond said, looking up with a quick, cold smile.

"I am not theorizing. Your daughter has spoken."

"Not to me," Osmond continued, bending forward a little and dropping his eyes to his boot-toes.

"I have her promise, sir!" cried Rosier, with the sharpness of exasperation.

As their voices had been pitched very low before, such a note attracted some attention from the company. Osmond waited till this little movement had subsided, then he said very quickly—

"I think she has no recollection of having given it."

They had been standing with their faces to the fire, and after he had uttered these last words Osmond turned round again to the room. Before Rosier had time to rejoin he perceived that a gentleman—a stranger—had just come in, unannounced, according to the Roman custom, and was about to present himself to the master of the house. The latter smiled blandly, but somewhat blankly; the visitor was a handsome man, with a large, fair beard—evidently an Englishman.

"You apparently don't recognize me," he said, with a smile that expressed more than Osmond's.

"Ah yes, now I do; I expected so little to see you."

Rosier departed, and went in direct pursuit of Pansy. He sought her, as usual, in the neighboring room, but he again encountered Mrs. Osmond in his path. He gave this gracious lady no greeting—he was too righteously indignant; but said to her crudely—

"Your husband is awfully cold-blooded."

She gave the same mystical smile that he had noticed before.

"You can't expect everyone to be as hot as yourself."

"I don't pretend to be cold, but I am cool. What has he been doing to his daughter?"

"I have no idea."

"Don't you take any interest?" Rosier demanded, feeling that she too was irritating.

For a moment she answered nothing. Then—

"No!" she said abruptly, and with a quickened light in her eye which directly contradicted the word.

"Excuse me if I don't believe that. Where is Miss Osmond?"

"In the corner, making tea. Please leave her there."

Rosier instantly discovered the young girl, who had been hidden by intervening groups. He watched her, but her own attention was entirely given to her occupation.

"What on earth has he done to her?" he asked again imploringly. "He declares to me that she has given me up."

"She has not given you up," Isabel said, in a low tone, without looking at him.

"Ah, thank you for that! Now I will leave her alone as long as you think proper!"

He had hardly spoken when he saw her change color, and became aware that Osmond was coming toward her, accompanied by the gentleman who had just entered. He thought the latter, in spite of the advantage of good looks and evident social experience, was a little embarrassed.

"Isabel," said Osmond, "I bring you an old friend."

Mrs. Osmond's face, though it wore a smile, was, like her old friend's, not perfectly confident. "I am very happy to see Lord Warburton," she said. Rosier turned away, and now that his talk with her had been interrupted, felt absolved from the little pledge he had just taken. He had a quick impression that Mrs. Osmond would not notice what he did.

To do him justice, Isabel for some time quite ceased to observe him. She had been startled; she hardly knew whether she were glad or not. Lord Warburton, however, now that he was face to face with her, was plainly very well pleased; his frank gray eye expressed a deep, if still somewhat shy, satisfaction. He was larger, stouter than of yore, and he looked older; he stood there very solidly and sensibly.

"I suppose you didn't expect to see me," he said; "I have only just arrived. Literally, I only got here this evening. You see I have lost no time in coming to pay you my respects; I knew you were at home on Thursdays."

"You see the fame of your Thursdays has spread to England," Osmond remarked, smiling, to his wife.

"It is very kind of Lord Warburton to come so soon; we are greatly flattered," Isabel said.

"Ah well, it's better than stopping in one of those horrible inns," Osmond went on.

"The hotel seems very good; I think it is the same one where I saw you four years ago. You know it was here in Rome that we first met; it is a long time ago. Do you remember where I bade you goodbye? It was in the Capitol, in the first room."

"I remember that myself," said Osmond; "I was there at the time."

"Yes, I remember that you were there. I was very sorry to leave Rome—so sorry that, somehow or other, it became a melancholy sort of memory, and I have never cared to come back till today. But I knew you were living here, and I assure you I have often thought of you. It must be a charming place to live in," said Lord Warburton, brightly, looking about him.

"We should have been glad to see you at any time," Osmond remarked with propriety.

"Thank you very much. I haven't been out of England since then. Till a month ago, I really supposed my travels were over."

"I have heard of you from time to time," said Isabel, who had now completely recovered her self-possession.

"I hope you have heard no harm. My life has been a blank."

"Like the good reigns in history," Osmond suggested. He appeared to think his duties as a host had now terminated, he had performed them very conscientiously. Nothing could have been more adequate, more nicely measured, than his courtesy to his wife's old friend. It was punctilious, it was explicit, it was everything but natural—a deficiency which Lord Warburton, who, himself, had on the whole a good deal of nature, may be supposed to have perceived. "I will leave you and Mrs. Osmond together," he added. "You have reminiscences into which I don't enter."

"I am afraid you lose a good deal!" said Lord Warburton, in a tone which perhaps betrayed over-much his appreciation of Osmond's generosity. He stood a moment, looking at Isabel with an eye that gradually became more serious. "I am really very glad to see you."

"It is very pleasant. You are very kind."

"Do you know that you are changed—a little?"

Isabel hesitated a moment.

"Yes—a good deal."

"I don't mean for the worse, of course; and yet how can I say for the better?"

"I think I shall have no scruple in saying that to you," said Isabel, smiling.

"Ah well, for me—it's a long time. It would be a pity that there shouldn't be something to show for it."

They sat down, and Isabel asked him about his sisters, with other inquiries of a somewhat perfunctory kind. He answered her questions as if they interested him, and in a few moments she saw—or believed she saw—that he would prove a more comfortable companion than of yore. Time had breathed upon his heart, and without chilling this organ, had freely ventilated it. Isabel felt her usual esteem for Time rise at a bound. Lord Warburton's manner was certainly that of a contented man who would rather like one to know it.

"There is something I must tell you without more delay," he said. "I have brought Ralph Touchett with me."

"Brought him with you?" Isabel's surprise was great.

"He is at the hotel; he was too tired to come out, and has gone to bed."

"I will go and see him," said Isabel, quickly.

"That is exactly what I hoped you would do. I had an idea that you hadn't seen much of him since your marriage—that in fact your relations were a—a little more formal. That's why I hesitated—like an awkward Englishman."

"I am as fond of Ralph as ever," Isabel answered. "But why has he come to Rome?" The declaration was very gentle; the question a little sharp.

"Because he is very far gone, Mrs. Osmond."

"Rome, then, is no place for him. I heard from him that he had determined to give up his custom of wintering abroad, and remain in England, indoors, in what he called an artificial climate."

"Poor fellow, he doesn't succeed with the artificial! I went to see him three weeks ago, at Gardencourt, and found him extremely ill. He has been getting worse every year, and now he has no strength left. He smokes no more cigarettes! He had got up an artificial climate indeed; the house was as hot as Calcutta. Nevertheless, he had suddenly taken it into his head to start for Sicily. I didn't believe in it—neither did the doctors, nor any of his friends. His mother, as I suppose you know, is in America, so there was no one to prevent him. He stuck to his idea that it would be the saving of him to spend the winter at Catania. He said he could take servants and furniture, and make himself comfortable; but in point of fact he hasn't brought anything. I wanted him at least to go by sea, to save fatigue; but he said he hated the sea, and wished to stop at Rome. After that, though I thought it all rubbish, I made up my mind to come with him. I am acting as—what do you call it in America?—as a kind of moderator. Poor Touchett's very moderate now. We left England a fortnight ago, and he has been very bad on the way. He can't keep warm, and the further south we come the more he feels the cold. He has got a rather good man, but I'm afraid he's beyond human help. If you don't mind my saying so, I think it was a most extraordinary time for Mrs. Touchett to choose for going to America."

Isabel had listened eagerly; her face was full of pain and wonder.

"My aunt does that at fixed periods, and she lets nothing turn her aside. When the date comes round she starts; I think she would have started if Ralph had been dying."

"I sometimes think he is dying," Lord Warburton said.

Isabel started up.

"I will go to him now!"

He checked her; he was a little disconcerted at the quick effect of his words.

"I don't mean that I thought so tonight. On the contrary, today, in the train, he seemed particularly well; the idea of our reaching Rome—he is very fond of Rome, you know—gave him strength. An hour ago, when I bade him goodnight, he told me that he was very tired, but very happy. Go to him in the morning; that's all I mean. I didn't tell him I was coming here; I didn't think of it till after we separated. Then I remembered that he had told me that you had an evening, and that it was this very Thursday. It occurred to me to come in and tell you that he was here, and let you know that you had perhaps better not wait for him to call. I think he said he had not written to you." There was no need of Isabel's declaring that she would act upon Lord Warburton's information; she looked, as she sat there, like a winged creature held back. "Let alone that I wanted to see you for myself," her visitor added, gallantly.

"I don't understand Ralph's plan; it seems to me very wild," she said. "I was glad to think of him between those thick walls at Gardencourt."

"He was completely alone there; the thick walls were his only company."

"You went to see him; you have been extremely kind."

"Oh dear, I had nothing to do," said Lord Warburton.

"We hear, on the contrary, that you are doing great things. Everyone speaks of you as a great statesman, and I am perpetually seeing your name in the *Times,* which, by the way, doesn't appear to hold it in reverence. You are apparently as bold a radical as ever."

"I don't feel nearly so bold; you know the world has come round to me. Touchett and I have kept up a sort of Parliamentary debate, all the way from London. I tell him he is the last of the Tories, and he calls me the head of the Communists. So you see there is life in him yet."

Isabel had many questions to ask about Ralph, but she abstained from asking them all. She would see for herself on the morrow. She perceived that after a little Lord Warburton would tire of that subject—that he had a consciousness of other possible topics. She was more and more able to say to herself that he had recovered, and, what is more to the point, she was able to say it without bitterness. He had been for her, of old, such an image of urgency, of insistence, of something to be resisted and reasoned with, that his reappearance at first menaced her with a new trouble. But she was now reassured; she could see that he only wished to live with her on good terms, that she was to understand that he had forgiven her and was incapable of the bad taste of making pointed allusions. This was not a form of revenge, of course; she had no suspicion that he wished to punish her by an exhibition of disillusionment; she did him the justice to believe that it had simply occurred to him that she would now take a good-natured interest in knowing that he was resigned. It was the resignation of a healthy, manly nature, in which sentimental wounds could never fester. British politics had cured him; she had known they would. She gave an envious thought to the happier lot of men, who are always free to plunge into the healing waters of action. Lord Warburton of course spoke of the past, but he spoke of it without implication; he even went so far as to allude to their former meeting in Rome as a very jolly time. And he told her that he had been immensely interested in hearing of her marriage—that it was a great pleasure to him to make Mr. Osmond's acquaintance—since he could hardly be said to have made it on the other occasion. He had not written to her when she married, but he did not apologize to her for that. The only thing he implied was that they were old friends, intimate friends. It was very much as an intimate friend that he said to her, suddenly, after a short pause which he had occupied in smiling, as he looked about him, like a man to whom everything suggested a cheerful interpretation—

"Well now, I suppose you are very happy, and all that sort of thing?"

Isabel answered with a quick laugh; the tone of his remark struck her almost as the accent of comedy.

"Do you suppose if I were not I would tell you?"

"Well, I don't know. I don't see why not."

"I do, then. Fortunately, however, I am very happy."

"You have got a very good house."

"Yes, it's very pleasant. But that's not my merit—it's my husband's."

"You mean that he has arranged it?"

"Yes, it was nothing when we came."

"He must be very clever."

"He has a genius for upholstery," said Isabel.

"There is a great rage for that sort of thing now. But you must have a taste of your own."

"I enjoy things when they are done; but I have no ideas. I can never propose anything."

"Do you mean that you accept what others propose?"

O

"Very willingly, for the most part."

"That's a good thing to know. I shall propose you something."

"It will be very kind. I must say, however, that I have in a few small ways a certain initiative. I should like, for instance, to introduce you to some of these people."

"Oh, please don't; I like sitting here. Unless it be to that young lady in the blue dress. She has a charming face."

"The one talking to the rosy young man? That's my husband's daughter."

"Lucky man, your husband. What a dear little maid!"

"You must make her acquaintance."

"In a moment, with pleasure. I like looking at her from here." He ceased to look at her, however, very soon; his eyes constantly reverted to Mrs. Osmond. "Do you know I was wrong just now in saying that you had changed?" he presently went on. "You seem to me, after all, very much the same."

"And yet I find it's a great change to be married," said Isabel, with gaiety.

"It affects most people more than it has affected you. You see I haven't gone in for that."

"It rather surprises me."

"You ought to understand it, Mrs. Osmond. But I want to marry," he added, more simply.

"It ought to be very easy," Isabel said, rising, and then blushing a little at the thought that she was hardly the person to say this. It was perhaps because Lord Warburton noticed her blush that he generously forbore to call her attention to the incongruity.

Edward Rosier meanwhile had seated himself on an ottoman beside Pansy's tea table. He pretended at first to talk to her about trifles, and she asked him who was the new gentleman conversing with her stepmother.

"He's an English lord," said Rosier. "I don't know more."

"I wonder if he will have some tea. The English are so fond of tea."

"Never mind that; I have something particular to say to you."

"Don't speak so loud, or everyone will hear us," said Pansy.

"They won't hear us if you continue to look that way: as if your only thought in life was the wish that the kettle would boil."

"It has just been filled; the servants never know!" the young girl exclaimed, with a little sigh.

"Do you know what your father said to me just now? That you didn't mean what you said a week ago."

"I don't mean everything I say. How can a young girl do that? But I mean what I say to you."

"He told me that you had forgotten me."

"Ah no, I don't forget," said Pansy, showing her pretty teeth in a fixed smile.

"Then everything is just the same?"

"Ah no, it's not just the same. Papa has been very severe."

"What has he done to you?"

"He asked me what *you* had done to me, and I told him everything. Then he forbade me to marry you."

"You needn't mind that."

"Oh yes, I must indeed. I can't disobey papa."

"Not for one who loves you as I do, and whom you pretend to love?"

Pansy raised the lid of the teapot, gazing into this vessel for a moment; then she dropped six words into its aromatic depths. "I love you just as much."

"What good will that do me?"

"Ah," said Pansy, raising her sweet, vague eyes, "I don't know that."

"You disappoint me," groaned poor Rosier.

Pansy was silent a moment; she handed a teacup to a servant.

"Please don't talk anymore."

"Is this to be all my satisfaction?"

"Papa said I was not to talk with you."

"Do you sacrifice me like that? Ah, it's too much!"

"I wish you would wait a little," said the young girl, in a voice just distinct enough to betray a quaver.

"Of course I will wait if you will give me hope. But you take my life away."

"I will not give you up—oh, no!" Pansy went on.

"He will try and make you marry someone else."

"I will never do that."

"What then are we to wait for?"

She hesitated a moment.

"I will speak to Mrs. Osmond, and she will help us." It was in this manner that she for the most part designated her step-mother.

"She won't help as much. She is afraid."

"Afraid of what?"

"Of your father, I suppose."

Pansy shook her little head.

"She is not afraid of anyone! We must have patience."

"Ah, that's an awful word," Rosier groaned; he was deeply disconcerted. Oblivious of the customs of good society, he dropped his head into his hands, and, supporting it with a melancholy grace, sat staring at the carpet. Presently he became aware of a good deal of movement about him, and when he looked up saw Pansy making a curtsey—it was still her little curtsey of the convent—to the English lord whom Mrs. Osmond had presented.

❧ 39 ❧

It probably will not be surprising to the reflective reader that Ralph Touchett should have seen less of his cousin since her marriage than he had done before that event—an event of which he took such a view as could hardly prove a confirmation of intimacy. He had uttered his thought, as we know, and after this he had held his peace, Isabel not having invited him to resume a discussion which marked an era in their relations. That discussion had made a difference—the difference that he feared, rather than the one he hoped. It had not chilled the girl's zeal in carrying out her engagement, but it had come dangerously near to spoiling a friendship. No reference was ever again made between them to Ralph's opinion of Gilbert Osmond; and by surrounding this topic with a sacred silence, they managed to preserve a semblance of reciprocal frankness. But there was a difference, as Ralph often said to himself—there was a difference. She had not forgiven him, she never would forgive him; that was all he had gained. She thought she had forgiven him; she believed she didn't care; and as she was both very generous and very proud, these convictions represented a certain reality. But whether or no the event should justify him, he would virtually have done her a wrong, and the wrong was of the sort that women remember best. As Osmond's wife, she could never again be his friend. If in this character she should enjoy the felicity she expected, she would have nothing but contempt for the man who had attempted, in advance, to undermine a blessing so dear; and if on the other hand his warning should be justified, the vow she had taken that he should never know it, would lay upon her spirit a burden that would make her hate him. Such had been, during the year that followed his cousin's marriage, Ralph's rather dismal prevision of the future; and if his meditations appear morbid, we must remember that he was not in the bloom of health. He consoled himself as he might by behaving (as he deemed) beautifully, and was present at the ceremony by which Isabel was united to Mr. Osmond, and which was performed in Florence in the month of June. He learned from his mother that Isabel at first had thoughts of celebrating her nuptials in her native land, but that as simplicity was what she chiefly desired to secure, she had finally decided, in spite of Osmond's professed willingness to make a journey of any length, that this characteristic would best be preserved by their being married by the nearest clergyman in the shortest time. The thing was done, therefore, at the little American chapel, on a very hot day, in the presence only of Mrs. Touchett and her son, of Pansy Osmond and the Countess Gemini. That severity in the proceedings of which I just spoke, was in part the result of the absence of two persons who might have been looked for on the occasion, and who would have lent it a certain richness. Madame Merle had been invited, but Madame Merle, who was unable to leave Rome, sent a gracious letter of excuses. Henrietta Stackpole had not been invited, as her departure from America, announced to Isabel by Mr. Goodwood, was in fact frustrated by the duties of her profession; but she had sent a letter, less gracious than Madame Merle's, intimating that had she been able to cross the Atlantic, she would have been present not only as a witness but as a critic. Her return to Europe took place somewhat later, and she effected a meeting with Isabel in the autumn, in Paris, when she indulged perhaps a trifle too freely—her critical genius. Poor Osmond, who was chiefly the subject of it, protested so sharply that Henrietta was obliged to declare to Isabel that she had taken a step which erected a barrier between them. "It isn't in the least that you have married—it is that you have married *him,*" she deemed it her duty to remark; agreeing, it will be seen, much more with Ralph Touchett than she suspected, though she had few of his hesitations and compunctions. Henrietta's second visit to Europe, however, was not made in vain; for just at the moment when Osmond had declared to Isabel that he really must object to that newspaperwoman, and Isabel had answered that it seemed to her he took Henrietta too hard, the good Mr. Bantling appeared upon the scene and proposed that they should take a run down to Spain. Henrietta's letters from Spain proved to be the most picturesque she had yet published, and there was one in especial, dated from the Alhambra, and entitled 'Moors and Moonlight,' which generally passed for her masterpiece. Isabel was secretly disappointed at her husband's not having been able to judge the poor girl more humorously. She even wondered whether his sense of humor were by chance defective. Of course she herself looked at the matter as a person whose present happiness had nothing to grudge to Henrietta's violated conscience. Osmond thought their alliance a kind of monstrosity; he couldn't imagine what they had in common. For him, Mr. Bantling's fellow-tourist was simply the most vulgar of women, and he also pronounced her the most abandoned. Against this latter clause of the verdict Isabel protested with an ardor which made him wonder afresh at the oddity of some of his wife's tastes. Isabel could explain it only by saying that she liked to know people who were as different as possible from herself. "Why then don't you make the acquaintance of your washerwoman?" Osmond had inquired; to which Isabel answered that she was afraid her washerwoman wouldn't care for her. Now Henrietta cared so much.

Ralph saw nothing of her for the greater part of the two years that followed her marriage; the winter that formed the beginning of her residence in Rome he spent again at San Remo, where he was joined in the spring by his mother, who after-wards went with him to England, to see what they were doing at the bank—an operation she could not induce him to perform. Ralph had taken a lease of his house at San Remo, a small villa, which he occupied still another winter; but late in the month of April of this second year he came down to Rome. It was the first time since her marriage that he had stood face to face with Isabel; his desire to see her again was of the keenest. She had written to him from time to time, but her letters told him nothing that he wanted to know. He had asked his mother what she was making of her life, and his mother had simply answered that she supposed she was making the best of it. Mrs. Touchett had not the imagination that communes with the unseen, and she now pretended to no intimacy with her niece, whom she rarely encountered. This young woman appeared to be living in a sufficiently honorable way, but Mrs. Touchett still remained of the opinion that her marriage was a shabby affair. It gave her no pleasure to think of Isabel's establishment, which she was sure was a very lame business. From time to time, in Florence, she rubbed against the Countess Gemini, doing her best, always, to minimize the contact; and the Count-ess reminded her of Osmond, who made her think of Isabel. The Countess was less talked about in these days; but Mrs. Touchett augured no good of that; it only proved how she had been talked about before. There was a more direct suggestion of Isabel in the person of Madame Merle; but Madame Merle's relations with Mrs. Touchett had undergone a perceptible change. Isabel's aunt had told her, without circumlocution, that she had played too ingenious a part; and Madame Merle, who never quarreled with anyone, who appeared to think no one worth it, and who had performed the miracle of living, more or less, for several years with Mrs. Touchett, without a symptom of irritation—Madame Merle now took a very high tone, and declared that this was an accusation from which she could not stoop to defend her-self. She added, however (without stooping), that her behavior had been only too simple, that she had believed only what she saw, that she saw that Isabel was not eager to marry, and that Osmond was not eager to please (his repeated visits were nothing; he was boring himself to death on his hilltop, and he came merely for amusement). Isabel had kept her sentiments to herself, and her journey to Greece and Egypt had effectually thrown dust in her companion's eyes. Madame Merle accepted the event—she was unprepared to think of it as a scandal; but that she had played any part in it, double or single, was an imputation against which she proudly protested. It was doubtless in consequence of Mrs. Touchett's attitude and of the injury it offered to habits consecrated by many charming seasons, that Madame Merle, after this, chose to pass many months in England, where her credit was quite unimpaired. Mrs. Touchett had done her a wrong; there are some things that can't be forgiven. But Madame Merle suffered in silence; there was always something exquisite in her dignity.

Ralph, as I say, had wished to see for himself; but while he was engaged in this pursuit he felt afresh what a fool he had been to put the girl on her guard. He had played the wrong card, and now he had lost the game. He should see nothing, he should learn nothing; for him she would always wear a mask. His true line would have been to profess delight in her marriage, so that later, when, as Ralph phrased it, the bottom should fall out of it, she might have the pleasure of saying to him that he had been a goose. He would gladly have consented to pass for a goose in order to know Isabel's real situation. But now she neither taunted him with his fallacies nor pretended that her own confidence was justified; if she wore a mask, it completely covered her face. There was something fixed and mechanical in the serenity painted upon it; this was not an expression, Ralph said—it was a representation. She had lost her child; that was a sorrow, but it was a sorrow she scarcely spoke of; there was more to say about it than she could say to Ralph. It belonged to the past, moreover; it had occurred six months before, and she had already laid aside the tokens of mourning. She seemed to be leading the life of the world; Ralph heard her spoken of as having a "charming position." He observed that she produced the impression of being peculiarly enviable, that it was supposed, among many people, to be a privilege even to know her. Her house was not open to everyone, and she had an evening in the week, to which people were not invited as a matter of course. She lived with a certain magnificence, but you needed to be a member of her circle to perceive it; for there was nothing to gape at, nothing to criticize, nothing even to admire, in the daily proceedings of Mr. and Mrs. Osmond. Ralph, in all this, recognized the hand of the master; for he knew that Isabel had no faculty for producing calculated impressions. She struck him as having a great love of movement, of gaiety, of late hours, of long drives, of fatigue; an eagerness to be entertained, to be interested, even to be bored, to make acquaintances, to see people that were talked about, to explore the neighborhood of Rome, to enter into relation with certain of the mustiest relics of its old society. In all this there was much less discrimination than in that desire for comprehensiveness of development on which he used to exercise his wit. There was a kind of violence in some of her impulses, of crudity in some of her experiments, which took him by surprise; it seemed to him that she even spoke faster, moved faster, than before her marriage. Certainly she had fallen into exaggerations—she who used to care so much for the pure truth; and whereas of old she had a great delight in good-humored argument, in intellectual play (she never looked so charming as when in the genial heat of discussion she received a crushing blow full in the face and brushed it away as a feather), she appeared now to think there was nothing worth people's either differing about or agreeing upon. Of old she had been curious, and now she was indifferent, and yet in spite of her indifference her activity was greater than ever. Slender still, but lovelier than before, she had gained no great maturity of aspect; but there was a kind of amplitude and brilliancy in her personal arrangements which gave a touch of insolence to her beauty. Poor human-hearted Isabel, what perversity had bitten her? Her light step drew a mass of drapery behind it; her intelligent head sustained a majesty of ornament. The free, keen girl had become quite another person; what he saw was the fine lady who was supposed to represent something. "What did Isabel represent?" Ralph asked himself; and he could only answer by saying that she represented Gilbert Osmond. "Good heavens, what a function!" he exclaimed. He was lost in wonder at the mystery of things. He recognized Osmond, as I say; he recognized him at every turn. He saw how he kept all things within limits; how he adjusted, regulated, animated their manner of life. Osmond was in his element; at last he had material to work with. He always had an eye to effect; and his effects were elaborately studied. They were produced by no vulgar means, but the motive was as vulgar as the art was great. To surround his interior with a sort of invidious sanctity, to tantalize society with a sense of exclusion, to make people believe his house was different from every other, to impart to the face that he presented to the world a cold originality—this was the ingenious effort of the personage to whom Isabel had attributed a superior morality. "He works with superior material," Ralph said to himself; "but it's rich abundance compared with his former resources." Ralph was a clever man; but Ralph had never—to his own sense—been so clever as when he observed, *in petto,* that under the guise of caring only for intrinsic values, Osmond lived exclusively for the world. Far from being its master, as he pretended to be, he was its very humble servant, and the degree of its attention was his only measure of success. He lived with his eye on it, from morning till night, and the world was so stupid it never suspected the trick. Everything he did was *pose*—*pose* so deeply calculated that if one were not on the lookout one mistook it for impulse. Ralph had never met a man who lived so much in the land of calculation. His tastes, his studies, his accomplishments, his collections, were all for a purpose. His life on his hilltop at Florence had been a *pose* of years. His solitude, his ennui, his love for his daughter, his good manners, his bad manners, were so many features of a mental image constantly present to him as a model of impertinence and mystification. His ambition was not to please the world, but to please himself by exciting the world's curiosity and then declining to satisfy it. It made him feel great to play the world a trick. The thing he had done in his life most directly to please himself was his marrying Isabel Archer; though in this case indeed the gullible world was in a manner embodied in poor Isabel, who had been mystified to the top of her bent. Ralph of course found a fitness in being consistent; he had embraced a creed, and as he had suffered for it he could not in honor forsake it. I give this little sketch of its articles for what they are worth. It was certain that he was very skillful in fitting the facts to his theory—even the fact that during the month he spent in Rome at this period Gilbert

Osmond appeared to regard him not in the least as an enemy. For Mr. Osmond Ralph had not now that importance. It was not that he had the importance of a friend; it was rather that he had none at all. He was Isabel's cousin, and he was rather unpleasantly ill—it was on this basis that Osmond treated with him. He made the proper inquiries, asked about his health, about Mrs. Touchett, about his opinion of winter climates, whether he was comfortable at his hotel. He addressed him, on the few occasions of their meeting, not a word that was not necessary; but his manner had always the urbanity proper to conscious success in the presence of conscious failure. For all this, Ralph had, toward the end, an inward conviction that Osmond had made it uncomfortable for his wife that she should continue to receive her cousin. He was not jealous—he had not that excuse; no one could be jealous of Ralph. But he made Isabel pay for her old-time kindness, of which so much was still left; and as Ralph had no idea of her paying too much, when his suspicion had become sharp, he took himself off. In doing so he deprived Isabel of a very interesting occupation: she had been constantly wondering what fine principle kept him alive. She decided that it was his love of conversation; his conversation was better than ever. He had given up walking; he was no longer a humorous stroller. He sat all day in a chair—almost any chair would do, and was so dependent on what you would do for him that, had not his talk been highly contemplative, you might have thought he was blind. The reader already knows more about him than Isabel was ever to know, and the reader may therefore be given the key to the mystery. What kept Ralph alive was simply the fact that he had not yet seen enough of his cousin; he was not yet satisfied. There was more to come; he couldn't make up his mind to lose that. He wished to see what she would make of her husband—or what he would make of her. This was only the first act of the drama, and he was determined to sit out the performance. His determination held good; it kept him going some eighteen months more, till the time of his return to Rome with Lord Warburton. It gave him indeed such an air of intending to live indefinitely that Mrs. Touchett, though more accessible to confusions of thought in the matter of this strange, unremunerative—and unremunerated—son of hers than she had ever been before, had, as we have learned, not scrupled to embark for a distant land. If Ralph had been kept alive by suspense, it was with a good deal of the same emotion—the excitement of wondering in what state she should find him—that Isabel ascended to his apartment the day after Lord Warburton had notified her of his arrival in Rome.

She spent an hour with him; it was the first of several visits. Gilbert Osmond called on him punctually, and on Isabel sending a carriage for him Ralph came more than once to the Palazzo Roccanera. A fortnight elapsed, at the end of which Ralph announced to Lord Warburton that he thought after all he wouldn't go to Sicily. The two men had been dining together after a day spent by the latter in rang-ing about the Campagna. They had left the table, and Warburton, before the chimney, was lighting a cigar, which he instantly removed from his lips.

"Won't go to Sicily? Where then will you go?"

"Well, I guess I won't go anywhere," said Ralph, from the sofa, in a tone of jocosity.

"Do you mean that you will return to England?"

"Oh dear no; I will stay in Rome."

"Rome won't do for you; it's not warm enough."

"It will have to do; I will make it do. See how well I have been."

Lord Warburton looked at him a while, puffing his cigar, as if he were trying to see it.

"You have been better than you were on the journey, certainly. I wonder how you lived through that. But I don't understand your condition. I recommend you to try Sicily."

"I can't try," said poor Ralph; "I can't move further. I can't face that journey. Fancy me between Scylla and Charybdis! I don't want to die on the Sicilian plains—to be snatched away, like Proserpine in the same locality, to the Plutonian shades."

"What the deuce then did you come for?" his lordship inquired.

"Because the idea took me. I see it won't do. It really doesn't matter where I am now. I've exhausted all remedies, I've swallowed all climates. As I'm here I'll stay; I haven't got any cousins in Sicily."

"Your cousin is certainly an inducement. But what does the doctor say?"

"I haven't asked him, and I don't care a fig. If I die here Mrs. Osmond will bury me. But I shall not die here."

"I hope not." Lord Warburton continued to smoke reflectively. "Well, I must say," he resumed, "for myself I am very glad you don't go to Sicily. I had a horror of that journey."

"Ah, but for you it needn't have mattered. I had no idea of dragging you in my train."

"I certainly didn't mean to let you go alone."

"My dear Warburton, I never expected you to come further than this," Ralph cried.

"I should have gone with you and seen you settled," said Lord Warburton.

"You are a very good fellow. You are very kind."

"Then I should have come back here."

"And then you would have gone to England."

"No, no; I should have stayed."

"Well," said Ralph, "if that's what we are both up to, I don't see where Sicily comes in!"

His companion was silent; he sat staring at the fire. At last, looking up—

"I say, tell me this," he broke out; "did you really mean to go to Sicily when we started?"

"Ah, *vous m'en demandez trop!* Let me put a question first. Did you come with me quite—platonically?"

"I don't know what you mean by that. I wanted to come abroad."

"I suspect we have each been playing our little game."

"Speak for yourself. I made no secret whatever of my wanting to be here a while."

"Yes, I remember you said you wished to see the Minister of Foreign Affairs."

"I have seen him three times; he is very amusing."

"I think you have forgotten what you came for," said Ralph.

"Perhaps I have," his companion answered, rather gravely.

These two gentlemen were children of a race which is not distinguished by the absence of reserve, and they had traveled together from London to Rome without an allusion to matters that were uppermost in the mind of each. There was an old subject that they had once discussed, but it had lost its recognized place in their attention, and even after their arrival in Rome, where many things led back to it, they had kept the same half-diffident, half-confident silence.

"I recommend you to get the doctor's consent, all the same," Lord Warburton went on, abruptly, after an interval.

"The doctor's consent will spoil it; I never have it when I can help it!"

"What does Mrs. Osmond think?"

"I have not told her. She will probably say that Rome is too cold, and even offer to go with me to Catania. She is capable of that."

"In your place I should like it."

"Her husband won't like it."

"Ah well, I can fancy that; though it seems to me you are not bound to mind it. It's his affair."

"I don't want to make any more trouble between them," said Ralph.

"Is there so much already?"

"There's complete preparation for it. Her going off with me would make the explosion. Osmond isn't fond of his wife's cousin."

"Then of course he would make a row. But won't he make a row if you stop here?"

"That's what I want to see. He made one the last time I was in Rome, and then I thought it my duty to go away. Now I think it's my duty to stop and defend her."

"My dear Touchett, your defensive powers—" Lord Warburton began, with a smile. But he saw something in his companion's face that checked him. "Your duty, in these premises, seems to me rather a nice question," he said.

Ralph for a short time answered nothing.

"It is true that my defensive powers are small," he remarked at last; "but as my aggressive ones are still smaller, Osmond may, after all, not think me worth his gunpowder. At any rate," he added, "there are things I am curious to see."

"You are sacrificing your health to your curiosity then?"

"I am not much interested in my health, and I am deeply interested in Mrs. Osmond."

"So am I. But not as I once was," Lord Warburton added quickly. This was one of the allusions he had not hitherto found occasion to make.

"Does she strike you as very happy?" Ralph inquired, emboldened by this confidence.

"Well, I don't know; I have hardly thought. She told me the other night that she was happy."

"Ah, she told *you*, of course," Ralph exclaimed, smiling.

"I don't know that. It seems to me I was rather the sort of person she might have complained to."

"Complain? She will never complain. She has done it, and she knows it. She will complain to you least of all. She is very careful."

"She needn't be. I don't mean to make love to her again."

"I am delighted to hear it; there can be no doubt at least of *your* duty."

"Ah no," said Lord Warburton, gravely; "none!"

"Permit me to ask," Ralph went on, "whether it is to bring out the fact that you don't mean to make love to her that you are so very civil to the little girl?"

Lord Warburton gave a slight start; he got up and stood before the fire, blushing a little.

"Does that strike you as very ridiculous?"

"Ridiculous? Not in the least, if you really like her."

"I think her a delightful little person. I don't know when a girl of that age has pleased me more."

"She's a charming creature. Ah, she at least is genuine."

"Of course there's the difference in our ages—more than twenty years."

"My dear Warburton," said Ralph, "are you serious?"

"Perfectly serious—as far as I've got."

"I am very glad. And, heaven help us," cried Ralph, "how tickled Gilbert Osmond will be!"

His companion frowned.

"I say, don't spoil it. I shan't marry his daughter to please him."

"He will have the perversity to be pleased all the same."

"He's not so fond of me as that," said his lordship.

"As that? My dear Warburton, the drawback of your position is that people needn't be fond of you at all to wish to be connected with you. Now, with me in such a case, I should have the happy confidence that they loved me."

Lord Warburton seemed scarcely to be in the mood for doing justice to general axioms; he was thinking of a special case.

"Do you think she'll be pleased?"

"The girl herself? Delighted, surely."

"No, no; I mean Mrs. Osmond."

Ralph looked at him a moment.

"My dear fellow, what has she to do with it?"

"Whatever she chooses. She is very fond of the girl."

"Very true—very true." And Ralph slowly got up. "It's an interesting question—how far her fondness for the girl will carry her." He stood there a moment with his hands in his pockets, with a rather somber eye. "I hope, you know, that you are very—very sure—The deuce!" he broke off, "I don't know how to say it."

"Yes, you do; you know how to say everything."

"Well, it's awkward. I hope you are sure that among Miss Osmond's merits her being a—so near her stepmother isn't a leading one?"

"Good heavens, Touchett!" cried Lord Warburton, angrily, "for what do you take me?"

❧ 40 ❧

Isabel had not seen much of Madame Merle since her marriage, this lady having indulged in frequent absences from Rome. At one time she had spent six months in England; at another she had passed a portion of a winter in Paris. She had made numerous visits to distant friends, and gave countenance to the idea that for the future she should be a less inveterate Roman than in the past. As she had been inveterate in the past only in the sense of constantly having an apartment in one of the sunniest niches of the Pincian—an apartment which often stood empty—this suggested a prospect of almost constant absence; a danger which Isabel at one period had been much inclined to deplore. Familiarity had modified in some degree her first impression of Madame Merle, but it had not essentially altered it; there was still a kind of wonder of admiration in it. Madame Merle was armed at all points; it was a pleasure to see a person so completely equipped for the social battle. She carried her flag discreetly, but her weapons were polished steel, and she used them with a skill which struck Isabel as more and more that of a veteran. She was never weary, never overcome with disgust; she never appeared to need rest or consolation. She had her own ideas; she had of old exposed a great many of them to Isabel, who knew also that under an appearance of extreme self-control her highly-cultivated friend concealed a rich sensibility. But her will was mistress of her life; there was something brilliant in the way she kept going. It was as if she had learned the secret of it—as if the art of life were some clever trick that she had guessed. Isabel, as she herself grew older, became acquainted with revulsions, with disgust; there were days when the world looked black, and she asked herself with some peremptoriness what it was that she was pretending to live for. Her old habit had been to live by enthusiasm, to fall in love with suddenly perceived possibilities, with the idea of a new attempt. As a young girl, she used to proceed from one little exaltation to the other; there were scarcely any dull places between. But Madame Merle had suppressed enthusiasm; she fell in love nowadays with nothing; she lived entirely by reason, by wisdom. There were hours when Isabel would have given anything for lessons in this art; if Madame Merle had been near, she would have made an appeal to her. She had become aware more than before of the advantage of being like that—of having made one's self a firm surface, a sort of corselet of silver. But, as I say, it was not till the winter, during which we lately renewed acquaintance with our heroine, that Madame Merle made a continuous stay in Rome. Isabel now saw more of her than she had done since her marriage; but by this time Isabel's needs and inclinations had considerably changed. It was not at present to Madame Merle that she would have applied for instruction; she had lost the desire to know this lady's clever trick. If she had troubles she must keep them to herself, and if life was difficult it would not make it easier to confess herself beaten. Madame Merle was doubtless of great use to herself, and an ornament to any circle; but was she—would she be—of use to others in periods of refined embarrassment? The best way to profit by Madame Merle—this indeed Isabel had always thought—was to imitate her; to be as firm and bright as she. She recognized no embarrassments, and Isabel, considering this fact, determined, for the fiftieth time, to brush aside her own. It seemed to her, too, on the renewal of an intercourse which had virtually been interrupted, that Madame Merle was changed—that she pushed to the extreme a certain rather artificial fear of being indiscreet. Ralph Touchett, we know, had been of the opinion that she was prone to exaggeration, to forcing the note—was apt, in the vulgar phrase, to overdo it. Isabel had never admitted this charge—had never, indeed, quite understood it; Madame Merle's conduct, to her perception, always bore the stamp of good taste, was always "quiet." But in this matter of not wishing to intrude upon the inner life of the Osmond family, it at last occurred to our heroine that she overdid it a little. That, of course, was not the best taste; that was rather violent. She remembered too much that Isabel was married; that she had now other interests; that though she, Madame Merle, had known Gilbert Osmond and his little Pansy very well, better almost than anyone, she was after all not one of them. She was on her guard; she never spoke of their affairs till she was asked, even pressed—as when her opinion was wanted; she had a dread of seeming to meddle. Madame Merle was as candid as we know, and one day she candidly expressed this dread to Isabel.

"I must be on my guard," she said; "I might so easily, without suspecting it, offend you. You would be right to be offended, even if my intention should have been of the purest. I must not forget that I knew your husband long before you did; I must not let that betray me. If you were a silly woman you might be jealous. You are not a silly woman; I know that perfectly. But neither am I; therefore I am determined not to get into trouble. A little harm is very soon done; a mistake is made before one knows it. Of course, if I had wished to make love to your husband, I had ten years to do it in, and nothing to prevent; so it isn't likely I shall begin today, when I am so much less attractive than I was. But if I were to annoy you by seeming to take a place that doesn't belong to me, you wouldn't make that reflection; you would simply say that I was forgetting certain differences. I am determined not to forget them. Of course a good friend isn't always thinking of that; one doesn't suspect one's friends of injustice. I don't suspect you, my dear, in the least; but I suspect human nature. Don't think I make myself uncomfortable; I am not always watching myself. I think I sufficiently prove it in talking to you as I do now. All I wish to say is, however, that if you were to be jealous—that is the form it would take—I should be sure to think it was a little my fault. It certainly wouldn't be your husband's."

Isabel had had three years to think over Mrs. Touchett's theory that Madame Merle had made Gilbert Osmond's marriage. We know how she had at first received it. Madame Merle might have made Gilbert Osmond's marriage, but she certainly had not made Isabel Archer's. That was the work of—Isabel scarcely knew what: of nature, of providence, of fortune, of the eternal mystery of things. It was true that her aunt's complaint had been not so much of Madame Merle's activity as of her duplicity; she had brought about the marriage and then she had denied her guilt. Such guilt would not have been great, to Isabel's mind; she couldn't make a crime of Madame Merle's having been the cause of the most fertile friendship she had ever formed. That occurred to her just before her marriage, after her little discussion with her aunt. If Madame Merle had desired the event, she could only say it had been a very happy thought. With her, moreover, she had been perfectly straightforward; she had never concealed her high opinion of Gilbert Osmond. After her marriage Isabel discovered that her husband took a less comfortable view of the matter; he seldom spoke of Madame Merle, and when his wife alluded to her he usually let the allusion drop.

"Don't you like her?" Isabel had once said to him. "She thinks a great deal of you."

"I will tell you once for all," Osmond had answered. "I liked her once better than I do today. I am tired of her, and I am rather ashamed of it. She is so good! I am glad she is not in Italy; it's a sort of rest. Don't talk of her too much; it seems to bring her back. She will come back in plenty of time."

Madame Merle, in fact, had come back before it was too late—too late, I mean, to recover whatever advantage she might have lost. But meantime, if, as I have said, she was somewhat changed, Isabel's feelings were also altered. Her consciousness of the situation was as acute as of old, but it was much less satisfying. A dissatisfied mind, whatever else it lack, is rarely in want of reasons; they bloom as thick as buttercups in June. The fact of Madame Merle having had a hand in Gilbert Osmond's marriage ceased to be one of her titles to consideration; it seemed, after all, that there was not so much to thank her for. As time went on there was less and less; and Isabel once said to herself that perhaps without her these things would not have been. This reflection, however, was instantly stifled; Isabel felt a sort of horror at having made it. "Whatever happens to me, let me not be unjust," she said; "let me bear my burdens myself, and not shift them upon others!" This disposition was tested, eventually, by that ingenious apology for her present conduct which Madame Merle saw fit to make, and of which I have given a sketch; for there was something irritating—there was almost an air of mockery— in her neat discriminations and clear convictions. In Isabel's mind today there was nothing clear; there was a confusion of regrets, a complication of fears. She felt helpless as she turned away from her brilliant friend, who had just made the statements I have quoted; Madame Merle knew so little what she was thinking of! Moreover, she herself was so unable to explain. Jealous of her—jealous of her with Gilbert? The idea just then suggested no near reality. She almost wished that jealousy had been possible; it would be a kind of refreshment. Jealousy, after all, was in a sense one of the symptoms of happiness. Madame Merle, however, was wise; it would seem that she knew Isabel better than Isabel knew herself. This young woman had always been fertile in resolutions—many of them of an elevated character; but at no period had they flourished (in the privacy of her heart) more richly than today. It is true that they all had a family likeness; they might have been summed up in the determination that if she was to be unhappy it should not be by a fault of her own. The poor girl had always had a great desire to do her best, and she had not as yet been seriously discouraged. She wished, therefore, to hold fast to justice—not to pay herself by petty revenges. To associate Madame Merle with her disappointment would be a petty revenge—especially as the pleasure she might derive from it would be perfectly insincere. It might feed her sense of bitterness, but it would not loosen her bonds. It was impossible to pretend that she had not acted with her eyes open; if ever a girl was a free agent, she had been. A girl in love was doubtless not a free agent; but the sole source of her mistake had been within herself. There had been no plot, no snare; she had looked, and considered, and chosen. When a woman had made such a mistake, there was only one way to repair it—to accept it. One folly was enough, especially when it was to last forever; a second one would not much set it off. In this vow of reticence there was a certain nobleness which kept Isabel going; but Madame Merle had been right, for all that, in taking her precautions.

One day, about a month after Ralph Touchett's arrival in Rome, Isabel came back from a walk with Pansy. It was not only a part of her general determination to be just that she was at present very thankful for Pansy. It was a part of her tenderness for things that were pure and weak. Pansy was dear to her, and there was nothing in her life so much as it should be as the young girl's attachment and the pleasantness of feeling it. It was like a soft presence—like a small hand in her own; on Pansy's part it was more than an affection—it was a kind of faith. On her own side her sense of Pansy's dependence was more than a pleasure; it operated as a command, as a definite reason when motives threatened to fail her. She had said to herself that we must take our duty where we find it, and that we must look for it as much as possible. Pansy's sympathy was a kind of admonition; it seemed to say that here was an opportunity. An opportunity for what, Isabel could hardly have said; in general, to be more for the child than the child was able to be for herself. Isabel could have smiled, in these days, to remember that her little companion had once been ambiguous; for she now perceived that Pansy's ambiguities were simply her own grossness of vision. She had been unable to believe that anyone could care so much—so extraordinarily much—to please. But since then she had seen this delicate faculty in operation, and she knew what to think of it. It was the whole creature—it was a sort of genius. Pansy had no pride to interfere with it, and though she was constantly extending her conquests she took no credit for them. The two were constantly together; Mrs. Osmond was rarely seen without her step-daughter. Isabel liked her company; it had the effect of one's carrying a nosegay composed all of the same flower. And then not to neglect Pansy—not under any provocation to neglect her; this she had made an article of religion. The young girl had every appearance of being happier in Isabel's society than in that of anyone save her father, whom she admired with an intensity justified by the fact that, as paternity was an exquisite pleasure to Gilbert Osmond, he had always been elaborately soft. Isabel knew that Pansy liked immensely to be with her and studied the means of pleasing her. She had decided that the best way of pleasing her was negative, and consisted in not giving her trouble—a conviction which certainly could not have had any reference to trouble already existing. She was therefore ingeniously passive and almost imaginatively docile; she was careful even to moderate the eagerness with which she assented to Isabel's propositions, and which might have implied that she thought otherwise. She never interrupted, never asked social questions, and though she delighted in approbation, to the point of turning pale when it came to her, never held out her hand for it. She only looked toward it wistfully—an attitude which, as she grew older, made her eyes the prettiest in the world. When during the second winter at the Palazzo Roccanera, she began to go to parties, to dances, she always, at a reasonable hour, lest Mrs. Osmond should be tired, was the first to propose departure. Isabel appreciated the sacrifice of the late dances, for she knew that

Pansy had a passionate pleasure in this exercise, taking her steps to the music like a conscientious fairy. Society, moreover, had no drawbacks for her; she liked even the tiresome parts—the heat of ballrooms, the dulness of dinners, the crush at the door, the awkward waiting for the carriage. During the day, in this vehicle, beside Isabel, she sat in a little fixed appreciative posture, bending forward and faintly smiling, as if she had been taken to drive for the first time.

On the day I speak of they had been driven out of one of the gates of the city, and at the end of half-an-hour had left the carriage to await them by the roadside, while they walked away over the short grass of the Campagna, which even in the winter months is sprinkled with delicate flowers. This was almost a daily habit with Isabel, who was fond of a walk, and stepped quickly, though not so quickly as when she first came to Europe. It was not the form of exercise that Pansy loved best, but she liked it, because she liked everything; and she moved with a shorter undulation beside her stepmother, who afterwards, on their return to Rome, paid a tribute to Pansy's preferences by making the circuit of the Pincian or the Villa Borghese. Pansy had gathered a handful of flowers in a sunny hollow, far from the walls of Rome, and on reaching the Palazzo Roccanera she went straight to her room, to put them into water. Isabel passed into the drawing room, the one she herself usually occupied, the second in order from the large antechamber which was entered from the stair-case, and in which even Gilbert Osmond's rich devices had not been able to correct a look of rather grand nudity. Just beyond the threshold of the drawing room she stopped short, the reason for her doing so being that she had received an impression. The impression had, in strictness, nothing unprecedented; but she felt it as something new, and the soundlessness of her step gave her time to take in the scene before she interrupted it. Madame Merle sat there in her bonnet, and Gilbert Osmond was talking to her; for a minute they were unaware that she had come in. Isabel had often seen that before, certainly; but what she had not seen, or at least had not noticed—was that their dialogue had for the moment converted itself into a sort of familiar silence, from which she instantly perceived that her entrance would startle them. Madame Merle was standing on the rug, a little way from the fire; Osmond was in a deep chair, leaning back and looking at her. Her head was erect, as usual, but her eyes were bent upon his. What struck Isabel first was that he was sitting while Madame Merle stood; there was an anomaly in this that arrested her. Then she perceived that they had arrived at a desultory pause in their exchange of ideas, and were musing, face to face, with the freedom of old friends who sometimes exchange ideas without uttering them. There was nothing shocking in this; they were old friends in fact. But the thing made an image, lasting only a moment, like a sudden flicker of light. Their relative position, their absorbed mutual gaze, struck her as something detected. But it was all over by the time she had fairly seen it. Madame Merle had seen her, and had welcomed her without moving; Gilbert Osmond, on the other hand, had instantly jumped up. He presently murmured something about wanting a walk, and after having asked Madame Merle to excuse him, he left the room.

"I came to see you, thinking you would have come in; and as you had not, I waited for you," Madame Merle said.

"Didn't he ask you to sit down?" asked Isabel, smiling.

Madame Merle looked about her.

"Ah, it's very true; I was going away."

"You must stay now."

"Certainly. I came for a reason; I have something on my mind."

"I have told you that before," Isabel said—"that it takes something extraordinary to bring you to this house."

"And you know what I have told you; that whether I come or whether I stay away, I have always the same motive—the affection I bear you."

"Yes, you have told me that."

"You look just now as if you didn't believe me," said Madame Merle.

"Ah," Isabel answered, "the profundity of your motives, that is the last thing I doubt!"

"You doubt sooner of the sincerity of my words."

Isabel shook her head gravely. "I know you have always been kind to me."

"As often as you would let me. You don't always take it; then one has to let you alone. It's not to do you a kindness, however, that I have come today; it's quite another affair. I have come to get rid of a trouble of my own—to make it over to you. I have been talking to your husband about it."

"I am surprised at that; he doesn't like troubles."

"Especially other people's; I know that. But neither do you, I suppose. At any rate, whether you do or not, you must help me. It's about poor Mr. Rosier."

"Ah," said Isabel, reflectively, "it's his trouble, then, not yours."

"He has succeeded in saddling me with it. He comes to see me ten times a week, to talk about Pansy."

"Yes, he wants to marry her. I know all about it."

Madame Merle hesitated a moment. "I gathered from your husband that perhaps you didn't."

"How should he know what I know? He has never spoken to me of the matter."

"It is probably because he doesn't know how to speak of it."

"It's nevertheless a sort of question in which he is rarely at fault."

"Yes, because as a general thing he knows perfectly well what to think. Today he doesn't."

"Haven't you been telling him?" Isabel asked.

Madame Merle gave a bright, voluntary smile. "Do you know you're a little dry?"

"Yes; I can't help it. Mr. Rosier has also talked to me."

"In that there is some reason. You are so near the child."

"Ah," said Isabel, "for all the comfort I have given him! If you think me dry, I wonder what he thinks."

"I believe he thinks you can do more than you have done."

"I can do nothing."

"You can do more at least than I. I don't know what mysterious connection he may have discovered between me and Pansy; but he came to me from the first, as if I held his fortune in my hand. Now he keeps coming back, to spur me up, to know what hope there is, to pour out his feelings."

"He is very much in love," said Isabel.

"Very much—for him."

"Very much for Pansy, you might say as well."

Madame Merle dropped her eyes a moment. "Don't you think she's attractive?"

"She is the dearest little person possible; but she is very limited."

"She ought to be all the easier for Mr. Rosier to love. Mr. Rosier is not unlimited."

"No," said Isabel, "he has about the extent of one's pocket-handkerchief—the small ones, with lace." Her humor had lately turned a good deal to sarcasm, but in a moment she was ashamed of exercising it on so innocent an object as Pansy's suitor. "He is very kind, very honest," she presently added; "and he is not such a fool as he seems."

"He assures me that she delights in him," said Madame Merle.

"I don't know; I have not asked her."

"You have never sounded her a little?"

"It's not my place; it's her father's."

"Ah, you are too literal!" said Madame Merle.

"I must judge for myself."

Madame Merle gave her smile again. "It isn't easy to help you."

"To help me?" said Isabel, very seriously. "What do you mean?"

"It's easy to displease you. Don't you see how wise I am to be careful? I notify you, at any rate, as I notified Osmond, that I wash my hands of the love-affairs of Miss Pansy and Mr. Edward Rosier. *Je n'y peux rien, moi!* I can't talk to Pansy about him. Especially," added Madame Merle, "as I don't think him a paragon of husbands."

Isabel reflected a little; after which, with a smile—"You don't wash your hands, then!" she said. Then she added, in another tone—"You can't—you are too much interested."

Madame Merle slowly rose; she had given Isabel a look as rapid as the intimation that had gleamed before our heroine a few moments before. Only, this time Isabel saw nothing. "Ask him the next time, and you will see."

"I can't ask him; he has ceased to come to the house. Gilbert has let him know that he is not welcome."

"Ah yes," said Madame Merle, "I forgot that, though it's the burden of his lamentation. He says Osmond has insulted him. All the same," she went on, "Osmond
doesn't dislike him as much as he thinks." She had got up, as if to close the conversation, but she lingered, looking about her, and had evidently more to say. Isabel
perceived this, and even saw the point she had in view; but Isabel also had her own
reasons for not opening the way.

"That must have pleased him, if you have told him," she answered, smiling.

"Certainly I have told him; as far as that goes, I have encouraged him. I have
preached patience, have said that his case is not desperate, if he will only hold his
tongue and be quiet. Unfortunately he has taken it into his head to be jealous."

"Jealous?"

"Jealous of Lord Warburton, who, he says, is always here."

Isabel, who was tired, had remained sitting; but at this she also rose. "Ah!" she
exclaimed simply, moving slowly to the fireplace. Madame Merle observed her as
she passed and as she stood a moment before the mantel-glass, pushing into its
place a wandering tress of hair.

"Poor Mr. Rosier keeps saying that there is nothing impossible in Lord Warburton falling in love with Pansy," Madame Merle went on.

Isabel was silent a little; she turned away from the glass. "It is true—there is
nothing impossible," she rejoined at last, gravely and more gently.

"So I have had to admit to Mr. Rosier. So, too, your husband thinks."

"That I don't know."

"Ask him, and you will see."

"I shall not ask him," said Isabel.

"Excuse me; I forgot that you had pointed that out. Of course," Madame Merle
added, "you have had infinitely more observation of Lord Warburton's behavior
than I."

"I see no reason why I shouldn't tell you that he likes my step-daughter very
much."

Madame Merle gave one of her quick looks again. "Likes her, you mean—as Mr.
Rosier means?"

"I don't know how Mr. Rosier means; but Lord Warburton has let me know that
he is charmed with Pansy."

"And you have never told Osmond?" This observation was immediate, precipitate; it almost burst from Madame Merle's lips.

Isabel smiled a little. "I suppose he will know in time; Lord Warburton has a
tongue, and knows how to express himself."

Madame Merle instantly became conscious that she had spoken more quickly
than usual, and the reflection brought the color to her cheek. She gave the treacherous impulse time to subside, and then she said, as if she had been thinking it over
a little: "That would be better than marrying poor Mr. Rosier."

"Much better, I think."

"It would be very delightful; it would be a great marriage. It is really very kind of him."

"Very kind of him?"

"To drop his eyes on a simple little girl."

"I don't see that."

"It's very good of you. But after all, Pansy Osmond—"

"After all, Pansy Osmond is the most attractive person he has ever known!" Isabel exclaimed.

Madame Merle stared, and indeed she was justly bewildered. "Ah, a moment ago, I thought you seemed rather to disparage her."

"I said she was limited. And so she is. And so is Lord Warburton."

"So are we all, if you come to that. If it's no more than Pansy deserves, all the better. But if she fixes her affections on Mr. Rosier, I won't admit that she deserves it. That will be too perverse."

"Mr. Rosier's a nuisance!" cried Isabel, abruptly.

"I quite agree with you, and I am delighted to know that I am not expected to feed his flame. For the future, when he calls on me, my door shall be closed to him." And gathering her mantle together, Madame Merle prepared to depart. She was checked, however, on her progress to the door, by an inconsequent request from Isabel.

"All the same, you know, be kind to him."

She lifted her shoulders and eyebrows, and stood looking at her friend. "I don't understand your contradictions! Decidedly, I shall not be kind to him, for it will be a false kindness. I wish to see her married to Lord Warburton."

"You had better wait till he asks her."

"If what you say is true, he will ask her. Especially," said Madame Merle in a moment, "if you make him."

"If I make him?"

"It's quite in your power. You have great influence with him."

Isabel frowned a little. "Where did you learn that?"

"Mrs. Touchett told me. Not you—never!" said Madame Merle, smiling.

"I certainly never told you that."

"You might have done so when we were by way of being confidential with each other. But you really told me very little; I have often thought so since."

Isabel had thought so too, sometimes with a certain satisfaction. But she did not admit it now—perhaps because she did not wish to appear to exult in it. "You seem to have had an excellent informant in my aunt," she simply said.

"She let me know that you had declined an offer of marriage from Lord Warburton, because she was greatly vexed, and was full of the subject. Of course I think you have done better in doing as you did. But if you wouldn't marry Lord Warburton yourself, make him the reparation of helping him to marry someone else."

Isabel listened to this with a face which persisted in not reflecting the bright expressiveness of Madame Merle's. But in a moment she said, reasonably and gently enough, "I should be very glad indeed if, as regards Pansy, it could be arranged." Upon which her companion, who seemed to regard this as a speech of good omen, embraced her more tenderly than might have been expected, and took her departure.

❊ 41 ❊

Osmond touched on this matter that evening for the first time; coming very late into the drawing room, where she was sitting alone. They had spent the evening at home, and Pansy had gone to bed; he himself had been sitting since dinner in a small apartment in which he had arranged his books and which he called his study. At ten o'clock Lord Warburton had come in, as he always did when he knew from Isabel that she was to be at home; he was going somewhere else, and he sat for half-an-hour. Isabel, after asking him for news of Ralph, said very little to him, on purpose; she wished him to talk with the young girl. She pretended to read; she even went after a little to the piano; she asked herself whether she might not leave the room. She had come little by little to think well of the idea of Pansy's becoming the wife of the master of beautiful Lockleigh, though at first it had not presented itself in a manner to excite her enthusiasm. Madame Merle, that afternoon, had applied the match to an accumulation of inflammable material. When Isabel was unhappy, she always looked about her—partly from impulse and partly by theory—for some form of exertion. She could never rid herself of the conviction that unhappiness was a state of disease; it was suffering as opposed to action. To act, to do something—it hardly mattered what—would therefore be an escape, perhaps in some degree a remedy. Besides, she wished to convince herself that she had done everything possible to content her husband; she was determined not to be haunted by images of a flat want of zeal. It would please him greatly to see Pansy married to an English nobleman, and justly please him, since this nobleman was such a fine fellow. It seemed to Isabel that if she could make it her duty to bring about such an event, she should play the part of a good wife. She wanted to be that; she wanted to be able to believe, sincerely, that she had been that. Then, such an undertaking had other recommendations. It would occupy her, and she desired occupation. It would even amuse her, and if she could really amuse herself she perhaps might be saved. Lastly, it would be a service to Lord Warburton, who evidently pleased himself greatly with the young girl. It was a little odd that he should—being what he was; but there was no accounting for such impressions. Pansy might captivate anyone—anyone, at least, but Lord Warburton. Isabel would have thought her too small, too slight, perhaps even too artificial for that. There was always a little of the doll about her, and that was not what Lord Warburton had been looking for. Still, who could say what men looked for? They looked for what they found; they knew what pleased them only when they saw it. No theory was valid in such matters, and nothing was more unaccountable or more natural than anything else. If he had cared for *her* it might seem odd that he cared for Pansy, who was so different; but he had not cared for her so much as he supposed. Or if he had, he had completely got over it, and it was natural that as that affair had failed, he should think that something of quite another sort might succeed. Enthusiasm, as I say, had not come at first to Isabel, but it came today and made her feel almost happy. It was astonishing what happiness she could still find in the idea of procuring a pleasure for her husband. It was a pity, however, that Edward Rosier had crossed their path!

At this reflection the light that had suddenly gleamed upon that path lost something of its brightness. Isabel was unfortunately as sure that Pansy thought Mr. Rosier the nicest of all the young men—as sure as if she had held an interview with her on the subject. It was very tiresome that she should be so sure, when she had carefully abstained from informing herself; almost as tiresome as that poor Mr. Rosier should have taken it into his own head. He was certainly very inferior to Lord Warburton. It was not the difference in fortune so much as the difference in the men; the young American was really so very flimsy. He was much more of the type of the useless fine gentleman than the English nobleman. It was true that there was no particular reason why Pansy should marry a statesman; still, if a statesman admired her, that was his affair, and she would make a very picturesque little peeress.

It may seem to the reader that Isabel had suddenly grown strangely cynical; for she ended by saying to herself that this difficulty could probably be arranged. Somehow, an impediment that was embodied in poor Rosier could not present itself as a dangerous one; there were always means of leveling secondary obstacles. Isabel was perfectly aware that she had not taken the measure of Pansy's tenacity, which might prove to be inconveniently great; but she inclined to think the young girl would not be tenacious, for she had the faculty of assent developed in a very much higher degree than that of resistance. She would cling, yes, she would cling; but it really mattered to her very little what she clung to. Lord Warburton would do as well as Mr. Rosier—especially as she seemed quite to like him. She had expressed this sentiment to Isabel without a single reservation; she said she thought his conversation most interesting—he had told her all about India. His manner to Pansy had been of the happiest; Isabel noticed that for herself, as she also observed that he talked to her not in the least in a patronising way, reminding himself of her youth and simplicity, but quite as if she could understand everything. He was careful only to be kind—he was as kind as he had been to Isabel herself at Gardencourt. A girl might well be touched by that; she remembered how she herself had been touched, and said to herself that if she had been as simple as Pansy, the impression would have been deeper still. She had not been simple when she refused him; that operation had been as complicated, as, later, her acceptance of Osmond. Pansy, however, in spite of *her* simplicity, really did understand, and was glad that Lord Warburton should talk to her, not about her partners and bouquets, but about the state of Italy, the condition of the peasantry, the famous grist-tax, the *pellagra,* his impressions of Roman society. She looked at him as she drew her needle through her tapestry, with sweet, attentive eyes, and when she lowered them she gave little quiet oblique glances at his person, his hands, his feet, his clothes, as if she were considering him. Even his person, Isabel might have reminded her, was better than Mr. Rosier's. But Isabel contented herself at such moments with wondering where this gentleman was; he came no more at all to the Palazzo Roccanera. It was surprising, as I say, the hold it had taken of her—the idea of assisting her husband to be pleased.

It was surprising for a variety of reasons, which I shall presently touch upon. On the evening I speak of, while Lord Warburton sat there, she had been on the point of taking the great step of going out of the room and leaving her companions alone. I say the great step, because it was in this light that Gilbert Osmond would have regarded it, and Isabel was trying as much as possible to take her husband's view. She succeeded after a fashion, but she did not succeed in coming to the point I mention. After all, she couldn't; something held her and made it impossible. It was not exactly that it would be base, insidious; for women as a general thing practice such maneuvers with a perfectly good conscience, and Isabel had all the qualities of her sex. It was a vague doubt that interposed—a sense that she was not quite sure. So she remained in the drawing room, and after a while Lord Warburton went off to his party, of which he promised to give Pansy a full account on the morrow. After he had gone, Isabel asked herself whether she had prevented something which would have happened if she had absented herself for a quarter of an hour; and then she exclaimed—always mentally—that when Lord Warburton wished her to go away he would easily find means to let her know it. Pansy said nothing whatever about him after he had gone, and Isabel said nothing, as she had taken a vow of reserve until after he should have declared himself. He was a little longer in coming to this than might seem to accord with the description he had given Isabel of his feelings. Pansy went to bed, and Isabel had to admit that she could not now guess what her step-daughter was thinking of. Her transparent little companion was for the moment rather opaque.

Isabel remained alone, looking at the fire, until, at the end of half-an-hour, her husband came in. He moved about a while in silence, and then sat down, looking at the fire like herself. But Isabel now had transferred her eyes from the flickering flame in the chimney to Osmond's face, and she watched him while he sat silent. Covert observation had become a habit with her; an instinct, of which it is not an exaggeration to say that it was allied to that of self-defence, had made it habitual. She wished as much as possible to know his thoughts, to know what he would say, beforehand, so that she might prepare her answer. Preparing answers had not been her strong point of old; she had rarely in this respect got further than thinking afterwards of clever things she might have said. But she had learned caution—learned it in a measure from her husband's very countenance. It was the same face she had looked into with eyes equally earnest perhaps, but less penetrating, on the terrace of a Florentine villa; except that Osmond had grown a little stouter since his marriage. He still, however, looked very distinguished.

"Has Lord Warburton been here?" he presently asked.

"Yes, he stayed for half-an-hour."

"Did he see Pansy?"

"Yes; he sat on the sofa beside her."

"Did he talk with her much?"

"He talked almost only to her."

"It seems to me he's attentive. Isn't that what you call it?"

"I don't call it anything," said Isabel; "I have waited for you to give it a name."

"That's a consideration you don't always show," Osmond answered, after a moment.

"I have determined, this time, to try and act as you would like. I have so often failed in that."

Osmond turned his head, slowly, looking at her.

"Are you trying to quarrel with me?"

"No, I am trying to live at peace."

"Nothing is more easy; you know I don't quarrel myself."

"What do you call it when you try to make me angry?" Isabel asked.

"I don't try; if I have done so, it has been the most natural thing in the world. Moreover, I am not in the least trying now."

Isabel smiled. "It doesn't matter. I have determined never to be angry again."

"That's an excellent resolve. Your temper isn't good."

"No—it's not good." She pushed away the book she had been reading, and took up the band of tapestry that Pansy had left on the table.

"That's partly why I have not spoken to you about this business of my daughter's," Osmond said, designating Pansy in the manner that was most frequent with him. "I was afraid I should encounter opposition—that you too would have views on the subject. I have sent little Rosier about his business."

"You were afraid that I would plead for Mr. Rosier? Haven't you noticed that I have never spoken to you of him?"

"I have never given you a chance. We have so little conversation in these days. I know he was an old friend of yours."

"Yes; he's an old friend of mine." Isabel cared little more for him than for the tapestry that she held in her hand; but it was true that he was an old friend, and with her husband she felt a desire not to extenuate such ties. He had a way of expressing contempt for them which fortified her loyalty to them, even when, as in the present case, they were in themselves insignificant. She sometimes felt a sort of passion of tenderness for memories which had no other merit than that they belonged to her unmarried life. "But as regards Pansy," she added in a moment, "I have given him no encouragement."

"That's fortunate," Osmond observed.

"Fortunate for me, I suppose you mean. For him it matters little."

"There is no use talking of him," Osmond said. "As I tell you, I have turned him out."

"Yes; but a lover outside is always a lover. He is sometimes even more of one. Mr. Rosier still has hope."

"He's welcome to the comfort of it! My daughter has only to sit still, to become Lady Warburton."

"Should you like that?" Isabel asked, with a simplicity which was not so affected as it may appear. She was resolved to assume nothing, for Osmond had a way of unexpectedly turning her assumptions against her. The intensity with which he would like his daughter to become Lady Warburton had been the very basis of her own recent reflections. But that was for herself; she would recognize nothing until Osmond should have put it into words; she would not take for granted with him that he thought Lord Warburton a prize worth an amount of effort that was unusual among the Osmonds. It was Gilbert's constant intimation that, for him, nothing was a prize; that he treated as from equal to equal with the most distinguished people in the world, and that his daughter had only to look about her to pick out a prince. It cost him therefore a lapse from consistency to say explicitly that he yearned for Lord Warburton, that if this nobleman should escape, his equivalent might not be found; and it was another of his customary implications that he was never inconsistent. He would have liked his wife to glide over the point. But strangely enough, now that she was face to face with him, though an hour before she had almost invented a scheme for pleasing him, Isabel was not accommodating, would not glide. And yet she knew exactly the effect on his mind of her question: it would operate as a humiliation. Never mind; he was terribly capable of humiliating her—all the more so that he was also capable of waiting for great opportunities and of showing, sometimes, an almost unaccountable indifference to small ones. Isabel perhaps took a small opportunity because she would not have availed herself of a great one.

Osmond at present acquitted himself very honorably. "I should like it extremely; it would be a great marriage. And then Lord Warburton has another advantage; he is an old friend of yours. It would be pleasant for him to come into the family. It is very singular that Pansy's admirers should all be your old friends."

"It is natural that they should come to see me. In coming to see me, they see Pansy. Seeing her, it is natural that they should fall in love with her."

"So I think. But you are not bound to do so."

"If she should marry Lord Warburton, I should be very glad," Isabel went on, frankly. "He's an excellent man. You say, however, that she has only to sit still. Perhaps she won't sit still; if she loses Mr. Rosier she may jump up!"

Osmond appeared to give no heed to this; he sat gazing at the fire. "Pansy would like to be a great lady," he remarked in a moment, with a certain tenderness of tone. "She wishes, above all, to please," he added.

"To please Mr. Rosier, perhaps."

"No, to please me."

"Me too a little, I think," said Isabel.

"Yes, she has a great opinion of you. But she will do what I like."

"If you are sure of that, it's very well," Isabel said.

"Meantime," said Osmond, "I should like our distinguished visitor to speak."

"He has spoken—to me. He has told me that it would be a great pleasure to him to believe she could care for him."

Osmond turned his head quickly; but at first he said nothing. Then—"Why didn't you tell me that?" he asked, quickly.

"There was no opportunity. You know how we live. I have taken the first chance that has offered."

"Did you speak to him of Rosier?"

"Oh yes, a little."

"That was hardly necessary."

"I thought it best he should know, so that, so that—" And Isabel paused.

"So that what?"

"So that he should act accordingly."

"So that he should back out, do you mean?"

"No, so that he should advance while there is yet time."

"That is not the effect it seems to have had."

"You should have patience," said Isabel. "You know Englishmen are shy."

"This one is not. He was not when he made love to you."

She had been afraid Osmond would speak of that; it was disagreeable to her. "I beg your pardon; he was extremely so," she said simply.

He answered nothing for some time; he took up a book and turned over the pages, while Isabel sat silent, occupying herself with Pansy's tapestry. "You must have a great deal of influence with him," Osmond went on at last. "The moment you really wish it, you can bring him to the point."

This was more disagreeable still; but Isabel felt it to be natural that her husband should say it, and it was after all something very much of the same sort that she had said to herself. "Why should I have influence?" she asked. "What have I ever done to put him under an obligation to me?"

"You refused to marry him," said Osmond, with his eyes on his book.

"I must not presume too much on that," Isabel answered, gently.

He threw down the book presently, and got up, standing before the fire with his hands behind him. "Well," he said, "I hold that it lies in your hands. I shall leave it there. With a little good-will you may manage it. Think that over and remember that I count upon you."

He waited a little, to give her time to answer; but she answered nothing, and he presently strolled out of the room.

42

She answered nothing, because his words had put the situation before her, and she was absorbed in looking at it. There was something in them that suddenly opened the door to agitation, so that she was afraid to trust herself to speak. After Osmond had gone, she leaned back in her chair and closed her eyes; and for a long time, far into the night, and still further, she sat in the silent drawing room, given up to her meditation. A servant came in to attend to the fire, and she bade him bring fresh candles and then go to bed. Osmond had told her to think of what he had said; and she did so indeed, and of many other things. The suggestion, from another, that she had a peculiar influence on Lord Warburton, had given her the start that accompanies unexpected recognition. Was it true that there was something still between them that might be a handle to make him declare himself to Pansy—a susceptibility, on his part, to approval, a desire to do what would please her? Isabel had hitherto not asked herself the question, because she had not been forced; but now that it was directly presented to her, she saw the answer, and the answer frightened her. Yes, there was something—something on Lord Warburton's part. When he first came to Rome she believed that the link which united them had completely snapped; but little by little she had been reminded that it still had a palpable existence. It was as thin as a hair, but there were moments when she seemed to hear it vibrate. For herself, nothing was changed; what she once thought of Lord Warburton she still thought; it was needless that feeling should change; on the contrary, it seemed to her a better feeling than ever. But he? had he still the idea that she might be more to him than other women? Had he the wish to profit by the memory of the few moments of intimacy through which they had once passed? Isabel knew that she had read some of the signs of such a disposition. But what were his hopes, his pretensions, and in what strange way were they mingled with his evidently very sincere appreciation of poor Pansy? Was he in love with Gilbert Osmond's wife, and if so, what comfort did he expect to derive from it? If he was in love with Pansy, he was not in love with her step-mother; and if he was in love with her step-mother, he was not in love with Pansy. Was she to cultivate the advantage she possessed, in order to make him commit himself to Pansy, knowing that he would do so for her sake, and not for the young girl's—was this the service her husband had asked of her? This at any rate was the duty with which Isabel found herself confronted from the moment that she admitted to herself that Lord Warburton had still an uneradicated predilection for her society. It was not an agreeable task; it was, in fact, a repulsive one. She asked herself with dismay whether Lord Warburton were pretending to be in love with Pansy in order to cultivate another satisfaction. Of this refinement of duplicity she presently acquitted him; she preferred to believe that he was in good faith. But if his admiration for Pansy was a delusion, this was scarcely better than its being an affectation. Isabel wandered among these ugly possibilities until she completely lost her way; some of them, as she suddenly encountered them, seemed ugly enough. Then she broke out of the labyrinth, rubbing her eyes, and declared that her imagination surely did her little honor, and that her husband's did him even less. Lord Warburton was as disinterested as he need be, and she was no more to him than she need wish. She would rest upon this until the contrary should be proved; proved more effectually than by a cynical intimation of Osmond's.

Such a resolution, however, brought her this evening but little peace, for her soul was haunted with terrors which crowded to the foreground of thought as quickly as a place was made for them. What had suddenly set them into livelier motion she hardly knew, unless it were the strange impression she had received in the afternoon of her husband and Madame Merle being in more direct communication than she suspected. This impression came back to her from time to time, and now she wondered that it had never come before. Besides this, her short interview with Osmond, half-an-hour before, was a striking example of his faculty for making everything wither that he touched, spoiling everything for her that he looked at. It was very well to undertake to give him a proof of loyalty; the real fact was that the knowledge of his expecting a thing raised a presumption against it. It was as if he had had the evil eye; as if his presence were a blight and his favor a misfortune. Was the fault in himself, or only in the deep mistrust she had conceived for him? This mistrust was the clearest result of their short married life; a gulf had opened between them over which they looked at each other with eyes that were on either side a declaration of the deception suffered. It was a strange opposition, of the like of which she had never dreamed—an opposition in which the vital principle of the one was a thing of contempt to the other. It was not her fault—she had practiced no deception; she had only admired and believed. She had taken all the first steps in the purest confidence, and then she had suddenly found the infinite vista of a multiplied life to be a dark, narrow alley, with a dead wall at the end. Instead of leading to the high places of happiness, from which the world would seem to lie below one, so that one could look down with a sense of exaltation and advantage, and judge and choose and pity, it led rather downward and earthward, into realms of restriction and depression, where the sound of other lives, easier and freer, was heard as from above, and served to deepen the feeling of failure. It was her deep distrust of her husband—this was what darkened the world. That is a sentiment easily indicated, but not so easily explained, and so composite in its character that much time and still more suffering had been needed to bring it to its actual perfection. Suffering, with Isabel, was an active condition; it was not a chill, a stupor, a despair; it was a passion of thought, of speculation, of response to every pressure. She flattered herself, however, that she had kept her failing faith to herself—that no one suspected it but Osmond. Oh, he knew it, and there were times when she thought that he enjoyed it. It had come gradually—it was not till the first year of her marriage had closed that she took the alarm. Then the shadows began to gather; it was as if Osmond deliberately, almost malignantly, had put the lights out one by one. The dusk at first was vague and thin, and she could still see her way in it. But it steadily increased, and if here and there it had occasionally lifted, there were certain corners of her life that were impenetrably black. These shadows were not an emanation from her own mind; she was very sure of that; she had done her best to be just and temperate, to see only the truth. They were a part of her husband's very presence. They were not his misdeeds, his turpitudes; she accused him of nothing—that is, of but one thing, which was not a crime. She knew of no wrong that he had done; he was not violent, he was not cruel; she simply believed that he hated her. That was all she accused him of, and the miserable part of it was precisely that it was not a crime, for against a crime she might have found redress. He had discovered that she was so different, that she was not what he had believed she would prove to be. He had thought at first he could change her, and she had done her best to be what he would like. But she was, after all, herself—she couldn't help that; and now there was no use pretending, playing a part, for he knew her and he had made up his mind. She was not afraid of him; she had no apprehension that he would hurt her; for the ill-will he bore her was not of that sort. He would, if possible, never give her a pretext, never put himself in the wrong. Isabel, scanning the future with dry, fixed eyes, saw that he would have the better of her there. She would give him many pretexts, she would often put herself in the wrong. There were times when she almost pitied him; for if she had not deceived him in intention she understood how completely she must have done so in fact. She had effaced herself, when he first knew her; she had made herself small, pretending there was less of her than there really was. It was because she had been under the extraordinary charm that he, on his side, had taken pains to put forth. He was not changed; he had not disguised himself, during the year of his courtship, any more than she. But she had seen only half his nature then, as one saw the disk of the moon when it was partly masked by the shadow of the earth. She saw the full moon now—she saw the whole man. She had kept still, as it were, so that he should have a free field, and yet in spite of this she had mistaken a part for the whole.

Ah, she had him immensely under the charm! It had not passed away; it was there still; she still knew perfectly what it was that made Osmond delightful when he chose to be. He had wished to be when he made love to her, and as she had wished to be charmed it was not wonderful that he succeeded. He succeeded because he was sincere; it never occurred to her to deny him that. He admired her—he had told her why; because she was the most imaginative woman he had known. It might very well have been true; for during those months she had imagined a world of things that had no substance. She had a vision of him—she had not read him right. A certain combination of features had touched her, and in them she had seen the most striking of portraits. That he was poor and lonely, and yet that somehow he was noble—that was what interested her and seemed to give her her opportunity. There was an indefinable beauty about him—in his situation, in his mind, in his face. She had felt at the same time that he was helpless and ineffectual, but the feeling had taken the form of a tenderness which was the very flower of respect. He was like a skeptical voyager, strolling on the beach while he waited for the tide, looking seaward yet not putting to sea. It was in all this that she found her occasion. She would launch his boat for him; she would be his providence; it would be a good thing to love him. And she loved him—a good deal for what she found in him, but a good deal also for what she brought him. As she looked back at the passion of those weeks she perceived in it a kind of maternal strain—the happiness of a woman who felt that she was a contributor, that she came with full hands. But for her money, as she saw today, she wouldn't have done it. And then her mind wandered off to poor Mr. Touchett, sleeping under English turf, the beneficent author of infinite woe! For this was a fact. At bottom her money had been a burden, had been on her mind, which was filled with the desire to transfer the weight of it to some other conscience. What would lighten her own conscience more effectually than to make it over to the man who had the best taste in the world? Unless she should give it to a hospital, there was nothing better she could do with it; and there was no charitable institution in which she was as much interested as in Gilbert Osmond. He would use her fortune in a way that would make her think better of it, and rub off a certain grossness which attached to the good luck of an unexpected inheritance. There had been nothing very delicate in inheriting seventy thousand pounds; the delicacy had been all in Mr. Touchett's leaving them to her. But to marry Gilbert Osmond and bring him such a portion—in that there would be delicacy for her as well. There would be less for him—that was true; but that was his affair, and if he loved her he would not object to her being rich. Had he not had the courage to say he was glad she was rich?

Isabel's cheek tingled when she asked herself if she had really married on a factitious theory, in order to do something finely appreciable with her money. But she was able to answer quickly enough that this was only half the story. It was because a certain feeling took possession of her—a sense of the earnestness of his affection and a delight in his personal qualities. He was better than anyone else. This supreme conviction had filled her life for months, and enough of it still remained to prove to her that she could not have done otherwise. The finest individual she had ever known was hers; the simple knowledge was a sort of act of devotion. She had not been mistaken about the beauty of his mind; she knew that organ perfectly now. She had lived with it, she had lived in it almost—it appeared to have become her habitation. If she had been captured, it had taken a firm hand to do it; that reflection perhaps had some worth. A mind more ingenious, more subtle, more cultivated, more trained to admirable exercises, she had not encountered; and it was this exquisite instrument that she had now to reckon with. She lost herself in infinite dismay when she thought of the magnitude of *his* deception. It was a wonder, perhaps, in view of this, that he didn't hate her more. She remembered perfectly the first sign he had given of it—it had been like the bell that was to ring up the curtain upon the real drama of their life. He said to her one day that she had too many ideas, and that she must get rid of them. He had told her that already, before their marriage; but then she had not noticed it; it came back to her only afterwards. This time she might well notice it, because he had really meant it. The words were nothing, superficially; but when in the light of deepening experience she looked into them, they appeared portentous. He really meant it—he would have liked her to have nothing of her own but her pretty appearance. She knew she had too many ideas; she had more even than he supposed, many more than she had expressed to him when he asked her to marry him. Yes, she *had* been hypocritical; she liked him so much. She had too many ideas for herself; but that was just what one married for, to share them with someone else. One couldn't pluck them up by the roots, though of course one might suppress them, be careful not to utter them. It was not that, however, his objecting to her opinions; that was nothing. She had no opinions— none that she would not have been eager to sacrifice in the satisfaction of feeling herself loved for it. What he meant was the whole thing—her character, the way she felt, the way she judged. This was what she had kept in reserve; this was what he had not known until he found himself—with the door closed behind, as it were—set down face to face with it. She had a certain way of looking at life which he took as a personal offence. Heaven knew that, now at least, it was a very humble, accommodating way! The strange thing was that she should not have suspected from the first that his own was so different. She had thought it so large, so enlight- ened, so perfectly that of an honest man and a gentleman. Had not he assured her that he had no superstitions, no dull limitations, no prejudices that had lost their freshness? Hadn't he all the appearance of a man living in the open air of the world, indifferent to small considerations, caring only for truth and knowledge, and believing that two intelligent people ought to look for them together, and whether they found them or not, to find at least some happiness in the search? He had told her that he loved the conventional; but there was a sense in which this seemed a noble declaration. In that sense, the love of harmony, and order, and decency, and all the stately offices of life, she went with him freely, and his warning had con- tained nothing ominous. But when, as the months elapsed, she followed him fur- ther and he led her into the mansion of his own habitation, then, then she had seen where she really was. She could live it over again, the incredulous terror with which she had taken the measure of her dwelling. Between those four walls she had lived ever since; they were to surround her for the rest of her life. It was the house of darkness, the house of dumbness, the house of suffocation. Osmond's beautiful mind gave it neither light nor air; Osmond's beautiful mind, indeed, seemed to peep down from a small high window and mock at her. Of course it was not physical suf- fering; for physical suffering there might have been a remedy. She could come and go; she had her liberty; her husband was perfectly polite. He took himself so seri- ously; it was something appalling. Under all his culture, his cleverness, his amenity, under his good-nature, his facility, his knowledge of life, his egotism lay hidden like a serpent in a bank of flowers. She had taken him seriously, but she had not taken him so seriously as that. How could she—especially when she knew him better? She was to think of him as he thought of himself—as the first gentleman in Europe. So it was that she had thought of him at first, and that indeed was the reason she had married him. But when she began to see what it implied, she drew back; there was more in the bond than she had meant to put her name to. It implied a sovereign contempt for everyone but some three or four very exalted people whom he envied, and for everything in the world but half-a-dozen ideas of his own. That was very well; she would have gone with him even there, a long distance; for he pointed out to her so much of the baseness and shabbiness of life, opened her eyes so wide to the stupidity, the depravity, the ignorance of mankind, that she had been properly impressed with the infinite vulgarity of things, and of the virtue of keeping one's self unspotted by it. But this base, ignoble world, it appeared, was after all what one was to live for; one was to keep it forever in one's eye, in order, not to enlighten, or convert, or redeem it, but to extract from it some recognition of one's own superiority. On the one hand it was despicable, but on the other it afforded a standard. Osmond had talked to Isabel about his renunciation, his indifference, the ease with which he dispensed with the usual aids to success; and all this had seemed to her admirable. She had thought it a noble indifference, an exquisite independence. But indifference was really the last of his qualities; she had never seen anyone who thought so much of others. For herself, the world had always interested her, and the study of her fellow-creatures was her constant passion. She would have been willing, however, to renounce all her curiosities and sympathies for the sake of a personal life, if the person concerned had only been able to make her believe it was a gain! This, at least, was her present conviction; and the thing certainly would have been easier than to care for society as Osmond cared for it.

He was unable to live without it, and she saw that he had never really done so; he had looked at it out of his window even when he appeared to be most detached from it. He had his ideal, just as she had tried to have hers; only it was strange that people should seek for justice in such different quarters. His ideal was a conception of high prosperity and propriety, of the aristocratic life, which she now saw that Osmond deemed himself always, in essence at least, to have led. He had never lapsed from it for an hour; he would never have recovered from the shame of doing so. That again was very well; here too she would have agreed; but they attached such different ideas, such different associations and desires, to the same formulas. Her notion of the aristocratic life was simply the union of great knowledge with great liberty; the knowledge would give one a sense of duty, and the liberty a sense of enjoyment. But for Osmond it was altogether a thing of forms, a conscious, cal-culated attitude. He was fond of the old, the consecrated, and transmitted; so was she, but she pretended to do what she chose with it. He had an immense esteem for tradition; he had told her once that the best thing in the world was to have it, but that if one was so unfortunate as not to have it, one must immediately proceed to make it. She knew that he meant by this that she hadn't it, but that he was better off; though where he had got his traditions she never learned. He had a very large collection of them, however; that was very certain; after a little she began to see.

The great thing was to act in accordance with them; the great thing not only for him but for her. Isabel had an undefined conviction that, to serve for another person than their proprietor, traditions must be of a thoroughly superior kind; but she nevertheless assented to this intimation that she too must march to the stately music that floated down from unknown periods in her husband's past; she who of old had been so free of step, so desultory, so devious, so much the reverse of processional. There were certain things they must do, a certain posture they must take, certain people they must know and not know. When Isabel saw this rigid system closing about her, draped though it was in pictured tapestries, that sense of darkness and suffocation of which I have spoken took possession of her; she seemed to be shut up with an odor of mold and decay. She had resisted, of course; at first very humorously, ironically, tenderly; then as the situation grew more serious, eagerly, passionately, pleadingly. She had pleaded the cause of freedom, of doing as they chose, of not caring for the aspect and denomination of their life—the cause of other instincts and longings, of quite another ideal. Then it was that her husband's personality, touched as it never had been, stepped forth and stood erect. The things that she had said were answered only by his scorn, and she could see that he was ineffably ashamed of her. What did he think of her—that she was base, vulgar, ignoble? He at least knew now that she had no traditions! It had not been in his prevision of things that she should reveal such flatness; her sentiments were worthy of a radical newspaper or of a Unitarian preacher. The real offense, as she ultimately perceived, was her having a mind of her own at all. Her mind was to be his—attached to his own like a small garden plot to a deer-park. He would rake the soil gently and water the flowers; he would weed the beds and gather an occasional nosegay. It would be a pretty piece of property for a proprietor already far-reaching. He didn't wish her to be stupid. On the contrary, it was because she was clever that she had pleased him. But he expected her intelligence to operate altogether in his favor, and so far from desiring her mind to be a blank, he had flattered himself that it would be richly receptive. He had expected his wife to feel with him and for him, to enter into his opinions, his ambitions, his preferences; and Isabel was obliged to confess that this was no very unwarrantable demand on the part of a husband. But there were certain things she could never take in. To begin with, they were hideously unclean. She was not a daughter of the Puritans, but for all that she believed in such a thing as purity. It would appear that Osmond didn't; some of his traditions made her push back her skirts. Did all women have lovers? Did they all lie, and even the best have their price? Were there only three or four that didn't deceive their husbands? When Isabel heard such things she felt a greater scorn for them than for the gossip of a village-parlor—a scorn that kept its freshness in a very tainted air. There was the taint of her sister-in-law; did her husband judge only by the Countess Gemini? This lady very often lied, and she had practiced decep-

THE PORTRAIT OF A LADY

tions which were not simply verbal. It was enough to find these facts assumed among Osmond's traditions, without giving them such a general extension. It was her scorn of his assumptions—it was that that made him draw himself up. He had plenty of contempt, and it was proper that his wife should be as well furnished; but that she should turn the hot light of her disdain upon his own conception of things—this was a danger he had not allowed for. He believed he should have regulated her emotions before she came to that; and Isabel could easily imagine how his ears scorched when he discovered that he had been too confident. When one had a wife who gave one that sensation there was nothing left but to hate her!

She was morally certain now that this feeling of hatred, which at first had been a refuge and a refreshment, had become the occupation and comfort of Osmond's life. The feeling was deep, because it was sincere; he had had a revelation that, after all, she could dispense with him. If to herself the idea was startling, if it presented itself at first as a kind of infidelity, a capacity for pollution, what infinite effect might it not be expected to have had upon him? It was very simple; he despised her; she had no traditions, and the moral horizon of a Unitarian minister. Poor Isabel, who had never been able to understand Unitarianism! This was the conviction that she had been living with now for a time that she had ceased to measure. What was coming—what was before them? That was her constant question. What would he do—what ought she to do? When a man hated his wife, what did it lead to? She didn't hate him, that she was sure of, for every little while she felt a passionate wish to give him a pleasant surprise. Very often, however, she felt afraid, and it used to come over her, as I have intimated, that she had deceived him at the very first. They were strangely married, at all events, and it was an awful life. Until that morning he had scarcely spoken to her for a week; his manner was as dry as a burned-out fire. She knew there was a special reason; he was displeased at Ralph Touchett's staying on in Rome. He thought she saw too much of her cousin—he had told her a week before that it was indecent she should go to him at his hotel. He would have said more than this if Ralph's invalid state had not appeared to make it brutal to denounce him; but having to contain himself only deepened Osmond's disgust. Isabel read all this as she would have read the hour on the clock-face; she was as perfectly aware that the sight of her interest in her cousin stirred her husband's rage, as if Osmond had locked her into her bedroom—which she was sure he wanted to do. It was her honest belief that on the whole she was not defiant; but she certainly could not pretend to be indifferent to Ralph. She believed he was dying, at last, and that she should never see him again, and this gave her a tenderness for him that she had never known before. Nothing was a pleasure to her now; how could anything be a pleasure to a woman who knew that she had thrown away her life? There was an everlasting weight upon her heart—there was a livid light upon everything. But Ralph's little visit was a lamp in the darkness; for the hour

that she sat with him her spirit rose. She felt today as if he had been her brother.
She had never had a brother, but if she had, and she were in trouble, and he were
dying, he would be dear to her as Ralph was. Ah yes, if Gilbert was jealous of her
there was perhaps some reason; it didn't make Gilbert look better to sit for half-an-
hour with Ralph. It was not that they talked of him—it was not that she complained. His name was never uttered between them. It was simply that Ralph was
generous and that her husband was not. There was something in Ralph's talk, in his
smile, in the mere fact of his being in Rome, that made the blasted circle round
which she walked more spacious. He made her feel the good of the world; he made
her feel what might have been. He was, after all, as intelligent as Osmond—quite
apart from his being better. And thus it seemed to her an act of devotion to conceal
her misery from him. She concealed it elaborately; in their talk she was perpetually
hanging out curtains and arranging screens. It lived before her again—it had never
had time to die—that morning in the garden at Florence, when he warned her
against Osmond. She had only to close her eyes to see the place, to hear his voice,
to feel the warm, sweet air. How could he have known? What a mystery! what a wonder of wisdom! As intelligent as Gilbert? He was much more intelligent, to arrive at
such a judgment as that. Gilbert had never been so deep, so just. She had told him
then that from her at least he should never know if he was right; and this was what
she was taking care of now. It gave her plenty to do; there was passion, exaltation,
religion in it. Women find their religion sometimes in strange exercises, and Isabel,
at present, in playing a part before her cousin, had an idea that she was doing him
a kindness. It would have been a kindness, perhaps, if he had been for a single
instant a dupe. As it was, the kindness consisted mainly in trying to make him
believe that he had once wounded her greatly and that the event had put him to
shame, but that as she was very generous and he was so ill, she bore him no grudge
and even considerately forbore to flaunt her happiness in his face. Ralph smiled to
himself, as he lay on his sofa, at this extraordinary form of consideration; but he forgave her for having forgiven him. She didn't wish him to have the pain of knowing
she was unhappy; that was the great thing, and it didn't matter that such knowledge would rather have righted him.

For herself, she lingered in the soundless drawing room long after the fire had
gone out. There was no danger of her feeling the cold; she was in a fever. She heard
the small hours strike, and then the great ones, but her vigil took no heed of time.
Her mind, assailed by visions, was in a state of extraordinary activity, and her
visions might as well come to her there, where she sat up to meet them, as on her
pillow, to make a mockery of rest. As I have said, she believed she was not defiant,
and what could be a better proof of it than that she should linger there half the
night, trying to persuade herself that there was no reason why Pansy shouldn't be
married as you would put a letter in the post-office? When the clock struck four she

got up; she was going to bed at last, for the lamp had long since gone out and the candles had burned down to their sockets. But even then she stopped again in the middle of the room, and stood there gazing at a remembered vision—that of her husband and Madame Merle, grouped unconsciously and familiarly.

❧ 43 ❧

Three nights after this she took Pansy to a great party, to which Osmond, who never went to dances, did not accompany them. Pansy was as ready for a dance as ever; she was not of a generalizing turn, and she had not extended to other pleasures the interdict that she had seen placed on those of love. If she was biding her time or hoping to circumvent her father, she must have had a prevision of success. Isabel thought that this was not likely; it was much more likely that Pansy had simply determined to be a good girl. She had never had such a chance, and she had a proper esteem for chances. She carried herself no less attentively than usual, and kept no less anxious an eye upon her vaporous skirts; she held her bouquet very tight, and counted over the flowers for the twentieth time. She made Isabel feel old; it seemed so long since she had been in a flutter about a ball. Pansy, who was greatly admired, was never in want of partners, and very soon after their arrival she gave Isabel, who was not dancing, her bouquet to hold. Isabel had rendered this service for some minutes when she became aware that Edward Rosier was standing before her. He had lost his affable smile, and wore a look of almost military resolution; the change in his appearance would have made Isabel smile if she had not felt that at bottom his case was a hard one; he had always smelt so much more of heliotrope than of gunpowder. He looked at her a moment somewhat fiercely, as if to notify her that he was dangerous, and then he dropped his eyes on her bouquet. After he had inspected it his glance softened, and he said quickly,

"It's all pansies; it must be hers!"

Isabel smiled kindly.

"Yes, it's hers; she gave it to me to hold."

"May I hold it a little, Mrs. Osmond?" the poor young man asked.

"No, I can't trust you; I am afraid you wouldn't give it back."

"I am not sure that I should; I should leave the house with it instantly. But may I not at least have a single flower?"

Isabel hesitated a moment, and then, smiling still, held out the bouquet.

"Choose one yourself. It's frightful what I am doing for you."

"Ah, if you do no more than this, Mrs. Osmond!" Rosier exclaimed, with his glass in one eye, carefully choosing his flower.

"Don't put it into your button-hole," she said. "Don't for the world!"

"I should like her to see it. She has refused to dance with me, but I wish to show her that I believe in her still."

"It's very well to show it to her, but it's out of place to show it to others. Her father has told her not to dance with you."

"And is that all *you* can do for me? I expected more from you, Mrs. Osmond," said the young man, in a tone of fine general reference. "You know that our acquaintance goes back very far—quite into the days of our innocent childhood."

"Don't make me out too old," Isabel answered, smiling. "You come back to that very often, and I have never denied it. But I must tell you that, old friends as we are, if you had done me the honor to ask me to marry you I should have refused you."

"Ah, you don't esteem me, then. Say at once that you think I'm a trifler!"

"I esteem you very much, but I'm not in love with you. What I mean by that, of course, is that I am not in love with you for Pansy."

"Very good; I see; you pity me, that's all."

And Edward Rosier looked all round, inconsequently, with his single glass. It was a revelation to him that people shouldn't be more pleased; but he was at least too proud to show that the movement struck him as general.

Isabel for a moment said nothing. His manner and appearance had not the dignity of the deepest tragedy; his little glass, among other things, was against that. But she suddenly felt touched; her own unhappiness, after all, had something in common with his, and it came over her, more than before, that here, in recognizable, if not in romantic form, was the most affecting thing in the world—young love struggling with adversity.

"Would you really be very kind to her?" she said, in a low tone.

He dropped his eyes, devoutly, and raised the little flower which he held in his fingers to his lips. Then he looked at her. "You pity me; but don't you pity her a little?"

"I don't know; I am not sure. She will always enjoy life."

"It will depend on what you call life!" Rosier exclaimed. "She won't enjoy being tortured."

"There will be nothing of that."

"I am glad to hear it. She knows what she is about. You will see."

"I think she does, and she will never disobey her father. But she is coming back to me," Isabel added, "and I must beg you to go away."

Rosier lingered a moment, till Pansy came in sight, on the arm of her cavalier; he stood just long enough to look her in the face. Then he walked away, holding up his head; and the manner in which he achieved this sacrifice to expediency convinced Isabel that he was very much in love.

Pansy, who seldom got disarranged in dancing, and looked perfectly fresh and cool after this exercise, waited a moment and then took back her bouquet. Isabel watched her and saw that she was counting the flowers; whereupon she said to herself that, decidedly, there were deeper forces at play than she had recognized. Pansy had seen Rosier turn away, but she said nothing to Isabel about him; she talked only of her partner, after he had made his bow and retired; of the music, the floor, the rare misfortune of having already torn her dress. Isabel was sure, however, that she perceived that her lover had abstracted a flower; though this knowledge was not needed to account for the dutiful grace with which she responded to the appeal of her next partner. That perfect amenity under acute constraint was part of a larger system. She was again led forth by a flushed young man, this time carrying her bouquet; and she had not been absent many minutes when Isabel saw Lord Warburton advancing through the crowd. He presently drew near and bade her good evening; she had not seen him since the day before. He looked about him, and then—"Where is the little maid?" he asked. It was in this manner that he formed the harmless habit of alluding to Miss Osmond.

"She is dancing," said Isabel; "you will see her somewhere."

He looked among the dancers, and at last caught Pansy's eye. "She sees me, but she won't notice me," he then remarked. "Are you not dancing?"

"As you see, I'm a wall-flower."

"Won't you dance with me?"

"Thank you; I would rather you should dance with my little maid."

"One needn't prevent the other; especially as she is engaged."

"She is not engaged for everything, and you can reserve yourself. She dances very hard, and you will be the fresher."

"She dances beautifully," said Lord Warburton, following her with his eyes. "Ah, at last," he added, "she has given me a smile." He stood there with his handsome, easy, important physiognomy; and as Isabel observed him it came over her, as it had done before, that it was strange a man of his importance should take an interest in a little maid. It struck her as a great incongruity; neither Pansy's small fascinations, nor his own kindness, his good-nature, not even his need for amusement, which was extreme and constant, were sufficient to account for it. "I shall like to dance with you," he went on in a moment, turning back to Isabel; "but I think I like even better to talk with you."

"Yes, it's better, and it's more worthy of your dignity. Great statesmen oughtn't to waltz."

"Don't be cruel. Why did you recommend me then to dance with Miss Osmond?"

"Ah, that's different. If you dance with her, it would look simply like a piece of kindness—as if you were doing it for her amusement. If you dance with me you will look as if you were doing it for your own."

"And pray haven't I a right to amuse myself?"

"No, not with the affairs of the British Empire on your hands."

"The British Empire be hanged! You are always laughing at it."

"Amuse yourself with talking to me," said Isabel.

"I am not sure that is a recreation. You are too pointed; I have always to be defending myself. And you strike me as more than usually dangerous tonight. Won't you really dance?"

"I can't leave my place. Pansy must find me here."

He was silent a moment. "You are wonderfully good to her," he said, suddenly.

Isabel stared a little, and smiled. "Can you imagine one's not being?"

"No, indeed. I know how one cares for her. But you must have done a great deal for her."

"I have taken her out with me," said Isabel, smiling still. "And I have seen that she has proper clothes."

"Your society must have been a great benefit to her. You have talked to her, advised her, helped her to develop."

"Ah, yes, if she isn't the rose, she has lived near it."

Isabel laughed, and her companion smiled; but there was a certain visible preoccupation in his face which interfered with complete hilarity. "We all try to live as near it as we can," he said, after a moment's hesitation.

Isabel turned away; Pansy was about to be restored to her, and she welcomed the diversion. We know how much she liked Lord Warburton; she thought him delightful; there was something in his friendship which appeared a kind of resource in case of indefinite need; it was like having a large balance at the bank. She felt happier when he was in the room; there was something reassuring in his approach; the sound of his voice reminded her of the beneficence of nature. Yet for all that it did not please her that he should be too near to her, that he should take too much of her good-will for granted. She was afraid of that; she averted herself from it; she wished he wouldn't. She felt that if he should come too near, as it were, it was in her to flash out and bid him keep his distance. Pansy came back to Isabel with another rent in her skirt, which was the inevitable consequence of the first, and which she displayed to Isabel with serious eyes. There were too many gentlemen in uniform; they wore those dreadful spurs, which were fatal to the dresses of young girls. It hereupon became apparent that the resources of women are innumerable. Isabel devoted herself to Pansy's desecrated drapery; she fumbled for a pin and repaired the injury; she smiled and listened to her account of her adventures. Her attention, her sympathy, were most active; and they were in direct proportion to a sentiment with which they were in no way connected—a lively conjecture as to whether Lord Warburton was trying to make love to her. It was not simply his words just then; it was others as well; it was the reference and the continuity. This was what she thought about while she pinned up Pansy's dress. If it were so, as she feared, he was of course unconscious; he himself had not taken account of his intention. But this made it none the more auspicious, made the situation none the less unacceptable. The sooner Lord Warburton should come to self-consciousness the better. He immediately began to talk to Pansy—on whom it was certainly mystifying to see that he dropped a smile of chastened devotion. Pansy replied as usual, with a little air of conscientious aspiration; he had to bend toward her a good deal in conversation, and her eyes, as usual, wandered up and down his robust person, as if he had offered it to her for exhibition. She always seemed a little frightened; yet her fright was not of the painful character that suggests dislike; on the contrary, she looked as if she knew that he knew that she liked him. Isabel left them together a little, and wandered toward a friend whom she saw near, and with whom she talked till the music of the following dance began, for which she knew that Pansy was also engaged. The young girl joined her presently, with a little fluttered look, and Isabel, who scrupulously took Osmond's view of his daughter's complete dependence, consigned her, as a precious and momentary loan, to her appointed partner. About all this matter she had her own imaginations, her own reserves; there were moments when Pansy's extreme adhesiveness made each of them, to her sense, look foolish. But Osmond had given her a sort of tableau of her position as his daughter's duenna, which consisted of gracious alternation of concession and contraction; and there were directions of his which she liked to think that she obeyed to the letter. Perhaps, as regards some of them, it was because her doing so appeared to reduce them to the absurd.

After Pansy had been led away, Isabel found Lord Warburton drawing near her again. She rested her eyes on him, steadily; she wished she could sound his thoughts. But he had no appearance of confusion.

"She has promised to dance with me later," he said.

"I am glad of that. I suppose you have engaged her for the cotillion."

At this he looked a little awkward. "No, I didn't ask her for that. It's a quadrille."

"Ah, you are not clever!" said Isabel, almost angrily. "I told her to keep the cotillion, in case you should ask for it."

"Poor little maid, fancy that!" And Lord Warburton laughed frankly. "Of course I will if you like."

"If I like? Oh, if you dance with her only because I like it!"

"I am afraid I bore her. She seems to have a lot of young fellows on her book."

Isabel dropped her eyes, reflecting rapidly; Lord Warburton stood there looking at her and she felt his eyes on her face. She felt much inclined to ask him to remove

them. She did not do so, however; she only said to him, after a minute, looking up—
"Please to let me understand."

"Understand what?"

"You told me ten days ago that you should like to marry my step-daughter. You have not forgotten it!"

"Forgotten it? I wrote to Mr. Osmond about it this morning."

"Ah," said Isabel, "he didn't mention to me that he had heard from you."

Lord Warburton stammered a little. "I—I didn't send my letter."

"Perhaps you forgot that."

"No, I wasn't satisfied with it. It's an awkward sort of letter to write, you know. But I shall send it tonight."

"At three o'clock in the morning?"

"I mean later, in the course of the day."

"Very good. You still wish, then, to marry her?"

"Very much indeed."

"Aren't you afraid that you will bore her?" And as her companion stared at this inquiry, Isabel added—"If she can't dance with you for half-an-hour, how will she be able to dance with you for life?"

"Ah," said Lord Warburton, readily, "I will let her dance with other people! About the cotillion, the fact is I thought that you—that you—"

"That I would dance with you? I told you I would dance nothing."

"Exactly; so that while it is going on I might find some quiet corner where we might sit down and talk."

"Oh," said Isabel gravely, "you are much too considerate of me."

When the cotillion came, Pansy was found to have engaged herself, thinking, in perfect humility, that Lord Warburton had no intentions. Isabel recommended him to seek another partner, but he assured her that he would dance with no one but herself. As, however, she had, in spite of the remonstrances of her hostess, declined other invitations on the ground that she was not dancing at all, it was not possible for her to make an exception in Lord Warburton's favor.

"After all, I don't care to dance," he said, "it's a barbarous amusement; I would much rather talk." And he intimated that he had discovered exactly the corner he had been looking for—a quiet nook in one of the smaller rooms, where the music would come to them faintly and not interfere with conversation. Isabel had decided to let him carry out his idea; she wished to be satisfied. She wandered away from the ballroom with him, though she knew that her husband desired she should not lose sight of his daughter. It was with his daughter's *prétendant*, however; that would make it right for Osmond. On her way out of the ballroom she came upon Edward Rosier, who was standing in a doorway, with folded arms, looking at the dance, in the attitude of a young man without illusions. She stopped a moment and asked him if he were not dancing.

"Certainly not, if I can't dance with her!" he answered.

"You had better go away, then," said Isabel, with the manner of good counsel.

"I shall not go till she does!" And he let Lord Warburton pass, without giving him a look.

This nobleman, however, had noticed the melancholy youth, and he asked Isabel who her dismal friend was, remarking that he had seen him somewhere before.

"It's the young man I have told you about, who is in love with Pansy," said Isabel.

"Ah yes, I remember. He looks rather bad."

"He has reason. My husband won't listen to him."

"What's the matter with him?" Lord Warburton inquired. "He seems very harmless."

"He hasn't money enough, and he isn't very clever."

Lord Warburton listened with interest; he seemed struck with this account of Edward Rosier. "Dear me; he looked a well-set-up young fellow."

"So he is, but my husband is very particular."

"Oh, I see." And Lord Warburton paused a moment. "How much money has he got?" he then ventured to ask.

"Some forty thousand francs a year."

"Sixteen hundred pounds? Ah, but that's very good, you know."

"So I think. But my husband has larger ideas."

"Yes; I have noticed that your husband has very large ideas. Is he really an idiot, the young man?"

"An idiot? Not in the least; he's charming. When he was twelve years old I myself was in love with him."

"He doesn't look much more than twelve today," Lord Warburton rejoined, vaguely, looking about him. Then, with more point—"Don't you think we might sit here?" he asked.

"Wherever you please." The room was a sort of boudoir, pervaded by a subdued, rose-colored light; a lady and gentleman moved out of it as our friends came in. "It's very kind of you to take such an interest in Mr. Rosier," Isabel said.

"He seems to me rather ill-treated. He had a face a yard long; I wondered what ailed him."

"You are a just man," said Isabel. "You have a kind thought even for a rival."

Lord Warburton turned, suddenly, with a stare. "A rival! Do you call him my rival?"

"Surely—if you both wish to marry the same person."

"Yes—but since he has no chance!"

"All the same, I like you for putting yourself in his place. It shows imagination."

"You like me for it?" And Lord Warburton looked at her with an uncertain eye. "I think you mean that you are laughing at me for it."

"Yes, I am laughing at you, a little. But I like you, too."

"Ah well, then, let me enter into his situation a little more. What do you suppose one could do for him?"

"Since I have been praising your imagination, I will leave you to imagine that yourself," Isabel said. "Pansy, too, would like you for that."

"Miss Osmond? Ah, she, I flatter myself, likes me already."

"Very much, I think."

He hesitated a little; he was still questioning her face. "Well, then, I don't understand you. You don't mean that she cares for him?"

"Surely, I have told you that I thought she did."

A sudden blush sprung to his face. "You told me that she would have no wish apart from her father's, and as I have gathered that he would favor me—" He paused a little, and then he added—"Don't you see?" suggestively, through his blush.

"Yes, I told you that she had an immense wish to please her father, and that it would probably take her very far."

"That seems to me a very proper feeling," said Lord Warburton.

"Certainly; it's a very proper feeling." Isabel remained silent for some moments; the room continued to be empty; the sound of the music reached them with its richness softened by the interposing apartments. Then at last she said—"But it hardly strikes me as the sort of feeling to which a man would wish to be indebted for a wife."

"I don't know; if the wife is a good one, and he thinks she does well!"

"Yes, of course you must think that."

"I do; I can't help it. You call that very British, of course."

"No, I don't. I think Pansy would do wonderfully well to marry you, and I don't know who should know it better than you. But you are not in love."

"Ah, yes I am, Mrs. Osmond!"

Isabel shook her head. "You like to think you are, while you sit here with me. But that's not how you strike me."

"I'm not like the young man in the doorway. I admit that. But what makes it so unnatural? Could anything in the world be more charming than Miss Osmond?"

"Nothing, possibly. But love has nothing to do with good reasons."

"I don't agree with you. I am delighted to have good reasons."

"Of course you are. If you were really in love you wouldn't care a straw for them."

"Ah, really in love—really in love!" Lord Warburton exclaimed, folding his arms, leaning back his head, and stretching himself a little. "You must remember that I am forty years old. I won't pretend that I am as I once was."

"Well, if you are sure," said Isabel, "it's all right."

He answered nothing; he sat there, with his head back, looking before him. Abruptly, however, he changed his position; he turned quickly to his companion. "Why, are you so unwilling, so skeptical?"

She met his eye, and for a moment they looked straight at each other. If she wished to be satisfied, she saw something that satisfied her; she saw in his eye the gleam of an idea that she was uneasy on her own account—that she was perhaps even frightened. It expressed a suspicion, not a hope, but such as it was it told her what she wished to know. Not for an instant should he suspect that she detected in his wish to marry her step-daughter an implication of increased nearness to herself, or that if she did detect it she thought it alarming or compromising. In that brief, extremely personal gaze, however, deeper meanings passed between them than they were conscious of at the moment.

"My dear Lord Warburton," she said, smiling, "you may do, as far as I am concerned, whatever comes into your head."

And with this she got up, and wandered into the adjoining room, where she encountered several acquaintances. While she talked with them she found herself regretting that she had moved; it looked a little like running away—all the more as Lord Warburton didn't follow her. She was glad of this, however, and, at any rate, she was satisfied. She was so well satisfied that when, in passing back into the ballroom, she found Edward Rosier still planted in the doorway, she stopped and spoke to him again.

"You did right not to go away. I have got some comfort for you."

"I need it," the young man murmured, "when I see you so awfully thick with *him!*"

"Don't speak of him, I will do what I can for you. I am afraid it won't be much, but what I can I will do."

He looked at her with gloomy obliqueness. "What has suddenly brought you round?"

"The sense that you are an inconvenience in the doorways!" she answered, smiling, as she passed him. Half-an-hour later she took leave, with Pansy, and at the foot of the staircase the two ladies, with many other departing guests, waited a while for their carriage. Just as it approached, Lord Warburton came out of the house, and assisted them to reach their vehicle. He stood a moment at the door, asking Pansy if she had amused herself; and she, having answered him, fell back with a little air of fatigue. Then Isabel, at the window, detaining him by a movement of her finger, murmured gently—"Don't forget to send your letter to her father!"

❧ 44 ❧

The Countess Gemini was often extremely bored—bored, in her own phrase, to extinction. She had not been extinguished, however, and she struggled bravely enough with her destiny, which had been to marry an unaccommodating Florentine who insisted upon living in his native town, where he enjoyed such consideration as might attach to a gentleman whose talent for losing at cards had not the merit of being incidental to an obliging disposition. The Count Gemini was not liked even by those who won from him; and he bore a name which, having a measurable value in Florence, was, like the local coin of the old Italian states, without currency in other parts of the peninsula. In Rome he was simply a very dull Florentine, and it is not remarkable that he should not have cared to pay frequent visits to a city where, to carry it off, his dullness needed more explanation than was convenient. The Countess lived with her eyes upon Rome, and it was the constant grievance of her life that she had not a habitation there. She was ashamed to say how seldom she had been allowed to go there; it scarcely made the matter better that there were other members of the Florentine nobility who never had been there at all. She went whenever she could; that was all she could say. Or rather, not all; but all she said she could say. In fact, she had much more to say about it, and had often set forth the reasons why she hated Florence and wished to end her days in the shadow of St. Peter's. They are reasons, however, which do not closely concern us, and were usually summed up in the declaration that Rome, in short, was the Eternal City, and that Florence was simply a pretty little place like any other. The Countess apparently needed to connect the idea of eternity with her amusements. She was convinced that society was infinitely more interesting in Rome, where you met celebrities all winter at evening parties. At Florence there were no celebrities; none at least one had heard of. Since her brother's marriage her impatience had greatly increased; she was so sure that his wife had a more brilliant life than herself. She was not so intellectual as Isabel, but she was intellectual enough to do justice to Rome—not to the ruins and the catacombs, not even perhaps to the church ceremonies and the scenery; but certainly to all the rest. She heard a great deal about her sister-in-law, and knew perfectly that Isabel was having a beautiful time. She had indeed seen it for herself on the only occasion on which she had enjoyed the hospitality of the Palazzo Roccanera. She had spent a week there during the first winter of her brother's marriage; but she had not been encouraged to renew this satisfaction. Osmond didn't want her—that she was perfectly aware of; but she would have gone all the same, for after all she didn't care two straws about Osmond. But her husband wouldn't let her, and the money question was always a trouble. Isabel had been very nice; the Countess, who had liked her sister-in-law from the first, had not been blinded by envy to Isabel's personal merits. She had always observed that she got on better with clever women than with silly ones, like herself; the silly ones could never understand her wisdom, whereas the clever ones—the really clever ones—always understood her silliness. It appeared to her that, different as they were in appearance and general style, Isabel and she had a patch of common ground somewhere, which they would set their feet upon at last. It was not very large, but it was firm, and they would both know it when once they touched it. And then she lived, with Mrs. Osmond, under the influence of a pleasant surprise; she was constantly expecting that Isabel would "look down" upon her, and she as constantly saw this operation postponed. She asked herself when it would begin; not that she cared much; but she wondered what kept it in abeyance. Her sister-in-law regarded her with none but level glances, and expressed for the poor Countess as little contempt as admiration. In reality, Isabel would as soon have thought of despising her as of passing a moral judgment on a grasshopper. She was not indifferent to her husband's sister, however; she was rather a little afraid of her. She wondered at her; she thought her very extraordinary. The Countess seemed to her to have no soul; she was like a bright shell, with a polished surface, in which something would rattle when you shook it. This rattle was apparently the Countess's spiritual principle; a little loose nut that tumbled about inside of her. She was too odd for disdain, too anomalous for comparisons. Isabel would have invited her again (there was no question of inviting the Count); but Osmond, after his marriage, had not scrupled to say frankly that Amy was a fool of the worst species—a fool whose folly had the irrepressibility of genius. He said at another time that she had no heart; and he added in a moment that she had given it all away—in small pieces, like a wedding cake. The fact of not having been asked was of course another obstacle to the Countess's going again to Rome; but at the period with which this history has now to deal, she was in receipt of an invitation to spend several weeks at the Palazzo Roccanera. The proposal had come from Osmond himself, who wrote to his sister that she must be prepared to be very quiet. Whether or no she found in this phrase all the meaning he had put into it, I am unable to say; but she accepted the invitation on any terms. She was curious, moreover; for one of the impressions of her former visit had been that her brother had found his match. Before the marriage she had been sorry for Isabel, so sorry as to have had serious thoughts—if any of the Countess's thoughts were serious—of putting her on her guard. But she had let that pass, and after a little she was reassured. Osmond was as lofty as ever, but his wife would not be an easy victim. The Countess was not very exact at measurements; but it seemed to her that if Isabel should draw herself up she would be the taller spirit of the two. What she wanted to learn now was whether Isabel had drawn herself up; it would give her immense pleasure to see Osmond overtopped.

Several days before she was to start for Rome a servant brought her the card of a visitor—a card with the simple superscription, "Henrietta C. Stackpole." The Countess pressed her fingertips to her forehead; she did not remember to have known any such Henrietta as that. The servant then remarked that the lady had requested him to say that if the Countess should not recognize her name, she would know her well enough on seeing her. By the time she appeared before her visitor she had in fact reminded herself that there was once a literary lady at Mrs. Touchett's; the only woman of letters she had ever encountered. That is, the only modern one, since she was the daughter of a defunct poetess. She recognized Miss Stackpole immediately; the more so that Miss Stackpole seemed perfectly unchanged; and the Countess, who was thoroughly good-natured, thought it rather fine to be called on by a person of that sort of distinction. She wondered whether Miss Stackpole had come on account of her mother—whether she had heard of the American Corinne. Her mother was not at all like Isabel's friend; the Countess could see at a glance that this lady was much more modern; and she received an impression of the improvements that were taking place—chiefly in distant countries—in the character (the professional character) of literary ladies. Her mother used to wear a Roman scarf thrown over a pair of bare shoulders, and a gold laurel-wreath set upon a multitude of glossy ringlets. She spoke softly and vaguely, with a kind of Southern accent; she sighed a great deal, and was not at all enterprising. But Henrietta, the Countess could see, was always closely buttoned and compactly braided; there was something brisk and businesslike in her appearance, and her manner was almost conscientiously familiar. The Countess could not but feel that the correspondent of the *Interviewer* was much more efficient than the American Corinne.

Henrietta explained that she had come to see the Countess because she was the only person she knew in Florence, and that when she visited a foreign city she liked to see something more than superficial travelers. She knew Mrs. Touchett, but Mrs. Touchett was in America, and even if she had been in Florence Henrietta would not have gone to see her, for Mrs. Touchett was not one of her admirations.

"Do you mean by that that I am?" the Countess asked, smiling graciously.

"Well, I like you better than I do her," said Miss Stackpole. "I seem to remember that when I saw you before you were very interesting. I don't know whether it was an accident, or whether it is your usual style. At any rate, I was a good deal struck with what you said. I made use of it afterwards in print."

"Dear me!" cried the Countess, staring and half-alarmed; "I had no idea I ever said anything remarkable! I wish I had known it."

"It was about the position of woman in this city," Miss Stackpole remarked. "You threw a good deal of light upon it."

"The position of woman is very uncomfortable. Is that what you mean? And you wrote it down and published it?" the Countess went on. "Ah, do let me see it!"

"I will write to them to send you the paper if you like," Henrietta said. "I didn't mention your name; I only said a lady of high rank. And then I quoted your views."

The Countess threw herself hastily backward, tossing up her clasped hands.

"Do you know I am rather sorry you didn't mention my name? I should have rather liked to see my name in the papers. I forget what my views were; I have so many! But I am not ashamed of them. I am not at all like my brother—I suppose you know my brother? He thinks it a kind of disgrace to be put into the papers; if you were to quote him he would never forgive you."

"He needn't be afraid; I shall never refer to him," said Miss Stackpole, with soft dryness. "That's another reason," she added, "why I wanted to come and see you. You know Mr. Osmond married my dearest friend."

"Ah, yes; you were a friend of Isabel's. I was trying to think what I knew about you."

"I am quite willing to be known by that," Henrietta declared. "But that isn't what your brother likes to know me by. He has tried to break up my relations with Isabel."

"Don't permit it," said the Countess.

"That's what I want to talk about. I am going to Rome."

"So am I!" the Countess cried. "We will go together."

"With great pleasure. And when I write about my journey I will mention you by name, as my companion."

The Countess sprang from her chair and came and sat on the sofa beside her visitor.

"Ah, you must send me the paper! My husband won't like it; but he need never see it. Besides, he doesn't know how to read."

Henrietta's large eyes became immense.

"Doesn't know how to read? May I put that into my letter?"

"Into your letter?"

"In the *Interviewer*. That's my paper."

"Oh yes, if you like; with his name. Are you going to stay with Isabel?"

Henrietta held up her head, gazing a little in silence at her hostess.

"She has not asked me. I wrote to her I was coming, and she answered that she would engage a room for me at a *pension.*"

The Countess listened with extreme interest.

"That's Osmond," she remarked, pregnantly.

"Isabel ought to resist," said Miss Stackpole. "I am afraid she has changed a great deal. I told her she would."

"I am sorry to hear it; I hoped she would have her own way. Why doesn't my brother like you?" the Countess added, ingenuously.

"I don't know, and I don't care. He is perfectly welcome not to like me; I don't want everone to like me; I should think less of myself if some people did. A journalist can't hope to do much good unless he gets a good deal hated; that's the way he knows how his work goes on. And it's just the same for a lady. But I didn't expect it of Isabel."

"Do you mean that she hates you?" the Countess inquired.

"I don't know; I want to see. That's what I am going to Rome for."

"Dear me, what a tiresome errand!" the Countess exclaimed.

"She doesn't write to me in the same way; it's easy to see there's a difference. If you know anything," Miss Stackpole went on, "I should like to hear it beforehand, so as to decide on the line I shall take."

The Countess thrust out her under lip and gave a gradual shrug.

"I know very little; I see and hear very little of Osmond. He doesn't like me any better than he appears to like you."

"Yet you are not a lady correspondent," said Henrietta, pensively.

"Oh, he has plenty of reasons. Nevertheless they have invited me—I am to stay in the house!" And the Countess smiled almost fiercely; her exultation, for the moment, took little account of Miss Stackpole's disappointment.

This lady, however, regarded it very placidly.

"I should not have gone if she had asked me. That is, I think I should not; and I am glad I hadn't to make up my mind. It would have been a very difficult question. I should not have liked to turn away from her, and yet I should not have been happy under her roof. A *pension* will suit me very well. But that is not all."

"Rome is very good just now," said the Countess; "there are all sorts of smart people. Did you ever hear of Lord Warburton?"

"Hear of him? I know him very well. Do you consider him very smart?" Henrietta inquired.

"I don't know him, but I am told he is extremely *grand seigneur*. He is making love to Isabel."

"Making love to her?"

"So I'm told; I don't know the details," said the Countess lightly. "But Isabel is pretty safe."

Henrietta gazed earnestly at her companion; for a moment she said nothing.

"When do you go to Rome?" she inquired, abruptly.

"Not for a week, I am afraid."

"I shall go tomorrow," Henrietta said. "I think I had better not wait."

"Dear me, I am sorry; I am having some dresses made. I am told Isabel receives immensely. But I shall see you there; I shall call on you at your *pension*." Henrietta sat still—she was lost in thought; and suddenly the Countess cried, "Ah, but if you don't go with me you can't describe our journey!"

Miss Stackpole seemed unmoved by this consideration; she was thinking of something else, and she presently expressed it.

"I am not sure that I understand you about Lord Warburton."

"Understand me? I mean he's very nice, that's all."

"Do you consider it nice to make love to married women?" Henrietta inquired, softly.

The Countess stared, and then, with a little violent laugh—

"It's certain that all the nice men do it. Get married and you'll see!" she added.

"That idea would be enough to prevent me," said Miss Stackpole. "I should want my own husband; I shouldn't want anyone else's. Do you mean that Isabel is guilty—is guilty—" and she paused a little, choosing her expression.

"Do I mean she's guilty? Oh dear no, not yet, I hope. I only mean that Osmond is very tiresome, and that Lord Warburton is, as I hear, a great deal at the house. I'm afraid you are scandalized."

"No, I am very anxious," Henrietta said.

"Ah, you are not very complimentary to Isabel! You should have more confidence. I tell you," the Countess added quickly, "if it will be a comfort to you I will engage to draw him off."

Miss Stackpole answered at first only with the deeper solemnity of her eyes.

"You don't understand me," she said after a while. "I haven't the idea that you seem to suppose. I am not afraid for Isabel—in that way. I am only afraid she is unhappy—that's what I want to get at."

The Countess gave a dozen turns of the head; she looked impatient and sarcastic.

"That may very well be; for my part I should like to know whether Osmond is."

Miss Stackpole had begun to bore her a little.

"If she is really changed that must be at the bottom of it," Henrietta went on.

"You will see; she will tell you," said the Countess.

"Ah, she may not tell me—that's what I am afraid of!"

"Well, if Osmond isn't enjoying himself I flatter myself I shall discover it," the Countess rejoined.

"I don't care for that," said Henrietta.

"I do immensely! If Isabel is unhappy I am very sorry for her, but I can't help it. I might tell her something that would make her worse, but I can't tell her anything that would console her. What did she go and marry him for? If she had listened to me she would have got rid of him. I will forgive her, however, if I find she has made things hot for him! If she has simply allowed him to trample upon her I don't know that I shall even pity her. But I don't think that's very likely. I count upon finding that if she is miserable she has at least made him so."

Henrietta got up; these seemed to her, naturally, very dreadful expectations. She honestly believed that she had no desire to see Mr. Osmond unhappy; and indeed he could not be for her the subject of a flight of fancy. She was on the whole rather disappointed in the Countess, whose mind moved in a narrower circle than she had imagined.

"It will be better if they love each other," she said, gravely.

"They can't. He can't love anyone."

"I presumed that was the case. But it only increases my fear for Isabel. I shall positively start tomorrow."

"Isabel certainly has devotees," said the Countess, smiling very vividly. "I declare I don't pity her."

"It may be that I can't assist her," said Miss Stackpole, as if it were well not to have illusions.

"You can have wanted to, at any rate; that's something. I believe that's what you came from America for," the Countess suddenly added.

"Yes, I wanted to look after her," Henrietta said, serenely.

Her hostess stood there smiling at her, with her small bright eyes and her eager-looking nose; a flush had come into each of her cheeks.

"Ah, that's very pretty—*c'est bien gentil!*" she said. "Isn't that what they call friendship?"

"I don't know what they call it. I thought I had better come."

"She is very happy—she is very fortunate," the Countess went on. "She has others besides." And then she broke out, passionately. "She is more fortunate than I! I am as unhappy as she—I have a very bad husband; he is a great deal worse than Osmond. And I have no friends. I thought I had, but they are gone. No one would do for me what you have done for her."

Henrietta was touched; there was nature in this bitter effusion. She gazed at her companion a moment, and then—

"Look here, Countess, I will do anything for you that you like. I will wait over and travel with you."

"Never mind," the Countess answered, with a quick change of tone; "only describe me in the newspaper!"

Henrietta, before leaving her, however, was obliged to make her understand that she could not give a fictitious representation of her journey to Rome. Miss Stackpole was a strictly veracious reporter.

On quitting the Countess she took her way to the Lung' Arno, the sunny quay beside the yellow river, where the bright-faced hotels familiar to tourists stand all in a row. She had learned her way before this through the streets of Florence (she was very quick in such matters), and was therefore able to turn with great decision of step out of the little square which forms the approach to the bridge of the Holy Trinity. She proceeded to the left, toward the Ponte Vecchio, and stopped in front of one of the hotels which overlook that delightful structure. Here she drew forth a small pocketbook, took from it a card and a pencil, and, after meditating a moment, wrote a few words. It is our privilege to look over her shoulder, and if we exercise it we may read the brief query—"Could I see you this evening for a few moments on a very important matter?" Henrietta added that she should start on the morrow for Rome. Armed with this little document she approached the porter, who now had taken up his station in the doorway, and asked if Mr. Goodwood were at home. The porter replied, as porters always reply, that he had gone out about twenty minutes before; whereupon Henrietta presented her card and begged it might be handed to him on his return. She left the inn and took her course along the quay to the severe portico of the Uffizi, through which she presently reached the entrance of the famous gallery of paintings. Making her way in, she ascended the high staircase which leads to the upper chambers. The long corridor, glazed on one side and decorated with antique busts, which gives admission to these apartments, presented an empty vista, in which the bright winter light twinkled upon the marble floor. The gallery is very cold, and during the midwinter weeks is but scantily visited. Miss Stackpole may appear more ardent in her quest of artistic beauty than she has hitherto struck us as being, but she had after all her preferences and admirations. One of the latter was the little Correggio of the Tribune— the Virgin kneeling down before the sacred infant, who lies in a litter of straw, and clapping her hands to him while he delightedly laughs and crows. Henrietta had taken a great fancy to this intimate scene—she thought it the most beautiful picture in the world. On her way, at present, from New York to Rome, she was spending but three days in Florence, but she had reminded herself that they must not elapse without her paying another visit to her favorite work of art. She had a great sense of beauty in all ways, and it involved a good many intellectual obligations. She was about to turn into the Tribune when a gentleman came out of it; whereupon she gave a little exclamation and stood before Caspar Goodwood.

"I have just been at your hotel," she said. "I left a card for you."

"I am very much honored," Caspar Goodwood answered, as if he really meant it.

"It was not to honor you I did it; I have called on you before, and I know you don't like it. It was to talk to you a little about something."

He looked for a moment at the buckle in her hat. "I shall be very glad to hear what you wish to say."

"You don't like to talk with me," said Henrietta. "But I don't care for that; I don't talk for your amusement. I wrote a word to ask you to come and see me; but since I have met you here this will do as well."

"I was just going away," Goodwood said; "but of course I will stop." He was civil, but he was not enthusiastic.

Henrietta, however, never looked for great professions, and she was so much in earnest that she was thankful he would listen to her on any terms. She asked him first, however, if he had seen all the pictures.

"All I want to. I have been here an hour."

"I wonder if you have seen my Correggio," said Henrietta. "I came up on purpose to have a look at it." She went into the Tribune, and he slowly accompanied her.

"I suppose I have seen it, but I didn't know it was yours. I don't remember pictures—especially that sort." She had pointed out her favorite work; and he asked her if it was about Correggio that she wished to talk with him.

"No," said Henrietta, "it's about something less harmonious!" They had the small, brilliant room, a splendid cabinet of treasures, to themselves; there was only a custode hovering about the Medicean Venus. "I want you to do me a favor," Miss Stackpole went on.

Caspar Goodwood frowned a little, but he expressed no embarrassment at the sense of not looking eager. His face was that of a much older man than our earlier friend. "I'm sure it's something I shan't like," he said, rather loud.

"No, I don't think you will like it. If you did, it would be no favor."

"Well, let us hear it," he said, in the tone of a man quite conscious of his own reasonableness.

"You may say there is no particular reason why you should do me a favor. Indeed, I only know of one: the fact that if you would let me I would gladly do you one." Her soft, exact tone, in which there was no attempt at effect, had an extreme sincerity; and her companion, though he presented rather a hard surface, could not help being touched by it. When he was touched he rarely showed it, however, by the usual signs; he neither blushed, nor looked away, nor looked conscious. He only fixed his attention more directly; he seemed to consider with added firmness. Henrietta went on therefore disinterestedly, without the sense of an advantage. "I may say now, indeed—it seems a good time—that if I have ever annoyed you (and I think sometimes that I have), it is because I knew that I was willing to suffer annoyance for you. I have troubled you—doubtless. But I would take trouble for you."

Goodwood hesitated. "You are taking trouble now."

"Yes, I am, some. I want you to consider whether it is better on the whole that you should go to Rome."

"I thought you were going to say that!" Goodwood exclaimed, rather artlessly.

"You *have* considered it, then?"

"Of course I have, very carefully. I have looked all round it. Otherwise I shouldn't have come as far as this. That's what I stayed in Paris two months for; I was thinking it over."

"I am afraid you decided as you liked. You decided it was best, because you were so much attracted."

"Best for whom, do you mean?" Goodwood inquired.

"Well, for yourself first. For Mrs. Osmond next."

"Oh, it won't do her any good! I don't flatter myself that."

"Won't it do her harm?—that's the question."

"I don't see what it will matter to her. I am nothing to Mrs. Osmond. But if you want to know, I do want to see her myself."

"Yes, and that's why you go."

"Of course it is. Could there be a better reason?"

"How will it help you? that's what I want to know," said Miss Stackpole.

"That's just what I can't tell you; it's just what I was thinking about in Paris."

"It will make you more discontented."

"Why do you say more so?" Goodwood asked, rather sternly. "How do you know I am discontented?"

"Well," said Henrietta, hesitating a little—"you seem never to have cared for another."

"How do you know what I care for?" he cried, with a big blush. "Just now I care to go to Rome."

Henrietta looked at him in silence, with a sad yet luminous expression. "Well," she observed, at last, "I only wanted to tell you what I think; I had it on my mind. Of course you think it's none of my business. But nothing is anyone's business, on that principle."

"It's very kind of you; I am greatly obliged to you for your interest," said Caspar Goodwood. "I shall go to Rome, and I shan't hurt Mrs. Osmond."

"You won't hurt her, perhaps. But will you help her?—that is the question."

"Is she in need of help?" he asked, slowly, with a penetrating look.

"Most women always are," said Henrietta, with conscientious evasiveness, and generalizing less hopefully than usual. "If you go to Rome," she added, "I hope you will be a true friend—not a selfish one!" And she turned away and began to look at the pictures.

Caspar Goodwood let her go, and stood watching her while she wandered round the room; then, after a moment, he rejoined her. "You have heard something about her here," he said in a moment. "I should like to know what you have heard."

Henrietta had never prevaricated in her life, and though on this occasion there might have been a fitness in doing so, she decided, after a moment's hesitation, to make no superficial exception. "Yes, I have heard," she answered; "but as I don't want you to go to Rome I won't tell you."

"Just as you please. I shall see for myself," said Goodwood. Then, inconsistently—for him, "You have heard she is unhappy!" he added.

"Oh, you won't see that!" Henrietta exclaimed.

"I hope not. When do you start?"

"Tomorrow, by the evening train. And you?"

Goodwood hesitated; he had no desire to make his journey to Rome in Miss Stackpole's company. His indifference to this advantage was not of the same character as Gilbert Osmond's, but it had at this moment an equal distinctness. It was rather a tribute to Miss Stackpole's virtues than a reference to her faults. He thought her very remarkable, very brilliant, and he had, in theory, no objection to the class to which she belonged. Lady correspondents appeared to him a part of the natural scheme of things in a progressive country, and though he never read their letters he supposed that they ministered somehow to social progress. But it was this very eminence of their position that made him wish that Miss Stackpole did not take so much for granted. She took for granted that he was always ready for some allusion to Mrs. Osmond; she had done so when they met in Paris, six weeks after his arrival in Europe, and she had repeated the assumption with every successive opportunity. He had no wish whatever to allude to Mrs. Osmond; he was *not* always thinking of her; he was perfectly sure of that. He was the most reserved, the least colloquial of men, and this inquiring authoress was constantly flashing her lantern into the quiet darkness of his soul. He wished she didn't care so much; he even wished, though it might seem rather brutal of him, that she would leave him alone. In spite of this, however, he just now made other reflections—which show how widely different, in effect, his ill-humor was from Gilbert Osmond's. He wished to go immediately to Rome; he would have liked to go alone, in the night-train. He hated the European railway-carriages, in which one sat for hours in a vice, knee to knee and nose to nose with a foreigner to whom one presently found one's self objecting with all the added vehemence of one's wish to have the window open; and if they were worse at night even than by day, at least at night one could sleep and dream of an American saloon-car. But he could not take a night-train when Miss Stackpole was starting in the morning; it seemed to him that this would be an insult to an unprotected woman. Nor could he wait until after she had gone, unless he should wait longer than he had patience for. It would not do to start the next day. She worried him; she oppressed him; the idea of spending the day in a European railway-carriage with her offered a complication of irritations. Still, she was a lady traveling alone; it was his duty to put himself out for her. There could be no two questions about that; it was a perfectly clear necessity. He looked extremely grave for some moments, and then he said, without any of the richness of gallantry, but in a tone of extreme distinctness—"Of course, if you are going tomorrow, I will go too, as I may be of assistance to you."

"Well, Mr. Goodwood, I should hope so!" Henrietta remarked, serenely.

❧ 45 ❧

I have already had reason to say that Isabel knew that her husband was displeased by the continuance of Ralph's visit to Rome. This knowledge was very present to her as she went to her cousin's hotel the day after she had invited Lord Warburton to give a tangible proof of his sincerity; and at this moment, as at others, she had a sufficient perception of the sources of Osmond's displeasure. He wished her to have no freedom of mind, and he knew perfectly well that Ralph was an apostle of freedom. It was just because he was this, Isabel said to herself, that it was a refreshment to go and see him. It will be perceived that she partook of this refreshment in spite of her husband's disapproval; that is, she partook of it, as she flattered herself, discreetly. She had not as yet undertaken to act in direct opposition to Osmond's wishes; he was her master; she gazed at moments with a sort of incredulous blankness at this fact. It weighed upon her imagination, however; constantly present to her mind were all the traditionary decencies and sanctities of marriage. The idea of violating them filled her with shame as well as with dread, for when she gave herself away she had lost sight of this contingency in the perfect belief that her husband's intentions were as generous as her own. She seemed to see, however, the rapid approach of the day when she should have to take back something that she had solemnly given. Such a ceremony would be odious and monstrous; she tried to shut her eyes to it meanwhile. Osmond would do nothing to help it by beginning first; he would put that burden upon her. He had not yet formally forbidden her to go and see Ralph; but she felt sure that unless Ralph should very soon depart this prohibition would come. How could poor Ralph depart? The weather as yet made it impossible. She could perfectly understand her husband's wish for the event; to be just, she didn't see how he could like her to be with her cousin. Ralph never said a word against him; but Osmond's objections were nonetheless founded. If Osmond should positively interpose, then she should have to decide, and that would not be easy. The prospect made her heart beat and her cheeks burn, as I say, in advance; there were moments when, in her wish to avoid an open rupture with her husband, she found herself wishing that Ralph would start even at a risk. And it was of no use that when catching herself in this state of mind, she called herself a feeble spirit, a coward. It was not that she loved Ralph

397

less, but that almost anything seemed preferable to repudiating the most serious act—the single sacred act—of her life. That appeared to make the whole future hideous. To break with Osmond once would be to break forever; any open acknowledgment of irreconcilable needs would be an admission that their whole attempt had proved a failure. For them there could be no condonement, no compromise, no easy forgetfulness, no formal readjustment. They had attempted only one thing, but that one thing was to have been exquisite. Once they missed it, nothing else would do; there is no substitute for that success. For the moment, Isabel went to the Hôtel de Paris as often as she thought well; the measure of expediency resided in her moral consciousness. It had been very liberal today, for in addition to the general truth that she couldn't leave Ralph to die alone, she had something important to ask of him. This indeed was Gilbert's business as well as her own.

She came very soon to what she wished to speak of.

"I want you to answer me a question," she said. "It's about Lord Warburton."

"I think I know it," Ralph answered from his armchair, out of which his thin legs protruded at greater length than ever.

"It's very possible," said Isabel. "Please then answer it."

"Oh, I don't say I can do that."

"You are intimate with him," said Isabel; "you have a great deal of observation of him."

"Very true. But think how he must dissimulate!"

"Why should he dissimulate? That's not his nature."

"Ah, you must remember that the circumstances are peculiar," said Ralph, with an air of private amusement.

"To a certain extent—yes. But is he really in love?"

"Very much, I think. I can make that out."

"Ah!" said Isabel, with a certain dryness.

Ralph looked at her a moment; a shade of perplexity mingled with his mild hilarity.

"You said that as if you were disappointed."

Isabel got up, slowly, smoothing her gloves, and eyeing them thoughtfully.

"It's after all no business of mine."

"You are very philosophic," said her cousin. And then in a moment—"May I inquire what you are talking about?"

Isabel stared a little. "I thought you knew. Lord Warburton tells me he desires to marry Pansy. I have told you that before, without eliciting a comment from you. You might risk one this morning, I think. Is it your belief that he really cares for her?"

"Ah, for Pansy, no!" cried Ralph, very positively.

"But you said just now that he did."

Ralph hesitated a moment. "That he cared for you, Mrs. Osmond."

Isabel shook her head, gravely. "That's nonsense, you know."

"Of course it is. But the nonsense is Warburton's, not mine."

"That would be very tiresome," Isabel said, speaking, as she flattered herself, with much subtlety.

"I ought to tell you indeed," Ralph went on, "that to me he has denied it."

"It's very good of you to talk about it together! Has he also told you that he is in love with Pansy?"

"He has spoken very well of her—very properly. He has let me know, of course, that he thinks she would do very well at Lockleigh."

"Does he really think it?"

"Ah, what Warburton really thinks—!" said Ralph.

Isabel fell to smoothing her gloves again; they were long, loose gloves upon which she could freely expend herself. Soon, however, she looked up, and then—

"Ah, Ralph, you give me no help!" she cried, abruptly, passionately.

It was the first time she had alluded to the need for help, and the words shook her cousin with their violence. He gave a long murmur of relief, of pity, of tenderness; it seemed to him that at last the gulf between them had been bridged. It was this that made him exclaim in a moment—

"How unhappy you must be!"

He had no sooner spoken than she recovered her self-possession, and the first use she made of it was to pretend she had not heard him.

"When I talk of your helping me, I talk great nonsense," she said, with a quick smile. "The idea of my troubling you with my domestic embarrassments! The matter is very simple; Lord Warburton must get on by himself. I can't undertake to help him."

"He ought to succeed easily," said Ralph.

Isabel hesitated a moment. "Yes—but he has not always succeeded."

"Very true. You know, however, how that always surprised me. Is Miss Osmond capable of giving us a surprise?"

"It will come from him, rather. I suspect that after all he will let the matter drop."

"He will do nothing dishonorable," said Ralph.

"I am very sure of that. Nothing can be more honorable than for him to leave the poor child alone. She cares for someone else, and it is cruel to attempt to bribe her by magnificent offers to give him up."

"Cruel to the other person perhaps—the one she cares for. But Warburton isn't obliged to mind that."

"No, cruel to her," said Isabel. "She would be very unhappy if she were to allow herself to be persuaded to desert poor Mr. Rosier. That idea seems to amuse you; of course you are not in love with him. He has the merit of being in love with her. She can see at a glance that Lord Warburton is not."

"He would be very good to her," said Ralph.

"He has been good to her already. Fortunately, however, he has not said a word to disturb her. He could come and bid her goodbye tomorrow with perfect propriety."

"How would your husband like that?"

"Not at all; and he may be right in not liking it. Only he must obtain satisfaction himself."

"Has he commissioned you to obtain it?" Ralph ventured to ask.

"It was natural that as an old friend of Lord Warburton's—an older friend, that is, than Osmond—I should take an interest in his intentions."

"Take an interest in his renouncing them, you mean."

Isabel hesitated, frowning a little. "Let me understand. Are you pleading his cause?"

"Not in the least. I am very glad he should not become your step-daughter's husband. It makes such a very queer relation to you!" said Ralph, smiling. "But I'm rather nervous lest your husband should think you haven't pushed him enough."

Isabel found herself able to smile as well as he.

"He knows me well enough not to have expected me to push. He himself has no intention of pushing, I presume. I am not afraid I shall not be able to justify myself!" she said, lightly.

Her mask had dropped for an instant, but she had put it on again, to Ralph's infinite disappointment. He had caught a glimpse of her natural face, and he wished immensely to look into it. He had an almost savage desire to hear her complain of her husband—hear her say that she should be held accountable for Lord Warburton's defection. Ralph was certain that this was her situation; he knew by instinct, in advance, the form that in such an event Osmond's displeasure would take. It could only take the meanest and cruellest. He would have liked to warn Isabel of it—to let her see at least that he knew it. It little mattered that Isabel would know it much better; it was for his own satisfaction more than for hers that he longed to show her that he was not deceived. He tried and tried again to make her betray Osmond; he felt cold-blooded, cruel, dishonorable almost, in doing so. But it scarcely mattered, for he only failed. What had she come for then, and why did she seem almost to offer him a chance to violate their tacit convention? Why did she ask him his advice, if she gave him no liberty to answer her? How could they talk of her domestic embarrassments, as it pleased her humorously to designate them, if the principal factor was not to be mentioned? These contradictions were themselves but an indication of her trouble, and her cry for help, just before, was the only thing he was bound to consider.

"You will be decidedly at variance, all the same," he said, in a moment. And as she answered nothing, looking as if she scarcely understood—"You will find yourselves thinking very differently," he continued.

"That may easily happen, among the most united couples!" She took up her parasol; he saw that she was nervous, afraid of what he might say. "It's a matter we can hardly quarrel about, however," she added; "for almost all the interest is on his side. That is very natural. Pansy is after all his daughter—not mine." And she put out her hand to wish him goodbye.

Ralph took an inward resolution that she should not leave him without his letting her know that he knew everything; it seemed too great an opportunity to lose. "Do you know what his interest will make him say?" he asked, as he took her hand. She shook her head, rather dryly—not discouragingly—and he went on, "It will make him say that your want of zeal is owing to jealousy." He stopped a moment; her face made him afraid.

"To jealousy?"

"To jealousy of his daughter."

She blushed red and threw back her head.

"You are not kind," she said, in a voice that he had never heard on her lips.

"Be frank with me, and you'll see," said Ralph.

But she made no answer; she only shook her hand out of his own, which he tried still to hold, and rapidly went out of the room. She made up her mind to speak to Pansy, and she took an occasion on the same day, going to the young girl's room before dinner. Pansy was already dressed; she was always in advance of the time; it seemed to illustrate her pretty patience and the graceful stillness with which she could sit and wait. At present she was seated in her fresh array, before the bedroom fire; she had blown out her candles on the completion of her toilet, in accordance with the economical habits in which she had been brought up and which she was now more careful than ever to observe; so that the room was lighted only by a couple of logs. The rooms in the Palazzo Roccanera were as spacious as they were numerous, and Pansy's virginal bower was an immense chamber with a dark, heavily timbered ceiling. Its diminutive mistress, in the midst of it, appeared but a speck of humanity, and as she got up, with quick deference, to welcome Isabel, the latter was more than ever struck with her shy sincerity. Isabel had a difficult task—the only thing was to perform it as simply as possible. She felt bitter and angry, but she warned herself against betraying it to Pansy. She was afraid even of looking too grave, or at least too stern; she was afraid of frightening her. But Pansy seemed to have guessed that she had come a little as a confessor; for after she had moved the chair in which she had been sitting a little nearer to the fire, and Isabel had taken her place in it, she kneeled down on a cushion in front of her, looking up and resting her clasped hands on her step-mother's knees. What Isabel wished to do was to hear from her own lips that her mind was not occupied with Lord Warburton; but if she desired the assurance, she felt herself by no means at liberty to provoke it. The girl's father would have qualified this as rank treachery; and indeed Isabel knew that if

Pansy should display the smallest germ of a disposition to encourage Lord Warburton, her own duty was to hold her tongue. It was difficult to interrogate without appearing to suggest; Pansy's supreme simplicity, an innocence even more complete than Isabel had yet judged it, gave to the most tentative inquiry something of the effect of an admonition. As she knelt there in the vague firelight, with her pretty dress vaguely shining, her hands folded half in appeal and half in submission, her soft eyes, raised and fixed, full of the seriousness of the situation, she looked to Isabel like a childish martyr decked out for sacrifice and scarcely presuming even to hope to avert it. When Isabel said to her that she had never yet spoken to her of what might have been going on in relation to her getting married, but that her silence had not been indifference or ignorance, had only been the desire to leave her at liberty, Pansy bent forward, raised her face nearer and nearer to Isabel's, and with a little murmur which evidently expressed a deep longing, answered that she had greatly wished her to speak, and that she begged her to advise her now.

"It's difficult for me to advise you," Isabel rejoined. "I don't know how I can undertake that. That's for your father; you must get his advice, and, above all, you must act upon it."

At this Pansy dropped her eyes; for a moment she said nothing.

"I think I should like your advice better than papa's," she presently remarked.

"That's not as it should be," said Isabel, coldly. "I love you very much, but your father loves you better."

"It isn't because you love me—it's because you're a lady," Pansy answered, with the air of saying something very reasonable. "A lady can advise a young girl better than a man."

"I advise you, then, to pay the greatest respect to your father's wishes."

"Ah, yes," said Pansy, eagerly, "I must do that."

"But if I speak to you now about your getting married, it's not for your own sake, it's for mine," Isabel went on. "If I try to learn from you what you expect, what you desire, it is only that I may act accordingly."

Pansy stared, and then, very quickly—

"Will you do everything I desire?" she asked.

"Before I say yes, I must know what such things are."

Pansy presently told her that the only thing she wished in life was to marry Mr. Rosier. He had asked her, and she had told him that she would do so if her papa would allow it. Now her papa wouldn't allow it.

"Very well, then, it's impossible," said Isabel.

"Yes, it's impossible," said Pansy, without a sigh, and with the same extreme attention in her clear little face.

"You must think of something else, then," Isabel went on; but Pansy, sighing then, told her that she had attempted this feat without the least success.

"You think of those that think of you," she said, with a faint smile. "I know that Mr. Rosier thinks of me."

"He ought not to," said Isabel, loftily. "Your father has expressly requested he shouldn't.".

"He can't help it, because he knows that I think of him."

"You shouldn't think of him. There is some excuse for him, perhaps; but there is none for you!"

"I wish you would try to find one," the girl exclaimed, as if she were praying to the Madonna.

"I should be very sorry to attempt it," said the Madonna, with unusual frigidity. "If you knew someone else was thinking of you, would you think of him?"

"No one can think of me as Mr. Rosier does; no one has the right."

"Ah, but I don't admit Mr. Rosier's right," Isabel cried, hypocritically.

Pansy only gazed at her; she was evidently deeply puzzled; and Isabel, taking advantage of it, began to represent to her the miserable consequences of disobeying her father. At this Pansy stopped her, with the assurance that she would never disobey him, would never marry without his consent. And she announced, in the serenest, simplest tone, that though she might never marry Mr. Rosier, she would never cease to think of him. She appeared to have accepted the idea of eternal singleness; but Isabel of course was free to reflect that she had no conception of its meaning. She was perfectly sincere; she was prepared to give up her lover. This might seem an important step toward taking another, but for Pansy, evidently, it did not lead in that direction. She felt no bitterness toward her father; there was no bitterness in her heart; there was only the sweetness of fidelity to Edward Rosier, and a strange, exquisite intimation that she could prove it better by remaining single than even by marrying him.

"Your father would like you to make a better marriage," said Isabel. "Mr. Rosier's fortune is not very large."

"How do you mean better—if that would be good enough? And I have very little money; why should I look for a fortune?"

"Your having so little is a reason for looking for more." Isabel was grateful for the dimness of the room; she felt as if her face were hideously insincere. She was doing this for Osmond; this was what one had to do for Osmond! Pansy's solemn eyes, fixed on her own, almost embarrassed her; she was ashamed to think that she had made so light of the girl's preference.

"What should you like me to do?" said Pansy, softly.

The question was a terrible one, and Isabel pusillanimously took refuge in a generalization.

"To remember all the pleasure it is in your power to give your father."

"To marry someone else, you mean—if he should ask me?"

For a moment Isabel's answer caused itself to be waited for; then she heard herself utter it, in the stillness that Pansy's attention seemed to make.

"Yes—to marry someone else."

Pansy's eyes grew more penetrating; Isabel believed that she was doubting her sincerity, and the impression took force from her slowly getting up from her cushion. She stood there a moment, with her small hands unclasped, and then she said, with a timorous sigh—

"Well, I hope no one will ask me!"

"There has been a question of that. Someone else would have been ready to ask you."

"I don't think he can have been ready," said Pansy.

"It would appear so—if he had been sure that he would succeed."

"If he had been sure? Then he was not ready!"

Isabel thought this rather sharp; she also got up, and stood a moment, looking into the fire. "Lord Warburton has shown you great attention," she said; "of course you know it's of him I speak." She found herself, against her expectation, almost placed in the position of justifying herself; which led her to introduce this nobleman more crudely than she had intended.

"He has been very kind to me, and I like him very much. But if you mean that he will ask me to marry him, I think you are mistaken."

"Perhaps I am. But your father would like it extremely."

Pansy shook her head, with a little wise smile. "Lord Warburton won't ask me simply to please papa."

"Your father would like you to encourage him," Isabel went on, mechanically.

"How can I encourage him?"

"I don't know. Your father must tell you that."

Pansy said nothing for a moment; she only continued to smile as if she were in possession of a bright assurance. "There is no danger—no danger!" she declared at last.

There was a conviction in the way she said this, and a felicity in her believing it, which made Isabel feel very awkward. She felt accused of dishonesty, and the idea was disgusting. To repair her self-respect, she was on the point of saying that Lord Warburton had let her know that there *was* a danger. But she did not; she only said—in her embarrassment rather wide of the mark—that he surely had been most kind, most friendly.

"Yes, he has been very kind," Pansy answered. "That's what I like him for."

"Why then is the difficulty so great?"

"I have always felt sure that he knows that I don't want—what did you say I should do?—to encourage him. He knows I don't want to marry, and he wants me to know that he therefore won't trouble me. That's the meaning of his kindness. It's as if he said to me, 'I like you very much, but if it doesn't please you I will never say it again.' I think that is very kind, very noble," Pansy went on, with deepening positiveness. "That is all we have said to each other. And he doesn't care for me, either. Ah no, there is no danger!"

Isabel was touched with wonder at the depths of perception of which this submissive little person was capable; she felt afraid of Pansy's wisdom—began almost to retreat before it. "You must tell your father that," she remarked, reservedly.

"I think I would rather not," Pansy answered.

"You ought not to let him have false hopes."

"Perhaps not; but it will be good for me that he should. So long as he believes that Lord Warburton intends anything of the kind you say, papa won't propose anyone else. And that will be an advantage for me," said Pansy, very lucidly.

There was something brilliant in her lucidity, and it made Isabel draw a long breath. It relieved her of a heavy responsibility. Pansy had a sufficient illumination of her own, and Isabel felt that she herself just now had no light to spare from her small stock. Nevertheless it still clung to her that she must be loyal to Osmond, that she was on her honor in dealing with his daughter. Under the influence of this sentiment she threw out another suggestion before she retired—a suggestion with which it seemed to her that she should have done her utmost. "Your father takes for granted at least that you would like to marry a nobleman."

Pansy stood in the open doorway; she had drawn back the curtain for Isabel to pass. "I think Mr. Rosier looks like one!" she remarked, very gravely.

❧ 46 ❧

Lord Warburton was not seen in Mrs. Osmond's drawing room for several days, and Isabel could not fail to observe that her husband said nothing to her about having received a letter from him. She could not fail to observe, either, that Osmond was in a state of expectancy, and that though it was not agreeable to him to betray it, he thought their distinguished friend kept him waiting quite too long. At the end of four days he alluded to his absence.

"What has become of Warburton? What does he mean by treating one like a tradesman with a bill?"

"I know nothing about him," Isabel said. "I saw him last Friday, at the German ball. He told me then that he meant to write to you."

"He has never written to me."

"So I supposed, from your not having told me."

"He's an odd fish," said Osmond, comprehensively. And on Isabel's making no rejoinder, he went on to inquire whether it took his lordship five days to indite a letter. "Does he form his words with such difficulty?"

"I don't know," said Isabel. "I have never had a letter from him."

"Never had a letter? I had an idea that you were at one time in intimate correspondence."

Isabel answered that this had not been the case, and let the conversation drop. On the morrow, however, coming into the drawing room late in the afternoon, her husband took it up again.

"When Lord Warburton told you of his intention of writing, what did you say to him?" he asked.

Isabel hesitated a moment. "I think I told him not to forget it."

"Did you believe there was a danger of that?"

"As you say, he's an odd fish."

"Apparently he has forgotten it," said Osmond. "Be so good as to remind him."

"Should you like me to write to him?" Isabel asked.

"I have no objection whatever."

"You expect too much of me."

"Ah yes, I expect a great deal of you."

"I am afraid I shall disappoint you," said Isabel.

"My expectations have survived a good deal of disappointment."

"Of course I know that. Think how I must have disappointed myself! If you really wish to capture Lord Warburton, you must do it yourself."

For a couple of minutes Osmond answered nothing; then he said—"That won't be easy, with you working against me."

Isabel started; she felt herself beginning to tremble. He had a way of looking at her through half-closed eyelids, as if he were thinking of her but scarcely saw her, which seemed to her to have a wonderfully cruel intention. It appeared to recognize her as a disagreeable necessity of thought, but to ignore her, for the time, as a presence. That was the expression of his eyes now. "I think you accuse me of something very base," she said.

"I accuse you of not being trustworthy. If he doesn't come up to the mark it will be because you have kept him off. I don't know that it's base; it is the kind of thing a woman always thinks she may do. I have no doubt you have the finest ideas about it."

"I told you I would do what I could," said Isabel.

"Yes, that gained you time."

It came over Isabel, after he had said this, that she had once thought him beautiful. "How much you must wish to capture him!" she exclaimed, in a moment.

She had no sooner spoken than she perceived the full reach of her words, of which she had not been conscious in uttering them. They made a comparison between Osmond and herself, recalled the fact that she had once held this coveted treasure in her hand and felt herself rich enough to let it fall. A momentary exultation took possession of her—a horrible delight in having wounded him; for his face instantly told her that none of the force of her exclamation was lost. Osmond expressed nothing otherwise, however; he only said, quickly, "Yes, I wish it very much."

At this moment a servant came in, as if to usher a visitor, and he was followed the next by Lord Warburton, who received a visible check on seeing Osmond. He looked rapidly from the master of the house to the mistress; a movement that seemed to denote a reluctance to interrupt or even a perception of ominous conditions. Then he advanced, with his English address, in which a vague shyness seemed to offer itself as an element of good breeding; in which the only defect was a difficulty in achieving transitions.

Osmond was embarrassed; he found nothing to say; but Isabel remarked, promptly enough, that they had been in the àct of talking about their visitor. Upon this her husband added that they hadn't known what was become of him—they had been afraid he had gone away.

"No," said Lord Warburton, smiling and looking at Osmond; "I am only on the point of going." And then he explained that he found himself suddenly recalled to England; he should start on the morrow or next day. "I am awfully sorry to leave poor Touchett!" he ended by exclaiming.

For a moment neither of his companions spoke; Osmond only leaned back in his chair, listening. Isabel didn't look at him; she could only fancy how he looked. Her eyes were upon Lord Warburton's face, where they were the more free to rest that those of his lordship carefully avoided them. Yet Isabel was sure that had she met her visitor's glance, she should have found it expressive. "You had better take poor Touchett with you," she heard her husband say, lightly enough, in a moment.

"He had better wait for warmer weather," Lord Warburton answered. "I shouldn't advise him to travel just now."

He sat there for a quarter of an hour, talking as if he might not soon see them again—unless indeed they should come to England, a course which he strongly recommended. Why shouldn't they come to England in the autumn? that struck him as a very happy thought. It would give him such pleasure to do what he could for them—to have them come and spend a month with him. Osmond, by his own admission, had been to England but once; which was an absurd state of things. It was just the country for him—he would be sure to get on well there. Then Lord Warburton asked Isabel if she remembered what a good time she had there, and if she didn't want to try it again. Didn't she want to see Gardencourt once more? Gardencourt was really very good. Touchett didn't take proper care of it, but it was the sort of place you could hardly spoil by letting it alone. Why didn't they come and pay Touchett a visit? He surely must have asked them. Hadn't asked them? What an ill-mannered wretch! and Lord Warburton promised to give the master of Gardencourt a piece of his mind. Of course it was a mere accident; he would be delighted to have them. Spending a month with Touchett and a month with himself, and seeing all the rest of the people they must know there, they really wouldn't find it half bad. Lord Warburton added that it would amuse Miss Osmond as well, who had told him that she had never been to England and whom he had assured it was a country she deserved to see. Of course she didn't need to go to England to be admired—that was her fate everywhere; but she would be immensely liked in England, Miss Osmond would, if that was any inducement. He asked if she were not at home: couldn't he say goodbye? Not that he liked goodbyes—he always funked them. When he left England the other day he had not said goodbye to anyone. He had had half a mind to leave Rome without troubling Mrs. Osmond for a final interview. What could be more dreary than a final interview? One never said the things one wanted to—one remembered them all an hour afterwards. On the other hand, one usually said a lot of things one shouldn't, simply from a sense that one had to say something. Such a sense was bewildering; it made one nervous. He had it at present, and that was the effect it produced on him. If Mrs. Osmond didn't think he spoke as he ought, she must set it down to agitation; it was no light thing to part with Mrs. Osmond. He was really very sorry to be going. He had thought of writing to her, instead of calling—but he would write to her at any rate, to tell her a lot of things that would be sure to occur to him as soon as he had left the house. They must think seriously about coming to Lockleigh.

If there was anything awkward in the circumstances of his visit or in the announcement of his departure, it failed to come to the surface. Lord Warburton talked about his agitation; but he showed it in no other manner, and Isabel saw that since he had determined on a retreat he was capable of executing it gallantly. She was very glad for him; she liked him quite well enough to wish him to appear to carry a thing off. He would do that on any occasion; not from impudence, but simply from the habit of success; and Isabel perceived that it was not in her husband's power to frustrate this faculty. A double operation, as she sat there, went on in her mind. On one side she listened to Lord Warburton; said what was proper to him; read, more or less, between the lines of what he said himself; and wondered how he would have spoken if he had found her alone. On the other she had a perfect consciousness of Osmond's emotion. She felt almost sorry for him; he was condemned to the sharp pain of loss without the relief of cursing. He had had a great hope, and now, as he saw it vanish into smoke, he was obliged to sit and smile and twirl his thumbs. Not that he troubled himself to smile very brightly; he treated Lord Warburton, on the whole, to as vacant a countenance as so clever a man could very well wear. It was indeed a part of Osmond's cleverness that he could look consummately uncompromised. His present appearance, however, was not a confession of disappointment; it was simply a part of Osmond's habitual system, which was to be inexpressive exactly in proportion as he was really intent. He had been intent upon Lord Warburton from the first; but he had never allowed his eagerness to irradiate his refined face. He had treated his possible son-in-law as he treated everyone—with an air of being interested in him only for his own advantage, not for Gilbert Osmond's. He would give no sign now of an inward rage which was the result of a vanished prospect of gain—not the faintest nor subtlest. Isabel could be sure of that, if it was any satisfaction to her. Strangely, very strangely, it was a satisfaction; she wished Lord Warburton to triumph before her husband, and at the same time she wished her husband to be very superior before Lord Warburton. Osmond, in his way, was admirable; he had, like their visitor, the advantage of an acquired habit. It was not that of succeeding, but it was something almost as good—that of not attempting. As he leaned back in his place, listening but vaguely to Lord Warburton's friendly offers and suppressed explanations—as if it were only proper to assume that they were addressed essentially to his wife—he had at least (since so little else was left him) the comfort of thinking how well he personally had kept out of it, and how the air of indifference, which he was now able to wear, had the added beauty of consistency. It was something to be able to look as if their visitor's movements had no relation to his own mind. Their visitor did well, certainly; but Osmond's performance was in its very nature more finished. Lord Warburton's position was after all an easy one; there was no reason in the world why he should not leave Rome. He had beneficent inclinations; but they had stopped short of fruition; he had never committed himself, and his honor was safe. Osmond appeared to take but a moderate interest in the proposal that they should go and stay with him, and in his allusion to the success Pansy might extract from their visit. He murmured a recognition, but left Isabel to say that it was a matter requiring grave consideration. Isabel, even while she made this remark, could see the great vista which had suddenly opened out in her husband's mind, with Pansy's little figure marching up the middle of it.

Lord Warburton had asked leave to bid goodbye to Pansy, but neither Isabel nor Osmond had made any motion to send for her. He had the air of giving out that his visit must be short; he sat on a small chair, as if it were only for a moment, keeping his hat in his hand. But he stayed and stayed; Isabel wondered what he was waiting for. She believed it was not to see Pansy; she had an impression that on the whole he would rather not see Pansy. It was of course to see herself alone—he had something to say to her. Isabel had no great wish to hear it, for she was afraid it would be an explanation, and she could perfectly dispense with explanations. Osmond, however, presently got up, like a man of good taste to whom it had occurred that so inveterate a visitor might wish to say just the last word of all to the ladies.

"I have a letter to write before dinner," he said; "you must excuse me. I will see if my daughter is disengaged, and if she is she shall know you are here. Of course when you come to Rome you will always look us up. Isabel will talk to you about the English expedition; she decides all those things."

The nod with which, instead of a handshake, he terminated this little speech, was perhaps a rather meager form of salutation; but on the whole it was all the occasion demanded. Isabel reflected that after he left the room Lord Warburton would have no pretext for saying—"Your husband is very angry;" which would have been extremely disagreeable to her. Nevertheless, if he had done so, she would have said—"Oh, don't be anxious. He doesn't hate *you:* it's me that he hates!"

It was only when they had been left alone together that Lord Warburton showed a certain vague awkwardness—sitting down in another chair, handling two or three of the objects that were near him. "I hope he will make Miss Osmond come," he presently remarked. "I want very much to see her."

"I'm glad it's the last time," said Isabel.

"So am I. She doesn't care for me."

"No, she doesn't care for you."

"I don't wonder at it," said Lord Warburton. Then he added, with inconsequence—"You will come to England, won't you?"

"I think we had better not."

"Ah, you owe me a visit. Don't you remember that you were to have come to Lockleigh once, and you never did?"

"Everything is changed since then," said Isabel.

"Not changed for the worse, surely—as far as we are concerned. To see you under my roof"—and he hesitated a moment—"would be a great satisfaction."

She had feared an explanation; but that was the only one that occurred. They talked a little of Ralph, and in another moment Pansy came in, already dressed for dinner and with a little red spot in either cheek. She shook hands with Lord Warburton and stood looking up into his face with a fixed smile—a smile that Isabel knew, though his lordship probably never suspected it, to be near akin to a burst of tears.

"I am going away," he said. "I want to bid you goodbye."

"Goodbye, Lord Warburton." The young girl's voice trembled a little.

"And I want to tell you how much I wish you may be very happy."

"Thank you, Lord Warburton," Pansy answered.

He lingered a moment, and gave a glance at Isabel. "You ought to be very happy—you have got a guardian angel."

"I am sure I shall be happy," said Pansy, in the tone of a person whose certainties were always cheerful.

"Such a conviction as that will take you a great way. But if it should ever fail you, remember—remember—" and Lord Warburton stammered a little. "Think of me sometimes, you know," he said with a vague laugh. Then he shook hands with Isabel, in silence, and presently he was gone.

When he had left the room Isabel expected an effusion of tears from her step-daughter; but Pansy in fact treated her to something very different.

"I think you *are* my guardian angel!" she exclaimed, very sweetly.

Isabel shook her head. "I am not an angel of any kind. I am at the most your good friend."

"You are a very good friend then—to have asked papa to be gentle with me."

"I have asked your father nothing," said Isabel, wondering.

"He told me just now to come to the drawing room, and then he gave me a very kind kiss."

"Ah," said Isabel, "that was quite his own idea!"

She recognized the idea perfectly; it was very characteristic, and she was to see a great deal more of it. Even with Pansy, Osmond could not put himself the least in the wrong. They were dining out that day, and after their dinner they went to another entertainment; so that it was not till late in the evening that Isabel saw him alone. When Pansy kissed him, before going to bed, he returned her embrace with even more than his usual munificence, and Isabel wondered whether he meant it as a hint that his daughter had been injured by the machinations of her step-mother. It was a partial expression, at any rate, of what he continued to expect of his wife. Isabel was about to follow Pansy, but he remarked that he wished she would remain; he had something to say to her. Then he walked about the drawing room a little, while she stood waiting, in her cloak.

"I don't understand what you wish to do," he said in a moment. "I should like to know—so that I may know how to act."

"Just now I wish to go to bed. I am very tired."

"Sit down and rest; I shall not keep you long. Not there—take a comfortable place." And he arranged a multitude of cushions that were scattered in picturesque disorder upon a vast divan. This was not, however, where she seated herself; she dropped into the nearest chair. The fire had gone out; the lights in the great room were few. She drew her cloak about her; she felt mortally cold. "I think you are trying to humiliate me," Osmond went on. "It's a most absurd undertaking."

"I haven't the least idea what you mean," said Isabel.

"You have played a very deep game; you have managed it beautifully."

"What is it that I have managed?"

"You have not quite settled it, however; we shall see him again." And he stopped in front of her, with his hands in his pockets, looking down at her thoughtfully, in his usual way, which seemed meant to let her know that she was not an object, but only a rather disagreeable incident, of thought.

"If you mean that Lord Warburton is under an obligation to come back, you are wrong," Isabel said. "He is under none whatever."

"That's just what I complain of. But when I say he will come back, I don't mean that he will come from a sense of duty."

"There is nothing else to make him. I think he has quite exhausted Rome."

"Ah no, that's a shallow judgment. Rome is inexhaustible." And Osmond began to walk about again. "However, about that, perhaps, there is no hurry," he added. "It's rather a good idea of his that we should go to England. If it were not for the fear of finding your cousin there, I think I should try to persuade you."

"It may be that you will not find my cousin," said Isabel.

"I should like to be sure of it. However, I shall be as sure as possible. At the same time I should like to see his house, that you told me so much about at one time: what do you call it?—Gardencourt. It must be a charming thing. And then, you know, I have a devotion to the memory of your uncle; you made me take a great fancy to him. I should like to see where he lived and died. That, however, is a detail. Your friend was right; Pansy ought to see England."

"I have no doubt she would enjoy it," said Isabel.

"But that's a long time hence; next autumn is far off," Osmond continued; "and meantime there are things that more nearly interest us. Do you think me so very proud?" he asked, suddenly.

"I think you very strange."

"You don't understand me."

"No, not even when you insult me."

"I don't insult you; I am incapable of it. I merely speak of certain facts, and if the allusion is an injury to you the fault is not mine. It is surely a fact that you have kept all this matter quite in your own hands."

"Are you going back to Lord Warburton?" Isabel asked. "I am very tired of his name."

"You shall hear it again before we have done with it."

She had spoken of his insulting her, but it suddenly seemed to her that this ceased to be a pain. He was going down—down; the vision of such a fall made her almost giddy; that was the only pain. He was too strange, too different; he didn't touch her. Still, the working of his morbid passion was extraordinary, and she felt a rising curiosity to know in what light he saw himself justified. "I might say to you that I judge you have nothing to say to me that is worth hearing," she rejoined in a moment. "But I should perhaps be wrong. There is a thing that would be worth my hearing—to know in the plainest words of what it is you accuse me."

"Of preventing Pansy's marriage to Warburton. Are those words plain enough?"

"On the contrary, I took a great interest in it. I told you so; and when you told me that you counted on me—that I think was what you said—I accepted the obligation. I was a fool to do so, but I did it."

"You pretended to do it, and you even pretended reluctance, to make me more willing to trust you. Then you began to use your ingenuity to get him out of the way."

"I think I see what you mean," said Isabel.

"Where is the letter that you told me he had written me?" her husband asked.

"I haven't the least idea; I haven't asked him."

"You stopped it on the way," said Osmond.

Isabel slowly got up; standing there, in her white cloak, which covered her to her feet, she might have represented the angel of disdain, first cousin to that of pity. "Oh, Osmond, for a man who was so fine!" she exclaimed, in a long murmur.

"I was never so fine as you! You have done everything you wanted. You have got him out of the way without appearing to do so, and you have placed me in the position in which you wished to see me—that of a man who tried to marry his daughter to a lord, but didn't succeed."

"Pansy doesn't care for him; she is very glad he is gone," said Isabel.

"That has nothing to do with the matter."

"And he doesn't care for Pansy."

"That won't do; you told me he did. I don't know why you wanted this particular satisfaction," Osmond continued; "you might have taken some other. It doesn't seem to me that I have been presumptuous—that I have taken too much for granted. I have been very modest about it, very quiet. The idea didn't originate with me. He began to show that he liked her before I ever thought of it. I left it all to you."

"Yes, you were very glad to leave it to me. After this you must attend to such things yourself."

He looked at her a moment, and then he turned away. "I thought you were very fond of my daughter."

"I have never been more so than today."

"Your affection is attended with immense limitations. However, that perhaps is natural."

"Is this all you wished to say to me?" Isabel asked, taking a candle that stood on one of the tables.

"Are you satisfied? Am I sufficiently disappointed?"

"I don't think that on the whole you are disappointed. You have had another opportunity to try to bewilder me."

"It's not that. It's proved that Pansy can aim high."

"Poor little Pansy!" said Isabel, turning away with her candle.

❧ 47 ❧

It was from Henrietta Stackpole that she learned that Caspar Goodwood had come to Rome; an event that took place three days after Lord Warburton's departure. This latter event had been preceded by an incident of some importance to Isabel—the temporary absence, once again, of Madame Merle, who had gone to Naples to stay with a friend, the happy possessor of a villa at Posilippo. Madame Merle had ceased to minister to Isabel's happiness, who found herself wondering whether the most discreet of women might not also by chance be the most dangerous. Sometimes, at night, she had strange visions; she seemed to see her husband and Madame Merle in dim, indistinguishable combination. It seemed to her that she had not done with her; this lady had something in reserve. Isabel's imagination applied itself actively to this elusive point, but every now and then it was checked by a nameless dread, so that when her brilliant friend was away from Rome she had almost a consciousness of respite. She had already learned from Miss Stackpole that Caspar Goodwood was in Europe, Henrietta having written to inform her of this fact immediately after meeting him in Paris. He himself never wrote to Isabel, and though he was in Europe she thought it very possible he might not desire to see her. Their last interview, before her marriage, had had quite the character of a complete rupture; if she remembered rightly he had said he wished to take his last look at her. Since then he had been the most inharmonious survival of her earlier time—the only one, in fact, with which a permanent pain was associated. He left her, that morning, with the sense of an unnecessary shock; it was like a collision between vessels in broad daylight. There had been no mist, no hidden current to excuse it, and she herself had only wished to steer skillfully. He had bumped against her prow, however, while her hand was on the tiller, and—to complete the metaphor—had given the lighter vessel a strain which still occasionally betrayed itself in a faint creaking. It had been painful to see him, because he represented the only serious harm that (to her belief) she had ever done in the world; he was the only person with an unsatisfied claim upon her. She had made him unhappy; she couldn't help it; and his unhappiness was a great reality. She cried with rage, after he had left her, at—she hardly knew what: she tried to think it was at his want of consideration. He had come to her with his unhappiness when her

414

own bliss was so perfect; he had done his best to darken the brightness of these pure rays. He had not been violent, and yet there was a violence in that. There was a violence at any rate in something, somewhere; perhaps it was only in her own fit of weeping and that after-sense of it which lasted for three or four days. The effect of Caspar Goodwood's visit faded away, and during the first year of Isabel's marriage he dropped out of her books. He was a thankless subject of reference; it was disagreeable to have to think of a person who was unhappy on your account and whom you could do nothing to relieve. It would have been different if she had been able to doubt, even a little, of his unhappiness, as she doubted of Lord Warburton's; unfortunately it was beyond question, and this aggressive, uncompromising look of it was just what made it unattractive. She could never say to herself that Caspar Goodwood had great compensations, as she was able to say in the case of her English suitor. She had no faith in his compensations, and no esteem for them. A cotton factory was not a compensation for anything—least of all for having failed to marry Isabel Archer. And yet, beyond that, she hardly knew what he had—save of course his intrinsic qualities. Oh, he was intrinsic enough; she never thought of his even looking for artificial aids. If he extended his business—that, to the best of her belief, was the only form exertion could take with him—it would be because it was an enterprising thing, or good for the business; not in the least because he might hope it would overlay the past. This gave his figure a kind of bareness and bleakness which made the accident of meeting it in one's meditations always a sort of shock; it was deficient in the social drapery which muffles the sharpness of human contact. His perfect silence, moreover, the fact that she never heard from him and very seldom heard any mention of him, deepened this impression of his loneliness. She asked Lily for news of him, from time to time; but Lily knew nothing about Boston; her imagination was confined within the limits of Manhattan. As time went on Isabel thought of him oftener, and with fewer restrictions; she had more than once the idea of writing to him. She had never told her husband about him—never let Osmond know of his visits to her in Florence; a reserve not dictated in the early period by a want of confidence in Osmond, but simply by the consideration that Caspar Goodwood's disappointment was not her secret but his own. It would be wrong of her, she believed, to convey it to another, and Mr. Goodwood's affairs could have, after all, but little interest for Gilbert. When it came to the point she never wrote to him; it seemed to her that, considering his grievance, the least she could do was to let him alone. Nevertheless she would have been glad to be in some way nearer to him. It was not that it ever occurred to her that she might have married him; even after the consequences of her marriage became vivid to her, that particular reflection, though she indulged in so many, had not the assurance to present itself. But when she found herself in trouble he became a member of that circle of things with which she wished to set herself right. I have related how passionately she desired to feel that her unhappiness should not have come to her through her own fault. She had no near prospect of dying, and yet she wished to make her peace with the world—to put her spiritual affairs in order. It came back to her from time to time that there was an account still to be settled with Caspar Goodwood; it seemed to her that she would settle it today on terms easy for him. Still, when she learned that he was coming to Rome she felt afraid; it would be more disagreeable for him than for anyone else to learn that she was unhappy. Deep in her breast she believed that he had invested all his in her happiness, while the others had invested only a part. He was one more person from whom she should have to conceal her misery. She was reassured, however, after he arrived in Rome, for he spent several days without coming to see her.

Henrietta Stackpole, it may well be imagined, was much more punctual, and Isabel was largely favored with the society of her friend. She threw herself into it, for now that she had made such a point of keeping her conscience clear, that was one way of proving that she had not been superficial—the more so that the years, in their flight, had rather enriched than blighted those peculiarities which had been humorously criticized by persons less interested than Isabel and were striking enough to give friendship a spice of heroism. Henrietta was as keen and quick and fresh as ever, and as neat and bright and fair. Her eye had lost none of its serenity, her toilet none of its crispness, her opinions none of their national flavor. She was by no means quite unchanged, however; it seemed to Isabel that she had grown restless. Of old she had never been restless; though she was perpetually in motion it was impossible to be more deliberate. She had a reason for everything she did; she fairly bristled with motives. Formerly, when she came to Europe it was because she wished to see it, but now, having already seen it, she had no such excuse. She did not for a moment pretend that the desire to examine decaying civilizations had anything to do with her present enterprise; her journey was rather an expression of her independence of the old world than of a sense of further obligations to it. "It's nothing to come to Europe," she said to Isabel; "it doesn't seem to me one needs so many reasons for that. It is something to stay at home; this is much more important." It was not therefore with a sense of doing anything very important that she treated herself to another pilgrimage to Rome; she had seen the place before and carefully inspected it; the actual episode was simply a sign of familiarity, of one's knowing all about it, of one's having as good a right as anyone else to be there. This was all very well, and Henrietta was restless; she had a perfect right to be restless, too, if one came to that. But she had after all a better reason for coming to Rome than that she cared for it so little. Isabel easily recognized it, and with it the worth of her friend's fidelity. She had crossed the stormy ocean in midwinter because she guessed that Isabel was sad. Henrietta guessed a great deal, but she had never guessed so happily as that. Isabel's satisfactions just now were few, but even if they had been more numerous, there would still have been something of individual joy in her sense of being justified in having always thought highly of Henrietta. She had made large concessions with regard to her, but she had insisted that, with all abatements, she was very valuable. It was not her own triumph, however, that Isabel found good; it was simply the relief of confessing to Henrietta, the first person to whom she had owned it, that she was not contented. Henrietta had herself approached this point with the smallest possible delay, and had accused her to her face of being miserable. She was a woman, she was a sister; she was not Ralph, nor Lord Warburton, nor Caspar Goodwood, and Isabel could speak.

"Yes, I am miserable," she said, very gently. She hated to hear herself say it; she tried to say it as judicially as possible.

"What does he do to you?" Henrietta asked, frowning as if she were inquiring into the operations of a quack doctor.

"He does nothing. But he doesn't like me."

"He's very difficult!" cried Miss Stackpole. "Why don't you leave him?"

"I can't change, that way," Isabel said.

"Why not, I should like to know? You won't confess that you have made a mistake. You are too proud."

"I don't know whether I am too proud. But I can't publish my mistake. I don't think that's decent. I would much rather die."

"You won't think so always," said Henrietta.

"I don't know what great unhappiness might bring me to; but it seems to me I shall always be ashamed. One must accept one's deeds. I married him before all the world; I was perfectly free; it was impossible to do anything more deliberate. One can't change, that way," Isabel repeated.

"You have changed, in spite of the impossibility. I hope you don't mean to say that you like him."

Isabel hesitated a moment. "No, I don't like him. I can tell you, because I am weary of my secret. But that's enough; I can't tell all the world."

Henrietta gave a rich laugh. "Don't you think you are rather too considerate?"

"It's not of him that I am considerate—it's of myself!" Isabel answered.

It was not surprising that Gilbert Osmond should not have taken comfort in Miss Stackpole; his instinct had naturally set him in opposition to a young lady capable of advising his wife to withdraw from the conjugal mansion. When she arrived in Rome he said to Isabel that he hoped she would leave her friend the interviewer, alone; and Isabel answered that he at least had nothing to fear from her. She said to Henrietta that as Osmond didn't like her she could not invite her to dine; but they could easily see each other in other ways. Isabel received Miss Stackpole freely in her own sitting room, and took her repeatedly to drive, face to face with Pansy, who, bending a little forward, on the opposite seat of the carriage, gazed at the celebrated authoress with a respectful attention which Henrietta occasionally found irritating. She complained to Isabel that Miss Osmond had a little look as if she should remember everything one said. "I don't want to be remembered that way," Miss Stackpole declared; "I consider that my conversation refers only to the moment, like the morning papers. Your step-daughter, as she sits there, looks as if she kept all the back numbers and would bring them out some day against me." She could not bring herself to think favorably of Pansy, whose absence of initiative, of conversation, of personal claims, seemed to her, in a girl of twenty, unnatural and even sinister. Isabel presently saw that Osmond would have liked her to urge a little the cause of her friend, insist a little upon his receiving her, so that he might appear to suffer for good manners' sake. Her immediate acceptance of his objections put him too much in the wrong—it being in effect one of the disadvantages of expressing contempt, that you cannot enjoy at the same time the credit of expressing sympathy. Osmond held to his credit, and yet he held to his objections—all of which were elements difficult to reconcile. The right thing would have been that Miss Stackpole should come to dine at the Palazzo Roccanera once or twice, so that (in spite of his superficial civility, always so great) she might judge for herself how little pleasure it gave him. From the moment, however, that both the ladies were so unaccommodating, there was nothing for Osmond but to wish that Henrietta would take herself off. It was surprising how little satisfaction he got from his wife's friends; he took occasion to call Isabel's attention to it.

"You are certainly not fortunate in your intimates; I wish you might make a new collection," he said to her one morning, in reference to nothing visible at the moment, but in a tone of ripe reflection which deprived the remark of all brutal abruptness. "It's as if you had taken the trouble to pick out the people in the world that I have least in common with. Your cousin I have always thought a conceited ass—besides his being the most ill-favored animal I know. Then it's insufferably tiresome that one can't tell him so; one must spare him on account of his health. His health seems to me the best part of him; it gives him privileges enjoyed by no one else. If he is so desperately ill there is only one way to prove it; but he seems to have no mind for that. I can't say much more for the great Warburton. When one really thinks of it, the cool insolence of that performance was something rare! He comes and looks at one's daughter as if she were a suite of apartments; he tries the door handles and looks out of the windows, raps on the walls and almost thinks he will take the place. Will you be so good as to draw up a lease? Then, on the whole, he decides that the rooms are too small; he doesn't think he could live on a third floor; he must look out for a *piano nobile*. And he goes away, after having got a month's lodging in the poor little apartment for nothing. Miss Stackpole, however, is your most wonderful invention. She strikes me as a kind of monster. One hasn't a nerve in one's body that she doesn't set quivering. You know I never have admitted

that she is a woman. Do you know what she reminds me of? Of a new steel pen—
the most odious thing in nature. She talks as a steel pen writes; aren't her letters,
by the way, on ruled paper? She thinks and moves, and walks and looks, exactly as
she talks. You may say that she doesn't hurt me, inasmuch as I don't see her. I don't
see her, but I hear her; I hear her all day long. Her voice is in my ears; I can't get rid
of it. I know exactly what she says, and every inflection of the tone in which she says
it. She says charming things about me, and they give you great comfort. I don't like
at all to think she talks about me—I feel as I should feel if I knew the footman were
wearing my hat!"

Henrietta talked about Gilbert Osmond, as his wife assured him, rather less than
he suspected. She had plenty of other subjects, in two of which the reader may be
supposed to be especially interested. She let Isabel know that Caspar Goodwood
had discovered for himself that she was unhappy, though indeed her ingenuity was
unable to suggest what comfort he hoped to give her by coming to Rome and yet not
calling on her. They met him twice in the street, but he had no appearance of seeing them; they were driving, and he had a habit of looking straight in front of him,
as if he proposed to contemplate but one object at a time. Isabel could have fancied
she had seen him the day before; it must have been with just that face and step that
he walked out of Mrs. Touchett's door at the close of their last interview. He was
dressed just as he had been dressed on that day; Isabel remembered the color of his
cravat; and yet in spite of this familiar look there was a strangeness in his figure
too; something that made her feel afresh that it was rather terrible he should have
come to Rome. He looked bigger and more over-topping than of old, and in those
days he certainly was lofty enough. She noticed that the people whom he passed
looked back after him; but he went straight forward, lifting above them a face like
a February sky.

Miss Stackpole's other topic was very different; she gave Isabel the latest news
about Mr. Bantling. He had been out in the United States the year before, and she
was happy to say she had been able to show him considerable attention. She didn't
know how much he had enjoyed it, but she would undertake to say it had done him
good; he wasn't the same man when he left that he was when he came. It had
opened his eyes and shown him that England was not everything. He was very much
liked over there, and thought extremely simple—more simple than the English
were commonly supposed to be. There were some people thought him affected; she
didn't know whether they meant that his simplicity was an affectation. Some of his
questions were too discouraging; he thought all the chamber-maids were farmers'
daughters—or all the farmers' daughters were chamber-maids—she couldn't
exactly remember which. He hadn't seemed able to grasp the school system; it
seemed really too much for him. On the whole he had appeared as if there were too
much—as if he could only take a small part. The part he had chosen was the hotel

system, and the river navigation. He seemed really fascinated with the hotels; he had a photograph of every one he had visited. But the river-steamers were his principal interest; he wanted to do nothing but sail on the big boats. They had traveled together from New York to Milwaukee, stopping at the most interesting cities on the route; and whenever they started afresh he had wanted to know if they could go by the steamer. He seemed to have no idea of geography—had an impression that Baltimore was a western city, and was perpetually expecting to arrive at the Mississippi. He appeared never to have heard of any river in America but the Mississippi, and was unprepared to recognize the existence of the Hudson, though he was obliged to confess at last that it was fully equal to the Rhine. They had spent some pleasant hours in the palace-cars; he was always ordering ice-cream from the colored man. He could never get used to that idea—that you could get ice-cream in the cars. Of course you couldn't, nor fans, nor candy, nor anything in the English cars! He found the heat quite overwhelming, and she had told him that she expected it was the greatest he had ever experienced. He was now in England, hunting—"hunting round," Henrietta called it. These amusements were those of the American red men; we had left that behind long ago, the pleasures of the chase. It seemed to be generally believed in England that we wore tomahawks and feathers; but such a costume was more in keeping with English habits. Mr. Bantling would not have time to join her in Italy, but when she should go to Paris again he expected to come over. He wanted very much to see Versailles again; he was very fond of the ancient *régime*. They didn't agree about that, but that was what she liked Versailles for, that you could see the ancient *régime* had been swept away. There were no dukes and marquises there now; on the contrary, she remembered one day when there were five American families, all walking round. Mr. Bantling was very anxious that she should take up the subject of England again, and he thought she might get on better with it now; England had changed a good deal within two or three years. He was determined that if she went there he should go to see his sister, Lady Pensil, and that this time the invitation should come to her straight. The mystery of that other one had never been explained.

Caspar Goodwood came at last to the Palazzo Roccanera; he had written Isabel a note beforehand, to ask leave. This was promptly granted; she would be at home at six o'clock that afternoon. She spent the day wondering what he was coming for—what good he expected to get of it. He had presented himself hitherto as a person destitute of the faculty of compromise, who would take what he had asked for or nothing. Isabel's hospitality, however, asked no questions, and she found no great difficulty in appearing happy enough to deceive him. It was her conviction, at least, that she deceived him, and made him say to himself that he had been misinformed. But she also saw, so she believed, that he was not disappointed, as some other men, she was sure, would have been; he had not come to Rome to look for an opportunity. She never found out what he had come for; he offered her no explanation; there could be none but the very simple one that he wanted to see her. In other words, he had come for his amusement. Isabel followed up this induction with a good deal of eagerness, and was delighted to have found a formula that would lay the ghost of this gentleman's ancient grievance. If he had come to Rome for his amusement this was exactly what she wanted; for if he cared for amusement he had got over his heartache. If he had got over his heartache everything was as it should be, and her responsibilities were at an end. It was true that he took his recreation a little stiffly, but he had never been demonstrative, and Isabel had every reason to believe that he was satisfied with what he saw. Henrietta was not in his confidence, though he was in hers, and Isabel consequently received no side-light upon his state of mind. He had little conversation upon general topics; it came back to her that she had said of him once, years before—"Mr. Goodwood speaks a good deal, but he doesn't talk." He spoke a good deal in Rome, but he talked, perhaps, as little as ever; considering, that is, how much there was to talk about. His arrival was not calculated to simplify her relations with her husband, for if Mr. Osmond didn't like her friends, Mr. Goodwood had no claim upon his attention save having been one of the first of them. There was nothing for her to say of him but that he was an old friend; this rather meager synthesis exhausted the facts. She had been obliged to introduce him to Osmond; it was impossible she should not ask him to dinner, to her Thursday evenings, of which she had grown very weary, but to which her husband still held for the sake not so much of inviting people as of not inviting them. To the Thursdays Mr. Goodwood came regularly, solemnly, rather early; he appeared to regard them with a good deal of gravity. Isabel every now and then had a moment of anger; there was something so literal about him; she thought he might know that she didn't know what to do with him. But she couldn't call him stupid; he was not that in the least; he was only extraordinarily honest. To be as honest as that made a man very different from most people; one had to be almost equally honest with him. Isabel made this latter reflection at the very time she was flattering herself that she had persuaded him that she was the most light-hearted of women. He never threw any doubt on this point, never asked her any personal questions. He got on much better with Osmond than had seemed probable. Osmond had a great dislike to being counted upon; in such a case he had an irresistible need of disappointing you. It was in virtue of this principle that he gave himself the entertainment of taking a fancy to a perpendicular Bostonian whom he had been depended upon to treat with coldness. He asked Isabel if Mr. Goodwood also had wanted to marry her, and expressed surprise at her not having accepted him. It would have been an excellent thing, like living under a tall belfry which would strike all the hours and make a queer vibration in the upper air. He declared he liked to talk with the great Goodwood; it wasn't easy at first, you had to climb up an interminable steep staircase up to the top of the tower; but when you got there you had a big view and felt a little fresh breeze. Osmond, as we know, had delightful qualities, and he gave Caspar Goodwood the benefit of them all. Isabel could see that Mr. Goodwood thought better of her husband than he had ever wished to; he had given her the impression that morning in Florence of being inaccessible to a good impression. Osmond asked him repeatedly to dinner, and Goodwood smoked a cigar with him afterwards, and even desired to be shown his collections. Osmond said to Isabel that he was very original; he was as strong as an English portmanteau. Caspar Goodwood took to riding on the Campagna, and devoted much time to this exercise; it was therefore mainly in the evening that Isabel saw him. She bethought herself of saying to him one day that if he were willing he could render her a service. And then she added smiling—

"I don't know, however, what right I have to ask a service of you."

"You are the person in the world who has most right," he answered. "I have given you assurances that I have never given anyone else."

The service was that he should go and see her cousin Ralph, who was ill at the Hôtel de Paris, alone, and be as kind to him as possible. Mr. Goodwood had never seen him, but he would know who the poor fellow was; if she was not mistaken, Ralph had once invited him to Gardencourt. Caspar remembered the invitation perfectly, and, though he was not supposed to be a man of imagination, had enough to put himself in the place of a poor gentleman who lay dying at a Roman inn. He called at the Hôtel de Paris, and on being shown into the presence of the master of Gardencourt, found Miss Stackpole sitting beside his sofa. A singular change had, in fact, occurred in this lady's relations with Ralph Touchett. She had not been asked by Isabel to go and see him, but on hearing that he was too ill to come out had immediately gone of her own motion. After this she had paid him a daily visit— always under the conviction that they were great enemies. "Oh yes, we are intimate enemies," Ralph used to say; and he accused her freely—as freely as the humor of it would allow—of coming to worry him to death. In reality they became excellent friends, and Henrietta wondered that she should never have liked him before. Ralph liked her exactly as much as he had always done; he had never doubted for a moment that she was an excellent fellow. They talked about everything, and always differed; about everything, that is, but Isabel—a topic as to which Ralph always had a thin forefinger on his lips. On the other hand, Mr. Bantling was a great resource; Ralph was capable of discussing Mr. Bantling with Henrietta for hours. Discussion was stimulated of course by their inevitable difference of view—Ralph having amused himself with taking the ground that the genial ex-guardsman was a regular Machiavelli. Caspar Goodwood could contribute nothing to such a debate; but after he had been left alone with Touchett, he found there were various other matters they could talk about. It must be admitted that the lady who had just gone out was not one of these; Caspar granted all Miss Stackpole's merits in advance, but had no further remark to make about her. Neither, after the first allusions, did the two men expatiate upon Mrs. Osmond—a theme in which Goodwood perceived as many dangers as his host. He felt very sorry for Ralph; he couldn't bear to see a pleasant man so helpless. There was help in Goodwood, when once the fountain had been tapped; and he repeated several times his visit to the Hôtel de Paris. It seemed to Isabel that she had been very clever; she had disposed of the superfluous Caspar. She had given him an occupation; she had converted him into a caretaker of Ralph. She had a plan of making him travel northward with her cousin as soon as the first mild weather should allow it. Lord Warburton had brought Ralph to Rome, and Mr. Goodwood should take him away. There seemed a happy symmetry in this, and she was now intensely eager that Ralph should leave Rome. She had a constant fear that he would die there, and a horror of this event occurring at an inn, at her door, which he had so rarely entered. Ralph must sink to his last rest in his own dear house, in one of those deep, dim chambers of Gardencourt, where the dark ivy would cluster round the edges of the glimmering window. There seemed to Isabel in these days something sacred about Gardencourt; no chapter of the past was more perfectly irrecoverable. When she thought of the months she had spent there the tears rose to her eyes. She flattered herself, as I say, upon her ingenuity, but she had need of all she could muster; for several events occurred which seemed to confront and defy her. The Countess Gemini arrived from Florence—arrived with her trunks, her dresses, her chatter, her little fibs, her frivolity, the strange memory of her lovers. Edward Rosïer, who had been away somewhere—no one, not even Pansy, knew where—reappeared in Rome and began to write her long letters, which she never answered. Madame Merle returned from Naples and said to her with a strange smile—"What on earth did you do with Lord Warburton?" As if it were any business of hers!

❦ 48 ❦

One day, toward the end of February, Ralph Touchett made up his mind to return to England. He had his own reasons for this decision, which he was not bound to communicate; but Henrietta Stackpole, to whom he mentioned his intention, flattered herself that she guessed them. She forbore to express them, however; she only said, after a moment, as she sat by his sofa—

"I suppose you know that you can't go alone?"

"I have no idea of doing that," Ralph answered. "I shall have people with me."

"What do you mean by 'people'? Servants, whom you pay?"

"Ah," said Ralph, jocosely, "after all, they are human beings."

"Are there any women among them?" Miss Stackpole inquired, calmly.

"You speak as if I had a dozen! No, I confess I haven't a soubrette in my employment."

"Well," said Henrietta, tranquilly, "you can't go to England that way. You must have a woman's care."

"I have had so much of yours for the past fortnight that it will last me a good while."

"You have not had enough of it yet. I guess I will go with you," said Henrietta.

"Go with me?" Ralph slowly raised himself from his sofa.

"Yes, I know you don't like me, but I will go with you all the same. It would be better for your health to lie down again."

Ralph looked at her a little; then he slowly resumed his former posture.

"I like you very much," he said in a moment.

Miss Stackpole gave one of her infrequent laughs.

"You needn't think that by saying that you can buy me off. I will go with you, and what is more I will take care of you."

"You are a very good woman," said Ralph.

"Wait till I get you safely home before you say that. It won't be easy. But you had better go, all the same."

Before she left him, Ralph said to her—

"Do you really mean to take care of me?"

"Well, I mean to try."

"I notify you, then, that I submit. Oh, I submit!" And it was perhaps a sign of submission that a few minutes after she had left him alone he burst into a loud fit of laughter. It seemed to him so inconsequent, such a conclusive proof of his having abdicated all functions and renounced all exercise, that he should start on a journey across Europe under the supervision of Miss Stackpole. And the great oddity was that the prospect pleased him; he was gratefully, luxuriously passive. He felt even impatient to start; and indeed he had an immense longing to see his own house again. The end of everything was at hand; it seemed to him that he could stretch out his arm and touch the goal. But he wished to die at home; it was the only wish he had left—to extend himself in the large quiet room where he had last seen his father lie, and close his eyes upon the summer dawn.

That same day Caspar Goodwood came to see him, and he informed his visitor that Miss Stackpole had taken him up and was to conduct him back to England.

"Ah then," said Caspar, "I am afraid I shall be a fifth wheel to the coach. Mrs. Osmond has made *me* promise to go with you."

"Good heavens—it's the golden age! You are all too kind."

"The kindness on my part is to her; it's hardly to you."

"Granting that, *she* is kind," said Ralph, smiling.

"To get people to go with you? Yes, that's a sort of kindness," Goodwood answered, without lending himself to the joke. "For myself, however," he added, "I will go so far as to say that I would much rather travel with you and Miss Stackpole than with Miss Stackpole alone."

"And you would rather stay here than do either," said Ralph. "There is really no need of your coming. Henrietta is extraordinarily efficient."

"I am sure of that. But I have promised Mrs. Osmond."

"You can easily get her to let you off."

"She wouldn't let me off for the world. She wants me to look after you, but that isn't the principal thing. The principal thing is that she wants me to leave Rome."

"Ah, you see too much in it," Ralph suggested.

"I bore her," Goodwood went on; "she has nothing to say to me, so she invented that."

"Oh then, if it's a convenience to her, I certainly will take you with me. Though I don't see why it should be a convenience," Ralph added in a moment.

"Well," said Caspar Goodwood, simply, "she thinks I am watching her."

"Watching her?"

"Trying to see whether she's happy."

"That's easy to see," said Ralph. "She's the most visibly happy woman I know."

"Exactly so; I am satisfied," Goodwood answered, dryly. For all his dryness, however, he had more to say. "I have been watching her; I was an old friend, and it seemed to me I had the right. She pretends to be happy; that was what she undertook to be; and I thought I should like to see for myself what it amounts to. I have seen," he continued, in a strange voice, "and I don't want to see anymore. I am now quite ready to go."

"Do you know it strikes me as about time you should?" Ralph rejoined. And this was the only conversation these gentlemen had about Isabel Osmond.

Henrietta made her preparations for departure, and among them she found it proper to say a few words to the Countess Gemini, who returned at Miss Stackpole's *pension* the visit which this lady had paid her in Florence.

"You were very wrong about Lord Warburton," she remarked, to the Countess. "I think it is right you should know that."

"About his making love to Isabel? My poor lady, he was at her house three times a day. He has left traces of his passage!" the Countess cried.

"He wished to marry your niece; that's why he came to the house."

The Countess stared, and then gave an inconsiderate laugh.

"Is that the story that Isabel tells? It isn't bad, as such things go. If he wishes to marry my niece, pray why doesn't he do it? Perhaps he has gone to buy the wedding ring, and will come back with it next month, after I am gone."

"No, he will not come back. Miss Osmond doesn't wish to marry him."

"She is very accommodating! I knew she was fond of Isabel, but I didn't know she carried it so far."

"I don't understand you," said Henrietta, coldly, and reflecting that the Countess was unpleasantly perverse. "I really must stick to my point—that Isabel never encouraged the attentions of Lord Warburton."

"My dear friend, what do you and I know about it? All we know is that my brother is capable of everything."

"I don't know what he is capable of," said Henrietta, with dignity.

"It's not her encouraging Lord Warburton that I complain of; it's her sending him away. I want particularly to see him. Do you suppose she thought I would make him faithless?" the Countess continued, with audacious insistence. "However, she is only keeping him, one can feel that. The house is full of him there; he is quite in the air. Oh yes, he has left traces; I am sure I shall see him yet."

"Well," said Henrietta, after a little, with one of those inspirations which had made the fortune of her letters to the *Interviewer*, "perhaps he will be more successful with you than with Isabel!"

When she told her friend of the offer she had made to Ralph, Isabel replied that she could have done nothing that would have pleased her more. It had always been her faith that, at bottom, Ralph and Henrietta were made to understand each other.

"I don't care whether he understands me or not," said Henrietta. "The great thing is that he shouldn't die in the cars."

"He won't do that," Isabel said, shaking her head, with an extension of faith.

"He won't if I can help it. I see you want us all to go. I don't know what you want to do."

"I want to be alone," said Isabel.

"You won't be that so long as you have got so much company at home."

"Ah, they are part of the comedy. You others are spectators."

"Do you call it a comedy, Isabel Archer?" Henrietta inquired, severely.

"The tragedy, then, if you like. You are all looking at me; it makes me uncomfortable."

Henrietta contemplated her a while.

"You are like the stricken deer, seeking the innermost shade. Oh, you do give me such a sense of helplessness!" she broke out.

"I am not at all helpless. There are many things I mean to do."

"It's not you I am speaking of; it's myself. It's too much, having come on purpose, to leave you just as I find you."

"You don't do that; you leave me much refreshed," Isabel said.

"Very mild refreshment—sour lemonade! I want you to promise me something."

"I can't do that. I shall never make another promise. I made such a solemn one four years ago, and I have succeeded so ill in keeping it."

"You have had no encouragement. In this case I should give you the greatest. Leave your husband before the worst comes; that's what I want you to promise."

"The worst? What do you call the worst?"

"Before your character gets spoiled."

"Do you mean my disposition? It won't get spoiled," Isabel answered, smiling. "I am taking very good care of it. I am extremely struck," she added, turning away, "with the offhand way in which you speak of a woman leaving her husband. It's easy to see you have never had one!"

"Well," said Henrietta, as if she were beginning an argument, "nothing is more common in our western cities, and it is to them, after all, that we must look in the future." Her argument, however, does not concern this history, which has too many other threads to unwind. She announced to Ralph Touchett that she was ready to leave Rome by any train that he might designate, and Ralph immediately pulled himself together for departure. Isabel went to see him at the last, and he made the same remark that Henrietta had made. It struck him that Isabel was uncommonly glad to get rid of them all.

For all answer to this she gently laid her hand on his, and said in a low tone, with a quick smile—

"My dear Ralph!"

It was answer enough, and he was quite contented. But he went on, in the same way, jocosely, ingenuously—"I've seen less of you than I might, but it's better than nothing. And then I have heard a great deal about you."

"I don't know from whom, leading the life you have done."

"From the voices of the air! Oh, from no one else; I never let other people speak of you. They always say you are 'charming,' and that's so flat."

"I might have seen more of you, certainly," Isabel said. "But when one is married one has so much occupation."

"Fortunately I am not married. When you come to see me in England, I shall be able to entertain you with all the freedom of a bachelor." He continued to talk as if they should certainly meet again, and succeeded in making the assumption appear almost just. He made no allusion to his term being near, to the probability that he should not outlast the summer. If he preferred it so, Isabel was willing enough; the reality was sufficiently distinct, without their erecting finger-posts in conversation. That had been well enough for the earlier time, though about this as about his other affairs Ralph had never been egotistic. Isabel spoke of his journey, of the stages into which he should divide it, of the precautions he should take.

"Henrietta is my greatest precaution," Ralph said. "The conscience of that woman is sublime."

"Certainly, she will be very conscientious."

"Will be? She has been! It's only because she thinks it's her duty that she goes with me. There's a conception of duty for you."

"Yes, it's a generous one," said Isabel, "and it makes me deeply ashamed. I ought to go with you, you know."

"Your husband wouldn't like that."

"No, he wouldn't like it. But I might go, all the same."

"I am startled by the boldness of your imagination. Fancy my being a cause of disagreement between a lady and her husband!"

"That's why I don't go," said Isabel, simply, but not very lucidly.

Ralph understood well enough, however. "I should think so, with all those occupations you speak of."

"It isn't that. I am afraid," said Isabel. After a pause she repeated, as if to make herself, rather than him, hear the words—"I am afraid."

Ralph could hardly tell what her tone meant; it was so strangely deliberate—apparently so void of emotion. Did she wish to do public penance for a fault of which she had not been convicted? or were her words simply an attempt at enlightened self-analysis? However this might be, Ralph could not resist so easy an opportunity. "Afraid of your husband?" he said, jocosely.

"Afraid of myself!" said Isabel, getting up. She stood there a moment, and then she added—"If I were afraid of my husband, that would be simply my duty. That is what women are expected to be."

"Ah, yes," said Ralph, laughing; "but to make up for it there is always some man awfully afraid of some woman!"

She gave no heed to this pleasantry, but suddenly took a different turn. "With Henrietta at the head of your little band," she exclaimed abruptly, "there will be nothing left for Mr. Goodwood!"

"Ah, my dear Isabel," Ralph answered, "he's used to that. There *is* nothing left for Mr. Goodwood!"

Isabel colored, and then she declared, quickly, that she must leave him. They stood together a moment; both her hands were in both of his. "You have been my best friend," she said.

"It was for you that I wanted—that I wanted to live. But I am of no use to you."

Then it came over her more poignantly that she should not see him again. She could not accept that; she could not part with him that way. "If you should send for me I would come," she said at last.

"Your husband won't consent to that."

"Oh yes, I can arrange it."

"I shall keep that for my last pleasure!" said Ralph.

In answer to which she simply kissed him.

It was a Thursday, and that evening Caspar Goodwood came to the Palazzo Roccanera. He was among the first to arrive, and he spent some time in conversation with Gilbert Osmond, who almost always was present when his wife received. They sat down together, and Osmond, talkative, communicative, expansive, seemed possessed with a kind of intellectual gaiety. He leaned back with his legs crossed, lounging and chatting, while Goodwood, more restless, but not at all lively, shifted his position, played with his hat, made the little sofa creak beneath him. Osmond's face wore a sharp, aggressive smile; he was like a man whose perceptions had been quickened by good news. He remarked to Goodwood that he was very sorry they were to lose him; he himself should particularly miss him. He saw so few intelligent men—they were surprisingly scarce in Rome. He must be sure to come back; there was something very refreshing, to an inveterate Italian like himself, in talking with a genuine outsider.

"I am very fond of Rome, you know," Osmond said; "but there is nothing I like better than to meet people who haven't that superstition. The modern world is after all very fine. Now you are thoroughly modern, and yet you are not at all flimsy. So many of the moderns we see are such very poor stuff. If they are the children of the future we are willing to die young. Of course the ancients too are often very tiresome. My wife and I like everything that is really new—not the mere pretence of it. There is nothing new, unfortunately, in ignorance and stupidity. We see plenty of that in forms that offer themselves as a revelation of progress, of light. A revelation of vulgarity! There is a certain kind of vulgarity which I believe is really new; I don't think there ever was anything like it before. Indeed I don't find vulgarity, at all, before the present century. You see a faint menace of it here and there in the last, but today the air has grown so dense that delicate things are literally not recognized. Now, we have liked you—" And Osmond hesitated a moment, laying his hand gently on Goodwood's knee and smiling with a mixture of assurance and embarrassment. "I am going to say something extremely offensive and patronising, but you must let me have the satisfaction of it. We have liked you because—because you have reconciled us a little to the future. If there are to be a certain number of people like you—*à la bonne heure!* I am talking for my wife as well as for myself, you see. She speaks for me; why shouldn't I speak for her? We are as united, you know, as the candlestick and the snuffers. Am I assuming too much when I say that I think I have understood from you that your occupations have been—a—commercial? There is a danger in that, you know; but it's the way you have escaped that strikes us. Excuse me if my little compliment seems in execrable taste; fortunately my wife doesn't hear me. What I mean is that you *might have been*—a—what I was mentioning just now. The whole American world was in a conspiracy to make you so. But you resisted, you have something that saved you. And yet you are so modern, so modern; the most modern man we know! We shall always be delighted to see you again."

I have said that Osmond was in good-humor, and these remarks will give ample evidence of the fact. They were infinitely more personal than he usually cared to be, and if Caspar Goodwood had attended to them more closely he might have thought that the defence of delicacy was in rather odd hands. We may believe, however, that Osmond knew very well what he was about, and that if he chose for once to be a little vulgar, he had an excellent reason for the escapade. Goodwood had only a vague sense that he was laying it on, somehow; he scarcely knew where the mixture was applied. Indeed he scarcely knew what Osmond was talking about; he wanted to be alone with Isabel, and that idea spoke louder to him than her husband's perfectly modulated voice. He watched her talking with other people, and wondered when she would be at liberty, and whether he might ask her to go into one of the other rooms. His humor was not, like Osmond's, of the best; there was an element of dull rage in his consciousness of things. Up to this time he had not disliked Osmond personally; he had only thought him very well informed and obliging, and more than he had supposed like the person whom Isabel Archer would naturally marry. Osmond had won in the open field a great advantage over him, and Goodwood had too strong a sense of fair play to have been moved to underrate him on that account. He had not tried positively to like him; this was a flight of sentimental benevolence of which, even in the days when he came nearest to reconciling himself to what had happened, Goodwood was quite incapable. He accepted him as a rather brilliant personage of the amateurish kind, afflicted with a redundancy of leisure which it amused him to work off in little refinements of conversation. But he only half trusted him; he could never make out why the deuce Osmond should lavish refinements of any sort upon *him*. It made him suspect that he found some private entertainment in it, and it ministered to a general impression that his successful rival had a fantastic streak in his composition. He knew indeed that Osmond could have no reason to wish him evil; he had nothing to fear from him. He had carried off a supreme advantage, and he could afford to be kind to a man who had lost everything. It was true that Goodwood at times had wished Osmond were dead, and would have liked to kill him; but Osmond had no means of knowing this, for practice had made Goodwood quite perfect in the art of appearing inaccessible today to any violent emotion. He cultivated this art in order to deceive himself, but it was others that he deceived first. He cultivated it, moreover, with very limited success; of which there could be no better proof than the deep, dumb irritation that reigned in his soul when he heard Osmond speak of his wife's feelings as if he were commissioned to answer for them. That was all he had an ear for in what his host said to him this evening; he was conscious that Osmond made more of a point even than usual of referring to the conjugal harmony which prevailed at the Palazzo Roccanera. He was more careful than ever to speak as if he and his wife had all things in sweet community, and it were as natural to each of them to say "we" as to say "I." In all this there was an air of intention which puzzled and angered our poor Bostonian, who could only reflect for his comfort that Mrs. Osmond's relations with her husband were none of his business. He had no proof whatever that her husband misrepresented her, and if he judged her by the surface of things was bound to believe that she liked her life. She had never given him the faintest sign of discontent. Miss Stackpole had told him that she had lost her illusions, but writing for the papers had made Miss Stackpole sensational. She was too fond of early news. Moreover, since her arrival in Rome she had been much on her guard; she had ceased to flash her lantern at him. This, indeed, it may be said for her, would have been quite against her conscience. She had now seen the reality of Isabel's situation, and it had inspired her with a just reserve. Whatever could be done to improve it, the most useful form of assistance would not be to inflame her former lovers with a sense of her wrongs. Miss Stackpole continued to take a deep interest in the state of Mr. Goodwood's feelings, but she showed it at present only by sending him choice extracts, humorous and other, from the American journals, of which she received several by every post and which she always perused with a pair of scissors in her hand. The articles she cut out she placed in an envelope addressed to Mr. Goodwood, which she left with her own hand at his hotel. He never asked her a question about Isabel; hadn't he come five thousand miles to see for himself? He was thus not in the least authorized to think Mrs. Osmond unhappy; but the very absence of authorization operated as an irritant, ministered to the angry pain with which, in spite of his theory that he had ceased to care, he now recognized that, as far as she was concerned, the future had nothing more for him. He had not even the satisfaction of knowing the truth; apparently he could not even be trusted to respect her if she *were* unhappy. He was hopeless, he was helpless, he was superfluous. To this last fact she had called his attention by her ingenious plan for making him leave Rome. He had no objection whatever to doing what he could for her cousin, but it made him grind his teeth to think that of all the services she might have asked of him this was the one she had been eager to select. There had been no danger of her choosing one that would have kept him in Rome!

Tonight what he was chiefly thinking of was that he was to leave her tomorrow, and that he had gained nothing by coming but the knowledge that he was as superfluous as ever. About herself he had gained no knowledge; she was imperturbable, impenetrable. He felt the old bitterness, which he had tried so hard to swallow, rise again in his throat, and he knew that there are disappointments which last as long as life. Osmond went on talking; Goodwood was vaguely aware that he was touching again upon his perfect intimacy with his wife. It seemed to him for a moment that Osmond had a kind of demoniac imagination; it was impossible that without malice he should have selected so unusual a topic. But what did it matter, after all, whether he were demoniac or not, and whether she loved him or hated him? She might hate him to the death without Goodwood's gaining by it.

"You travel, by the by, with Touchett," Osmond said. "I suppose that means that you will move slowly?"

"I don't know; I shall do just as he likes."

"You are very accommodating. We are immensely obliged to you; you must really let me say it. My wife has probably expressed to you what we feel. Touchett has been on our minds all winter; it has looked more than once as if he would never leave Rome. He ought never to have come; it's worse than an imprudence for people in that state to travel; it's a kind of indelicacy. I wouldn't for the world be under such an obligation to Touchett as he has been to—to my wife and me. Other people inevitably have to look after him, and everyone isn't so generous as you."

"I have nothing else to do," said Caspar, dryly.

Osmond looked at him a moment, askance. "You ought to marry, and then you would have plenty to do! It is true that in that case you wouldn't be quite so available for deeds of mercy."

"Do you find that as a married man you are so much occupied?"

"Ah, you see, being married is in itself an occupation. It isn't always active; it's often passive; but that takes even more attention. Then my wife and I do so many things together. We read, we study, we make music, we walk, we drive—we talk even, as when we first knew each other. I delight, to this hour, in my wife's conversation. If you are ever bored, get married. Your wife indeed may bore you, in that case; but you will never bore yourself. You will always have something to say to yourself—always have a subject of reflection."

"I am not bored," said Goodwood. "I have plenty to think about and to say to myself."

"More than to say to others!" Osmond exclaimed, with a light laugh. "Where shall you go next? I mean after you have consigned Touchett to his natural caretakers—I believe his mother is at last coming back to look after him. That little lady is superb; she neglects her duties with a finish! Perhaps you will spend the summer in England?"

"I don't know; I have no plans."

"Happy man! That's a little nude, but it's very free."

"Oh yes, I am very free."

"Free to come back to Rome, I hope," said Osmond, as he saw a group of new visitors enter the room. "Remember that when you do come we count upon you!"

Goodwood had meant to go away early, but the evening elapsed without his having a chance to speak to Isabel otherwise than as one of several associated interlocutors. There was something perverse in the inveteracy with which she avoided him; Goodwood's unquenchable rancor discovered an intention where there was certainly no appearance of one. There was absolutely no appearance of one. She met his eye with her sweet hospitable smile, which seemed almost to ask that he would come and help her to entertain some of her visitors. To such suggestions, however, he only opposed a stiff impatience. He wandered about and waited; he talked to the few people he knew, who found him for the first time rather self-contradictory. This was indeed rare with Caspar Goodwood, though he often contradicted others. There was often music at the Palazzo Roccanera, and it was usually very good. Under cover of the music he managed to contain himself; but toward the end, when he saw the people beginning to go, he drew near to Isabel and asked her in a low tone if he might not speak to her in one of the other rooms, which he had just assured himself was empty.

She smiled as if she wished to oblige him, but found herself absolutely prevented. "I'm afraid it's impossible. People are saying goodnight, and I must be where they can see me."

"I shall wait till they are all gone, then!"

She hesitated a moment. "Ah, that will be delightful!" she exclaimed.

And he waited, though it took a long time yet. There were several people, at the end, who seemed tethered to the carpet. The Countess Gemini, who was never herself till midnight, as she said, displayed no consciousness that the entertainment was over; she had still a little circle of gentlemen in front of the fire, who every now and then broke into a united laugh. Osmond had disappeared—he never bade goodbye to people; and as the Countess was extending her range, according to her custom at this period of the evening, Isabel had sent Pansy to bed. Isabel sat a little apart; she too appeared to wish that her sister-in-law would sound a lower note and let the last loiterers depart in peace.

"May I not say a word to you now?" Goodwood presently asked her.

She got up immediately, smiling. "Certainly, we will go somewhere else, if you like."

They went together, leaving the Countess with her little circle, and for a moment after they had crossed the threshold neither of them spoke. Isabel would not sit down; she stood in the middle of the room slowly fanning herself, with the same familiar grace. She seemed to be waiting for him to speak. Now that he was alone with her, all the passion that he had never stifled surged into his senses; it hummed in his eyes and made things swim around him. The bright, empty room grew dim and blurred, and through the rustling tissue he saw Isabel hover before him with gleaming eyes and parted lips. If he had seen more distinctly he would have perceived that her smile was fixed and a trifle forced—that she was frightened at what she saw in his own face.

"I suppose you wish to bid me goodbye?" she said.

"Yes—but I don't like it. I don't want to leave Rome," he answered, with almost plaintive honesty.

"I can well imagine. It is wonderfully good of you. I can't tell you how kind I think you."

For a moment more he said nothing. "With a few words like that you make me go."

"You must come back some day," Isabel rejoined, brightly.

"Some day? You mean as long a time hence as possible."

"Oh no; I don't mean all that."

"What *do* you mean? I don't understand! But I said I would go, and I will go," Goodwood added.

"Come back whenever you like," said Isabel, with attempted lightness.

"I don't care a straw for your cousin!" Caspar broke out.

"Is that what you wished to tell me?"

"No, no; I didn't want to tell you anything; I wanted to ask you—" he paused a moment, and then—"what have you really made of your life?" he said, in a low, quick tone. He paused again, as if for an answer; but she said nothing, and he went on—"I can't understand, I can't penetrate you! What am I to believe—what do you want me to think?" Still she said nothing; she only stood looking at him, now quite without pretending to smile. "I am told you are unhappy, and if you are I should like to know it. That would be something for me. But you yourself say you are happy, and you are somehow so still, so smooth. You are completely changed. You conceal everything; I haven't really come near you."

"You come very near," Isabel said, gently, but in a tone of warning.

"And yet I don't touch you! I want to know the truth. Have you done well?"

"You ask a great deal."

"Yes—I have always asked a great deal. Of course you won't tell me. I shall never know, if you can help it. And then it's none of my business." He had spoken with a visible effort to control himself, to give a considerate form to an inconsiderate state of mind. But the sense that it was his last chance, that he loved her and had lost her, that she would think him a fool whatever he should say, suddenly gave him a lash and added a deep vibration to his low voice: "You are perfectly inscrutable, and that's what makes me think you have something to hide. I say that I don't care a straw for your cousin, but I don't mean that I don't like him. I mean that it isn't because I like him that I go away with him. I would go if he were an idiot, and you should have asked me. If you should ask me, I would go to Siberia tomorrow. Why do you want me to leave the place? You must have some reason for that; if you were as contented as you pretend you are, you wouldn't care. I would rather know the truth about you, even if it's damnable, than have come here for nothing. That isn't what I came for. I thought I shouldn't care. I came because I wanted to assure myself that I needn't think of you anymore. I haven't thought of anything else, and you are quite right to wish me to go away. But if I must go, there is no harm in my letting myself out for a single moment, is there? If you are really hurt—if *he* hurts you—nothing *I* say will hurt you. When I tell you I love you, it's simply what I came for. I thought it was for something else; but it was for that. I shouldn't say it if I didn't believe I should never see you again. It's the last time—let me pluck a single flower! I have no right to say that, I know; and you have no right to listen. But you don't listen; you never listen, you are always thinking of something else. After this I must go, of course; so I shall at least have a reason. Your asking me is no reason, not a real one. I can't judge by your husband," he went on, irrelevantly, almost incoherently, "I don't understand him; he tells me you adore each other. Why does he tell me that? What business is it of mine? When I say that to you, you look strange. But you always look strange. Yes, you have something to hide. It's none of my business—very true. But I love you," said Caspar Goodwood.

As he said, she looked strange. She turned her eyes to the door by which they had entered, and raised her fan as if in warning.

"You have behaved so well; don't spoil it," she said, softly.

"No one hears me. It's wonderful what you tried to put me off with. I love you as I have never loved you."

"I know it. I knew it as soon as you consented to go."

"You can't help it—of course not. You would if you could, but you can't, unfortunately. Unfortunately for me, I mean. I ask nothing—nothing, that is, that I shouldn't. But I do ask one sole satisfaction—that you tell me—that you tell me——"

"That I tell you what?"

"Whether I may pity you."

"Should you like that?" Isabel asked, trying to smile again.

"To pity you? Most assuredly! That at least would be doing something. I would give my life to it."

She raised her fan to her face, which it covered, all except her eyes. They rested a moment on his.

"Don't give your life to it; but give a thought to it every now and then."

And with that Isabel went back to the Countess Gemini.

❧ 49 ❧

Madame Merle had not made her appearance at the Palazzo Roccanera on the evening of that Thursday of which I have narrated some of the incidents, and Isabel, though she observed her absence, was not surprised by it. Things had passed between them which added no stimulus to sociability, and to appreciate which we must glance a little backward. It has been mentioned that

Madame Merle returned from Naples shortly after Lord Warburton had left Rome, and that on her first meeting with Isabel (whom, to do her justice, she came immediately to see) her first utterance was an inquiry as to the whereabouts of this nobleman, for whom she appeared to hold her dear friend accountable.

"Please don't talk of him," said Isabel, for answer; "we have heard so much of him of late."

Madame Merle bent her head on one side a little, protestingly, and smiled in the left corner of her mouth.

"You have heard, yes. But you must remember that I have not, in Naples. I hoped to find him here, and to be able to congratulate Pansy."

"You may congratulate Pansy still; but not on marrying Lord Warburton."

"How you say that! Don't you know I had set my heart on it?" Madame Merle asked, with a great deal of spirit, but still with the intonation of good-humor.

Isabel was discomposed, but she was determined to be good-humored too.

"You shouldn't have gone to Naples, then. You should have stayed here to watch the affair."

"I had too much confidence in you. But do you think it is too late?"

"You had better ask Pansy," said Isabel.

"I shall ask her what you have said to her."

These words seemed to justify the impulse of self-defence aroused on Isabel's part by her perceiving that her visitor's attitude was a critical one. Madame Merle, as we know, had been very discreet hitherto; she had never criticized; she had been excessively afraid of intermeddling. But apparently she had only reserved herself for this occasion; for she had a dangerous quickness in her eye, and an air of irritation which even her admirable smile was not able to transmute. She had suffered a disappointment which excited Isabel's surprise—our heroine having no knowledge of her zealous interest in Pansy's marriage; and she betrayed it in a manner which quickened Mrs. Osmond's alarm. More clearly than ever before, Isabel heard a cold, mocking voice proceed from she knew not where, in the dim void that surrounded her, and declare that this bright, strong, definite, worldly woman, this incarnation of the practical, the personal, the immediate, was a powerful agent in her destiny. She was nearer to her than Isabel had yet discovered, and her nearness was not the charming accident that she had so long thought. The sense of accident indeed had died within her that day when she happened to be struck with the manner in which Madame Merle and her own husband sat together in private. No definite suspicion had as yet taken its place; but it was enough to make her look at this lady with a different eye, to have been led to reflect that there was more intention in her past behavior than she had allowed for at the time. Ah, yes, there had been intention, there had been intention, Isabel said to herself; and she seemed to wake from a long, pernicious dream. What was it that brought it home to her that Madame

Merle's intention had not been good? Nothing but the mistrust which had lately taken body, and which married itself now to the fruitful wonder produced by her visitor's challenge on behalf of poor Pansy. There was something in this challenge which at the very outset excited an answering defiance; a nameless vitality which Isabel now saw to have been absent from her friend's professions of delicacy and caution. Madame Merle had been unwilling to interfere, certainly, but only so long as there was nothing to interfere with. It will perhaps seem to the reader that Isabel went fast in casting doubt, on mere suspicion, on a sincerity proved by several years of good offices. She moved quickly, indeed, and with reason, for a strange truth was filtering into her soul. Madame Merle's interest was identical with Osmond's; that was enough.

"I think Pansy will tell you nothing that will make you more angry," she said, in answer to her companion's last remark.

"I am not in the least angry. I have only a great desire to retrieve the situation. Do you think his lordship has left us forever?"

"I can't tell you; I don't understand you. It's all over; please let it rest. Osmond has talked to me a great deal about it, and I have nothing more to say or to hear. I have no doubt," Isabel added, "that he will be very happy to discuss the subject with you."

"I know what he thinks; he came to see me last evening."

"As soon as you had arrived? Then you know all about it, and you needn't apply to me for information."

"It isn't information I want. At bottom, it's sympathy. I had set my heart on that marriage; the idea did what so few things do—it satisfied the imagination."

"Your imagination, yes. But not that of the persons concerned."

"You mean by that of course that I am not concerned. Of course not directly. But when one is such an old friend, one can't help having something at stake. You forget how long I have known Pansy. You mean, of course," Madame Merle added, "that *you* are one of the persons concerned."

"No; that's the last thing I mean. I am very weary of it all."

Madame Merle hesitated a little. "Ah yes, your work's done."

"Take care what you say," said Isabel, very gravely.

"Oh, I take care; never perhaps more than when it appears least. Your husband judges you severely."

Isabel made for a moment no answer to this; she felt choked with bitterness. It was not the insolence of Madame Merle's informing her that Osmond had been taking her into his confidence as against his wife that struck her most: for she was not quick to believe that this was meant for insolence. Madame Merle was very rarely insolent, and only when it was exactly right. It was not right now, or at least it was not right yet. What touched Isabel like a drop of corrosive acid upon an open wound, was the knowledge that Osmond dishonored her in his words as well as in his thoughts.

"Should you like to know how I judge him?" she asked at last.

"No, because you would never tell me. And it would be painful for me to know."

There was a pause, and for the first time since she had known her, Isabel thought Madame Merle disagreeable. She wished she would leave her.

"Remember how attractive Pansy is, and don't despair," she said abruptly, with a desire that this should close their interview.

But Madame Merle's expansive presence underwent no contraction. She only gathered her mantle about her, and, with the movement, scattered upon the air a faint, agreeable fragrance.

"I don't despair," she answered; "I feel encouraged. And I didn't come to scold you; I came if possible to learn the truth. I know you will tell it if I ask you. It's an immense blessing with you, that one can count upon that. No, you won't believe what a comfort I take in it."

"What truth do you speak of?" Isabel asked, wondering.

"Just this: whether Lord Warburton changed his mind quite of his own movement, or because you recommended it. To please himself, I mean; or to please you. Think of the confidence I must still have in you, in spite of having lost a little of it," Madame Merle continued with a smile, "to ask such a question as that!" She sat looking at Isabel a moment, to judge of the effect of her words, and then she went on— "Now don't be heroic, don't be unreasonable, don't take offence. It seems to me I do you an honor in speaking so. I don't know another woman to whom I would do it. I haven't the least idea that any other woman would tell me the truth. And don't you see how well it is that your husband should know it? It is true that he doesn't appear to have had any tact whatever in trying to extract it; he has indulged in gratuitous suppositions. But that doesn't alter the fact that it would make a difference in his view of his daughter's prospects to know distinctly what really occurred. If Lord Warburton simply got tired of the poor child, that's one thing; it's a pity. If he gave her up to please you, it's another. That's a pity, too; but in a different way. Then, in the latter case, you would perhaps resign yourself to not being pleased—to simply seeing your step-daughter married. Let him off—let us have him!"

Madame Merle had proceeded very deliberately, watching her companion and apparently thinking she could proceed safely. As she went on, Isabel grew pale; she clasped her hands more tightly in her lap. It was not that Madame Merle had at last thought it the right time to be insolent; for this was not what was most apparent. It was a worse horror than that. "Who are you—what are you?" Isabel murmured. "What have you to do with my husband?" It was strange that, for the moment, she drew as near to him as if she had loved him.

"Ah, then you take it heroically! I am very sorry. Don't think, however, that I shall do so."

"What have you to do with me?" Isabel went on.

Madame Merle slowly got up, stroking her muff, but not removing her eyes from Isabel's face.

"Everything!" she answered.

Isabel sat there looking up at her, without rising; her face was almost a prayer to be enlightened. But the light of her visitor's eyes seemed only a darkness.

"Oh, misery!" she murmured at last; and she fell back, covering her face with her hands. It had come over her like a high-surging wave that Mrs. Touchett was right. Madame Merle had married her! Before she uncovered her face again, this lady had left the room.

Isabel took a drive, alone, that afternoon; she wished to be far away, under the sky, where she could descend from her carriage and tread upon the daisies. She had long before this taken old Rome into her confidence, for in a world of ruins the ruin of her happiness seemed a less unnatural catastrophe. She rested her weariness upon things that had crumbled for centuries and yet still were upright; she dropped her secret sadness into the silence of lonely places, where its very modern quality detached itself and grew objective, so that as she sat in a sun-warmed angle on a winter's day, or stood in a mouldy church to which no one came, she could almost smile at it and think of its smallness. Small it was, in the large Roman record, and her haunting sense of the continuity of the human lot easily carried her from the less to the greater. She had become deeply, tenderly acquainted with Rome; it interfused and moderated her passion. But she had grown to think of it chiefly as the place where people had suffered. This was what came to her in the starved churches, where the marble columns, transferred from pagan ruins, seemed to offer her a companionship in endurance, and the musty incense to be a compound of long-unanswered prayers. There was no gentler nor less consistent heretic than Isabel; the firmest of worshippers, gazing at dark altar-pictures or clustered candles, could not have felt more intimately the suggestiveness of these objects nor have been more liable at such moments to a spiritual visitation. Pansy, as we know, was almost always her companion, and of late the Countess Gemini, balancing a pink parasol, had lent brilliancy to their equipage; but she still occasionally found herself alone when it suited her mood, and where it suited the place. On such occasions she had several resorts; the most accessible of which perhaps was a seat on the low parapet which edges the wide grassy space lying before the high, cold front of St. John Lateran; where you look across the Campagna at the far-trailing outline of the Alban Mount, and at that mighty plain between, which is still so full of all that has vanished from it. After the departure of her cousin and his companions she wandered about more than usual; she carried her somber spirit from one familiar shrine to the other. Even when Pansy and the Countess were with her, she felt the touch of a vanished world. The carriage, passing out of the walls of Rome, rolled through narrow lanes, where the wild honeysuckle had begun to tangle itself in the hedges, or waited for her in quiet places where the fields lay near, while she strolled further and further over the flower-freckled turf, or sat on a stone that had once had a use, and gazed through the veil of her personal sadness at the splendid sadness of the scene—at the dense, warm light, the far gradations and soft confusions of color, the motionless shepherds in lonely attitudes, the hills where the cloud-shadows had the lightness of a blush.

On the afternoon I began with speaking of, she had taken a resolution not to think of Madame Merle; but the resolution proved vain, and this lady's image hovered constantly before her. She asked herself, with an almost childlike horror of the supposition, whether to this intimate friend of several years the great historical epithet of *wicked* were to be applied. She knew the idea only by the Bible and other literary works; to the best of her belief she had no personal acquaintance with wickedness. She had desired a large acquaintance with human life, and in spite of her having flattered herself that she cultivated it with some success, this elementary privilege had been denied her. Perhaps it was not wicked—in the historic sense—to be false; for that was what Madame Merle had been. Isabel's Aunt Lydia had made this discovery long before, and had mentioned it to her niece; but Isabel had flattered herself at this time that she had a much richer view of things, especially of the spontaneity of her own career and the nobleness of her own interpretations, than poor stiffly reasoning Mrs. Touchett. Madame Merle had done what she wanted; she had brought about the union of her two friends; a reflection which could not fail to make it a matter of wonder that she should have desired such an event. There were people who had the match-making passion, like the votaries of art for art; but Madame Merle, great artist as she was, was scarcely one of these. She thought too ill of marriage, too ill even of life; she had desired that marriage, but she had not desired others. She therefore had had an idea of gain, and Isabel asked herself where she had found her profit. It took her, naturally, a long time to discover, and even then her discovery was very incomplete. It came back to her that Madame Merle, though she had seemed to like her from their first meeting at Gardencourt, had been doubly affectionate after Mr. Touchett's death, and after learning that her young friend was a victim of the good old man's benevolence. She had found her profit not in the gross device of borrowing money from Isabel, but in the more refined idea of introducing one of her intimates to the young girl's fortune. She had naturally chosen her closest intimate, and it was already vivid enough to Isabel that Gilbert Osmond occupied this position. She found herself confronted in this manner with the conviction that the man in the world whom she had supposed to be the least sordid, had married her for her money. Strange to say, it had never before occurred to her; if she had thought a good deal of harm of Osmond, she had not done him this particular injury. This was the worst she could think of, and she had been saying to herself that the worst was still to come. A man might marry a woman for her money, very well; the thing was often done. But at least he should let her know! She wondered whether, if he wanted her money, her money today would satisfy him. Would he take her money and let her go? Ah, if Mr. Touchett's great charity would help her today, it would be blessed indeed! It was not slow to occur to her that if Madame Merle had wished to do Osmond a service, his recognition of the fact must have lost its warmth. What must be his feelings today in regard to his too zealous benefactress, and what expression must they have found on the part of such a master of irony? It is a singular, but a characteristic, fact that before Isabel returned from her silent drive she had broken its silence by the soft exclamation—

"Poor Madame Merle!"

Her exclamation would perhaps have been justified if on this same afternoon she had been concealed behind one of the valuable curtains of time-softened damask which dressed the interesting little *salon* of the lady to whom it referred; the carefully arranged apartment to which we once paid a visit in company with the discreet Mr. Rosier. In that apartment, toward six o'clock, Gilbert Osmond was seated, and his hostess stood before him as Isabel had seen her stand on an occasion commemorated in this history with an emphasis appropriate not so much to its apparent as to its real importance.

"I don't believe you are unhappy; I believe you like it," said Madame Merle.

"Did I say I was unhappy?" Osmond asked, with a face grave enough to suggest that he might have been so.

"No, but you don't say the contrary, as you ought in common gratitude."

"Don't talk about gratitude," Osmond returned, dryly. "And don't aggravate me," he added in a moment.

Madame Merle slowly seated herself, with her arms folded and her white hands arranged as a support to one of them and an ornament, as it were, to the other. She looked exquisitely calm, but impressively sad.

"On your side, don't try to frighten me," she said. "I wonder whether you know some of my thoughts."

"No more than I can help. I have quite enough of my own."

"That's because they are so delightful."

Osmond rested his head against the back of his chair and looked at his companion for a long time, with a kind of cynical directness which seemed also partly an expression of fatigue. "You do aggravate me," he remarked in a moment. "I am very tired."

"*Eh moi, donc!*" cried Madame Merle.

"With you, it's because you fatigue yourself. With me, it's not my own fault."

"When I fatigue myself it's for you. I have given you an interest; that's a great gift."

"Do you call it an interest?" Osmond inquired, languidly.

"Certainly, since it helps you to pass your time."

"The time has never seemed longer to me than this winter."

"You have never looked better; you have never been so agreeable, so brilliant."

"Damn my brilliancy!" Osmond murmured, thoughtfully. "How little, after all, you know me!"

"If I don't know you, I know nothing," said Madame Merle, smiling. "You have the feeling of complete success."

"No, I shall not have that till I have made you stop judging me."

"I did that long ago. I speak from old knowledge. But you express yourself more, too."

Osmond hesitated a moment. "I wish you would express yourself less!"

"You wish to condemn me to silence? Remember that I have never been a chatterbox. At any rate, there are three or four things that I should like to say to you first.—Your wife doesn't know what to do with herself," she went on, with a change of tone.

"Excuse me; she knows perfectly. She has a line sharply marked out. She means to carry out her ideas."

"Her ideas, today, must be remarkable."

"Certainly they are. She has more of them than ever."

"She was unable to show me any this morning," said Madame Merle. "She seemed in a very simple, almost in a stupid, state of mind. She was completely bewildered."

"You had better say at once that she was pathetic."

"Ah no, I don't want to encourage you too much."

Osmond still had his head against the cushion behind him; the ankle of one foot rested on the other knee. So he sat for a while. "I should like to know what is the matter with you," he said, at last.

"The matter—the matter—" And here Madame Merle stopped. Then she went on, with a sudden outbreak of passion, a burst of summer thunder in a clear sky—"The matter is that I would give my right hand to be able to weep, and that I can't!"

"What good would it do you to weep?"

"It would make me feel as I felt before I knew you."

"If I have dried your tears, that's something. But I have seen you shed them."

"Oh, I believe you will make me cry still. I have a great hope of that. I was vile this morning; I was horrid," said Madame Merle.

"If Isabel was in the stupid state of mind you mention, she probably didn't perceive it," Osmond answered.

"It was precisely my devilry that stupefied her. I couldn't help it; I was full of something bad. Perhaps it was something good; I don't know. You have not only dried up my tears; you have dried up my soul."

"It is not I then that am responsible for my wife's condition," Osmond said. "It is pleasant to think that I shall get the benefit of your influence upon her. Don't you know the soul is an immortal principle? How can it suffer alteration?"

"I don't believe at all that it's an immortal principle. I believe it can perfectly be destroyed. That's what has happened to mine, which was a very good one to start with; and it's you I have to thank for it.—You are very bad," Madame Merle added, gravely.

"Is this the way we are to end?" Osmond asked, with the same studied coldness.

"I don't know how we are to end. I wish I did! How do bad people end? You have made me bad."

"I don't understand you. You seem to me quite good enough," said Osmond, his conscious indifference giving an extreme effect to the words.

Madame Merle's self-possession tended on the contrary to diminish, and she was nearer losing it than on any occasion on which we have had the pleasure of meeting her. Her eye brightened, even flashed; her smile betrayed a painful effort. "Good enough for anything that I have done with myself? I suppose that's what you mean."

"Good enough to be always charming!" Osmond exclaimed, smiling too.

"Oh God!" his companion murmured; and, sitting there in her ripe freshness, she had recourse to the same gesture that she had provoked on Isabel's part in the morning; she bent her face and covered it with her hands.

"Are you going to weep, after all?" Osmond asked; and on her remaining motionless he went on—"Have I ever complained to you?"

She dropped her hands quickly. "No, you have taken your revenge otherwise— you have taken it on *her.*"

Osmond threw back his head further; he looked a while at the ceiling, and might have been supposed to be appealing, in an informal way, to the heavenly powers. "Oh, the imagination of women! It's always vulgar, at bottom. You talk of revenge like a third-rate novelist."

"Of course you haven't complained. You have enjoyed your triumph too much."

"I am rather curious to know what you call my triumph."

"You have made your wife afraid of you."

Osmond changed his position; he leaned forward, resting his elbows on his knees and looking a while at a beautiful old Persian rug, at his feet. He had an air of refusing to accept anyone's valuation of anything, even of time, and of preferring to abide by his own; a peculiarity which made him at moments an irritating person to converse with. "Isabel is not afraid of me, and it's not what I wish," he said at last. "To what do you wish to provoke me when you say such things as that?"

"I have thought over all the harm you can do me," Madame Merle answered. "Your wife was afraid of me this morning, but in me it was really you she feared."

"You may have said things that were in very bad taste; I am not responsible for that. I didn't see the use of your going to see her at all; you are capable of acting without her. I have not made you afraid of me, that I can see," Osmond went on; "how then should I have made her? You are at least as brave. I can't think where you have picked up such rubbish; one might suppose you knew me by this time." He got up, as he spoke, and walked to the chimney, where he stood a moment bending his eye, as if he had seen them for the first time, on the delicate specimens of rare porcelain with which it was covered. He took up a small cup and held it in his hand; then, still holding it and leaning his arm on the mantel, he continued: "You always see too much in everything; you overdo it; you lose sight of the real. I am much simpler than you think."

"I think you are very simple." And Madame Merle kept her eye upon her cup. "I have come to that with time. I judged you, as I say, of old; but it is only since your marriage that I have understood you. I have seen better what you have been to your wife than I ever saw what you were for me. Please be very careful of that precious object."

"It already has a small crack," said Osmond, dryly, as he put it down. "If you didn't understand me before I married, it was cruelly rash of you to put me into such a box. However, I took a fancy to my box myself; I thought it would be a comfortable fit. I asked very little; I only asked that she should like me."

"That she should like you so much!"

"So much, of course; in such a case one asks the maximum. That she should adore me, if you will. Oh yes, I wanted that."

"I never adored you," said Madame Merle.

"Ah, but you pretended to!"

"It is true that you never accused me of being a comfortable fit," Madame Merle went on.

"My wife has declined—declined to do anything of the sort," said Osmond. "If you are determined to make a tragedy of that, the tragedy is hardly for her."

"The tragedy is for me!" Madame Merle exclaimed, rising, with a long low sigh, but giving a glance at the same time at the contents of her mantel shelf. "It appears that I am to be severely taught the disadvantages of a false position."

"You express yourself like a sentence in a copybook. We must look for our comfort where we can find it. If my wife doesn't like me, at least my child does. I shall look for compensations in Pansy. Fortunately I haven't a fault to find with her."

"Ah," said Madame Merle, softly, "if I had a child—"

Osmond hesitated a moment; and then, with a little formal air—"The children of others may be a great interest!" he announced.

"You are more like a copybook than I. There is something, after all, that holds us together."

"Is it the idea of the harm I may do you?" Osmond asked.

"No; it's the idea of the good I may do for you. It is that," said Madame Merle, "that made me so jealous of Isabel. I want it to be *my* work," she added, with her face, which had grown hard and bitter, relaxing into its usual social expression.

Osmond took up his hat and his umbrella, and after giving the former article two or three strokes with his coat-cuff—"On the whole, I think," he said, "you had better leave it to me."

After he had left her, Madame Merle went and lifted from the mantel shelf the attenuated coffee cup in which he had mentioned the existence of a crack; but she looked at it rather abstractedly. "Have I been so vile all for nothing?" she murmured to herself.

❧ 50 ❧

As the Countess Gemini was not acquainted with the ancient monuments, Isabel occasionally offered to introduce her to these interesting relics and to give their afternoon drive an antiquarian aim. The Countess, who professed to think her sister-in-law a prodigy of learning, never made an objection, and gazed at masses of Roman brickwork as patiently as if they had been mounds of modern drapery. She was not an antiquarian; but she was so delighted to be in Rome that she only desired to float with the current. She would gladly have passed an hour every day in the damp darkness of the Baths of Titus, if it had been a condition of her remaining at the Palazzo Roccanera. Isabel, however, was not a severe cicerone; she used to visit the ruins chiefly because they offered an excuse for talking about other matters than the love-affairs of the ladies of Florence, as to which her companion was never weary of offering information. It must be added that during these visits the Countess was not very active; her preference was to sit in the carriage and exclaim that everything was most interesting. It was in this manner that she had hitherto examined the Coliseum, to the infinite regret of her niece, who—with all the respect that she owed her—could not see why she should not descend from the vehicle and enter the building. Pansy had so little chance to ramble that her view of the case was not wholly disinterested; it may be divined that she had a secret hope that, once inside, her aunt might be induced to climb to the upper tiers. There came a day when the Countess announced her willingness to undertake this feat—a mild afternoon in March, when the windy month expressed itself in occasional puffs of spring. The three ladies went into the Coliseum together, but Isabel left her companions to wander over the place. She had often ascended to those desolate ledges from which the Roman crowd used to bellow applause, and where now the wildflowers (when they are allowed), bloom in the deep crevices; and today she felt weary, and preferred to sit in the despoiled arena. It made an intermission, too, for the Countess often asked more from one's attention than she gave in return; and Isabel believed that when she was alone with her niece she let the dust gather for a moment upon the ancient scandals of Florence. She remained below, therefore, while Pansy guided her undiscriminating aunt to the steep brick staircase at the foot of which the custodian unlocks the tall wooden gate. The great inclosure was half in shadow; the western sun brought out the pale red tone of the great blocks of travertine—the latent color which is the only living element in the immense ruin. Here and there wandered a peasant or a tourist, looking up at the far skyline where in the clear stillness a multitude of swallows kept circling and plunging. Isabel presently became aware that one of the other visitors, planted in the middle of the arena, had turned his attention to her own person, and was looking at her with a certain little poise of the head, which she had some weeks before perceived to be characteristic of baffled but indestructible purpose. Such an attitude, today, could belong only to Mr. Edward Rosier; and this gentleman proved in fact to have been considering the question of speaking to her. When he had assured himself that she was unaccompanied he drew near, remarking that though she would not answer his letters she would perhaps not wholly close her ears to his spoken eloquence. She replied that her step-daughter was close at hand and she could only give him five minutes; whereupon he took out his watch and sat down upon a broken block.

"It's very soon told," said Edward Rosier. "I have sold all my bibelots!"

Isabel gave, instinctively, an exclamation of horror; it was as if he had told her he had had all his teeth drawn.

"I have sold them by auction at the Hôtel Drouot," he went on. "The sale took place three days ago, and they have telegraphed me the result. It's magnificent."

"I am glad to hear it; but I wish you had kept your pretty things."

"I have the money instead—forty thousand dollars. Will Mr. Osmond think me rich enough now?"

"Is it for that you did it?" Isabel asked, gently.

"For what else in the world could it be? That is the only thing I think of. I went to Paris and made my arrangements. I couldn't stop for the sale; I couldn't have seen them going off; I think it would have killed me. But I put them into good hands, and they brought high prices. I should tell you I have kept my enamels. Now I have got the money in my pocket, and he can't say I'm poor!" the young man exclaimed, defiantly.

"He will say now that you are not wise," said Isabel, as if Gilbert Osmond had never said this before.

Rosier gave her a sharp look.

"Do you mean that without my bibelots I am nothing? Do you mean that they were the best thing about me? That's what they told me in Paris; oh, they were very frank about it. But they hadn't seen *her!*"

"My dear friend, you deserve to succeed," said Isabel, very kindly.

"You say that so sadly that it's the same as if you said I shouldn't." And he questioned her eye with the clear trepidation of his own. He had the air of a man who knows he has been the talk of Paris for a week and is full half a head taller in consequence; but who also has a painful suspicion that in spite of this increase of stature one or two persons still have the perversity to think him diminutive. "I know what happened here while I was away," he went on. "What does Mr. Osmond expect, after she has refused Lord Warburton?"

Isabel hesitated a moment.

"That she will marry another nobleman."

"What other nobleman?"

"One that he will pick out."

Rosier slowly got up, putting his watch into his waistcoat pocket.

"You are laughing at someone; but this time I don't think it's at me."

"I didn't mean to laugh," said Isabel. "I laugh very seldom. Now you had better go away."

"I feel very safe!" Rosier declared, without moving. This might be; but it evidently made him feel more so to make the announcement in rather a loud voice, balancing himself a little complacently, on his toes, and looking all around the Coliseum, as if it were filled with an audience. Suddenly Isabel saw him change color; there was more of an audience than he had suspected. She turned, and perceived that her two companions had returned from their excursion.

"You must really go away," she said, quickly.

"Ah, my dear lady, pity me!" Edward Rosier murmured, in a voice strangely at variance with the announcement I have just quoted. And then he added, eagerly, like a man who in the midst of his misery is seized by a happy thought—"Is that lady the Countess Gemini? I have a great desire to be presented to her."

Isabel looked at him a moment.

"She has no influence with her brother."

"Ah, what a monster you make him out!" Rosier exclaimed, glancing at the Countess, who advanced, in front of Pansy, with an animation partly due perhaps to the fact that she perceived her sister-in-law to be engaged in conversation with a very pretty young man.

"I am glad you have kept your enamels!" Isabel exclaimed, leaving him. She went straight to Pansy, who, on seeing Edward Rosier, had stopped short, with lowered eyes. "We will go back to the carriage," said Isabel gently.

"Yes, it is getting late," Pansy answered, more gently still. And she went on without a murmur, without faltering or glancing back.

Isabel, however, allowed herself this last liberty, and saw that a meeting had immediately taken place between the Countess and Mr. Rosier. He had removed his hat, and was bowing and smiling; he had evidently introduced himself; while the Countess's expressive back displayed to Isabel's eye a gracious inclination. These facts, however, were presently lost to sight, for Isabel and Pansy took their places again in the carriage. Pansy, who faced her step-mother, at first kept her eyes fixed on her lap; then she raised them and rested them on Isabel's. There shone out of each of them a little melancholy ray—a spark of timid passion which touched Isabel to the heart. At the same time a wave of envy passed over her soul, as she compared the tremulous longing, the definite ideal, of the young girl with her own dry despair.

"Poor little Pansy!" she said, affectionately.

"Oh, never mind!" Pansy answered, in the tone of eager apology.

And then there was a silence; the Countess was a long time coming.

"Did you show your aunt everything, and did she enjoy it?" Isabel asked at last.

"Yes, I showed her everything. I think she was very much pleased."

"And you are not tired, I hope."

"Oh no, thank you, I am not tired."

The Countess still remained behind, so that Isabel requested the footman to go into the Coliseum and tell her that they were waiting. He presently returned with the announcement that the Signora Contessa begged them not to wait—she would come home in a cab!

About a week after this lady's quick sympathies had enlisted themselves with Mr. Rosier, Isabel, going rather late to dress for dinner, found Pansy sitting in her room. The girl seemed to have been waiting for her; she got up from her low chair.

"Excuse my taking the liberty," she said, in a small voice. "It will be the last—for some time."

Her voice was strange, and her eyes, widely opened, had an excited, frightened look.

"You are not going away!" Isabel exclaimed.

"I am going to the convent."

"To the convent?"

Pansy drew nearer, till she was near enough to put her arms round Isabel and rest her head on her shoulder. She stood this way a moment, perfectly still; but Isabel could feel her trembling. The tremor of her little body expressed everything that she was unable to say.

Nevertheless, Isabel went on in a moment—

"Why are you going to the convent?"

"Because papa thinks it best. He says a young girl is better, every now and then, for making a little retreat. He says the world, always the world, is very bad for a young girl. This is just a chance for a little seclusion—a little reflection." Pansy spoke in short detached sentences, as if she could not trust herself. And then she added, with a triumph of self-control—"I think papa is right; I have been so much in the world this winter."

Her announcement had a strange effect upon Isabel; it seemed to carry a larger meaning than the girl herself knew.

"When was this decided?" she asked. "I have heard nothing of it."

"Papa told me half-an-hour ago; he thought it better it shouldn't be too much talked about in advance. Madame Catherine is to come for me at a quarter past seven, and I am only to take two dresses. It is only for a few weeks; I am sure it will be very good. I shall find all those ladies who used to be so kind to me, and I shall see the little girls who are being educated. I am very fond of little girls," said Pansy, with a sort of diminutive grandeur. "And I am also very fond of Mother Catherine. I shall be very quiet, and think a great deal."

Isabel listened to her, holding her breath; she was almost awe-struck.

"Think of *me*, sometimes," she said.

"Ah, come and see me soon!" cried Pansy; and the cry was very different from the heroic remarks of which she had just delivered herself.

Isabel could say nothing more; she understood nothing; she only felt that she did not know her husband yet. Her answer to Pansy was a long tender kiss.

Half-an-hour later she learned from her maid that Madame Catherine had arrived in a cab, and had departed again with the Signorina. On going to the drawing room before dinner she found the Countess Gemini alone, and this lady characterized the incident by exclaiming, with a wonderful toss of the head—*"En voilà, ma chère, une pose!"* But if it was an affectation, she was at a loss to see what her husband affected. She could only dimly perceive that he had more traditions than she supposed. It had become her habit to be so careful as to what she said to him that, strange as it may appear, she hesitated, for several minutes after he had come in, to allude to his daughter's sudden departure; she spoke of it only after they were seated at table. But she had forbidden herself ever to ask Osmond a question. All she could do was to make a declaration, and there was one that came very naturally.

"I shall miss Pansy very much."

Osmond looked a while, with his head inclined a little, at the basket of flowers in the middle of the table.

"Ah, yes," he said at last, "I had thought of that. You must go and see her, you know; but not too often. I dare say you wonder why I sent her to the good sisters; but I doubt whether I can make you understand. It doesn't matter; don't trouble yourself about it. That's why I had not spoken of it. I didn't believe you would enter into it. But I have always had the idea; I have always thought it a part of the education of a young girl. A young girl should be fresh and fair; she should be innocent and gentle. With the manners of the present time she is liable to become so dusty and crumpled! Pansy is a little dusty, a little dishevelled; she has knocked about too much. This bustling, pushing rabble, that calls itself society—one should take her out of it occasionally. Convents are very quiet, very convenient, very salutary. I like to think of her there, in the old garden, under the arcade, among those tranquil, virtuous women. Many of them are gentlewomen born; several of them are noble. She will have her books and her drawing; she will have her piano. I have made the most liberal arrangements. There is to be nothing ascetic; there is just to be a certain little feeling. She will have time to think, and there is something I want her to think about." Osmond spoke deliberately, reasonably, still with his head on one side, as if he were looking at the basket of flowers. His tone, however, was that of a man not so much offering an explanation as putting a thing into words—almost into pictures—to see, himself, how it would look. He contemplated a while the picture he had evoked, and seemed greatly pleased with it. And then he went on—"The Catholics are very wise, after all. The convent is a great institution; we can't do without it; it corresponds to an essential need in families, in society. It's a school of good manners; it's a school of repose. Oh, I don't want to detach my daughter from the world," he added; "I don't want to make her fix her thoughts on the other one. This one is very well, after all, and she may think of it as much as she chooses. Only she must think of it in the right way."

Isabel gave an extreme attention to this little sketch; she found it indeed intensely interesting. It seemed to show her how far her husband's desire to be effective was capable of going—to the point of playing picturesque tricks upon the delicate organism of his daughter. She could not understand his purpose, no—not wholly; but she understood it better than he supposed or desired, inasmuch as she was convinced that the whole proceeding was an elaborate mystification, addressed to herself and destined to act upon her imagination. He wished to do something sudden and arbitrary, something unexpected and refined; to mark the difference between his sympathies and her own, and to show that if he regarded his daughter as a precious work of art, it was natural he should be more and more careful about the finishing touches. If he wished to be effective he had succeeded; the incident struck a chill into Isabel's heart. Pansy had known the convent in her childhood and had found a happy home there; she was fond of the good sisters, who were very fond of her, and there was therefore, for the moment, no definite hardship in her lot. But all the same, the girl had taken fright; the impression her father wanted to make would evidently be sharp enough. The old Protestant tradition had never faded from Isabel's imagination, and as her thoughts attached themselves to this striking example of her husband's genius—she sat looking, like him, at the basket of flowers—poor little Pansy became the heroine of a tragedy. Osmond wished it to be known that he shrank from nothing, and Isabel found it hard to pretend to eat her dinner. There was a certain relief, presently, in hearing the high, bright voice of her sister-in-law. The Countess, too, apparently, had been thinking the thing out; but she had arrived at a different conclusion from Isabel.

"It is very absurd, my dear Osmond," she said, "to invent so many pretty reasons for poor Pansy's banishment. Why don't you say at once that you want to get her out of my way? Haven't you discovered that I think very well of Mr. Rosier? I do indeed; he seems to me a delightful young man. He has made me believe in true love; I never did before! Of course you have made up your mind that with those convictions I am dreadful company for Pansy."

Osmond took a sip of a glass of wine; he looked perfectly good-humored.

"My dear Amy," he answered, smiling as if he were uttering a piece of gallantry, "I don't know anything about your convictions, but if I suspected that they interfere with mine it would be much simpler to banish you."

❧ 51 ❧

The Countess was not banished, but she felt the insecurity of her tenure of her brother's hospitality. A week after this incident Isabel received a telegram from England, dated from Gardencourt, and bearing the stamp of Mrs. Touchett's authorship. "Ralph cannot last many days," it ran, "and if convenient would like to see you. Wishes me to say that you must come only if you have not other duties. Say, for myself, that you used to talk a good deal about your duty and to wonder what it was; shall be curious to see whether you have found it out. Ralph is dying, and there is no other company." Isabel was prepared for this news, having received from Henrietta Stackpole a detailed account of her journey to England with her appreciative patient. Ralph had arrived more dead than alive, but she had managed to convey him to Gardencourt, where he had taken to his bed, which, as Miss Stackpole wrote, he evidently would never leave again. "I like him much better sick than when he used to be well," said Henrietta, who, it will be remembered, had taken a few years before a skeptical view of Ralph's disabilities. She added that she had really had two patients on her hands instead of one, for that Mr. Goodwood, who had been of no earthly use, was quite as sick, in a different way, as

Mr. Touchett. Afterwards she wrote that she had been obliged to surrender the field to Mrs. Touchett, who had just returned from America, and had promptly given her to understand that she didn't wish any interviewing at Gardencourt. Isabel had written to her aunt shortly after Ralph came to Rome, letting her know of his critical condition, and suggesting that she should lose no time in returning to Europe. Mrs. Touchett had telegraphed an acknowledgment of this admonition, and the only further news Isabel received from her was the second telegram which I have just quoted.

Isabel stood a moment looking at the latter missive, then, thrusting it into her pocket, she went straight to the door of her husband's study. Here she again paused an instant, after which she opened the door and went in. Osmond was seated at the table near the window with a folio volume before him, propped against a pile of books. This volume was open at a page of small colored plates, and Isabel presently saw that he had been copying from it the drawing of an antique coin. A box of watercolors and fine brushes lay before him, and he had already transferred to a sheet of immaculate paper the delicate, finely tinted disk. His back was turned toward the door, but without looking round he recognized his wife.

"Excuse me for disturbing you," she said.

"When I come to your room I always knock," he answered, going on with his work.

"I forgot; I had something else to think of. My cousin is dying."

"Ah, I don't believe that," said Osmond, looking at his drawing through a magnifying glass. "He was dying when we married; he will outlive us all."

Isabel gave herself no time, no thought, to appreciate the careful cynicism of this declaration; she simply went on quickly, full of her own intention—

"My aunt has telegraphed for me; I must go to Gardencourt."

"Why must you go to Gardencourt?" Osmond asked, in the tone of impartial curiosity.

"To see Ralph before he dies."

To this, for some time, Osmond made no rejoinder; he continued to give his chief attention to his work, which was of a sort that would brook no negligence.

"I don't see the need of it," he said at last. "He came to see you here. I didn't like that; I thought his being in Rome a great mistake. But I tolerated it, because it was to be the last time you should see him. Now you tell me it is not to have been the last. Ah, you are not grateful!"

"What am I to be grateful for?"

Gilbert Osmond laid down his little implements, blew a speck of dust from his drawing, slowly got up, and for the first time looked at his wife.

"For my not having interfered while he was here."

"Oh yes, I am. I remember perfectly how distinctly you let me know you didn't like it. I was very glad when he went away."

"Leave him alone then. Don't run after him."

Isabel turned her eyes away from him; they rested upon his little drawing.

"I must go to England," she said, with a full consciousness that her tone might strike an irritable man of taste as stupidly obstinate.

"I shall not like it if you do," Osmond remarked.

"Why should I mind that? You won't like it if I don't. You like nothing I do or don't do. You pretend to think I lie."

Osmond turned slightly pale; he gave a cold smile.

"That's why you must go then? Not to see your cousin, but to take a revenge on me."

"I know nothing about revenge."

"I do," said Osmond. "Don't give me an occasion."

"You are only too eager to take one. You wish immensely that I would commit some folly."

"I shall be gratified then if you disobey me."

"If I disobey you?" said Isabel, in a low tone, which had the effect of gentleness.

"Let it be clear. If you leave Rome today it will be a piece of the most deliberate, the most calculated, opposition."

"How can you call it calculated? I received my aunt's telegram but three minutes ago."

"You calculate rapidly; it's a great accomplishment. I don't see why we should prolong our discussion; you know my wish." And he stood there as if he expected to see her withdraw.

But she never moved; she couldn't move, strange as it may seem; she still wished to justify herself; he had the power, in an extraordinary degree, of making her feel this need. There was something in her imagination that he could always appeal to against her judgment.

"You have no reason for such a wish," said Isabel, "and I have every reason for going. I can't tell you how unjust you seem to me. But I think you know. It is your own opposition that is calculated. It is malignant."

She had never uttered her worst thought to her husband before, and the sensation of hearing it was evidently new to Osmond. But he showed no surprise, and his coolness was apparently a proof that he had believed his wife would in fact be unable to resist forever his ingenious endeavor to draw her out.

"It is all the more intense, then," he answered. And he added, almost as if he were giving her a friendly counsel—"This is a very important matter." She recognized this; she was fully conscious of the weight of the occasion; she knew that between them they had arrived at a crisis. Its gravity made her careful; she said nothing, and he went on. "You say I have no reason? I have the very best. I dislike, from the bottom of my soul, what you intend to do. It's dishonorable; it's indelicate;

it's indecent. Your cousin is nothing whatever to me, and I am under no obligation to make concessions to him. I have already made the very handsomest. Your relations with him, while he was here, kept me on pins and needles; but I let that pass, because from week to week I expected him to go. I have never liked him and he has never liked me. That's why you like him—because he hates me," said Osmond, with a quick, barely audible tremor in his voice. "I have an ideal of what my wife should do and should not do. She should not travel across Europe alone, in defiance of my deepest desire, to sit at the bedside of other men. Your cousin is nothing to you; he is nothing to us. You smile most expressively when I talk about *us;* but I assure you that *we, we,* is all that I know. I take our marriage seriously; you appear to have found a way of not doing so. I am not aware that we are divorced or separated; for me we are indissolubly united. You are nearer to me than any human creature, and I am nearer to you. It may be a disagreeable proximity; it's one, at any rate, of our own deliberate making. You don't like to be reminded of that, I know; but I am perfectly willing, because—because—" And Osmond paused a moment, looking as if he had something to say which would be very much to the point. "Because I think we should accept the consequences of our actions, and what I value most in life is the honor of a thing!"

He spoke gravely and almost gently; the accent of sarcasm had dropped out of his tone. It had a gravity which checked his wife's quick emotion; the resolution with which she had entered the room found itself caught in a mesh of fine threads. His last words were not a command, they constituted a kind of appeal; and though she felt that any expression of respect on Osmond's part could only be a refinement of egotism, they represented something transcendent and absolute, like the sign of the cross or the flag of one's country. He spoke in the name of something sacred and precious—the observance of a magnificent form. They were as perfectly apart in feeling as two disillusioned lovers had ever been; but they had never yet separated in act. Isabel had not changed; her old passion for justice still abode within her; and now, in the very thick of her sense of her husband's blasphemous sophistry, it began to throb to a tune which for a moment promised him the victory. It came over her that in his wish to preserve appearances he was after all sincere, and that this, as far as it went, was a merit. Ten minutes before, she had felt all the joy of irreflective action—a joy to which she had so long been a stranger; but action had been suddenly changed to slow renunciation, transformed by the blight of her husband's touch. If she must renounce, however, she would let him know that she was a victim rather than a dupe. "I know you are a master of the art of mockery," she said. "How can you speak of an indissoluble union—how can you speak of your being contented? Where is our union when you accuse me of falsity? Where is your contentment when you have nothing but hideous suspicion in your heart?"

"It is in our living decently together, in spite of such drawbacks."

"We don't live decently together!" Isabel cried.

"Indeed we don't, if you go to England."

"That's very little; that's nothing. I might do much more."

Osmond raised his eyebrows and even his shoulders a little; he had lived long enough in Italy to catch this trick. "Ah, if you have come to threaten me, I prefer my drawing," he said, walking back to his table, where he took up the sheet of paper on which he had been working and stood a moment examining his work.

"I suppose that if I go you will not expect me to come back," said Isabel.

He turned quickly round, and she could see that this movement at least was not studied. He looked at her a little, and then—"Are you out of your mind?" he inquired.

"How can it be anything but a rupture?" she went on; "especially if all you say is true?" She was unable to see how it could be anything but a rupture; she sincerely wished to know what else it might be.

Osmond sat down before his table. "I really can't argue with you on the hypothesis of your defying me," he said. And he took up one of his little brushes again.

Isabel lingered but a moment longer; long enough to embrace with her eye his whole deliberately indifferent, yet most expressive, figure; after which she quickly left the room. Her faculties, her energy, her passion, were all dispersed again; she felt as if a cold, dark mist had suddenly encompassed her. Osmond possessed in a supreme degree the art of eliciting one's weakness.

On her way back to her room she found the Countess Gemini standing in the open doorway of a little parlor in which a small collection of heterogeneous books had been arranged. The Countess had an open volume in her hand; she appeared to have been glancing down a page which failed to strike her as interesting. At the sound of Isabel's step she raised her head.

"Ah my dear," she said, "you, who are so literary, do tell me some amusing book to read! Everything here is so fearfully edifying. Do you think this would do me any good?"

Isabel glanced at the title of the volume she held out, but without reading or understanding it. "I am afraid I can't advise you. I have had bad news. My cousin, Ralph Touchett, is dying."

The Countess threw down her book. "Ah, he was so nice! I am sorry for you," she said.

"You would be sorrier still if you knew."

"What is there to know? You look very badly," the Countess added. "You must have been with Osmond."

Half-an-hour before, Isabel would have listened very coldly to an intimation that she should ever feel a desire for the sympathy of her sister-in-law, and there can be no better proof of her present embarrassment than the fact that she almost clutched at this lady's fluttering attention. "I have been with Osmond," she said, while the Countess's bright eyes glittered at her.

"I am sure he has been odious!" the Countess cried. "Did he say he was glad poor Mr. Touchett is dying?"

"He said it is impossible I should go to England."

The Countess's mind, when her interests were concerned, was agile; she already foresaw the extinction of any further brightness in her visit to Rome. Ralph Touchett would die, Isabel would go into mourning, and then there would be no more dinner-parties. Such a prospect produced for a moment in her countenance an expressive grimace; but this rapid, picturesque play of feature was her only tribute to disappointment. After all, she reflected, the game was almost played out; she had already overstayed her invitation. And then she cared enough for Isabel's trouble to forget her own, and she saw that Isabel's trouble was deep. It seemed deeper than the mere death of a cousin, and the Countess had no hesitation in connecting her exasperating brother with the expression of her sister-in-law's eyes. Her heart beat with an almost joyous expectation; for if she had wished to see Osmond overtopped, the conditions looked favorable now. Of course, if Isabel should go to England, she herself would immediately leave the Palazzo Roccanera; nothing would induce her to remain there with Osmond. Nevertheless she felt an immense desire to hear that Isabel would go to England. "Nothing is impossible for you, my dear," she said, caressingly. "Why else are you rich and clever and good?"

"Why indeed? I feel stupidly weak."

"Why does Osmond say it's impossible?" the Countess asked, in a tone which sufficiently declared that she couldn't imagine.

From the moment that she began to question her, however, Isabel drew back; she disengaged her hand, which the Countess had affectionately taken. But she answered this inquiry with frank bitterness. "Because we are so happy together that we cannot separate even for a fortnight."

"Ah," cried the Countess, while Isabel turned away; "when I want to make a journey my husband simply tells me I can have no money!"

Isabel went to her room, where she walked up and down for an hour. It may seem to some readers that she took things very hard, and it is certain that for a woman of a high spirit she had allowed herself easily to be arrested. It seemed to her that only now she fully measured the great undertaking of matrimony. Marriage meant that in such a case as this, when one had to choose, one chose as a matter of course for one's husband. "I am afraid—yes, I am afraid," she said to herself more than once, stopping short in her walk. But what she was afraid of was not her husband—his displeasure, his hatred, his revenge; it was not even her own later judgment of her conduct—a consideration which had often held her in check; it was simply the violence there would be in going when Osmond wished her to remain. A gulf of difference had opened between them, but nevertheless it was his desire that she should stay, it was a horror to him that she should go. She knew the nervous fineness with which he could feel an objection. What he thought of her she knew; what he was capable of saying to her she had felt; yet they were married, for all that, and marriage meant that a woman should abide with her husband. She sank down on her sofa at last, and buried her head in a pile of cushions.

When she raised her head again, the Countess Gemini stood before her. She had come in noiselessly, unperceived; she had a strange smile on her thin lips, and a still stranger glitter in her small dark eye.

"I knocked," she said, "but you didn't answer me. So I ventured in. I have been looking at you for the last five minutes. You are very unhappy."

"Yes; but I don't think you can comfort me."

"Will you give me leave to try?" And the Countess sat down on the sofa beside her. She continued to smile, and there was something communicative and exultant in her expression. She appeared to have something to say, and it occurred to Isabel for the first time that her sister-in-law might say something important. She fixed her brilliant eyes upon Isabel, who found at last a disagreeable fascination in her gaze. "After all," the Countess went on, "I must tell you, to begin with, that I don't understand your state of mind. You seem to have so many scruples, so many reasons, so many ties. When I discovered, ten years ago, that my husband's dearest wish was to make me miserable—of late he has simply let me alone—ah, it was a wonderful simplification! My poor Isabel, you are not simple enough."

"No, I am not simple enough," said Isabel.

"There is something I want you to know," the Countess declared—"because I think you ought to know it. Perhaps you do; perhaps you have guessed it. But if you have, all I can say is that I understand still less why you shouldn't do as you like."

"What do you wish me to know?" Isabel felt a foreboding which made her heart beat. The Countess was about to justify herself, and this alone was portentous.

But the Countess seemed disposed to play a little with her subject. "In your place I should have guessed it ages ago. Have you never really suspected?"

"I have guessed nothing. What should I have suspected? I don't know what you mean."

"That's because you have got such a pure mind. I never saw a woman with such a pure mind!" cried the Countess.

Isabel slowly got up. "You are going to tell me something horrible."

"You can call it by whatever name you will!" And the Countess rose also, while the sharp animation of her bright, capricious face emitted a kind of flash. She stood a moment looking at Isabel, and then she said—"My first sister-in-law had no children!"

Isabel stared back at her; the announcement was an anticlimax. "Your first sister-in-law?" she murmured.

"I suppose you know that Osmond has been married before? I have never spoken to you of his wife; I didn't suppose it was proper. But others, less particular, must have done so. The poor little woman lived but two years and died childless. It was after her death that Pansy made her appearance."

Isabel's brow had gathered itself into a frown; her lips were parted in pale, vague wonder. She was trying to follow; there seemed to be more to follow than she could see. "Pansy is not my husband's child, then?"

"Your husband's—in perfection! But no one else's husband's. Someone else's wife's. Ah, my good Isabel," cried the Countess, "with you one must dot one's *i*'s!"

"I don't understand; whose wife's?" said Isabel.

"The wife of a horrid little Swiss, who died twelve years ago. He never recognized Miss Pansy, and there was no reason he should. Osmond did, and that was better."

Isabel stayed the name which rose in a sudden question to her lips; she sank down on her seat again, hanging her head. "Why have you told me this?" she asked, in a voice which the Countess hardly recognized.

"Because I was so tired of your not knowing! I was tired of not having told you. It seemed to me so dull. It's not a lie, you know; it's exactly as I say."

"I never knew," said Isabel, looking up at her, simply.

"So I believed—though it was hard to believe. Has it never occurred to you that he has been her lover?"

"I don't know. Something has occurred to me. Perhaps it was that."

"She has been wonderfully clever about Pansy!" cried the Countess.

"That thing has never occurred to me," said Isabel. "And as it is—I don't understand."

She spoke in a low, thoughtful tone, and the poor Countess was equally surprised and disappointed at the effect of her revelation. She had expected to kindle a conflagration, and as yet she had barely extracted a spark. Isabel seemed more awe-stricken than anything else.

"Don't you perceive that the child could never pass for her husband's?" the Countess asked. "They had been separated too long for that, and M. Merle had gone to some far country; I think to South America. If she had ever had children—which I am not sure of—she had lost them. On the other hand, circumstances made it convenient enough for Osmond to acknowledge the little girl. His wife was dead—very true; but she had only been dead a year, and what was more natural than that she should have left behind a pledge of their affection? With the aid of a change of residence—he had been living at Naples, and he left it forever—the little fable was easily set going. My poor sister-in-law, who was in her grave, couldn't help herself, and the real mother, to save her reputation, renounced all visible property in the child."

"Ah, poor creature!" cried Isabel, bursting into tears. It was a long time since she had shed any; she had suffered a reaction from weeping. But now they gushed with an abundance in which the Countess Gemini found only another discomfiture.

"It's very kind of you to pity her!" she cried, with a discordant laugh. "Yes, indeed, you have a pure mind!"

"He must have been false to his wife," said Isabel, suddenly controlling herself.

"That's all that's wanting—that you should take up *her* cause!" the Countess went on.

"But to me—to me—" And Isabel hesitated, though there was a question in her eyes.

"To you he has been faithful? It depends upon what you call faithful. When he married you, he was no longer the lover of another woman. That state of things had passed away; the lady had repented; and she had a worship of appearances so intense that even Osmond himself got tired of it. You may therefore imagine what it was! But the whole past was between them."

"Yes," said Isabel, "the whole past is between them."

"Ah, this later past is nothing. But for five years they were very intimate."

"Why then did she want him to marry me?"

"Ah, my dear, that's her superiority! Because you had money; and because she thought you would be good to Pansy."

"Poor woman—and Pansy who doesn't like her!" cried Isabel.

"That's the reason she wanted someone whom Pansy would like. She knows it; she knows everything."

"Will she know that you have told me this?"

"That will depend upon whether you tell her. She is prepared for it, and do you know what she counts upon for her defense? On your thinking that I lie. Perhaps you do; don't make yourself uncomfortable to hide it. Only, as it happens this time, I don't. I have told little fibs; but they have never hurt anyone but myself."

Isabel sat staring at her companion's story as at a bale of fantastic wares that some strolling gypsy might have unpacked on the carpet at her feet. "Why did Osmond never marry her?" she asked, at last.

"Because she had no money." The Countess had an answer for everything, and if she lied she lied well. "No one knows, no one has ever known, what she lives on, or how she has got all those beautiful things. I don't believe Osmond himself knows. Besides, she wouldn't have married him."

"How can she have loved him then?"

"She doesn't love him, in that way. She did at first, and then, I suppose, she would have married him; but at that time her husband was living. By the time M. Merle had rejoined—I won't say his ancestors, because he never had any—her relations with Osmond had changed, and she had grown more ambitious. She hoped she might marry a great man; that has always been her idea. She has waited and watched and plotted and prayed; but she has never succeeded. I don't call Madame Merle a success, you know. I don't know what she may accomplish yet, but at present she has very little to show. The only tangible result she has ever achieved—except, of course, getting to know everyone and staying with them free of expense—has been her bringing you and Osmond together. Oh, she did that, my dear; you needn't look as if you doubted it. I have watched them for years; I know everything—everything. I am thought a great scatterbrain, but I have had enough application of mind to follow up those two. She hates me, and her way of showing it is to pretend to be forever defending me. When people say I have had fifteen lovers, she looks horrified, and declares that quite half of them were never proved. She has been afraid of me for years, and she has taken great comfort in the vile, false things that people have said about me. She has been afraid I would expose her, and she threatened me one day, when Osmond began to pay his court to you. It was at his house in Florence; do you remember that afternoon when she brought you there and we had tea in the garden? She let me know then that if I should tell tales, two could play at that game. She pretends there is a good deal more to tell about me than about her. It would be an interesting comparison! I don't care a fig what she may say, simply because I know you don't care a fig. You can't trouble your head about me less than you do already. So she may take her revenge as she chooses; I don't think she will frighten you very much. Her great idea has been to be tremendously irreproachable—a kind of full-blown lily—the incarnation of propriety. She has always worshipped that god. There should be no scandal about Caesar's wife, you know; and, as I say, she has always hoped to marry Caesar. That was one reason she wouldn't marry Osmond; the fear that on seeing her with Pansy people would put things together—would even see a resemblance. She has had a terror lest the mother should betray herself. She has been awfully careful; the mother has never done so."

"Yes, yes, the mother has done so," said Isabel, who had listened to all this with a face of deepening dreariness. "She betrayed herself to me the other day, though I didn't recognize her. There appeared to have been a chance of Pansy's making a great marriage, and in her disappointment at its not coming off she almost dropped the mask."

"Ah, that's where she would stumble!" cried the Countess. "She has failed so dreadfully herself that she is determined her daughter shall make it up."

Isabel started at the words "her daughter," which the Countess threw off so familiarly. "It seems very wonderful," she murmured; and in this bewildering impression she had almost lost her sense of being personally touched by the story.

"Now don't go and turn against the poor innocent child!" the Countess went on. "She is very nice, in spite of her lamentable parentage. I have liked Pansy, not because she was hers—but because she had become yours."

"Yes, she has become mine. And how the poor woman must have suffered at seeing me——!" Isabel exclaimed, flushing quickly at the thought.

"I don't believe she has suffered; on the contrary, she has enjoyed. Osmond's marriage has given Pansy a great lift. Before that she lived in a hole. And do you know what the mother thought? That you might take such a fancy to the child that you would do something for her. Osmond, of course, could never give her a portion. Osmond was really extremely poor; but of course you know all about that.—Ah, my dear," cried the Countess, "why did you ever inherit money?" She stopped a moment, as if she saw something singular in Isabel's face. "Don't tell me now that you will give her a dowry. You are capable of that, but I shouldn't believe it. Don't try to be too good. Be a little wicked, feel a little wicked, for once in your life!"

"It's very strange. I suppose I ought to know, but I am sorry," Isabel said. "I am much obliged to you."

"Yes, you seem to be!" cried the Countess, with a mocking laugh. "Perhaps you are—perhaps you are not. You don't take it as I should have thought."

"How should I take it?" Isabel asked.

"Well, I should say as a woman who has been made use of." Isabel made no answer to this; she only listened, and the Countess went on. "They have always been bound to each other; they remained so even after she became proper. But he has always been more for her than she has been for him. When their little carnival was over they made a bargain that each should give the other complete liberty, but that each should also do everything possible to help the other on. You may ask me how I know such a thing as that. I know it by the way they have behaved. Now see how much better women are than men! She has found a wife for Osmond, but Osmond has never lifted a little finger for her. She has worked for him, plotted for him, suffered for him; she has even more than once found money for him; and the end of it is that he is tired of her. She is an old habit; there are moments when he needs her; but on the whole he wouldn't miss her if she were removed. And, what's more, today she knows it. So you needn't be jealous!" the Countess added, humorously.

Isabel rose from her sofa again; she felt bruised and short of breath; her head was humming with new knowledge. "I am much obliged to you," she repeated. And then she added, abruptly, in quite a different tone—"How do you know all this?"

This inquiry appeared to ruffle the Countess more than Isabel's expression of gratitude pleased her. She gave her companion a bold stare, with which—"Let us assume that I have invented it!" she cried. She too, however, suddenly changed her tone, and, laying her hand on Isabel's arm, said softly, with her sharp, bright smile—"Now will you give up your journey?"

Isabel started a little; she turned away. But she felt weak and in a moment had to lay her arm upon the mantel shelf for support. She stood a minute so, and then upon her arm she dropped her dizzy head, with closed eyes and pale lips.

"I have done wrong to speak—I have made you ill!" the Countess cried.

"Ah, I must see Ralph!" Isabel murmured; not in resentment, not in the quick passion her companion had looked for; but in a tone of exquisite far-reaching sadness.

❧ 52 ❧

There was a train for Turin and Paris that evening; and after the Countess had left her, Isabel had a rapid and decisive conference with her maid, who was discreet, devoted, and active. After this, she thought (except of her journey) of only one thing. She must go and see Pansy; from her she could not turn away. She had not seen her yet, as Osmond had given her to understand that it was too soon to begin. She drove at five o'clock to a high door in a narrow street in the quarter of the Piazza Navona, and was admitted by the portress of the convent, a genial and obsequious person. Isabel had been at this institution before; she had come with Pansy to see the sisters. She knew they were good women, and she saw that the large rooms were clean and cheerful, and that the well-used garden had sun for winter and shade for spring. But she disliked the place, and it made her horribly sad; not for the world would she have spent a night there. It produced today more than before the impression of a well-appointed prison; for it was not possible to pretend that Pansy was free to leave it. This innocent creature had been presented to her in a new and violent light, but the secondary effect of the revelation was to make Isabel reach out her hand to her.

The portress left her to wait in the parlor of the convent, while she went to make it known that there was a visitor for the dear young lady. The parlor was a vast, cold apartment, with new-looking furniture; a large clean stove of white porcelain, unlighted; a collection of wax flowers, under glass; and a series of engravings from religious pictures on the walls. On the other occasion Isabel had thought it less like Rome than like Philadelphia; but today she made no reflections; the apartment only seemed to her very empty and very soundless. The portress returned at the end of some five minutes, ushering in another person. Isabel got up, expecting to see one of the ladies of the sisterhood; but to her extreme surprise she found herself confronted with Madame Merle. The effect was strange, for Madame Merle was already so present to her vision that her appearance in the flesh was a sort of reduplication. Isabel had been thinking all day of her falsity, her audacity, her ability, her probable suffering; and these dark things seemed to flash with a sudden light as she entered the room. Her being there at all was a kind of vivid proof. It made Isabel feel faint; if it had been necessary to speak on the spot, she would have been quite unable. But no such necessity was distinct to her; it seemed to her indeed that she had absolutely nothing to say to Madame Merle. In one's relations with this lady, however, there were never any absolute necessities; she had a manner which carried off not only her own deficiencies, but those of other people. But she was different from usual; she came in slowly, behind the portress, and Isabel instantly perceived that she was not likely to depend upon her habitual resources. For her, too, the occasion was exceptional, and she had undertaken to treat it by the light of the moment. This gave her a peculiar gravity; she did not even pretend to smile, and though Isabel saw that she was more than ever playing a part, it seemed to her that on the whole the wonderful woman had never been so natural. She looked at Isabel from head to foot, but not harshly nor defiantly; with a cold gentleness rather, and an absence of any air of allusion to their last meeting. It was as if she had wished to mark a difference; she had been irritated then—she was reconciled now.

"You can leave us alone," she said to the portress; "in five minutes this lady will ring for you." And then she turned to Isabel, who, after noting what has just been mentioned, had ceased to look at her, and had let her eyes wander as far as the limits of the room would allow. She wished never to look at Madame Merle again. "You are surprised to find me here, and I am afraid you are not pleased," this lady went on. "You don't see why I should have come; it's as if I had anticipated you. I confess I have been rather indiscreet—I ought to have asked your permission." There was none of the oblique movement of irony in this; it was said simply and softly; but Isabel, far afloat on a sea of wonder and pain, could not have told herself with what intention it was uttered. "But I have not been sitting long," Madame Merle continued; "that is, I have not been long with Pansy. I came to see her because it occurred to me this afternoon that she must be rather lonely, and perhaps even a little miserable. It may be good for a young girl; I know so little about young girls, I can't tell. At any rate it's a little dismal. Therefore I came—on the chance. I knew of course that you would come, and her father as well; still, I had not been told that other visitors were forbidden. The good woman—what's her name? Madame Catherine—made no objection whatever. I stayed twenty minutes with Pansy; she has a charming little room, not in the least conventual, with a piano and flowers. She has arranged it delightfully; she has so much taste. Of course it's all none of my business, but I feel happier since I have seen her. She may even have a maid if she likes;

but of course she has no occasion to dress. She wears a little black dress; she looks so charming. I went afterwards to see Mother Catherine, who has a very good room too; I assure you I don't find the poor sisters at all monastic. Mother Catherine has a most coquettish little toilet-table, with something that looked uncommonly like a bottle of eau-de-Cologne. She speaks delightfully of Pansy; says it's a great happiness for them to have her. She is a little saint of heaven, and a model to the oldest of them. Just as I was leaving Madame Catherine, the portress came to say to her that there was a lady for the Signorina. Of course I knew it must be you, and I asked her to let me go and receive you in her place. She demurred greatly—I must tell you that—and said it was her duty to notify the Superior; it was of such high importance that you should be treated with respect. I requested her to let the poor Superior alone, and asked her how she supposed I would treat you!"

So Madame Merle went on, with much of the brilliancy of a woman who had long been a mistress of the art of conversation. But there were phases and gradations in her speech, not one of which was lost upon Isabel's ear, though her eyes were absent from her companion's face. She had not proceeded far before Isabel noted a sudden rupture in her voice, which was in itself a complete drama. This subtle modulation marked a momentous discovery—the perception of an entirely new attitude on the part of her listener. Madame Merle had guessed in the space of an instant that everything was at end between them, and in the space of another instant she had guessed the reason why. The person who stood there was not the same one she had seen hitherto; it was a very different person—a person who knew her secret. This discovery was tremendous, and for the moment she made it the most accomplished of women faltered and lost her courage. But only for that moment. Then the conscious stream of her perfect manner gathered itself again and flowed on as smoothly as might be to the end. But it was only because she had the end in view that she was able to go on. She had been touched with a point that made her quiver, and she needed all the alertness of her will to repress her agitation. Her only safety was in not betraying herself. She did not betray herself; but the startled quality of her voice refused to improve—she couldn't help it—while she heard herself say she hardly knew what. The tide of her confidence ebbed, and she was able only just to glide into port, faintly grazing the bottom.

Isabel saw all this as distinctly as if it had been a picture on the wall. It might have been a great moment for her, for it might have been a moment of triumph. That Madame Merle had lost her pluck and saw before her the phantom of exposure—this in itself was a revenge, this in itself was almost a symptom of a brighter day. And for a moment while she stood apparently looking out of the window, with her back half turned, Isabel enjoyed her knowledge. On the other side of the window lay the garden of the convent; but this is not what Isabel saw; she saw nothing of the budding plants and the glowing afternoon. She saw, in the crude light of that revelation which had already become a part of experience and to which the very frailty of the vessel in which it had been offered her only gave an intrinsic price, the dry, staring fact that she had been a dull unreverenced tool. All the bitterness of this knowledge surged into her soul again; it was as if she felt on her lips the taste of dishonor. There was a moment during which, if she had turned and spoken, she would have said something that would hiss like a lash. But she closed her eyes, and then the hideous vision died away. What remained was the cleverest woman in the world, standing there within a few feet of her and knowing as little what to think as the meanest. Isabel's only revenge was to be silent still—to leave Madame Merle in this unprecedented situation. She left her there for a period which must have seemed long to this lady, who at last seated herself with a movement which was in itself a confession of helplessness. Then Isabel turned her eyes and looked down at her. Madame Merle was very pale; her own eyes covered Isabel's face. She might see what she would, but her danger was over. Isabel would never accuse her, never reproach her; perhaps because she never would give her the opportunity to defend herself.

"I am come to bid Pansy goodbye," Isabel said at last. "I am going to England tonight."

"Going to England tonight!" Madame Merle repeated, sitting there and looking up at her.

"I am going to Gardencourt. Ralph Touchett is dying."

"Ah, you will feel that." Madame Merle recovered herself; she had a chance to express sympathy. "Do you go alone?" she asked.

"Yes; without my husband."

Madame Merle gave a low, vague murmur; a sort of recognition of the general sadness of things.

"Mr. Touchett never liked me; but I am sorry he is dying. Shall you see his mother?"

"Yes; she has returned from America."

"She used to be very kind to me; but she has changed. Others, too, have changed," said Madame Merle, with a quiet, noble pathos. She paused a moment, and then she said, "And you will see dear old Gardencourt again!"

"I shall not enjoy it much," Isabel answered.

"Naturally—in your grief. But it is on the whole, of all the houses I know, and I know many, the one I should have liked best to live in. I don't venture to send a message to the people," Madame Merle added; "but I should like to give my love to the place."

Isabel turned away.

"I had better go to Pansy," she said. "I have not much time."

And while she looked about her for the proper egress, the door opened and admitted one of the ladies of the house, who advanced with a discreet smile, gently rubbing, under her long loose sleeves, a pair of plump white hands. Isabel recognized her as Madame Catherine, whose acquaintance she had already made, and begged that she would immediately let her see Miss Osmond. Madame Catherine looked doubly discreet, but smiled very blandly and said—

"It will be good for her to see you. I will take you to her myself." Then she directed her pleasant, cautious little eye toward Madame Merle.

"Will you let me remain a little?" this lady asked. "It is so good to be here."

"You may remain always, if you like!" And the good sister gave a knowing laugh. She led Isabel out of the room, through several corridors, and up a long staircase. All these departments were solid and bare, light and clean; so, thought Isabel, are the great penal establishments. Madame Catherine gently pushed open the door of Pansy's room and ushered in the visitor; then stood smiling, with folded hands, while the two others met and embraced.

"She is glad to see you," she repeated; "it will do her good." And she placed the best chair carefully for Isabel. But she made no movement to seat herself; she seemed ready to retire. "How does this dear child look?" she asked of Isabel, lingering a moment.

"She looks pale," Isabel answered.

"That is the pleasure of seeing you. She is very happy. *Elle éclaire la maison,*" said the good sister.

Pansy wore, as Madame Merle had said, a little black dress; it was perhaps this that made her look pale.

"They are very good to me—they think of everything!" she exclaimed, with all her customary eagerness to say something agreeable.

"We think of you always—you are a precious charge," Madame Catherine remarked, in the tone of a woman with whom benevolence was a habit, and whose conception of duty was the acceptance of every care. It fell with a leaden weight upon Isabel's ears; it seemed to represent the surrender of a personality, the authority of the Church.

When Madame Catherine had left them together, Pansy kneeled down before Isabel and hid her head in her step-mother's lap. So she remained some moments, while Isabel gently stroked her hair. Then she got up, averting her face and looking about the room.

"Don't you think I have arranged it well? I have everything I have at home."

"It is very pretty; you are very comfortable." Isabel scarcely knew what she could say to her. On the one hand she could not let her think she had come to pity her, and on the other it would be a dull mockery to pretend to rejoice with her. So she simply added, after a moment, "I have come to bid you goodbye. I am going to England."

Pansy's white little face turned red.

"To England! Not to come back?"

"I don't know when I shall come back."

"Ah; I'm sorry," said Pansy, faintly. She spoke as if she had no right to criticize; but her tone expressed a depth of disappointment.

"My cousin, Mr. Touchett, is very ill; he will probably die. I wish to see him," Isabel said.

"Ah, yes; you told me he would die. Of course you must go. And will papa go?"

"No; I shall go alone."

For a moment, Pansy said nothing. Isabel had often wondered what she thought of the apparent relations of her father with his wife; but never by a glance, by an intimation, had she let it be seen that she deemed them deficient in the quality of intimacy. She made her reflections, Isabel was sure; and she must have had a conviction that there were husbands and wives who were more intimate than that. But Pansy was not indiscreet even in thought; she would as little have ventured to judge her gentle step-mother as to criticize her magnificent father. Her heart may almost have stood still, as it would have done if she had seen two of the saints in the great picture in the convent chapel turn their painted heads and shake them at each other; but as in this latter case she would (for very solemnity's sake), never have mentioned the awful phenomenon, so she put away all knowledge of the secrets of larger lives than her own.

"You will be very far away," she said presently.

"Yes; I shall be far away. But it will scarcely matter," Isabel answered; "for so long as you are here I am very far away from you."

"Yes; but you can come and see me; though you have not come very often."

"I have not come because your father forbade it. Today I bring nothing with me. I can't amuse you."

"I am not to be amused. That's not what papa wishes."

"Then it hardly matters whether I am in Rome or in England."

"You are not happy, Mrs. Osmond," said Pansy.

"Not very. But it doesn't matter."

"That's what I say to myself. What does it matter? But I should like to come out."

"I wish indeed you might."

"Don't leave me here," Pansy went on, gently.

Isabel was silent a moment; her heart beat fast.

"Will you come away with me now?" she asked.

Pansy looked at her pleadingly.

"Did papa tell you to bring me?"

"No; it's my own proposal."

"I think I had better wait, then. Did papa send me no message?"

"I don't think he knew I was coming."

"He thinks I have not had enough," said Pansy. "But I have. The ladies are very kind to me, and the little girls come to see me. There are some very little ones— such charming children. Then my room—you can see for yourself. All that is very delightful. But I have had enough. Papa wished me to think a little—and I have thought a great deal."

"What have you thought?"

"Well, that I must never displease papa."

"You knew that before."

"Yes; but I know it better. I will do anything—I will do anything," said Pansy. Then, as she heard her own words, a deep, pure blush came into her face. Isabel read the meaning of it; she saw that the poor girl had been vanquished. It was well that Mr. Edward Rosier had kept his enamels! Isabel looked into her eyes and saw there mainly a prayer to be treated easily. She laid her hand on Pansy's, as if to let her know that her look conveyed no diminution of esteem; for the collapse of the girl's momentary resistance (mute and modest though it had been), seemed only her tribute to the truth of things. She didn't presume to judge others, but she had judged herself; she had seen the reality. She had no vocation for struggling with combinations; in the solemnity of sequestration there was something that overwhelmed her. She bowed her pretty head to authority, and only asked of authority to be merciful. Yes; it was very well that Edward Rosier had reserved a few articles!

Isabel got up; her time was rapidly shortening.

"Goodbye, then," she said; "I leave Rome tonight."

Pansy took hold of her dress; there was a sudden change in the girl's face.

"You look strange; you frighten me."

"Oh, I am very harmless," said Isabel.

"Perhaps you won't come back?"

"Perhaps not. I can't tell."

"Ah, Mrs. Osmond, you won't leave me!"

Isabel now saw that she had guessed everything.

"My dear child, what can I do for you?" she asked.

"I don't know—but I am happier when I think of you."

"You can always think of me."

"Not when you are so far. I am a little afraid," said Pansy.

"What are you afraid of?"

"Of papa—a little. And of Madame Merle. She has just been to see me."

"You must not say that," Isabel observed.

"Oh, I will do everything they want. Only if you are here I shall do it more easily."

Isabel reflected a little.

"I won't desert you," she said at last. "Goodbye, my child."

Then they held each other a moment in a silent embrace, like two sisters; and afterwards Pansy walked along the corridor with her visitor to the top of the staircase.

"Madame Merle has been here," Pansy remarked as they went; and as Isabel answered nothing she added, abruptly, "I don't like Madame Merle!"

Isabel hesitated a moment; then she stopped.

"You must never say that—that you don't like Madame Merle."

Pansy looked at her in wonder; but wonder with Pansy had never been a reason for noncompliance.

"I never will again," she said, with exquisite gentleness.

At the top of the staircase they had to separate, as it appeared to be part of the mild but very definite discipline under which Pansy lived that she should not go down. Isabel descended, and when she reached the bottom the girl was standing above.

"You will come back?" she called out in a voice that Isabel remembered afterwards.

"Yes—I will come back."

Madame Catherine met Isabel below, and conducted her to the door of the parlor, outside of which the two stood talking a minute.

"I won't go in," said the good sister. "Madame Merle is waiting for you."

At this announcement Isabel gave a start, and she was on the point of asking if there were no other egress from the convent. But a moment's reflection assured her that she would do well not to betray to the worthy nun her desire to avoid Pansy's other visitor. Her companion laid her hand very gently on her arm, and fixing her a moment with a wise, benevolent eye, said to her, speaking French, almost familiarly—

"*Eh bien, chère Madame, qu'en pensez-vous?*"

"About my step-daughter? Oh, it would take long to tell you."

"We think it's enough," said Madame Catherine, significantly. And she pushed open the door of the parlor.

Madame Merle was sitting just as Isabel had left her, like a woman so absorbed in thought that she had not moved a little finger. As Madame Catherine closed the door behind Isabel, she got up, and Isabel saw that she had been thinking to some purpose. She had recovered her balance; she was in full possession of her resources.

"I found that I wished to wait for you," she said, urbanely. "But it's not to talk about Pansy."

Isabel wondered what it could be to talk about, and in spite of Madame Merle's declaration she answered after a moment—

"Madame Catherine says it's enough."

"Yes; it also seems to me enough. I wanted to ask you another word about poor Mr. Touchett," Madame Merle added. "Have you reason to believe that he is really at his last?"

"I have no information but a telegram. Unfortunately it only confirms a probability."

"I am going to ask you a strange question," said Madame Merle. "Are you very fond of your cousin?" And she gave a smile as strange as her question.

"Yes, I am very fond of him. But I don't understand you."

Madame Merle hesitated a moment.

"It is difficult to explain. Something has occurred to me which may not have occurred to you, and I give you the benefit of my idea. Your cousin did you once a great service. Have you never guessed it?"

"He has done me many services."

"Yes; but one was much above the rest. He made you a rich woman."

"*He* made me——?"

Madame Merle appeared to see herself successful, and she went on, more triumphantly—

"He imparted to you that extra luster which was required to make you a brilliant match. At bottom, it is him that you have to thank." She stopped; there was something in Isabel's eyes.

"I don't understand you. It was my uncle's money."

"Yes; it was your uncle's money; but it was your cousin's idea. He brought his father over to it. Ah, my dear, the sum was large!"

Isabel stood staring; she seemed today to be living in a world illumined by lurid flashes.

"I don't know why you say such things! I don't know what you know."

"I know nothing but what I have guessed. But I have guessed that."

Isabel went to the door, and when she had opened it stood a moment with her hand on the latch. Then she said—it was her only revenge—

"I believed it was you I had to thank!"

Madame Merle dropped her eyes; she stood there in a kind of proud penance.

"You are very unhappy, I know. But I am more so."

"Yes; I can believe that. I think I should like never to see you again."

Madame Merle raised her eyes.

"I shall go to America," she announced, while Isabel passed out.

❧ 53 ❧

It was not with surprise, it was with a feeling which in other circumstances would have had much of the effect of joy, that as Isabel descended from the Paris mail at Charing Cross, she stepped into the arms, as it were—or at any rate into the hands—of Henrietta Stackpole. She had telegraphed to her friend from Turin, and though she had not definitely said to herself that Henrietta would meet her, she had felt that her telegram would produce some helpful result. On her long journey from Rome her mind had been given up to vagueness; she was unable to question the future. She performed this journey with sightless eyes, and took little pleasure in the countries she traversed, decked out though they were in the richest freshness of spring. Her thoughts followed their course through other countries—strange-looking, dimly lighted, pathless lands, in which there was no change of seasons, but only, as it seemed, a perpetual dreariness of winter. She had plenty to think about; but it was not reflection, nor conscious purpose, that filled her mind. Disconnected visions passed through it, and sudden dull gleams of memory, of expectation. The past and the future alternated at their will, but she saw them only in fitful images, which came and went by a logic of their own. It was extraordinary the things she remembered. Now that she was in the secret, now that she knew something that so much concerned her, and the eclipse of which had made life resemble an attempt to play whist with an imperfect pack of cards, the truth of things, their mutual relations, their meaning, and for the most part their horror, rose before her with a kind of architectural vastness. She remembered a thousand trifles; they started to life with the spontaneity of a shiver. That is, she had thought them trifles at the time; now she saw that they were leaden-weighted. Yet even now they were trifles, after all; for of what use was it to her to understand them? Nothing seemed of use to her today. All purpose, all intention, was suspended; all desire, too, save the single desire to reach her richly constituted refuge. Gardencourt had been her starting point, and to those muffled chambers it was at least a temporary solution to return. She had gone forth in her strength; she would come back in her weakness; and if the place had been a rest to her before, it would be a positive sanctuary now. She envied Ralph his dying; for if one were thinking of rest, that was the most perfect of all. To cease utterly, to give it all up and not know

471

anything more—this idea was as sweet as the vision of a cool bath in a marble tank, in a darkened chamber, in a hot land. She had moments, indeed, in her journey from Rome, which were almost as good as being dead. She sat in her corner, so motionless, so passive, simply with the sense of being carried, so detached from hope and regret, that if her spirit was haunted with sudden pictures, it might have been the spirit disembarrassed of the flesh. There was nothing to regret now—that was all over. Not only the time of her folly, but the time of her repentance seemed far away. The only thing to regret was that Madame Merle had been so—so strange. Just here Isabel's imagination paused, from literal inability to say what it was that Madame Merle had been. Whatever it was, it was for Madame Merle herself to regret it; and doubtless she would do so in America, where she was going. It concerned Isabel no more; she only had an impression that she should never again see Madame Merle. This impression carried her into the future, of which from time to time she had a mutilated glimpse. She saw herself, in the distant years, still in the attitude of a woman who had her life to live, and these intimations contradicted the spirit of the present hour. It might be desirable to die; but this privilege was evidently to be denied her. Deep in her soul—deeper than any appetite for renunciation—was the sense that life would be her business for a long time to come. And at moments there was something inspiring, almost exhilarating, in the conviction. It was a proof of strength—it was a proof that she should some day be happy again. It couldn't be that she was to live only to suffer; she was still young, after all, and a great many things might happen to her yet. To live only to suffer—only to feel the injury of life repeated and enlarged—it seemed to her that she was too valuable, too capable, for that. Then she wondered whether it were vain and stupid to think so well of herself. When had it ever been a guarantee to be valuable? Was not all history full of the destruction of precious things? Was it not much more probable that if one were delicate one would suffer? It involved then, perhaps, an admission that one had a certain grossness; but Isabel recognized, as it passed before her eyes, the quick, vague shadow of a long future. She should not escape; she should last. Then the middle years wrapped her about again, and the gray curtain of her indifference closed her in.

Henrietta kissed her, as Henrietta usually kissed, as if she were afraid she should be caught doing it; and then Isabel stood there in the crowd, looking about her, looking for her servant. She asked nothing; she wished to wait. She had a sudden perception that she should be helped. She was so glad Henrietta was there; there was something terrible in an arrival in London. The dusky, smoky, far-arching vault of the station, the strange, livid light, the dense, dark, pushing crowd, filled her with a nervous fear and made her put her arm into her friend's. She remembered that she had once liked these things; they seemed part of a mighty spectacle, in which there was something that touched her. She remembered how she walked away from Euston, in the winter dusk, in the crowded streets, five years before. She could not have done that today, and the incident came before her as the deed of another person.

"It's too beautiful that you should have come," said Henrietta, looking at her as if she thought Isabel might be prepared to challenge the proposition. "If you hadn't—if you hadn't; well, I don't know," remarked Miss Stackpole, hinting ominously at her powers of disapproval.

Isabel looked about, without seeing her maid. Her eyes rested on another figure, however, which she felt that she had seen before; and in a moment she recognized the genial countenance of Mr. Bantling. He stood a little apart, and it was not in the power of the multitude that pressed about him to make him yield an inch of the ground he had taken—that of abstracting himself, discreetly, while the two ladies performed their embraces.

"There's Mr. Bantling," said Isabel, gently, irrelevantly, scarcely caring much now whether she should find her maid or not.

"Oh yes, he goes everywhere with me. Come here, Mr. Bantling!" Henrietta exclaimed. Whereupon the gallant bachelor advanced with a smile—a smile tempered, however, by the gravity of the occasion. "Isn't it lovely that she has come?" Henrietta asked. "He knows all about it," she added; "we had quite a discussion; he said you wouldn't; I said you would."

"I thought you always agreed," Isabel answered, smiling. She found she could smile now; she had seen in an instant, in Mr. Bantling's excellent eye, that he had good news for her. It seemed to say that he wished her to remember that he was an old friend of her cousin—that he understood—that it was all right. Isabel gave him her hand; she thought him so kind.

"Oh, I always agree," said Mr. Bantling. "But she doesn't, you know."

"Didn't I tell you that a maid was a nuisance?" Henrietta inquired. "Your young lady has probably remained at Calais."

"I don't care," said Isabel, looking at Mr. Bantling, whom she had never thought so interesting.

"Stay with her while I go and see," Henrietta commanded, leaving the two for a moment together.

They stood there at first in silence, and then Mr. Bantling asked Isabel how it had been on the Channel.

"Very fine. No, I think it was rather rough," said Isabel, to her companion's obvious surprise. After which she added, "You have been to Gardencourt, I know."

"Now how do you know that?"

"I can't tell you—except that you look like a person who has been there."

"Do you think I look sad? It's very sad there, you know."

"I don't believe you ever look sad. You look kind," said Isabel, with a frankness that cost her no effort. It seemed to her that she should never again feel a superficial embarrassment.

Poor Mr. Bantling, however, was still in this inferior stage. He blushed a good deal, and laughed, and assured her that he was often very blue, and that when he was blue he was awfully fierce.

"You can ask Miss Stackpole, you know," he said. "I was at Gardencourt two days ago."

"Did you see my cousin?"

"Only for a little. But he had been seeing people; Warburton was there the day before. Touchett was just the same as usual, except that he was in bed, and that he looks tremendously ill, and that he can't speak," Mr. Bantling pursued. "He was immensely friendly all the same. He was just as clever as ever. It's awfully sad."

Even in the crowded, noisy station this simple picture was vivid. "Was that late in the day?"

"Yes; I went on purpose; we thought you would like to know."

"I am very much obliged to you. Can I go down tonight?"

"Ah, I don't think *she*'ll let you go," said Mr. Bantling. "She wants you to stop with her. I made Touchett's man promise to telegraph me today, and I found the telegram an hour ago at my club. 'Quiet and easy,' that's what it says, and it's dated two o'clock. So you see you can wait till tomorrow. You must be very tired."

"Yes, I am very tired. And I thank you again."

"Oh," said Mr. Bantling, "we were certain you would like the last news." While Isabel vaguely noted that after all he and Henrietta seemed to agree.

Miss Stackpole came back with Isabel's maid, whom she had caught in the act of proving her utility. This excellent person, instead of losing herself in the crowd, had simply attended to her mistress's luggage, so that now Isabel was at liberty to leave the station.

"You know you are not to think of going to the country tonight," Henrietta remarked to her. "It doesn't matter whether there is a train or not. You are to come straight to me, in Wimpole Street. There isn't a corner to be had in London, but I have got you one all the same. It isn't a Roman palace, but it will do for a night."

"I will do whatever you wish," Isabel said.

"You will come and answer a few questions; that's what I wish."

"She doesn't say anything about dinner, does she, Mrs. Osmond?" Mr. Bantling inquired jocosely.

Henrietta fixed him a moment with her speculative gaze. "I see you are in a great hurry to get to your own. You will be at the Paddington station tomorrow morning at ten."

"Don't come for my sake, Mr. Bantling," said Isabel.

"He will come for mine," Henrietta declared, as she ushered Isabel into a cab.

Later, in a large, dusky parlor in Wimpole Street—to do her justice, there had been dinner enough—she asked Isabel those questions to which she had alluded at the station.

"Did your husband make a scene about your coming?" That was Miss Stackpole's first inquiry.

"No; I can't say he made a scene."

"He didn't object then?"

"Yes; he objected very much. But it was not what you would call a scene."

"What was it then?"

"It was a very quiet conversation."

Henrietta for a moment contemplated her friend.

"It must have been awful," she then remarked. And Isabel did not deny that it had been awful. But she confined herself to answering Henrietta's questions, which was easy, as they were tolerably definite. For the present she offered her no new information. "Well," said Miss Stackpole at last, "I have only one criticism to make. I don't see why you promised little Miss Osmond to go back."

"I am not sure that I see myself, now," Isabel replied. "But I did then."

"If you have forgotten your reason perhaps you won't return."

Isabel for a moment said nothing, then—

"Perhaps I shall find another," she rejoined.

"You will certainly never find a good one."

"In default of a better, my having promised will do," Isabel suggested.

"Yes; that's why I hate it."

"Don't speak of it now. I have a little time. Coming away was hard; but going back will be harder still."

"You must remember, after all, that he won't make a scene!" said Henrietta, with much intention.

"He will, though," Isabel answered gravely. "It will not be the scene of a moment; it will be a scene that will last always."

For some minutes the two women sat gazing at this prospect; and then Miss Stackpole, to change the subject, as Isabel had requested, announced abruptly—

"I have been to stay with Lady Pensil!"

"Ah, the letter came at last!"

"Yes; it took five years. But this time she wanted to see me."

"Naturally enough."

"It was more natural than I think you know," said Henrietta, fixing her eyes on a distant point. And then she added, turning suddenly: "Isabel Archer, I beg your pardon. You don't know why? Because I criticized you, and yet I have gone further than you. Mr. Osmond, at least, was born on the other side!"

It was a moment before Isabel perceived her meaning; it was so modestly, or at least so ingeniously, veiled. Isabel's mind was not possessed at present with the comicality of things; but she greeted with a quick laugh the image that her companion had raised. She immediately recovered herself, however, and with a gravity too pathetic to be real—

"Henrietta Stackpole," she asked, "are you going to give up your country?"

"Yes, my poor Isabel, I am. I won't pretend to deny it; I look the fact in the face. I am going to marry Mr. Bantling, and I am going to reside in London."

"It seems very strange," said Isabel, smiling now.

"Well yes, I suppose it does. I have come to it little by little. I think I know what I am doing; but I don't know that I can explain."

"One can't explain one's marriage," Isabel answered. "And yours doesn't need to be explained. Mr. Bantling is very good."

Henrietta said nothing; she seemed lost in reflection.

"He has a beautiful nature," she remarked at last. "I have studied him for many years, and I see right through him. He's as clear as glass—there's no mystery about him. He is not intellectual, but he appreciates intellect. On the other hand, he doesn't exaggerate its claims. I sometimes think we do in the United States."

"Ah," said Isabel, "you are changed indeed! It's the first time I have ever heard you say anything against your native land."

"I only say that we are too intellectual; that, after all, is a glorious fault. But I *am* changed; a woman has to change a good deal to marry."

"I hope you will be very happy. You will at last—over here—see something of the inner life."

Henrietta gave a little significant sigh. "That's the key to the mystery, I believe. I couldn't endure to be kept off. Now I have as good a right as anyone!" she added, with artless elation.

Isabel was deeply diverted, but there was a certain melancholy in her view. Henrietta, after all, was human and feminine, Henrietta whom she had hitherto regarded as a light keen flame, a disembodied voice. It was rather a disappointment to find that she had personal susceptibilities, that she was subject to common passions, and that her intimacy with Mr. Bantling had not been completely original. There was a want of originality in her marrying him—there was even a kind of stupidity; and for a moment, to Isabel's sense, the dreariness of the world took on a deeper tinge. A little later, indeed, she reflected that Mr. Bantling, after all, was original. But she didn't see how Henrietta could give up her country. She herself had relaxed her hold of it, but it had never been her country as it had been Henrietta's. She presently asked her if she had enjoyed her visit to Lady Pensil.

"Oh, yes," said Henrietta, "she didn't know what to make of me."

"And was that very enjoyable?"

"Very much so, because she is supposed to be very talented. She thinks she knows everything; but she doesn't understand a lady correspondent! It would be so much easier for her if I were only a little better or a little worse. She's so puzzled; I believe she thinks it's my duty to go and do something immoral. She thinks it's immoral that I should marry her brother; but, after all, that isn't immoral enough. And she will never understand—never!"

"She is not so intelligent as her brother, then," said Isabel. "He appears to have understood."

"Oh no, he hasn't!" cried Miss Stackpole, with decision. "I really believe that's what he wants to marry me for—just to find out. It's a fixed idea—a kind of fascination."

"It's very good in you to humor it."

"Oh well," said Henrietta, "I have something to find out too!" And Isabel saw that she had not renounced an allegiance, but planned an attack. She was at last about to grapple in earnest with England.

Isabel also perceived, however, on the morrow, at the Paddington station, where she found herself, at ten o'clock, in the company both of Miss Stackpole and Mr. Bantling, that the gentleman bore his perplexities lightly. If he had not found out everything, he had found out at least the great point—that Miss Stackpole would not be wanting in initiative. It was evident that in the selection of a wife he had been on his guard against this deficiency.

"Henrietta has told me, and I am very glad," Isabel said, as she gave him her hand.

"I dare say you think it's very odd," Mr. Bantling replied, resting on his neat umbrella.

"Yes, I think it's very odd."

"You can't think it's so odd as I do. But I have always rather liked striking out a line," said Mr. Bantling, serenely.

❊ 54 ❊

Isabel's arrival at Gardencourt on this second occasion was even quieter than it had been on the first. Ralph Touchett kept but a small household, and to the new servants Mrs. Osmond was a stranger; so that Isabel, instead of being conducted to her own apartment, was coldly shown into the drawing room, and left to wait while her name was carried up to her aunt. She waited a long time; Mrs.

Touchett appeared to be in no hurry to come to her. She grew impatient at last; she grew nervous and even frightened. The day was dark and cold; the dusk was thick in the corners of the wide brown rooms. The house was perfectly still—a stillness that Isabel remembered; it had filled all the place for days before the death of her uncle. She left the drawing room and wandered about—strolled into the library and along the gallery of pictures, where, in the deep silence, her footstep made an echo. Nothing was changed; she recognized everything that she had seen years before; it might have been only yesterday that she stood there. She reflected that things change but little, while people change so much, and she became aware that she was walking about as her aunt had done on the day that she came to see her in Albany. She was changed enough since then—that had been the beginning. It suddenly struck her that if her Aunt Lydia had not come that day in just that way and found her alone, everything might have been different. She might have had another life, and today she might have been a happier woman. She stopped in the gallery in front of a small picture—a beautiful and valuable Bonington—upon which her eyes rested for a long time. But she was not looking at the picture; she was wondering whether if her aunt had not come that day in Albany she would have married Caspar Goodwood.

Mrs. Touchett appeared at last, just after Isabel had returned to the big uninhabited drawing room. She looked a good deal older, but her eye was as bright as ever and her head as erect; her thin lips seemed a repository of latent meanings. She wore a little gray dress, of the most undecorated fashion, and Isabel wondered, as she had wondered the first time, whether her remarkable kinswoman resembled more a queen-regent or the matron of a gaol. Her lips felt very thin indeed as Isabel kissed her.

"I have kept you waiting because I have been sitting with Ralph," Mrs. Touchett said. "The nurse had gone to her lunch and I had taken her place. He has a man who is supposed to look after him, but the man is good for nothing; he is always looking out of the window—as if there were anything to see! I didn't wish to move, because Ralph seemed to be sleeping, and I was afraid the sound would disturb him. I waited till the nurse came back; I remembered that you knew the house."

"I find I know it better even than I thought; I have been walking," Isabel answered. And then she asked whether Ralph slept much.

"He lies with his eyes closed; he doesn't move. But I am not sure that it's always sleep."

"Will he see me? Can he speak to me?"

Mrs. Touchett hesitated a moment. "You can try him," she said. And then she offered to conduct Isabel to her room. "I thought they had taken you there; but it's not my house, it's Ralph's; and I don't know what they do. They must at least have taken your luggage; I don't suppose you have brought much. Not that I care, however. I believe they have given you the same room you had before; when Ralph heard you were coming he said you must have that one."

"Did he say anything else?"

"Ah, my dear, he doesn't chatter as he used!" cried Mrs. Touchett, as she preceded her niece up the staircase.

It was the same room, and something told Isabel that it had not been slept in since she occupied it. Her luggage was there, and it was not voluminous; Mrs. Touchett sat down a moment, with her eyes upon it.

"Is there really no hope?" Isabel asked, standing before her aunt.

"None whatever. There never has been. It has not been a successful life."

"No—it has only been a beautiful one." Isabel found herself already contradicting her aunt; she was irritated by her dryness.

"I don't know what you mean by that; there is no beauty without health. That is a very odd dress to travel in."

Isabel glanced at her garment. "I left Rome at an hour's notice; I took the first that came."

"Your sisters, in America, wished to know how you dress. That seemed to be their principal interest. I wasn't able to tell them—but they seemed to have the right idea: that you never wear anything less than black brocade."

"They think I am more brilliant than I am; I am afraid to tell them the truth," said Isabel. "Lily wrote me that you had dined with her."

"She invited me four times, and I went once. After the second time she should have let me alone. The dinner was very good; it must have been expensive. Her husband has a very bad manner. Did I enjoy my visit to America? Why should I have enjoyed it? I didn't go for my pleasure."

These were interesting items, but Mrs. Touchett soon left her niece, whom she was to meet in half-an-hour at the midday meal. At this repast the two ladies faced each other at an abbreviated table in the melancholy dining room. Here, after a little, Isabel saw that her aunt was not so dry as she appeared, and her old pity for the poor woman's inexpressiveness, her want of regret, of disappointment, came back to her. It seemed to her she would find it a blessing today to be able to indulge a regret. She wondered whether Mrs. Touchett were not trying, whether she had not a desire for the recreation of grief. On the other hand, perhaps, she was afraid; if she began to regret, it might take her too far. Isabel could perceive, however, that it had come over her that she had missed something, that she saw herself in the future as an old woman without memories. Her little sharp face looked tragical. She told her niece that Ralph as yet had not moved, but that he probably would be able to see her before dinner. And then in a moment she added that he had seen Lord Warburton the day before; an announcement which startled Isabel a little, as it seemed an intimation that this personage was in the neighborhood and that an accident might bring them together. Such an accident would not be happy; she had not come to England to converse with Lord Warburton. She presently said to her aunt that he had been very kind to Ralph; she had seen something of that in Rome.

"He has something else to think of now," Mrs. Touchett rejoined. And she paused, with a gaze like a gimlet.

Isabel saw that she meant something, and instantly guessed what she meant. But her reply concealed her guess; her heart beat faster, and she wished to gain a moment. "Ah yes—the House of Lords, and all that."

"He is not thinking of the Lords; he is thinking of the ladies. At least he is thinking of one of them; he told Ralph he was engaged to be married."

"Ah, to be married!" Isabel gently exclaimed.

"Unless he breaks it off. He seemed to think Ralph would like to know. Poor Ralph can't go to the wedding, though I believe it is to take place very soon."

"And who is the young lady?"

"A member of the aristocracy; Lady Flora, Lady Felicia—something of that sort."

"I am very glad," Isabel said. "It must be a sudden decision."

"Sudden enough, I believe; a courtship of three weeks. It has only just been made public."

"I am very glad," Isabel repeated, with a larger emphasis. She knew her aunt was watching her—looking for the signs of some curious emotion, and the desire to prevent her companion from seeing anything of this kind enabled her to speak in the tone of quick satisfaction—the tone, almost, of relief. Mrs. Touchett of course followed the tradition that ladies, even married ones, regard the marriage of their old lovers as an offence to themselves. Isabel's first care therefore was to show that however that might be in general, she was not offended now. But meanwhile, as I say, her heart beat faster; and if she sat for some moments thoughtful—she presently forgot Mrs. Touchett's observation—it was not because she had lost an admirer. Her imagination had traversed half Europe; it halted, panting, and even trembling a little, in the city of Rome. She figured herself announcing to her husband that Lord Warburton was to lead a bride to the altar, and she was of course not aware how extremely sad she looked while she made this intellectual effort. But at last she collected herself, and said to her aunt—"He was sure to do it some time or other."

Mrs. Touchett was silent; then she gave a sharp little shake of the head. "Ah, my dear, you're beyond me!" she cried, suddenly. They went on with their luncheon in silence; Isabel felt as if she had heard of Lord Warburton's death. She had known him only as a suitor, and now that was all over. He was dead for poor Pansy; by Pansy he might have lived. A servant had been hovering about; at last Mrs. Touchett requested him to leave them alone. She had finished her lunch; she sat with her hands folded on the edge of the table. "I should like to ask you three questions," she said to Isabel, when the servant had gone.

"Three are a great many."

"I can't do with less; I have been thinking. They are all very good ones."

"That's what I am afraid of. The best questions are the worst," Isabel answered. Mrs. Touchett had pushed back her chair, and Isabel left the table and walked, rather consciously, to one of the deep windows, while her aunt followed her with her eyes.

"Have you ever been sorry you didn't marry Lord Warburton?" Mrs. Touchett inquired.

Isabel shook her head slowly, smiling. "No, dear aunt."

"Good. I ought to tell you that I propose to believe what you say."

"Your believing me is an immense temptation," Isabel replied, smiling still.

"A temptation to lie? I don't recommend you to do that, for when I'm misinformed I'm as dangerous as a poisoned rat. I don't mean to crow over you."

"It is my husband that doesn't get on with me," said Isabel.

"I could have told him that. I don't call that crowing over *you*," Mrs. Touchett added. "Do you still like Serena Merle?" she went on.

"Not as I once did. But it doesn't matter, for she is going to America."

"To America? She must have done something very bad."

"Yes—very bad."

"May I ask what it is?"

"She made a convenience of me."

"Ah," cried Mrs. Touchett, "so she did of me! She does of everyone."

"She will make a convenience of America," said Isabel, smiling again, and glad that her aunt's questions were over.

It was not till the evening that she was able to see Ralph. He had been dozing all day; at least he had been lying unconscious. The doctor was there, but after a while he went away; the local doctor, who had attended his father, and whom Ralph liked. He came three or four times a day; he was deeply interested in his patient. Ralph had had Sir Matthew Hope, but he had got tired of this celebrated man, to whom he had asked his mother to send word that he was now dead, and was therefore without further need of medical advice. Mrs. Touchett had simply written to Sir Matthew that her son disliked him. On the day of Isabel's arrival Ralph gave no sign, as I have related, for many hours; but toward evening he raised himself and said he knew that she had come. How he knew it was not apparent; inasmuch as, for fear of exciting him, no one had offered the information. Isabel came in and sat by his bed in the dim light; there was only a shaded candle in a corner of the room. She told the nurse that she might go—that she herself would sit with him for the rest of the evening. He had opened his eyes and recognized her, and had moved his hand, which lay very helpless beside him, so that she might take it. But he was unable to speak; he closed his eyes again and remained perfectly still, only keeping her hand in his own. She sat with him a long time—till the nurse came back; but he gave no further sign. He might have passed away while she looked at him; he was already the figure and pattern of death. She had thought him far gone in Rome, but this was worse; there was only one change possible now. There was a strange tranquility in his face; it was as still as the lid of a box. With this, he was a mere lattice of bones; when he opened his eyes to greet her, it was as if she were looking into immeasurable space. It was not till midnight that the nurse came back; but the hours, to Isabel, had not seemed long; it was exactly what she had come for. If she had come simply to wait, she found ample occasion, for he lay for three days in a kind of grateful silence. He recognized her, and at moments he seemed to wish to speak; but he found no voice. Then he closed his eyes again, as if he too were waiting for something—for something that certainly would come. He was so absolutely quiet that it seemed to her what was coming had already arrived; and yet she never lost the sense that they were still together. But they were not always together; there were other hours that she passed in wandering through the empty house and listening for a voice that was not poor Ralph's. She had a constant fear; she thought it possible her husband would write to her. But he remained silent, and she only got a letter from Florence from the Countess Gemini. Ralph, however, spoke at last, on the evening of the third day.

"I feel better tonight," he murmured, abruptly, in the soundless dimness of her vigil; "I think I can say something."

She sank upon her knees beside his pillow; took his thin hand in her own; begged him not to make an effort—not to tire himself.

His face was of necessity serious—it was incapable of the muscular play of a smile; but its owner apparently had not lost a perception of incongruities. "What does it matter if I am tired, when I have all eternity to rest?" he asked. "There is no harm in making an effort when it is the very last. Don't people always feel better just before the end? I have often heard of that; it's what I was waiting for. Ever since you have been here; I thought it would come. I tried two or three times; I was afraid you would get tired of sitting there." He spoke slowly, with painful breaks and long pauses; his voice seemed to come from a distance. When he ceased, he lay with his face turned to Isabel, and his large unwinking eyes open into her own. "It was very good of you to come," he went on. "I thought you would; but I wasn't sure."

"I was not sure either, till I came," said Isabel.

"You have been like an angel beside my bed. You know they talk about the angel of death. It's the most beautiful of all. You have been like that; as if you were waiting for me."

"I was not waiting for your death; I was waiting for—for this. This is not death, dear Ralph."

"Not for you—no. There is nothing makes us feel so much alive as to see others die. That's the sensation of life—the sense that we remain. I have had it—even I. But now I am of no use but to give it to others. With me it's all over." And then he paused. Isabel bowed her head further, till it rested on the two hands that were clasped upon his own. She could not see him now; but his far-away voice was close to her ear. "Isabel," he went on, suddenly, "I wish it were over for you." She answered nothing; she had burst into sobs; she remained so, with her buried face. He lay silent, listening to her sobs; at last he gave a long groan. "Ah, what is it you have done for me?"

"What is it you did for me?" she cried, her now extreme agitation half smothered by her attitude. She had lost all her shame, all wish to hide things. Now he might know; she wished him to know, for it brought them supremely together, and he was beyond the reach of pain. "You did something once—you know it. Oh Ralph, you have been everything! What have I done for you—what can I do today? I would die if you could live. But I don't wish you to live; I would die myself, not to lose you." Her voice was as broken as his own, and full of tears and anguish.

"You won't lose me—you will keep me. Keep me in your heart; I shall be nearer to you than I have ever been. Dear Isabel, life is better; for in life there is love. Death is good—but there is no love."

"I never thanked you—I never spoke—I never was what I should be!" Isabel went on. She felt a passionate need to cry out and accuse herself, to let her sorrow possess her. All her troubles, for the moment, became single and melted together into this present pain. "What must you have thought of me? Yet how could I know? I never knew, and I only know today because there are people less stupid than I."

"Don't mind people," said Ralph. "I think I am glad to leave people."

She raised her head and her clasped hands; she seemed for a moment to pray to him.

"Is it true—is it true?" she asked.

"True that you have been stupid? Oh no," said Ralph, with a sensible intention of wit.

"That you made me rich—that all I have is yours?"

He turned away his head, and for some time said nothing. Then at last—

"Ah, don't speak of that—that was not happy." Slowly he moved his face toward her again, and they once more saw each other. "But for that—but for that—" And he paused. "I believe I ruined you," he added softly.

She was full of the sense that he was beyond the reach of pain; he seemed already so little of this world. But even if she had not had it she would still have spoken, for nothing mattered now but the only knowledge that was not pure anguish—the knowledge that they were looking at the truth together.

"He married me for my money," she said.

She wished to say everything; she was afraid he might die before she had done so.

He gazed at her a little, and for the first time his fixed eyes lowered their lids. But he raised them in a moment, and then—

"He was greatly in love with you," he answered.

"Yes, he was in love with me. But he would not have married me if I had been poor. I don't hurt you in saying that. How can I? I only want you to understand. I always tried to keep you from understanding; but that's all over."

"I always understood," said Ralph.

"I thought you did, and I didn't like it. But now I like it."

"You don't hurt me—you make me very happy." And as Ralph said this there was an extraordinary gladness in his voice. She bent her head again, and pressed her lips to the back of his hand. "I always understood," he continued, "though it was so strange—so pitiful. You wanted to look at life for yourself—but you were not allowed; you were punished for your wish. You were ground in the very mill of the conventional!"

"Oh yes, I have been punished," Isabel sobbed.

He listened to her a little, and then continued—

"Was he very bad about your coming?"

"He made it very hard for me. But I don't care."

"It is all over, then, between you?"

"Oh no; I don't think anything is over."

"Are you going back to him?" Ralph stammered.

"I don't know—I can't tell. I shall stay here as long as I may. I don't want to think—I needn't think. I don't care for anything but you, and that is enough for the present. It will last a little yet. Here on my knees, with you dying in my arms, I am happier than I have been for a long time. And I want you to be happy—not to think of anything sad; only to feel that I am near you and I love you. Why should there be pain? In such hours as this what have we to do with pain? That is not the deepest thing; there is something deeper."

Ralph evidently found, from moment to moment, greater difficulty in speaking; he had to wait longer to collect himself. At first he appeared to make no response to these last words; he let a long time elapse. Then he murmured simply—

"You must stay here."

"I should like to stay, as long as seems right."

"As seems right—as seems right?" He repeated her words. "Yes, you think a great deal about that."

"Of course one must. You are very tired," said Isabel.

"I am very tired. You said just now that pain is not the deepest thing. No—no. But it is very deep. If I could stay——"

"For me you will always be here," she softly interrupted. It was easy to interrupt him.

But he went on, after a moment—

"It passes, after all; it's passing now. But love remains. I don't know why we should suffer so much. Perhaps I shall find out. There are many things in life; you are very young."

"I feel very old," said Isabel.

"You will grow young again. That's how I see you. I don't believe—I don't believe——" And he stopped again; his strength failed him.

She begged him to be quiet now. "We needn't speak to understand each other," she said.

"I don't believe that such a generous mistake as yours—can hurt you for more than a little."

"Oh, Ralph, I am very happy now," she cried, through her tears.

"And remember this," he continued, "that if you have been hated, you have also been loved."

"Ah, my brother!" she cried, with a movement of still deeper prostration.

55

He had told her, the first evening she ever spent at Gardencourt, that if she should live to suffer enough she might some day see the ghost with which the old house was duly provided. She apparently had fulfilled the necessary condition; for the next morning, in the cold, faint dawn, she knew that a spirit was standing by her bed. She had lain down without undressing, for it was her belief that Ralph would not outlast the night. She had no inclination to sleep; she was waiting, and such waiting was wakeful. But she closed her eyes; she believed that as the night wore on she should hear a knock at her door. She heard no knock, but at the time the darkness began vaguely to grow gray, she started up from her pillow as abruptly as if she had received a summons. It seemed to her for an instant that Ralph was standing there—a dim, hovering figure in the dimness of the room. She stared a moment; she saw his white face—his kind eyes; then she saw there was nothing. She was not afraid; she was only sure. She went out of her room, and in her certainty passed through dark corridors and down a flight of oaken steps that shone in the vague light of a hall window. Outside of Ralph's door she stopped a moment, listening; but she seemed to hear only the hush that filled it. She opened the door with a hand as gentle as if she were lifting a veil from the face of the dead, and saw Mrs. Touchett sitting motionless and upright beside the couch of her son, with one of his hands in her own. The doctor was on the other side, with poor Ralph's further wrist resting in his professional fingers. The nurse was at the foot, between them. Mrs. Touchett took no notice of Isabel, but the doctor looked at her very hard; then he gently placed Ralph's hand in a proper position, close beside him. The nurse looked at her very hard too, and no one said a word; but Isabel only looked at what she had come to see. It was fairer than Ralph had ever been in life, and there was a strange resemblance to the face of his father, which, six years before, she had seen lying on the same pillow. She went to her aunt and put her arm round her; and Mrs. Touchett, who as a general thing neither invited nor enjoyed caresses, submitted for a moment to this one, rising, as it were, to take it. But she was stiff and dry-eyed; her acute white face was terrible.

"Poor Aunt Lydia," Isabel murmured.

"Go and thank God you have no child," said Mrs. Touchett, disengaging herself.

Three days after this a considerable number of people found time, in the height of the London "season," to take a morning train down to a quiet station in Berkshire and spend half-an-hour in a small gray church, which stood within an easy walk. It was in the green burial-place of this edifice that Mrs. Touchett consigned her son to earth. She stood herself at the edge of the grave, and Isabel stood beside her; the sexton himself had not a more practical interest in the scene than Mrs. Touchett. It was a solemn occasion, but it was not a disagreeable one; there was a certain geniality in the appearance of things. The weather had changed to fair; the day, one of the last of the treacherous May-time, was warm and windless, and the air had the brightness of the hawthorn and the blackbird. If it was sad to think of poor Touchett, it was not too sad, since death, for him, had had no violence. He had been dying so long; he was so ready; everything had been so expected and prepared. There were tears in Isabel's eyes, but they were not tears that blinded. She looked through them at the beauty of the day, the splendor of nature, the sweetness of the old English churchyard, the bowed heads of good friends. Lord Warburton was there, and a group of gentlemen unknown to Isabel, several of whom, as she afterwards learned, were connected with the bank; and there were others whom she knew. Miss Stackpole was among the first, with honest Mr. Bantling beside her; and Caspar Goodwood, lifting his head higher than the rest—bowing it rather less. During much of the time Isabel was conscious of Mr. Goodwood's gaze; he looked at her somewhat harder than he usually looked in public, while the others had fixed their eyes upon the churchyard turf. But she never let him see that she saw him; she thought of him only to wonder that he was still in England. She found that she had taken for granted that after accompanying Ralph to Gardencourt he had gone away; she remembered that it was not a country that pleased him. He was there, however, very distinctly there; and something in his attitude seemed to say that he was there with a complex intention. She would not meet his eyes, though there was doubtless sympathy in them; he made her rather uneasy. With the dispersal of the little group he disappeared, and the only person who came to speak to her—though several spoke to Mrs. Touchett—was Henrietta Stackpole. Henrietta had been crying.

Ralph had said to Isabel that he hoped she would remain at Gardencourt, and she made no immediate motion to leave the place. She said to herself that it was but common charity to stay a little with her aunt. It was fortunate she had so good a formula; otherwise she might have been greatly in want of one. Her errand was over; she had done what she left her husband for. She had a husband in a foreign city, counting the hours of her absence; in such a case one needed an excellent motive. He was not one of the best husbands; but that didn't alter the case. Certain obligations were involved in the very fact of marriage, and were quite independent of the quantity of enjoyment extracted from it. Isabel thought of her husband as little as might be; but now that she was at a distance, beyond its spell, she thought with a kind of spiritual shudder of Rome. There was a deadly sadness in the thought, and she drew back into the deepest shade of Gardencourt. She lived from day to day, postponing, closing her eyes, trying not to think. She knew she must decide, but she decided nothing; her coming itself had not been a decision. On that occasion she had simply started. Osmond gave no sound, and now evidently he would give none; he would leave it all to her. From Pansy she heard nothing, but that was very simple; her father had told her not to write.

Mrs. Touchett accepted Isabel's company, but offered her no assistance; she appeared to be absorbed in considering, without enthusiasm, but with perfect lucidity, the new conveniences of her own situation. Mrs. Touchett was not an optimist, but even from painful occurrences she managed to extract a certain satisfaction. This consisted in the reflection that, after all, such things happened to other people and not to herself. Death was disagreeable, but in this case it was her son's death, not her own; she had never flattered herself that her own would be disagreeable to anyone but Mrs. Touchett. She was better off than poor Ralph, who had left all the commodities of life behind him, and indeed all the security; for the worst of dying was, to Mrs. Touchett's mind, that it exposed one to be taken advantage of. For herself, she was on the spot; there was nothing so good as that. She made known to Isabel very punctually—it was the evening her son was buried—several of Ralph's testamentary arrangements. He had told her everything, had consulted her about everything. He left her no money; of course she had no need of money. He left her the furniture of Gardencourt, exclusive of the pictures and books, and the use of the place for a year; after which it was to be sold. The money produced by the sale was to constitute an endowment for a hospital for poor persons suffering from the malady of which he died; and of this portion of the will Lord Warburton was appointed executor. The rest of his property, which was to be withdrawn from the bank, was disposed of in various bequests, several of them to those cousins in Vermont to whom his father had already been so bountiful. Then there were a number of small legacies.

"Some of them are extremely peculiar," said Mrs. Touchett; "He has left considerable sums to persons I never heard of. He gave me a list, and I asked then who some of them were, and he told me they were people who at various times had seemed to like him. Apparently he thought you didn't like him, for he has not left you a penny. It was his opinion that you were handsomely treated by his father, which I am bound to say I think you were—though I don't mean that I ever heard him complain of it. The pictures are to be dispersed; he has distributed them about, one by one, as little keepsakes. The most valuable of the collection goes to Lord Warburton. And what do you think he has done with his library? It sounds like a practical joke. He has left it to your friend Miss Stackpole—'in recognition of her services to literature.' Does he mean her following him up from Rome? Was that a service to literature? It contains a great many rare and valuable books, and as she can't carry it about the world in her trunk, he recommends her to sell it at auction. She will sell it of course at Christie's, and with the proceeds she will set up a newspaper. Will that be a service to literature?"

This question Isabel forbore to answer, as it exceeded the little interrogatory to which she had deemed it necessary to submit on her arrival. Besides, she had never been less interested in literature than today, as she found when she occasionally took down from the shelf one of the rare and valuable volumes of which Mrs. Touchett had spoken. She was quite unable to read; her attention had never been so little at her command. One afternoon, in the library, about a week after the ceremony in the churchyard, she was trying to fix it a little; but her eyes often wandered from the book in her hand to the open window, which looked down the long avenue. It was in this way that she saw a modest vehicle approach the door, and perceived Lord Warburton sitting, in rather an uncomfortable attitude, in a corner of it. He had always had a high standard of courtesy, and it was therefore not remarkable, under the circumstances, that he should have taken the trouble to come down from London to call upon Mrs. Touchett. It was of course Mrs. Touchett that he had come to see, and not Mrs. Osmond; and to prove to herself the validity of this theory, Isabel presently stepped out of the house and wandered away into the park. Since her arrival at Gardencourt she had been but little out of doors, the weather being unfavorable for visiting the grounds. This evening, however, was fine, and at first it struck her as a happy thought to have come out. The theory I have just mentioned was plausible enough, but it brought her little rest, and if you had seen her pacing about, you would have said she had a bad conscience. She was not pacified when at the end of a quarter of an hour, finding herself in view of the house, she saw Mrs. Touchett emerge from the portico, accompanied by her visitor. Her aunt had evidently proposed to Lord Warburton that they should come in search of her.

She was in no humor for visitors, and if she had had time she would have drawn back, behind one of the great trees. But she saw that she had been seen and that nothing was left her but to advance. As the lawn at Gardencourt was a vast expanse, this took some time; during which she observed that, as he walked beside his hostess, Lord Warburton kept his hands rather stiffly behind him and his eyes upon the ground. Both persons apparently were silent; but Mrs. Touchett's thin little glance, as she directed it toward Isabel, had even at a distance an expression. It seemed to say, with cutting sharpness, "Here is the eminently amenable nobleman whom you might have married!" When Lord Warburton lifted his own eyes, however, that was not what they said. They only said, "This is rather awkward, you know, and I depend upon you to help me." He was very grave, very proper, and for the first time since Isabel had known him, he greeted her without a smile. Even in his days of distress he had always begun with a smile. He looked extremely self-conscious.

"Lord Warburton has been so good as to come out to see me," said Mrs. Touchett. "He tells me he didn't know you were still here. I know he's an old friend of yours, and as I was told you were not in the house, I brought him out to see for himself."

"Oh, I saw there was a good train at 6:40, that would get me back in time for dinner," Mrs. Touchett's companion explained, rather irrelevantly. "I am so glad to find you have not gone."

"I am not here for long, you know," Isabel said, with a certain eagerness.

"I suppose not; but I hope it's for some weeks. You came to England sooner than—a—than you thought?"

"Yes, I came very suddenly."

Mrs. Touchett turned away, as if she were looking at the condition of the grounds, which indeed was not what it should be; while Lord Warburton hesitated a little. Isabel fancied he had been on the point of asking about her husband—rather confusedly—and then had checked himself. He continued immitigably grave, either because he thought it becoming in a place over which death had just passed, or for more personal reasons. If he was conscious of personal reasons, it was very fortunate that he had the cover of the former motive; he could make the most of that. Isabel thought of all this. It was not that his face was sad, for that was another matter; but it was strangely inexpressive.

"My sisters would have been so glad to come if they had known you were still here—if they had thought you would see them," Lord Warburton went on. "Do kindly let them see you before you leave England."

"It would give me great pleasure; I have such a friendly recollection of them."

"I don't know whether you would come to Lockleigh for a day or two? You know there is always that old promise." And his lordship blushed a little as he made this suggestion, which gave his face a somewhat more familiar air. "Perhaps I'm not right in saying that just now; of course you are not thinking of visiting. But I meant what would hardly be a visit. My sisters are to be at Lockleigh at Whitsuntide for three days; and if you could come then—as you say you are not to be very long in England—I would see that there should be literally no one else."

Isabel wondered whether not even the young lady he was to marry would be there with her mamma; but she did not express this idea. "Thank you extremely," she contented herself with saying; "I'm afraid I hardly know about Whitsuntide."

"But I have your promise—haven't I?—for some other time."

There was an interrogation in this; but Isabel let it pass. She looked at her interlocutor a moment, and the result of her observation was that—as had happened before—she felt sorry for him. "Take care you don't miss your train," she said. And then she added, "I wish you every happiness."

He blushed again, more than before, and he looked at his watch.

"Ah yes, 6:40; I haven't much time, but I have a fly at the door. Thank you very much." It was not apparent whether the thanks applied to her having reminded him of his train, or to the more sentimental remark. "Goodbye, Mrs. Osmond; goodbye." He shook hands with her, without meeting her eye, and then he turned to Mrs. Touchett, who had wandered back to them. With her his parting was equally brief; and in a moment the two ladies saw him move with long steps across the lawn.

"Are you very sure he is to be married?" Isabel asked of her aunt.

"I can't be surer than he; but he seems sure. I congratulated him, and he accepted it."

"Ah," said Isabel, "I give it up!"—while her aunt returned to the house and to those avocations which the visitor had interrupted.

She gave it up, but she still thought of it—thought of it while she strolled again under the great oaks whose shadows were long upon the acres of turf. At the end of a few minutes she found herself near a rustic bench, which, a moment after she had looked at it, struck her as an object recognized. It was not simply that she had seen it before, nor even that she had sat upon it; it was that in this spot something important had happened to her—that the place had an air of association. Then she remembered that she had been sitting there six years before, when a servant brought her from the house the letter in which Caspar Goodwood informed her that he had followed her to Europe; and that when she had read that letter she looked up to hear Lord Warburton announcing that he should like to marry her. It was indeed an historical, an interesting, bench; she stood and looked at it as if it might have something to say to her. She would not sit down on it now—she felt rather afraid of it. She only stood before it, and while she stood, the past came back to her in one of those rushing waves of emotion by which people of sensibility are visited at odd hours. The effect of this agitation was a sudden sense of being very tired, under the influence of which she overcame her scruples and sank into the rustic seat. I have said that she was restless and unable to occupy herself; and whether or

no, if you had seen her there, you would have admitted the justice of the former epithet, you would at least have allowed that at this moment she was the image of a victim of idleness. Her attitude had a singular absence of purpose; her hands, hanging at her sides, lost themselves in the folds of her black dress; her eyes gazed vaguely before her. There was nothing to recall her to the house, the two ladies, in their seclusion, dined early and had tea at an indefinite hour. How long she had sat in this position she could not have told you; but the twilight had grown thick when she became aware that she was not alone. She quickly straightened herself, glancing about, and then saw what had become of her solitude. She was sharing it with Caspar Goodwood, who stood looking at her, a few feet off, and whose footfall, on the unresonant turf, as he came near, she had not heard. It occurred to her, in the midst of this, that it was just so Lord Warburton had surprised her of old.

She instantly rose, and as soon as Goodwood saw that he was seen he started forward. She had had time only to rise, when with a motion that looked like violence, but felt like—she knew not what—he grasped her by the wrist and made her sink again into the seat. She closed her eyes; he had not hurt her, it was only a touch that she had obeyed. But there was something in his face that she wished not to see. That was the way he had looked at her the other day in the churchyard; only to-day it was worse. He said nothing at first; she only felt him close to her. It almost seemed to her that no one had ever been so close to her as that. All this, however, took but a moment, at the end of which she had disengaged her wrist, turning her eyes upon her visitant.

"You have frightened me," she said.

"I didn't mean to," he answered, "but if I did a little, no matter. I came from London a while ago by the train, but I couldn't come here directly. There was a man at the station who got ahead of me. He took a fly that was there, and I heard him give the order to drive here. I don't know who he was, but I didn't want to come with him; I wanted to see you alone. So I have been waiting and walking about. I have walked all over, and I was just coming to the house when I saw you here. There was a keeper, or someone, who met me; but that was all right, because I had made his acquaintance when I came here with your cousin. Is that gentleman gone? are you really alone? I want to speak to you." Goodwood spoke very fast; he was as excited as when they parted in Rome. Isabel had hoped that condition would subside; and she shrank into herself as she perceived that, on the contrary, he had only let out sail. She had a new sensation; he had never produced it before; it was a feeling of danger. There was indeed something awful in his persistency. Isabel gazed straight before her; he with a hand on each knee, leaned forward, looking deeply into her face. The twilight seemed to darken around them. "I want to speak to you," he repeated; "I have something particular to say. I don't want to trouble you—as I did the other day, in Rome. That was no use; it only distressed you. I couldn't help it; I knew I was wrong. But I am not wrong now; please don't think I am," he went on, with his hard, deep voice melting a moment into entreaty. "I came here today for a purpose! it's very different. It was no use for me to speak to you then; but now I can help you."

She could not have told you whether it was because she was afraid, or because such a voice in the darkness seemed of necessity a boon; but she listened to him as she had never listened before; his words dropped deep into her soul. They produced a sort of stillness in all her being; and it was with an effort, in a moment, that she answered him.

"How can you help me?" she asked, in a low tone; as if she were taking what he had said seriously enough to make the inquiry in confidence.

"By inducing you to trust me. Now I know—today I know.—Do you remember what I asked you in Rome? Then I was quite in the dark. But today I know on good authority; everything is clear to me today. It was a good thing, when you made me come away with your cousin. He was a good fellow—he was a noble fellow—he told me how the case stands. He explained everything; he guessed what I thought of you. He was a member of your family, and he left you—so long as you should be in England—to my care," said Goodwood, as if he were making a great point. "Do you know what he said to me the last time I saw him—as he lay there where he died? He said—'Do everything you can for her; do everything she will let you.' "

Isabel suddenly got up. "You had no business to talk about me!"

"Why not—why not, when we talked in that way?" he demanded, following her fast. "And he was dying—when a man's dying it's different." She checked the movement she had made to leave him; she was listening more than ever; it was true that he was not the same as that last time. That had been aimless, fruitless passion; but at present he had an idea. Isabel scented his idea in all her being. "But it doesn't matter!" he exclaimed, pressing her close, though now without touching a hem of her garment. "If Touchett had never opened his mouth, I should have known all the same. I had only to look at you at your cousin's funeral to see what's the matter with you. You can't deceive me anymore; for God's sake be honest with a man who is so honest with you. You are the most unhappy of women, and your husband's a devil!"

She turned on him as if he had struck her. "Are you mad?" she cried.

"I have never been so sane; I see the whole thing. Don't think it's necessary to defend him. But I won't say another word against him; I will speak only of you," Goodwood added, quickly. "How can you pretend you are not heartbroken? You don't know what to do—you don't know where to turn. It's too late to play a part; didn't you leave all that behind you in Rome? Touchett knew all about it—and I knew it too—what it would cost you to come here. It will cost you your life! When I know that, how can I keep myself from wishing to save you? What would you think of me if I should stand still and see you go back to your reward? 'It's awful, what she'll have to pay for it!'—that's what Touchett said to me. I may tell you that, mayn't I? He was such a near relation!" cried Goodwood, making his point again. "I would sooner have been shot than let another man say those things to me; but he was different; he seemed to me to have the right. It was after he got home—when he saw he was dying, and when I saw it too. I understand all about it: you are afraid to go back. You are perfectly alone; you don't know where to turn. Now it is that I want you to think of me."

"To think of you?" Isabel said, standing before him in the dusk. The idea of which she had caught a glimpse a few moments before now loomed large. She threw back her head a little; she stared at it as if it had been a comet in the sky.

"You don't know where to turn; turn to me! I want to persuade you to trust me," Goodwood repeated. And then he paused a moment, with his shining eyes. "Why should you go back—why should you go through that ghastly form?"

"To get away from you!" she answered. But this expressed only a little of what she felt. The rest was that she had never been loved before. It wrapped her about; it lifted her off her feet.

At first, in rejoinder to what she had said, it seemed to her that he would break out into greater violence. But after an instant he was perfectly quiet; he wished to prove that he was sane, that he had reasoned it all out. "I wish to prevent that, and I think I may, if you will only listen to me. It's too monstrous to think of sinking back into that misery. It's you that are out of your mind. Trust me as if I had the care of you. Why shouldn't we be happy—when it's here before us, when it's so easy? I am yours forever—forever and ever. Here I stand; I'm as firm as a rock. What have you to care about? You have no children; that perhaps would be an obstacle. As it is, you have nothing to consider. You must save what you can of your life; you mustn't lose it all simply because you have lost a part. It would be an insult to you to assume that you care for the look of the thing—for what people will say—for the bottomless idiocy of the world! We have nothing to do with all that; we are quite out of it; we look at things as they are. You took the great step in coming away; the next is nothing; it's the natural one. I swear, as I stand here, that a woman deliberately made to suffer is justified in anything in life—in going down into the streets, if that will help her! I know how you suffer, and that's why I am here. We can do absolutely as we please; to whom under the sun do we owe anything? What is it that holds us— what is it that has the smallest right to interfere in such a question as this? Such a question is between ourselves—and to say that is to settle it! Were we born to rot in our misery—were we born to be afraid? I never knew *you* afraid! If you only trust me, how little you will be disappointed! The world is all before us—and the world is very large. I know something about that."

Isabel gave a long murmur, like a creature in pain; it was as if he were pressing something that hurt her. "The world is very small," she said, at random; she had an immense desire to appear to resist. She said it at random, to hear herself say something; but it was not what she meant. The world, in truth, had never seemed so large; it seemed to open out, all round her, to take the form of a mighty sea, where she floated in fathomless waters. She had wanted help, and here was help; it had come in a rushing torrent. I know not whether she believed everything that he said; but she believed that to let him take her in his arms would be the next best thing to dying. This belief, for a moment, was a kind of rapture, in which she felt herself sinking and sinking. In the movement she seemed to beat with her feet, in order to catch herself, to feel something to rest on.

"Ah, be mine as I am yours!" she heard her companion cry. He had suddenly given up argument, and his voice seemed to come through a confusion of sound.

This however, of course, was but a subjective fact, as the metaphysicians say; the confusion, the noise of waters, and all the rest of it, were in her own head. In an instant she became aware of this. "Do me the greatest kindness of all," she said. "I beseech you to go away!"

"Ah, don't say that. Don't kill me!" he cried.

She clasped her hands; her eyes were streaming with tears.

"As you love me, as you pity me, leave me alone!"

He glared at her a moment through the dusk, and the next instant she felt his arms about her, and his lips on her own lips. His kiss was like a flash of lightning; when it was dark again she was free. She never looked about her; she only darted away from the spot. There were lights in the windows of the house; they shone far across the lawn. In an extraordinarily short time—for the distance was considerable—she had moved through the darkness (for she saw nothing) and reached the door. Here only she paused. She looked all about her; she listened a little; then she put her hand on the latch. She had not known where to turn; but she knew now. There was a very straight path.

Two days afterwards, Caspar Goodwood knocked at the door of the house in Wimpole Street in which Henrietta Stackpole occupied furnished lodgings. He had hardly removed his hand from the knocker when the door was opened, and Miss Stackpole herself stood before him. She had on her bonnet and jacket; she was on the point of going out.

"Oh, good morning," he said, "I was in hope I should find Mrs. Osmond."

Henrietta kept him waiting a moment for her reply; but there was a good deal of expression about Miss Stackpole even when she was silent.

"Pray what led you to suppose she was here?"

"I went down to Gardencourt this morning, and the servant told me she had come to London. He believed she was to come to you."

Again Miss Stackpole held him—with an intention of perfect kindness—in suspense.

"She came here yesterday, and spent the night. But this morning she started for Rome."

Caspar Goodwood was not looking at her; his eyes were fastened on the doorstep.

"Oh, she started—" he stammered. And without finishing his phrase, or looking up, he turned away.

Henrietta had come out, closing the door behind her, and now she put out her hand and grasped his arm.

"Look here, Mr. Goodwood," she said, "just you wait!"

On which he looked up at her.

THE END.

THE ASPERN PAPERS

I

I had taken Mrs. Prest into my confidence; in truth without her I should have made but little advance, for the fruitful idea in the whole business dropped from her friendly lips. It was she who invented the short cut, who severed the Gordian knot. It is not supposed to be the nature of women to rise as a general thing to the largest and most liberal view—I mean of a practical scheme, but it has struck me that they sometimes throw off a bold conception—such as a man would not have risen to—with singular serenity. "Simply ask them to take you in on the footing of a lodger"—I don't think that unaided I should have risen to that. I was beating about the bush, trying to be ingenious, wondering by what combination of arts I might become an acquaintance, when she offered this happy suggestion that the way to become an acquaintance was first to become an inmate. Her actual knowledge of the Misses Bordereau was scarcely larger than mine, and indeed I had brought with me from England some definite facts that were new to her. Their name had been mixed up ages before with one of the greatest names of the century, and they lived now in Venice in obscurity, on very small means, unvisited, unapproachable, in a dilapidated old palace on an out-of-the-way canal: this was the substance of my friend's impression of them. She herself had been established in Venice for fifteen years and had done a great deal of good there, but the circle of her benevolence did not include the two shy, mysterious, and, as it was somehow supposed, scarcely respectable Americans (they were believed to have lost in their long exile all national quality, besides having had, as their name implied, some French strain in their origin), who asked no favors and desired no attention. In the early years of her residence she had made an attempt to see them, but this had been successful only as regards the little one, as Mrs. Prest called the niece; though in reality, as I afterward learned, she was considerably the bigger of the two. She had heard Miss Bordereau was ill and had a suspicion that she was in want, and she had gone to the house to offer assistance, so that if there were suffering (and American suffering), she should at least not have it on her conscience. The "little one" received her in the great cold, tarnished Venetian *sala*, the central hall of the house, paved with marble and roofed with dim crossbeams, and did not even ask her to sit down. This was not encouraging for me, who wished to sit so fast, and I remarked as much to Mrs. Prest. She, however, replied with profundity, "Ah, but there's all the difference: I went to confer a favor and you will go to ask one. If they are proud you will be on the right side." And she offered to show me their house to begin with—to row me thither in her gondola. I let her know that I had already been to look at it half-a-dozen times, but I accepted her invitation, for it charmed me to hover about the place. I had made my way to it the day after my arrival in Venice (it had been described to me in advance by the friend in England to whom I owed definite information as to their possession of the papers), and I had besieged it with my eyes while I considered my plan of campaign. Jeffrey Aspern had never been in it that I knew of, but some note of his voice seemed to abide there by a roundabout implication, a faint reverberation.

Mrs. Prest knew nothing about the papers, but she was interested in my curiosity, as she was always interested in the joys and sorrows of her friends. As we went, however, in her gondola, gliding there under the sociable hood with the bright Venetian picture framed on either side by the movable window, I could see that she was amused by my infatuation, the way my interest in the papers had become a fixed idea. "One would think you expected to find in them the answer to the riddle of the universe," she said; and I denied the impeachment only by replying that if I had to choose between that precious solution and a bundle of Jeffrey Aspern's letters I knew indeed which would appear to me the greater boon. She pretended to make light of his genius and I took no pains to defend him. One doesn't defend one's god: one's god is in himself a defence. Besides, today, after his long comparative obscuration, he hangs high in the heaven of our literature, for all the world to see; he is a part of the light by which we walk. The most I said was that he was no doubt not a woman's poet; to which she rejoined aptly enough that he had been at least Miss Bordereau's. The strange thing had been for me to discover in England that she was still alive; it was as if I had been told Mrs. Siddons was, or Queen Caroline, or the famous Lady Hamilton, for it seemed to me that she belonged to a generation as extinct. "Why, she must be tremendously old—at least a hundred," I had said, but on coming to consider dates I saw that it was not strictly necessary that she should have exceeded by very much the common span. Nonetheless she was very far advanced in life and her relations with Jeffrey Aspern had occurred in her early womanhood. "That is her excuse," said Mrs. Prest, half sententiously and yet also somewhat as if she were ashamed of making a speech so little in the real tone of Venice. As if a woman needed an excuse for having loved the divine poet! He had been not only one of the most brilliant minds of his day (and in those years, when the century was young, there were, as every one knows, many), but one of the most genial men and one of the handsomest.

The niece, according to Mrs. Prest, was not so old, and she risked the conjecture that she was only a grand-niece. This was possible; I had nothing but my share in the very limited knowledge of my English fellow-worshipper John Cumnor, who had never seen the couple. The world, as I say, had recognized Jeffrey Aspern, but

Cumnor and I had recognized him most. The multitude, today, flocked to his temple, but of that temple he and I regarded ourselves as the ministers. We held, justly, as I think, that we had done more for his memory than anyone else, and we had done it by opening lights into his life. He had nothing to fear from us because he had nothing to fear from the truth, which alone at such a distance of time we could be interested in establishing. His early death had been the only dark spot in his life, unless the papers in Miss Bordereau's hands should perversely bring out others. There had been an impression about 1825 that he had "treated her badly," just as there had been an impression that he had "served," as the London populace says, several other ladies in the same way. Each of these cases Cumnor and I had been able to investigate, and we had never failed to acquit him conscientiously of shabby behavior. I judged him perhaps more indulgently than my friend; certainly, at any rate, it appeared to me that no man could have walked straighter in the given circumstances. These were almost always awkward. Half the women of his time, to speak liberally, had flung themselves at his head, and out of this pernicious fashion many complications, some of them grave, had not failed to arise. He was not a woman's poet, as I had said to Mrs. Prest, in the modern phase of his reputation, but the situation had been different when the man's own voice was mingled with his song. That voice, by every testimony, was one of the sweetest ever heard. "Orpheus and the Mænads!" was the exclamation that rose to my lips when I first turned over his correspondence. Almost all the Mænads were unreasonable and many of them insupportable; it struck me in short that he was kinder, more considerate than, in his place (if I could imagine myself in such a place!) I should have been.

It was certainly strange beyond all strangeness, and I shall not take up space with attempting to explain it, that whereas in all these other lines of research we had to deal with phantoms and dust, the mere echoes of echoes, the one living source of information that had lingered on into our time had been unheeded by us. Every one of Aspern's contemporaries had, according to our belief, passed away; we had not been able to look into a single pair of eyes into which his had looked or to feel a transmitted contact in any aged hand that his had touched. Most dead of all did poor Miss Bordereau appear, and yet she alone had survived. We exhausted in the course of months our wonder that we had not found her out sooner, and the substance of our explanation was that she had kept so quiet. The poor lady on the whole had had reason for doing so. But it was a revelation to us that it was possible to keep so quiet as that in the latter half of the nineteenth century—the age of newspapers and telegrams and photographs and interviewers. And she had taken no great trouble about it either: she had not hidden herself away in an undiscoverable hole; she had boldly settled down in a city of exhibition. The only secret of her safety that we could perceive was that Venice contained so many curiosities that were greater than she. And then accident had somehow favored her, as was shown for example in the fact that Mrs. Prest had never happened to mention her to me, though I had spent three weeks in Venice—under her nose, as it were—five years before. Mrs. Prest had not mentioned this much to any one; she appeared almost to have forgotten she was there. Of course she had not the responsibilities of an editor. It was no explanation of the old woman's having eluded us to say that she lived abroad, for our researches had again and again taken us (not only by correspondence but by personal inquiry) to France, to Germany, to Italy, in which countries, not counting his important stay in England, so many of the too few years of Aspern's career were spent. We were glad to think at least that in all our publishings (some people consider, I believe, that we have overdone them), we had only touched in passing and in the most discreet manner on Miss Bordereau's connection. Oddly enough, even if we had had the material (and we often wondered what had become of it), it would have been the most difficult episode to handle.

The gondola stopped, the old palace was there. It was a house of the class which in Venice carries even in extreme dilapidation the dignified name. "How charming! It's gray and pink!" my companion exclaimed, and that is the most comprehensive description of it. It was not particularly old, only two or three centuries, and it had an air not so much of decay as of quiet discouragement, as if it had rather missed its career. But its wide front, with a stone balcony from end to end of the *piano nobile*, or most important floor, was architectural enough, with the aid of various pilasters and arches, and the stucco with which in the intervals it had long ago been endued was rosy in the April afternoon. It overlooked a clean, melancholy, unfrequented canal, which had a narrow *riva*, or convenient footway, on either side. "I don't know why—there are no brick gables," said Mrs. Prest, "but this corner has seemed to me before more Dutch than Italian, more like Amsterdam than like Venice. It's perversely clean, for reasons of its own, and though you can pass on foot scarcely anyone ever thinks of doing so. It has the air of a Protestant Sunday. Perhaps the people are afraid of the Misses Bordereau. I daresay they have the reputation of witches."

I forget what answer I made to this—I was given up to two other reflections. The first of these was that if the old lady lived in such a big, imposing house she could not be in any sort of misery and therefore would not be tempted by a chance to let a couple of rooms. I expressed this idea to Mrs. Prest, who gave me a very logical reply. "If she didn't live in a big house, how could it be a question of her having rooms to spare? If she were not amply lodged herself, you would lack ground to approach her. Besides, a big house here, and especially in this *quartier perdu*, proves nothing at all: it is perfectly compatible with a state of penury. Dilapidated old palazzi, if you will go out of the way for them, are to be had for five shillings a year. And as for the people who live in them—no, until you have explored Venice socially as much as I have you can form no idea of their domestic desolation. They live on nothing, for they have nothing to live on." The other idea that had come into my head was connected with a high blank wall which appeared to confine an expanse of ground on one side of the house. Blank I call it, but it was figured over with the patches that please a painter, repaired breaches, crumblings of plaster, extrusions of brick that had turned pink with time. A few thin trees, with the poles of certain rickety trellises, were visible over the top. The place was a garden and apparently it belonged to the house. It suddenly occurred to me that if it did belong to the house I had my pretext.

I sat looking out on all this with Mrs. Prest (it was covered with the golden glow of Venice) from the shade of our *felze,* and she asked me if I would go in then, while she waited for me, or come back another time. At first I could not decide—it was doubtless very weak of me. I wanted still to think I *might* get a footing, and I was afraid to meet failure, for it would leave me, as I remarked to my companion, without another arrow for my bow. "Why not another?" she inquired, as I sat there hesitating and thinking it over, and she wished to know why even now and before taking the trouble of becoming an inmate (which might be wretchedly uncomfortable after all, even if it succeeded), I had not the resource of simply offering them a sum of money down. In that way, I might obtain the documents without bad nights.

"Dearest lady," I exclaimed, "excuse the impatience of my tone when I suggest that you must have forgotten the very fact (surely I communicated it to you) which pushed me to throw myself upon your ingenuity. The old woman won't have the documents spoken of; they are personal, delicate, intimate, and she hasn't modern notions, God bless her! If I should sound that note first I should certainly spoil the game. I can arrive at the papers only by putting her off her guard, and I can put her off her guard only by ingratiating diplomatic practices. Hypocrisy, duplicity are my only chance. I am sorry for it, but for Jeffrey Aspern's sake I would do worse still. First I must take tea with her, then tackle the main job." And I told over what had happened to John Cumnor when he wrote to her. No notice whatever had been taken of his first letter, and the second had been answered very sharply, in six lines, by the niece. "Miss Bordereau requested her to say that she could not imagine what he meant by troubling them. They had none of Mr. Aspern's papers, and if they had should never think of showing them to any one on any account whatever. She didn't know what he was talking about and begged he would let her alone." I certainly did not want to be met that way.

"Well," said Mrs. Prest, after a moment, provokingly, "perhaps after all they haven't any of his things. If they deny it flat how are you sure?"

"John Cumnor is sure, and it would take me long to tell you how his conviction, or his very strong presumption—strong enough to stand against the old lady's not unnatural fib—has built itself up. Besides, he makes much of the internal evidence of the niece's letter."

"The internal evidence?"

"Her calling him 'Mr. Aspern.' "

"I don't see what that proves."

"It proves familiarity, and familiarity implies the possession of mementos, of relics. I can't tell you how that 'Mr.' touches me—how it bridges over the gulf of time and brings our hero near to me—not what an edge it gives to my desire to see Juliana. You don't say 'Mr.' Shakespeare."

"Would I, anymore, if I had a box full of his letters?"

"Yes, if he had been your lover and someone wanted them!" And I added that John Cumnor was so convinced, and so all the more convinced by Miss Bordereau's tone, that he would have come himself to Venice on the business were it not that for him there was the obstacle that it would be difficult to disprove his identity with the person who had written to them, which the old ladies would be sure to suspect in spite of dissimulation and a change of name. If they were to ask him point blank if he were not their correspondent it would be too awkward for him to lie; whereas I was fortunately not tied in that way. I was a fresh hand and could say no without lying.

"But you will have to change your name," said Mrs. Prest. "Juliana lives out of the world as much as it is possible to live, but nonetheless she has probably heard of Mr. Aspern's editors; she perhaps possesses what you have published."

"I have thought of that," I returned, and I drew out of my pocketbook a visiting card, neatly engraved with a name that was not my own.

"You are very extravagant; you might have written it," said my companion.

"This looks more genuine."

"Certainly, you are prepared to go far! But it will be awkward about your letters; they won't come to you in that mask."

"My banker will take them in and I will go every day to fetch them. It will give me a little walk."

"Shall you only depend upon that?" asked Mrs. Prest. "Aren't you coming to see me?"

"Oh, you will have left Venice, for the hot months, long before there are any results. I am prepared to roast all summer—as well as hereafter, perhaps you'll say! Meanwhile, John Cumnor will bombard me with letters addressed, in my feigned name, to the care of the *padrona*."

"She will recognize his hand," my companion suggested.

"On the envelope he can disguise it."

"Well, you're a precious pair! Doesn't it occur to you that even if you are able to say you are not Mr. Cumnor in person they may still suspect you of being his emissary?"

"Certainly, and I see only one way to parry that."

"And what may that be?"

I hesitated a moment. "To make love to the niece."

"Ah," cried Mrs. Prest, "wait till you see her!"

II

"I must work the garden—I must work the garden," I said to myself, five minutes later, as I waited, upstairs, in the long, dusky *sala,* where the bare scagliola floor gleamed vaguely in a chink of the closed shutters. The place was impressive, but it looked cold and cautious. Mrs. Prest had floated away, giving me a rendezvous at the end of half an hour by some neighboring watersteps, and I had been let into the house, after pulling the rusty bell wire, by a little red-headed, white-faced maidservant, who was very young and not ugly and wore clicking pattens and a shawl in the fashion of a hood. She had not contented herself with opening the door from above by the usual arrangement of a creaking pulley, though she had looked down at me first from an upper window, dropping the inevitable challenge which in Italy precedes the hospitable act. As a general thing I was irritated by this survival of mediæval manners, though as I liked the old I suppose I ought to have liked it, but I was so determined to be genial that I took my false card out of my pocket and held it up to her, smiling as if it were a magic token. It had the effect of one indeed, for it brought her, as I say, all the way down. I begged her to hand it to her mistress, having first written on it in Italian the words, "Could you very kindly see a gentleman, an American, for a moment?" The little maid was not hostile, and I reflected that even that was perhaps something gained. She colored, she smiled and looked both frightened and pleased. I could see that my arrival was a great affair, that visits were rare in that house, and that she was a person who would have liked a sociable place. When she pushed forward the heavy door behind me I felt that I had a foot in the citadel. She pattered across the damp, stony lower hall and I followed her up the high staircase—stonier still, as it seemed—without an invitation. I think she had meant I should wait for her below, but such was not my idea, and I took up my station in the *sala.* She flitted, at the far end of it, into impenetrable regions, and I looked at the place with my heart beating as I had known it to do in the dentist's parlor. It was gloomy and stately, but it owed its character almost entirely to its noble shape and to the fine architectural doors—as high as the doors of houses—which, leading into the various rooms, repeated themselves on either side at intervals. They were surmounted with old faded painted escutcheons, and here and there, in the spaces between them, brown pictures, which I perceived to be bad, in battered frames, were suspended. With the exception of several straw-bottomed chairs with their backs to the wall, the grand obscure vista contained nothing else to minister to effect. It was evidently never used save as a passage, and little even as that. I may add that by the time the door opened again through which the maidservant had escaped, my eyes had grown used to the want of light.

I had not meant by my private ejaculation that I must myself cultivate the soil of the tangled enclosure which lay beneath the windows, but the lady who came toward me from the distance over the hard, shining floor might have supposed as much from the way in which, as I went rapidly to meet her, I exclaimed, taking care to speak Italian: "The garden, the garden—do me the pleasure to tell me if it's yours!"

She stopped short, looking at me with wonder; and then, "Nothing here is mine," she answered in English, coldly and sadly.

"Oh, you are English; how delightful!" I remarked, ingenuously. "But surely the garden belongs to the house?"

"Yes, but the house doesn't belong to me." She was a long, lean, pale person, habited apparently in a dull-colored dressing gown, and she spoke with a kind of mild literalness. She did not ask me to sit down, any more than years before (if she were the niece) she had asked Mrs. Prest, and we stood face to face in the empty pompous hall.

"Well then, would you kindly tell me to whom I must address myself? I'm afraid you'll think me odiously intrusive, but you know I *must* have a garden—upon my honor I must!"

Her face was not young, but it was simple; it was not fresh, but it was mild. She had large eyes, which were not bright, and a great deal of hair, which was not "dressed," and long fine hands, which were—possibly—not clean. She clasped these members almost convulsively as, with a confused, alarmed look, she broke out, "Oh, don't take it away from us; we like it ourselves!"

"You have the use of it then?"

"Oh yes. If it wasn't for that!" And she gave a shy, melancholy smile.

"Isn't it a luxury, precisely? That's why, intending to be in Venice some weeks, possibly all summer, and having some literary work, some reading and writing to do, so that I must be quiet, and yet if possible a great deal in the open air—that's why I have felt that a garden is really indispensable. I appeal to your own experience," I went on, smiling. "Now can't I look at yours?"

"I don't know, I don't understand," the poor woman murmured, planted there and letting her embarrassed eyes wander all over my strangeness.

"I mean only from one of those windows—such grand ones as you have here—if you will let me open the shutters." And I walked toward the back of the house. When I had advanced halfway I stopped and waited, as if I took it for granted she would accompany me. I had been of necessity very abrupt, but I strove at the same time to give her the impression of extreme courtesy. "I have been looking at furnished rooms all over the place, and it seems impossible to find any with a garden attached. Naturally in a place like Venice gardens are rare. It's absurd if you like, for a man, but I can't live without flowers."

"There are none to speak of down there." She came nearer to me, as if, though she mistrusted me, I had drawn her by an invisible thread. I went on again, and she continued as she followed me: "We have a few, but they are very common. It costs too much to cultivate them; one has to have a man."

"Why shouldn't I be the man?" I asked. "I'll work without wages, or rather I'll put in a gardener. You shall have the sweetest flowers in Venice."

She protested at this, with a queer little sigh which might also have been a gush of rapture at the picture I presented. Then she observed, "We don't know you—we don't know you."

"You know me as much as I know you; that is, much more, because you know my name. And if you are English I am almost a countryman."

"We are not English," said my companion, watching me helplessly while I threw open the shutters of one of the divisions of the wide high window.

"You speak the language so beautifully: might I ask what you are?" Seen from above the garden was certainly shabby, but I perceived at a glance that it had great capabilities. She made no rejoinder, she was so lost in staring at me, and I exclaimed, "You don't mean to say you are also by chance American?"

"I don't know; we used to be."

"Used to be? Surely you haven't changed?"

"It's so many years ago—we are nothing."

"So many years that you have been living here? Well, I don't wonder at that; it's a grand old house. I suppose you all use the garden," I went on, "but I assure you I shouldn't be in your way. I would be very quiet and stay in one corner."

"We all use it?" she repeated after me, vaguely, not coming close to the window but looking at my shoes. She appeared to think me capable of throwing her out.

"I mean all your family, as many as you are."

"There is only one other; she is very old—she never goes down."

"Only one other, in all this great house!" I feigned to be not only amazed but almost scandalized. "Dear lady, you must have space then to spare!"

"To spare?" she repeated, in the same dazed way.

"Why, you surely don't live (two quiet women—I see *you* are quiet, at any rate) in fifty rooms!" Then with a burst of hope and cheer I demanded: "Couldn't you let me two or three? That would set me up!"

I had now struck the note that translated my purpose and I need not reproduce the whole of the tune I played. I ended by making my interlocutress believe that I was an honorable person, though of course I did not even attempt to persuade her that I was not an eccentric one. I repeated that I had studies to pursue; that I wanted quiet; that I delighted in a garden and had vainly sought one up and down the city; that I would undertake that before another month was over the dear old house should be smothered in flowers. I think it was the flowers that won my suit, for I afterward found that Miss Tita (for such the name of this high tremulous spinster proved somewhat incongruously to be) had an insatiable appetite for them. When I speak of my suit as won I mean that before I left her she had promised that she would refer the question to her aunt. I inquired who her aunt might be and she answered, "Why, Miss Bordereau!" with an air of surprise, as if I might have been expected to know. There were contradictions like this in Tita Bordereau which, as I observed later, contributed to make her an odd and affecting person. It was the study of the two ladies to live so that the world should not touch them, and yet they had never altogether accepted the idea that it never heard of them. In Tita at any rate a grateful susceptibility to human contact had not died out, and contact of a limited order there would be if I should come to live in the house.

"We have never done anything of the sort; we have never had a lodger or any kind of inmate." So much as this she made a point of saying to me. "We are very poor, we live very badly. The rooms are very bare—that you might take; they have nothing in them. I don't know how you would sleep, how you would eat."

"With your permission, I could easily put in a bed and a few tables and chairs. *C'est la moindre des choses* and the affair of an hour or two. I know a little man from whom I can hire what I should want for a few months, for a trifle, and my gondolier can bring the things round in his boat. Of course in this great house you must have a second kitchen, and my servant, who is a wonderfully handy fellow" (this personage was an evocation of the moment), "can easily cook me a chop there. My tastes and habits are of the simplest; I live on flowers!" And then I ventured to add that if they were very poor it was all the more reason they should let their rooms. They were bad economists—I had never heard of such a waste of material.

I saw in a moment that the good lady had never before been spoken to in that way, with a kind of humorous firmness which did not exclude sympathy but was on the contrary founded on it. She might easily have told me that my sympathy was impertinent, but this by good fortune did not occur to her. I left her with the understanding that she would consider the matter with her aunt and that I might come back the next day for their decision.

"The aunt will refuse; she will think the whole proceeding very *louche!*" Mrs. Prest declared shortly after this, when I had resumed my place in her gondola. She had put the idea into my head and now (so little are women to be counted on) she appeared to take a despondent view of it. Her pessimism provoked me and I pretended to have the best hopes; I went so far as to say that I had a distinct presentiment that I should succeed. Upon this Mrs. Prest broke out, "Oh, I see what's in your head! You fancy you have made such an impression in a quarter of an hour that she is dying for you to come and can be depended upon to bring the old one round. If you do get in you'll count it as a triumph."

I did count it as a triumph, but only for the editor (in the last analysis), not for the man, who had not the tradition of personal conquest. When I went back on the morrow the little maidservant conducted me straight through the long *sala* (it opened there as before in perfect perspective and was lighter now, which I thought a good omen) into the apartment from which the recipient of my former visit had emerged on that occasion. It was a large shabby parlor, with a fine old painted ceiling and a strange figure sitting alone at one of the windows. They come back to me now almost with the palpitation they caused, the successive feelings that accompanied my consciousness that as the door of the room closed behind me I was really face to face with the Juliana of some of Aspern's most exquisite and most renowned lyrics. I grew used to her afterward, though never completely, but as she sat there before me my heart beat as fast as if the miracle of resurrection had taken place for my benefit. Her presence seemed somehow to contain his, and I felt nearer to him at that first moment of seeing her than I ever had been before or ever have been since. Yes, I remember my emotions in their order, even including a curious little tremor that took me when I saw that the niece was not there. With her, the day before, I had become sufficiently familiar, but it almost exceeded my courage (much as I had longed for the event) to be left alone with such a terrible relic as the aunt. She was too strange, too literally resurgent. Then came a check, with the perception that we were not really face to face, inasmuch as she had over her eyes a horrible green shade which, for her, served almost as a mask. I believed for the instant that she had put it on expressly, so that from underneath it she might scrutinize me without being scrutinized herself. At the same time it increased the presumption that there was a ghastly death's-head lurking behind it. The divine Juliana as a grinning skull—the vision hung there until it passed. Then it came to me that she *was* tremendously old—so old that death might take her at any moment, before I had time to get what I wanted from her. The next thought was a correction to that; it lighted up the situation. She would die next week, she would die tomorrow—then I could seize her papers. Meanwhile she sat there neither moving nor speaking. She was very small and shrunken, bent forward, with her hands in her lap. She was dressed in black and her head was wrapped in a piece of old black lace which showed no hair.

My emotion keeping me silent she spoke first, and the remark she made was exactly the most unexpected.

III

"Our house is very far from the center, but the little canal is very *comme il faut.*"

"It's the sweetest corner of Venice and I can imagine nothing more charming," I hastened to reply. The old lady's voice was very thin and weak, but it had an agreeable, cultivated murmur and there was wonder in the thought that that individual note had been in Jeffrey Aspern's ear.

"Please to sit down there. I hear very well," she said quietly, as if perhaps I had been shouting at her, and the chair she pointed to was at a certain distance. I took possession of it, telling her that I was perfectly aware that I had intruded, that I had not been properly introduced and could only throw myself upon her indulgence. Perhaps the other lady, the one I had had the honor of seeing the day before, would have explained to her about the garden. That was literally what had given me courage to take a step so unconventional. I had fallen in love at sight with the whole place (she herself probably was so used to it that she did not know the impression it was capable of making on a stranger), and I had felt it was really a case to risk something. Was her own kindness in receiving me a sign that I was not wholly out in my calculation? It would render me extremely happy to think so. I could give her my word of honor that I was a most respectable, inoffensive person and that as an inmate they would be barely conscious of my existence. I would conform to any regulations, any restrictions if they would only let me enjoy the garden. Moreover I should be delighted to give her references, guarantees; they would be of the very best, both in Venice and in England as well as in America.

She listened to me in perfect stillness and I felt that she was looking at me with great attention, though I could see only the lower part of her bleached and shrivelled face. Independently of the refining process of old age it had a delicacy which once must have been great. She had been very fair, she had had a wonderful complexion. She was silent a little after I had ceased speaking, then she inquired, "If you are so fond of a garden why don't you go to *terra firma,* where there are so many far better than this?"

"Oh, it's the combination!" I answered, smiling; and then, with rather a flight of fancy, "It's the idea of a garden in the middle of the sea."

"It's not in the middle of the sea; you can't see the water."

I stared a moment, wondering whether she wished to convict me of fraud. "Can't see the water? Why, dear madam, I can come up to the very gate in my boat."

She appeared inconsequent, for she said vaguely in reply to this, "Yes, if you have got a boat. I haven't any; it's many years since I have been in one of the gondolas." She uttered these words as if the gondolas were a curious far-away craft which she knew only by hearsay.

"Let me assure you of the pleasure with which I would put mine at your service!" I exclaimed. I had scarcely said this, however, before I became aware that the speech was in questionable taste and might also do me the injury of making me appear too eager, too possessed of a hidden motive. But the old woman remained impenetrable and her attitude bothered me by suggesting that she had a fuller vision of me than I had of her. She gave me no thanks for my somewhat extravagant offer but remarked that the lady I had seen the day before was her niece; she would presently come in. She had asked her to stay away a little on purpose, because she herself wished to see me at first alone. She relapsed into silence and I asked myself why she had judged this necessary and what was coming yet; also whether I might venture on some judicious remark in praise of her companion. I went so far as to say that I should be delighted to see her again: she had been so very courteous to me, considering how odd she must have thought me—a declaration which drew from Miss Bordereau another of her whimsical speeches.

"She has very good manners; I bred her up myself!" I was on the point of saying that that accounted for the easy grace of the niece, but I arrested myself in time, and the next moment the old woman went on: "I don't care who you may be—I don't want to know; it signifies very little today." This had all the air of being a formula of dismissal, as if her next words would be that I might take myself off now that she had had the amusement of looking on the face of such a monster of indiscretion. Therefore I was all the more surprised when she added, with her soft, venerable quaver, "You may have as many rooms as you like—if you will pay a good deal of money."

I hesitated but for a single instant, long enough to ask myself what she meant in particular by this condition. First it struck me that she must have really a large sum in her mind; then I reasoned quickly that her idea of a large sum would probably not correspond to my own. My deliberation, I think, was not so visible as to diminish the promptitude with which I replied, "I will pay with pleasure and, of course, in advance whatever you may think it proper to ask me."

"Well then, a thousand francs a month," she rejoined instantly, while her baffling green shade continued to cover her attitude.

The figure, as they say, was startling and my logic had been at fault. The sum she had mentioned was, by the Venetian measure of such matters, exceedingly large;

there was many an old palace in an out-of-the-way corner that I might on such terms have enjoyed by the year. But so far as my small means allowed I was prepared to spend money, and my decision was quickly taken. I would pay her with a smiling face what she asked, but in that case I would give myself the compensation of extracting the papers from her for nothing. Moreover if she had asked five times as much I should have risen to the occasion, so odious would it have appeared to me to stand chaffering with Aspern's Juliana. It was queer enough to have a question of money with her at all. I assured her that her views perfectly met my own and that on the morrow I should have the pleasure of putting three months' rent into her hand. She received this announcement with serenity and with no apparent sense that after all it would be becoming of her to say that I ought to see the rooms first. This did not occur to her and indeed her serenity was mainly what I wanted. Our little bargain was just concluded when the door opened and the younger lady appeared on the threshold. As soon as Miss Bordereau saw her niece she cried out almost gaily, "He will give three thousand—three thousand tomorrow!"

Miss Tita stood still, with her patient eyes turning from one of us to the other; then she inquired, scarcely above her breath, "Do you mean francs?"

"Did you mean francs or dollars?" the old woman asked of me at this.

"I think francs were what you said," I answered, smiling.

"That is very good," said Miss Tita, as if she had become conscious that her own question might have looked over-reaching.

"What do *you* know? You are ignorant," Miss Bordereau remarked; not with acerbity but with a strange, soft coldness.

"Yes, of money—certainly of money!" Miss Tita hastened to exclaim.

"I am sure you have your own branches of knowledge," I took the liberty of saying, genially. There was something painful to me, somehow, in the turn the conversation had taken, in the discussion of the rent.

"She had a very good education when she was young. I looked into that myself," said Miss Bordereau. Then she added, "But she has learned nothing since."

"I have always been with you," Miss Tita rejoined very mildly, and evidently with no intention of making an epigram.

"Yes, but for that!" her aunt declared, with more satirical force. She evidently meant that but for this her niece would never have got on at all; the point of the observation however being lost on Miss Tita, though she blushed at hearing her history revealed to a stranger. Miss Bordereau went on, addressing herself to me: "And what time will you come tomorrow with the money?"

"The sooner the better. If it suits you I will come at noon."

"I am always here but I have my hours," said the old woman, as if her convenience were not to be taken for granted.

"You mean the times when you receive?"

"I never receive. But I will see you at noon, when you come with the money."

"Very good, I shall be punctual;" and I added, "May I shake hands with you, on our contract?" I thought there ought to be some little form, it would make me really feel easier, for I foresaw that there would be no other. Besides, though Miss Bordereau could not today be called personally attractive and there was something even in her wasted antiquity that bade one stand at one's distance, I felt an irresistible desire to hold in my own for a moment the hand that Jeffrey Aspern had pressed.

For a minute she made no answer and I saw that my proposal failed to meet with her approbation. She indulged in no movement of withdrawal, which I half expected, she only said coldly, "I belong to a time when that was not the custom."

I felt rather snubbed but I exclaimed good-humoredly to Miss Tita, "Oh, you will do as well!" I shook hands with her while she replied, with a small flutter, "Yes, yes, to show it's all arranged!"

"Shall you bring the money in gold?" Miss Bordereau demanded, as I was turning to the door.

I looked at her a moment. "Aren't you a little afraid, after all, of keeping such a sum as that in the house?" It was not that I was annoyed at her avidity but I was really struck with the disparity between such a treasure and such scanty means of guarding it.

"Whom should I be afraid of if I am not afraid of you?" she asked with her shrunken grimness.

"Ah well," said I, laughing, "I shall be in point of fact a protector and I will bring gold if you prefer."

"Thank you," the old woman returned with dignity and with an inclination of her head which evidently signified that I might depart. I passed out of the room, reflecting that it would not be easy to circumvent her. As I stood in the *sala* again I saw that Miss Tita had followed me and I supposed that, as her aunt had neglected to suggest that I should take a look at my quarters, it was her purpose to repair the omission. But she made no such suggestion; she only stood there with a dim, though not a languid smile, and with an effect of irresponsible, incompetent youth which was almost comically at variance with the faded facts of her person. She was not infirm, like her aunt, but she struck me as still more helpless, because her inefficiency was spiritual, which was not the case with Miss Bordereau's. I waited to see if she would offer to show me the rest of the house, but I did not precipitate the question, inasmuch as my plan was from this moment to spend as much of my time as possible in her society. I only observed at the end of a minute:

"I have had better fortune than I hoped. It was very kind of her to see me. Perhaps you said a good word for me."

"It was the idea of the money," said Miss Tita.

"And did you suggest that?"

"I told her that you would perhaps give a good deal."

"What made you think that?"

"I told her I thought you were rich."

"And what put that idea into your head?"

"I don't know; the way you talked."

"Dear me, I must talk differently now," I declared. "I'm sorry to say it's not the case."

"Well," said Miss Tita, "I think that in Venice the *forestieri*, in general, often give a great deal for something that after all isn't much." She appeared to make this remark with a comforting intention, to wish to remind me that if I had been extravagant I was not really foolishly singular. We walked together along the *sala*, and as I took its magnificent measure I said to her that I was afraid it would not form a part of my *quartiere*. Were my rooms by chance to be among those that opened into it? "Not if you go above, on the second floor," she answered with a little startled air, as if she had rather taken for granted I would know my proper place.

"And I infer that that's where your aunt would like me to be."

"She said your apartments ought to be very distinct."

"That certainly would be best." And I listened with respect while she told me that up above I was free to take whatever I liked; that there was another staircase, but only from the floor on which we stood, and that to pass from it to the garden-story or to come up to my lodging I should have in effect to cross the great hall. This was an immense point gained; I foresaw that it would constitute my whole leverage in my relations with the two ladies. When I asked Miss Tita how I was to manage at present to find my way up she replied with an access of that sociable shyness which constantly marked her manner.

"Perhaps you can't. I don't see—unless I should go with you." She evidently had not thought of this before.

We ascended to the upper floor and visited a long succession of empty rooms. The best of them looked over the garden; some of the others had a view of the blue lagoon, above the opposite rough-tiled housetops. They were all dusty and even a little disfigured with long neglect, but I saw that by spending a few hundred francs I should be able to convert three or four of them into a convenient habitation. My experiment was turning out costly, yet now that I had all but taken possession I ceased to allow this to trouble me. I mentioned to my companion a few of the things that I should put in, but she replied rather more precipitately than usual that I might do exactly what I liked; she seemed to wish to notify me that the Misses Bordereau would take no overt interest in my proceedings. I guessed that her aunt had instructed her to adopt this tone, and I may as well say now that I came afterward to distinguish perfectly (as I believed) between the speeches she made on her own responsibility and those the old lady imposed upon her. She took no notice of the unswept condition of the rooms and indulged in no explanations nor apologies. I said to myself that this was a sign that Juliana and her niece (disenchanting idea!) were untidy persons, with a low Italian standard, but I afterward recognized that a lodger who had forced an entrance had no *locus standi* as a critic. We looked out of a good many windows, for there was nothing within the rooms to look at, and still I wanted to linger. I asked her what several different objects in the prospect might be, but in no case did she appear to know. She was evidently not familiar with the view—it was if she had not looked at it for years—and I presently saw that she was too preoccupied with something else to pretend to care for it. Suddenly she said—the remark was not suggested:

"I don't know whether it will make any difference to you, but the money is for me."

"The money?"

"The money you are going to bring."

"Why, you'll make me wish to stay here two or three years." I spoke as benevolently as possible, though it had begun to act on my nerves that with these women so associated with Aspern the pecuniary question should constantly come back.

"That would be very good for me," she replied, smiling.

"You put me on my honor!"

She looked as if she failed to understand this, but went on: "She wants me to have more. She thinks she is going to die."

"Ah, not soon, I hope!" I exclaimed, with genuine feeling. I had perfectly considered the possibility that she would destroy her papers on the day she should feel her end really approach. I believed that she would cling to them till then and I think I had an idea that she read Aspern's letters over every night or at least pressed them to her withered lips. I would have given a good deal to have a glimpse of the latter spectacle. I asked Miss Tita if the old lady were seriously ill and she replied that she was only very tired—she had lived so very, very long. That was what she said herself—she wanted to die for a change. Besides, all her friends were dead long ago; either they ought to have remained or she ought to have gone. That was another thing her aunt often said—she was not at all content.

"But people don't die when they like, do they?" Miss Tita inquired. I took the liberty of asking why, if there was actually enough money to maintain both of them, there would not be more than enough in case of her being left alone. She considered this difficult problem a moment and then she said, "Oh, well, you know, she takes care of me. She thinks that when I'm alone I shall be a great fool, I shall not know how to manage."

"I should have supposed rather that you took care of her. I'm afraid she is very proud."

"Why, have you discovered that already?" Miss Tita cried, with the glimmer of an illumination in her face.

"I was shut up with her there for a considerable time, and she struck me, she interested me extremely. It didn't take me long to make my discovery. She won't have much to say to me while I'm here."

"No, I don't think she will," my companion averred.

"Do you suppose she has some suspicion of me?"

Miss Tita's honest eyes gave me no sign that I had touched a mark. "I shouldn't think so—letting you in after all so easily."

"Oh, so easily! she has covered her risk. But where is it that one could take an advantage of her?"

"I oughtn't to tell you if I knew, ought I?" And Miss Tita added, before I had time to reply to this, smiling dolefully, "Do you think we have any weak points?"

"That's exactly what I'm asking. You would only have to mention them for me to respect them religiously."

She looked at me, at this, with that air of timid but candid and even gratified curiosity with which she had confronted me from the first; and then she said, "There is nothing to tell. We are terribly quiet. I don't know how the days pass. We have no life."

"I wish I might think that I should bring you a little."

"Oh, we know what we want," she went on. "It's all right."

There were various things I desired to ask her: how in the world they did live; whether they had any friends or visitors, any relations in America or in other countries. But I judged such an inquiry would be premature; I must leave it to a later chance. "Well, don't *you* be proud," I contented myself with saying. "Don't hide from me altogether."

"Oh, I must stay with my aunt," she returned, without looking at me. And at the same moment, abruptly, without any ceremony of parting, she quitted me and disappeared, leaving me to make my own way downstairs. I remained a while longer, wandering about the bright desert (the sun was pouring in) of the old house, thinking the situation over on the spot. Not even the pattering little *serva* came to look after me and I reflected that after all this treatment showed confidence.

IV

Perhaps it did, but all the same, six weeks later, toward the middle of June, the moment when Mrs. Prest undertook her annual migration, I had made no measureable advance. I was obliged to confess to her that I had no results to speak of. My first step had been unexpectedly rapid, but there was no appearance that it would be followed by a second. I was a thousand miles from taking tea with my hostesses—that privilege of which, as I reminded Mrs. Prest, we both had had a vision. She reproached me with wanting boldness and I answered that even to be bold you must have an opportunity: you may push on through a breach but you can't batter down a dead wall. She answered that the breach I had already made was big enough to admit an army and accused me of wasting precious hours in whimpering in her salon when I ought to have been carrying on the struggle in the field. It is true that I went to see her very often, on the theory that it would console me (I freely expressed my discouragement) for my want of success on my own premises. But I began to perceive that it did not console me to be perpetually chaffed for my scruples, especially when I was really so vigilant, and I was rather glad when my derisive friend closed her house for the summer. She had expected to gather amusement from the drama of my intercourse with the Misses Bordereau and she was disappointed that the intercourse, and consequently the drama, had not come off. "They'll lead you on to your ruin," she said before she left Venice. "They'll get all your money without showing you a scrap." I think I settled down to my business with more concentration after she had gone away.

It was a fact that up to that time I had not, save on a single brief occasion, had even a moment's contact with my queer hostesses. The exception had occurred when I carried them according to my promise the terrible three thousand francs. Then I found Miss Tita waiting for me in the hall, and she took the money from my hand so that I did not see her aunt. The old lady had promised to receive me, but she apparently thought nothing of breaking that vow. The money was contained in a bag of chamois leather, of respectable dimensions, which my banker had given me, and Miss Tita had to make a big fist to receive it. This she did with extreme solemnity, though I tried to treat the affair a little as a joke. It was in no jocular strain, yet it was with simplicity, that she inquired, weighing the money in her two palms: "Don't you think it's too much?" To which I replied that that would depend upon the amount of pleasure I should get for it. Hereupon she turned away from me quickly, as she had done the day before, murmuring in a tone different from any she had used hitherto: "Oh, pleasure, pleasure—there's no pleasure in this house!"

After this, for a long time, I never saw her, and I wondered that the common chances of the day should not have helped us to meet. It could only be evident that she was immensely on her guard against them and, in addition to this, the house was so big that for each other we were lost in it. I used to look out for her hopefully as I crossed the *sala* in my comings and goings, but I was not rewarded with a glimpse of the tail of her dress. It was as if she never peeped out of her aunt's apartment. I used to wonder what she did there week after week and year after year. I had never encountered such a violent *parti pris* of seclusion; it was more than keeping quiet— it was like hunted creatures feigning death. The two ladies appeared to have no visitors whatever and no sort of contact with the world. I judged at least that people could not have come to the house and that Miss Tita could not have gone out without my having some observation of it. I did what I disliked myself for doing (reflecting that it was only once in a way): I questioned my servant about their habits and let him divine that I should be interested in any information he could pick up. But he picked up amazingly little for a knowing Venetian: it must be added that where there is a perpetual fast there are very few crumbs on the floor. His cleverness in other ways was sufficient, if it was not quite all that I had attributed to him on the occasion of my first interview with Miss Tita. He had helped my gondolier to bring me round a boat-load of furniture, and when these articles had been carried to the top of the palace and distributed according to our associated wisdom he organized my household with such promptitude as was consistent with the fact that it was composed exclusively of himself. He made me in short as comfortable as I could be with my indifferent prospects. I should have been glad if he had fallen in love with Miss Bordereau's maid or, failing this, had taken her in aversion; either event might have brought about some kind of catastrophe and a catastrophe might have led to some parley. It was my idea that she would have been sociable, and I myself on various occasions saw her flit to and fro on domestic errands, so that I was sure she was accessible. But I tasted of no gossip from that fountain, and I afterward learned that Pasquale's affections were fixed upon an object that made him heedless of other women. This was a young lady with a powdered face, a yellow cotton gown and much leisure, who used often to come to see him. She practiced, at her convenience, the art of a stringer of beads (these ornaments are made in Venice, in profusion; she had her pocket full of them and I used to find them on the floor of my apartment), and kept an eye on the maiden in the house. It was not for me, of course, to make the domestics tattle, and I never said a word to Miss Bordereau's cook.

It seemed to me a proof of the old lady's determination to have nothing to do with me that she should never have sent me a receipt for my three months' rent. For some days I looked out for it and then, when I had given it up, I wasted a good deal of time in wondering what her reason had been for neglecting so indispensable and familiar a form. At first I was tempted to send her a reminder, after which I relinquished the idea (against my judgment as to what was right in the particular case), on the general ground of wishing to keep quiet. If Miss Bordereau suspected me of ulterior aims she would suspect me less if I should be businesslike, and yet I consented not to be so. It was possible she intended her omission as an impertinence, a visible irony, to show how she could overreach people who attempted to overreach her. On that hypothesis it was well to let her see that one did not notice her little tricks. The real reading of the matter, I afterward perceived, was simply the poor old woman's desire to emphasize the fact that I was in the enjoyment of a favor as rigidly limited as it had been liberally bestowed. She had given me part of her house and now she would not give me even a morsel of paper with her name on it. Let me say that even at first this did not make me too miserable, for the whole episode was essentially delightful to me. I foresaw that I should have a summer after my own literary heart, and the sense of holding my opportunity was much greater than the sense of losing it. There could be no Venetian business without patience, and since I adored the place I was much more in the spirit of it for having laid in a large provision. That spirit kept me perpetual company and seemed to look out at me from the revived immortal face—in which all his genius shone—of the great poet who was my prompter. I had invoked him and he had come; he hovered before me half the time; it was as if his bright ghost had returned to earth to tell me that he regarded the affair as his own no less than mine and that we should see it fraternally, cheerfully to a conclusion. It was as if he had said, "Poor dear, be easy with her; she has some natural prejudices; only give her time. Strange as it may appear to you she was very attractive in 1820. Meanwhile, are we not in Venice together, and what better place is there for the meeting of dear friends? See how it glows with the advancing summer; how the sky and the sea and the rosy air and the marble of the palaces all shimmer and melt together." My eccentric private errand became a part of the general romance and the general glory—I felt even a mystic companionship, a moral fraternity with all those who in the past had been in the service of art. They had worked for beauty, for a devotion—and what else was I doing? That element was in everything that Jeffrey Aspern had written and I was only bringing it to the light.

I lingered in the *sala* when I went to and fro; I used to watch—as long as I thought decent—the door that led to Miss Bordereau's part of the house. A person observing me might have supposed I was trying to cast a spell upon it or attempting some odd experiment in hypnotism. But I was only praying it would open or thinking what treasure probably lurked behind it. I hold it singular, as I look back, that I should never have doubted for a moment that the sacred relics were there, never have failed to feel a certain joy at being under the same roof with them. After all they were under my hand—they had not escaped me yet, and they made my life continuous, in a fashion, with the illustrious life they had touched at the other end. I lost myself in this satisfaction to the point of assuming—in my quiet extravagance—that poor Miss Tita also went back, went back, as I used to phrase it. She did indeed, the gentle spinster, but not quite so far as Jeffrey Aspern, who was simple hearsay to her, quite as he was to me. Only she had lived for years with Juliana, she had seen and handled the papers and (even though she was stupid) some esoteric knowledge had rubbed off on her. That was what the old woman represented—esoteric knowledge; and this was the idea with which my editorial heart used to thrill. It literally beat faster often, of an evening, when I had been out, as I stopped with my candle in the reechoing hall on my way up to bed. It was as if at such a moment as that, in the stillness, after the long contradiction of the day, Miss Bordereau's secrets were in the air, the wonder of her survival more palpable. These were the acute impressions. I had them in another form, with more of a certain sort of reciprocity, during the hours that I sat in the garden looking up over the top of my book at the closed windows of my hostess. In these windows no sign of life ever appeared; it was as if, for fear of my catching a glimpse of them, the two ladies passed their days in the dark. But this only proved to me that they had something to conceal, which was what I had wished to demonstrate. Their motionless shutters became as expressive as eyes consciously closed, and I took comfort in thinking that at all events though invisible themselves they saw me between the lashes.

I made a point of spending as much time as possible in the garden, to justify the picture I had originally given of my horticultural passion. And I not only spent time, but (hang it! as I said) I spent money. As soon as I had got my rooms arranged and could give the proper thought to the matter I surveyed the place with a clever expert and made terms for having it put in order. I was sorry to do this, for personally I liked it better as it was, with its weeds and its wild, rough tangle, its sweet, char-acteristic Venetian shabbiness. I had to be consistent, to keep my promise that I would smother the house in flowers. Moreover I formed this graceful project that by flowers I would make my way—I would succeed by big nosegays. I would batter the old women with lilies—I would bombard their citadel with roses. Their door would have to yield to the pressure when a mountain of carnations should be piled up against it. The place in truth had been brutally neglected. The Venetian capacity for dawdling is of the largest, and for a good many days unlimited litter was all my gardener had to show for his ministrations. There was a great digging of holes and carting about of earth, and after a while I grew so impatient that I had thoughts of sending for my bouquets to the nearest stand. But I reflected that the ladies would see through the chinks of their shutters that they must have been bought and might make up their minds from this that I was a humbug. So I composed myself and finally, though the delay was long, perceived some appearances of bloom. This encouraged me and I waited serenely enough till they multiplied. Meanwhile the real summer days arrived and began to pass, and as I look back upon them they seem to me almost the happiest of my life. I took more and more care to be in the garden whenever it was not too hot. I had an arbor arranged and a low table and an armchair put into it, and I carried out books and portfolios (I had always some busi-ness of writing in hand), and worked and waited and mused and hoped, while the golden hours elapsed and the plants drank in the light and the inscrutable old palace turned pale and then, as the day waned, began to flush in it and my papers rustled in the wandering breeze of the Adriatic.

Considering how little satisfaction I got from it at first it is remarkable that I should not have grown more tired of wondering what mystic rites of ennui the Misses Bordereau celebrated in their darkened rooms; whether this had always been the tenor of their life and how in previous years they had escaped elbowing their neighbors. It was clear that they must have had other habits and other circumstances; that they must once have been young or at least middle-aged. There was no end to the questions it was possible to ask about them and no end to the answers it was not possible to frame. I had known many of my country people in Europe and was familiar with the strange ways they were liable to take up there, but the Misses Bordereau formed altogether a new type of the American absentee. Indeed it was plain that the American name had ceased to have any application to them—I had seen this in the ten minutes I spent in the old woman's room. You could never have said whence they came, from the appearance of either of them; wherever it was, they had long ago dropped the local accent and fashion. There was nothing in them that one recognized, and putting the question of speech aside they might have been Norwegians or Spaniards. Miss Bordereau, after all, had been in Europe nearly three-quarters of a century; it appeared by some verses addressed to her by Aspern on the occasion of his own second absence from America—verses of which Cumnor and I had after infinite conjecture established solidly enough the date—that she was even then, as a girl of twenty, on the foreign side of the sea. There was an implication in the poem (I hope not just for the phrase) that he had come back for her sake. We had no real light upon her circumstances at that moment, anymore than we had upon her origin, which we believed to be of the sort usually spoken of as modest. Cumnor had a theory that she had been a governess in some family in which the poet visited and that, in consequence of her position, there was from the first something unavowed, or rather something positively clandestine, in their relations. I, on the other hand, had hatched a little romance according to which she was the daughter of an artist, a painter or a sculptor, who had left the western world when the century was fresh, to study in the ancient schools. It was essential to my hypothesis that this amiable man should have lost his wife, should have been poor and unsuccessful and should have had a second daughter, of a disposition quite different from Juliana's. It was also indispensable that he should have been accompanied to Europe by these young ladies and should have established himself there for the remainder of a strug-gling, saddened life. There was a further implication that Miss Bordereau had had in her youth a perverse and adventurous, albeit a generous and fascinating character, and that she had passed through some singular vicissitudes. By what passions had she been ravaged, by what sufferings had she been blanched, what store of memories had she laid away for the monotonous future?

I asked myself these things as I sat spinning theories about her in my arbor and the bees droned in the flowers. It was incontestable that, whether for right or for wrong, most readers of certain of Aspern's poems (poems not as ambiguous as the sonnets—scarcely more divine, I think—of Shakespeare) had taken for granted that Juliana had not always adhered to the steep footway of renunciation. There hovered about her name a perfume of reckless passion, an intimation that she had not been exactly as the respectable young person in general. Was this a sign that her singer had betrayed her, had given her away, as we say nowadays, to posterity?

Certain it is that it would have been difficult to put one's finger on the passage in which her fair fame suffered an imputation. Moreover was not any fame fair enough that was so sure of duration and was associated with works immortal through their beauty? It was a part of my idea that the young lady had had a foreign lover (and an unedifying tragical rupture) before her meeting with Jeffrey Aspern. She had lived with her father and sister in a queer old-fashioned, expatriated, artistic Bohemia, in the days when the æsthetic was only the academic and the painters who knew the best models for a *contadina* and *pifferaro* wore peaked hats and long hair. It was a society less furnished than the coteries of today (in its ignorance of the wonderful chances, the opportunities of the early bird, with which its path was strewn), with tatters of old stuff and fragments of old crockery, so that Miss Bordereau appeared not to have picked up or have inherited many objects of importance. There was no enviable *bric-à-brac*, with its provoking legend of cheapness, in the room in which I had seen her. Such a fact as that suggested bareness, but nonetheless it worked happily into the sentimental interest I had always taken in the early movements of my countrymen as visitors to Europe. When Americans went abroad in 1820, there was something romantic, almost heroic in it, as compared with the perpetual ferryings of the present hour, when photography and other conveniences have annihilated surprise. Miss Bordereau sailed with her family on a tossing brig, in the days of long voyages and sharp differences; she had her emotions on the top of yellow diligences, passed the night at inns where she dreamed of travelers' tales, and was struck, on reaching the eternal city, with the elegance of Roman pearls and scarfs. There was something touching to me in all that and my imagination frequently went back to the period. If Miss Bordereau carried it there of course Jeffrey Aspern at other times had done so a great deal more. It was a much more important fact, if one were looking at his genius critically, that he had lived in the days before the general transfusion. It had happened to me to regret that he had known Europe at all; I should have liked to see what he would have written without that experience, by which he had incontestably been enriched. But as his fate had ordered otherwise, I went with him—I tried to judge how the old world would have struck him. It was not only there, however, that I watched him: the relations he had entertained with the new had even a livelier interest. His own country, after all, had had most of his life, and his muse, as they said at that time, was essentially American. That was originally what I had loved him for: that at a period when our native land was nude and crude and provincial, when the famous "atmosphere" it is supposed to lack was not even missed, when literature was lonely there and art and form almost impossible, he had found means to live and write like one of the first; to be free and general and not at all afraid; to feel, understand and express everything.

V

I was seldom at home in the evening, for when I attempted to occupy myself in my apartments the lamplight brought in a swarm of noxious insects, and it was too hot for closed windows. Accordingly I spent the late hours either on the water (the moonlight of Venice is famous), or in the splendid square which serves as a vast forecourt to the strange old basilica of Saint Mark. I sat in front of Florian's *café*, eating ices, listening to music, talking with acquaintances: the traveler will remember how the immense cluster of tables and little chairs stretches like a promontory into the smooth lake of the Piazza. The whole place, of a summer's evening, under the stars and with all the lamps, all the voices and light footsteps on marble (the only sounds of the arcades that enclose it), is like an open-air saloon dedicated to cooling drinks and to a still finer degustation—that of the exquisite impressions received during the day. When I did not prefer to keep mine to myself there was always a stray tourist, disencumbered of his Bädeker, to discuss them with, or some domesticated painter rejoicing in the return of the season of strong effects. The wonderful church, with its low domes and bristling embroideries, the mystery of its mosaic and sculpture, looked ghostly in the tempered gloom, and the sea breeze passed between the twin columns of the Piazzetta, the lintels of a door no longer guarded, as gently as if a rich curtain were swaying there. I used sometimes on these occasions to think of the Misses Bordereau and of the pity of their being shut up in apartments, which in the Venetian July even Venetian vastness did not prevent from being stuffy. Their life seemed miles away from the life of the Piazza, and no doubt it was really too late to make the austere Juliana change her habits. But poor Miss Tita would have enjoyed one of Florian's ices, I was sure; sometimes I even had thoughts of carrying one home to her. Fortunately my patience bore fruit and I was not obliged to do anything so ridiculous.

One evening about the middle of July, I came in earlier than usual—I forget what chance had led to this—and instead of going up to my quarters made my way into the garden. The temperature was very high; it was such a night as one would gladly have spent in the open air and I was in no hurry to go to bed. I had floated home in my gondola, listening to the slow splash of the oar in the narrow dark canals, and now the only thought that solicited me was the vague reflection that it would be pleasant to recline at one's length in the fragrant darkness on a garden bench. The odor of the canal was doubtless at the bottom of that aspiration and the breath of the garden, as I entered it, gave consistency to my purpose. It was delicious—just such an air as must have trembled with Romeo's vows when he stood among the flowers and raised his arms to his mistress's balcony. I looked at the windows of the palace to see if by chance the example of Verona (Verona being not far off) had been followed, but everything was dim, as usual, and everything was still. Juliana, on summer nights in her youth, might have murmured down from open windows at Jeffrey Aspern, but Miss Tita was not a poet's mistress any more than I was a poet. This, however, did not prevent my gratification from being great as I became aware on reaching the end of the garden that Miss Tita was seated in my little bower. At first I only made out an indistinct figure, not in the least counting on such an overture from one of my hostesses; it even occurred to me that some sentimental maidservant had stolen in to keep a tryst with her sweetheart. I was going to turn away, not to frighten her, when the figure rose to its height and I recognized Miss Bordereau's niece. I must do myself the justice to say that I did not wish to frighten her either, and, much as I had longed for some such accident, I should have been capable of retreating. It was as if I had laid a trap for her by coming home earlier than usual and adding to that eccentricity by creeping into the garden. As she rose she spoke to me, and then I reflected that perhaps, secure in my almost inveterate absence, it was her nightly practice to take a lonely airing. There was no trap, in truth, because I had had no suspicion. At first I took for granted that the words she uttered expressed discomfiture at my arrival, but as she repeated them—I had not caught them clearly—I had the surprise of hearing her say, "Oh, dear, I'm so very glad you've come!" She and her aunt had in common the property of unexpected speeches. She came out of the arbor almost as if she were going to throw herself into my arms.

I hasten to add that she did nothing of the kind; she did not even shake hands with me. It was a gratification to her to see me and presently she told me why—because she was nervous when she was out-of-doors at night alone. The plants and bushes looked so strange in the dark, and there were all sorts of queer sounds—she could not tell what they were—like the noises of animals. She stood close to me, looking about her with an air of greater security, but without any demonstration of interest in me as an individual. Then I guessed that nocturnal prowlings were not in the least her habit, and I was also reminded (I had been struck with the circumstance in talking with her before I took possession) that it was impossible to over-estimate her simplicity.

"You speak as if you were lost in the backwoods," I said, laughing. "How you manage to keep out of this charming place when you have only three steps to take to get into it, is more than I have yet been able to discover. You hide away mighty well so long as I am on the premises, I know, but I had a hope that you peeped out a little at other times. You and your poor aunt are worse off than Carmelite nuns in their cells. Should you mind telling me how you exist without air, without exercise, without any sort of human contact? I don't see how you carry on the common business of life."

She looked at me as if I were talking some strange tongue and her answer was so little of an answer that I was considerably irritated.

"We go to bed very early—earlier than you would believe." I was on the point of saying that this only deepened the mystery when she gave me some relief by adding, "Before you came we were not so private. But I never have been out at night."

"Never in these fragrant alleys, blooming here under your nose?"

"Ah," said Miss Tita, "they were never nice till now!" There was an unmistakable reference in this and a flattering comparison, so that it seemed to me I had gained a small advantage. As it would help me to follow it up to establish a sort of grievance I asked her why, since she thought my garden nice, she had never thanked me in any way for the flowers I had been sending up in such quantities for the previous three weeks. I had not been discouraged—there had been, as she would have observed, a daily armful, but I had been brought up in the common forms and a word of recognition now and then would have touched me in the right place.

"Why I didn't know they were for me!"

"They were for both of you. Why should I make a difference?"

Miss Tita reflected as if she might be thinking of a reason for that, but she failed to produce one. Instead of this, she asked abruptly, "Why in the world do you want to know us?"

"I ought after all to make a difference," I replied. "That question is your aunt's; it isn't yours. You wouldn't ask it if you hadn't been put up to it."

"She didn't tell me to ask you," Miss Tita replied, without confusion; she was the oddest mixture of the shrinking and the direct.

"Well, she has often wondered about it herself and expressed her wonder to you. She has insisted on it, so that she has put the idea into your head that I am insufferably pushing. Upon my word I think I have been very discreet. And how completely your aunt must have lost every tradition of sociability, to see anything out of the way in the idea that respectable intelligent people, living as we do under the same roof, should occasionally exchange a remark! What could be more natural? We are of the same country and we have at least some of the same tastes, since, like you, I am intensely fond of Venice."

My interlocutress appeared incapable of grasping more than one clause in any proposition, and she declared quickly, eagerly, as if she were answering my whole speech: "I am not in the least fond of Venice. I should like to go far away!"

"Has she always kept you back so?" I went on, to show her that I could be as irrelevant as herself.

"She told me to come out tonight; she has told me very often," said Miss Tita. "It is I who wouldn't come. I don't like to leave her."

"Is she too weak, is she failing?" I demanded, with more emotion, I think, than I intended to show. I judged this by the way her eyes rested upon me in the darkness. It embarrassed me a little, and to turn the matter off I continued genially: "Do let us sit down together comfortably somewhere and you will tell me all about her."

Miss Tita made no resistance to this. We found a bench less secluded, less confidential, as it were, than the one in the arbor, and we were still sitting there when I heard midnight ring out from those clear bells of Venice which vibrate with a solemnity of their own over the lagoon and hold the air so much more than the chimes of other places. We were together more than an hour and our interview gave, as it struck me, a great lift to my undertaking. Miss Tita accepted the situation without a protest; she had avoided me for three months, yet now she treated me almost as if these three months had made me an old friend. If I had chosen I might have inferred from this that though she had avoided me she had given a good deal of consideration to doing so. She paid no attention to the flight of time—never worried at my keeping her so long away from her aunt. She talked freely, answering questions and asking them and not even taking advantage of certain longish pauses with which they inevitably alternated to say she thought she had better go in. It was almost as if she were waiting for something—something I might say to her—and intended to give me my opportunity. I was the more struck by this as she told me that her aunt had been less well for a good many days and in a way that was rather new. She was weaker—at moments it seemed as if she had no strength at all—yet more than ever before she wished to be left alone. That was why she had told her to come out—not even to remain in her own room, which was alongside; she said her niece irritated her, made her nervous. She sat still for hours together, as if she were asleep; she had always done that, musing and dozing, but at such times formerly she gave at intervals some small sign of life, of interest, liking her companion to be near her with her work. Miss Tita confided to me that at present her aunt was so motionless that she sometimes feared she was dead; moreover she took hardly any food—one couldn't see what she lived on. The great thing was that she still on most days got up; the serious job was to dress her, to wheel her out of her bedroom. She clung to as many of her old habits as possible and she had always, little company as they had received for years, made a point of sitting in the parlor.

I scarcely knew what to think of all this—of Miss Tita's sudden conversion to sociability and of the strange circumstance that the more the old lady appeared to decline toward her end the less she should desire to be looked after. The story did not hang together, and I even asked myself whether it were not a trap laid for me, the result of a design to make me show my hand. I could not have told why my companions (as they could only by courtesy be called) should have this purpose—why they should try to trip up so lucrative a lodger. At any rate, I kept on my guard, so that Miss Tita should not have occasion again to ask me if I had an *arrière-pensée*. Poor woman, before we parted for the night my mind was at rest as to *her* capacity for entertaining one.

She told me more about their affairs than I had hoped; there was no need to be prying, for it evidently drew her out simply to feel that I listened, that I cared. She ceased wondering why I cared, and at last, as she spoke of the brilliant life they had led years before, she almost chattered. It was Miss Tita who judged it brilliant; she said that when they first came to live in Venice, years and years before (I saw that her mind was essentially vague about dates and the order in which events had occurred), there was scarcely a week that they had not some visitor or did not make some delightful *passeggio* in the city. They had seen all the curiosities; they had even been to the Lido in a boat (she spoke as if I might think there was a way on foot); they had had a collation there, brought in three baskets and spread out on the grass. I asked her what people they had known and she said, Oh! very nice ones—the Cavaliere Bombicci and the Contessa Altemura, with whom they had had a great friendship. Also English people—the Churtons and the Goldies and Mrs. Stock-Stock, whom they had loved dearly; she was dead and gone, poor dear. That was the case with most of their pleasant circle (this expression was Miss Tita's own), though a few were left, which was a wonder considering how they had neglected them. She mentioned the names of two or three Venetian old women; of a certain doctor, very clever, who was so kind—he came as a friend, he had really given up practice; of the *avvocato* Pochintesta, who wrote beautiful poems and had addressed one to her aunt. These people came to see them without fail every year, usually at the *capo d'anno*, and of old her aunt used to make them some little present—her aunt and she together: small things that she, Miss Tita, made herself, like paper lampshades or mats for the decanters of wine at dinner or those woolen things that in cold weather were worn on the wrists. The last few years there had not been many presents; she could not think what to make and her aunt had lost her interest and never suggested. But the people came all the same; if the Venetians liked you once they liked you for ever.

There was something affecting in the good faith of this sketch of former social glories; the picnic at the Lido had remained vivid through the ages and poor Miss Tita evidently was of the impression that she had had a brilliant youth. She had in fact had a glimpse of the Venetian world in its gossiping, home-keeping, parsimonious, professional walks, for I observed for the first time that she had acquired by contact something of the trick of the familiar, soft-sounding, almost infantile speech of the place. I judged that she had imbibed this invertebrate dialect, from the natural way the names of things and people—mostly purely local—rose to her lips. If she knew little of what they represented, she knew still less of anything else. Her aunt had drawn in—her failing interest in the table mats and lampshades was a sign of that—and she had not been able to mingle in society or to entertain it alone, so that the matter of her reminiscences struck one as an old world altogether. If she had not been so decent, her references would have seemed to carry one back to the queer rococo Venice of Casanova. I found myself falling into the error of thinking of her too as one of Jeffrey Aspern's contemporaries; this came from her having so little in common with my own. It was possible, I said to myself, that she had not even heard of him; it might very well be that Juliana had not cared to lift even for her the veil that covered the temple of her youth. In this case she perhaps would not know of the existence of the papers, and I welcomed that presumption—it made me feel more safe with her—until I remembered that we had believed the letter of disavowal received by Cumnor to be in the handwriting of the niece. If it had been dictated to her she had of course to know what it was about, yet after all the effect of it was to repudiate the idea of any connection with the poet. I held it probable at all events that Miss Tita had not read a word of his poetry. Moreover if, with her companion, she had always escaped the interviewer, there was little occasion for her having got it into her head that people were "after" the letters. People had not been after them, inasmuch as they had not heard of them, and Cumnor's fruitless feeler would have been a solitary accident.

When midnight sounded Miss Tita got up, but she stopped at the door of the house only after she had wandered two or three times with me round the garden. "When shall I see you again?" I asked, before she went in; to which she replied with promptness that she should like to come out the next night. She added however that she should not come—she was so far from doing everything she liked.

"You might do a few things that *I* like," I said with a sigh.

"Oh, you—I don't believe you!" she murmured, at this, looking at me with her simple solemnity.

"Why don't you believe me?"

"Because I don't understand you."

"That is just the sort of occasion to have faith." I could not say more, though I should have liked to, as I saw that I only mystified her; for I had no wish to have it on my conscience that I might pass for having made love to her. Nothing less should I have seemed to do had I continued to beg a lady to "believe in me" in an Italian garden on a midsummer night. There was some merit in my scruples, for Miss Tita lingered and lingered: I perceived that she felt that she should not really soon come down again and wished therefore to protract the present. She insisted too on making the talk between us personal to ourselves and altogether her behaviour was such as would have been possible only to a completely innocent woman.

"I shall like the flowers better now that I know they are also meant for me."

"How could you have doubted it? If you will tell me the kind you like best I will send a double lot of them."

"Oh, I like them all best!" Then she went on, familiarly: "Shall you study—shall you read and write—when you go up to your rooms?"

"I don't do that at night, at this season. The lamplight brings in the animals."

"You might have known that when you came."

"I did know it!"

"And in winter do you work at night?"

"I read a good deal, but I don't often write." She listened as if these details had a rare interest, and suddenly a temptation quite at variance with the prudence I had been teaching myself associated itself with her plain, mild face. Ah yes, she was safe and I could make her safer! It seemed to me from one moment to another that I could not wait longer—that I really must take a sounding. So I went on: "In general before I go to sleep—very often in bed (it's a bad habit, but I confess to it), I read some great poet. In nine cases out of ten it's a volume of Jeffrey Aspern."

I watched her well as I pronounced that name but I saw nothing wonderful. Why should I indeed—was not Jeffrey Aspern the property of the human race?

"Oh, we read him—we *have* read him," she quietly replied.

"He is my poet of poets—I know him almost by heart."

For an instant Miss Tita hesitated; then her sociability was too much for her.

"Oh, by heart—that's nothing!" she murmured, smiling. "My aunt used to know him—to know him"—she paused an instant and I wondered what she was going to say—"to know him as a visitor."

"As a visitor?" I repeated, staring.

"He used to call on her and take her out."

I continued to stare. "My dear lady, he died a hundred years ago!"

"Well," she said, mirthfully, "my aunt is a hundred and fifty."

"Mercy on us!" I exclaimed; "why didn't you tell me before? I should like so to ask her about him."

"She wouldn't care for that—she wouldn't tell you," Miss Tita replied.

"I don't care what she cares for! She *must* tell me—it's not a chance to be lost."

"Oh, you should have come twenty years ago: then she still talked about him."

"And what did she say?" I asked, eagerly.

"I don't know—that he liked her immensely."

"And she—didn't she like him?"

"She said he was a god." Miss Tita gave me this information flatly, without expression; her tone might have made it a piece of trivial gossip. But it stirred me deeply as she dropped the words into the summer night; it seemed such a direct testimony.

"Fancy, fancy!" I murmured. And then, "Tell me this, please—has she got a portrait of him? They are distressingly rare."

"A portrait? I don't know," said Miss Tita, and now there was discomfiture in her face. "Well, goodnight!" she added, and she turned into the house.

I accompanied her into the wide, dusky, stone-paved passage, which on the ground floor corresponded with our grand *sala*. It opened at one end into the garden, at the other upon the canal, and was lighted now only by the small lamp that was always left for me to take up as I went to bed. An extinguished candle, which Miss Tita apparently had brought down with her, stood on the same table with it. "Goodnight, goodnight!" I replied, keeping beside her as she went to get her light. "Surely you would know, shouldn't you, if she had one?"

"If she had what?" the poor lady asked, looking at me queerly over the flame of her candle.

"A portrait of the god. I don't know what I wouldn't give to see it."

"I don't know what she has got. She keeps her things locked up." And Miss Tita went away, toward the staircase, with the sense evidently that she had said too much.

I let her go—I wished not to frighten her—and I contented myself with remarking that Miss Bordereau would not have locked up such a glorious possession as that—a thing a person would be proud of and hang up in a prominent place on the parlor wall. Therefore, of course, she had not any portrait. Miss Tita made no direct answer to this and candle in hand, with her back to me, ascended two or three stairs. Then she stopped short and turned round looking at me across the dusky space.

"Do you write—do you write?" There was a shake in her voice—she could scarcely bring out what she wanted to ask.

"Do I write? Oh, don't speak of my writing on the same day with Aspern's!"

"Do you write about *him*—do you pry into his life?"

"Ah, that's your aunt's question; it can't be yours!" I said, in a tone of slightly wounded sensibility.

"All the more reason then that you should answer it. Do you, please?"

I thought I had allowed for the falsehoods I should have to tell, but I found that in fact when it came to the point I had not. Besides, now that I had an opening there was a kind of relief in being frank. Lastly (it was perhaps fanciful, even fatuous), I guessed that Miss Tita personally would not in the last resort be less my friend. So after a moment's hesitation I answered, "Yes, I have written about him and I am looking for more material. In heaven's name have you got any?"

"*Santo Dio!*" she exclaimed, without heeding my question, and she hurried upstairs and out of sight. I might count upon her in the last resort, but for the present she was visibly alarmed. The proof of it was that she began to hide again, so that for a fortnight I never beheld her. I found my patience ebbing and after four or five days of this I told the gardener to stop the flowers.

VI

One afternoon, as I came down from my quarters to go out, I found Miss Tita in the *sala*. It was our first encounter on that ground since I had come to the house. She put on no air of being there by accident; there was an ignorance of such arts in her angular, diffident directness. That I might be quite sure she was waiting for me, she informed me of the fact and told me that Miss Bordereau wished to see me: she would take me into the room at that moment if I had time. If I had been late for a love tryst I would have stayed for this, and I quickly signified that I should be delighted to wait upon the old lady. "She wants to talk with you—to know you," Miss Tita said, smiling as if she herself appreciated that idea, and she led me to the door of her aunt's apartment. I stopped her a moment before she had opened it, looking at her with some curiosity. I told her that this was a great satisfaction to me and a great honor, but all the same I should like to ask what had made Miss Bordereau change so suddenly. It was only the other day that she wouldn't suffer me near her. Miss Tita was not embarrassed by my question; she had as many little unexpected serenities as if she told fibs, but the odd part of them was that they had on the contrary their source in her truthfulness. "Oh, my aunt changes," she answered; "it's so terribly dull—I suppose she's tired."

"But you told me that she wanted more and more to be alone."

Poor Miss Tita colored, as if she found me overinsistent. "Well, if you don't believe she wants to see you—I haven't invented it! I think people often are capricious when they are very old."

"That's perfectly true. I only wanted to be clear as to whether you have repeated to her what I told you the other night."

"What you told me?"

"About Jeffrey Aspern—that I am looking for materials."

"If I had told her do you think she would have sent for you?"

"That's exactly what I want to know. If she wants to keep him to herself she might have sent for me to tell me so."

"She won't speak of him," said Miss Tita. Then as she opened the door she added in a lower tone, "I have told her nothing."

The old woman was sitting in the same place in which I had seen her last, in the same position, with the same mystifying bandage over her eyes. Her welcome was to turn her almost invisible face to me and show me that while she sat silent she

531

saw me clearly. I made no motion to shake hands with her; I felt too well on this occasion that that was out of place for ever. It had been sufficiently enjoined upon me that she was too sacred for that sort of reciprocity—too venerable to touch. There was something so grim in her aspect (it was partly the accident of her green shade), as I stood there to be measured, that I ceased on the spot to feel any doubt as to her knowing my secret, though I did not in the least suspect that Miss Tita had not just spoken the truth. She had not betrayed me, but the old woman's brooding instinct had served her; she had turned me over and over in the long, still hours and she had guessed. The worst of it was that she looked terribly like an old woman who at a pinch would burn her papers. Miss Tita pushed a chair forward, saying to me, "This will be a good place for you to sit." As I took possession of it, I asked after Miss Bordereau's health and expressed the hope that in spite of the very hot weather it was satisfactory. She replied that it was good enough—good enough; that it was a great thing to be alive.

"Oh, as to that, it depends upon what you compare it with!" I exclaimed, laughing.

"I don't compare—I don't compare. If I did that I should have given everything up long ago."

I liked to think that this was a subtle allusion to the rapture she had known in the society of Jeffrey Aspern—though it was true that such an allusion would have accorded ill with the wish I imputed to her to keep him buried in her soul. What it accorded with was my constant conviction that no human being had ever had a more delightful social gift than his, and what it seemed to convey was that nothing in the world was worth speaking of if one pretended to speak of that. But one did not! Miss Tita sat down beside her aunt, looking as if she had reason to believe some very remarkable conversation would come off between us.

"It's about the beautiful flowers," said the old lady; "you sent us so many—I ought to have thanked you for them before. But I don't write letters and I receive only at long intervals."

She had not thanked me while the flowers continued to come, but she departed from her custom so far as to send for me as soon as she began to fear that they would not come any more. I noted this; I remembered what an acquisitive propensity she had shown when it was a question of extracting gold from me, and I privately rejoiced at the happy thought I had had in suspending my tribute. She had missed it and she was willing to make a concession to bring it back. At the first sign of this concession I could only go to meet her. "I am afraid you have not had many, of late, but they shall begin again immediately—tomorrow, tonight."

"Oh, do send us some tonight!" Miss Tita cried, as if it were an immense circumstance.

"What else should you do with them? It isn't a manly taste to make a bower of your room," the old woman remarked.

"I don't make a bower of my room, but I am exceedingly fond of growing flowers, of watching their ways. There is nothing unmanly in that: it has been the amusement of philosophers, of statesmen in retirement, even I think of great captains."

"I suppose you know you can sell them—those you don't use," Miss Bordereau went on. "I daresay they wouldn't give you much for them; still, you could make a bargain."

"Oh, I have never made a bargain, as you ought to know. My gardener disposes of them and I ask no questions."

"I would ask a few, I can promise you!" said Miss Bordereau, and it was the first time I had heard her laugh. I could not get used to the idea that this vision of pecuniary profit was what drew out the divine Juliana most.

"Come into the garden yourself and pick them; come as often as you like; come every day. They are all for you," I pursued, addressing Miss Tita and carrying off this veracious statement by treating it as an innocent joke. "I can't imagine why she doesn't come down," I added, for Miss Bordereau's benefit.

"You must make her come; you must come up and fetch her," said the old woman, to my stupefaction. "That odd thing you have made in the corner would be a capital place for her to sit."

The allusion to my arbor was irreverent; it confirmed the impression I had already received that there was a flicker of impertinence in Miss Bordereau's talk, a strange mocking lambency which must have been a part of her adventurous youth and which had outlived passions and faculties. Nonetheless I asked, "Wouldn't it be possible for you to come down there yourself? Wouldn't it do you good to sit there in the shade, in the sweet air?"

"Oh, sir, when I move out of this it won't be to sit in the air, and I'm afraid that any that may be stirring around me won't be particularly sweet! It will be a very dark shade indeed. But that won't be just yet," Miss Bordereau continued, cannily, as if to correct any hopes that this courageous allusion to the last receptacle of her mortality might lead me to entertain. "I have sat here many a day and I have had enough of arbors in my time. But I'm not afraid to wait till I'm called."

Miss Tita had expected some interesting talk, but perhaps she found it less genial on her aunt's side (considering that I had been sent for with a civil intention) than she had hoped. As if to give the conversation a turn that would put our companion in a light more favorable she said to me, "Didn't I tell you the other night that she had sent me out? You see that I can do what I like!"

"Do you pity her—do you teach her to pity herself?" Miss Bordereau demanded, before I had time to answer this appeal. "She has a much easier life than I had when I was her age."

"You must remember that it has been quite open to me to think you rather inhuman."

"Inhuman? That's what the poets used to call the women a hundred years ago. Don't try that; you won't do as well as they!" Juliana declared. "There is no more poetry in the world—that I know of at least. But I won't bandy words with you," she pursued, and I well remember the old-fashioned, artificial sound she gave to the speech. "You have made me talk, talk! It isn't good for me at all." I got up at this and told her I would take no more of her time; but she detained me to ask, "Do you remember, the day I saw you about the rooms, that you offered us the use of your gondola?" And when I assented, promptly, struck again with her disposition to make a "good thing" of my being there and wondering what she now had in her eye, she broke out, "Why don't you take that girl out in it and show her the place?"

"Oh dear aunt, what do you want to do with me?" cried the "girl," with a piteous quaver. "I know all about the place!"

"Well then, go with him as a *cicerone!*" said Miss Bordereau, with an effect of something like cruelty in her implacable power of retort—an incongruous suggestion that she was a sarcastic, profane, cynical old woman. "Haven't we heard that there have been all sorts of changes in all these years? You ought to see them and at your age (I don't mean because you're so young), you ought to take the chances that come. You're old enough, my dear, and this gentleman won't hurt you. He will show you the famous sunsets, if they still go on—*do* they go on? The sun set for me so long ago. But that's not a reason. Besides, I shall never miss you; you think you are too important. Take her to the Piazza; it used to be very pretty," Miss Bordereau continued, addressing herself to me. "What have they done with the funny old church? I hope it hasn't tumbled down. Let her look at the shops; she may take some money, she may buy what she likes."

Poor Miss Tita had got up, discountenanced and helpless, and as we stood there before her aunt it would certainly have seemed to a spectator of the scene that the old woman was amusing herself at our expense. Miss Tita protested, in a confusion of exclamations and murmurs, but I lost no time in saying that if she would do me the honor to accept the hospitality of my boat I would engage that she should not be bored. Or if she did not want so much of my company the boat itself, with the gondolier, was at her service; he was a capital oar and she might have every confidence. Miss Tita, without definitely answering this speech, looked away from me, out of the window, as if she were going to cry, and I remarked that once we had Miss Bordereau's approval we could easily come to an understanding. We would take an hour, whichever she liked, one of the very next days. As I made my obeisance to the old lady, I asked her if she would kindly permit me to see her again.

For a moment she said nothing; then she inquired, "Is it very necessary to your happiness?"

"It diverts me more than I can say."

"You are wonderfully civil. Don't you know it almost kills *me?*"

"How can I believe that when I see you more animated, more brilliant than when I came in?"

"That is very true, aunt," said Miss Tita. "I think it does you good."

"Isn't it touching, the solicitude we each have that the other shall enjoy herself?" sneered Miss Bordereau. "If you think me brilliant today you don't know what you are talking about; you have never seen an agreeable woman. Don't try to pay me a compliment; I have been spoiled," she went on. "My door is shut, but you may sometimes knock."

With this she dismissed me and I left the room. The latch closed behind me, but Miss Tita, contrary to my hope, had remained within. I passed slowly across the hall and before taking my way downstairs I waited a little. My hope was answered; after a minute Miss Tita followed me. "That's a delightful idea about the Piazza," I said. "When will you go—tonight, tomorrow?"

She had been disconcerted, as I have mentioned, but I had already perceived and I was to observe again that when Miss Tita was embarrassed she did not (as most women would have done) turn away from you and try to escape, but came closer, as it were, with a deprecating, clinging appeal to be spared, to be protected. Her attitude was perpetually a sort of prayer for assistance, for explanation, and yet no woman in the world could have been less of a comedian. From the moment you were kind to her she depended on you absolutely; her self-consciousness dropped from her and she took the greatest intimacy, the innocent intimacy which was the only thing she could conceive, for granted. She told me she did not know what had got into her aunt; she had changed so quickly, she had got some idea. I replied that she must find out what the idea was and then let me know; we would go and have an ice together at Florian's and she should tell me while we listened to the band.

"Oh, it will take me a long time to find out!" she said, rather ruefully, and she could promise me this satisfaction neither for that night nor for the next. I was patient now, however, for I felt that I had only to wait and, in fact, at the end of the week, one lovely evening after dinner, she stepped into my gondola, to which in honor of the occasion I had attached a second oar.

We swept in the course of five minutes into the Grand Canal, whereupon she uttered a murmur of ecstasy as fresh as if she had been a tourist just arrived. She had forgotten how splendid the great waterway looked on a clear, hot summer evening, and how the sense of floating between marble palaces and reflected lights disposed the mind to sympathetic talk. We floated long and far, and though Miss Tita gave no high-pitched voice to her satisfaction, I felt that she surrendered herself. She was more than pleased, she was transported; the whole thing was an immense liberation. The gondola moved with slow strokes, to give her time to enjoy it, and she listened to the plash of the oars, which grew louder and more musically liquid as we passed into narrow canals, as if it were a revelation of Venice. When I asked her how long it was since she had been in a boat she answered, "Oh, I don't know; a long time—not since my aunt began to be ill." This was not the only example she gave me of her extreme vagueness about the previous years and the line which marked off the period when Miss Bordereau flourished. I was not at liberty to keep her out too long, but we took a considerable *giro* before going to the Piazza. I asked her no questions, keeping the conversation on purpose away from her domestic situation and the things I wanted to know; I poured treasures of information about Venice into her ears, described Florence and Rome, discoursed to her on the charms and advantages of travel. She reclined, receptive, on the deep leather cushions, turned her eyes conscientiously to everything I pointed out to her, and never mentioned to me till some time afterward that she might be supposed to know Florence better than I, as she had lived there for years with Miss Bordereau. At last she asked, with the shy impatience of a child, "Are we not really going to the Piazza? That's what I want to see!" I immediately gave the order that we should go straight, and then we sat silent with the expectation of arrival. As some time still passed, however, she said suddenly, of her own movement, "I have found out what is the matter with my aunt: she is afraid you will go!"

"What has put that into her head?"

"She has had an idea you have not been happy. That is why she is different now."

"You mean she wants to make me happier?"

"Well, she wants you not to go; she wants you to stay."

"I suppose you mean on account of the rent," I remarked candidly.

Miss Tita's candor showed itself a match for my own. "Yes, you know; so that I shall have more."

"How much does she want you to have?" I asked, laughing. "She ought to fix the sum, so that I may stay till it's made up."

"Oh, that wouldn't please me," said Miss Tita. "It would be unheard of, your taking that trouble."

"But suppose I should have my own reasons for staying in Venice?"

"Then it would be better for you to stay in some other house."

"And what would your aunt say to that?"

"She wouldn't like it at all. But I should think you would do well to give up your reasons and go away altogether."

"Dear Miss Tita," I said, "it's not so easy to give them up!"

She made no immediate answer to this, but after a moment she broke out: "I think I know what your reasons are!"

"I daresay, because the other night I almost told you how I wish you would help me to make them good."

"I can't do that without being false to my aunt."

"What do you mean, being false to her?"

"Why, she would never consent to what you want. She has been asked, she has been written to. It made her fearfully angry."

"Then she *has* got papers of value?" I demanded, quickly.

"Oh, she has got everything!" sighed Miss Tita, with a curious weariness, a sudden lapse into gloom.

These words caused all my pulses to throb, for I regarded them as precious evidence. For some minutes I was too agitated to speak, and in the interval the gondola approached the Piazzetta. After we had disembarked I asked my companion whether she would rather walk round the square or go and sit at the door of the café; to which she replied that she would do whichever I liked best—I must only remember again how little time she had. I assured her there was plenty to do both, and we made the circuit of the long arcades. Her spirits revived at the sight of the bright shopwindows, and she lingered and stopped, admiring or disapproving of their contents, asking me what I thought of things, theorizing about prices. My attention wandered from her; her words of a while before, "Oh, she has got everything!" echoed so in my consciousness. We sat down at last in the crowded circle at Florian's, finding an unoccupied table among those that were ranged in the square. It was a splendid night and all the world was out-of-doors; Miss Tita could not have wished the elements more auspicious for her return to society. I saw that she enjoyed it even more than she told; she was agitated with the multitude of her impressions. She had forgotten what an attractive thing the world is, and it was coming over her that somehow she had for the best years of her life been cheated of it. This did not make her angry, but as she looked all over the charming scene her face had, in spite of its smile of appreciation, the flush of a sort of wounded surprise. She became silent, as if she were thinking with a secret sadness of opportunities, forever lost, which ought to have been easy, and this gave me a chance to say to her, "Did you mean a while ago that your aunt has a plan of keeping me on by admitting me occasionally to her presence?"

"She thinks it will make a difference with you if you sometimes see her. She wants you so much to stay that she is willing to make that concession."

"And what good does she consider that I think it will do me to see her?"

"I don't know; she thinks it's interesting," said Miss Tita, simply. "You told her you found it so."

"So I did; but everyone doesn't think so."

"No, of course not, or more people would try."

"Well, if she is capable of making that reflection she is capable also of making this further one," I went on: "that I must have a particular reason for not doing as others do, in spite of the interest she offers—for not leaving her alone." Miss Tita looked as if she failed to grasp this rather complicated proposition, so I continued, "If you have not told her what I said to you the other night, may she not at least have guessed it?"

"I don't know; she is very suspicious."

"But she has not been made so by indiscreet curiosity, by persecution?"

"No, no; it isn't that," said Miss Tita, turning on me a somewhat troubled face. "I don't know how to say it: it's on account of something—ages ago, before I was born—in her life."

"Something? What sort of thing?" I asked, as if I myself could have no idea.

"Oh, she has never told me," Miss Tita answered, and I was sure she was speaking the truth.

Her extreme limpidity was almost provoking, and I felt for the moment that she would have been more satisfactory if she had been less ingenuous. "Do you suppose it's something to which Jeffrey Aspern's letters and papers—I mean the things in her possession—have reference?"

"I daresay it is!" my companion exclaimed, as if this were a very happy suggestion. "I have never looked at any of those things."

"None of them? Then how do you know what they are?"

"I don't," said Miss Tita, placidly. "I have never had them in my hands. But I have seen them when she has had them out."

"Does she have them out often?"

"Not now, but she used to. She is very fond of them."

"In spite of their being compromising?"

"Compromising?" Miss Tita repeated, as if she was ignorant of the meaning of the word. I felt almost as one who corrupts the innocence of youth.

"I mean their containing painful memories."

"Oh, I don't think they are painful."

"You mean you don't think they affect her reputation?"

At this a singular look came into the face of Miss Bordereau's niece—a kind of confession of helplessness, an appeal to me to deal fairly, generously with her. I had brought her to the Piazza, placed her among charming influences, paid her an attention she appreciated, and now I seemed to let her perceive that all this had been a bribe—a bribe to make her turn in some way against her aunt. She was of a yielding nature and capable of doing almost anything to please a person who was kind to her, but the greatest kindness of all would be not to presume too much on this. It was strange enough, as I afterward thought, that she had not the least air of resenting my want of consideration for her aunt's character, which would have been in the worst possible taste if anything less vital (from my point of view) had been at stake. I don't think she really measured it. "Do you mean that she did something bad?" she asked in a moment.

"Heaven forbid I should say so, and it's none of my business. Besides, if she did," I added, laughing, "it was in other ages, in another world. But why should she not destroy her papers?"

"Oh, she loves them too much."

"Even now, when she may be near her end?"

"Perhaps when she's sure of that she will."

"Well, Miss Tita," I said, "it's just what I should like you to prevent."

"How can I prevent it?"

"Couldn't you get them away from her?"

"And give them to you?"

This put the case very crudely, though I am sure there was no irony in her intention. "Oh, I mean that you might let me see them and look them over. It isn't for myself; there is no personal avidity in my desire. It is simply that they would be of such immense interest to the public, such immeasurable importance as a contribution to Jeffrey Aspern's history."

She listened to me in her usual manner, as if my speech were full of reference to things she had never heard of, and I felt particularly like the reporter of a newspaper who forces his way into a house of mourning. This was especially the case when after a moment she said, "There was a gentleman who some time ago wrote to her in very much those words. He also wanted her papers."

"And did she answer him?" I asked, rather ashamed of myself for not having her rectitude.

"Only when he had written two or three times. He made her very angry."

"And what did she say?"

"She said he was a devil," Miss Tita replied, simply.

"She used that expression in her letter?"

"Oh no, she said it to me. She made me write to him."

"And what did you say?"

"I told him there were no papers at all."

"Ah, poor gentleman!" I exclaimed.

"I knew there were, but I wrote what she bade me."

"Of course you had to do that. But I hope I shall not pass for a devil."

"It will depend upon what you ask me to do for you," said Miss Tita, smiling.

"Oh, if there is a chance of *your* thinking so my affair is in a bad way! I shan't ask you to steal for me, nor even to fib—for you can't fib, unless on paper. But the principal thing is this—to prevent her from destroying the papers."

"Why, I have no control of her," said Miss Tita. "It's she who controls me."

"But she doesn't control her own arms and legs, does she? The way she would naturally destroy her letters would be to burn them. Now she can't burn them without fire, and she can't get fire unless you give it to her."

"I have always done everything she has asked," my companion rejoined. "Besides, there's Olimpia."

I was on the point of saying that Olimpia was probably corruptible, but I thought it best not to sound that note. So I simply inquired if that faithful domestic could not be managed.

"Everyone can be managed by my aunt," said Miss Tita. And then she observed that her holiday was over; she must go home.

I laid my hand on her arm, across the table, to stay her a moment. "What I want of you is a general promise to help me."

"Oh, how can I—how can I?" she asked, wondering and troubled. She was half surprised, half frightened at my wishing to make her play an active part.

"This is the main thing: to watch her carefully and warn me in time, before she commits that horrible sacrilege."

"I can't watch her when she makes me go out."

"That's very true."

"And when you do too."

"Mercy on us; do you think she will have done anything tonight?"

"I don't know; she is very cunning."

"Are you trying to frighten me?" I asked.

I felt this inquiry sufficiently answered when my companion murmured in a musing, almost envious way, "Oh, but she loves them—she loves them!"

This reflection, repeated with such emphasis, gave me great comfort, but to obtain more of that balm I said, "If she shouldn't intend to destroy the objects we speak of before her death she will probably have made some disposition by will."

"By will?"

"Hasn't she made a will for your benefit?"

"Why, she has so little to leave. That's why she likes money," said Miss Tita.

"Might I ask, since we are really talking things over, what you and she live on?"

"On some money that comes from America, from a lawyer. He sends it every quarter. It isn't much!"

"And won't she have disposed of that?"

My companion hesitated—I saw she was blushing. "I believe it's mine," she said; and the look and tone which accompanied these words betrayed so the absence of the habit of thinking of herself that I almost thought her charming. The next instant she added, "But she had a lawyer once, ever so long ago. And some people came and signed something."

"They were probably witnesses. And you were not asked to sign? Well then," I argued, rapidly and hopefully, "it is because you are the legatee; she has left all her documents to you!"

"If she has, it's with very strict conditions," Miss Tita responded, rising quickly, while the movement gave the words a little character of decision. They seemed to imply that the bequest would be accompanied with a command that the articles bequeathed should remain concealed from every inquisitive eye and that I was very much mistaken if I thought she was the person to depart from an injunction so solemn.

"Oh, of course you will have to abide by the terms," I said, and she uttered nothing to mitigate the severity of this conclusion. Nonetheless, later, just before we disembarked at her own door, on our return, which had taken place almost in silence, she said to me abruptly, "I will do what I can to help you." I was grateful for this—it was very well so far as it went, but it did not keep me from remembering that night in a worried waking hour that I now had her word for it to reinforce my own impression that the old woman was very cunning.

VII

The fear of what this side of her character might have led her to do made me nervous for days afterward. I waited for an intimation from Miss Tita; I almost figured to myself that it was her duty to keep me informed, to let me know definitely whether or not Miss Bordereau had sacrificed her treasures. But as she gave no sign I lost patience and determined to judge so far as was possible with my own senses. I sent late one afternoon to ask if I might pay the ladies a visit, and my servant came back with surprising news. Miss Bordereau could be approached without the least difficulty; she had been moved out into the *sala* and was sitting by the window that overlooked the garden. I descended and found this picture correct; the old lady had been wheeled forth into the world and had a certain air, which came mainly perhaps from some brighter element in her dress, of being prepared again to have converse with it. It had not yet, however, begun to flock about her; she was perfectly alone and, though the door leading to her own quarters stood open, I had at first no glimpse of Miss Tita. The window at which she sat had the afternoon shade and, one of the shutters having been pushed back, she could see the pleasant garden, where the summer sun had by this time dried up too many of the plants—she could see the yellow light and the long shadows.

"Have you come to tell me that you will take the rooms for six months more?" she asked, as I approached her, startling me by something coarse in her cupidity almost as much as if she had not already given me a specimen of it. Juliana's desire to make our acquaintance lucrative had been, as I have sufficiently indicated, a false note in my image of the woman who had inspired a great poet with immortal lines, but I may say here definitely that I recognized after all that it behooved me to make a large allowance for her. It was I who had kindled the unholy flame; it was I who had put into her head that she had the means of making money. She appeared never to have thought of that; she had been living wastefully for years, in a house five times too big for her, on a footing that I could explain only by the presumption that, excessive as it was, the space she enjoyed cost her next to nothing and that small as were her revenues they left her, for Venice, an appreciable margin. I had descended on her one day and taught her to calculate, and my almost extravagant comedy on the subject of the garden had presented me irresistibly in the light of a victim. Like all persons who achieve the miracle of changing their point of view when they are old, she had been intensely converted; she had seized my hint with a desperate, tremulous clutch.

I invited myself to go and get one of the chairs that stood, at a distance, against the wall (she had given herself no concern as to whether I should sit or stand), and while I placed it near her I began, gaily, "Oh, dear madam, what an imagination you have, what an intellectual sweep! I am a poor devil of a man of letters who lives from day to day. How can I take palaces by the year? My existence is precarious. I don't know whether six months hence I shall have bread to put in my mouth. I have treated myself for once; it has been an immense luxury. But when it comes to going on—!"

"Are your rooms too dear? if they are you can have more for the same money," Juliana responded. "We can arrange, we can *combinare*, as they say here."

"Well yes, since you ask me, they are too dear," I said. "Evidently you suppose me richer than I am."

She looked at me in her barricaded way. "If you write books don't you sell them?"

"Do you mean don't people buy them? A little—not so much as I could wish. Writing books, unless one be a great genius—and even then!—is the last road to fortune. I think there is no more money to be made by literature."

"Perhaps you don't choose good subjects. What do you write about?" Miss Bordereau inquired.

"About the books of other people. I'm a critic, an historian, in a small way." I wondered what she was coming to.

"And what other people, now?"

"Oh, better ones than myself: the great writers mainly—the great philosophers and poets of the past; those who are dead and gone and can't speak for themselves."

"And what do you say about them?"

"I say they sometimes attached themselves to very clever women!" I answered, laughing. I spoke with great deliberation, but as my words fell upon the air they struck me as imprudent. However, I risked them and I was not sorry, for perhaps after all the old woman would be willing to treat. It seemed to be tolerably obvious that she knew my secret: why therefore drag the matter out? But she did not take what I had said as a confession; she only asked:

"Do you think it's right to rake up the past?"

"I don't know that I know what you mean by raking it up, but how can we get at it unless we dig a little? The present has such a rough way of treading it down."

"Oh, I like the past, but I don't like critics," the old woman declared, with her fine tranquility.

"Neither do I, but I like their discoveries."

"Aren't they mostly lies?"

"The lies are what they sometimes discover," I said, smiling at the quiet impertinence of this. "They often lay bare the truth."

"The truth is God's, it isn't man's; we had better leave it alone. Who can judge of it—who can say?"

"We are terribly in the dark, I know," I admitted; "but if we give up trying what becomes of all the fine things? What becomes of the work I just mentioned, that of the great philosophers and poets? It is all vain words if there is nothing to measure it by!"

"You talk as if you were a tailor," said Miss Bordereau, whimsically, and then she added quickly, in a different manner, "This house is very fine; the proportions are magnificent. Today I wanted to look at this place again. I made them bring me out here. When your man came, just now, to learn if I would see you, I was on the point of sending for you, to ask if you didn't mean to go on. I wanted to judge what I'm letting you have. This *sala* is very grand," she pursued, like an auctioneer, moving a little, as I guessed, her invisible eyes. "I don't believe you often have lived in such a house, eh?"

"I can't often afford to!" I said.

"Well then, how much will you give for six months?"

I was on the point of exclaiming—and the air of excrucation in my face would have denoted a moral fact—"Don't, Juliana; for *his* sake, don't!" But I controlled myself and asked less passionately: "Why should I remain so long as that?"

"I thought you liked it," said Miss Bordereau, with her shriveled dignity.

"So I thought I should."

For a moment she said nothing more, and I left my own words to suggest to her what they might. I half expected her to say, coldly enough, that if I had been disappointed we need not continue the discussion, and this in spite of the fact that I believed her now to have in her mind (however it had come there), what would have told her that my disappointment was natural. But to my extreme surprise she ended by observing: "If you don't think we have treated you well enough perhaps we can discover some way of treating you better." This speech was somehow so incongruous that it made me laugh again, and I excused myself by saying that she talked as if I were a sulky boy, pouting in the corner, to be "brought round." I had not a grain of complaint to make, and could anything have exceeded Miss Tita's graciousness in accompanying me a few nights before to the Piazza? At this the old woman went on: "Well, you brought it on yourself!" And then in a different tone, "She is a very nice girl." I assented cordially to this proposition, and she expressed the hope that I did so not merely to be obliging, but that I really liked her. Meanwhile I wondered still more what Miss Bordereau was coming to. "Except for me, today," she said, "she has not a relation in the world." Did she by describing her niece as amiable and unencumbered wish to represent her as a *parti*?

It was perfectly true that I could not afford to go on with my rooms at a fancy price and that I had already devoted to my undertaking almost all the hard cash I had set apart for it. My patience and my time were by no means exhausted, but I should be able to draw upon them only on a more usual Venetian basis. I was willing to pay the venerable woman with whom my pecuniary dealings were such a discord twice as much as any other *padrona di casa* would have asked, but I was not willing to pay her twenty times as much. I told her so plainly, and my plainness appeared to have some success, for she exclaimed, "Very good; you have done what I asked—you have made an offer!"

"Yes, but not for half a year. Only by the month."

"Oh, I must think of that then." She seemed disappointed that I would not tie myself to a period, and I guessed that she wished both to secure me and to discourage me; to say, severely, "Do you dream that you can get off with less than six months? Do you dream that even by the end of that time you will be appreciably nearer your victory?" What was more in my mind was that she had a fancy to play me the trick of making me engage myself when in fact she had annihilated the papers. There was a moment when my suspense on this point was so acute that I all but broke out with the question, and what kept it back was but a kind of instinctive recoil (lest it should be a mistake), from the last violence of self-exposure. She was such a subtle old witch that one could never tell where one stood with her. You may imagine whether it cleared up the puzzle when, just after she had said she would think of my proposal and without any formal transition, she drew out of her pocket with an embarrassed hand a small object wrapped in crumpled white paper. She held it there a moment and then she asked, "Do you know much about curiosities?"

"About curiosities?"

"About antiquities, the old gimcracks that people pay so much for today. Do you know the kind of price they bring?"

I thought I saw what was coming, but I said ingenuously, "Do you want to buy something?"

"No, I want to sell. What would an amateur give me for that?" She unfolded the white paper and made a motion for me to take from her a small oval portrait. I possessed myself of it with a hand of which I could only hope that she did not perceive the tremor, and she added, "I would part with it only for a good price."

At the first glance I recognized Jeffrey Aspern, and I was well aware that I flushed with the act. As she was watching me, however, I had the consistency to exclaim, "What a striking face! Do tell me who it is."

"It's an old friend of mine, a very distinguished man in his day. He gave it to me himself, but I'm afraid to mention his name, lest you never should have heard of him, critic and historian as you are. I know the world goes fast and one generation forgets another. He was all the fashion when I was young."

She was perhaps amazed at my assurance, but I was surprised at hers; at her having the energy, in her state of health and at her time of life, to wish to sport with me that way simply for her private entertainment—the humor to test me and practice on me. This, at least, was the interpretation that I put upon her production of the portrait, for I could not believe that she really desired to sell it or cared for any information I might give her. What she wished was to dangle it before my eyes and put a prohibitive price on it. "The face comes back to me, it torments me," I said, turning the object this way and that and looking at it very critically. It was a careful but not a supreme work of art, larger than the ordinary miniature and representing a young man with a remarkably handsome face, in a high-collared green coat and a buff waistcoat. I judged the picture to have a valuable quality of resemblance and to have been painted when the model was about twenty-five years old. There are, as all the world knows, three other portraits of the poet in existence, but none of them is of so early a date as this elegant production. "I have never seen the original but I have seen other likenesses," I went on. "You expressed doubt of this generation having heard of the gentleman, but he strikes me for all the world as a celebrity. Now who is he? I can't put my finger on him—I can't give him a label. Wasn't he a writer? Surely he's a poet." I was determined that it should be she, not I, who should first pronounce Jeffrey Aspern's name.

My resolution was taken in ignorance of Miss Bordereau's extremely resolute character, and her lips never formed in my hearing the syllables that meant so much for her. She neglected to answer my question but raised her hand to take back the picture, with a gesture which, though ineffectual, was in a high degree peremptory. "It's only a person who should know for himself that would give me my price," she said with a certain dryness.

"Oh, then, you have a price?" I did not restore the precious thing; not from any vindictive purpose but because I instinctively clung to it. We looked at each other hard while I retained it.

"I know the least I would take. What it occurred to me to ask you about is the most I shall be able to get."

She made a movement, drawing herself together as if, in a spasm of dread at having lost her treasure, she were going to attempt the immense effort of rising to snatch it from me. I instantly placed it in her hand again, saying as I did so, "I should like to have it myself, but with your ideas I could never afford it."

She turned the small oval plate over in her lap, with its face down, and I thought I saw her catch her breath a little, as if she had had a strain or an escape. This, however, did not prevent her saying in a moment, "You would buy a likeness of a person you don't know, by an artist who has no reputation?"

"The artist may have no reputation, but that thing is wonderfully well painted," I replied, to give myself a reason.

"It's lucky you thought of saying that, because the painter was my father."

"That makes the picture indeed precious!" I exclaimed, laughing, and I may add that a part of my laughter came from my satisfaction in finding that I had been right in my theory of Miss Bordereau's origin. Aspern had of course met the young lady when he went to her father's studio as a sitter. I observed to Miss Bordereau that if she would entrust me with her property for twenty-four hours I should be happy to take advice upon it, but she made no answer to this save to slip it in silence into her pocket. This convinced me still more that she had no sincere intention of selling it during her lifetime, though she may have desired to satisfy herself as to the sum her niece, should she leave it to her, might expect eventually to obtain for it. "Well, at any rate I hope you will not offer it without giving me notice," I said, as she remained irresponsive. "Remember that I am a possible purchaser."

"I should want your money first!" she returned, with unexpected rudeness, and then, as if she bethought herself that I had just cause to complain of such an insinuation and wished to turn the matter off, asked abruptly what I talked about with her niece when I went out with her that way in the evening.

"You speak as if we had set up the habit," I replied. "Certainly I should be very glad if it were to become a habit. But in that case I should feel a still greater scruple at betraying a lady's confidence."

"Her confidence? Has she got confidence?"

"Here she is—she can tell you herself," I said, for Miss Tita now appeared on the threshold of the old woman's parlor. "Have you got confidence, Miss Tita? Your aunt wants very much to know."

"Not in her, not in her!" the younger lady declared, shaking her head with a dolefulness that was neither jocular nor affected. "I don't know what to do with her; she has fits of horrid imprudence. She is so easily tired—and yet she has begun to roam—to drag herself about the house." And she stood looking down at her immemorial companion with a sort of helpless wonder, as if all their years of familiarity had not made her perversities, on occasion, any more easy to follow.

"I know what I'm about. I'm not losing my mind. I daresay you would like to think so," said Miss Bordereau, with a cynical little sigh.

"I don't suppose you came out here yourself. Miss Tita must have had to lend you a hand," I interposed, with a pacifying intention.

"Oh, she insisted that we should push her—and when she insists!" said Miss Tita, in the same tone of apprehension, as if there were no knowing what service that she disapproved of her aunt might force her next to render.

"I have always got most things done I wanted, thank God! The people I have lived with have humored me," the old woman continued, speaking out of the gray ashes of her vanity.

"I suppose you mean that they have obeyed you."

"Well, whatever it is, when they like you."

"It's just because I like you that I want to resist," said Miss Tita, with a nervous laugh.

"Oh, I suspect you'll bring Miss Bordereau upstairs next, to pay me a visit," I went on, to which the old lady replied:

"Oh no; I can keep an eye on you from here!"

"You are very tired; you will certainly be ill tonight!" cried Miss Tita.

"Nonsense, my dear; I feel better at this moment than I have done for a month. Tomorrow I shall come out again. I want to be where I can see this clever gentleman."

"Shouldn't you perhaps see me better in your sitting room?" I inquired.

"Don't you mean shouldn't you have a better chance at me?" she returned, fixing me a moment with her green shade.

"Ah, I haven't that anywhere! I look at you but I don't see you."

"You excite her dreadfully—and that is not good," said Miss Tita, giving me a reproachful, appealing look.

"I want to watch you—I want to watch you!" the old lady went on.

"Well then, let us spend as much of our time together as possible—I don't care where—and that will give you every facility."

"Oh, I've seen you enough for today. I'm satisfied. Now I'll go home." Miss Tita laid her hands on the back of her aunt's chair and began to push, but I begged her to let me take her place. "Oh yes, you may move me this way—you shan't in any other!" Miss Bordereau exclaimed, as she felt herself propelled firmly and easily over the smooth, hard floor. Before we reached the door of her own apartment she commanded me to stop, and she took a long, last look up and down the noble *sala*. "Oh, it's a magnificent house!" she murmured, after which I pushed her forward. When we had entered the parlor Miss Tita told me that she should now be able to manage, and at the same moment the little redhaired *donna* came to meet her mistress. Miss Tita's idea was evidently to get her aunt immediately back to bed. I confess that in spite of this urgency I was guilty of the indiscretion of lingering; it held me there to think that I was nearer the documents I coveted—that they were probably put away somewhere in the faded, unsociable room. The place had indeed a bareness which did not suggest hidden treasures; there were no dusky nooks nor curtained corners, no massive cabinets nor chests with iron bands. Moreover it was possible, it was perhaps even probable that the old lady had consigned her relics to her bedroom, to some battered box that was shoved under the bed, to the drawer of some lame dressing table, where they would be in the range of vision by the dim night lamp. Nonetheless I scrutinized every article of furniture, every conceivable cover for a hoard, and noticed that there were half a dozen things with drawers, and in particular a tall old secretary, with brass ornaments of the style of the Empire—a receptacle somewhat rickety but still capable of keeping a great many secrets. I don't know why this article fascinated me so, inasmuch as I certainly had no definite purpose of breaking into it, but I stared at it so hard that Miss Tita noticed me and changed color. Her doing this made me think I was right and that wherever they might have been before, the Aspern papers at that moment languished behind the peevish little lock of the secretary. It was hard to remove my eyes from the dull mahogany front when I reflected that a simple panel divided me from the goal of my hopes, but I remembered my prudence and with an effort took leave of Miss Bordereau. To make the effort graceful I said to her that I should certainly bring her an opinion about the little picture.

"The little picture?" Miss Tita asked, surprised.

"What do *you* know about it, my dear?" the old woman demanded. "You needn't mind. I have fixed my price."

"And what may that be?"

"A thousand pounds."

"Oh Lord!" cried poor Miss Tita, irrepressibly.

"Is that what she talks to you about?" said Miss Bordereau.

"Imagine your aunt's wanting to know!" I had to separate from Miss Tita with only those words, though I should have liked immensely to add, "For heaven's sake meet me tonight in the garden!"

VIII

As it turned out the precaution had not been needed, for three hours later, just as I had finished my dinner, Miss Bordereau's niece appeared, unannounced, in the open doorway of the room in which my simple repasts were served. I remember well that I felt no surprise at seeing her, which is not a proof that I did not believe in her timidity. It was immense, but in a case in which there was a particular reason for boldness it never would have prevented her from running up to my rooms. I saw that she was now quite full of a particular reason; it threw her forward—made her seize me, as I rose to meet her, by the arm.

"My aunt is very ill; I think she is dying!"

"Never in the world," I answered, bitterly. "Don't you be afraid!"

"Do go for a doctor—do, do! Olimpia is gone for the one we always have, but she doesn't come back; I don't know what has happened to her. I told her that if he was not at home she was to follow him where he had gone; but apparently she is following him all over Venice. I don't know what to do—she looks so as if she were sinking."

"May I see her, may I judge?" I asked. "Of course I shall be delighted to bring someone; but hadn't we better send my man instead, so that I may stay with you?"

Miss Tita assented to this and I despatched my servant for the best doctor in the neighborhood. I hurried downstairs with her, and on the way she told me that an hour after I quitted them in the afternoon Miss Bordereau had had an attack of "oppression," a terrible difficulty in breathing. This had subsided but had left her so exhausted that she did not come up: she seemed all gone. I repeated that she was not gone, that she would not go yet; whereupon Miss Tita gave me a sharper sidelong glance than she had ever directed at me and said, "Really, what do you mean? I suppose you don't accuse her of making believe!" I forget what reply I made to this, but I grant that in my heart I thought the old woman capable of any weird manœuvre. Miss Tita wanted to know what I had done to her; her aunt had told her that I had made her so angry. I declared I had done nothing—I had been exceedingly careful, to which my companion rejoined that Miss Bordereau had assured her she had had a scene with me—a scene that had upset her. I answered with some resentment that it was a scene of her own making—that I couldn't think what she was angry with me for unless for not seeing my way to give a thousand pounds for the portrait of Jeffrey Aspern. "And did she show you that? Oh gracious—oh deary me!" groaned Miss Tita, who appeared to feel that the situation was passing out of her control and that the elements of her fate were thickening around her. I said that I would give anything to possess it, yet that I had not a thousand pounds, but I stopped when we came to the door of Miss Bordereau's room. I had an immense curiosity to pass it, but I thought it my duty to represent to Miss Tita that if I made the invalid angry she ought perhaps to be spared the sight of me. "The sight of you? Do you think she can *see?*" my companion demanded, almost with indignation. I did think so but forbore to say it, and I softly followed my conductress.

I remember that what I said to her as I stood for a moment beside the old woman's bed was, "Does she never show you her eyes then? Have you never seen them?" Miss Bordereau had been divested of her green shade, but (it was not my fortune to behold Juliana in her nightcap) the upper half of her face was covered by the fall of a piece of dingy lacelike muslin, a sort of extemporized hood which, wound round her head, descended to the end of her nose, leaving nothing visible but her white withered cheeks and puckered mouth, closed tightly and, as it were, consciously. Miss Tita gave me a glance of surprise, evidently not seeing a reason for my impatience. "You mean that she always wears something? She does it to preserve them."

"Because they are so fine?"

"Oh, today, today!" And Miss Tita shook her head, speaking very low. "But they used to be magnificent!"

"Yes indeed, we have Aspern's word for that." And as I looked again at the old woman's wrappings I could imagine that she had not wished to allow people a reason to say that the great poet had overdone it. But I did not waste my time in considering

Miss Bordereau, in whom the appearance of respiration was so slight as to suggest that no human attention could ever help her more. I turned my eyes all over the room, rummaging with them the closets, the chests of drawers, the tables. Miss Tita met them quickly and read, I think, what was in them, but she did not answer it, turning away restlessly, anxiously, so that I felt rebuked, with reason, for a preoccupation that was almost profane in the presence of our dying companion. All the same I took another look, endeavoring to pick out mentally the place to try first, for a person who should wish to put his hand on Miss Bordereau's papers directly after her death. The room was a dire confusion; it looked like the room of an old actress. There were clothes hanging over chairs, odd-looking, shabby bundles here and there, and various pasteboard boxes piled together, battered, bulging and discolored, which might have been fifty years old. Miss Tita after a moment noticed the direction of my eyes again and, as if she guessed how I judged the air of the place (forgetting I had no business to judge it at all), said, perhaps to defend herself from the imputation of complicity in such untidiness:

"She likes it this way; we can't move things. There are old bandboxes she has had most of her life." Then she added, half taking pity on my real thought, "Those things were *there*." And she pointed to a small, low trunk which stood under a sofa where there was just room for it. It appeared to be a queer, superannuated coffer, of painted wood, with elaborate handles and shriveled straps and with the color (it had last been endued with a coat of light green) much rubbed off. It evidently had traveled with Juliana in the olden time—in the days of her adventures, which it had shared. It would have made a strange figure arriving at a modern hotel.

"*Were* there—they aren't now?" I asked, startled by Miss Tita's implication.

She was going to answer, but at that moment the doctor came in—the doctor whom the little maid had been sent to fetch and whom she had at last overtaken. My servant, going on his own errand, had met her with her companion in tow, and in the sociable Venetian spirit, retracing his steps with them, had also come up to the threshold of Miss Bordereau's room, where I saw him peeping over the doctor's shoulder. I motioned him away the more instantly that the sight of his prying face reminded me that I myself had almost as little to do there—an admonition confirmed by the sharp way the little doctor looked at me, appearing to take me for a rival who had the field before him. He was a short, fat, brisk gentleman who wore the tall hat of his profession and seemed to look at everything but his patient. He looked particularly at me, as if it struck him that I should be better for a dose, so that I bowed to him and left him with the women, going down to smoke a cigar in the garden. I was nervous; I could not go further; I could not leave the place. I don't know exactly what I thought might happen, but it seemed to me important to be there. I wandered about in the alleys—the warm night had come on—smoking cigar after cigar and looking at the light in Miss Bordereau's windows. They were open now, I could see; the situation was different. Sometimes the light moved, but not quickly; it did not suggest the hurry of a crisis. Was the old woman dying or was she already dead? Had the doctor said that there was nothing to be done at her tremendous age but to let her quietly pass away, or had he simply announced with a look a little more conventional that the end of the end had come? Were the other two women moving about to perform the offices that follow in such a case? It made me uneasy not to be nearer, as if I thought the doctor himself might carry away the papers with him. I bit my cigar hard as it came over me again that perhaps there were now no papers to carry!

I wandered about for an hour—for an hour and a half. I looked out for Miss Tita at one of the windows, having a vague idea that she might come there to give me some sign. Would she not see the red tip of my cigar moving about in the dark and feel that I wanted eminently to know what the doctor had said? I am afraid it is a proof my anxieties had made me gross that I should have taken in some degree for granted that at such an hour, in the midst of the greatest change that could take place in her life, they were uppermost also in poor Miss Tita's mind. My servant came down and spoke to me; he knew nothing save that the doctor had gone after a visit of half an hour. If he had stayed half an hour then Miss Bordereau was still alive: it could not have taken so much time as that to enunciate the contrary. I sent the man out of the house; there were moments when the sense of his curiosity annoyed me and this was one of them. *He* had been watching my cigar tip from an upper window, if Miss Tita had not; he could not know what I was after and I could not tell him, though I was conscious he had fantastic private theories about me which he thought fine and which I, had I known them, should have thought offensive.

I went upstairs at last but I ascended no higher than the *sala*. The door of Miss Bordereau's apartment was open, showing from the parlor the dimness of a poor candle. I went toward it with a light tread and at the same moment Miss Tita appeared and stood looking at me as I approached. "She's better—she's better," she said, even before I had asked. "The doctor has given her something; she woke up, came back to life while he was there. He says there is no immediate danger."

"No immediate danger? Surely he thinks her condition strange!"

"Yes, because she had been excited. That affects her dreadfully."

"It will do so again then, because she excites herself. She did so this afternoon."

"Yes, she mustn't come out any more," said Miss Tita, with one of her lapses into a deeper placidity.

"What is the use of making such a remark as that if you begin to rattle her about again the first time she bids you?"

"I won't—I won't do it any more."

"You must learn to resist her," I went on.

"Oh yes, I shall; I shall do so better if you tell me it's right."

"You mustn't do it for me; you must do it for yourself. It all comes back to you, if you are frightened."

"Well, I am not frightened now," said Miss Tita cheerfully. "She is very quiet."

"Is she conscious again—does she speak?"

"No, she doesn't speak, but she takes my hand. She holds it fast."

"Yes," I rejoined, "I can see what force she still has by the way she grabbed that picture this afternoon. But if she holds you fast how comes it that you are here?"

Miss Tita hesitated a moment; though her face was in deep shadow (she had her back to the light in the parlor and I had put down my own candle far off, near the door of the *sala*), I thought I saw her smile ingenuously. "I came on purpose—I heard your step."

"Why, I came on tiptoe, as inaudibly as possible."

"Well, I heard you," said Miss Tita.

"And is your aunt alone now?"

"Oh no, Olimpia is sitting there."

On my side I hesitated. "Shall we then step in there?" And I nodded at the parlor; I wanted more and more to be on the spot.

"We can't talk there—she will hear us."

I was on the point of replying that in that case we would sit silent, but I was too conscious that this would not do, as there was something I desired immensely to ask her. So I proposed that we should walk a little in the *sala*, keeping more at the other end, where we should not disturb the old lady. Miss Tita assented unconditionally; the doctor was coming again, she said, and she would be there to meet him at the door. We strolled through the fine superfluous hall, where on the marble floor—particularly as at first we said nothing—our footsteps were more audible than I had expected. When we reached the other end—the wide window, inveterately closed, connecting with the balcony that overhung the canal—I suggested that we should remain there, as she would see the doctor arrive still better. I opened the window and we passed out on the balcony. The air of the canal seemed even heavier, hotter, than that of the *sala*. The place was hushed and void; the quiet neighborhood had gone to sleep. A lamp, here and there, over the narrow black water, glimmered in double; the voice of a man going homeward singing, with his jacket on his shoulder and his hat on his ear, came to us from a distance. This did not prevent the scene from being very *comme il faut*, as Miss Bordereau had called it the first time I saw her. Presently a gondola passed along the canal with its slow rhythmical plash, and as we listened we watched it in silence. It did not stop, it did not carry the doctor, and after it had gone on I said to Miss Tita:

"And where are they now—the things that were in the trunk?"

"In the trunk?"

"That green box you pointed out to me in her room. You said her papers had been there; you seemed to imply that she had transferred them."

"Oh yes, they are not in the trunk," said Miss Tita.

"May I ask if you have looked?"

"Yes, I have looked—for you."

"How for me, dear Miss Tita? Do you mean you would have given them to me if you had found them?" I asked, almost trembling.

She delayed to reply and I waited. Suddenly she broke out, "I don't know what I would do—what I wouldn't!"

"Would you look again—somewhere else?"

She had spoken with a strange, unexpected emotion, and she went on in the same tone: "I can't—I can't—while she lies there. It isn't decent."

"No, it isn't decent," I replied, gravely. "Let the poor lady rest in peace." And the words, on my lips, were not hypocritical, for I felt reprimanded and shamed.

Miss Tita added in a moment, as if she had guessed this and were sorry for me, but at the same time wished to explain that I did drive her on or at least did insist too much: "I can't deceive her that way. I can't deceive her—perhaps on her deathbed."

"Heaven forbid I should ask you, though I have been guilty myself!"

"You have been guilty?"

"I have sailed under false colors." I felt now as if I must tell her that I had given her an invented name, on account of my fear that her aunt would have heard of me and would refuse to take me in. I explained this and also that I had really been a party to the letter written to them by John Cumnor months before.

She listened with great attention, looking at me with parted lips, and when I had made my confession she said, "Then your real name—what is it?" She repeated it over twice when I had told her, accompanying it with the exclamation "Gracious, gracious!" Then she added, "I like your own best."

"So do I," I said, laughing. "Ouf! it's a relief to get rid of the other."

"So it was a regular plot—a kind of conspiracy?"

"Oh, a conspiracy—we were only two," I replied, leaving out Mrs. Prest of course.

She hesitated; I thought she was perhaps going to say that we had been very base. But she remarked after a moment, in a candid, wondering way, "How much you must want them!"

"Oh, I do, passionately!" I conceded, smiling. And this chance made me go on, forgetting my compunction of a moment before. "How can she possibly have changed their place herself? How can she walk? How can she arrive at that sort of muscular exertion? How can she lift and carry things?"

"Oh, when one wants and when one has so much will!" said Miss Tita, as if she had thought over my question already herself and had simply had no choice but that answer—the idea that in the dead of night, or at some moment when the coast was clear, the old woman had been capable of a miraculous effort.

"Have you questioned Olimpia? Hasn't she helped her—hasn't she done it for her?" I asked; to which Miss Tita replied promptly and positively that their servant had had nothing to do with the matter, though without admitting definitely that she had spoken to her. It was as if she were a little shy, a little ashamed now of letting me see how much she had entered into my uneasiness and had me on her mind. Suddenly she said to me, without any immediate relevance:

"I feel as if you were a new person, now that you have got a new name."

"It isn't a new one; it is a very good old one, thank heaven!"

She looked at me a moment. "I do like it better."

"Oh, if you didn't I would almost go on with the other!"

"Would you really?"

I laughed again, but for all answer to this inquiry I said, "Of course if she can rummage about that way she can perfectly have burned them."

"You must wait—you must wait," Miss Tita moralized mournfully, and her tone ministered little to my patience, for it seemed after all to accept that wretched possibility. I would teach myself to wait, I declared nevertheless, because in the first place I could not do otherwise and in the second I had her promise, given me the other night, that she would help me.

"Of course if the papers are gone that's no use," she said, not as if she wished to recede, but only to be conscientious.

"Naturally. But if you could only find out!" I groaned, quivering again.

"I thought you said you would wait."

"Oh, you mean wait even for that?"

"For what then?"

"Oh, nothing," I replied, rather foolishly, being ashamed to tell her what had been implied in my submission to delay—the idea that she would do more than merely find out. I know not whether she guessed this; at all events she appeared to become aware of the necessity for being a little more rigid.

"I didn't promise to deceive, did I? I don't think I did."

"It doesn't much matter whether you did or not, for you couldn't!"

I don't think Miss Tita would have contested this even had she not been diverted by our seeing the doctor's gondola shoot into the little canal and approach the house. I noted that he came as fast as if he believed that Miss Bordereau was still in danger. We looked down at him while he disembarked and then went back into the *sala* to meet him. When he came up, however, I naturally left Miss Tita to go off with him alone, only asking her leave to come back later for news.

I went out of the house and took a long walk, as far as the Piazza, where my restlessness declined to quit me. I was unable to sit down (it was very late now but there were people still at the little tables in front of the cafés); I could only walk round and round, and I did so half a dozen times. I was uncomfortable, but it gave me a certain pleasure to have told Miss Tita who I really was. At last I took my way home again, slowly getting all but inextricably lost, as I did whenever I went out in

Venice: so that it was considerably past midnight when I reached my door. The *sala*, upstairs, was as dark as usual and my lamp as I crossed it found nothing satisfactory to show me. I was disappointed, for I had notified Miss Tita that I would come back for a report, and I thought she might have left a light there as a sign. The door of the ladies' apartment was closed, which seemed an intimation that my faltering friend had gone to bed, tired of waiting for me. I stood in the middle of the place, considering, hoping she would hear me and perhaps peep out, saying to myself too that she would never go to bed with her aunt in a state so critical; she would sit up and watch—she would be in a chair, in her dressing gown. I went nearer the door; I stopped there and listened. I heard nothing at all and at last I tapped gently. No answer came and after another minute I turned the handle. There was no light in the room; this ought to have prevented me from going in, but it had no such effect. If I have candidly narrated the importunities, the indelicacies, of which my desire to possess myself of Jeffrey Aspern's papers had rendered me capable I need not shrink from confessing this last indiscretion. I think it was the worst thing I did, yet there were extenuating circumstances. I was deeply though doubtless not disinterestedly anxious for more news of the old lady, and Miss Tita had accepted from me, as it were, a rendezvous which it might have been a point of honor with me to keep. It may be said that her leaving the place dark was a positive sign that she released me, and to this I can only reply that I desired not to be released.

The door of Miss Bordereau's room was open and I could see beyond it the faintness of a taper. There was no sound—my footstep caused no one to stir. I came further into the room; I lingered there with my lamp in my hand. I wanted to give Miss Tita a chance to come to me if she were with her aunt, as she must be. I made no noise to call her; I only waited to see if she would not notice my light. She did not, and I explained this (I found afterward I was right) by the idea that she had fallen asleep. If she had fallen asleep her aunt was not on her mind, and by explanation ought to have led me to go out as I had come. I must repeat again that it did not, for I found myself at the same moment thinking of something else. I had no definite purpose, no bad intention, but I felt myself held to the spot by an acute, though absurd, sense of opportunity. For what I could not have said, inasmuch as it was not in my mind that I might commit a theft. Even if it had been I was confronted with the evident fact that Miss Bordereau did not leave her secretary, her cupboard and the drawers of her tables gaping. I had no keys, no tools and no ambition to smash her furniture. Nonetheless it came to me that I was now, perhaps alone, unmolested, at the hour of temptation and secrecy, nearer to the tormenting treasure than I had ever been. I held up my lamp, let the light play on the different objects as if it could tell me something. Still there came no movement from the other room. If Miss Tita was sleeping she was sleeping sound. Was she doing so— generous creature—on purpose to leave me the field? Did she know I was there and was she just keeping quiet to see what I would do—what I *could* do? But what could I do, when it came to that? She herself knew even better than I how little.

I stopped in front of the secretary, looking at it very idiotically; for what had it to say to me after all? In the first place it was locked, and in the second it almost surely contained nothing in which I was interested. Ten to one the papers had been destroyed, and even if they had not been destroyed the old woman would not have put them in such a place as that after removing them from the green trunk—would not have transferred them, if she had the idea of their safety on her brain, from the better hiding place to the worse. The secretary was more conspicuous, more accessible in a room in which she could no longer mount guard. It opened with a key, but there was a little brass handle, like a button, as well; I saw this as I played my lamp over it. I did something more than this at that moment: I caught a glimpse of the possibility that Miss Tita wished me really to understand. If she did not wish me to understand, if she wished me to keep away, why had she not locked the door of communication between the sitting room and the sala? That would have been a definite sign that I was to leave them alone. If I did not leave them alone she meant me to come for a purpose—a purpose now indicated by the quick, fantastic idea that to oblige me she had unlocked the secretary. She had not left the key, but the lid would probably move if I touched the button. This theory fascinated me, and I bent over very close to judge. I did not propose to do anything, not even—not in the least—to let down the lid; I only wanted to test my theory, to see if the cover *would* move. I touched the button with my hand—a mere touch would tell me, and as I did so (it is embarrassing for me to relate it), I looked over my shoulder. It was a chance, an instinct, for I had not heard anything. I almost let my luminary drop and certainly I stepped back, straightening myself up at what I saw. Miss Bordereau stood there in her nightdress, in the doorway of her room, watching me; her hands were raised, she had lifted the everlasting curtain that covered half her face, and for the first, the last, the only time I beheld her extraordinary eyes. They glared at me, they made me horribly ashamed. I never shall forget her strange little bent white tottering figure, with its lifted head, her attitude, her expression; neither shall I forget the tone in which as I turned, looking at her, she hissed out passionately, furiously:

"Ah, you publishing scoundrel!"

I know not what I stammered, to excuse myself, to explain, but I went toward her, to tell her I meant no harm. She waved me off with her old hands, retreating before me in horror, and the next thing I knew she had fallen back with a quick spasm, as if death had descended on her, into Miss Tita's arms.

IX

I left Venice the next morning, as soon as I learnt that the old lady had not succumbed, as I feared at the moment, to the shock I had given her—the shock I may
also say she had given me. How in the world could I have supposed her capable of
getting out of bed by herself? I failed to see Miss Tita before going; I only saw the
donna, whom I entrusted with a note for her younger mistress. In this note I mentioned that I should be absent but for a few days. I went to Treviso, to Bassano, to
Castelfranco; I took walks and drives and looked at musty old churches with
ill-lighted pictures and spent hours seated smoking at the doors of cafés, where
there were flies and yellow curtains, on the shady side of sleepy little squares. In
spite of these pastimes, which were mechanical and perfunctory, I scantily enjoyed
my journey: there was too strong a taste of the disagreeable in my life. It had been
devilish awkward, as the young men say, to be found by Miss Bordereau in the dead
of night examining the attachment of her bureau, and it had not been less so to
have to believe for a good many hours afterward that it was highly probable I had
killed her. In writing to Miss Tita I attempted to minimize these irregularities, but
as she gave me no word of answer I could not know what impression I made upon
her. It rankled in my mind that I had been called a publishing scoundrel, for
certainly I did publish and certainly I had not been very delicate. There was a
moment when I stood convinced that the only way to make up for this latter fault
was to take myself away altogether on the instant; to sacrifice my hopes and relieve
the two poor women for ever of the oppression of my intercourse. Then I reflected
that I had better try a short absence first, for I must already have had a sense
(unexpressed and dim) that in disappearing completely it would not be merely my
own hopes that I should condemn to extinction. It would perhaps be sufficient if I
stayed away long enough to give the elder lady time to think she was rid of me. That
she would wish to be rid of me after this (if I was not rid of her) was now not to be
doubted: that nocturnal scene would have cured her of the disposition to put up
with my company for the sake of my dollars. I said to myself that after all I could not
abandon Miss Tita, and I continued to say this even while I observed that she quite
failed to comply with my earnest request (I had given her two or three addresses,
at little towns, *poste restante*) that she would let me know how she was getting on.
I would have made my servant write to me but that he was unable to manage a pen.

It struck me there was a kind of scorn in Miss Tita's silence (little disdainful as she had ever been), so that I was uncomfortable and sore. I had scruples about going back and yet I had others about not doing so, for I wanted to put myself on a better footing. The end of it was that I did return to Venice on the twelfth day, and as my gondola gently bumped against Miss Bordereau's steps a certain palpitation of suspense told me that I had done myself a violence in holding off so long.

I had faced about so abruptly that I had not telegraphed to my servant. He was therefore not at the station to meet me, but he poked out his head from an upper window when I reached the house. "They have put her into the earth, *la vecchia,*" he said to me in the lower hall, while he shouldered my valise, and he grinned and almost winked, as if he knew I should be pleased at the news.

"She's dead!" I exclaimed, giving him a very different look.

"So it appears, since they have buried her."

"It's all over? When was the funeral?"

"The other yesterday. But a funeral you could scarcely call it, signore: it was a dull little *passeggio* of two gondolas. *Poveretta!*" the man continued, referring apparently to Miss Tita. His conception of funerals was apparently that they were mainly to amuse the living.

I wanted to know about Miss Tita—how she was and where she was—but I asked him no more questions till we had got upstairs. Now that the fact had met me I took a bad view of it, especially of the idea that poor Miss Tita had had to manage by herself after the end. What did she know about arrangements, about the steps to take in such a case? *Poveretta* indeed! I could only hope that the doctor had given her assistance and that she had not been neglected by the old friends of whom she had told me, the little band of the faithful whose fidelity con- sisted in coming to the house once a year. I elicited from my servant that two old ladies and an old gentleman had in fact rallied round Miss Tita and had supported her (they had come for her in a gondola of their own) during the journey to the cemetery, the little red-walled island of tombs which lies to the north of the town, on the way to Murano. It appeared from these circumstances that the Misses Bor- dereau were Catholics, a discovery I had never made, as the old woman could not go to church and her niece, so far as I perceived, either did not or went only to early mass in the parish, before I was stirring. Certainly even the priests respected their seclusion; I had never caught the whisk of the *curato's* skirt. That evening, an hour later, I sent my servant down with five words written on a card, to ask Miss Tita if she would see me for a few moments. She was not in the house, where he had sought her, he told me when he came back, but in the garden walk- ing about to refresh herself and gathering flowers. He had found her there and she would be very happy to see me.

I went down and passed half an hour with poor Miss Tita. She had always had a look of musty mourning (as if she were wearing out old robes of sorrow that would

not come to an end), and in this respect there was no appreciable change in her appearance. But she evidently had been crying, crying a great deal—simply, satisfyingly, refreshingly, with a sort of primitive, retarded sense of loneliness and violence. But she had none of the formalism or the self-consciousness of grief, and I was almost surprised to see her standing there in the first dusk with her hands full of flowers, smiling at me with her reddened eyes. Her white face, in the frame of her mantilla, looked longer, leaner than usual. I had had an idea that she would be a good deal disgusted with me—would consider that I ought to have been on the spot to advise her, to help her; and, though I was sure there was no rancor in her composition and no great conviction of the importance of her affairs, I had prepared myself for a difference in her manner, for some little injured look, half familiar, half estranged, which should say to my conscience, "Well, you are a nice person to have professed things!" But historic truth compels me to declare that Tita Bordereau's countenance expressed unqualified pleasure in seeing her late aunt's lodger. That touched him extremely and he thought it simplified his situation until he found it did not. I was as kind to her that evening as I knew how to be, and I walked about the garden with her for half an hour. There was no explanation of any sort between us; I did not ask her why she had not answered my letter. Still less did I repeat what I had said to her in that communication: if she chose to let me suppose that she had forgotten the position in which Miss Bordereau surprised me that night and the effect of the discovery on the old woman I was quite willing to take it that way: I was grateful to her for not treating me as if I had killed her aunt.

We strolled and strolled and really not much passed between us save the recognition of her bereavement, conveyed in my manner and in a visible air that she had of depending on me now, since I let her see that I took an interest in her. Miss Tita had none of the pride that makes a person wish to preserve the look of independence; she did not in the least pretend that she knew at present what would become of her. I forbore to touch particularly on that, however, for I certainly was not prepared to say that I would take charge of her. I was cautious; not ignobly, I think, for I felt that her knowledge of life was so small that in her unsophisticated vision there would be no reason why—since I seemed to pity her—I should not look after her. She told me how her aunt had died, very peacefully at the last, and how everything had been done afterward by the care of her good friends (fortunately, thanks to me, she said, smiling, there was money in the house, and she repeated that when once the Italians like you they are your friends for life), and when we had gone into this she asked me about my *giro,* my impressions, the places I had seen. I told her what I could, making it up partly, I am afraid, as in my depression I had not seen much, and after she had heard me she exclaimed, quite as if she had forgotten her aunt and her sorrow, "Dear, dear, how much I should like to do such things—to take a little journey!" It came over me for the moment that I ought to propose some tour, say I would take her anywhere she liked, and I remarked at any rate that some excursion—to give her a change—

might be managed: we would think of it, talk it over. I said never a word to her about the Aspern documents; asked no questions as to what she had ascertained or what had otherwise happened with regard to them before Miss Bordereau's death. It was not that I was not on pins and needles to know, but that I thought it more decent not to betray my anxiety so soon after the catastrophe. I hoped she herself would say something, but she never glanced that way, and I thought this natural at the time. Later however, that night, it occurred to me that her silence was somewhat strange, for if she had talked of my movements, of anything so detached as the Giorgione at Castelfranco, she might have alluded to what she could easily remember was in my mind. It was not to be supposed that the emotion produced by her aunt's death had blotted out the recollection that I was interested in that lady's relics, and I fidgeted afterward as it came to me that her reticence might very possibly mean simply that nothing had been found. We separated in the garden (it was she who said she must go in); now that she was alone in the rooms I felt that (judged, at any rate, by Venetian ideas) I was on rather a different footing in regard to visiting her there. As I shook hands with her for goodnight I asked her if she had any general plan—had thought over what she had better do. "Oh yes, oh yes, but I haven't settled anything yet," she replied, quite cheerfully. Was her cheerfulness explained by the impression that I would settle for her?

I was glad the next morning that we had neglected practical questions, for this gave me a pretext for seeing her again immediately. There was a very practical question to be touched upon. I owed it to her to let her know formally that of course I did not expect her to keep me on as a lodger, and also to show some interest in her own tenure, what she might have on her hands in the way of a lease. But I was not destined, as it happened, to converse with her for more than an instant on either of these points. I sent her no message; I simply went down to the *sala* and walked to and fro there. I knew she would come out; she would very soon discover I was there. Somehow I preferred not to be shut up with her; gardens and big halls seemed better places to talk. It was a splendid morning, with something in the air that told of the waning of the long Venetian summer: a freshness from the sea which stirred the flowers in the garden and made a pleasant draft in the house, less shuttered and darkened now than when the old woman was alive. It was the beginning of autumn, of the end of the golden months. With this it was the end of my experiment—or would be in the course of half an hour, when I should really have learned that the papers had been reduced to ashes. After that there would be nothing left for me but to go to the station, for seriously (and as it struck me in the morning light) I could not linger there to act as guardian to a piece of middle-aged female helplessness. If she had not saved the papers wherein should I be indebted to her? I think I winced a little as I asked myself how much, if she *had* saved them, I should have to recognize and, as it were, to reward such a courtesy. Might not that circumstance after all saddle me with a guardianship? If this idea did not make me more uncomfortable as I walked up and down it was because I was convinced I had nothing to look to. If the old woman had not destroyed everything before she pounced upon me in the parlor she had done so afterward.

It took Miss Tita rather longer than I had expected to guess that I was there, but when at last she came out she looked at me without surprise. I said to her that I had been waiting for her and she asked why I had not let her know. I was glad the next day that I had checked myself before remarking that I had wished to see if a friendly intuition would not tell her: it became a satisfaction to me that I had not indulged in that rather tender joke. What I did say was virtually the truth—that I was too nervous, since I expected her now to settle my fate.

"Your fate?" said Miss Tita, giving me a queer look, and as she spoke I noticed a rare change in her. She was different from what she had been the evening before—less natural, less quiet. She had been crying the day before and she was not crying now, and yet she struck me as less confident. It was as if something had happened to her during the night, or at least as if she had thought of something that troubled her—something in particular that affected her relations with me, made them more embarrassing and complicated. Had she simply perceived that her aunt's not being there now altered my position?

"I mean about our papers. *Are* there any? You must know now."

"Yes, there are a great many; more than I supposed." I was struck with the way her voice trembled as she told me this.

"Do you mean that you have got them in there—and that I may see them?"

"I don't think you can see them," said Miss Tita, with an extraordinary expression of entreaty in her eyes, as if the dearest hope she had in the world now was that I would not take them from her. But how could she expect me to make such a sacrifice as that after all that had passed between us? What had I come back to Venice for but to see them, to take them? My delight at learning they were still in existence was such that if the poor woman had gone down on her knees to beseech me never to mention them again I would have treated the proceeding as a bad joke. "I have got them but I can't show them," she added.

"Not even to me? Ah, Miss Tita!" I groaned, with a voice of infinite remonstrance and reproach.

She colored and the tears came back to her eyes; I saw that it cost her a kind of anguish to take such a stand but that a dreadful sense of duty had descended upon her. It made me quite sick to find myself confronted with that particular obstacle; all the more that it appeared to me I had been extremely encouraged to leave it out of account. I almost considered that Miss Tita had assured me that if she had no greater hindrance than that—! "You don't mean to say you made her a deathbed promise? It was precisely against your doing anything of that sort that I thought I was safe. Oh, I would rather she had burned the papers outright than that!"

"No, it isn't a promise," said Miss Tita.

"Pray what is it then?"

She hesitated and then she said, "She tried to burn them, but I prevented it. She had hid them in her bed."

"In her bed?"

"Between the mattresses. That's where she put them when she took them out of the trunk. I can't understand how she did it, because Olimpia didn't help her. She tells me so and I believe her. My aunt only told her afterward so that she shouldn't touch the bed—anything but the sheets. So it was badly made," added Miss Tita, simply.

"I should think so! And how did she try to burn them?"

"She didn't try much; she was too weak, those last days. But she told me—she charged me. Oh, it was terrible! She couldn't speak after that night; she could only make signs."

"And what did you do?"

"I took them away. I locked them up."

"In the secretary?"

"Yes, in the secretary," said Miss Tita, reddening again.

"Did you tell her you would burn them?"

"No, I didn't—on purpose."

"On purpose to gratify me?"

"Yes, only for that."

"And what good will you have done me if after all you won't show them?"

"Oh, none; I know that—I know that."

"And did she believe you had destroyed them?"

"I don't know what she believed at the last. I couldn't tell—she was too far gone."

"Then if there was no promise and no assurance I can't see what ties you."

"Oh, she hated it so—she hated it so! She was so jealous. But here's the portrait—you may have that," Miss Tita announced, taking the little picture, wrapped up in the same manner in which her aunt had wrapped it, out of her pocket.

"I may have it—do you mean you give it to me?" I questioned, staring, as it passed into my hand.

"Oh yes."

"But it's worth money—a large sum."

"Well!" said Miss Tita, still with her strange look.

I did not know what to make of it, for it could scarcely mean that she wanted to bargain like her aunt. She spoke as if she wished to make me a present. "I can't take it from you as a gift," I said, "and yet I can't afford to pay you for it according to the ideas Miss Bordereau had of its value. She rated it at a thousand pounds."

"Couldn't we sell it?" asked Miss Tita.

"God forbid! I prefer the picture to the money."

"Well then keep it."

"You are very generous."

"So are you."

"I don't know why you should think so," I replied, and this was a truthful speech, for the singular creature appeared to have some very fine reference in her mind, which I did not in the least seize.

"Well, you have made a great difference for me," said Miss Tita.

I looked at Jeffrey Aspern's face in the little picture, partly in order not to look at that of my interlocutress, which had begun to trouble me, even to frighten me a little—it was so self-conscious, so unnatural. I made no answer to this last declaration; I only privately consulted Jeffrey Aspern's delightful eyes with my own (they were so young and brilliant, and yet so wise, so full of vision); I asked him what on earth was the matter with Miss Tita. He seemed to smile at me with friendly mockery, as if he were amused at my case. I had got into a pickle for him—as if he needed it! He was unsatisfactory, for the only moment since I had known him. Nevertheless, now that I held the little picture in my hand I felt that it would be a precious possession. "Is this a bribe to make me give up the papers?" I demanded in a moment, perversely. "Much as I value it, if I were to be obliged to choose, the papers are what I should prefer. Ah, but ever so much!"

"How can you choose—how can you choose?" Miss Tita asked, slowly, lamentably.

"I see! Of course there is nothing to be said, if you regard the interdiction that rests upon you as quite insurmountable. In this case it must seem to you that to part with them would be an impiety of the worst kind, a simple sacrilege!"

Miss Tita shook her head, full of her dolefulness. "You would understand if you had known her. I'm afraid," she quavered suddenly—"I'm afraid! She was terrible when she was angry."

"Yes, I saw something of that, that night. She was terrible. Then I saw her eyes. Lord, they were fine!"

"I see them—they stare at me in the dark!" said Miss Tita.

"You are nervous, with all you have been through."

"Oh yes, very—very!"

"You mustn't mind; that will pass away," I said, kindly. Then I added, resignedly, for it really seemed to me that I must accept the situation, "Well, so it is, and it can't be helped. I must renounce." Miss Tita, at this, looking at me, gave a low, soft moan, and I went on: "I only wish to heaven she had destroyed them; then there would be nothing more to say. And I can't understand why, with her ideas, she didn't."

"Oh, she lived on them!" said Miss Tita.

"You can imagine whether that makes me want less to see them," I answered, smiling. "But don't let me stand here as if I had it in my soul to tempt you to do anything base. Naturally you will understand I give up my rooms. I leave Venice immediately." And I took up my hat, which I had placed on a chair. We were still there rather awkwardly, on our feet, in the middle of the *sala*. She had left the door of the apartments open behind her but she had not led me that way.

A kind of spasm came into her face as she saw me take my hat. "Immediately—do you mean today?" The tone of the words was tragical—they were a cry of desolation.

"Oh no, not so long as I can be of the least service to you."

"Well, just a day or two more—just two or three days," she panted. Then controlling herself she added in another manner, "She wanted to say something to me—the last day—something very particular, but she couldn't."

"Something very particular?"

"Something more about the papers."

"And did you guess—have you any idea?"

"No, I have thought—but I don't know. I have thought all kinds of things."

"And for instance?"

"Well, that if you were a relation it would be different."

"If I were a relation?"

"If you were not a stranger. Then it would be the same for you as for me. Anything that is mine—would be yours, and you could do what you like. I couldn't prevent you—and you would have no responsibility."

She brought out this droll explanation with a little nervous rush, as if she were speaking words she had got by heart. They gave me an impression of subtlety and at first I failed to follow. But after a moment her face helped me to see further, and then a light came into my mind. It was embarrassing, and I bent my head over Jeffrey Aspern's portrait. What an odd expression was in his face! "Get out of it as you can, my dear fellow!" I put the picture into the pocket of my coat and said to Miss Tita, "Yes, I'll sell it for you. I shan't get a thousand pounds by any means, but I shall get something good."

She looked at me with tears in her eyes, but she seemed to try to smile as she remarked, "We can divide the money."

"No, no, it shall be all yours." Then I went on, "I think I know what your poor aunt wanted to say. She wanted to give directions that her papers should be buried with her."

Miss Tita appeared to consider this suggestion for a moment, after which she declared, with striking decision, "Oh no, she wouldn't have thought that safe!"

"It seems to me nothing could be safer."

"She had an idea that when people want to publish they are capable—" And she paused, blushing.

"Of violating a tomb? Mercy on us, what must she have thought of me!"

"She was not just, she was not generous!" Miss Tita cried with sudden passion.

The light that had come into my mind a moment before increased. "Ah, don't say that, for we *are* a dreadful race." Then I pursued, "If she left a will, that may give you some idea."

"I have found nothing of the sort—she destroyed it. She was very fond of me," Miss Tita added, incongruously. "She wanted me to be happy. And if any person should be kind to me—she wanted to speak of that."

I was almost awestricken at the astuteness with which the good lady found herself inspired, transparent astuteness as it was and sewn, as the phrase is, with white thread. "Depend upon it she didn't want to make any provision that would be agreeable to me."

"No, not to you but to me. She knew I should like it if you could carry out your idea. Not because she cared for you but because she did think of me," Miss Tita went on, with her unexpected, persuasive volubility. "You could see them—you could use them." She stopped, seeing that I perceived the sense of that conditional—stopped long enough for me to give some sign which I did not give. She must have been conscious, however, that though my face showed the greatest embarrassment that was ever painted on a human countenance it was not set as a stone, it was also full of compassion. It was a comfort to me a long time afterward to consider that she could not have seen in me the smallest symptom of disrespect. "I don't know what to do; I'm too tormented, I'm too ashamed!" she continued, with vehemence. Then turning away from me and burying her face in her hands she burst into a flood of tears. If she did not know what to do it may be imagined whether I did any better. I stood there dumb, watching her while her sobs resounded in the great empty hall. In a moment she was facing me again, with her streaming eyes. "I would give you everything—and she would understand, where she is—she would forgive me!"

"Ah, Miss Tita—ah, Miss Tita," I stammered, for all reply. I did not know what to do, as I say, but at a venture I made a wild, vague movement, in consequence of which I found myself at the door. I remember standing there and saying, "It wouldn't do—it wouldn't do!" pensively, awkwardly, grotesquely, while I looked away to the opposite end of the *sala* as if there were a beautiful view there. The next thing I remember is that I was downstairs and out of the house. My gondola was there and my gondolier, reclining on the cushions, sprang up as soon as he saw me. I jumped in and to his usual "*Dove commanda?*" I replied, in a tone that made him stare, "Anywhere, anywhere; out into the lagoon!"

He rowed me away and I sat there prostrate, groaning softly to myself, with my hat pulled over my face. What in the name of the preposterous did she mean if she did not mean to offer me her hand? That was the price—that was the price! And did she think I wanted it, poor deluded, infatuated, extravagant lady? My gondolier, behind me, must have seen my ears red as I wondered, sitting there under the fluttering *tenda,* with my hidden face, noticing nothing as we passed—wondered whether her delusion, her infatuation had been my own reckless work. Did she think I had made love to her, even to get the papers? I had not, I had not; I repeated that over to myself for an hour, for two hours, till I was wearied if not convinced. I don't know where my gondolier took me; we floated aimlessly about on the lagoon, with slow, rare strokes. At last I became conscious that we were near the Lido, far up, on the right hand, as you turn your back to Venice, and I made him put me ashore. I wanted to walk, to move, to shed some of my bewilderment. I crossed the narrow strip and got to the sea beach—I took my way toward Malamocco. But presently I flung myself down again on the warm sand, in the breeze, on the coarse dry grass. It took it out of me to think I had been so much at fault, that I had unwittingly but nonetheless deplorably trifled. But I had not given her cause—distinctly I had not. I had said to Mrs. Prest that I would make love to her, but it had been a joke without consequences and I had never said it to Tita Bordereau. I had been as kind as possible, because I really liked her, but since when had that become a crime where a woman of such an age and such an appearance was concerned? I am far from remembering clearly the succession of events and feelings during this long day of confusion, which I spent entirely in wandering about, without going home, until late at night; it only comes back to me that there were moments when I pacified my conscience and others when I lashed it into pain. I did not laugh all day—that I do recollect; the case, however it might have struck others, seemed to me so little amusing. It would have been better perhaps for me to feel the comic side of it. At any rate, whether I had given cause or not, it went without saying that I could not pay the price. I could not accept. I could not, for a bundle of tattered papers, marry a ridiculous, pathetic, provincial old woman. It was a proof that she did not think the idea would come to me, her having determined to suggest it herself in that practical, argumentative, heroic way, in which the timidity, however, had been so much more striking than the boldness that her reasons appeared to come first and her feelings afterward.

As the day went on I grew to wish that I had never heard of Aspern's relics, and I cursed the extravagant curiosity that had put John Cumnor on the scent of them. We had more than enough material without them and my predicament was the just punishment of that most fatal of human follies, our not having known when to stop. It was very well to say it was no predicament, that the way out was simple, that I had only to leave Venice by the first train in the morning, after writing a note to Miss Tita, to be placed in her hand as soon as I got clear of the house; for it was a strong sign that I was embarrassed that when I tried to make up the note in my mind in advance (I would put it on paper as soon as I got home, before going to bed), I could not think of anything but "How can I thank you for the rare confidence you have placed in me?" That would never do; it sounded exactly as if an acceptance were to follow. Of course I might go away without writing a word, but that would be brutal and my idea was still to exclude brutal solutions. As my confusion cooled I was lost in wonder at the importance I had attached to Miss Bordereau's crumpled scraps; the thought of them became odious to me and I was as vexed with the old witch for the superstition that had prevented her from destroying them as I was with myself for having already spent more money than I could afford in attempting to control their fate. I forget what I did, where I went after leaving the Lido and at what hour or with what recovery of composure I made my way back to my boat. I only know that in the afternoon, when the air was aglow with the sunset, I was standing before the church of Saints John and Paul and looking up at the small square-jawed face of Bartolommeo Colleoni, the terrible *condottiere* who sits so sturdily astride of his huge bronze horse, on the high pedestal on which Venetian gratitude maintains him. The statue is incomparable, the finest of all mounted figures, unless that of Marcus Aurelius, who rides benignant before the Roman Capitol, be finer: but I was not thinking of that; I only found myself staring at the triumphant captain as if he had an oracle on his lips. The western light shines into all his grimness at that hour and makes it wonderfully personal. But he continued to look far over my head, at the red immersion of another day—he had seen so many go down into the lagoon through the centuries—and if he were thinking of battles and stratagems, they were of a different quality from any I had to tell him of. He could not direct me what to do, gaze up at him as I might. Was it before this or after that I wandered about for an hour in the small canals, to the continued stupefaction of my gondolier, who had never seen me so restless and yet so void of a purpose and could extract from me no order but "Go anywhere—everywhere—all over the place"? He reminded me that I had not lunched and expressed therefore respectfully the hope that I would dine earlier. He had had long periods of leisure during the day, when I had left the boat and rambled, so that I was not obliged to consider him, and I told him that that day, for a change, I would touch no meat. It was an effect of poor Miss Tita's proposal, not altogether auspicious, that I had quite lost my appetite. I don't know why it happened that on this occasion I was more than ever struck with that queer air of sociability, of cousinship and family life, which makes up half the expression of Venice. Without streets and vehicles, the uproar of wheels, the brutality of horses, and with its little winding ways where people crowd together, where voices sound as in the corridors of a house, where the human step circulates as if it skirted the angles of furniture and shoes never wear out, the place has the character of an immense collective apartment, in which Piazza San Marco is the most ornamented corner and palaces and churches, for the rest, play the part of great divans of repose, tables of entertainment, expanses of decoration. And somehow the splendid common domicile, familiar, domestic and resonant, also resembles a theater, with actors clicking over bridges and, in straggling processions, tripping along *fondamentas*. As you sit in your gondola, the footways that in certain parts edge the canals assume to the eye the importance of a stage, meeting it at the same angle, and the Venetian figures, moving to and fro against the battered scenery of their little houses of comedy, strike you as members of an endless dramatic troupe.

I went to bed that night very tired, without being able to compose a letter to Miss Tita. Was this failure the reason why I became conscious the next morning as soon as I awoke of a determination to see the poor lady again the first moment she would receive me? That had something to do with it, but what had still more was the fact that during my sleep a very odd revulsion had taken place in my spirit. I found myself aware of this almost as soon as I opened my eyes; it made me jump out of my bed with the movement of a man who remembers that he has left the house door ajar or a candle burning under a shelf. Was I still in time to save my goods? That question was in my heart, for what had now come to pass was that in the unconscious cerebration of sleep I had swung back to a passionate appreciation of Miss Bordereau's papers. They were now more precious than ever and a kind of ferocity had come into my desire to possess them. The condition Miss Tita had attached to the possession of them no longer appeared an obstacle worth thinking of, and for an hour, that morning, my repentant imagination brushed it aside. It was absurd that I should be able to invent nothing; absurd to renounce so easily and turn away helpless from the idea that the only way to get hold of the papers was to unite myself to her for life. I would not unite myself and yet I would have them. I must add that by the time I sent down to ask if she would see me I had invented no alternative, though to do so I had had all the time that I was dressing. This failure was humiliating, yet what could the alternative be? Miss Tita sent back word that I might come, and as I descended the stairs and crossed the *sala* to her door—this time she received me in her aunt's forlorn parlor—I hoped she would not think my errand was to tell her I accepted her hand. She certainly would have made the day before the reflection that I declined it.

As soon as I came into the room I saw that she had drawn this inference, but I also saw something which had not been in my forecast. Poor Miss Tita's sense of her failure had produced an extraordinary alteration in her, but I had been too full of my literary concupiscence to think of that. Now I perceived it; I can scarcely tell how it startled me. She stood in the middle of the room with a face of mildness bent upon me, and her look of forgiveness, of absolution made her angelic. It beautified her; she was younger; she was not a ridiculous old woman. This optical trick gave her a sort of phantasmagoric brightness, and while I was still the victim of it I heard a whisper somewhere in the depths of my conscience: "Why not, after all—why not?" It seemed to me I was ready to pay the price. Still more distinctly, however, than the whisper I heard Miss Tita's own voice. I was so struck with the different effect she made upon me that at first I was not clearly aware of what she was saying; then I perceived she had bade me goodbye—she said something about hoping I should be very happy.

"Goodbye—goodbye?" I repeated, with an inflection interrogative and probably foolish.

I saw she did not feel the interrogation, she only heard the words; she had strung herself up to accepting our separation and they fell upon her ear as a proof. "Are you going today?" she asked. "But it doesn't matter, for whenever you go I shall not see you again. I don't want to." And she smiled strangely, with an infinite gentleness. She had never doubted that I had left her the day before in horror. How could she, since I had not come back before night to contradict, even as a simple form, such an idea? And now she had the force of soul—Miss Tita with force of soul was a new conception—to smile at me in her humiliation.

"What shall you do—where shall you go?" I asked.

"Oh, I don't know. I have done the great thing. I have destroyed the papers."

"Destroyed them?" I faltered.

"Yes, what was I to keep them for? I burned them last night, one by one, in the kitchen."

"One by one?" I repeated, mechanically.

"It took a long time—there were so many." The room seemed to go round me as she said this and a real darkness for a moment descended upon my eyes. When it passed, Miss Tita was there still, but the transfiguration was over and she had changed back to a plain, dingy, elderly person. It was in this character she spoke as she said, "I can't stay with you longer, I can't"; and it was in this character that she turned her back upon me, as I had turned mine upon her twenty-four hours before, and moved to the door of her room. Here she did what I had not done when I quitted her—she paused long enough to give me one look. I have never forgotten it and I sometimes still suffer from it, though it was not resentful. No, there was no resentment, nothing hard or vindictive in poor Miss Tita; for when, later, I sent her in exchange for the portrait of Jeffrey Aspern a larger sum of money than I had hoped to be able to gather for her, writing to her that I had sold the picture, she kept it with thanks; she never sent it back. I wrote to her that I had sold the picture, but I admitted to Mrs. Prest, at the time (I met her in London, in the autumn), that it hangs above my writing table. When I look at it my chagrin at the loss of the letters becomes almost intolerable.

THE TURN OF
THE SCREW

The story had held us, round the fire, sufficiently breathless, but except the obvious remark that it was gruesome, as on Christmas Eve in an old house a strange tale should essentially be, I remember no comment uttered till somebody happened to note it as the only case he had met in which such a visitation had fallen on a child. The case, I may mention, was that of an apparition in just such an old house as had gathered us for the occasion—an appearance, of a dreadful kind, to a little boy sleeping in the room with his mother and waking her up in the terror of it; waking her not to dissipate his dread and soothe him to sleep again, but to encounter also herself, before she had succeeded in doing so, the same sight that had shocked him. It was this observation that drew from Douglas—not immediately, but later in the evening—a reply that had the interesting consequence to which I call attention. Someone else told a story not particularly effective, which I saw he was not following. This I took for a sign that he had himself something to produce and that we should only have to wait. We waited in fact till two nights later, but that same evening, before we scattered, he brought out what was in his mind.

"I quite agree—in regard to Griffin's ghost, or whatever it was—that its appearing first to the little boy, at so tender an age, adds a particular touch. But it's not the first occurrence of its charming kind that I know to have been concerned with a child. If the child gives the effect another turn of the screw, what do you say to *two* children—?"

"We say of course," somebody exclaimed, "that two children give two turns! Also that we want to hear about them."

I can see Douglas there before the fire, to which he had got up to present his back, looking down at this converser with his hands in his pockets. "Nobody but me, till now, has ever heard. It's quite too horrible." This was naturally declared by several voices to give the thing the utmost price, and our friend, with quiet art, prepared his triumph by turning his eyes over the rest of us and going on: "It's beyond everything. Nothing at all that I know touches it."

"For sheer terror?" I remember asking.

He seemed to say it wasn't so simple as that; to be really at a loss how to qualify it. He passed his hand over his eyes, made a little wincing grimace. "For dreadful—dreadfulness!"

"Oh how delicious!" cried one of the women.

He took no notice of her; he looked at me, but as if, instead of me, he saw what he spoke of. "For general uncanny ugliness and horror and pain."

"Well then," I said, "just sit right down and begin."

He turned round to the fire, gave a kick to a log, watched it an instant. Then as he faced us again: "I can't begin. I shall have to send to town." There was a unanimous groan at this, and much reproach; after which, in his preoccupied way, he explained. "The story's written. It's in a locked drawer—it has not been out for years. I could write to my man and enclose the key; he could send down the packet as he finds it." It was to me in particular that he appeared to propound this—appeared almost to appeal for aid not to hesitate. He had broken a thickness of ice, the formation of many a winter; had had his reasons for a long silence. The others resented postponement, but it was just his scruples that charmed me. I adjured him to write by the first post and to agree with us for an early hearing; then I asked him if the experience in question had been his own. To this his answer was prompt. "Oh thank God, no!"

"And is the record yours? You took the thing down?"

"Nothing but the impression. I took that *here*"—he tapped his heart. "I've never lost it."

"Then your manuscript—?"

"Is in old faded ink and in the most beautiful hand." He hung fire again. "A woman's. She has been dead these twenty years. She sent me the pages in question before she died." They were all listening now, and of course there was somebody to be arch, or at any rate to draw the inference. But if he put the inference by without a smile it was also without irritation. "She was a most charming person, but she was ten years older than I. She was my sister's governess," he quietly said. "She was the most agreeable woman I've ever known in her position; she'd have been worthy of any whatever. It was long ago, and this episode was long before. I was at Trinity, and I found her at home on my coming down the second summer. I was much there that year—it was a beautiful one, and we had, in her off-hours, some strolls and talks in the garden—talks in which she struck me as awfully clever and nice. Oh yes, don't grin: I liked her extremely and am glad to this day to think she liked me too. If she hadn't she wouldn't have told me. She had never told any one. It wasn't simply that she said so, but that I knew she hadn't. I was sure; I could see. You'll easily judge why when you hear."

"Because the thing had been such a scare?"

He continued to fix me. "You'll easily judge," he repeated: "*you* will."

I fixed him too. "I see. She was in love."

He laughed for the first time. "You *are* acute. Yes, she was in love. That is she *had* been. That came out—she couldn't tell her story without its coming out. I saw it, and she saw I saw it, but neither of us spoke of it. I remember the time and the place—the corner of the lawn, the shade of the great beeches and the long hot summer afternoon. It wasn't a scene for a shudder, but oh—!" He quitted the fire and dropped back into his chair.

"You'll receive the packet Thursday morning?" I said.

"Probably not till the second post."

"Well then, after dinner—"

"You'll all meet me here?" He looked us round again. "Isn't anybody going?" It was almost the tone of hope.

"Everybody will stay!"

"*I* will—and *I* will!" cried the ladies whose departure had been fixed. Mrs. Griffin, however, expressed the need for a little more light. "Who was it she was in love with?"

"The story will tell," I took upon myself to reply.

"Oh I can't wait for the story!"

"The story *won't* tell," said Douglas; "not in any literal vulgar way."

"More's the pity then. That's the only way I ever understand."

"Won't *you* tell, Douglas?" somebody else required.

He sprang to his feet again. "Yes—tomorrow. Now I must go to bed. Goodnight." And, quickly catching up a candlestick, he left us slightly bewildered. From our end of the great brown hall we heard his step on the stair, whereupon Mrs. Griffin spoke. "Well, if I don't know who she was in love with I know who *he* was."

"She was ten years older," said her husband.

"*Raison de plus*—at that age! But it's rather nice, his long reticence."

"Forty years!" Griffin put in.

"With this outbreak at last."

"The outbreak," I returned, "will make a tremendous occasion of Thursday night"; and everyone so agreed with me that in the light of it we lost all attention for everything else. The last story, however incomplete and like the mere opening of a serial, had been told; we handshook and "candlestuck," as somebody said, and went to bed.

I knew the next day that a letter containing the key had, by the first post, gone off to his London apartments, but in spite of—or perhaps just on account of—the eventual diffusion of this knowledge we quite let him alone till after dinner, till such an hour of the evening in fact as might best accord with the kind of emotion on which our hopes were fixed. Then he became as communicative as we could desire, and indeed gave us his best reason for being so. We had it from him again before the fire in the hall, as we had had our mild wonders of the previous night. It appeared that the narrative he had promised to read us really required for a proper intelligence a few words of prologue. Let me say here distinctly, to have done with it, that this narrative, from an exact transcript of my own made much later, is what I shall presently give. Poor Douglas, before his death—when it was in sight—committed to me the manuscript that reached him on the third of these days and that, on the same spot, with immense effect, he began to read to our hushed little circle on the night of the fourth. The departing ladies who had said they would stay didn't, of course, thank heaven, stay: they departed, in consequence of arrangements made, in a rage of curiosity, as they professed, produced by the touches with which he had already worked us up. But that only made his little final auditory more compact and select, kept it, round the hearth, subject to a common thrill.

The first of these touches conveyed that the written statement took up the tale at a point after it had, in a manner, begun. The fact to be in possession of was therefore that his old friend, the youngest of several daughters of a poor country parson, had at the age of twenty, on taking service for the first time in the schoolroom, come up to London, in trepidation, to answer in person an advertisement that had already placed her in brief correspondence with the advertiser. This person proved, on her presenting herself for judgment at a house in Harley Street that impressed her as vast and imposing—this prospective patron proved a gentleman, a bachelor in the prime of life, such a figure as had never risen, save in a dream or an old novel, before a fluttered anxious girl out of a Hampshire vicarage. One could easily fix his type; it never, happily, dies out. He was handsome and bold and pleasant, off-hand and gay and kind. He struck her, inevitably, as gallant and splendid, but what took her most of all and gave her the courage she afterward showed was that he put the whole thing to her as a favor, an obligation he should gratefully incur. She figured him as rich, but as fearfully extravagant—saw him all in a glow of high fashion, of good looks, of expensive habits, of charming ways with women. He had for his town residence a big house filled with the spoils of travel and the trophies of the chase, but it was to his country home, an old family place in Essex, that he wished her immediately to proceed.

He had been left, by the death of his parents in India, guardian to a small nephew and a small niece, children of a younger, a military brother whom he had lost two years before. These children were, by the strangest of chances for a man in his position—a lone man without the right sort of experience or a grain of patience—very heavy on his hands. It had all been a great worry and, on his own part doubtless, a series of blunders, but he immensely pitied the poor chicks and had done all he could; had in particular sent them down to his other house, the proper place for them being of course the country, and kept them there from the first with the best people he could find to look after them, parting even with his own servants to wait on them and going down himself, whenever he might, to see how they were doing. The awkward thing was that they had practically no other relations and that his own affairs took up all his time. He had put them in possession of Bly, which was healthy and secure, and had placed at the head of their little establishment—but belowstairs only—an excellent woman, Mrs. Grose, whom he was sure his visitor would like and who had formerly been maid to his mother. She was now housekeeper and was also acting for the time as superintendent to the little girl, of whom, without children of her own, she was by good luck extremely fond. There were plenty of people to help, but of course the young lady who should go down as governess would be in supreme authority. She would also have, in holidays, to look after the small boy, who had been for a term at school—young as he was to be sent, but what else could be done?—and who, as the holidays were about to begin, would be back from one day to the other. There had been for the two children at first a young lady whom they had had the misfortune to lose. She had done for them quite beautifully—she was a most respectable person—till her death, the great awkwardness of which had, precisely, left no alternative but the school for little Miles. Mrs. Grose, since then, in the way of manners and things, had done as she could for Flora; and there were, further, a cook, a housemaid, a dairywoman, an old pony, an old groom and an old gardener, all likewise thoroughly respectable.

So far had Douglas presented his picture when some one put a question. "And what did the former governess die of? Of so much respectability?"

Our friend's answer was prompt. "That will come out. I don't anticipate."

"Pardon me—I thought that was just what you *are* doing."

"In her successor's place," I suggested, "I should have wished to learn if the office brought with it—"

"Necessary danger to life?" Douglas completed my thought. "She did wish to learn, and she did learn. You shall hear tomorrow what she learnt. Meanwhile of course the prospect struck her as slightly grim. She was young, untried, nervous: it was a vision of serious duties and little company, of really great loneliness. She hesitated—took a couple of days to consult and consider. But the salary offered much exceeded her modest measure, and on a second interview she faced the music, she engaged." And Douglas, with this, made a pause that, for the benefit of the company, moved me to throw in—

"The moral of which was of course the seduction exercised by the splendid young man. She succumbed to it."

He got up and, as he had done the night before, went to the fire, gave a stir to a log with his foot, then stood a moment with his back to us. "She saw him only twice."

"Yes, but that's just the beauty of her passion."

A little to my surprise, on this, Douglas turned round to me. "It *was* the beauty of it. There were others," he went on, "who hadn't succumbed. He told her frankly all his difficulty—that for several applicants the conditions had been prohibitive. They were somehow simply afraid. It sounded dull—it sounded strange; and all the more so because of his main condition."

"Which was—?"

"That she should never trouble him—but never, never: neither appeal nor complain nor write about anything; only meet all questions herself, receive all moneys from his solicitor, take the whole thing over and let him alone. She promised to do this, and she mentioned to me that when, for a moment, disburdened, delighted, he held her hand, thanking her for the sacrifice, she already felt rewarded."

"But was that all her reward?" one of the ladies asked.

"She never saw him again."

"Oh!" said the lady, which, as our friend immediately again left us, was the only other word of importance contributed to the subject till, the next night, by the corner of the hearth, in the best chair, he opened the faded red cover of a thin old-fashioned gilt-edged album. The whole thing took indeed more nights than one, but on the first occasion the same lady put another question. "What's your title?"

"I haven't one."

"Oh *I* have!" I said. But Douglas, without heeding me, had begun to read with a fine clearness that was like a rendering to the ear of the beauty of his author's hand.

I

I remember the whole beginning as a succession of flights and drops, a little see-saw of the right throbs and the wrong. After rising, in town, to met his appeal I had at all events a couple of very bad days—found all my doubts bristle again, felt indeed sure I had made a mistake. In this state of mind I spent the long hours of bumping swinging coach that carried me to the stopping place at which I was to be met by a vehicle from the house. This convenience, I was told, had been ordered, and I found, toward the close of the June afternoon, a commodious fly in waiting for me. Driving at that hour, on a lovely day, through a country the summer sweetness of which served as a friendly welcome, my fortitude revived and, as we turned into the avenue, took a flight that was probably but a proof of the point to which it had sunk. I suppose I had expected, or had dreaded, something so dreary that what greeted me was a good surprise. I remember as a thoroughly pleasant impression the broad clear front, its open windows and fresh curtains and the pair of maids looking out; I remember the lawn and the bright flowers and the crunch of my wheels on the gravel and the clustered treetops over which the rooks circled and cawed in the golden sky. The scene had a greatness that made a different affair from my own scant home, and there immediately appeared at the door, with a little girl in her hand, a civil person who dropped me as decent a curtsey as if I had been the mistress or a distinguished visitor. I had received in Harley Street a narrower notion of the place, and that, as I recalled it, made me think the proprietor still more of a gentleman, suggested that what I was to enjoy might be a matter beyond his promise.

I had no drop again till the next day, for I was carried triumphantly through the following hours by my introduction to the younger of my pupils. The little girl who accompanied Mrs. Grose affected me on the spot as a creature too charming not to make it a great fortune to have to do with her. She was the most beautiful child I had ever seen, and I afterward wondered why my employer hadn't made more of a point to me of this. I slept little that night—I was too much excited, and this astonished me too, I recollect, remained with me, adding to my sense of the liberality with which I was treated. The large impressive room, one of the best in the house, the great state bed, as I almost felt it, the figured full draperies, the long glasses in which, for the first time, I could see myself from head to foot, all struck me—like the wonderful appeal of my small charge—as so many things thrown in. It was thrown in as well, from the first moment, that I should get on with Mrs. Grose in a relation over which, on my way, in the coach, I fear I had rather brooded. The one appearance indeed that in this early outlook might have made me shrink again was that of her being so inordinately glad to see me. I felt within half an hour that she was so glad—stout simple plain clean wholesome woman—as to be positively on her guard against showing it too much. I wondered even then a little why she should wish *not* to show it, and that, with reflexion, with suspicion, might of course have made me uneasy.

But it was a comfort that there could be no uneasiness in a connection with anything so beatific as the radiant image of my little girl, the vision of whose angelic beauty had probably more than anything else to do with the restlessness that, before morning, made me several times rise and wander about my room to take in the whole picture and prospect; to watch from my open window the faint summer dawn, to look at such stretches of the rest of the house as I could catch, and to listen, while in the fading dusk the first birds began to twitter, for the possible recurrence of a sound or two, less natural and not without but within, that I had fancied I heard. There had been a moment when I believed I recognized, faint and far, the cry of a child; there had been another when I found myself just consciously starting as at the passage, before my door, of a light footstep. But these fancies were not marked enough not to be thrown off, and it is only in the light, or the gloom, I should rather say, of other and subsequent matters that they now come back to me. To watch, teach, "form" little Flora would too evidently be the making of a happy and useful life. It had been agreed between us downstairs that after this first occasion I should have her as a matter of course at night, her small white bed being already arranged, to that end, in my room. What I had undertaken was the whole care of her, and she had remained just this last time with Mrs. Grose only as an effect of our consideration for my inevitable strangeness and her natural timidity.

In spite of this timidity—which the child herself, in the oddest way in the world, had been perfectly frank and brave about, allowing it, without a sign of uncomfortable consciousness, with the deep sweet serenity indeed of one of Raphael's holy infants, to be discussed, to be imputed to her and to determine us—I felt quite sure she would presently like me. It was part of what I already liked Mrs. Grose herself for, the pleasure I could see her feel in my admiration and wonder as I sat at supper with four tall candles and with my pupil, in a high chair and a bib, brightly facing me between them over bread and milk. There were naturally things that in Flora's presence could pass between us only as prodigious and gratified looks, obscure and roundabout allusions.

"And the little boy—does he look like her? Is he too so very remarkable?"

One wouldn't, it was already conveyed between us, too grossly flatter a child. "Oh Miss, *most* remarkable. If you think well of this one!"—and she stood there with a plate in her hand, beaming at our companion, who looked from one of us to the other with placid heavenly eyes that contained nothing to check us.

"Yes, if I do—?"

"You *will* be carried away by the little gentleman!"

"Well, that, I think, is what I came for—to be carried away I'm afraid, however," I remember feeling the impulse to add, "I'm rather easily carried away. I was carried away in London!"

I can still see Mrs. Grose's broad face as she took this in. "In Harley Street?"

"In Harley Street."

"Well, Miss, you're not the first—and you won't be the last."

"Oh I've no pretensions," I could laugh, "to being the only one. My other pupil, at any rate, as I understand, comes back tomorrow?"

"Not tomorrow—Friday, Miss. He arrives, as you did, by the coach, under care of the guard, and is to be met by the same carriage."

I forthwith wanted to know if the proper as well as the pleasant and friendly thing wouldn't therefore be that on the arrival of the public conveyance I should await him with his little sister; a proposition to which Mrs. Grose assented so heartily that I somehow took her manner as a kind of comforting pledge—never falsified, thank heaven!—that we should on every question be quite at one. Oh she was glad I was there!

What I felt the next day was, I suppose, nothing that could be fairly called a reaction from the cheer of my arrival; it was probably at the most only a slight oppression produced by a fuller measure of the scale, as I walked round them, gazed up at them, took them in, of my new circumstances. They had, as it were, an extent and mass for which I had not been prepared and in the presence of which I found myself, freshly, a little scared not less than a little proud. Regular lessons, in this agitation, certainly suffered some wrong; I reflected that my first duty was, by the gentlest arts I could contrive, to win the child into the sense of knowing me. I spent the day with her out of doors; I arranged with her, to her great satisfaction, that it should be she, she only, who might show me the place. She showed it step by step and room by room and secret by secret, with droll delightful childish talk about it and with the result, in half an hour, of our becoming tremendous friends. Young as she was I was struck, throughout our little tour, with her confidence and courage, with the way, in empty chambers and dull corridors, on crooked staircases that made me pause and even on the summit of an old machicolated square tower that made me dizzy, her morning music, her disposition to tell me so many more things than she asked, rang out and led me on. I have not seen Bly since the day I left it, and I dare say that to my present older and more informed eyes it would show a very reduced importance. But as my little conductress, with her hair of gold and her frock of blue, danced before me round corners and pattered down passages, I had the view of a castle of romance inhabited by a rosy sprite, such a place as would somehow, for diversion of the young idea, take all color out of story books and fairy tales. Wasn't it just a storybook over which I had fallen a-doze and a-dream? No, it was a big ugly antique but convenient house, embodying a few features of a building still older, half-displaced and half-utilized, in which I had the fancy of our being almost as lost as a handful of passengers in a great drifting ship. Well, I was strangely at the helm!

II

This came home to me when, two days later, I drove over with Flora to meet, as Mrs. Grose said, the little gentleman, and all the more for an incident that, presenting itself the second evening, had deeply disconcerted me. The first day had been, on the whole, as I have expressed, reassuring, but I was to see it wind up to a change of note. The postbag that evening—it came late—contained a letter for me which, however, in the hand of my employer, I found to be composed but of a few words enclosing another, addressed to himself, with a seal still unbroken. "This, I recognize, is from the headmaster, and the headmaster's an awful bore. Read him please; deal with him; but mind you don't report. Not a word. I'm off!" I broke the seal with a great effort—so great a one that I was a long time coming to it; took the unopened missive at last up to my room and only attacked it just before going to bed. I had better have let it wait till morning, for it gave me a second sleepless night. With no counsel to take, the next day, I was full of distress, and it finally got so the better of me that I determined to open myself at least to Mrs. Grose.

"What does it mean? The child's dismissed his school."

She gave me a look that I remarked at the moment; then, visibly, with a quick blankness, seemed to try to take it back. "But aren't they all—?"

"Sent home—yes. But only for the holidays. Miles may never go back at all."

Consciously, under my attention, she reddened. "They won't take him?"

"They absolutely decline."

At this she raised her eyes, which she had turned from me; I saw them fill with good tears. "What has he done?"

I cast about, then I judged best simply to hand her my document—which, however, had the effect of making her, without taking it, simply put her hands behind her. She shook her head sadly. "Such things are not for me, Miss."

My counselor couldn't read! I winced at my mistake, which I attenuated as I could, and opened the letter again to repeat it to her; then, faltering in the act and folding it up once more, I put it back in my pocket. "Is he really *bad?*"

The tears were still in her eyes. "Do the gentlemen say so?"

"They go into no particulars. They simply express their regret that it should be impossible to keep him. That can have but one meaning." Mrs. Grose listened with dumb emotion; she forbore to ask me what this meaning might be, so that, presently, to put the thing with some coherence and with the mere aid of her presence to my own mind, I went on: "That he's an injury to the others."

At this, with one of the quick turns of simple folk, she suddenly flamed up. "Master Miles!—*him* an injury?"

There was such a flood of good faith in it that, though I had not yet seen the child, my very fears made me jump to the absurdity of the idea. I found myself, to meet my friend the better, offering it, on the spot, sarcastically. "To his poor little innocent mates!"

"It's too dreadful," cried Mrs. Grose, "to say such cruel things! Why he's scarce ten years old."

"Yes, yes, it would be incredible."

She was evidently grateful for such a profession. "See him, Miss, first. *Then* believe it!" I felt forthwith a new impatience to see him; it was the beginning of a curiosity that, all the next hours, was to deepen almost to pain. Mrs. Grose was aware, I could judge, of what she had produced in me, and she followed it up with assurance. "You might as well believe it of the little lady. Bless her," she added the next moment—"*look* at her!"

I turned and saw that Flora, whom, ten minutes before, I had established in the schoolroom with a sheet of white paper, a pencil and a copy of nice "round O's," now presented herself to view at the open door. She expressed in her little way an extraordinary detachment from disagreeable duties, looking at me, however, with a great childish light that seemed to offer it as a mere result of the affection she had conceived for my person, which had rendered necessary that she should follow me. I needed nothing more than this to feel the full force of Mrs. Grose's comparison, and, catching my pupil in my arms, covered her with kisses in which there was a sob of atonement.

Nonetheless, the rest of the day, I watched for further occasion to approach my colleague, especially as, toward evening, I began to fancy she rather sought to avoid me. I overtook her, I remember, on the staircase; we went down together and at the bottom I detained her, holding her there with a hand on her arm. "I take what you said to me at noon as a declaration that *you've* never known him to be bad."

She threw back her head; she had clearly by this time, and very honestly, adopted an attitude. "Oh never known him—I don't pretend *that!*"

I was upset again. "Then you *have* known him—?"

"Yes indeed, Miss, thank God!"

On reflexion I accepted this. "You mean that a boy who never is—?"

"Is no boy for *me!*"

I held her tighter. "You like them with the spirit to be naughty?" Then, keeping pace with her answer, "So do I!" I eagerly brought out. "But not to the degree to contaminate—"

"To contaminate?"—my big word left her at a loss.

I explained it. "To corrupt."

She stared, taking my meaning in; but it produced in her an odd laugh. "Are you afraid he'll corrupt *you?*" She put the question with such a fine bold humor that with a laugh, a little silly doubtless, to match her own, I gave way for the time to the apprehension of ridicule.

But the next day, as the hour for my drive approached, I cropped up in another place. "What was the lady who was here before?"

"The last governess? She was also young and pretty—almost as young and almost as pretty, Miss, even as you."

"Ah then I hope her youth and her beauty helped her!" I recollect throwing off. "He seems to like us young and pretty!"

"Oh he *did*," Mrs. Grose assented: "it was the way he liked everyone!" She had no sooner spoken indeed than she caught herself up. "I mean that's *his* way—the master's."

I was struck. "But of whom did you speak first?"

She looked blank, but she colored. "Why of *him*."

"Of the master?"

"Of who else?"

There was so obviously no one else that the next moment I had lost my impression of her having accidentally said more than she meant, and I merely asked what I wanted to know. "Did *she* see anything in the boy—?"

"That wasn't right? She never told me."

I had a scruple, but I overcame it. "Was she careful—particular?"

Mrs. Grose appeared to try to be conscientious. "About some things—yes."

"But not about all?"

Again she considered. "Well, Miss—she's gone. I won't tell tales."

"I quite understand your feeling," I hastened to reply, but I thought it after an instant not opposed to this concession to pursue: "Did she die here?"

"No—she went off."

I don't know what there was in this brevity of Mrs. Grose's that struck me as ambiguous. "Went off to die?" Mrs. Grose looked straight out of the window, but I felt that, hypothetically, I had a right to know what young persons engaged for Bly were expected to do. "She was taken ill, you mean, and went home?"

"She was not taken ill, so far as appeared, in this house. She left it, at the end of the year, to go home, as she said, for a short holiday, to which the time she had put in had certainly given her a right. We had then a young woman—a nursemaid who had stayed on and who was a good girl and clever; and *she* took the children altogether for the interval. But our young lady never came back, and at the very moment I was expecting her I heard from the master that she was dead."

I turned this over. "But of what?"

"He never told me! But please, Miss," said Mrs. Grose, "I must get to my work."

III

Her thus turning her back on me was fortunately not, for my just preoccupations, a snub that could check the growth of our mutual esteem. We met, after I had brought home little Miles, more intimately than ever on the ground of my stupefaction, my general emotion: so monstrous was I then ready to pronounce it that such a child as had now been revealed to me should be under an interdict. I was a little late on the scene of his arrival, and I felt, as he stood wistfully looking out for me before the door of the inn at which the coach had put him down, that I had seen him on the instant, without and within, in the great glow of freshness, the same positive fragrance of purity, in which I had from the first moment seen his little sister. He was incredibly beautiful, and Mrs. Grose had put her finger on it: everything but a sort of passion of tenderness for him was swept away by his presence. What I then and there took him to my heart for was something divine that I have never found to the same degree in any child—his indescribable little air of knowing nothing in the world but love. It would have been impossible to carry a bad name with a greater sweetness of innocence, and by the time I had got back to Bly with him I remained merely bewildered—so far, that is, as I was not outraged—by the sense of the horrible letter locked up in one of the drawers of my room. As soon as I could compass a private word with Mrs. Grose I declared to her that it was grotesque.

She promptly understood me. "You mean the cruel charge—?"

"It doesn't live an instant. My dear woman, *look* at him!"

She smiled at my pretension to have discovered his charm. "I assure you, Miss, I do nothing else! What will you say then?" she immediately added.

"In answer to the letter?" I had made up my mind. "Nothing at all."

"And to his uncle?"

I was incisive. "Nothing at all."

"And to the boy himself?"

I was wonderful. "Nothing at all."

She gave with her apron a great wipe to her mouth. "Then I'll stand by you. We'll see it out."

"We'll see it out!" I ardently echoed, giving her my hand to make it a vow.

She held me there a moment, then whisked up her apron again with her detached hand. "Would you mind, Miss, if I used the freedom—"

"To kiss me? No!" I took the good creature in my arms and after we had embraced like sisters felt still more fortified and indignant.

This at all events was for the time: a time so full that as I recall the way it went it reminds me of all the art I now need to make it a little distinct. What I look back at with amazement is the situation I accepted. I had undertaken, with my companion, to see it out, and I was under a charm apparently that could smooth away the extent and the far and difficult connections of such an effort. I was lifted aloft on a great wave of infatuation and pity. I found it simple, in my ignorance, my confusion and perhaps my conceit, to assume that I could deal with a boy whose education for the world was all on the point of beginning. I am unable even to remember at this day what proposal I framed for the end of his holidays and the resumption of his studies. Lessons with me indeed, that charming summer, we all had a theory that he was to have, but I now feel that for weeks the lessons must have been rather my own. I learnt something—at first certainly—that had not been one of the teachings of my small smothered life; learnt to be amused, and even amusing, and not to think for the morrow. It was the first time, in a manner, that I had known space and air and freedom, all the music of summer and all the mystery of nature. And then there was consideration—and consideration was sweet. Oh it was a trap—not designed but deep—to my imagination, to my delicacy, perhaps to my vanity—to whatever in me was most excitable. The best way to picture it all is to say that I was off my guard. They gave me so little trouble—they were of a gentleness so extraordinary. I used to speculate—but even this with a dim disconnectedness—as to how the rough future (for all futures are rough!) would handle them and might bruise them. They had the bloom of health and happiness, and yet, as if I had been in charge of a pair of little grandees, of princes of the blood, for whom everything, to be right, would have to be fenced about and ordered and arranged, the only form that in my fancy the afteryears could take for them was that of a romantic, a really royal extension of the garden and the park. It may be of course above all that what suddenly broke into this gives the previous time a charm of stillness—that hush in which something gathers or crouches. The change was actually like the spring of a beast.

In the first weeks the days were long; they often, at their finest, gave me what I used to call my own hour, the hour when, for my pupils, teatime and bedtime having come and gone, I had before my final retirement a small interval alone. Much as I liked my companions this hour was the thing in the day I liked most, and I liked it best of all when, as the light faded—or rather, I should say, the day lingered and the last calls of the last birds sounded, in a flushed sky, from the old trees—I could take a turn into the grounds and enjoy, almost with a sense of property that amused and flattered me, the beauty and dignity of the place. It was a pleasure at these moments to feel myself tranquil and justified; doubtless perhaps also to reflect that by my discretion, my quiet good sense and general high propriety, I was giving pleasure—if he ever thought of it!—to the person to whose pressure I had yielded. What I was doing was what he had earnestly hoped and directly asked of me, and that I *could*, after all, do it proved even a greater joy than I had expected. I dare say I fancied myself in short a remarkable young woman and took comfort in the faith that this would more publicly appear. Well, I needed to be remarkable to offer a front to the remarkable things that presently gave their first sign.

It was plump, one afternoon, in the middle of my very hour: the children were tucked away and I had come out for my stroll. One of the thoughts that, as I don't in the least shrink now from noting, used to be with me in these wanderings was that it would be as charming as a charming story suddenly to meet someone. Someone would appear there at the turn of a path and would stand before me and smile and approve. I didn't ask more than that—I only asked that he should *know*, and the only way to be sure he knew would be to see it, and the kind light of it, in his handsome face. That was exactly present to me—by which I mean the face was—when, on the first of these occasions, at the end of a long June day, I stopped short on emerging from one of the plantations and coming into view of the house. What arrested me on the spot—and with a shock much greater than any vision had allowed for—was the sense that my imagination had, in a flash, turned real. He did stand there!—but high up, beyond the lawn and at the very top of the tower to which, on that first morning, little Flora had conducted me. This tower was one of a pair—square incongruous crenellated structures—that were distinguished, for some reason, though I could see little difference, as the new and the old. They flanked opposite ends of the house and were probably architectural absurdities, redeemed in a measure indeed by not being wholly disengaged nor of a height too pretentious, dating, in their gingerbread antiquity, from a romantic revival that was already a respectable past. I admired them, had fancies about them, for we could all profit in a degree, especially when they loomed through the dusk, by the grandeur of their actual battlements, yet it was not at such an elevation that the figure I had so often invoked seemed most in place.

It produced in me, this figure, in the clear twilight, I remember, two distinct gasps of emotion, which were, sharply, the shock of my first and that of my second surprise. My second was a violent perception of the mistake of my first: the man who met my eyes was not the person I had precipitately supposed. There came to me thus a bewilderment of vision of which, after these years, there is no living view that I can hope to give. An unknown man in a lonely place is a permitted object of fear to a young woman privately bred, and the figure that faced me was—a few more seconds assured me—as little anyone else I knew as it was the image that had been in my mind. I had not seen it in Harley Street—I had not seen it anywhere. The place moreover, in the strangest way in the world, had on the instant and by the very fact of its appearance become a solitude. To me at least, making my statement here with a deliberation with which I have never made it, the whole feeling of the moment returns. It was as if, while I took in, what I did take in, all the rest of the scene had been stricken with death. I can hear again, as I write, the intense hush in which the sounds of evening dropped. The rooks stopped cawing in the golden sky and the friendly hour lost for the unspeakable minute all its voice. But there was no other change in nature, unless indeed it were a change that I saw with a stranger sharpness. The gold was still in the sky, the clearness in the air, and the man who looked at me over the battlements was as definite as a picture in a frame. That's how I thought, with extraordinary quickness, of each person he might have been and that he wasn't. We were confronted across our distance quite long enough for me to ask myself with intensity who then he was and to feel, as an effect of my inability to say, a wonder that in a few seconds more became intense.

The great question, or one of these, is afterward, I know, with regard to certain matters, the question of how long they have lasted. Well, this matter of mine, think what you will of it, lasted while I caught at a dozen possibilities, none of which made a difference for the better, that I could see, in there having been in the house—and for how long, above all?—a person of whom I was in ignorance. It lasted while I just bridled a little with the sense of how my office seemed to require that there should be no such ignorance and no such person. It lasted while this visitant, at all events—and there was a touch of the strange freedom, as I remember, in the sign of familiarity of his wearing no hat—seemed to fix me, from his position, with just the question, just the scrutiny through the fading light, that his own presence provoked. We were too far apart to call to each other, but there was a moment at which, at shorter range, some challenge between us, breaking the hush, would have been the right result of our straight mutual stare. He was in one of the angles, the one away from the house, very erect, as it struck me, and with both hands on the ledge. So I saw him as I see the letters I form on this page, then, exactly, after a minute, as if to add to the spectacle, he slowly changed his place—passed, looking at me hard all the while, to the opposite corner of the platform. Yes, it was intense to me that during this transit he never took his eyes from me, and I can see at this moment the way his hand, as he went, moved from one of the crenellations to the next. He stopped at the other corner, but less long, and even as he turned away still markedly fixed me. He turned away; that was all I knew.

IV

It was not that I didn't wait, on this occasion, for more, since I was as deeply rooted as shaken. Was there a "secret" at Bly—a mystery of Udolpho or an insane, an unmentionable relative kept in unsuspected confinement? I can't say how long I turned it over, or how long, in a confusion of curiosity and dread, I remained where I had had my collision; I only recall that when I re-entered the house darkness had quite closed in. Agitation, in the interval, certainly had held me and driven me, for I must, in circling about the place, have walked three miles, but I was to be later on so much more overwhelmed that this mere dawn of alarm was a comparatively human chill. The most singular part of it in fact—singular as the rest had been— was the part I became, in the hall, aware of in meeting Mrs. Grose. This picture comes back to me in the general train—the impression, as I received it on my return, of the wide white paneled space, bright in the lamplight and with its portraits and red carpet, and of the good surprised look of my friend, which immediately told me she had missed me. It came to me straightway, under her contact, that, with plain heartiness, mere relieved anxiety at my appearance, she knew nothing whatever that could bear upon the incident I had there ready for her. I had not suspected in advance that her comfortable face would pull me up, and I somehow measured the importance of what I had seen by my thus finding myself hesitate to mention it. Scarce anything in the whole history seems to me so odd as this fact that my real beginning of fear was one, as I may say, with the instinct of sparing my companion. On the spot, accordingly, in the pleasant hall and with her eyes on me, I, for a reason that I couldn't then have phrased, achieved an inward revolution—offered a vague pretext for my lateness and, with the plea of the beauty of the night and of the heavy dew and wet feet, went as soon as possible to my room.

Here it was another affair; here, for many days after, it was a queer affair enough. There were hours, from day to day—or at least there were moments, snatched even from clear duties—when I had to shut myself up to think. It wasn't so much yet that I was more nervous than I could bear to be as that I was remarkably afraid of becoming so, for the truth I had now to turn over was simply and clearly the truth that I could arrive at no account whatever of the visitor with whom I had been so inexplicably and yet, as it seemed to me, so intimately concerned. It took me little time to see that I might easily sound, without forms of enquiry and without exciting remark, any domestic complication. The shock I had suffered must have sharpened all my senses; I felt sure, at the end of three days and as the result of mere closer attention, that I had not been practiced upon by the servants nor made the object of any "game." Of whatever it was that I knew nothing was known around me. There was but one sane inference: someone had taken a liberty rather monstrous. That was what, repeatedly, I dipped into my room and locked the door to say to myself. We had been, collectively, subject to an intrusion; some unscrupulous traveler, curious in old houses, had made his way in unobserved, enjoyed the prospect from the best point of view and then stolen out as he came. If he had given me such a bold hard stare, that was but a part of his indiscretion. The good thing, after all, was that we should surely see no more of him.

This was not so good a thing, I admit, as not to leave me to judge that what, essentially, made nothing else much signify was simply my charming work. My charming work was just my life with Miles and Flora, and through nothing could I so like it as through feeling that to throw myself into it was to throw myself out of my trouble. The attraction of my small charges was a constant joy, leading me to wonder afresh at the vanity of my original fears, the distaste I had begun by entertaining for the probable gray prose of my office. There was to be no gray prose, it appeared, and no long grind, so how could work not be charming that presented itself as daily beauty? It was all the romance of the nursery and the poetry of the schoolroom. I don't mean by this of course that we studied only fiction and verse; I mean that I can express not otherwise the sort of interest my companions inspired. How can I describe that except by saying that instead of growing deadly used to them—and it's a marvel for a governess: I call the sisterhood to witness!—I made constant fresh discoveries. There was one direction, assuredly, in which these discoveries stopped: deep obscurity continued to cover the region of the boy's conduct at school. It had been promptly given me, I have noted, to face that mystery without a pang. Perhaps even it would be nearer the truth to say that—without a word—he himself had cleared it up. He had made the whole charge absurd. My conclusion bloomed there with the real rose-flush of his innocence: he was only too fine and fair for the little horrid unclean school world, and he had paid a price for it. I reflected acutely that the sense of such individual differences, such superiorities of quality, always, on the part of the majority—which could include even stupid sordid headmasters—turns infallibly to the vindictive.

Both the children had a gentleness—it was their only fault, and it never made Miles a muff—that kept them (how shall I express it?) almost impersonal and certainly quite unpunishable. They were like those cherubs of the anecdote who had—morally at any rate—nothing to whack! I remember feeling with Miles in especial as if he had had, as it were, nothing to call even an infinitesimal history. We expect of a small child scant enough "antecedents," but there was in this beautiful little boy something extraordinarily sensitive, yet extraordinarily happy, that, more than in any creature of his age I have seen, struck me as beginning anew each day. He had never for a second suffered. I took this as a direct disproof of his having really been chastised. If he had been wicked he would have "caught" it, and I should have caught it by the rebound—I should have found the trace, should have felt the wound and the dishonor. I could reconstitute nothing at all, and he was therefore an angel. He never spoke of his school, never mentioned a comrade or a master, and I, for my part, was quite too much disgusted to allude to them. Of course I was under the spell, and the wonderful part is that, even at the time, I perfectly knew I was. But I gave myself up to it; it was an antidote to any pain, and I had more pains than one. I was in receipt in these days of disturbing letters from home, where things were not going well. But with this joy of my children what things in the world mattered? That was the question I used to put to my scrappy retirements. I was dazzled by their loveliness.

There was a Sunday—to get on—when it rained with such force and for so many hours that there could be no procession to church, in consequence of which, as the day declined, I had arranged with Mrs. Grose that, should the evening show improvement, we would attend together the late service. The rain happily stopped, and I prepared for our walk, which, through the park and by the good road to the village, would be a matter of twenty minutes. Coming downstairs to meet my colleague in the hall, I remembered a pair of gloves that had required three stitches and that had received them—with a publicity perhaps not edifying—while I sat with the children at their tea, served on Sundays, by exception, in that cold clean temple of mahogany and brass, the "grownup" dining room. The gloves had been dropped there, and I turned in to recover them. The day was gray enough, but the afternoon light still lingered, and it enabled me, on crossing the threshold, not only to recognize, on a chair near the wide window, then closed, the articles I wanted, but to become aware of a person on the other side of the window and looking straight in. One step into the room had sufficed; my vision was instantaneous; it was all there. The person looking straight in was the person who had already appeared to me. He appeared thus again with I won't say greater distinctness, for that was impossible, but with a nearness that represented a forward stride in our intercourse and made me, as I met him, catch my breath and turn cold. He was the same—he was the same, and seen, this time, as he had been seen before, from the waist up, the window, though the dining room was on the ground floor, not going down to the terrace on which he stood. His face was close to the glass, yet the effect of this better view was, strangely, just to show me how intense the former had been. He remained but a few seconds—long enough to convince me he also saw and recognized, but it was as if I had been looking at him for years and had known him always. Something, however, happened this time that had not happened before; his stare into my face, through the glass and across the room, was as deep and hard as then, but it quitted me for a moment during which I could still watch it, see it fix successively several other things. On the spot there came to me the added shock of a certitude that it was not for me he had come. He had come for someone else.

The flash of this knowledge—for it was knowledge in the midst of dread—produced in me the most extraordinary effect, starting, as I stood there, a sudden vibration of duty and courage. I say courage because I was beyond all doubt already far gone. I bounded straight out of the door again, reached that of the house, got in an instant upon the drive and, passing along the terrace as fast as I could rush, turned a corner and came full in sight. But it was in sight of nothing now—my visitor had vanished. I stopped, almost dropped, with the real relief of this, but I took in the whole scene—I gave him time to reappear. I call it time, but how long was it? I can't speak to the purpose today of the duration of these things. That kind of measure must have left me: they couldn't have lasted as they actually appeared to me to last. The terrace and the whole place, the lawn and the garden beyond it, all I could see of the park, were empty with a great emptiness. There were shrubberies and big trees, but I remember the clear assurance I felt that none of them concealed him. He was there or was not there: not there if I didn't see him. I got hold of this, then, instinctively, instead of returning as I had come, went to the window. It was confusedly present to me that I ought to place myself where he had stood. I did so: I applied my face to the pane and looked, as he had looked, into the room. As if, at this moment, to show me exactly what his range had been, Mrs. Grose, as I had done for himself just before, came in from the hall. With this I had the full image of a repetition of what had already occurred. She saw me as I had seen my own visitant; she pulled up short as I had done; I gave her something of the shock that I had received. She turned white, and this made me ask myself if I had blanched as much. She stared, in short, and retreated just on *my* lines, and I knew she had then passed out and come round to me and that I should presently meet her. I remained where I was, and while I waited I thought of more things than one. But there's only one I take space to mention. I wondered why *she* should be scared.

V

Oh she let me know as soon as, round the corner of the house, she loomed again into view. "What in the name of goodness is the matter—?" She was now flushed and out of breath.

I said nothing till she came quite near. "With me?" I must have made a wonderful face. "Do I show it?"

"You're as white as a sheet. You look awful."

I considered; I could meet on this, without scruple, any degree of innocence. My need to respect the bloom of Mrs. Grose's had dropped, without a rustle, from my shoulders, and if I wavered for the instant it was not with what I kept back. I put out my hand to her and she took it; I held her hard a little, liking to feel her close to me. There was a kind of support in the shy heave of her surprise. "You came for me for church, of course, but I can't go."

"Has anything happened?"

"Yes. You must know now. Did I look very queer?"

"Through this window? Dreadful!"

"Well," I said, "I've been frightened." Mrs. Grose's eyes expressed plainly that *she* had no wish to be, yet also that she knew too well her place not to be ready to share with me any marked inconvenience. Oh it was quite settled that she *must* share! "Just what you saw from the dining room a minute ago was the effect of that. What *I* saw—just before—was much worse."

Her hand tightened. "What was it?"

"An extraordinary man. Looking in."

"What extraordinary man?"

"I haven't the least idea."

Mrs. Grose gazed round us in vain. "Then where is he gone?"

"I know still less."

"Have you see him before?"

"Yes—once. On the old tower."

She could only look at me harder. "Do you mean he's a stranger?"

"Oh very much!"

"Yet you didn't tell me?"

"No—for reasons. But now that you 've guessed—"

Mrs. Grose's round eyes encountered this charge. "Ah I haven't guessed!" she said very simply. "How can I if *you* don't imagine?"

"I don't in the very least."

"You've seen him nowhere but on the tower?"

"And on this spot just now."

Mrs. Grose looked round again. "What was he doing on the tower?"

"Only standing there and looking down at me."

She thought a minute. "Was he a gentleman?"

I found I had no need to think. "No." She gazed in deeper wonder. "No."

"Then nobody about the place? Nobody from the village?"

"Nobody—nobody. I didn't tell you, but I made sure."

She breathed a vague relief: this was, oddly, so much to the good. It only went indeed a little way. "But if he isn't a gentleman—"

"What *is* he? He's a horror."

"A horror?"

"He's—God help me if I know *what* he is!"

Mrs. Grose looked round once more; she fixed her eyes on the duskier distance and then, pulling herself together, turned to me with full inconsequence. "It's time we should be at church."

"Oh I'm not fit for church!"

"Won't it do you good?"

"It won't do *them*—!" I nodded at the house.

"The children?"

"I can't leave them now."

"You're afraid—"

I spoke boldly "I'm afraid of *him.*"

Mrs. Grose's large face showed me, at this, for the first time, the far-away faint glimmer of a consciousness more acute: I somehow made out in it the delayed dawn of an idea I myself had not given her and that was as yet quite obscure to me. It comes back to me that I thought instantly of this as something I could get from her, and I felt it to be connected with the desire she presently showed to know more. "When was it—on the tower?"

"About the middle of the month. At this same hour."

"Almost at dark," said Mrs. Grose.

"Oh no, not nearly. I saw him as I see you."

"Then how did he get in?"

"And how did he get out?" I laughed. "I had no opportunity to ask him! This evening, you see," I pursued, "he has not been able to get in."

"He only peeps?"

"I hope it will be confined to that!" She had now let go my hand; she turned away a little. I waited an instant; then I brought out: "Go to church. Goodbye. I must watch."

Slowly she faced me again. "Do you fear for them?"

We met in another long look. "Don't *you?*" Instead of answering she came nearer to the window and, for a minute, applied her face to the glass. "You see how he could see," I meanwhile went on.

She didn't move. "How long was he here?"

"Till I came out. I came to meet him."

Mrs. Grose at last turned round, and there was still more in her face. "*I* couldn't have come out."

"Neither could I!" I laughed again. "But I did come. I've my duty."

"So have I mine," she replied, after which she added: What's he like?"

"I've been dying to tell you. But he's like nobody."

"Nobody?" she echoed.

"He has no hat." Then seeing in her face that she already, in this, with a deeper dismay, found a touch of picture, I quickly added stroke to stroke. "He has red hair, very red, close-curling, and a pale face, long in shape, with straight good features and little rather queer whiskers that are as red as his hair. His eyebrows are somehow darker; they look particularly arched and as if they might move a good deal. His eyes are sharp, strange—awfully, but I only know clearly that they're rather small and very fixed. His mouth's wide, and his lips are thin, except for his little whiskers he's quite clean-shaven. He gives me a sort of sense of looking like an actor."

"An actor!" It was impossible to resemble one less, at least, than Mrs. Grose at that moment.

"I've never seen one, but so I suppose them. He's tall, active, erect," I continued, "but never—no, never!—a gentleman."

My companion's face had blanched as I went on; her round eyes started and her mild mouth gaped. "A gentleman?" she gasped, confounded, stupefied: "a gentleman *he?*"

"You know him then?"

She visibly tried to hold herself. "But he *is* handsome?"

I saw the way to help her. "Remarkably!"

"And dressed—?"

"In somebody's clothes. They're smart, but they're not his own."

She broke into a breathless affirmative groan. "They're the master's!"

I caught it up. "You *do* know him?"

She faltered but a second. "Quint!" she cried.

"Quint?"

"Peter Quint—his own man, his valet, when he was here!"

"When the master was?"

Gaping still, but meeting me, she pieced it all together. "He never wore his hat, but he did wear—well, there were waistcoats missed! They were both here—last year. Then the master went, and Quint was alone."

I followed, but halting a little. "Alone?"

"Alone with *us*." Then as from a deeper depth, "In charge," she added.

"And what became of him?"

She hung fire so long that I was still more mystified. "He went too," she brought out at last.

"Went where?"

Her expression, at this, became extraordinary. "God knows where! He died."

"Died?" I almost shrieked.

She seemed fairly to square herself, plant herself more firmly to express the wonder of it. "Yes. Mr. Quint's dead."

VI

It took of course more than that particular passage to place us together in presence of what we had now to live with as we could, my dreadful liability to impressions of the order so vividly exemplified, and my companion's knowledge henceforth—a knowledge half consternation and half compassion—of that liability. There had been this evening, after the revelation that left me for an hour so prostrate—there had been for either of us no attendance on any service but a little service of tears and vows, of prayers and promises, a climax to the series of mutual challenges and pledges that had straightway ensued on our retreating together to the schoolroom and shutting ourselves up there to have everything out. The result of our having everything out was simply to reduce our situation to the last rigor of its elements. She herself had seen nothing, not the shadow of a shadow, and nobody in the house but the governess was in the governess's plight, yet she accepted without directly impugning my sanity the truth as I gave it to her, and ended by showing me on this ground an awestricken tenderness, a deference to my more than questionable privilege, of which the very breath has remained with me as that of the sweetest of human charities.

What was settled between us accordingly that night was that we thought we might bear things together, and I was not even sure that in spite of her exemption it was she who had the best of the burden. I knew at this hour, I think, as well as I knew later, what I was capable of meeting to shelter my pupils, but it took me some time to be wholly sure of what my honest comrade was prepared for to keep terms with so stiff an agreement. I was queer company enough—quite as queer as the company I received; but as I trace over what we went through I see how much common ground we must have found in the one idea that, by good fortune, *could* steady us. It was the idea, the second movement, that led me straight out, as I may say, of the inner chamber of my dread. I could take the air in the court, at least, and there Mrs. Grose could join me. Perfectly can I recall now the particular way strength came to me before we separated for the night. We had gone over and over every feature of what I had seen.

"He was looking for someone else, you say—someone who was not you?"

"He was looking for little Miles." A portentous clearness now possessed me. "*That's* whom he was looking for."

"But how do you know?"

"I know, I know, I know!" My exaltation grew. "And *you* know, my dear!"

She didn't deny this, but I required, I felt, not even so much telling as that. She took it up again in a moment. "What if *he* should see him?"

"Little Miles? That's what he wants!"

She looked immensely scared again. "The child?"

"Heaven forbid! The man. He wants to appear to *them*." That he might was an awful conception, and yet somehow I could keep it at bay, which moreover, as we lingered there, was what I succeeded in practically proving. I had an absolute certainty that I should see again what I had already seen, but something within me said that by offering myself bravely as the sole subject of such experience, by accepting, by inviting, by surmounting it all, I should serve as an expiatory victim and guard the tranquility of the rest of the household. The children in special I should thus fence about and absolutely save. I recall one of the last things I said that night to Mrs. Grose.

"It does strike me that my pupils have never mentioned—!"

She looked at me hard as I musingly pulled up. "His having been here and the time they were with him?"

"The time they were with him, and his name, his presence, his history, in any way. They've never alluded to it."

"Oh the little lady doesn't remember. She never heard or knew."

"The circumstances of his death?" I thought with some intensity. "Perhaps not. But Miles would remember—Miles would know."

"Ah don't try him!" broke from Mrs. Grose.

I returned her the look she had given me. "Don't be afraid." I continued to think. "It *is* rather odd."

"That he has never spoken of him?"

"Never by the least reference. And you tell me they were 'great friends.' "

"Oh it wasn't *him!*" Mrs. Grose with emphasis declared. "It was Quint's own fancy. To play with him, I mean—to spoil him." She paused a moment; then she added: "Quint was much too free."

This gave me, straight from my vision of his face—*such* a face!—a sudden sickness of disgust. "Too free with *my* boy?"

"Too free with everyone!"

I forbore for the moment to analyze this description further than by the reflexion that a part of it applied to several of the members of the household, of the half-dozen maids and men who were still of our small colony. But there was everything, for our apprehension, in the lucky fact that no discomfortable legend, no perturbation of scullions, had ever, within any one's memory, attached to the kind old place. It had neither bad name nor ill fame, and Mrs. Grose, most apparently, only desired to cling to me and to quake in silence. I even put her, the very last thing of all, to the test. It was when, at midnight, she had her hand on the schoolroom door to take leave. "I *have it* from you then—for it's of great importance—that he was definitely and admittedly bad?"

"Oh not admittedly. *I* knew it—but the master didn't."

"And you never told him?"

"Well, he didn't like tale-bearing—he hated complaints. He was terribly short with anything of that kind, and if people were all right to *him*—"

"He wouldn't be bothered with more?" This squared well enough with my impression of him: he was not a trouble-loving gentleman, nor so very particular perhaps about some of the company he himself kept. All the same, I pressed my informant. "I promise you *I* would have told!"

She felt my discrimination. "I dare say I was wrong. But really I was afraid."

"Afraid of what?"

"Of things that man could do. Quint was so clever—he was so deep."

I took this in still more than I probably showed. "You weren't afraid of anything else? Not of his effect—?"

"His effect?" she repeated with a face of anguish and waiting while I faltered.

"On innocent little precious lives. They were in your charge."

"No, they weren't in mine!" she roundly and distressfully returned. "The master believed in him and placed him here because he was supposed not to be quite in health and the country air so good for him. So he had everything to say. Yes"—she let me have it—"even about *them.*"

"Them—that creature?" I had to smother a kind of howl. "And you could bear it?"

"No. I couldn't—and I can't now!" And the poor woman burst into tears.

A rigid control, from the next day, was, as I have said, to follow them; yet how often and how passionately, for a week, we came back together to the subject! Much as we had discussed it that Sunday night, I was, in the immediate later hours in especial—for it may be imagined whether I slept—still haunted with the shadow of something she had not told me. I myself had kept back nothing, but there was a word Mrs. Grose had kept back. I was sure moreover by morning that this was not from a failure of frankness, but because on every side there were fears. It seems to me indeed, in raking it all over, that by the time the morrow's sun was high I had restlessly read into the facts before us almost all the meaning they were to receive from subsequent and more cruel occurrences. What they gave me above all was just the sinister figure of the living man—the dead one would keep a while!—and of the months he had continuously passed at Bly, which, added up, made a formidable stretch. The limit of this evil time had arrived only when, on the dawn of a winter's morning, Peter Quint was found, by a laborer going to early work, stone dead on the road from the village: a catastrophe explained—superficially at least—by a visible wound to his head; such a wound as might have been produced (and as, on the final evidence, *had* been) by a fatal slip, in the dark and after leaving the public-house, on the steepish icy slope, a wrong path altogether, at the bottom of which he lay. The icy slope, the turn mistaken at night and in liquor, accounted for much—practically, in the end and after the inquest and boundless chatter, for everything, but there had been matters in his life, strange passages and perils, secret disorders, vices more than suspected, that would have accounted for a good deal more.

I scarce know how to put my story into words that shall be a credible picture of my state of mind, but I was in these days literally able to find a joy in the extraordinary flight of heroism the occasion demanded of me. I now saw that I had been asked for a service admirable and difficult, and there would be a greatness in letting it be seen—oh in the right quarter!—that I could succeed where many another girl might have failed. It was an immense help to me—I confess I rather applaud myself as I look back!—that I saw my response so strongly and so simply. I was there to protect and defend the little creatures in the world the most bereaved and the most loveable, the appeal of whose helplessness had suddenly become only too explicit, a deep constant ache of one's own engaged affection. We were cut off, really, together; we were united in our danger. They had nothing but me, and I—well, I had *them*. It was in short a magnificent chance. This chance presented itself to me in an image richly material. I was a screen—I was to stand before them. The more I saw the less they would. I began to watch them in a stifled suspense, a disguised tension, that might well, had it continued too long, have turned to something like madness. What saved me, as I now see, was that it turned to another matter altogether. It didn't last as suspense—it was superseded by horrible proofs. Proofs, I say, yes—from the moment I really took hold.

This moment dated from an afternoon hour that I happened to spend in the grounds with the younger of my pupils alone. We had left Miles indoors, on the red cushion of a deep window seat; he had wished to finish a book, and I had been glad to encourage a purpose so laudable in a young man whose only defect was a certain ingenuity of restlessness. His sister, on the contrary, had been alert to come out, and I strolled with her half an hour, seeking the shade, for the sun was still high and the day exceptionally warm. I was aware afresh with her, as we went, of how, like her brother, she contrived—it was the charming thing in both children—to let me alone without appearing to drop me and to accompany me without appearing to oppress. They were never importunate and yet never listless. My attention to them all really went to seeing them amuse themselves immensely without me: this was a spectacle they seemed actively to prepare and that employed me as an active admirer. I walked in a world of their invention—they had no occasion whatever to draw upon mine, so that my time was taken only with being for them some remarkable person or thing that the game of the moment required and that was merely, thanks to my superior, my exalted stamp, a happy and highly distinguished sinecure. I forget what I was on the present occasion; I only remember that I was something very important and very quiet and that Flora was playing very hard. We were on the edge of the lake, and, as we had lately begun geography, the lake was the Sea of Azof.

Suddenly, amid these elements, I became aware that on the other side of the Sea of Azof we had an interested spectator. The way this knowledge gathered in me was the strangest thing in the world—the strangest, that is, except the very much stranger in which it quickly merged itself. I had sat down with a piece of work—for I was something or other that could sit—on the old stone bench which overlooked the pond, and in this position I began to take in with certitude and yet without direct vision the presence, a good way off, of a third person. The old trees, the thick shrubbery, made a great and pleasant shade, but it was all suffused with the brightness of the hot still hour. There was no ambiguity in anything; none whatever at least in the conviction I from one moment to another found myself forming as to what I should see straight before me and across the lake as a consequence of raising my eyes. They were attached at this juncture to the stitching in which I was engaged, and I can feel once more the spasm of my effort not to move them till I should so have steadied myself as to be able to make up my mind what to do. There was an alien object in view—a figure whose right of presence I instantly and passionately questioned. I recollect counting over perfectly the possibilities, reminding myself that nothing was more natural for instance than the appearance of one of the men about the place, or even of a messenger, a postman or a tradesman's boy, from the village. That reminder had as little effect on my practical certitude as I was conscious—still even without looking—of its having upon the character and attitude of our visitor. Nothing was more natural than that these things should be the other things they absolutely were not.

Of the positive identity of the apparition I would assure myself as soon as the small clock of my courage should have ticked out the right second; meanwhile, with an effort that was already sharp enough, I transferred my eyes straight to little Flora, who, at the moment, was about ten yards away. My heart had stood still for an instant with the wonder and terror of the question whether she too would see, and I held my breath while I waited for what a cry from her, what some sudden innocent sign either of interest or of alarm, would tell me. I waited, but nothing came; then in the first place—and there is something more dire in this, I feel, than in anything I have to relate—I was determined by a sense that within a minute all spontaneous sounds from her had dropped, and in the second by the circumstance that also within the minute she had, in her play, turned her back to the water. This was her attitude when I at last looked at her—looked with the confirmed conviction that we were still, together, under direct personal notice. She had picked up a small flat piece of wood which happened to have in it a little hole that had evidently suggested to her the idea of sticking in another fragment that might figure as a mast and make the thing a boat. This second morsel, as I watched her, she was very markedly and intently attempting to tighten in its place. My apprehension of what she was doing sustained me so that after some seconds I felt I was ready for more. Then I again shifted my eyes—I faced what I had to face.

VII

I got hold of Mrs. Grose as soon after this as I could, and I can give no intelligible account of how I fought out the interval. Yet I still hear myself cry as I fairly threw myself into her arms: "They *know*—it's too monstrous: they know, they know!"

"And what on earth—?" I felt her incredulity as she held me.

"Why all that *we* know—and heaven knows what more besides!" Then as she released me I made it out to her, made it out perhaps only now with full coherency even to myself. "Two hours ago, in the garden"—I could scarce articulate—"Flora *saw!*"

Mrs. Grose took it as she might have taken a blow in the stomach. "She has told you?" she panted.

"Not a word—that's the horror. She kept it to herself! The child of eight, *that* child!" Unutterable still for me was the stupefaction of it.

Mrs. Grose, of course, could only gape the wider. "Then how do you know?"

"I was there—I saw with my eyes: saw she was perfectly aware."

"Do you mean aware of *him?*"

"No—of *her.*" I was conscious as I spoke that I looked prodigious things, for I got the slow reflexion of them in my companion's face. "Another person—this time, but a figure of quite as unmistakeable horror and evil: a woman in black, pale and dreadful—with such an air also, and such a face!—on the other side of the lake. I was there with the child—quiet for the hour, and in the midst of it she came."

"Came how—from where?"

"From where they come from! She just appeared and stood there—but not so near."

"And without coming nearer?"

"Oh for the effect and the feeling she might have been as close as you!"

My friend, with an odd impulse, fell back a step. "Was she someone you've never seen?"

"Never. But someone the child has. Someone *you* have." Then to show how I had thought it all out: "My predecessor—the one who died."

"Miss Jessel?"

"Miss Jessel. You don't believe me?" I pressed.

She turned right and left in her distress. "How can you be sure?"

This drew from me, in the state of my nerves, a flash of impatience. "Then ask Flora—*she's* sure!" But I had no sooner spoken than I caught myself up. "No, for God's sake *don't!* She'll say she isn't—she'll lie!"

Mrs. Grose was not too bewildered instinctively to protest. "Ah how *can* you?"

"Because I'm clear. Flora doesn't want me to know."

"It's only then to spare you."

"No, no—there are depths, depths! The more I go over it the more I see in it, and the more I see in it the more I fear. I don't know what I *don't* see, what I *don't* fear!"

Mrs. Grose tried to keep up with me. "You mean you're afraid of seeing her again?"

"Oh no, that's nothing—now!" Then I explained. "It's of *not* seeing her."

But my companion only looked wan. "I don't understand."

"Why, it's that the child may keep it up—and that the child assuredly *will*—without my knowing it."

At the image of this possibility Mrs. Grose for a moment collapsed, yet presently to pull herself together again as from the positive force of the sense of what, should we yield an inch, there would really be to give way to. "Dear, dear—we must keep our heads! And after all, if she doesn't mind it—!" She even tried a grim joke. "Perhaps she likes it!"

"Like *such* things—a scrap of an infant!"

"Isn't it just a proof of her blest innocence?" my friend bravely enquired.

She brought me, for the instant, almost round. "Oh we must clutch at *that*—we must cling to it! If it isn't a proof of what you say, it's a proof of—God knows what! For the woman's a horror of horrors."

Mrs. Grose, at this, fixed her eyes a minute on the ground, then at last raising them, "Tell me how you know," she said.

"Then you admit it's what she was?" I cried.

"Tell me how you know," my friend simply repeated.

"Know? By seeing her! By the way she looked."

"At you, do you mean—so wickedly?"

"Dear me, no—I could have borne that. She gave me never a glance. She only fixed the child."

Mrs. Grose tried to see it. "Fixed her?"

"Ah with such awful eyes!"

She stared at mine as if they might really have resembled them. "Do you mean of dislike?"

"God help us, no. Of something much worse."

"Worse than dislike?"—this left her indeed at a loss.

"With a determination—indescribable. With a kind of fury of intention."

I made her turn pale. "Intention?"

"To get hold of her." Mrs. Grose—her eyes just lingering on mine—gave a shudder and walked to the window, and while she stood there looking out I completed my statement. "*That's* what Flora knows."

After a little she turned round. "The person was in black, you say?"

"In mourning—rather poor, almost shabby. But—yes—with extraordinary beauty." I now recognized to what I had at last, stroke by stroke, brought the victim of my confidence, for she quite visibly weighed this. "Oh handsome—very, very," I insisted; "wonderfully handsome. But infamous."

She slowly came back to me. "Miss Jessel—*was* infamous." She once more took my hand in both her own, holding it as tight as if to fortify me against the increase of alarm I might draw from this disclosure. "They were both infamous," she finally said.

So for a little we faced it once more together, and I found absolutely a degree of help in seeing it now so straight. "I appreciate," I said, "the great decency of your not having hitherto spoken, but the time has certainly come to give me the whole thing." She appeared to assent to this, but still only in silence, seeing which I went on: "I must have it now. Of what did she die? Come, there was something between them."

"There was everything."

"In spite of the difference—?"

"Oh of their rank, their condition"—she brought it woefully out. "*She* was a lady."

I turned it over; I again saw. "Yes—she was a lady."

"And he so dreadfully below," said Mrs. Grose.

I felt that I doubtless needn't press too hard, in such company, on the place of a servant in the scale, but there was nothing to prevent an acceptance of my companion's own measure of my predecessor's abasement. There was a way to deal with that, and I dealt; the more readily for my full vision—on the evidence—of our employer's late clever good-looking "own" man; impudent, assured, spoiled, depraved. "The fellow was a hound."

Mrs. Grose considered as if it were perhaps a little a case for a sense of shades. "I've never seen one like him. He did what he wished."

"With *her?*"

"With them all."

It was as if now in my friend's own eyes Miss Jessel had again appeared. I seemed at any rate for an instant to trace their evocation of her as distinctly as I had seen her by the pond, and I brought out with decision: "It must have been also what *she* wished!"

Mrs. Grose's face signified that it had been indeed, but she said at the same time: "Poor woman—she paid for it!"

"Then you do know what she died of?" I asked.

"No—I know nothing. I wanted not to know; I was glad enough I didn't, and I thanked heaven she was well out of this!"

"Yet you had then your idea—"

"Of her real reason for leaving? Oh yes—as to that. She couldn't have stayed. Fancy it here—for a governess! And afterward I imagined—and I still imagine. And what I imagine is dreadful."

"Not so dreadful as what *I* do," I replied, on which I must have shown her—as I was indeed but too conscious—a front of miserable defeat. It brought out again all her compassion for me, and at the renewed touch of her kindness my power to resist broke down. I burst, as I had the other time made her burst, into tears; she took me to her motherly breast, where my lamentation overflowed. "I don't do it!" I sobbed in despair; "I don't save or shield them! It's far worse than I dreamed. They're lost"

VIII

What I had said to Mrs. Grose was true enough: there were in the matter I had put before her depths and possibilities that I lacked resolution to sound, so that when we met once more in the wonder of it we were of a common mind about the duty of resistance to extravagant fancies. We were to keep our heads if we should keep nothing else—difficult indeed as that might be in the face of all that, in our prodigious experience, seemed least to be questioned. Late that night, while the house slept, we had another talk in my room; when she went all the way with me as to its being beyond doubt that I had seen exactly what I had seen. I found that to keep her thoroughly in the grip of this I had only to ask her how, if I had "made it up," I came to be able to give, of each of the persons appearing to me, a picture disclosing, to the last detail, their special marks—a portrait on the exhibition of which she had instantly recognized and named them. She wished, of course—small blame to her!—to sink the whole subject, and I was quick to assure her that my own interest in it had now violently taken the form of a search for the way to escape from it. I closed with her cordially on the article of the likelihood that with recurrence—for recurrence we took for granted—I should get used to my danger; distinctly professing that my personal exposure had suddenly become the least of my discomforts. It was my new suspicion that was intolerable, and yet even to this complication the later hours of the day had brought a little ease.

On leaving her, after my first outbreak, I had of course returned to my pupils, associating the right remedy for my dismay with that sense of their charm which I had already recognized as a resource I could positively cultivate and which had never failed me yet. I had simply, in other words, plunged afresh into Flora's special society and there become aware—it was almost a luxury!—that she could put her little conscious hand straight upon the spot that ached. She had looked at me in sweet speculation and then had accused me to my face of having "cried." I had supposed the ugly signs of it brushed away, but I could literally—for the time at all events—rejoice, under this fathomless charity, that they had not entirely disappeared. To gaze into the depths of blue of the child's eyes and pronounce their loveliness a trick of premature cunning was to be guilty of a cynicism in preference to which I naturally preferred to abjure my judgement and, so far as might be, my agitation. I couldn't abjure for merely wanting to, but I could repeat to Mrs. Grose—as I did there, over and over, in the small hours—that with our small friends' voices in the air, their pressure on one's heart and their fragrant faces against one's cheek, everything fell to the ground but their incapacity and their beauty. It was a pity that, somehow, to settle this once for all, I had equally to re-enumerate the signs of subtlety that, in the afternoon, by the lake, had made a miracle of my show of self-possession. It was a pity to be obliged to re-investigate the certitude of the moment itself and repeat how it had come to me as a revelation that the inconceivable communion I then surprised must have been for both parties a matter of habit. It was a pity I should have had to quaver out again the reasons for my not having, in my delusion, so much as questioned that the little girl saw our visitant even as I actually saw Mrs. Grose herself, and that she wanted, by just so much as she did thus see, to make me suppose she didn't, and at the same time, without showing anything, arrive at a guess as to whether I myself did! It was a pity I needed to recapitulate the portentous little activities by which she sought to divert my attention—the perceptible increase of movement, the greater intensity of play, the singing, the gabbling of nonsense and the invitation to romp.

Yet if I had not indulged, to prove there was nothing in it, in this review, I should have missed the two or three dim elements of comfort that still remained to me. I shouldn't for instance have been able to asseverate to my friend that I was certain—which was so much to the good—that *I* at least had not betrayed myself. I shouldn't have been prompted, by stress of need, by desperation of mind—I scarce know what to call it—to invoke such further aid to intelligence as might spring from pushing my colleague fairly to the wall. She had told me, bit by bit, under pressure, a great deal, but a small shifty spot on the wrong side of it all still sometimes brushed my brow like the wing of a bat, and I remember how on this occasion—for the sleeping house and the concentration alike of our danger and our watch seemed to help—I felt the importance of giving the last jerk to the curtain. "I don't believe anything so horrible," I recollect saying; "no, let us put it definitely, my dear, that I don't. But if I did, you know, there's a thing I should require now, just without sparing you the least bit more—oh not a scrap, come!—to get out of you. What was it you had in mind when, in our distress, before Miles came back, over the letter from his school, you said, under my insistence, that you didn't pretend for him he hadn't literally *ever* been 'bad'? He has *not,* truly, 'ever,' in these weeks that I myself have lived with him and so closely watched him; he has been an imperturbable little prodigy of delightful loveable goodness. Therefore you might perfectly have made the claim for him if you had not, as it happened, seen an exception to take. What was your exception, and to what passage in your personal observation of him did you refer?"

It was a straight question enough, but levity was not our note, and in any case I had before the gray dawn admonished us to separate got my answer. What my friend had had in mind proved immensely to the purpose. It was neither more nor less than the particular fact that for a period of several months Quint and the boy had been perpetually together. It was indeed the very appropriate item of evidence of her having ventured to criticize the propriety, to hint at the incongruity, of so close an alliance, and even to go so far on the subject as a frank overture to Miss Jessel would take her. Miss Jessel had, with a very high manner about it, requested her to mind her business, and the good woman had on this directly approached little Miles. What she had said to him, since I pressed, was that *she* liked to see young gentlemen not forget their station.

I pressed again, of course, the closer for that. "You reminded him that Quint was only a base menial?"

"As you might say! And it was his answer, for one thing, that was bad."

"And for another thing?" I waited. "He repeated your words to Quint?"

"No, not that. It's just what he *wouldn't!*" she could still impress on me. "I was sure, at any rate," she added, "that he didn't. But he denied certain occasions."

"What occasions?"

"When they had been about together quite as if Quint were his tutor—and a very grand one—and Miss Jessel only for the little lady. When he had gone off with the fellow, I mean, and spent hours with him."

"He then prevaricated about it—he said he hadn't?" Her assent was clear enough to cause me to add in a moment: "I see. He lied."

"Oh!" Mrs. Grose mumbled. This was a suggestion that it didn't matter, which indeed she backed up by a further remark. "You see, after all, Miss Jessel didn't mind. She didn't forbid him."

I considered. "Did he put that to you as a justification?"

At this she dropped again. "No, he never spoke of it."

"Never mentioned her in connection with Quint?"

She saw, visibly flushing, where I was coming out. "Well, he didn't show anything. He denied," she repeated; "he denied."

Lord, how I pressed her now! "So that you could see he knew what was between the two wretches?"

"I don't know—I don't know!" the poor woman wailed.

"You do know, you dear thing," I replied; "only you haven't my dreadful boldness of mind, and you keep back, out of timidity and modesty and delicacy, even the impression that in the past, when you had, without my aid, to flounder about in silence, most of all made you miserable. But I shall get it out of you yet! There was something in the boy that suggested to you," I continued, "his covering and concealing their relation."

"Oh he couldn't prevent—"

"Your learning the truth? I dare say! But, heavens," I fell, with vehemence, a-thinking, "what it shows that they must, to that extent, have succeeded in making of him!"

"Ah nothing that's not nice *now!*" Mrs. Grose lugubriously pleaded.

"I don't wonder you looked queer," I persisted, "when I mentioned to you the letter from his school!"

"I doubt if I looked as queer as you!" she retorted with homely force. "And if he was so bad then as that comes to, how is he such an angel now?"

"Yes indeed—and if he was a fiend at school! How, how, how? Well," I said in my torment, "you must put it to me again, though I shall not be able to tell you for some days. Only put it to me again!" I cried in a way that made my friend stare. "There are directions in which I mustn't for the present let myself go." Meanwhile I returned to her first example—the one to which she had just previously referred—of the boy's happy capacity for an occasional slip. "If Quint—on your remonstrance at the time you speak of—was a base menial, one of the things Miles said to you, I find myself guessing, was that you were another." Again her admission was so adequate that I continued: "And you forgave him that?"

"Wouldn't *you*?"

"Oh yes!" And we exchanged there, in the stillness, a sound of the oddest amusement. Then I went on: "At all events, while he was with the man—"

"Miss Flora was with the woman. It suited them all!"

It suited me too, I felt, only too well; by which I mean that it suited exactly the particular deadly view I was in the very act of forbidding myself to entertain. But I so far succeeded in checking the expression of this view that I will throw, just here, no further light on it than may be offered by the mention of my final observation to Mrs. Grose. "His having lied and been impudent are, I confess, less engaging specimens than I had hoped to have from you of the outbreak in him of the little natural man. Still," I mused, "they must do, for they make me feel more than ever that I must watch."

It made me blush, the next minute, to see in my friend's face how much more unreservedly she had forgiven him than her anecdote struck me as pointing out to my own tenderness any way to do. This was marked when, at the schoolroom door, she quitted me. "Surely you don't accuse *him*—"

"Of carrying on an intercourse that he conceals from me? Ah remember that, until further evidence, I now accuse nobody." Then before shutting her out to go by another passage to her own place, "I must just wait," I wound up.

<h1 style="text-align:center">IX</h1>

I waited and waited, and the days took as they elapsed something from my consternation. A very few of them, in fact, passing, in constant sight of my pupils, without a fresh incident, sufficed to give to grievous fancies and even to odious memories a kind of brush of the sponge. I have spoken of the surrender to their extraordinary childish grace as a thing I could actively promote in myself, and it may be imagined if I neglected now to apply at this source for whatever balm it would yield. Strange than I can express certainly, was the effort to struggle against my new lights. It would doubtless have been a greater tension still, however, had it not been so frequently successful. I used to wonder how my little charges could help guessing that I thought strange things about them, and the circumstance that these things only made them more intersting was not by itself a direct aid to keeping them in the dark. I trembled lest they should see that they *were* so immensely more interesting. Putting things at the worst, at all events, as in meditation I so often did, any clouding of their innocence could only be—blameless and foredoomed as they were—a reason the more for taking risks. There were moments when I knew myself to catch them up by an irresistible impulse and press them to my heart. As soon as I had done so I used to wonder—"What will they think of that? Doesn't it betray too much?" It would have been easy to get into a sad wild tangle about how much I might betray, but the real account, I feel, of the hours of peace I could still enjoy was that the immediate charm of my companions was a beguilement still effective even under the shadow of the possibility that it was studied. For if it occurred to me that I might occasionally excite suspicion by the little outbreaks of my sharper passion for them, so too I remember asking if I mightn't see a queerness in the traceable increase of their own demonstrations.

They were at this period extravagantly and preternaturally fond of me, which, after all, I could reflect, was no more than a graceful response in children perpetually bowed down over and hugged. The homage of which they were so lavish succeeded in truth for my nerves quite as well as if I never appeared to myself, as I may say, literally to catch them at a purpose in it. They had never, I think, wanted to do so many things for their poor protectress; I mean—though they got their lessons better and better, which was naturally what would please her most—in the way of diverting, entertaining, surprising her; reading her passages, telling her stories, acting her charades, pouncing out at her, in disguises, as animals and historical characters, and above all astonishing her by the "pieces" they had secretly got by heart and could interminably recite. I should never get to the bottom—were I to let myself go even now—of the prodigious private commentary, all under still more private correction, with which I in these days overscored their full hours. They had shown me from the first a facility for everything, a general faculty which, taking a fresh start, achieved remarkable flights. They got their little tasks as if they loved them; they indulged, from the mere exuberance of the gift, in the most unimposed little miracles of memory. They not only popped out at me as tigers and as Romans, but as Shakespeareans, astronomers and navigators. This was so singularly the case that it had presumably much to do with the fact as to which, at the present day, I am at a loss for a different explanation: I allude to my unnatural composure on the subject of another school for Miles. What I remember is that I was content for the time not to open the question, and that contentment must have sprung from the sense of his perpetually striking show of cleverness. He was too clever for a bad governess, for a parson's daughter, to spoil, and the strangest if not the brightest thread in the pensive embroidery I just spoke of was the impression I might have got, if I had dared to work it out, that he was under some influence operating in his small intellectual life as a tremendous incitement.

If it was easy to reflect, however, that such a boy could postpone school, it was at least as marked that for such a boy to have been "kicked out" by a schoolmaster was a mystification without end. Let me add that in their company now—and I was careful almost never to be out of it—I could follow no scent very far. We lived in a cloud of music and affection and success and private theatricals. The musical sense in each of the children was of the quickest, but the elder in especial had a marvelous knack of catching and repeating. The schoolroom piano broke into all gruesome fancies, and when that failed there were confabulations in corners, with a sequel of one of them going out in the highest spirits in order to "come in" as something new. I had had brothers myself, and it was no revelation to me that little girls could be slavish idolaters of little boys. What surpassed everything was that there was a little boy in the world who could have for the inferior age, sex and intelligence so fine a consideration. They were extraordinarily at one, and to say that they never either quarrelled or complained is to make the note of praise coarse for their quality of sweetness. Sometimes perhaps indeed (when I dropped into coarseness) I came across traces of little understandings between them by which one of them should keep me occupied while the other slipped away. There is a naive side, I suppose, in all diplomacy, but if my pupils practiced upon me it was surely with the minimum of grossness. It was all in the other quarter that, after a lull, the grossness broke out.

I find that I really hang back, but I must take my horrid plunge. In going on with the record of what was hideous at Bly I not only challenge the most liberal faith—for which I little care, but (and this is another matter) I renew what I myself suffered, I again push my dreadful way through it to the end. There came suddenly an hour after which, as I look back, the business seems to me to have been all pure suffering, but I have at least reached the heart of it, and the straightest road out is doubtless to advance. One evening—with nothing to lead up or prepare it—I felt the cold touch of the impression that had breathed on me the night of my arrival and which, much lighter then as I have mentioned, I should probably have made little of in memory had my subsequent sojourn been less agitated. I had not gone to bed; I sat reading by a couple of candles. There was a roomful of old books at Bly—last-century fiction some of it, which, to the extent of a distinctly deprecated renown, but never to so much as that of a stray specimen, had reached the sequestered home and appealed to the unavowed curiosity of my youth. I remember that the book I had in my hand was Fielding's *Amelia*; also that I was wholly awake. I recall further both a general conviction that it was horribly late and a particular objection to looking at my watch. I figure finally that the white curtain draping, in the fashion of those days, the head of Flora's little bed, shrouded, as I had assured myself long before, the perfection of childish rest. I recollect in short that though I was deeply interested in my author I found myself, at the turn of a page and with his spell all scattered, looking straight up from him and hard at the door of my room. There was a moment during which I listened, reminded of the faint sense I had had, the first night, of there being something undefinably astir in the house, and noted the soft breath of the open casement just move the half-drawn blind. Then, with all the marks of a deliberation that must have seemed magnificent had there been any one to admire it, I laid down my book, rose to my feet and, taking a candle, went straight out of the room and, from the passage, on which my light made little impression, noiselessly closed and locked the door.

I can say now neither what determined nor what guided me, but I went straight along the lobby, holding my candle high, till I came within sight of the tall window that presided over the great turn of the staircase. At this point I precipitately found myself aware of three things. They were practically simultaneous, yet they had flashes of succession. My candle, under a bold flourish, went out, and I perceived, by the uncovered window, that the yielding dusk of earliest morning rendered it unnecessary. Without it, the next instant, I knew that there was a figure on the stair. I speak of sequences, but I require no lapse of seconds to stiffen myself for a third encounter with Quint. The apparition had reached the landing halfway up and was therefore on the spot nearest the window, where, at sight of me, it stopped short and fixed me exactly as it had fixed me from the tower and from the garden. He knew me as well as I knew him, and so, in the cold faint twilight, with a glimmer in the high glass and another on the polish of the oak stair below, we faced each other in our common intensity. He was absolutely, on this occasion, a living detestable dangerous presence. But that was not the wonder of wonders; I reserve this distinction for quite another circumstance: the circumstance that dread had unmistakeably quitted me and that there was nothing in me unable to meet and measure him.

I had plenty of anguish after that extraordinary moment, but I had, thank God, no terror. And he knew I hadn't—I found myself at the end of an instant magnificently aware of this. I felt, in a fierce rigor of confidence, that if I stood my ground a minute I should cease—for the time at least—to have him to reckon with, and during the minute, accordingly, the thing was as human and hideous as a real interview: hideous just because it *was* human, as human as to have met alone, in the small hours, in a sleeping house, some enemy, some adventurer, some criminal. It was the dead silence of our long gaze at such close quarters that gave the whole horror, huge as it was, its only note of the unnatural. If I had met a murderer in such a place and at such an hour we still at least would have spoken. Something would have passed, in life, between us; if nothing had passed one of us would have moved. The moment was so prolonged that it would have taken but little more to make me doubt if even *I* were in life. I can't express what followed it save by saying that the silence itself—which was indeed in a manner an attestation of my strength—became the element into which I saw the figure disappear; in which I definitely saw it turn, as I might have seen the low wretch to which it had once belonged turn on receipt of an order, and pass, with my eyes on the villainous back that no hunch could have more disfigured, straight down the staircase and into the darkness in which the next bend was lost.

X

I remained a while at the top of the stair, but with the effect presently of understanding that when my visitor had gone, he had gone; then I returned to my room.
The foremost thing I saw there by the light of the candle I had left burning was that
Flora's little bed was empty, and on this I caught my breath with all the terror that,
five minutes before, I had been able to resist. I dashed at the place in which I had
left her lying and over which—for the small silk counterpane and the sheets were
disarranged—the white curtains had been deceivingly pulled forward. Then my
step, to my unutterable relief, produced an answering sound: I noticed an agitation
of the window-blind, and the child, ducking down, emerged rosily from the other
side of it. She stood there in so much of her candor and so little of her nightgown,
with her pink bare feet and the golden glow of her curls. She looked intensely
grave, and I had never had such a sense of losing an advantage acquired (the thrill
of which had just been so prodigious) as on my consciousness that she addressed
me with a reproach—"You naughty: where *have* you been?" Instead of challenging
her own irregularity I found myself arraigned and explaining. She herself
explained, for that matter, with the loveliest eagerest simplicity. She had known
suddenly, as she lay there, that I was out of the room, and had jumped up to see
what had become of me. I had dropped, with the joy of her reappearance, back into
my chair—feeling then, and then only, a little faint, and she had pattered straight
over to me, thrown herself upon my knee, given herself to be held with the flame of
the candle full in the wonderful little face that was still flushed with sleep. I
remember closing my eyes an instant, yieldingly, consciously, as before the excess
of something beautiful that shone out of the blue of her own. "You were looking for
me out of the window?" I said. "You thought I might be walking in the grounds?"

"Well, you know, I thought some one was"—she never blanched as she smiled
out that at me.

Oh how I looked at her now! "And did you see any one?"

"Ah *no!*" she returned almost (with the full privilege of childish inconsequence)
resentfully, though with a long sweetness in her little drawl of the negative.

At that moment, in the state of my nerves, I absolutely believed she lied, and if I
once more closed my eyes it was before the dazzle of the three or four possible ways
in which I might take this up. One of these for a moment tempted me with such sin-

gular force that, to resist it, I must have gripped my little girl with a spasm that, wonderfully, she submitted to without a cry or a sign of fright. Why not break out at her on the spot and have it all over?—give it to her straight in her lovely little lighted face? "You see, you see, you *know* that you do and that you already quite suspect I believe it, therefore why not frankly confess it to me, so that we may at least live with it together and learn perhaps, in the strangeness of our fate, where we are and what it means?" This solicitation dropped, alas, as it came: if I could immediately have succumbed to it I might have spared myself—well, you'll see what. Instead of succumbing I sprang again to my feet, looked at her bed and took a helpless middle way. "Why did you pull the curtain over the place to make me think you were still there?"

Flora luminously considered; after which, with her little divine smile: "Because I don't like to frighten you!"

"But if I had, by your idea, gone out—?"

She absolutely declined to be puzzled; she turned her eyes to the flame of the candle as if the question were as irrelevant, or at any rate as impersonal, as Mrs. Marcet or nine-times-nine. "Oh but you know," she quite adequately answered, "that you might come back, you dear, and that you *have!*" And after a little, when she had got into bed, I had, a long time, by almost sitting on her for the retention of her hand, to show how I recognized the pertinence of my return.

You may imagine the general complexion, from that moment, of my nights. I repeatedly sat up till I didn't know when; I selected moments when my roommate unmistakeably slept, and, stealing out, took noiseless turns in the passage. I even pushed as far as to where I had last met Quint. But I never met him there again, and I may as well say at once that I on no other occasion saw him in the house. I just missed, on the staircase, nevertheless, a different adventure. Looking down it from the top I once recognized the presence of a woman seated on one of the lower steps with her back presented to me, her body half-bowed and her head, in an attitude of woe, in her hands. I had been there but an instant, however, when she vanished without looking round at me. I knew, for all that, exactly what dreadful face she had to show; and I wondered whether, if instead of being above I had been below, I should have had the same nerve for going up that I had lately shown Quint. Well, there continued to be plenty of call for nerve. On the eleventh night after my latest encounter with that gentleman—they were all numbered now—I had an alarm that perilously skirted it and that indeed, from the particular quality of its unexpectedness, proved quite my sharpest shock. It was precisely the first night during this series that, weary with vigils, I had conceived I might again without laxity lay myself down at my old hour. I slept immediately and, as I afterward knew, till about one o'clock; but when I woke it was to sit straight up, as completely roused as if a hand had shaken me. I had left a light burning, but it was now out, and I felt an instant certainty that Flora had extinguished it. This brought me to my feet and straight, in the darkness, to her bed, which I found she had left. A glance at the window enlightened me further, and the striking of a match completed the picture.

The child had again got up—this time blowing out the taper, and had again, for some purpose of observation or response, squeezed in behind the blind and was peering out into the night. That she now saw—as she had not, I had satisfied myself, the previous time—was proved to me by the fact that she was disturbed neither by my re-illumination nor by the haste I made to get into slippers and into a wrap. Hidden, protected, absorbed, she evidently rested on the sill—the casement opened forward—and gave herself up. There was a great still moon to help her, and this fact had counted in my quick decision. She was face to face with the apparition we had met at the lake, and could now communicate with it as she had not then been able to do. What I, on my side, had to care for was, without disturbing her, to reach, from the corridor, some other window turned to the same quarter. I got to the door without her hearing me; I got out of it, closed it and listened, from the other side, for some sound from her. While I stood in the passage I had my eyes on her brother's door, which was but ten steps off and which, indescribably, produced in me a renewal of the strange impulse that I lately spoke of as my temptation. What if I should go straight in and march to *his* window?—what if, by risking to his boyish bewilderment a revelation of my motive, I should throw across the rest of the mystery the long halter of my boldness?

This thought held me sufficiently to make me cross to his threshold and pause again. I preternaturally listened; I figured to myself what might portentously be; I wondered if his bed were also empty and he also secretly at watch. It was a deep soundless minute, at the end of which my impulse failed. He was quiet; he might be innocent; the risk was hideous; I turned away. There was a figure in the grounds— a figure prowling for a sight, the visitor with whom Flora was engaged, but it wasn't the visitor most concerned with my boy. I hesitated afresh, but on other grounds and only a few seconds; then I had made my choice. There were empty rooms enough at Bly, and it was only a question of choosing the right one. The right one suddenly presented itself to me as the lower one—though high above the gardens—in the solid corner of the house that I have spoken of as the old tower. This was a large square chamber, arranged with some state as a bedroom, the extravagant size of which made it so inconvenient that it had not for years, though kept by Mrs. Grose in exemplary order, been occupied. I had often admired it and I knew my way about in it; I had only, after just faltering at the first chill gloom of its disuse, to pass across it and unbolt in all quietness one of the shutters. Achieving this transit I uncovered the glass without a sound and, applying my face to the pane, was able, the darkness without being much less than within, to see that I commanded the right direction. Then I saw something more. The moon made the night extraordinarily penetrable and showed me on the lawn a person, diminished by distance, who stood there motionless as if fascinated, looking up to where I had appeared—looking, that is, not so much straight at me as at something that was apparently above me. There was clearly another person above me—there was a person on the tower, but the presence on the lawn was not in the least what I had conceived and had confidently hurried to meet. The presence on the lawn—I felt sick as I made it out—was poor little Miles himself.

XI

It was not till late next day that I spoke to Mrs. Grose; the rigor with which I kept my pupils in sight making it often difficult to meet her privately: the more as we each felt the importance of not provoking—on the part of the servants quite as much as on that of the children—any suspicion of a secret flurry or of a discussion of mysteries. I drew a great security in this particular from her mere smooth aspect. There was nothing in her fresh face to pass on to others the least of my horrible confidences. She believed me, I was sure, absolutely: if she hadn't I don't know what would have become of me, for I couldn't have borne the strain alone. But she was a magnificent monument to the blessing of a want of imagination, and if she could see in our little charges nothing but their beauty and amiability, their happiness and cleverness, she had no direct communication with the sources of my trouble. If they had been at all visibly blighted or battered she would doubtless have grown, on tracing it back, haggard enough to match them; as matters stood, however, I could feel her, when she surveyed them with her large white arms folded and the habit of serenity in all her look, thank the Lord's mercy that if they were ruined the pieces would still serve. Flights of fancy gave place, in her mind, to a steady fireside glow, and I had already begun to perceive how, with the development of the conviction that—as time went on without a public accident—our young things could, after all, look out for themselves, she addressed her greatest solicitude to the sad case presented by their deputy guardian. That, for myself, was a sound simplication: I could engage that, to the world, my face should tell no tales, but it would have been, in the conditions, an immense added worry to find myself anxious about hers.

At the hour I now speak of she had joined me, under pressure, on the terrace, where, with the lapse of the season, the afternoon sun was now agreeable, and we sat there together while before us and at a distance, yet within call if we wished, the children strolled to and fro in one of their most manageable moods. They moved slowly, in unison, below us, over the lawn, the boy, as they went, reading aloud from a storybook and passing his arm round his sister to keep her quite in touch. Mrs. Grose watched them with positive placidity, then I caught the suppressed intellectual creak with which she conscientiously turned to take from me a view of the back of the tapestry. I had made her a receptacle of lurid things, but there was an odd recognition of my superiority—my accomplishments and my function—in her patience under my pain. She offered her mind to my disclosures as, had I wished to mix a witch's broth and propose it with assurance, she would have held out a large clean saucepan. This had become thoroughly her attitude by the time that, in my recital of the events of the night, I reached the point of what Miles had said to me when, after seeing him, at such a monstrous hour, almost on the very spot where he happened now to be, I had gone down to bring him in; choosing then, at the window, with a concentrated need of not alarming the house, rather that method than any noisier process. I had left her meanwhile in little doubt of my small hope of representing with success even to her actual sympathy my sense of the real splendor of the little inspiration with which, after I had got him into the house, the boy met my final articulate challenge. As soon as I appeared in the moonlight on the terrace he had come to me as straight as possible; on which I had taken his hand without a word and led him, through the dark spaces, up the staircase where Quint had so hungrily hovered for him, along the lobby where I had listened and trembled, and so to his forsaken room.

Not a sound, on the way, had passed between us, and I had wondered—oh *how* I had wondered!—if he were groping about in his dreadful little mind for something plausible and not too grotesque. It would tax his invention certainly, and I felt, this time, over his real embarrassment, a curious thrill of triumph. It was a sharp trap for any game hitherto successful. He could play no longer at perfect propriety, nor could he pretend to it, so how the deuce would he get out of the scrape? There beat in me indeed, with the passionate throb of this question, an equal dumb appeal as to how the deuce *I* should. I was confronted at last, as never yet, with all the risk attached even now to sounding my own horrid note. I remember in fact that as we pushed into his little chamber, where the bed had not been slept in at all and the window, uncovered to the moonlight, made the place so clear that there was no need of striking a match—I remember how I suddenly dropped, sank upon the edge of the bed from the force of the idea that he must know how he really, as they say, "had" me. He could do what he liked, with all his cleverness to help him, so long as I should continue to defer to the old tradition of the criminality of those caretakers of the young who minister to superstitions and fears. He "had" me indeed, and in a cleft stick, for who would ever absolve me, who would consent that I should go unhung, if, by the faintest tremor of an overture, I were the first to introduce into our perfect intercourse an element so dire? No, no: it was useless to attempt to convey to Mrs. Grose, just as it is scarcely less so to attempt to suggest here, how, during our short stiff brush there in the dark, he fairly shook me with admiration. I was of course thoroughly kind and merciful; never, never yet had I placed on his small shoulders hands of such tenderness as those with which, while I rested against the bed, I held him there well under fire. I had no alternative but, in form at least, to put it to him.

"You must tell me now—and all the truth. What did you go out for? What were you doing there?"

I can still see his wonderful smile, the whites of his beautiful eyes and the uncovering of his clear teeth, shine to me in the dusk. "If I tell you why, will you understand?" My heart, at this, leaped into my mouth. *Would* he tell me why? I found no sound on my lips to press it, and I was aware of answering only with a vague repeated grimacing nod. He was gentleness itself, and while I wagged my head at him he stood there more than ever a little fairy prince. It was his brightness indeed that gave me a respite. Would it be so great if he were really going to tell me? "Well," he said at last, "just exactly in order that you should do this."

"Do what?"

"Think me—for a change—*bad!*" I shall never forget the sweetness and gaiety with which he brought out the word, nor how, on top of it, he bent forward and kissed me. It was practically the end of everything. I met his kiss and I had to make, while I folded him for a minute in my arms, the most stupendous effort not to cry. He had given exactly the account of himself that permitted least my going behind it, and it was only with the effect of confirming my acceptance of it that, as I presently glanced about the room, I could say—

"Then you didn't undress at all?"

He fairly glittered in the gloom. "Not at all. I sat up and read."

"And when did you go down?"

"At midnight. When I'm bad I *am* bad!"

"I see, I see—it's charming. But how could you be sure I should know it?"

"Oh I arranged that with Flora." His answers rang out with a readiness! "She was to get up and look out."

"Which is what she did do." It was I who fell into the trap!

"So she disturbed you, and, to see what she was looking at, you also looked—you saw."

"While you," I concurred, "caught your death in the night air!"

He literally bloomed so from this exploit that he could afford radiantly to assent. "How otherwise should I have been bad enough?" he asked. Then, after another embrace, the incident and our interview closed on my recognition of all the reserves of goodness that, for his joke, he had been able to draw upon.

XII

The particular impression I had received proved in the morning light, I repeat, not quite successfully presentable to Mrs. Grose, though I re-enforced it with the mention of still another remark that he had made before we separated. "It all lies in half a dozen words," I said to her, "words that really settle the matter. 'Think, you know, what I *might* do!' He threw that off to show me how good he is. He knows down to the ground what he 'might do.' That's what he gave them a taste of at school."

"Lord, you do change!" cried my friend.

"I don't change—I simply make it out. The four, depend upon it, perpetually meet. If on either of these last nights you had been with either child you'd clearly have understood. The more I've watched and waited the more I've felt that if there were nothing else to make it sure it would be made so by the systematic silence of each. *Never,* by a slip of the tongue, have they so much as alluded to either of their old friends, any more than Miles has alluded to his expulsion. Oh yes, we may sit here and look at them, and they may show off to us there to their fill, but even while they pretend to be lost in their fairy tale they're steeped in their vision of the dead restored to them. He's not reading to her," I declared; "they're talking of *them*— they're talking horrors! I go on, I know, as if I were crazy, and it's a wonder I'm not. What I've seen would have made *you* so, but it has only made me more lucid, made me get hold of still other things."

My lucidity must have seemed awful, but the charming creatures who were victims of it, passing and repassing in their interlocked sweetness, gave my colleague something to hold on by, and I felt how tight she held as, without stirring in the breath of my passion, she covered them still with her eyes. "Of what other things have you got hold?"

"Why of the very things that have delighted, fascinated and yet, at bottom, as I now so strangely see, mystified and troubled me. Their more than earthly beauty, their absolutely unnatural goodness. It's a game," I went on; "it's a policy and a fraud!"

"On the part of little darlings—"

"As yet mere lovely babies? Yes, mad as that seems!" The very act of bringing it out really helped me to trace it—follow it all up and piece it all together. "They haven't been good—they've only been absent. It has been easy to live with them

617

because they're simply leading a life of their own. They're not mine—they're not ours. They're his and they're hers!"

"Quint's and that woman's?"

"Quint's and that woman's. They want to get to them."

Oh how, at this, poor Mrs. Grose appeared to study them! "But for what?"

"For the love of all the evil that, in those dreadful days, the pair put into them. And to ply them with that evil still, to keep up the work of demons, is what brings the others back."

"Laws!" said my friend under her breath. The exclamation was homely, but it revealed a real acceptance of my further proof of what, in the bad time—for there had been a worse even than this!—must have occurred. There could have been no such justification for me as the plain assent of her experience to whatever depth of depravity I found credible in our brace of scoundrels. It was in obvious submission of memory that she brought out after a moment: "They *were* rascals! But what can they now do?" she pursued.

"Do?" I echoed so loud that Miles and Flora, as they passed at their distance, paused an instant in their walk and looked at us. "Don't they do enough?" I demanded in a lower tone, while the children, having smiled and nodded and kissed hands to us, resumed their exhibition. We were held by it a minute, then I answered: "They can destroy them!" At this my companion did turn, but the appeal she launched was a silent one, the effect of which was to make me more explicit. "They don't know as yet quite how—but they're trying hard. They're seen only across, as it were, and beyond—in strange places and on high places, the top of towers, the roof of houses, the outside of windows, the further edge of pools, but there's a deep design, on either side, to shorten the distance and overcome the obstacle: so the success of the tempters is only a question of time. They've only to keep to their suggestions of danger."

"For the children to come?"

"And perish in the attempt!" Mrs. Grose slowly got up, and I scrupulously added: "Unless, of course, we can prevent!"

Standing there before me while I kept my seat she visibly turned things over. "Their uncle must do the preventing. He must take them away."

"And who's to make him?"

She had been scanning the distance, but she now dropped on me a foolish face. "You, Miss."

"By writing to him that his house is poisoned and his little nephew and niece mad?"

"But if they *are*, Miss?"

"And if I am myself, you mean? That's charming news to be sent him by a person enjoying his confidence and whose prime undertaking was to give him no worry."

Mrs. Grose considered, following the children again. "Yes, he do hate worry. That was the great reason—"

"Why those fiends took him in so long? No doubt, though his indifference must have been awful. As I'm not a fiend, at any rate, I shouldn't take him in."

My companion, after an instant and for all answer, sat down again and grasped my arm. "Make him at any rate come to you."

I stared. "To *me?*" I had a sudden fear of what she might do. " 'Him'?"

"He ought to *be* here—he ought to help."

I quickly rose and I think I must have shown her a queerer face than ever yet. "You see me asking him for a visit?" No, with her eyes on my face she evidently couldn't. Instead of it even—as a woman reads another—she could see what I myself saw: his derision, his amusement, his contempt for the breakdown of my resignation at being left alone and for the fine machinery I had set in motion to attract his attention to my slighted charms. She didn't know—no one knew—how proud I had been to serve him and to stick to our terms, yet she nonetheless took the measure, I think, of the warning I now gave her. "If you should so lose your head as to appeal to him for me—"

She was really frightened. "Yes, Miss?"

"I would leave, on the spot, both him and you."

XIII

It was all very well to join them, but speaking to them proved quite as much as ever an effort beyond my strength—offered, in close quarters, difficulties as insurmountable as before. This situation continued a month, and with new aggravations and particular notes, the note above all, sharper and sharper, of the small ironic consciousness on the part of my pupils. It was not, I am as sure today as I was sure then, my mere infernal imagination: it was absolutely traceable that they were aware of my predicament and that this strange relation made, in a manner, for a long time, the air in which we moved. I don't mean that they had their tongues in their cheeks or did anything vulgar, for that was not one of their dangers: I do mean, on the other hand, that the element of the unnamed and untouched became, between us, greater than any other, and that so much avoidance couldn't have been made successful without a great deal of tacit arrangement. It was as if, at moments, we were perpetually coming into sight of subjects before which we must stop short, turning suddenly out of alleys that we perceived to be blind, closing with a little bang that made us look at each other—for, like all bangs, it was something louder than we had intended—the doors we had indiscreetly opened. All roads lead to Rome, and there were times when it might have struck us that almost every branch of study or subject of conversation skirted forbidden ground. Forbidden ground was the question of the return of the dead in general and of whatever, in especial, might survive, for memory, of the friends little children had lost. There were days when I could have sworn that one of them had, with a small invisible nudge, said to the other: "She thinks she'll do it this time—but she *won't!*" To "do it" would have been to indulge for instance—and for once in a way—in some direct reference to the lady who had prepared them for my discipline. They had a delightful endless appetite for passages in my own history to which I had again and again treated them; they were in possession of everything that had ever happened to me, had had, with every circumstance, the story of my smallest adventures and of those of my brothers and sisters and of the cat and the dog at home, as well as many particulars of the whimsical bent of my father, of the furniture and arrangement of our house and of the conversation of the old women of our village. There were things enough, taking one with another, to chatter about, if one went very fast and knew by instinct when to go round. They pulled with an art of their own the strings of my invention and my memory, and nothing else perhaps, when I thought of such occasions afterward, gave me so the suspicion of being watched from under cover. It was in any case over *my* life, *my* past and *my* friends alone that we could take anything like our ease; a state of affairs that led them sometimes without the least pertinence to break out into sociable reminders. I was invited—with no visible connection—to repeat afresh Goody Gosling's celebrated *mot* or to confirm the details already supplied as to the cleverness of the vicarage pony.

It was partly at such junctures as these and partly at quite different ones that, with the turn my matters had now taken, my predicament, as I have called it, grew most sensible. The fact that the days passed for me without another encounter ought, it would have appeared, to have done something toward soothing my nerves. Since the light brush, that second night on the upper landing, of the presence of a woman at the foot of the stair, I had seen nothing, whether in or out of the house, that one had better not have seen. There was many a corner round which I expected to come upon Quint, and many a situation that, in a merely sinister way, would have favored the appearance of Miss Jessel. The summer had turned, the summer had gone; the autumn had dropped upon Bly and had blown out half our lights. The place, with its gray sky and withered garlands, its bared spaces and scattered dead leaves, was like a theater after the performance—all strewn with crumpled playbills. There were exactly states of the air, conditions of sound and of stillness, unspeakable impressions of the *kind* of ministering moment, that brought back to me, long enough to catch it, the feeling of the medium in which, that June evening out of doors, I had had my first sight of Quint, and in which too, at those other instants, I had, after seeing him through the window, looked for him in vain in the circle of shrubbery. I recognized the signs, the portents—I recognized the moment, the spot. But they remained unaccompanied and empty, and I continued unmolested; if unmolested one could call a young woman whose sensibility had, in the most extraordinary fashion, not declined but deepened. I had said in my talk with Mrs. Grose on that horrid scene of Flora's by the lake—and had perplexed her by so saying—that it would from that moment distress me much more to lose my power than to keep it. I had then expressed what was vividly in my mind: the truth that, whether the children really saw or not—since, that is, it was not yet definitely proved—I greatly preferred, as a safeguard, the fullness of my own exposure. I was ready to know the very worst that was to be known. What I had then had an ugly glimpse of was that my eyes might be sealed just while theirs were most opened. Well, my eyes *were* sealed, it appeared, at present—a consummation for which it seemed blasphemous not to thank God. There was, alas, a difficulty about that: I would have thanked him with all my soul had I not had in a proportionate measure this conviction of the secret of my pupils.

How can I retrace today the strange steps of my obsession? There were times of our being together when I would have been ready to swear that, literally, in my presence, but with my direct sense of it closed, they had visitors who were known and were welcome. Then it was that, had I not been deterred by the very chance that such an injury might prove greater than the injury to be averted, my exaltation would have broken out. "They're here, they're here, you little wretches," I would have cried, "and you can't deny it now!" The little wretches denied it with all the added volume of their sociability and their tenderness, just in the crystal depths of which—like the flash of a fish in a stream—the mockery of their advantage peeped up. The shock had in truth sunk into me still deeper than I knew on the night when, looking out either for Quint or for Miss Jessel under the stars, I had seen there the boy over whose rest I watched and who had immediately brought in with him—had straightway there turned on me—the lovely upward look with which, from the battlements above us, the hideous apparition of Quint had played. If it was a question of a scare, my discovery on this occasion had scared me more than any other, and it was essentially in the scared state that I drew my actual conclusions. They harassed me so that sometimes, at odd moments, I shut myself up audibly to rehearse—it was at once a fantastic relief and a renewed despair—the manner in which I might come to the point. I approached it from one side and the other while, in my room, I flung myself about, but I always broke down in the monstrous utterance of names. As they died away on my lips I said to myself that I should indeed help them to represent something infamous if by pronouncing them I should violate as rare a little case of instinctive delicacy as any schoolroom probably had ever known. When I said to myself: "*They* have the manners to be silent, and you, trusted as you are, the baseness to speak!" I felt myself crimson and covered my face with my hands. After these secret scenes I chattered more than ever, going on volubly enough till one of our prodigious palpable hushes occurred—I can call them nothing else—the strange dizzy lift or swim (I try for terms!) into a stillness, a pause of all life, that had nothing to do with the more or less noise we at the moment might be engaged in making and that I could hear through any intensified mirth or quickened recitation or louder strum of the piano. Then it was that the others, the outsiders, were there. Though they were not angels they "passed," as the French say, causing me, while they stayed, to tremble with the fear of their addressing to their younger victims some yet more infernal message or more vivid image than they had thought good enough for myself.

What it was least possible to get rid of was the cruel idea that, whatever I had seen, Miles and Flora saw *more*—things terrible and unguessable and that sprang from dreadful passages of intercourse in the past. Such things naturally left on the surface, for the time, a chill that we vociferously denied we felt, and we had all three, with repetition, got into such splendid training that we went, each time, to mark the close of the incident, almost automatically through the very same movements. It was striking of the children at all events to kiss me inveterately with a wild irrelevance and never to fail—one or the other—of the precious question that had helped us through many a peril. "When do you think he *will* come? Don't you think we *ought* to write?"—there was nothing like that enquiry, we found by experience, for carrying off an awkwardness. "He" of course was their uncle in Harley Street, and we lived in much profusion of theory that he might at any moment arrive to mingle in our circle. It was impossible to have given less encouragement than he had administered to such a doctrine, but if we had not had the doctrine to fall back upon we should have deprived each other of some of our finest exhibitions. He never wrote to them—that may have been selfish, but it was a part of the flattery of his trust of myself, for the way in which a man pays his highest tribute to a woman is apt to be but by the more festal celebration of one of the sacred laws of his comfort. So I held that I carried out the spirit of the pledge given not to appeal to him when I let our young friends understand that their own letters were but charming literary exercises. They were too beautiful to be posted; I kept them myself; I have them all to this hour. This was a rule indeed which only added to the satiric effect of my being plied with the supposition that he might at any moment be among us. It was exactly as if our young friends knew how almost more awkward than anything else that might be for me. There appears to me moreover as I look back no note in all this more extraordinary than the mere fact that, in spite of my tension and of their triumph, I never lost patience with them. Adorable they must in truth have been, I now feel, since I didn't in these days hate them! Would exasperation, however, if relief had longer been postponed, finally have betrayed me? It little matters, for relief arrived. I call it relief though it was only the relief that a snap brings to a strain or the burst of a thunderstorm to a day of suffocation. It was at least change, and it came with a rush.

XIV

Walking to church a certain Sunday morning, I had little Miles at my side and his sister, in advance of us and at Mrs. Grose's, well in sight. It was a crisp clear day, the first of its order for some time; the night had brought a touch of frost and the autumn air, bright and sharp, made the church bells almost gay. It was an odd accident of thought that I should have happened at such a moment to be particularly and very gratefully struck with the obedience of my little charges. Why did they never resent my inexorable, my perpetual society? Something or other had brought nearer home to me that I had all but pinned the boy to my shawl, and that in the way our companions were marshalled before me I might have appeared to provide against some danger of rebellion. I was like a jailer with an eye to possible surprises and escapes. But all this belonged—I mean their magnificent little surrender—just to the special array of the facts that were most abysmal. Turned out for Sunday by his uncle's tailor, who had had a free hand and a notion of pretty waistcoats and of his grand little air, Miles's whole title to independence, the rights of his sex and situation, were so stamped upon him that if he had suddenly struck for freedom I should have had nothing to say. I was by the strangest of chances wondering how I should meet him when the revolution unmistakeably occurred. I call it a revolution because I now see how, with the word he spoke, the curtain rose on the last act of my dreadful drama and the catastrophe was precipitated. "Look here, my dear, you know," he charmingly said, "when in the world, please, am I going back to school?"

Transcribed here the speech sounds harmless enough, particularly as uttered in the sweet, high, casual pipe with which, at all interlocutors, but above all at his eternal governess, he threw off intonations as if he were tossing roses. There was something in them that always made one "catch," and I caught at any rate now so effectually that I stopped as short as if one of the trees of the park had fallen across the road. There was something new, on the spot, between us, and he was perfectly aware I recognized it, though to enable me to do so he had no need to look a whit less candid and charming than usual. I could feel in him how he already, from my at first finding nothing to reply, perceived the advantage he had gained. I was so slow to find anything that he had plenty of time, after a minute, to continue with his suggestive but inconclusive smile: "You know, my dear, that for a fellow to be with a lady *always*—!" His "my dear" was constantly on his lips for me, and nothing could have expressed more the exact shade of the sentiment with which I desired to inspire my pupils than its fond familiarity. It was so respectfully easy.

But oh how I felt that at present I must pick my own phrases! I remember that, to gain time, I tried to laugh, and I seemed to see in the beautiful face with which he watched me how ugly and queer I looked. "And always with the same lady?" I returned.

He neither blanched nor winked. The whole thing was virtually out between us. "Ah of course she's a jolly 'perfect' lady, but after all I'm a fellow, don't you see? who's—well, getting on."

I lingered there with him an instant ever so kindly. "Yes, you're getting on." Oh but I felt helpless!

I have kept to this day the heartbreaking little idea of how he seemed to know that and to play with it. "And you can't say I've not been awfully good, can you?"

I laid my hand on his shoulder, for though I felt how much better it would have been to walk on I was not yet quite able. "No, I can't say that, Miles."

"Except just that one night, you know—!"

"That one night?" I couldn't look as straight as he.

"Why when I went down—went out of the house."

"Oh yes. But I forget what you did it for."

"You forget?"—he spoke with the sweet extravagance of childish reproach. "Why it was just to show you I could!"

"Oh yes—you could."

"And I can again."

I felt I might perhaps after all succeed in keeping my wits about me. "Certainly. But you won't."

"No, not *that* again. It was nothing."

"It was nothing," I said. "But we must go on."

He resumed our walk with me, passing his hand into my arm. "Then when *am* I going back?"

I wore, in turning it over, my most responsible air. "Were you very happy at school?"

He just considered. "Oh I'm happy enough anywhere!"

"Well then," I quavered, "if you're just as happy here—!"

"Ah but that isn't everything! Of course *you* know a lot—"

"But you hint that you know almost as much?" I risked as he paused.

"Not half I want to!" Miles honestly professed. "But it isn't so much that."

"What is it then?"

"Well—I want to see more life."

"I see, I see." We had arrived within sight of the church and of various persons, including several of the household of Bly, on their way to it and clustered about the door to see us go in. I quickened our step; I wanted to get there before the question between us opened up much further; I reflected hungrily that he would have for more than an hour to be silent; and I thought with envy of the comparative dusk of the pew and of the almost spiritual help of the hassock on which I might bend my knees. I seemed literally to be running a race with some confusion to which he was about to reduce me, but I felt he had got in first when, before we had even entered the churchyard, he threw out—

"I want my own sort!"

It literally made me bound forward. "There aren't many of your own sort, Miles!" I laughed. "Unless perhaps dear little Flora!"

"You really compare me to a baby girl?"

This found me singularly weak. "Don't you then *love* our sweet Flora?"

"If I didn't—and you too; if I didn't—!" he repeated as if retreating for a jump, yet leaving his thought so unfinished that, after we had come into the gate, another stop, which he imposed on me by the pressure of his arm, had become inevitable. Mrs. Grose and Flora had passed into the church, the other worshippers had followed and we were, for the minute, alone among the old thick graves. We had paused, on the path from the gate, by a low oblong table-like tomb.

"Yes, if you didn't—?"

He looked, while I waited, about at the graves. "Well, you know what!" But he didn't move, and he presently produced something that made me drop straight down on the stone slab as if suddenly to rest. "Does my uncle think what *you* think?"

I markedly rested. "How do you know what I think?"

"Ah well, of course I don't; for it strikes me you never tell me. But I mean does *he* know?"

"Know what, Miles?"

"Why the way I'm going on."

I recognized quickly enough that I could make, to this enquiry, no answer that wouldn't involve something of a sacrifice of my employer. Yet it struck me that we were all, at Bly, sufficiently sacrificed to make that venial. "I don't think your uncle much cares."

Miles, on this, stood looking at me. "Then don't you think he can be made to?"

"In what way?"

"Why by his coming down."

"But who'll get him to come down?"

"*I* will!" the boy said with extraordinary brightness and emphasis. He gave me another look charged with that expression and then marched off alone into church.

XV

The business was practically settled from the moment I never followed him. It was a pitiful surrender to agitation, but my being aware of this had somehow no power to restore me. I only sat there on my tomb and read into what our young friend had said to me the fullness of its meaning; by the time I had grasped the whole of which, I had also embraced, for absence, the pretext that I was ashamed to offer my pupils and the rest of the congregation such an example of delay. What I said to myself above all was that Miles had got something out of me and that the gage of it for him would be just this awkward collapse. He had got out of me that there was something I was much afraid of, and that he should probably be able to make use of my fear to gain, for his own purpose, more freedom. My fear was of having to deal with the intolerable question of the grounds of his dismissal from school, since that was really but the question of the horrors gathered behind. That his uncle should arrive to treat with me of these things was a solution that, strictly speaking, I ought now to have desired to bring on, but I could so little face the ugliness and the pain of it that I simply procrastinated and lived from hand to mouth. The boy, to my deep discomposure, was immensely in the right, was in a position to say to me: "Either you clear up with my guardian the mystery of this interruption of my studies, or you cease to expect me to lead with you a life that's so unnatural for a boy." What was so unnatural for the particular boy I was concerned with was this sudden revelation of a consciousness and a plan.

That was what really overcame me, what prevented my going in. I walked round the church, hesitating, hovering; I reflected that I had already, with him, hurt myself beyond repair. Therefore I could patch up nothing and it was too extreme an effort to squeeze beside him into the pew: he would be so much more sure than ever to pass his arm into mine and make me sit there for an hour in close mute contact with his commentary on our talk. For the first minute since his arrival I wanted to get away from him. As I paused beneath the high east window and listened to the sounds of worship I was taken with an impulse that might master me, I felt, and completely, should I give it the least encouragement. I might easily put an end to my ordeal by getting away altogether. Here was my chance; there was no one to stop me; I could give the whole thing up—turn my back and bolt. It was only a question of hurrying again, for a few preparations, to the house which the attendance at church of so many of the servants would practically have left unoccupied. No one, in short, could blame me if I should just drive desperately off. What was it to get away if I should get away only till dinner? That would be in a couple of hours, at the end of which—I had the acute prevision—my little pupils would play at innocent wonder about my non-appearance in their train.

"What *did* you do, you naughty bad thing? Why in the world, to worry us so—and take our thoughts off too, don't you know?—did you desert us at the very door?" I couldn't meet such questions nor, as they asked them, their false little lovely eyes, yet it was all so exactly what I should have to meet that, as the prospect grew sharp to me, I at last let myself go.

I got, so far as the immediate moment was concerned, away; I came straight out of the churchyard and, thinking hard, retraced my steps through the park. It seemed to me that by the time I reached the house I had made up my mind to cynical flight. The Sunday stillness both of the approaches and of the interior, in which I met no one, fairly stirred me with a sense of opportunity. Were I to get off quickly this way I should get off without a scene, without a word. My quickness would have to be remarkable, however, and the question of a conveyance was the great one to settle. Tormented, in the hall, with difficulties and obstacles, I remember sinking down at the foot of the staircase—suddenly collapsing there on the lowest step and then, with a revulsion, recalling that it was exactly where, more than a month before, in the darkness of night and just so bowed with evil things, I had seen the specter of the most horrible of women. At this I was able to straighten myself; I went the rest of the way up; I made, in my turmoil, for the schoolroom, where there were objects belonging to me that I should have to take. But I opened the door to find again, in a flash, my eyes unsealed. In the presence of what I saw I reeled straight back upon resistance.

Seated at my own table in the clear noonday light I saw a person whom, without my previous experience, I should have taken at the first blush for some housemaid who might have stayed at home to look after the place and who, availing herself of rare relief from observation and of the schoolroom table and my pens, ink and paper, had applied herself to the considerable effort of a letter to her sweetheart. There was an effort in the way that, while her arms rested on the table, her hands, with evident weariness, supported her head, but at the moment I took this in I had already become aware that, in spite of my entrance, her attitude strangely persisted. Then it was—with the very act of its announcing itself—that her identity flared up in a change of posture. She rose, not as if she had heard me, but with an indescribable grand melancholy of indifference and detachment, and, within a dozen feet of me, stood there as my vile predecessor. Dishonored and tragic, she was all before me, but even as I fixed and, for memory, secured it, the awful image passed away. Dark as midnight in her black dress, her haggard beauty and her unutterable woe, she had looked at me long enough to appear to say that her right to sit at my table was as good as mine to sit at hers. While these instants lasted indeed I had the extraordinary chill of a feeling that it was I who was the intruder. It was as a wild protest against it that, actually addressing her—"You terrible miserable woman!"—I heard myself break into a sound that, by the open door, rang through the long passage and the empty house. She looked at me as if she heard me, but I had recovered myself and cleared the air. There was nothing in the room the next minute but the sunshine and the sense that I must stay.

XVI

I had so perfectly expected the return of the others to be marked by a demonstration that I was freshly upset at having to find them merely dumb and discreet about my desertion. Instead of gaily denouncing and caressing me they made no allusion to my having failed them, and I was left, for the time, on perceiving that she too said nothing, to study Mrs. Grose's odd face. I did this to such purpose that I made sure they had in some way bribed her to silence; a silence that, however, I would engage to break down on the first private opportunity. This opportunity came before tea: I secured five minutes with her in the housekeeper's room, where, in the twilight, amid a smell of lately baked bread, but with the place all swept and garnished, I found her sitting in pained placidity before the fire. So I see her still, so I see her best: facing the flame from her straight chair in the dusky shining room, a large clean picture of the "put away"—of drawers closed and locked and rest without a remedy.

"Oh yes, they asked me to say nothing, and to please them—so long as they were there—of course I promised. But what had happened to you?"

"I only went with you for the walk," I said. "I had then to come back to meet a friend."

She showed her surprise. "A friend—you?"

"Oh yes, I've a couple!" I laughed. "But did the children give you a reason?"

"For not alluding to your leaving us? Yes, they said you'd like it better. Do you like it better?"

My face had made her rueful. "No, I like it worse!" But after an instant I added: "Did they say why I should like it better?"

"No, Master Miles only said 'We must do nothing but what she likes!' "

"I wish indeed he would! And what did Flora say?"

"Miss Flora was too sweet. She said 'Oh of course, of course!'—and I said the same."

I thought a moment. "You were too sweet too—I can hear you all. But none the less, between Miles and me, it's now all out."

"All out?" My companion stared. "But what, Miss?"

"Everything. It doesn't matter. I've made up my mind. I came home, my dear," I went on, "for a talk with Miss Jessel."

I had by this time formed the habit of having Mrs. Grose literally well in hand in advance of my sounding that note, so that even now, as she bravely blinked under the signal of my word, I could keep her comparatively firm. "A talk! Do you mean she spoke?"

"It came to that. I found her, on my return, in the schoolroom."

"And what did she say?" I can hear the good woman still, and the candor of her stupefaction.

"That she suffers the torments—!"

It was this, of a truth, that made her, as she filled out my picture, gape. "Do you mean," she faltered "—of the lost?"

"Of the lost. Of the damned. And that's why, to share them—" I faltered myself with the horror of it.

But my companion, with less imagination, kept me up. "To share them—?"

"She wants Flora." Mrs. Grose might, as I gave it to her, fairly have fallen away from me had I not been prepared. I still held her there, to show I was. "As I've told you, however, it doesn't matter."

"Because you've made up your mind? But to what?"

"To everything."

"And what do you call 'everything'?"

"Why to sending for their uncle."

"Oh Miss, in pity do," my friend broke out.

"Ah but I will, I *will*! I see it's the only way. What's 'out,' as I told you, with Miles is that if he thinks I'm afraid to—and has ideas of what he gains by that—he shall see he's mistaken. Yes, yes; his uncle shall have it here from me on the spot (and before the boy himself if necessary) that if I'm to be reproached with having done nothing again about more school—"

"Yes, Miss—" my companion pressed me.

"Well, there's that awful reason."

There were now clearly so many of these for my poor colleague that she was excusable for being vague. "But—a—which?"

"Why the letter from his old place."

"You'll show it to the master?"

"I ought to have done so on the instant."

"Oh no!" said Mrs. Grose with decision.

"I'll put it before him," I went on inexorably, "that I can't undertake to work the question on behalf of a child who has been expelled—"

"For we've never in the least known what!" Mrs. Grose declared.

"For wickedness. For what else—when he's so clever and beautiful and perfect? Is he stupid? Is he untidy? Is he infirm? Is he ill-natured? He's exquisite—so it can be only *that,* and that would open up the whole thing. After all," I said, "it's their uncle's fault. If he left here such people—!"

"He didn't really in the least know them. The fault's mine." She had turned quite pale.

"Well, you shan't suffer," I answered.

"The children shan't!" she emphatically returned.

I was silent a while; we looked at each other. "Then what am I to tell him?"

"You needn't tell him anything. *I'll* tell him."

I measured this. "Do you mean you'll write—?" Remembering she couldn't, I caught myself up. "How do you communicate?"

"I tell the bailiff. *He* writes."

"And should you like him to write our story?"

My question had a sarcastic force that I had not fully intended, and it made her after a moment inconsequently break down. The tears were again in her eyes. "Ah Miss, *you* write!"

"Well—tonight," I at last returned, and on this we separated.

XVII

I went so far, in the evening, as to make a beginning. The weather had changed back, a great wind was abroad, and beneath the lamp, in my room, with Flora at peace beside me, I sat for a long time before a blank sheet of paper and listened to the lash of the rain and the batter of the gusts. Finally I went out, taking a candle; I crossed the passage and listened a minute at Miles's door. What, under my endless obsession, I had been impelled to listen for was some betrayal of his not being at rest, and I presently caught one, but not in the form I had expected. His voice tinkled out. "I say, you there—come in." It was gaiety in the gloom!

I went in with my light and found him in bed, very wide awake but very much at his ease. "Well, what are *you* up to?" he asked with a grace of sociability in which it occurred to me that Mrs. Grose, had she been present, might have looked in vain for proof that anything was "out."

I stood over him with my candle. "How did you know I was there?"

"Why of course I heard you. Did you fancy you made no noise? You're like a troop of cavalry!" he beautifully laughed.

"Then you weren't asleep?"

"Not much! I lie awake and think."

I had put my candle, designedly, a short way off, and then, as he held out his friendly old hand to me, had sat down on the edge of his bed. "What is it," I asked, "that you think of?"

"What in the world, my dear, but *you?*"

"Ah the pride I take in your appreciation doesn't insist on that! I had so far rather you slept."

"Well, I think also, you know, of this queer business of ours."

I marked the coolness of his firm little hand. "Of what queer business, Miles?"

"Why the way you bring me up. And all the rest!"

I fairly held my breath a minute, and even from my glimmering taper there was light enough to show how he smiled up at me from his pillow. "What do you mean by all the rest?"

"Oh you know, you know!"

I could say nothing for a minute, though I felt as I held his hand and our eyes continued to meet that my silence had all the air of admitting his charge and that nothing in the whole world of reality was perhaps at that moment so fabulous as our actual relation. "Certainly you shall go back to school," I said, "if it be that that troubles you. But not to the old place—we must find another, a better. How could I know it did trouble you, this question, when you never told me so, never spoke of it at all?" His clear listening face, framed in its smooth whiteness, made him for the minute as appealing as some wistful patient in a children's hospital, and I would have given, as the resemblance came to me, all I possessed on earth really to be the nurse or the sister of charity who might have helped to cure him. Well, even as it was I perhaps might help! "Do you know you've never said a word to me about your school—I mean the old one; never mentioned it in any way?"

He seemed to wonder; he smiled with the same loveliness. But he clearly gained time; he waited, he called for guidance. "Haven't I?" It wasn't for *me* to help him—it was for the thing I had met!

Something in his tone and the expression of his face, as I got this from him, set my heart aching with such a pang as it had never yet known; so unutterably touching was it to see his little brain puzzled and his little resources taxed to play, under the spell laid on him, a part of innocence and consistency. "No, never—from the hour you came back. You've never mentioned to me one of your masters, one of your comrades, nor the least little thing that ever happened to you at school. Never, little Miles—no never—have you given me an inkling of anything that *may* have happened there. Therefore you can fancy how much I'm in the dark. Until you came out, that way, this morning, you had since the first hour I saw you scarce even made a reference to anything in your previous life. You seemed so perfectly to accept the present." It was extraordinary how my absolute conviction of his secret precocity—

or whatever I might call the poison of an influence that I dared but half-phrase—made him, in spite of the faint breath of his inward trouble, appear as accessible as an older person, forced me to treat him as an intelligent equal. "I thought you wanted to go on as you are."

It struck me that at this he just faintly coloured. He gave, at any rate, like a convalescent slightly fatigued, a languid shake of his head. "I don't—I don't. I want to get away."

"You're tired of Bly?"

"Oh no, I like Bly."

"Well then—?"

"Oh *you* know what a boy wants!"

I felt I didn't know so well as Miles, and I took temporary refuge. "You want to go to your uncle?"

Again, at this, with his sweet ironic face, he made a movement on the pillow. "Ah you can't get off with that!"

I was silent a little, and it was I now, I think, who changed color. "My dear, I don't want to get off!"

"You can't even if you do. You can't, you can't!"—he lay beautifully staring. "My uncle must come down and you must completely settle things."

"If we do," I returned with some spirit, "you may be sure it will be to take you quite away."

"Well, don't you understand that that's exactly what I'm working for? You'll have to *tell* him—about the way you've let it all drop: you'll have to tell him a tremendous lot!"

The exultation with which he uttered this helped me somehow for the instant to meet him rather more. "And how much will *you*, Miles, have to tell him? There are things he'll ask you!"

He turned it over. "Very likely. But what things?"

"The things you've never told me. To make up his mind what to do with you. He can't send you back—"

"I don't want to go back!" he broke in. "I want a new field."

He said it with admirable serenity, with positive unimpeachable gaiety, and doubtless it was that very note that most evoked for me the poignancy, the unnatural childish tragedy, of his probable reappearance at the end of three months with all this bravado and still more dishonor. It overwhelmed me now that I should never be able to bear that, and it made me let myself go. I threw myself upon him and in the tenderness of my pity I embraced him. "Dear little Miles, dear little Miles—!"

My face was close to his, and he let me kiss him, simply taking it with indulgent good humor. "Well, old lady?"

"Is there nothing—nothing at all that you want to tell me?"

He turned off a little, facing round toward the wall and holding up his hand to look at as one had seen sick children look. "I've told you—I told you this morning."

Oh I was sorry for him! "That you just want me not to worry you?"

He looked round at me now as if in recognition of my understanding him, then ever so gently, "To let me alone," he replied.

There was even a strange little dignity in it, something that made me release him, yet, when I had slowly risen, linger beside him. God knows *I* never wished to harass him, but I felt that merely, at this, to turn my back on him was to abandon or, to put it more truly, lose him. "I've just begun a letter to your uncle," I said.

"Well then, finish it!"

I waited a minute. "What happened before?"

He gazed up at me again. "Before what?"

"Before you came back. And before you went away."

For some time he was silent, but he continued to meet my eyes. "What happened?"

It made me, the sound of the words, in which it seemed to me I caught for the very first time a small faint quaver of consenting consciousness—it made me drop on my knees beside the bed and seize once more the chance of possessing him. "Dear little Miles, dear little Miles, if you *knew* how I want to help you! It's only that, it's nothing but that, and I'd rather die than give you a pain or do you a wrong—I'd rather die than hurt a hair of you. Dear little Miles"—oh I brought it out now even if I *should* go too far—"I just want you to help me to save you!" But I knew in a moment after this that I had gone too far. The answer to my appeal was instantaneous, but it came in the form of an extraordinary blast and chill, a gust of frozen air and a shake of the room as great as if, in the wild wind, the casement had crashed in. The boy gave a loud high shriek, which, lost in the rest of the shock of sound, might have seemed, indistinctly, though I was so close to him, a note either of jubilation or of terror. I jumped to my feet again and was conscious of darkness. So for a moment we remained, while I stared about me and saw the drawn curtains unstirred and the window still tight. "Why the candle's out!" I then cried.

"It was I who blew it, dear!" said Miles.

XVIII

The next day, after lessons, Mrs. Grose found a moment to say to me quietly: "Have you written, Miss?"

"Yes—I've written." But I didn't add—for the hour—that my letter, sealed and directed, was still in my pocket. There would be time enough to send it before the messenger should go to the village. Meanwhile there had been on the part of my pupils no more brilliant, more exemplary morning. It was exactly as if they had both had at heart to gloss over any recent little friction. They performed the dizziest feats of arithmetic, soaring quite out of *my* feeble range, and perpetrated, in higher spirits than ever, geographical and historical jokes. It was conspicuous of course in Miles in particular that he appeared to wish to show how easily he could let me down. This child, to my memory, really lives in a setting of beauty and misery that no words can translate. There was a distinction all his own in every impulse he revealed; never was a small natural creature, to the uninformed eye all frankness and freedom, a more ingenious, a more extraordinary little gentleman. I had perpetually to guard against the wonder of contemplation into which my initiated view betrayed me; to check the irrelevant gaze and discouraged sigh in which I constantly both attacked and renounced the enigma of what such a little gentleman could have done that deserved a penalty. Say that, by the dark prodigy I knew, the imagination of all evil *had* been opened up to him: all the justice within me ached for the proof that it could ever have flowered into an act.

He had never at any rate been such a little gentleman as when, after our early dinner on this dreadful day, he came round to me and asked if I shouldn't like him for half an hour to play to me. David playing to Saul could never have shown a finer sense of the occasion. It was literally a charming exhibition of tact, of magnanimity, and quite tantamount to his saying outright: "The true knights we love to read about never push an advantage too far. I know what you mean now: you mean that—to be let alone yourself and not followed up—you'll cease to worry and spy upon me, won't keep me so close to you, will let me go and come. Well, I 'come,' you see—but I don't go! There'll be plenty of time for that. I do really delight in your society and I only want to show you that I contended for a principle." It may be imagined whether I resisted this appeal or failed to accompany him again, hand in hand, to the schoolroom. He sat down at the old piano and played as he had never

634

played, and if there are those who think he had better have been kicking a football I can only say that I wholly agree with them. For at the end of a time that under his influence I had quite ceased to measure I started up with a strange sense of having literally slept at my post. It was after luncheon, and by the schoolroom fire, and yet I hadn't really in the least slept; I had only done something much worse—I had forgotten. Where all this time was Flora? When I put the question to Miles he played on a minute before answering, and then could only say: "Why, my dear, how do *I* know?"—breaking moreover into a happy laugh which immediately after, as if it were a vocal accompaniment, he prolonged into incoherent extravagant song.

I went straight to my room, but his sister was not there; then, before going downstairs, I looked into several others. As she was nowhere about she would surely be with Mrs. Grose, whom in the comfort of that theory I accordingly proceeded in quest of. I found her where I had found her the evening before, but she met my quick challenge with blank scared ignorance. She had only supposed that, after the repast, I had carried off both the children; as to which she was quite in her right, for it was the very first time I had allowed the little girl out of my sight without some special provision. Of course now indeed she might be with the maids, so that the immediate thing was to look for her without an air of alarm. This we promptly arranged between us, but when, ten minutes later and in pursuance of our arrangement, we met in the hall, it was only to report on either side that after guarded enquiries we had altogether failed to trace her. For a minute there, apart from observation, we exchanged mute alarms, and I could feel with what high interest my friend returned me all those I had from the first given her.

"She'll be above," she presently said—"in one of the rooms you haven't searched."

"No, she's at a distance." I had made up my mind. "She has gone out."

Mrs. Grose stared. "Without a hat?"

I naturally also looked volumes. "Isn't that woman always without one?"

"She's with *her?*"

"She's with *her!*" I declared. "We must find them."

My hand was on my friend's arm, but she failed for the moment, confronted with such an account of the matter, to respond to my pressure. She communed, on the contrary, where she stood, with her uneasiness. "And where's Master Miles?"

"Oh *he's* with Quint. They'll be in the schoolroom."

"Lord, Miss!" My view, I was myself aware—and therefore I suppose my tone—had never yet reached so calm an assurance.

"The trick's played," I went on; "they've successfully worked their plan. He found the most divine little way to keep me quiet while she went off."

" 'Divine'?" Mrs. Grose bewilderedly echoed.

"Infernal then!" I almost cheerfully rejoined. "He has provided for himself as well. But come!"

She had helplessly gloomed at the upper regions. "You leave him—?"

"So long with Quint? Yes—I don't mind that now."

She always ended at these moments by getting possession of my hand, and in this manner she could at present still stay me. But after gasping an instant at my sudden resignation, "Because of your letter?" she eagerly brought out.

I quickly, by way of answer, felt for my letter, drew it forth, held it up, and then, freeing myself, went and laid it on the great hall table. "Luke will take it," I said as I came back. I reached the house door and opened it; I was already on the steps.

My companion still demurred: the storm of the night and the early morning had dropped, but the afternoon was damp and gray. I came down to the drive while she stood in the doorway. "You go with nothing on?"

"What do I care when the child has nothing? I can't wait to dress," I cried, "and if you must do so I leave you. Try meanwhile yourself upstairs."

"With *them?*" Oh on this the poor woman promptly joined me!

XIX

We went straight to the lake, as it was called at Bly, and I dare say rightly called, though it may have been a sheet of water less remarkable than my untraveled eyes supposed it. My acquaintance with sheets of water was small, and the pool of Bly, at all events on the few occasions of my consenting, under the protection of my pupils, to affront its surface in the old flat-bottomed boat moored there for our use, had impressed me both with its extent and its agitation. The usual place of embarkation was half a mile from the house, but I had an intimate conviction that, wherever Flora might be, she was not near home. She had not given me the slip for any small adventure, and, since the day of the very great one that I had shared with her by the pond, I had been aware, in our walks, of the quarter to which she most inclined. This was why I had now given to Mrs. Grose's steps so marked a direction—a direction making her, when she perceived it, oppose a resistance that showed me she was freshly mystified. "You're going to the water, Miss?—you think she's *in*—?"

"She may be, though the depth is, I believe, nowhere very great. But what I judge most likely is that she's on the spot from which, the other day, we saw together what I told you."

"When she pretended not to see—?"

"With that astounding self-possession! I've always been sure she wanted to go back alone. And now her brother has managed it for her."

Mrs. Grose still stood where she had stopped. "You suppose they really *talk* of them?"

I could meet this with an assurance! "They say things that, if we heard them, would simply appall us."

"And if she *is* there—?"

"Yes?"

"Then Miss Jessel is?"

"Beyond a doubt. You shall see."

"Oh thank you!" my friend cried, planted so firm that, taking it in, I went straight on without her. By the time I reached the pool, however, she was close behind me, and I knew that, whatever, to her apprehension, might befall me, the exposure of sticking to me struck her as her least danger. She exhaled a moan of relief as we at last came in sight of the greater part of the water without a sight of the child. There was no trace of Flora on that nearer side of the bank where my observation of her had been most startling, and none on the opposite edge, where, save for a margin of some twenty yards, a thick copse came down to the pond. This expanse, oblong in shape, was so narrow compared to its length that, with its ends out of view, it might have been taken for a scant river. We looked at the empty stretch, and then I felt the suggestion in my friend's eyes. I knew what she meant and I replied with a negative headshake.

"No, no; wait! She has taken the boat."

My companion stared at the vacant mooring place and then again across the lake. "Then where is it?"

"Our not seeing it is the strongest of proofs. She has used it to go over, and then has managed to hide it."

"All alone—that child?"

"She's not alone, and at such times she's not a child: she's an old, old woman." I scanned all the visible shore while Mrs. Grose took again, into the queer element I offered her, one of her plunges of submission; then I pointed out that the boat might perfectly be in a small refuge formed by one of the recesses of the pool, an indentation masked, for the hither side, by a projection of the bank and by a clump of trees growing close to the water.

"But if the boat's there, where on earth's *she?*" my colleague anxiously asked.

"That's exactly what we must learn." And I started to walk further.

"By going all the way round?"

"Certainly, far as it is. It will take us but ten minutes, yet it's far enough to have made the child prefer not to walk. She went straight over."

"Laws!" cried my friend again: the chain of my logic was ever too strong for her. It dragged her at my heels even now, and when we had got halfway round—a devious tiresome process, on ground much broken and by a path choked with overgrowth—I paused to give her breath. I sustained her with a grateful arm, assuring her that she might hugely help me, and this started us afresh, so that in the course of but few minutes more we reached a point from which we found the boat to be where I had supposed it. It had been intentionally left as much as possible out of sight and was tied to one of the stakes of a fence that came, just there, down to the brink and that had been an assistance to disembarking. I recognized, as I looked at the pair of short thick oars, quite safely drawn up, the prodigious character of the feat for a little girl, but I had by this time lived too long among wonders and had panted to too many livelier measures. There was a gate in the fence, through which we passed, and that brought us after a trifling interval more into the open. Then "There she is!" we both exclaimed at once.

Flora, a short way off, stood before us on the grass and smiled as if her performance had now become complete. The next thing she did, however, was to stoop straight down and pluck—quite as if it were all she was there for—a big ugly spray of withered fern. I at once felt sure she had just come out of the copse. She waited for us, not herself taking a step, and I was conscious of the rare solemnity with which we presently approached her. She smiled and smiled, and we met, but it was all done in a silence by this time flagrantly ominous. Mrs. Grose was the first to break the spell: she threw herself on her knees and, drawing the child to her breast, clasped in a long embrace the little tender yielding body. While this dumb convulsion lasted I could only watch it—which I did the more intently when I saw Flora's face peep at me over our companion's shoulder. It was serious now—the flicker had left it, but it strengthened the pang with which I at that moment envied Mrs. Grose the simplicity of *her* relation. Still, all this while, nothing more passed between us save that Flora had let her foolish fern again drop to the ground. What she and I had virtually said to each other was that pretexts were useless now. When Mrs. Grose finally got up she kept the child's hand, so that the two were still before me, and the singular reticence of our communion was even more marked in the frank look she addressed me. "I'll be hanged," it said, "if *I'll* speak!"

It was Flora who, gazing all over me in candid wonder, was the first. She was struck with our bareheaded aspect. "Why where are your things?"

"Where yours are, my dear!" I promptly returned.

She had already got back her gaiety and appeared to take this as an answer quite sufficient. "And where's Miles?" she went on.

There was something in the small valor of it that quite finished me: these three words from her were, in a flash like the glitter of a drawn blade, the jostle of the cup that my hand for weeks and weeks had held high and full to the brim and that now, even before speaking, I felt overflow in a deluge. "I'll tell you if you'll tell *me*—" I heard myself say, then heard the tremor in which it broke.

"Well, what?"

Mrs. Grose's suspense blazed at me, but it was too late now, and I brought the thing out handsomely. "Where, my pet, is Miss Jessel?"

XX

Just as in the churchyard with Miles, the whole thing was upon us. Much as I had made of the fact that this name had never once, between us, been sounded, the quick smitten glare with which the child's face now received it fairly likened my breach of the silence to the smash of a pane of glass. It added to the interposing cry, as if to stay the blow, that Mrs. Grose at the same instant uttered over my violence—the shriek of a creature scared, or rather wounded, which, in turn, within a few seconds, was completed by a gasp of my own. I seized my colleague's arm. "She's there, she's there!"

Miss Jessel stood before us on the opposite bank exactly as she had stood the other time, and I remember, strangely, as the first feeling now produced in me, my thrill of joy at having brought on a proof. She was there, so I was justified; she was there, so I was neither cruel nor mad. She was there for poor scared Mrs. Grose, but she was there most for Flora, and no moment of my monstrous time was perhaps so extraordinary as that in which I consciously threw out to her—with the sense that, pale and ravenous demon as she was, she would catch and understand it—an inarticulate message of gratitude. She rose erect on the spot my friend and I had lately quitted, and there wasn't in all the long reach of her desire an inch of her evil that fell short. This first vividness of vision and emotion were things of a few seconds, during which Mrs. Grose's dazed blink across to where I pointed struck me as showing that she too at last saw, just as it carried my own eyes precipitately to the child. The revelation then of the manner in which Flora was affected startled me in truth far more than it would have done to find her also merely agitated, for direct dismay was of course not what I had expected. Prepared and on her guard as our pursuit had actually made her, she would repress every betrayal, and I was therefore at once shaken by my first glimpse of the particular one for which I had not allowed. To see her, without a convulsion of her small pink face, not even feign to glance in the direction of the prodigy I announced, but only, instead of that, turn at *me* an expression of hard still gravity, an expression absolutely new and unprecedented and that appeared to read and accuse and judge me—this was a stroke that somehow converted the little girl herself into a figure portentous. I gaped at her coolness even though my certitude of her thoroughly seeing was never greater than at that instant, and then, in the immediate need to defend myself, I called her passionately to witness. "She's there, you little unhappy thing—there, there, *there*, and you know it as well as you know me!" I had said shortly before to Mrs. Grose that she was not at these times a child, but an old, old woman, and my description of her couldn't have been more strikingly confirmed than in the way in which, for all notice of this, she simply showed me, without an expressional concession or admission, a countenance of deeper and deeper, of indeed suddenly quite fixed reprobation. I was by this time—if I can put the whole thing at all together—more appalled at what I may properly call her manner than at anything else, though it was quite simultaneously that I became aware of having Mrs. Grose also, and very formidably, to reckon with. My elder companion, the next moment, at any rate, blotted out everything but her own flushed face and her loud shocked protest, a burst of high disapproval. "What a dreadful turn, to be sure, Miss! Where on earth do you see anything?"

I could only grasp her more quickly yet, for even while she spoke the hideous plain presence stood undimmed and undaunted. It had already lasted a minute, and it lasted while I continued, seizing my colleague, quite thrusting her at it and presenting her to it, to insist with my pointing hand. "You don't see her exactly as *we* see?—you mean to say you don't now—*now?* She's as big as a blazing fire! Only look, dearest woman, *look*—!" She looked, just as I did, and gave me, with her deep groan of negation, repulsion, compassion—the mixture with her pity of her relief at her exemption—a sense, touching to me even then, that she would have backed me up if she had been able. I might well have needed that, for with this hard blow of the proof that her eyes were hopelessly sealed I felt my own situation horribly crumble, I felt—I *saw*—my livid predecessor press, from her position, on my defeat, and I took the measure, more than all, of what I should have from this instant to deal with in the astounding little attitude of Flora. Into this attitude Mrs. Grose immediately and violently entered, breaking, even while there pierced through my sense of ruin a prodigious private triumph, into breathless reassurance.

"She isn't there, little lady, and nobody's there—and you never see nothing, my sweet! How can poor Miss Jessel—when poor Miss Jessel's dead and buried? *We* know, don't we love?"—and she appealed, blundering in, to the child. "It's all a mere mistake and a worry and a joke—and we'll go home as fast as we can!"

Our companion, on this, had responded with a strange quick primness of propriety, and they were again, with Mrs. Grose on her feet, united, as it were, in shocked opposition to me. Flora continued to fix me with her small mask of disaffection, and even at that minute I prayed God to forgive me for seeming to see that, as she stood there holding tight to our friend's dress, her incomparable childish beauty had suddenly failed, had quite vanished. I've said it already—she was literally, she was hideously hard; she had turned common and almost ugly. "I don't know what you mean. I see nobody. I see nothing. I never *have*. I think you're cruel. I don't like you!" Then, after this deliverance, which might have been that of a vulgarly pert little girl in the street, she hugged Mrs. Grose more closely and buried in her skirts the dreadful little face. In this position she launched an almost furious wail. "Take me away, take me away—oh take me away from *her!*"

"From *me?*" I panted.

"From you—from you!" she cried.

Even Mrs. Grose looked across at me dismayed, while I had nothing to do but communicate again with the figure that, on the opposite bank, without a movement, as rigidly still as if catching, beyond the interval, our voices, was as vividly there for my disaster as it was not there for my service. The wretched child had spoken exactly as if she had got from some outside source each of her stabbing little words, and I could therefore, in the full despair of all I had to accept, but sadly shake my head at her. "If I had ever doubted all my doubt would at present have gone. I've been living with the miserable truth, and now it has only too much closed round me. Of course I've lost you: I've interfered, and you've seen, under *her* dictation"—with which I faced, over the pool again, our infernal witness—"the easy and perfect way to meet it. I've done my best, but I've lost you. Goodbye." For Mrs. Grose I had an imperative, an almost frantic "Go, go!" before which, in infinite distress, but mutely possessed of the little girl and clearly convinced, in spite of her blindness, that something awful had occurred and some collapse engulfed us, she retreated, by the way we had come, as fast as she could move.

Of what first happened when I was left alone I had no subsequent memory. I only knew that at the end of, I suppose, a quarter of an hour, an odorous dampness and roughness, chilling and piercing my trouble, had made me understand that I must have thrown myself, on my face, to the ground and given way to a wildness of grief. I must have lain there long and cried and wailed, for when I raised my head the day was almost done. I got up and looked a moment, through the twilight, at the gray pool and its blank haunted edge, and then I took, back to the house, my dreary and difficult course. When I reached the gate in the fence the boat, to my surprise, was gone, so that I had a fresh reflexion to make on Flora's extraordinary command of the situation. She passed that night, by the most tacit and, I should add, were not the word so grotesque a false note, the happiest of arrangements, with Mrs. Grose. I saw neither of them on my return, but on the other hand I saw, as by an ambiguous compensation, a great deal of Miles. I saw—I can use no other phrase—so much of him that it fairly measured more than it had ever measured. No evening I had passed at Bly was to have had the portentous quality of this one; in spite of which—and in spite also of the deeper depths of consternation that had opened beneath my feet—there was literally, in the ebbing actual, an extraordinarily sweet sadness. On reaching the house I had never so much as looked for the boy; I had simply gone straight to my room to change what I was wearing and to take in, at a glance, much material testimony to Flora's rupture. Her little belongings had all been removed. When later, by the schoolroom fire, I was served with tea by the usual maid, I indulged, on the article of my other pupil, in no enquiry whatever. He had his freedom now—he might have it to the end! Well, he did have it, and it consisted—in part at least—of his coming in at about eight o'clock and sitting down with me in silence. On the removal of the tea things I had blown out the candles and drawn my chair closer: I was conscious of a mortal coldness and felt as if I should never again be warm. So when he appeared I was sitting in the glow with my thoughts. He paused a moment by the door as if to look at me, then—as if to share them—came to the other side of the hearth and sank into a chair. We sat there in absolute stillness, yet he wanted, I felt, to be with me.

XXI

Before a new day, in my room, had fully broken, my eyes opened to Mrs. Grose, who had come to my bedside with worse news. Flora was so markedly feverish that an illness was perhaps at hand; she had passed a night of extreme unrest, a night agitated above all by fears that had for their subject not in the least her former but wholly her present governess. It was not against the possible re-entrance of Miss Jessel on the scene that she protested—it was conspicuously and passionately against mine. I was at once on my feet, and with an immense deal to ask; the more that my friend had discernibly now girded her loins to meet me afresh. This I felt as soon as I had put to her the question of her sense of the child's sincerity as against my own. "She persists in denying to you that she saw, or has ever seen, anything?"

My visitor's trouble truly was great. "Ah Miss, it isn't a matter on which I can push her! Yet it isn't either, I must say, as if I much needed to. It has made her, every inch of her, quite old."

"Oh I see her perfectly from here. She resents, for all the world like some high little personage, the imputation on her truthfulness and, as it were, her respectability. 'Miss Jessel indeed—*she!*' Ah she's 'respectable,' the chit! The impression she gave me there yesterday was, I assure you, the very strangest of all: it was quite beyond any of the others. I *did* put my foot in it! She'll never speak to me again."

Hideous and obscure as it all was, it held Mrs. Grose briefly silent, then she granted my point with a frankness which, I made sure, had more behind it. "I think indeed, Miss, she never will. She do have a grand manner about it!"

"And that manner"—I summed it up—"is practically what's the matter with her now."

Oh that manner, I could see in my visitor's face, and not a little else besides! "She asks me every three minutes if I think you're coming in."

"I see—I see." I too, on my side, had so much more than worked it out. "Has she said to you since yesterday—except to repudiate her familiarity with anything so dreadful—a single other word about Miss Jessel?"

"Not one, Miss. And of course, you know," my friend added, "I took it from her by the lake that just then and there at least there *was* nobody."

"Rather! And naturally you take it from her still."

"I don't contradict her. What else can I do?"

"Nothing in the world! You've the cleverest little person to deal with. They've made them—their two friends, I mean—still cleverer even than nature did, for it was wondrous material to play on! Flora has now her grievance, and she'll work it to the end."

"Yes, Miss; but to *what* end?"

"Why that of dealing with me to her uncle. She'll make me out to him the lowest creature—!"

I winced at the fair show of the scene in Mrs. Grose's face; she looked for a minute as if she sharply saw them together. "And him who thinks so well of you!"

"He has an odd way—it comes over me now," I laughed, "—of proving it! But that doesn't matter. What Flora wants of course is to get rid of me."

My companion bravely concurred. "Never again to so much as look at you."

"So that what you've come to me now for," I asked, "is to speed me on my way?" Before she had time to reply, however, I had her in check. "I've a better idea—the result of my reflections. My going *would* seem the right thing, and on Sunday I was terribly near it. Yet that won't do. It's *you* who must go. You must take Flora."

My visitor, at this, did speculate. "But where in the world—?"

"Away from here. Away from *them.* Away, even most of all, now, from me. Straight to her uncle."

"Only to tell on you—?"

"No, not 'only'! To leave me, in addition, with my remedy."

She was still vague. "And what *is* your remedy?"

"Your loyalty, to begin with. And then Miles's."

She looked at me hard. "Do you think he—?"

"Won't, if he has the chance, turn on me? Yes, I venture still to think it. At all events I want to try. Get off with his sister as soon as possible and leave me with him alone." I was amazed, myself, at the spirit I had still in reserve, and therefore perhaps a trifle the more disconcerted at the way in which, in spite of this fine example of it, she hesitated. "There's one thing, of course," I went on: "they mustn't, before she goes, see each other for three seconds." Then it came over me that, in spite of Flora's presumable sequestration from the instant of her return from the pool, it might already be too late. "Do you mean," I anxiously asked, "that they *have* met?"

At this she quite flushed. "Ah, Miss, I'm not such a fool as that! If I've been obliged to leave her three or four times, it has been each time with one of the maids, and at present, though she's alone, she's locked in safe. And yet—and yet!" There were too many things.

"And yet what?"

"Well, are you so sure of the little gentleman?"

"I'm not sure of anything but *you*. But I have, since last evening, a new hope. I think he wants to give me an opening. I do believe that—poor little exquisite wretch!—he wants to speak. Last evening, in the firelight and the silence, he sat with me for two hours as if it were just coming."

Mrs. Grose looked hard through the window at the gray gathering day. "And did it come?"

"No, though I waited and waited I confess it didn't, and it was without a breach of the silence, or so much as a faint allusion to his sister's condition and absence, that we at last kissed for goodnight. All the same," I continued, "I can't, if her uncle sees her, consent to his seeing her brother without my having given the boy—and most of all because things have got so bad—a little more time."

My friend appeared on this ground more reluctant than I could quite understand. "What do you mean by more time?"

"Well, a day or two—really to bring it out. He'll then be on *my* side—of which you see the importance. If nothing comes I shall only fail, and you at the worst have helped me by doing on your arrival in town whatever you may have found possible." So I put it before her, but she continued for a little so lost in other reasons that I came again to her aid. "Unless indeed," I wound up, "you really want *not* to go."

I could see it, in her face, at last clear itself: she put out her hand to me as a pledge. "I'll go—I'll go. I'll go this morning."

I wanted to be very just. "If you *should* wish still to wait I'd engage she shouldn't see me."

"No, no: it's the place itself. She must leave it." She held me a moment with heavy eyes, then brought out the rest. "Your idea's the right one. I myself, Miss—"

"Well?"

"I can't stay."

The look she gave me with it made me jump at possibilities. "You mean that, since yesterday, you *have* seen—?"

She shook her head with dignity. "I've *heard*—!"

"Heard?"

"From that child—horrors! There!" she sighed with tragic relief. "On my honor, Miss, she says things—!" But at this evocation she broke down; she dropped with a sudden cry upon my sofa and, as I had seen her do before, gave way to all the anguish of it.

It was quite in another manner that I for my part let myself go. "Oh thank God!"

She sprang up again at this, drying her eyes with a groan. " 'Thank God'?"

"It so justifies me!"

"It does that, Miss!"

I couldn't have desired more emphasis, but I just waited "She's so horrible?"

I saw my colleague scarce knew how to put it. "Really shocking."

"And about me?"

"About you, Miss—since you must have it. It's beyond everything, for a young lady, and I can't think wherever she must have picked up—"

"The appalling language she applies to me? I can then!" I broke in with a laugh that was doubtless significant enough.

It only in truth left my friend still more grave. "Well, perhaps I ought to also—since I've heard some of it before! Yet I can't bear it," the poor woman went on while with the same movement she glanced, on my dressing table, at the face of my watch. "But I must go back."

I kept her, however. "Ah if you can't bear it—!"

"How can I stop with her, you mean? Why just *for* that: to get her away. Far from this," she pursued, "far from *them*—"

"She may be different? she may be free?" I seized her almost with joy. "Then in spite of yesterday you *believe*—"

"In such doings?" Her simple description of them required, in the light of her expression, to be carried no further, and she gave me the whole thing as she had never done. "I believe."

Yes, it was a joy, and we were still shoulder to shoulder: if I might continue sure of that I should care but little what else happened. My support in the presence of disaster would be the same as it had been in my early need of confidence, and if my friend would answer for my honesty I would answer for all the rest. On the point of taking leave of her, nonetheless, I was to some extent embarrassed. "There's one thing of course—it occurs to me—to remember. My letter giving the alarm will have reached town before you."

I now felt still more how she had been beating about the bush and how weary at last it had made her. "Your letter won't have got there. Your letter never went."

"What then became of it?"

"Goodness knows! Master Miles—"

"Do you mean *he* took it?" I gasped.

She hung fire, but she overcame her reluctance. "I mean that I saw yesterday, when I came back with Miss Flora, that it wasn't where you had put it. Later in the evening I had the chance to question Luke, and he declared that he had neither noticed nor touched it." We could only exchange, on this, one of our deeper mutual soundings, and it was Mrs. Grose who first brought up the plumb with an almost elate "You see!"

"Yes, I see that if Miles took it instead he probably will have read it and destroyed it."

"And don't you see anything else?"

I faced her a moment with a sad smile. "It strikes me that by this time your eyes are open even wider than mine."

They proved to be so indeed, but she could still almost blush to show it. "I make out now what he must have done at school." And she gave, in her simple sharpness, an almost droll disillusioned nod. "He stole!"

I turned it over—I tried to be more judicial. "Well—perhaps."

She looked as if she found me unexpectedly calm. "He stole *letters!*"

She couldn't know my reasons for a calmness after all pretty shallow, so I showed them off as I might. "I hope then it was to more purpose than in this case! The note, at all events, that I put on the table yesterday," I pursued, "will have given him so scant an advantage—for it contained only the bare demand for an interview—that he's already much ashamed of having gone so far for so little, and that what he had on his mind last evening was precisely the need of confession." I seemed to myself for the instant to have mastered it, to see it all. "Leave us, leave us"—I was already, at the door, hurrying her off. "I'll get it out of him. He'll meet me. He'll confess. If he confesses he's saved. And if he's saved—"

"Then *you* are?" The dear woman kissed me on this, and I took her farewell. "I'll save you without him!" she cried as she went.

XXII

Yet it was when she had gone off—and I missed her on the spot—that the great pinch really came. If I had counted on what it would give me to find myself alone with Miles I quickly recognized that it would give me at least a measure. No hour of my stay in fact was so assailed with apprehensions as that of my coming down to learn that the carriage containing Mrs. Grose and my younger pupil had already rolled out of the gates. Now I *was,* I said to myself, face to face with the elements, and for much of the rest of the day, while I fought my weakness, I could consider that I had been supremely rash. It was a tighter place still than I had yet turned round in; all the more that, for the first time, I could see in the aspect of others a confused reflection of the crisis. What had happened naturally caused them all to stare; there was too little of the explained, throw out whatever we might, in the suddenness of my colleague's act. The maids and the men looked blank; the effect of which on my nerves was an aggravation until I saw the necessity of making it a positive aid. It was in short by just clutching the helm that I avoided total wreck, and I dare say that, to bear up at all, I became that morning very grand and very dry. I welcomed the consciousness that I was charged with much to do, and I caused it to be known as well that, left thus to myself, I was quite remarkably firm. I wandered with that manner, for the next hour or two, all over the place and looked, I have no doubt, as if I were ready for any onset. So, for the benefit of whom it might concern, I paraded with a sick heart.

The person it appeared least to concern proved to be, till dinner, little Miles himself. My perambulations had given me meanwhile no glimpse of him, but they had tended to make more public the change taking place in our relation as a consequence of his having at the piano, the day before, kept me, in Flora's interest, so beguiled and befooled. The stamp of publicity had of course been fully given by her confinement and departure, and the change itself was now ushered in by our non-observance of the regular custom of the schoolroom. He had already disappeared when, on my way down, I pushed open his door, and I learned below that he had breakfasted—in the presence of a couple of the maids—with Mrs. Grose and his sister. He had then gone out, as he said, for a stroll; than which nothing, I reflected, could better have expressed his frank view of the abrupt transformation of my office. What he would now permit this office to consist of was yet to be settled: there was at the least a queer relief—I mean for myself in especial—in the renouncement of one pretension. If so much had sprung to the surface I scarce put it too strongly in saying that what had perhaps sprung highest was the absurdity of our prolonging the fiction that I had anything more to teach him. It sufficiently stuck out that, by tacit little tricks in which even more than myself he carried out the care for my dignity, I had had to appeal to him to let me off straining to meet him on the ground of his true capacity. He had at any rate his freedom now; I was never to touch it again: as I had amply shown, moreover, when, on his joining me in the schoolroom the previous night, I uttered, in reference to the interval just concluded, neither challenge nor hint. I had too much, from this moment, my other ideas. Yet when he at last arrived the difficulty of applying them, the accumulations of my problem, were brought straight home to me by the beautiful little presence on which what had occurred had as yet, for the eye, dropped neither stain nor shadow.

To mark, for the house, the high state I cultivated I decreed that my meals with the boy should be served, as we called it, downstairs, so that I had been awaiting him in the ponderous pomp of the room outside the window of which I had had from Mrs. Grose, that first scared Sunday, my flash of something it would scarce have done to call light. Here at present I felt afresh—for I had felt it again and again—how my equilibrium depended on the success of my rigid will, the will to shut my eyes as tight as possible to the truth that what I had to deal with was, revoltingly, against nature. I could only get on at all by taking "nature" into my confidence and my account, by treating my monstrous ordeal as a push in a direction unusual, of course, and unpleasant, but demanding after all, for a fair front, only another turn of the screw of ordinary human virtue. No attempt, none the less, could well require more tact than just this attempt to supply, one's self, *all* the nature. How could I put even a little of that article into a suppression of reference to what had occurred? How on the other hand could I make a reference to what had occurred? How on the other hand could I make a reference without a new plunge into the hideous obscure? Well, a sort of answer, after a time, had come to me, and it was so far confirmed as that I was met, incontestably, by the quickened vision of what was rare in my little companion. It was indeed as if he had found even now—as he had so often found at lessons—still some other delicate way to ease me off. Wasn't there light in the fact which, as we shared our solitude, broke out with a specious glitter it had never yet quite worn?—the fact that (opportunity aiding, precious opportunity which had now come) it would be pre-posterous, with a child so endowed, to forego the help one might wrest from absolute intelligence? What had his intelligence been given him for but to save him? Mightn't one, to reach his mind, risk the stretch of a stiff arm across his character? It was as if, when we were face to face in the dining room, he had literally shown me the way. The roast mutton was on the table and I had dispensed with attendance. Miles, before he sat down, stood a moment with his hands in his pockets and looked at the joint, on which he seemed on the point of passing some humorous judgement. But what he presently produced was: "I say, my dear, is she really very awfully ill?"

"Little Flora? Not so bad but that she'll presently be better. London will set her up. Bly had ceased to agree with her. Come here and take your mutton."

He alertly obeyed me, carried the plate carefully to his seat and, when he was established, went on. "Did Bly disagree with her so terribly all at once?"

"Not so suddenly as you might think. One had seen it coming on."

"Then why didn't you get her off before?"

"Before what?"

"Before she became too ill to travel."

I found myself prompt. "She's *not too* ill to travel; she only might have become so if she had stayed. This was just the moment to seize. The journey will dissipate the influence"—oh I was grand!—"and carry it off."

"I see, I see"—Miles, for that matter, was grand too. He settled to his repast with the charming little "table manner" that, from the day of his arrival, had relieved me of all grossness of admonition. Whatever he had been expelled from school for, it wasn't for ugly feeding. He was irreproachable, as always, today, but was unmistakably more conscious. He was discernibly trying to take for granted more things than he found, without assistance, quite easy, and he dropped into peaceful silence while he felt his situation. Our meal was of the briefest—mine a vain pretence, and I had the things immediately removed. While this was done Miles stood again with his hands in his little pockets and his back to me—stood and looked out of the wide window through which, that other day, I had seen what pulled me up. We continued silent while the maid was with us—as silent, it whimsically occurred to me, as some young couple who, on their wedding journey, at the inn, feel shy in the presence of the waiter. He turned round only when the waiter had left us. "Well—so we're alone!"

XXIII

"Oh more or less." I imagine my smile was pale. "Not absolutely. We shouldn't like that!" I went on.

"No—I suppose we shouldn't. Of course we've the others."

"We've the others—we've indeed the others," I concurred.

"Yet even though we have them," he returned, still with his hands in his pockets and planted there in front of me, "they don't much count, do they?"

I made the best of it, but I felt wan. "It depends on what you call 'much'!"

"Yes"—with all accommodation—"everything depends!" On this, however, he faced to the window again and presently reached it with his vague restless cogitating step. He remained there a while with his forehead against the glass, in contemplation of the stupid shrubs I knew and the dull things of November. I had always my hypocrisy of "work," behind which I now gained the sofa. Steadying myself with it there as I had repeatedly done at those moments of torment that I have described as the moments of my knowing the children to be given to something from which I was barred, I sufficiently obeyed my habit of being prepared for the worst. But an extraordinary impression dropped on me as I extracted a meaning from the boy's embarrassed back—none other than the impression that I was not barred now. This inference grew in a few minutes to sharp intensity and seemed bound up with the direct perception that it was positively *he* who was. The frames and squares of the great window were a kind of image, for him, of a kind of failure. I felt that I saw him, in any case, shut in or shut out. He was admirable but not comfortable: I took it in with a throb of hope. Wasn't he looking through the haunted pane for something he couldn't see?—and wasn't it the first time in the whole business that he had known such a lapse? The first, the very first: I found it a splendid portent. It made him anxious, though he watched himself; he had been anxious all day and, even while in his usual sweet little manner he sat at table, had needed all his small strange genius to give it a gloss. When he at last turned round to meet me it was almost as if this genius had succumbed. "Well, I think I'm glad Bly agrees with *me!*"

"You'd certainly seem to have seen, these twenty-four hours, a good deal more of it than some time before. I hope," I went on bravely, "that you've been enjoying yourself."

"Oh yes, I've been ever so far; all round about—miles and miles away. I've never been so free."

He had really a manner of his own, and I could only try to keep up with him. "Well, do you like it?"

He stood there smiling, then at last he put into two words—"Do *you?*"—more discrimination than I had ever heard two words contain. Before I had time to deal with that, however, he continued as if with the sense that this was an impertinence to be softened. "Nothing could be more charming than the way you take it, for of course, if we're alone together now it's you that are alone most. But I hope," he threw in, "you don't particularly mind!"

"Having to do with you?" I asked. "My dear child, how can I help minding? Though I've renounced all claim to your company—you're so beyond me—I at least greatly enjoy it. What else should I stay on for?"

He looked at me more directly, and the expression of his face, graver now, struck me as the most beautiful I had ever found in it. "You stay on just for *that?*"

"Certainly. I stay on as your friend and from the tremendous interest I take in you till something can be done for you that may be more worth your while. That needn't surprise you." My voice trembled so that I felt it impossible to suppress the shake. "Don't you remember how I told you, when I came and sat on your bed the night of the storm, that there was nothing in the world I wouldn't do for you?"

"Yes, yes!" He, on his side, more and more visibly nervous, had a tone to master; but he was so much more successful than I that, laughing out through his gravity, he could pretend we were pleasantly jesting. "Only that, I think, was to get me to do something for *you!*"

"It was partly to get you to do something," I conceded. "But, you know, you didn't do it."

"Oh yes," he said with the brightest superficial eagerness, "you wanted me to tell you something."

"That's it. Out, straight out. What you have on your mind, you know."

"Ah then is *that* what you've stayed over for?"

He spoke with a gaiety through which I could still catch the finest little quiver of resentful passion, but I can't begin to express the effect upon me of an implication of surrender even so faint. It was as if what I had yearned for had come at last only to astonish me. "Well, yes—I may as well make a clean breast of it. It was precisely for that."

He waited so long that I supposed it for the purpose of repudiating the assumption on which my action had been founded, but what he finally said was: "Do you mean now—here?"

"There couldn't be a better place or time." He looked round him uneasily, and I had the rare—oh the queer!—impression of the very first symptom I had seen in him of the approach of immediate fear. It was as if he were suddenly afraid of me—which struck me indeed as perhaps the best thing to make him. Yet in the very pang of the effort I felt it vain to try sternness, and I heard myself the next instant so gentle as to be almost grotesque. "You want so to go out again?"

"Awfully!" He smiled at me heroically, and the touching little bravery of it was enhanced by his actually flushing with pain. He had picked up his hat, which he had brought in, and stood twirling it in a way that gave me, even as I was just nearly reaching port, a perverse horror of what I was doing. To do it in *any* way was an act of violence, for what did it consist of but the obtrusion of the idea of grossness and guilt on a small helpless creature who had been for me a revelation of the possibilities of beautiful intercourse? Wasn't it base to create for a being so exquisite a mere alien awkwardness? I suppose I now read into our situation a clearness it couldn't have had at the time, for I seem to see our poor eyes already lighted with some spark of a prevision of the anguish that was to come. So we circled about with terrors and scruples, fighters not daring to close. But it was for each other we feared! That kept us a little longer suspended and unbruised. "I'll tell you everything," Miles said—"I mean I'll tell you anything you like. You'll stay on with me, and we shall both be all right, and I *will* tell you—I *will*. But not now."

"Why not now?"

My insistence turned him from me and kept him once more at his window in a silence during which, between us, you might have heard a pin drop. Then he was before me again with the air of a person for whom, outside, someone who had frankly to be reckoned with was waiting. "I have to see Luke."

I had not yet reduced him to quite so vulgar a lie, and I felt proportionately ashamed. But, horrible as it was, his lies made up my truth. I achieved thoughtfully a few loops of my knitting. "Well then go to Luke, and I'll wait for what you promise. Only in return for that satisfy, before you leave me, one very much smaller request."

He looked as if he felt he had succeeded enough to be able still a little to bargain. "Very much smaller—?"

"Yes, a mere fraction of the whole. Tell me"—oh my work preoccupied me, and I was off-hand!—"if, yesterday afternoon, from the table in the hall, you took, you know, my letter."

XXIV

My grasp of how he received this suffered for a minute from something that I can describe only as a fierce split of my attention—a stroke that at first, as I sprang straight up, reduced me to the mere blind movement of getting hold of him, drawing him close and, while I just fell for support against the nearest piece of furniture, instinctively keeping him with his back to the window. The appearance was full upon us that I had already had to deal with here: Peter Quint had come into view like a sentinel before a prison. The next thing I saw was that, from outside, he had reached the window, and then I knew that, close to the glass and glaring in through it, he offered once more to the room his white face of damnation. It represents but grossly what took place within me at the sight to say that on the second my decision was made, yet I believe that no woman so overwhelmed ever in so short a time recovered her command of the *act.* It came to me in the very horror of the immediate presence that the act would be, seeing and facing what I saw and faced, to keep the boy himself unaware. The inspiration—I can call it by no other name—was that I felt how voluntarily, how transcendently, I *might.* It was like fighting with a demon for a human soul, and when I had fairly so appraised it I saw how the human soul—held out, in the tremor of my hands, at arms' length—had a perfect dew of sweat on a lovely childish forehead. The face that was close to mine was as white as the face against the glass, and out of it presently came a sound, not low nor weak, but as if from much further away, that I drank like a waft of fragrance.

"Yes—I took it."

At this, with a moan of joy, I enfolded, I drew him close, and while I held him to my breast, where I could feel in the sudden fever of his little body the tremendous pulse of his little heart, I kept my eyes on the thing at the window and saw it move and shift its posture. I have likened it to a sentinel, but its slow wheel, for a moment, was rather the prowl of a baffled beast. My present quickened courage, however, was such that, not too much to let it through, I had to shade, as it were, my flame. Meanwhile the glare of the face was again at the window, the scoundrel fixed as if to watch and wait. It was the very confidence that I might now defy him, as well as the positive certitude, by this time, of the child's unconsciousness, that made me go on. "What did you take it for?"

"To see what you said about me."

"You opened the letter?"

"I opened it."

My eyes were now, as I held him off a little again, on Miles's own face, in which the collapse of mockery showed me how complete was the ravage of uneasiness. What was prodigious was that at last, by my success, his sense was sealed and his communication stopped: he knew that he was in presence, but knew not of what, and knew still less that I also was and that I did know. And what did this strain of trouble matter when my eyes went back to the window only to see that the air was clear again and—by my personal triumph—the influence quenched? There was nothing there. I felt that the cause was mine and that I should surely get *all*. "And you found nothing!"—I let my elation out.

He gave the most mournful, thoughtful little headshake. "Nothing."

"Nothing, nothing!" I almost shouted in my joy.

"Nothing, nothing," he sadly repeated.

I kissed his forehead; it was drenched. "So what have you done with it?"

"I've burnt it."

"Burnt it?" It was now or never. "Is that what you did at school?"

Oh what this brought up! "At school?"

"Did you take letters?—or other things?"

"Other things?" He appeared now to be thinking of something far off and that reached him only through the pressure of his anxiety. Yet it did reach him. "Did I *steal?*"

I felt myself redden to the roots of my hair as well as wonder if it were more strange to put to a gentleman such a question or to see him take it with allowances that gave the very distance of his fall in the world. "Was it for that you mightn't go back?"

The only thing he felt was rather a dreary little surprise. "Did you know I mightn't go back?"

"I know everything."

He gave me at this the longest and strangest look. "Everything?"

"Everything. Therefore *did* you—?" But I couldn't say it again.

Miles could, very simply. "No. I didn't steal."

My face must have shown him I believed him utterly; yet my hands—but it was for pure tenderness—shook him as if to ask him why, if it was all for nothing, he had condemned me to months of torment. "What then did you do?"

He looked in vague pain all round the top of the room and drew his breath, two or three times over, as if with difficulty. He might have been standing at the bottom of the sea and raising his eyes to some faint green twilight. "Well—I said things."

"Only that?"

"They thought it was enough!"

"To turn you out for?"

Never, truly, had a person "turned out" shown so little to explain it as this little person! He appeared to weigh my question, but in a manner quite detached and almost helpless. "Well, I suppose I oughtn't."

"But to whom did you say them?"

He evidently tried to remember, but it dropped—he had lost it. "I don't know!"

He almost smiled at me in the desolation of his surrender, which was indeed practically, by this time, so complete that I ought to have left it there. But I was infatuated—I was blind with victory, though even then the very effect that was to have brought him so much nearer was already that of added separation. "Was it to every one?" I asked.

"No; it was only to—" But he gave a sick little headshake. "I don't remember their names."

"Were they then so many?"

"No—only a few. Those I liked."

Those he liked? I seemed to float not into clearness, but into a darker obscure, and within a minute there had come to me out of my very pity the appalling alarm of his being perhaps innocent. It was for the instant confounding and bottomless, for if he *were* innocent what then on earth was I? Paralyzed, while it lasted, by the mere brush of the question, I let him go a little, so that, with a deep-drawn sigh, he turned away from me again, which, as he faced toward the clear window, I suffered, feeling that I had nothing now there to keep him from. "And did they repeat what you said?" I went on after a moment.

He was soon at some distance from me, still breathing hard and again with the air, though now without anger for it, of being confined against his will. Once more, as he had done before, he looked up at the dim day as if, of what had hitherto sustained him, nothing was left but an unspeakable anxiety. "Oh yes," he nevertheless replied—"they must have repeated them. To those *they* liked," he added.

There was somehow less of it than I had expected; but I turned it over. "And these things came round—?"

"To the masters? Oh yes!" he answered very simply. "But I didn't know they'd tell."

"The masters? They didn't—they've never told. That's why I ask you."

He turned to me again his little beautiful fevered face. "Yes, it was too bad."

"Too bad?"

"What I suppose I sometimes said. To write home."

I can't name the exquisite pathos of the contradiction given to such a speech by such a speaker; I only know that the next instant I heard myself throw off with homely force: "Stuff and nonsense!" But the next after that I must have sounded stern enough. "What *were* these things?"

My sternness was all for his judge, his executioner, yet it made him avert himself again, and that movement made *me,* with a single bound and an irrepressible cry, spring straight upon him. For there again, against the glass, as if to blight his confession and stay his answer, was the hideous author of our woe—the white face of damnation. I felt a sick swim at the drop of my victory and all the return of my battle, so that the wildness of my veritable leap only served as a great betrayal. I saw him, from the midst of my act, meet it with a divination, and on the perception that even now he only guessed, and that the window was still to his own eyes free, I let the impulse flame up to convert the climax of his dismay into the very proof of his liberation. "No more, no more, no more!" I shrieked to my visitant as I tried to press him against me.

"Is she *here?*" Miles panted as he caught with his sealed eyes the direction of my words. Then as his strange "she" staggered me and, with a gasp, I echoed it, "Miss Jessel, Miss Jessel!" he with sudden fury gave me back.

I seized, stupefied, his supposition—some sequel to what we had done to Flora, but this made me only want to show him that it was better still than that. "It's not Miss Jessel! But it's at the window—straight before us. It's *there*—the coward horror, there for the last time!"

At this, after a second in which his head made the movement of a baffled dog's on a scent and then gave a frantic little shake for air and light, he was at me in a white rage, bewildered, glaring vainly over the place and missing wholly, though it now, to my sense, filled the room like the taste of poison, the wide overwhelming presence. "It's *he?*"

I was so determined to have all my proof that I flashed into ice to challenge him. "Whom do you mean by 'he'?"

"Peter Quint—you devil!" His face gave again, round the room, its convulsed supplication. "*Where?*"

They are in my ears still, his supreme surrender of the name and his tribute to my devotion. "What does he matter now, my own?—what will he *ever* matter? *I* have you," I launched at the beast, "but he has lost you forever!" Then for the demonstration of my work, "There, *there!*" I said to Miles.

But he had already jerked straight round, stared, glared again, and seen but the quiet day. With the stroke of the loss I was so proud of he uttered the cry of a creature hurled over an abyss, and the grasp with which I recovered him might have been that of catching him in his fall. I caught him, yes, I held him—it may be imagined with what a passion, but at the end of a minute I began to feel what it truly was that I held. We were alone with the quiet day, and his little heart, dispossessed, had stopped.